T[illegible]
TRIBES

TWO TRIBES

EMILY BOWEN COHEN
WITH COLORS BY LARK PIEN

Heartdrum
Imprints of HarperCollinsPublishers

HARPER
alley

FOR MY FAMILY

Heartdrum is an imprint of HarperCollins Publishers.
HarperAlley is an imprint of HarperCollins Publishers.

Two Tribes
Copyright © 2023 by Emily Bowen Cohen
All rights reserved. Manufactured in Bosnia and Herzegovina.
No part of this book may be used or reproduced in any manner whatsoever without
written permission except in the case of brief quotations embodied in critical articles
and reviews. For information address HarperCollins Children's Books, a division of
HarperCollins Publishers, 195 Broadway, New York, NY 10007.
www.harperalley.com

Library of Congress Control Number: 2022946865
ISBN 978-0-06-298358-9 (pbk.) — ISBN 978-0-06-298359-6

The artist used ink, brush, Micron pen, and Photoshop
to create the illustrations for this book.
Colors by Lark Pien
Lettering by Emily Bowen Cohen
Design by Laura Mock
23 24 25 26 27   GPS   10 9 8 7 6 5 4 3 2 1

First Edition

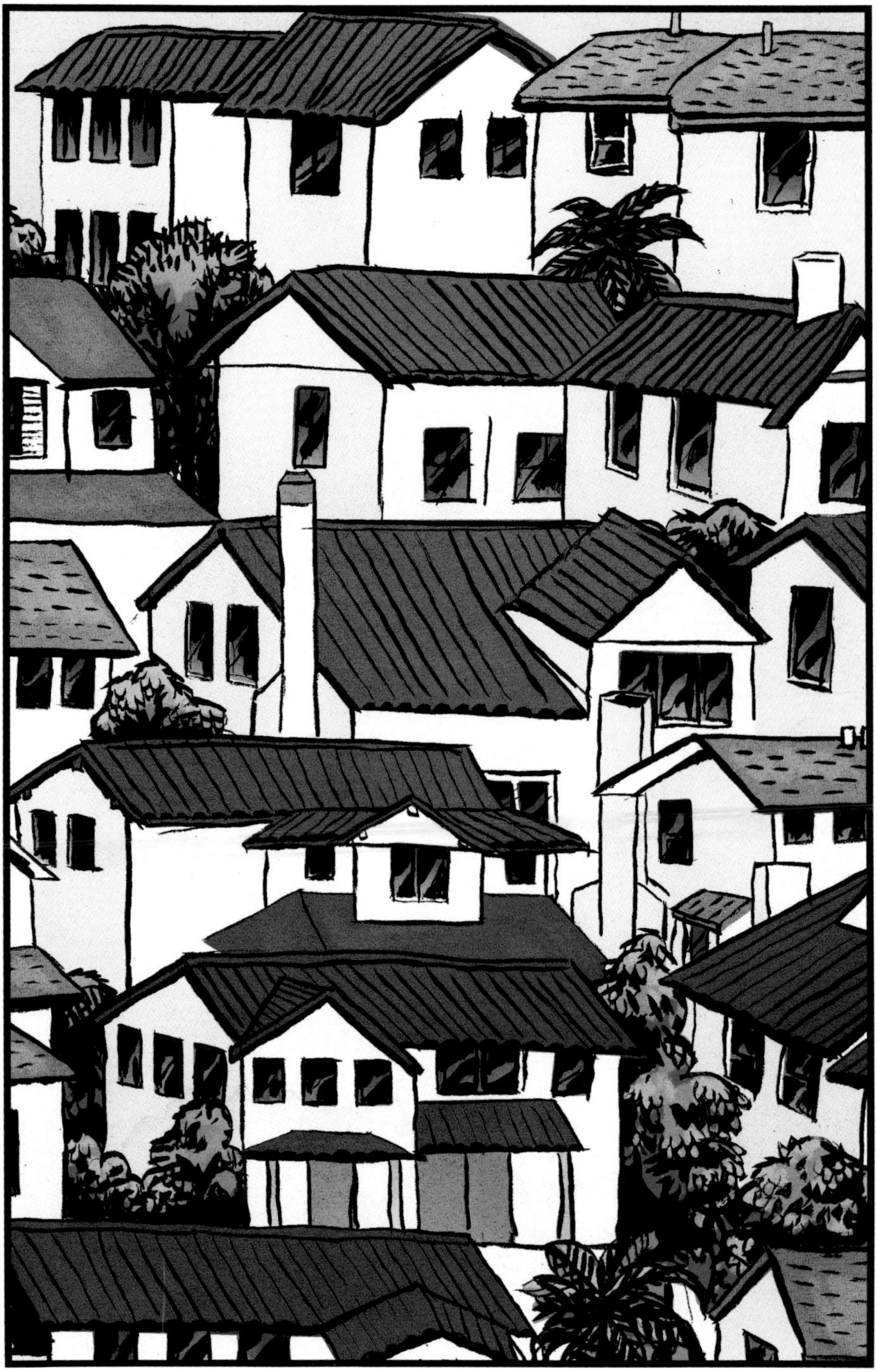

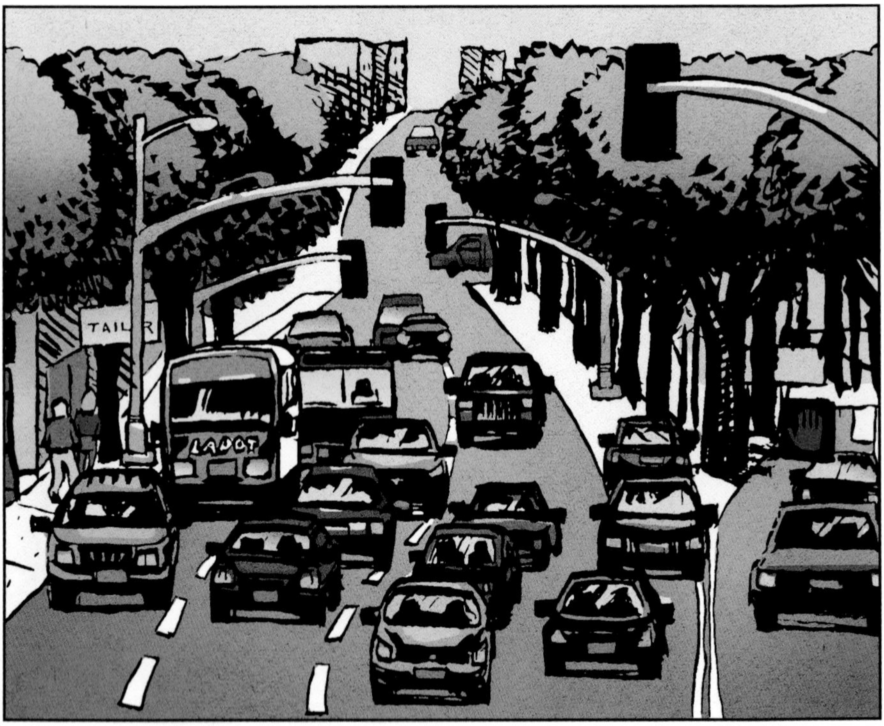
LADOT

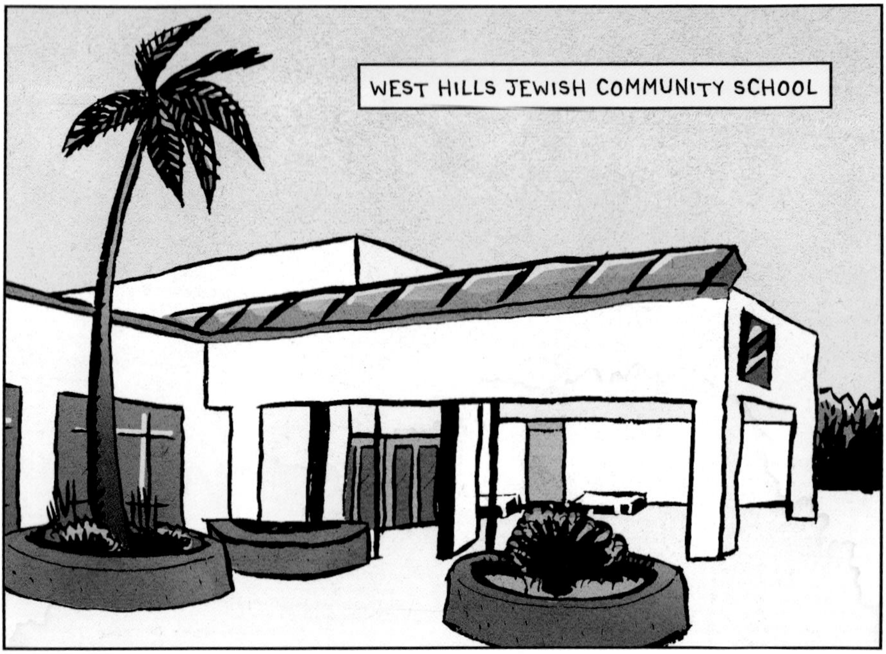
WEST HILLS JEWISH COMMUNITY SCHOOL

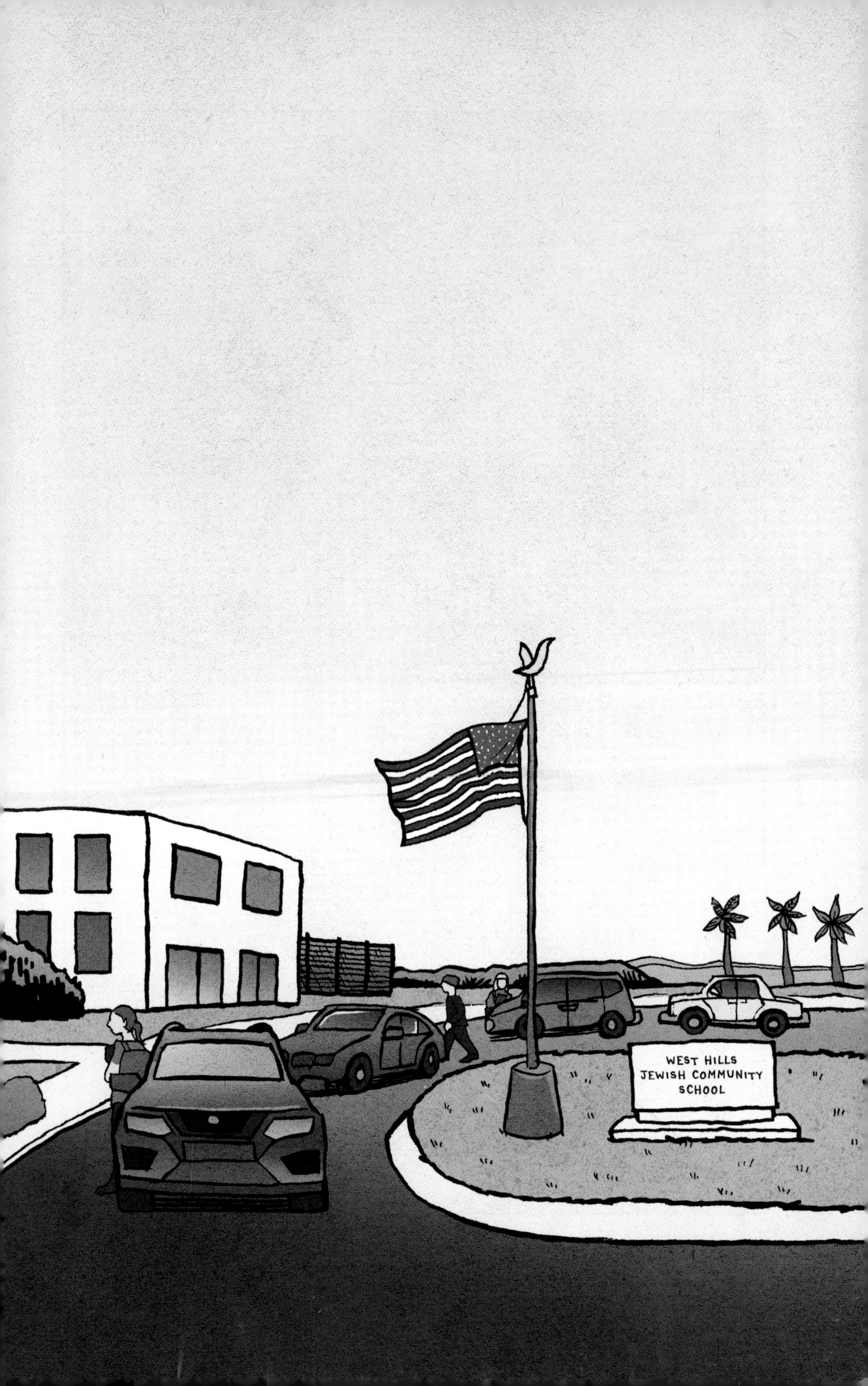
WEST HILLS
JEWISH COMMUNITY
SCHOOL

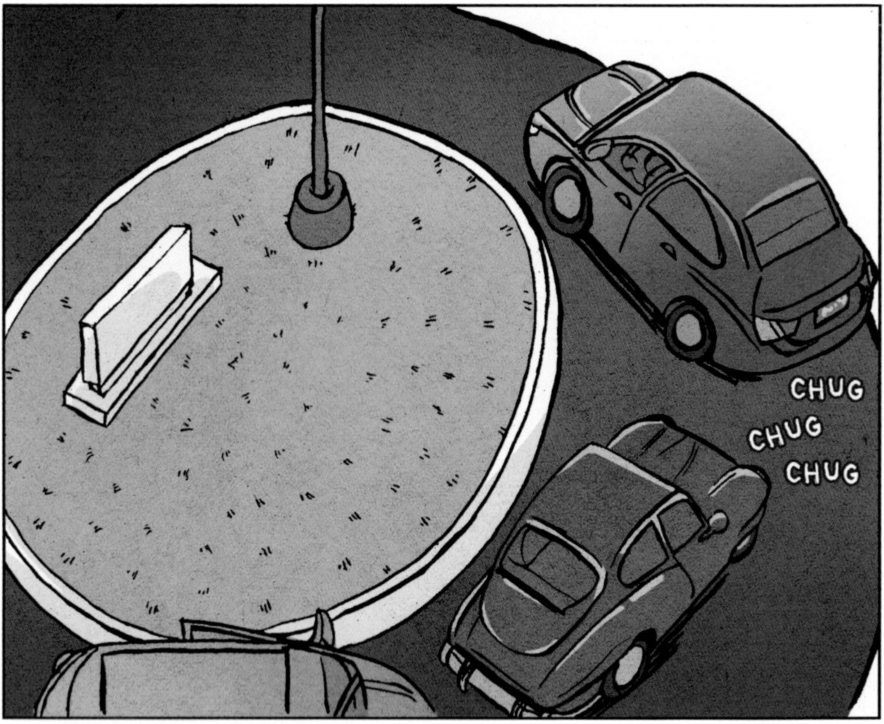
CHUG
CHUG
CHUG

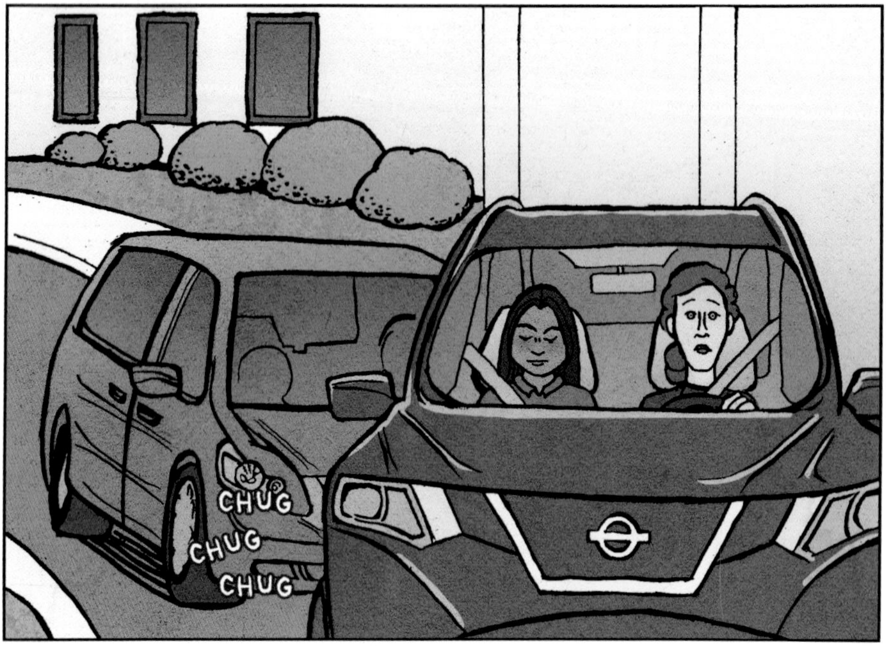
CHUG
CHUG
CHUG

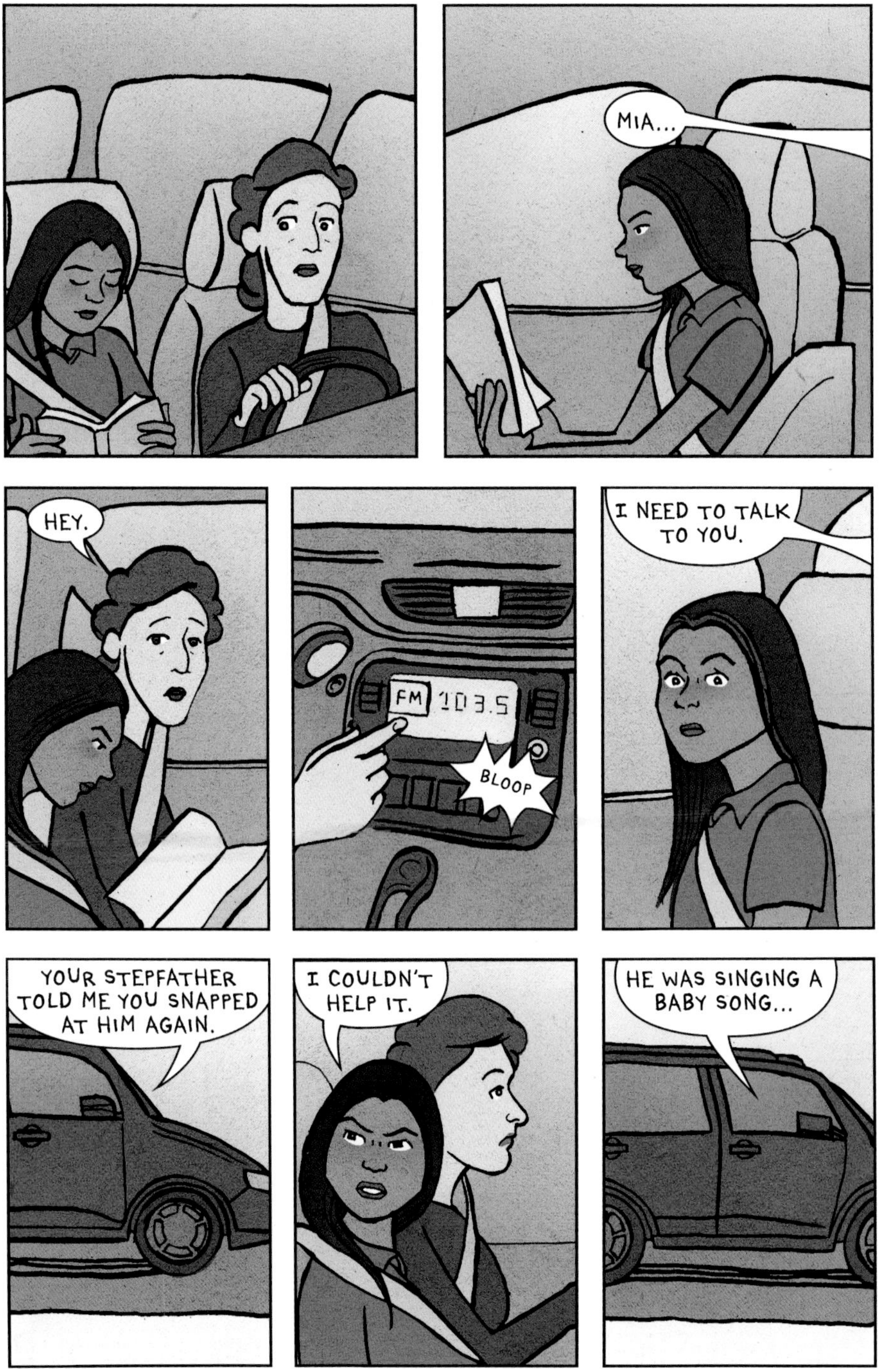
MIA...
HEY.
FM 103.5
BLOOP
I NEED TO TALK TO YOU.
YOUR STEPFATHER TOLD ME YOU SNAPPED AT HIM AGAIN.
I COULDN'T HELP IT.
HE WAS SINGING A BABY SONG...

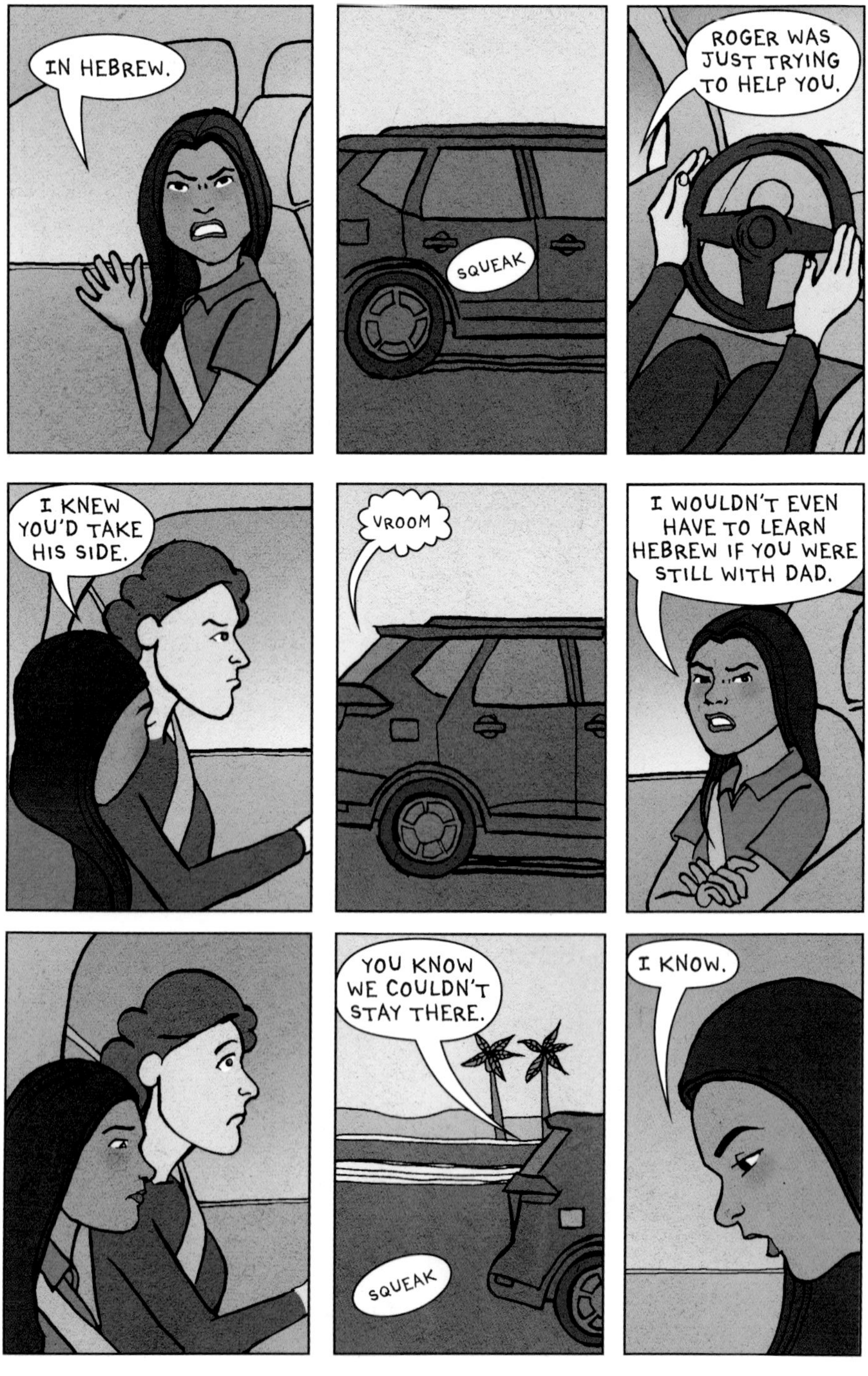
IN HEBREW.
SQUEAK
ROGER WAS JUST TRYING TO HELP YOU.
I KNEW YOU'D TAKE HIS SIDE.
VROOM
I WOULDN'T EVEN HAVE TO LEARN HEBREW IF YOU WERE STILL WITH DAD.
YOU KNOW WE COULDN'T STAY THERE.
SQUEAK
I KNOW.

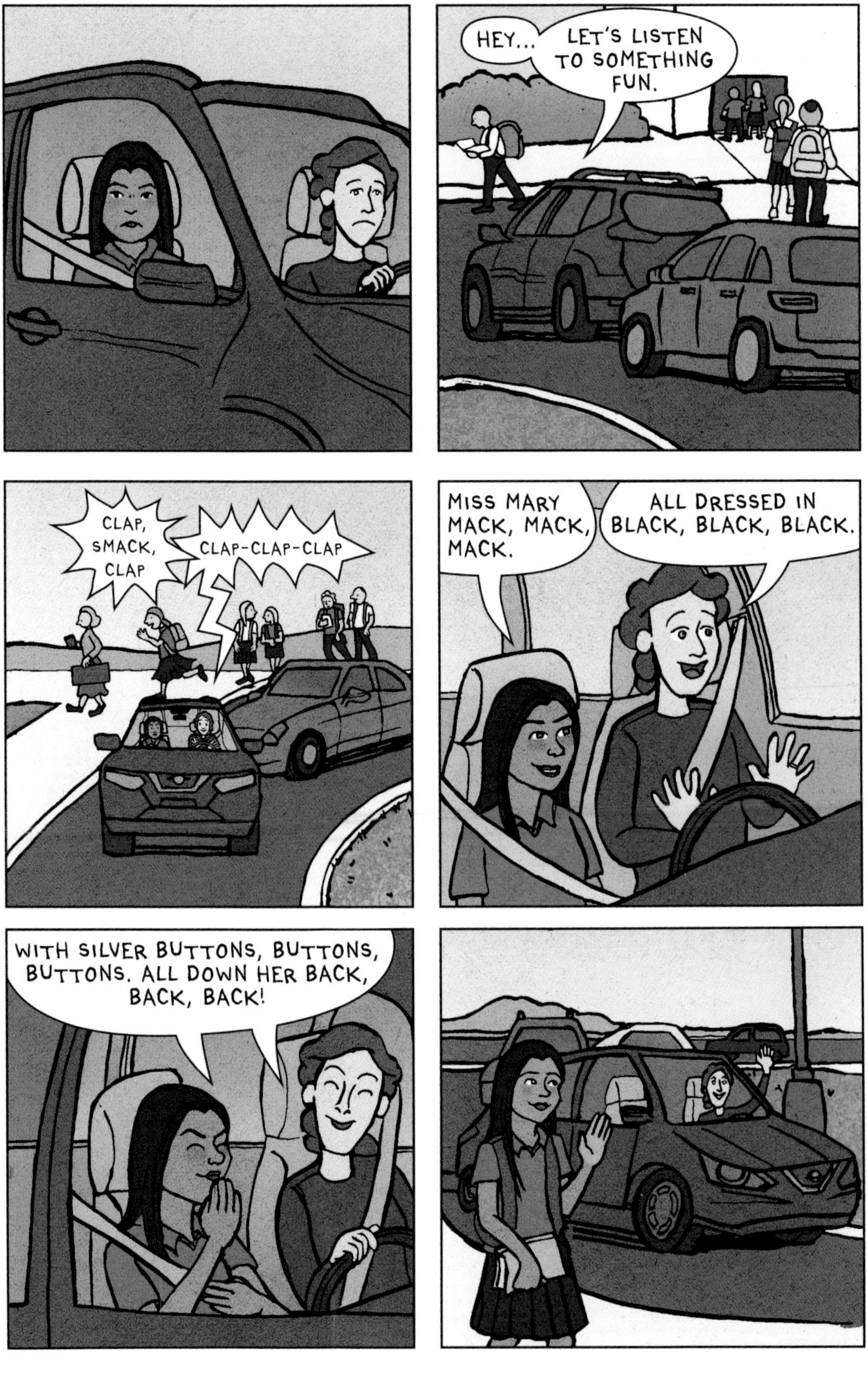
HEY...
LET'S LISTEN TO SOMETHING FUN.
CLAP, SMACK, CLAP
CLAP-CLAP-CLAP
MISS MARY MACK, MACK, MACK.
ALL DRESSED IN BLACK, BLACK, BLACK.
WITH SILVER BUTTONS, BUTTONS, BUTTONS. ALL DOWN HER BACK, BACK, BACK!

THE SEEDS

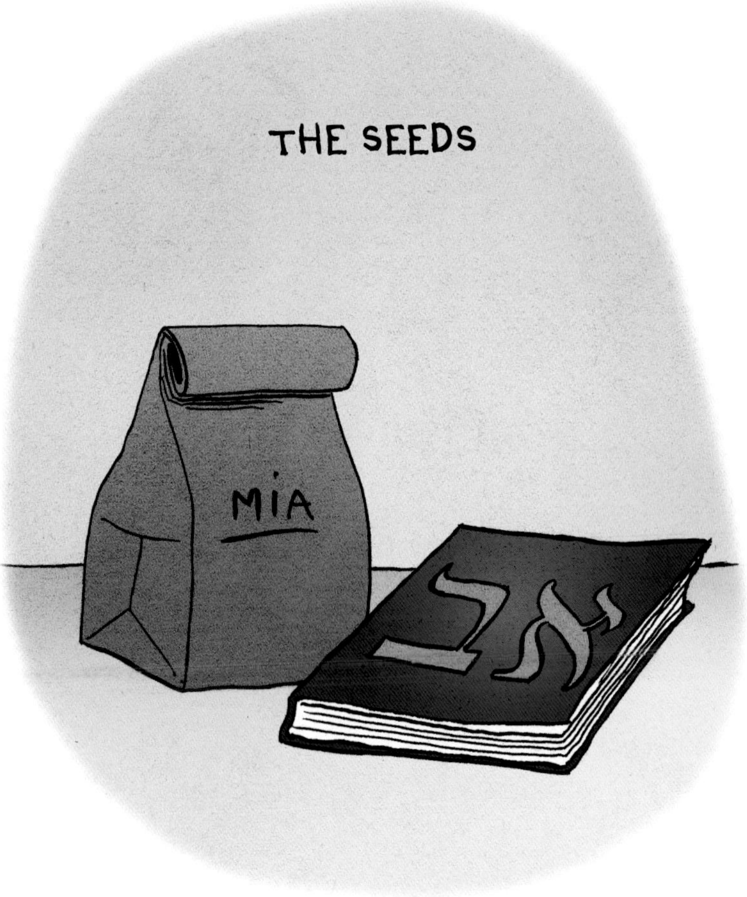
MIA

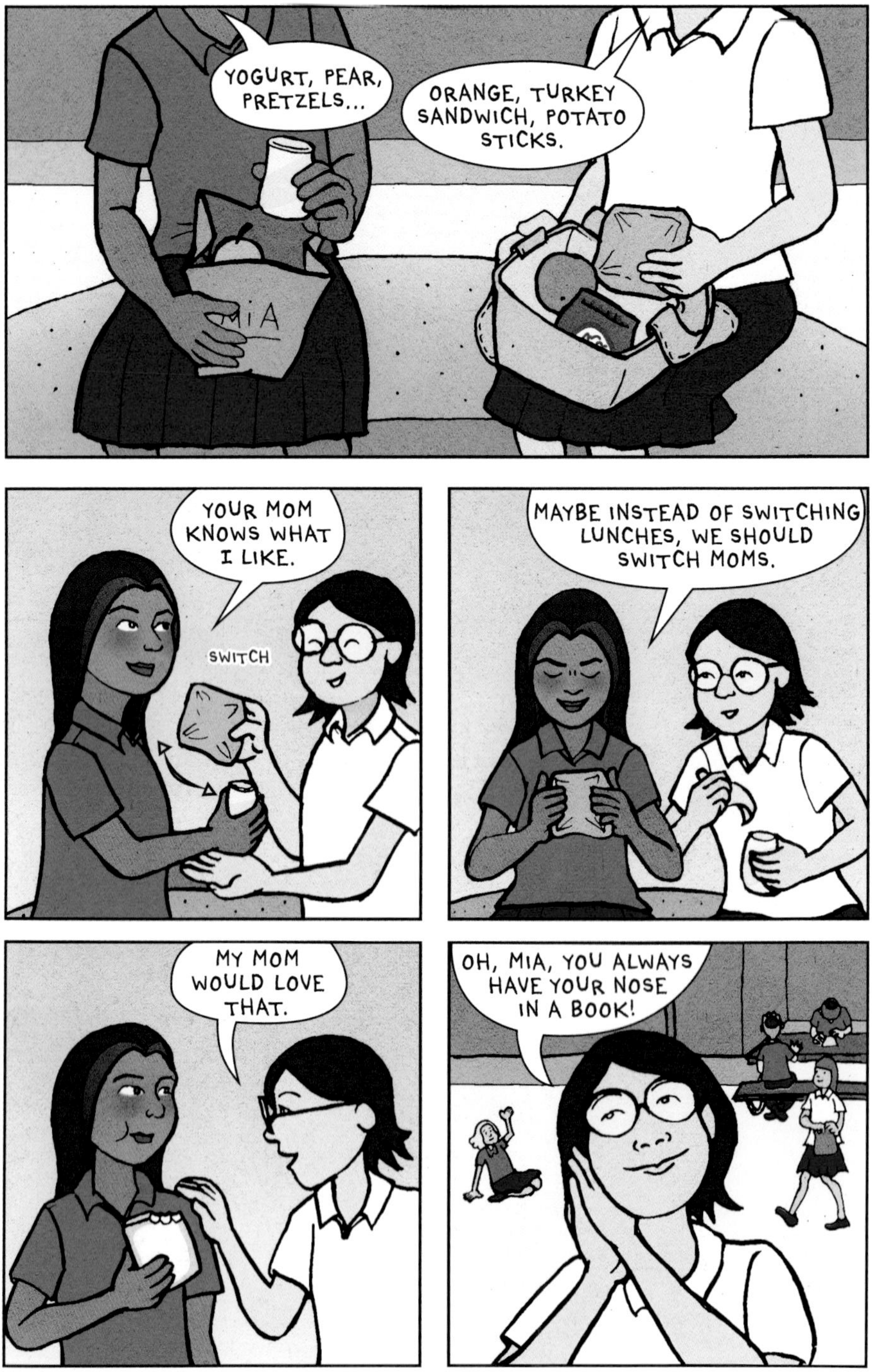
YOGURT, PEAR, PRETZELS...
ORANGE, TURKEY SANDWICH, POTATO STICKS.
MIA
YOUR MOM KNOWS WHAT I LIKE.
SWITCH
MAYBE INSTEAD OF SWITCHING LUNCHES, WE SHOULD SWITCH MOMS.
MY MOM WOULD LOVE THAT.
OH, MIA, YOU ALWAYS HAVE YOUR NOSE IN A BOOK!

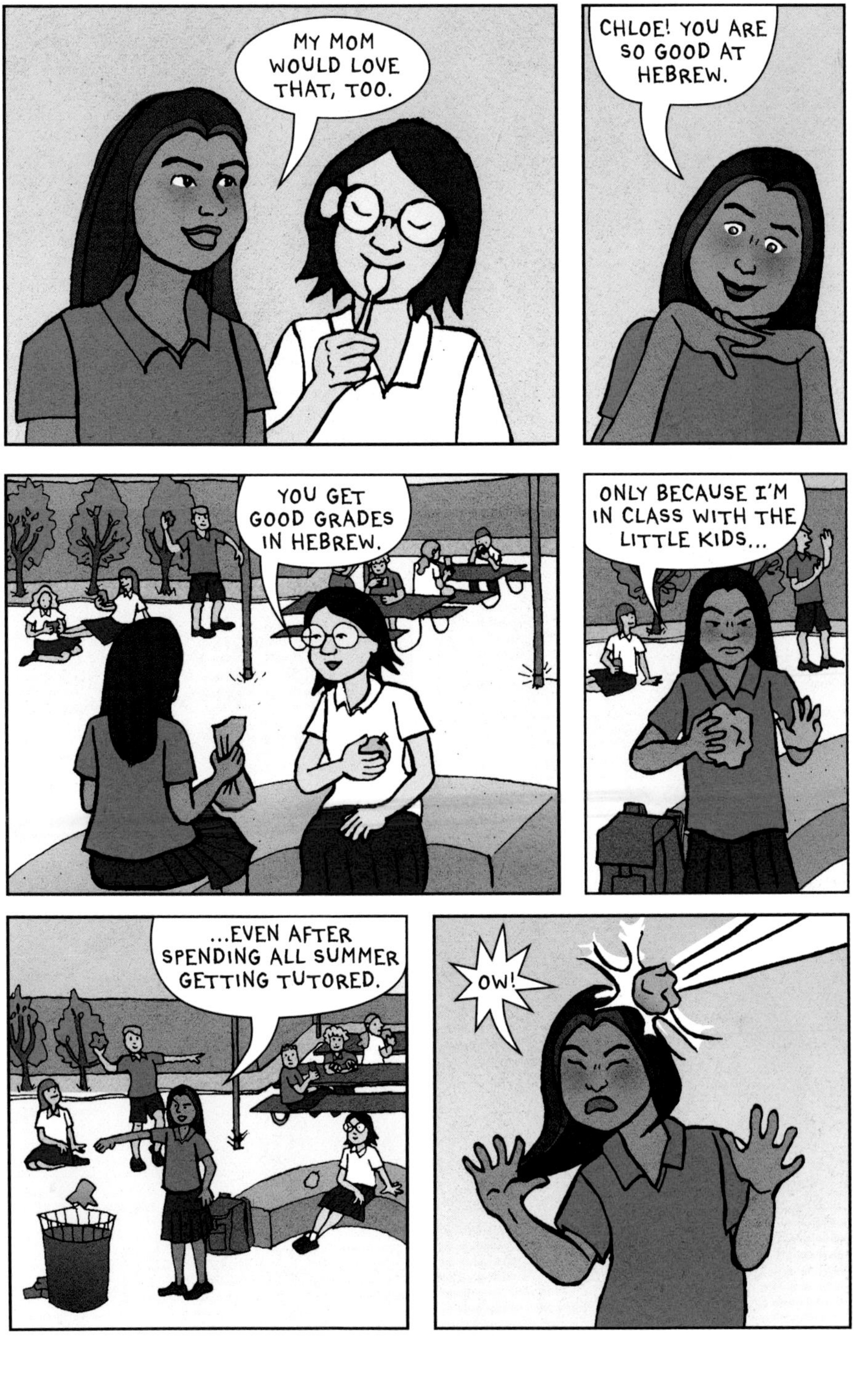
MY MOM WOULD LOVE THAT, TOO.
CHLOE! YOU ARE SO GOOD AT HEBREW.
YOU GET GOOD GRADES IN HEBREW.
ONLY BECAUSE I'M IN CLASS WITH THE LITTLE KIDS...
...EVEN AFTER SPENDING ALL SUMMER GETTING TUTORED.
OW!

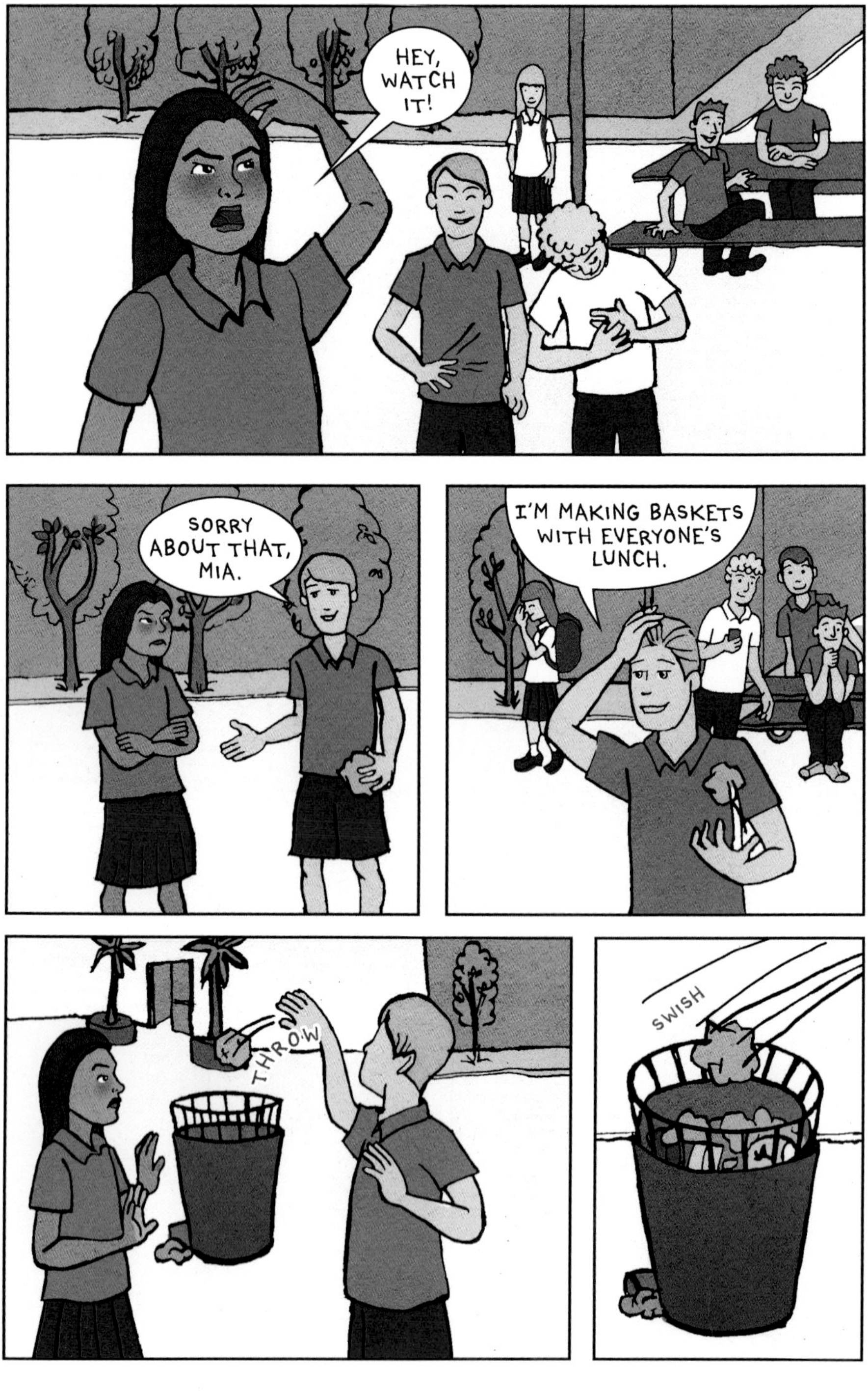
HEY, WATCH IT!
SORRY ABOUT THAT, MIA.
I'M MAKING BASKETS WITH EVERYONE'S LUNCH.
THROW
SWISH

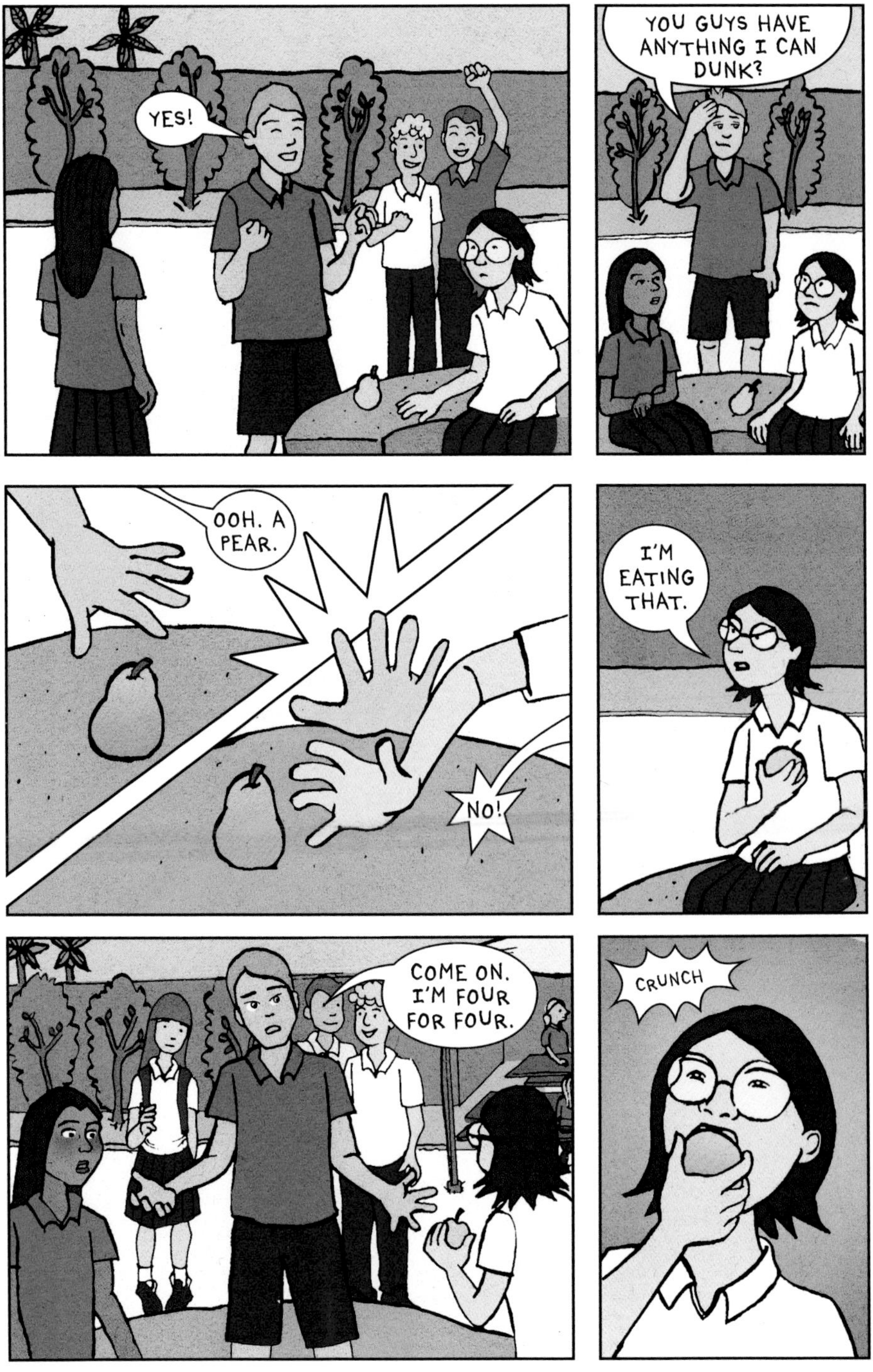
YES!
YOU GUYS HAVE ANYTHING I CAN DUNK?
OOH. A PEAR.
NO!
I'M EATING THAT.
COME ON. I'M FOUR FOR FOUR.
CRUNCH

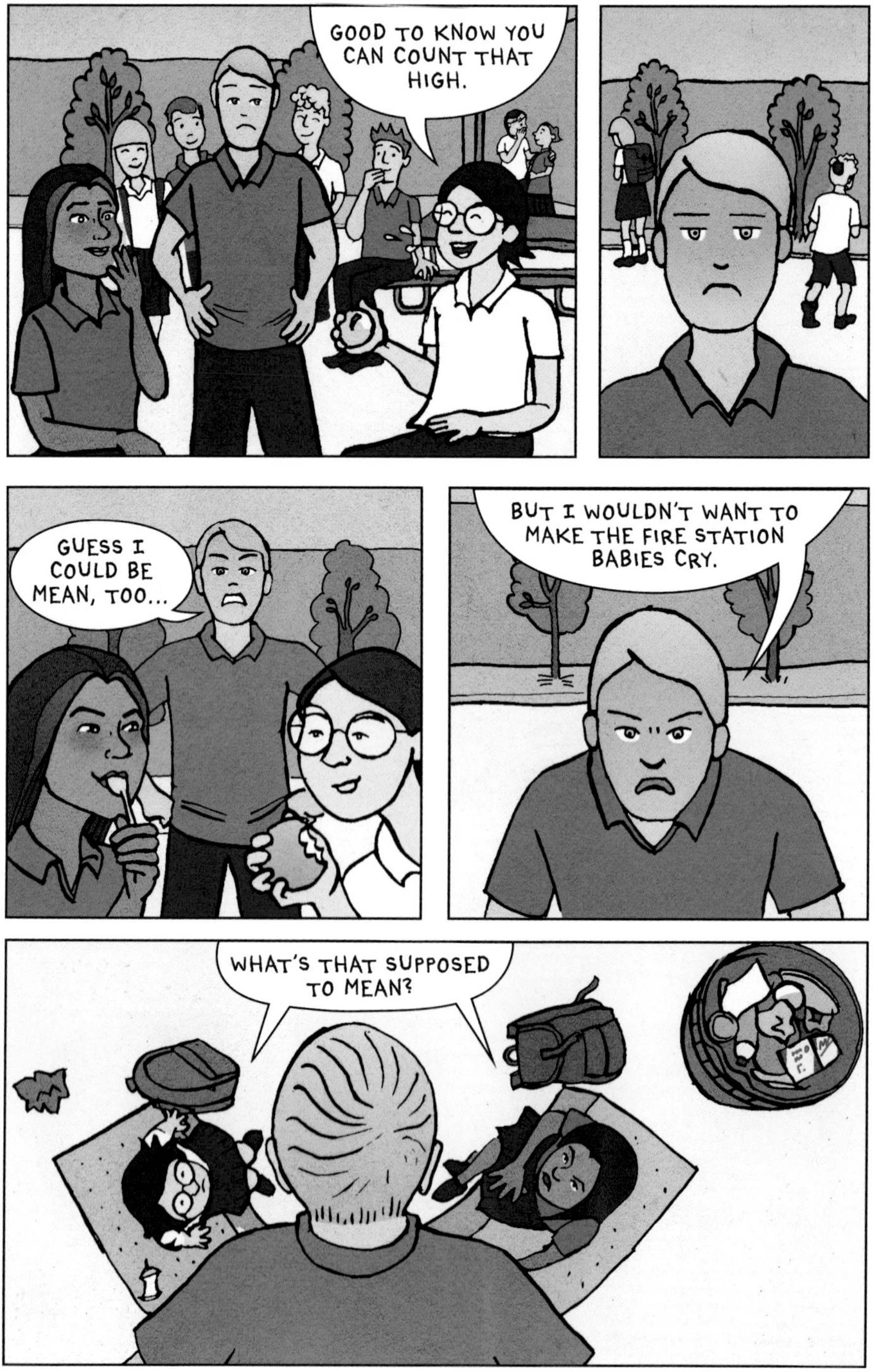
GOOD TO KNOW YOU CAN COUNT THAT HIGH.
GUESS I COULD BE MEAN, TOO...
BUT I WOULDN'T WANT TO MAKE THE FIRE STATION BABIES CRY.
WHAT'S THAT SUPPOSED TO MEAN?

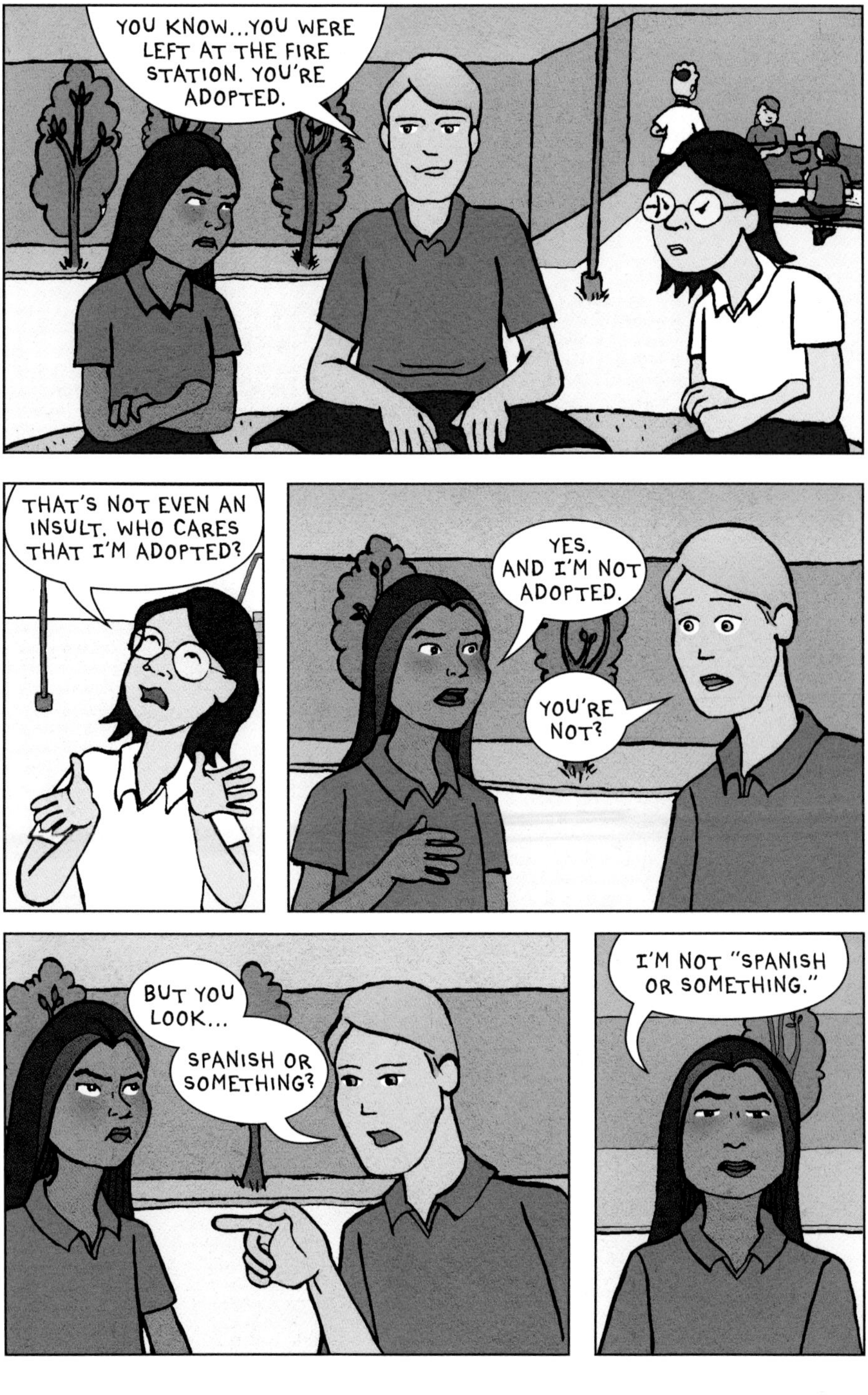
YOU KNOW...YOU WERE LEFT AT THE FIRE STATION. YOU'RE ADOPTED.
THAT'S NOT EVEN AN INSULT. WHO CARES THAT I'M ADOPTED?
YES. AND I'M NOT ADOPTED.
YOU'RE NOT?
BUT YOU LOOK...
SPANISH OR SOMETHING?
I'M NOT "SPANISH OR SOMETHING."

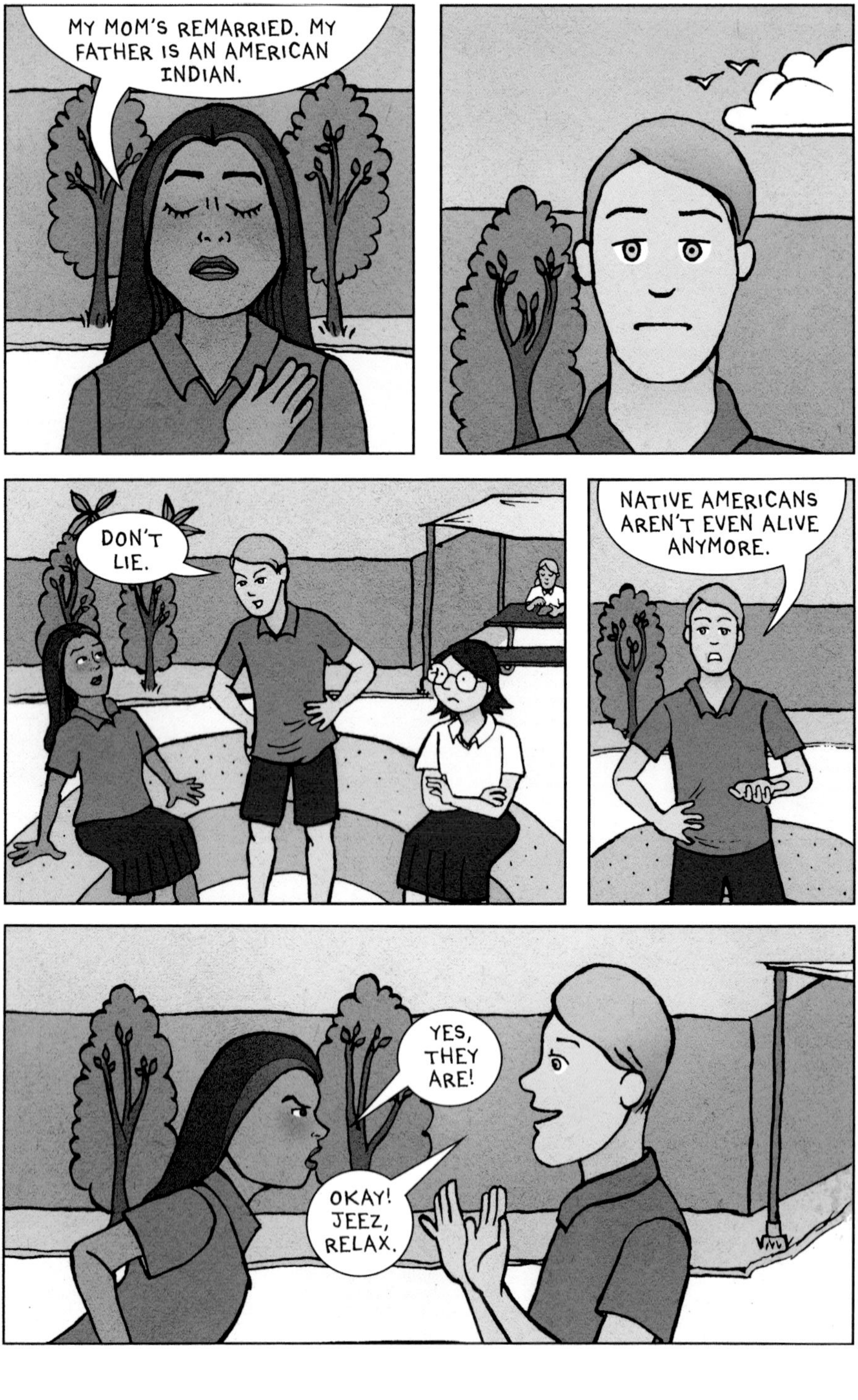
MY MOM'S REMARRIED. MY FATHER IS AN AMERICAN INDIAN.
DON'T LIE.
NATIVE AMERICANS AREN'T EVEN ALIVE ANYMORE.
YES, THEY ARE!
OKAY! JEEZ, RELAX.

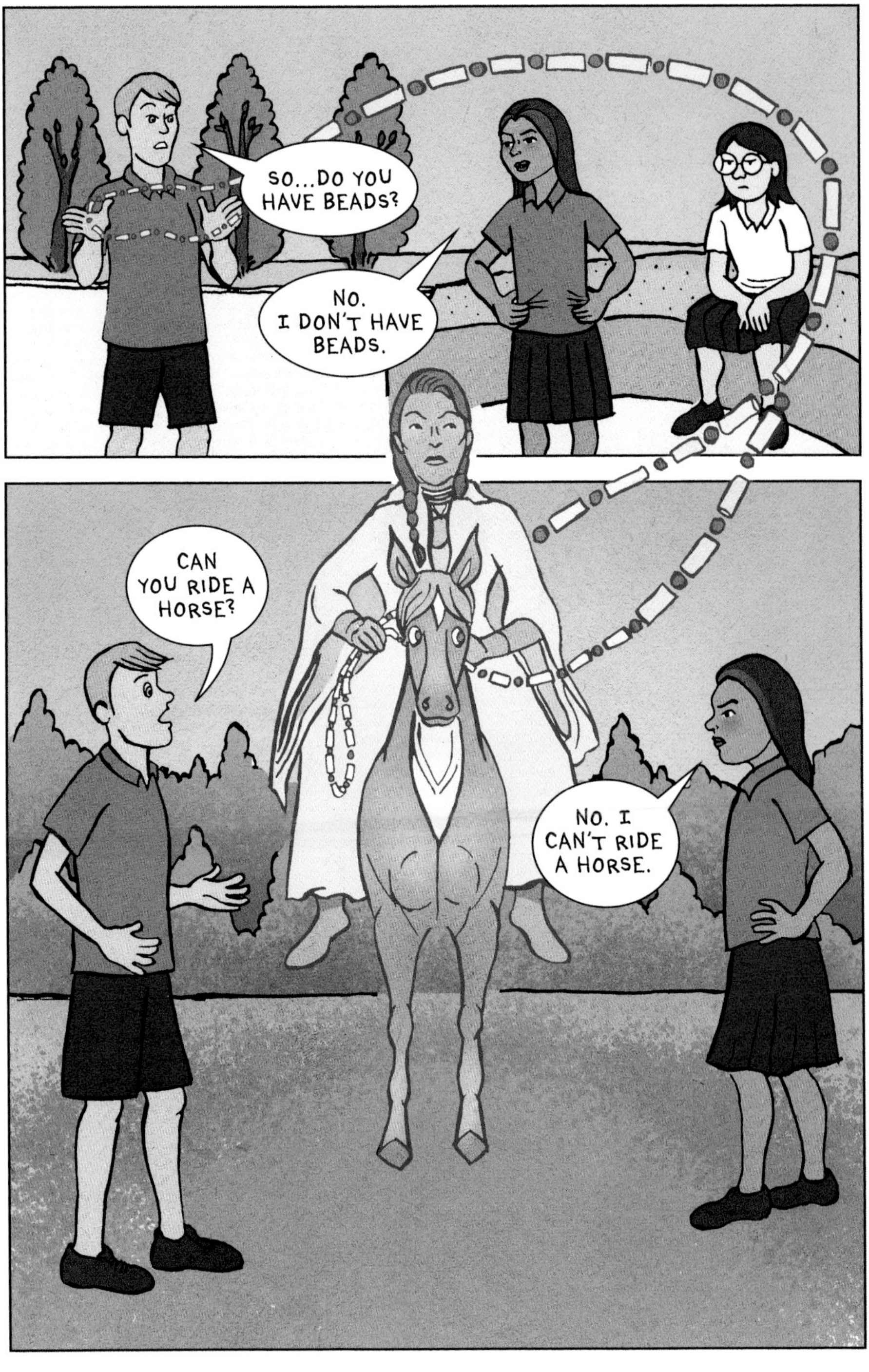
SO...DO YOU HAVE BEADS?
NO. I DON'T HAVE BEADS.
CAN YOU RIDE A HORSE?
NO. I CAN'T RIDE A HORSE.

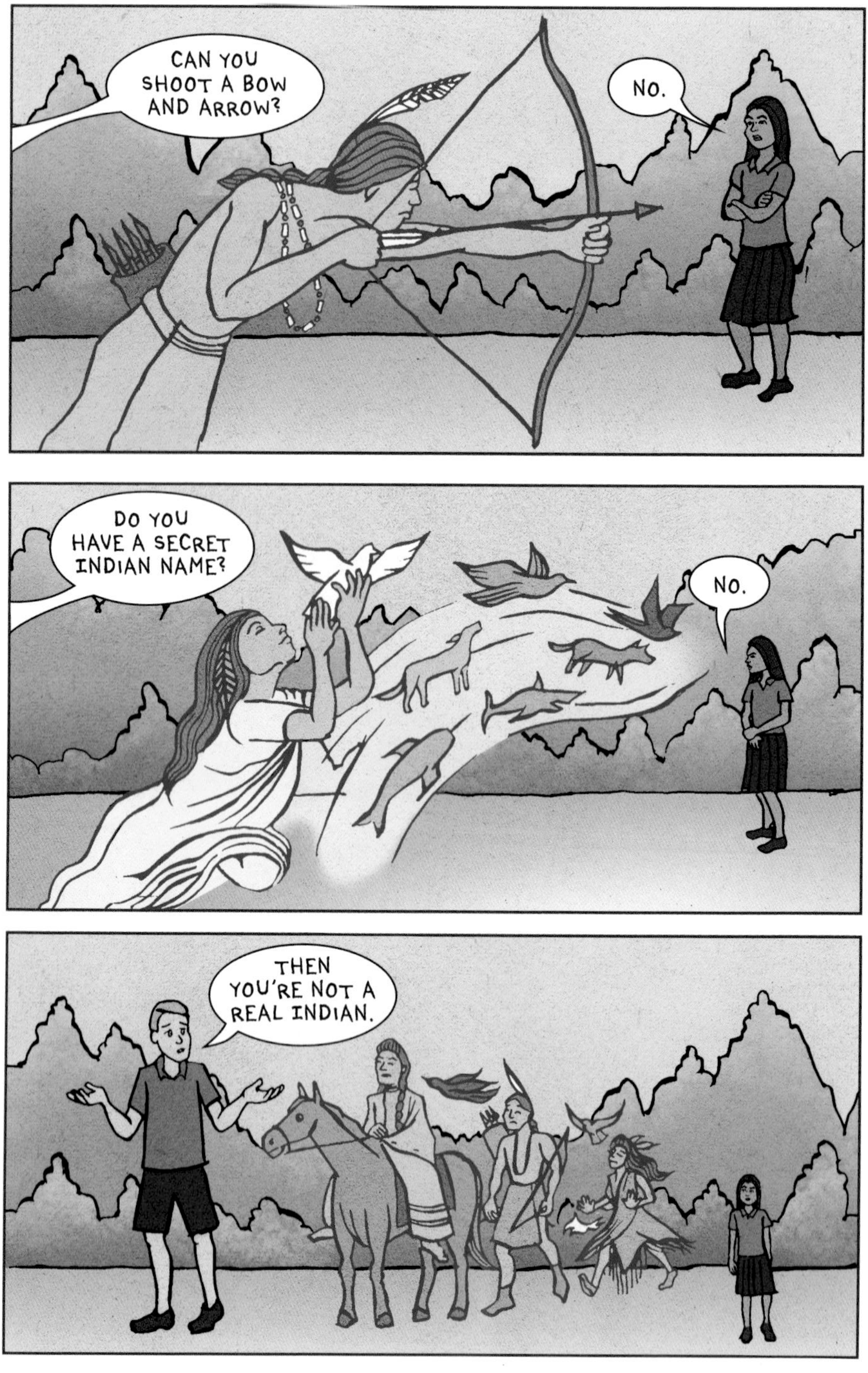
CAN YOU SHOOT A BOW AND ARROW?
NO.
DO YOU HAVE A SECRET INDIAN NAME?
NO.
THEN YOU'RE NOT A REAL INDIAN.

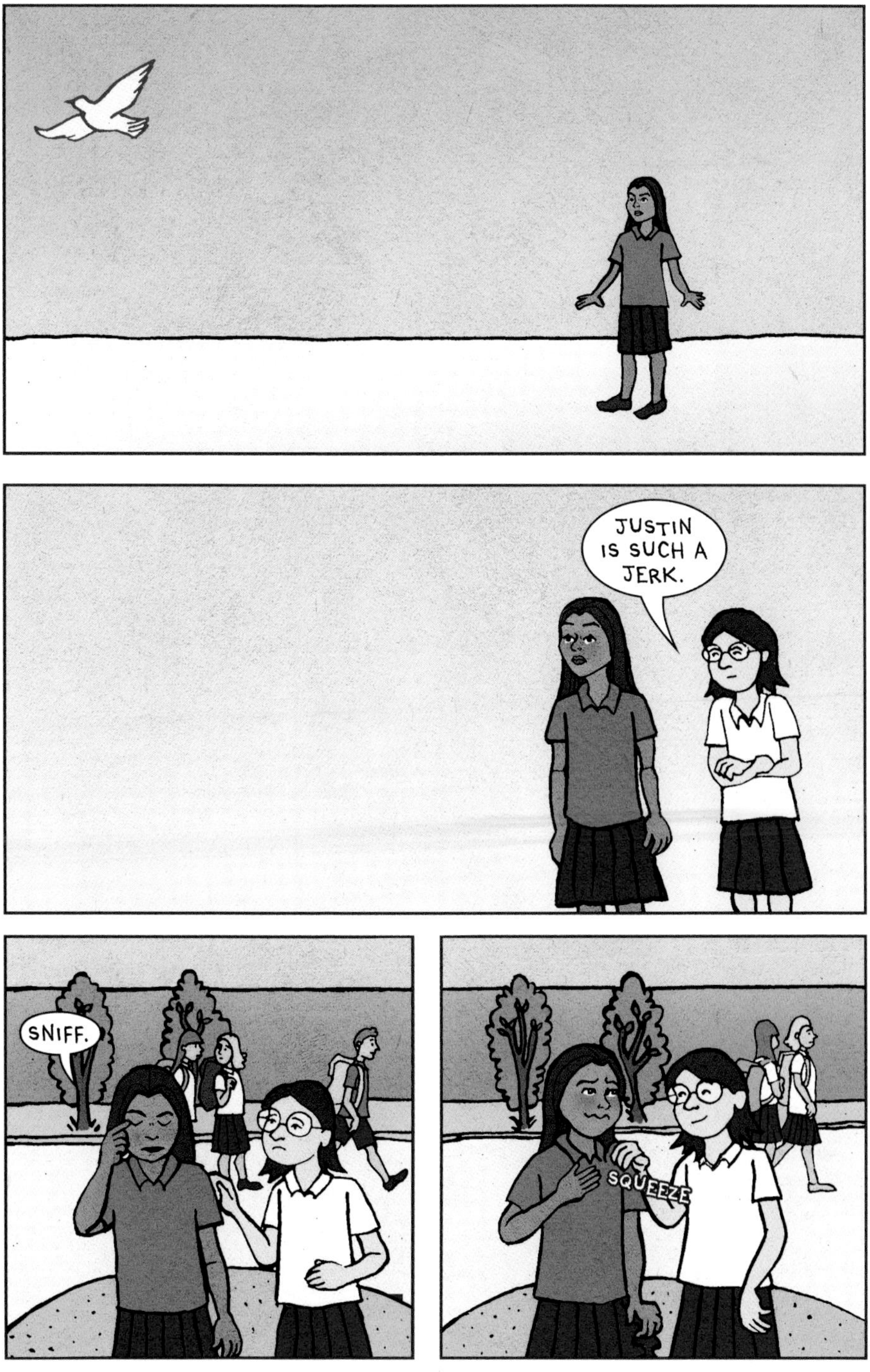
JUSTIN IS SUCH A JERK.
SNIFF.
SQUEEZE

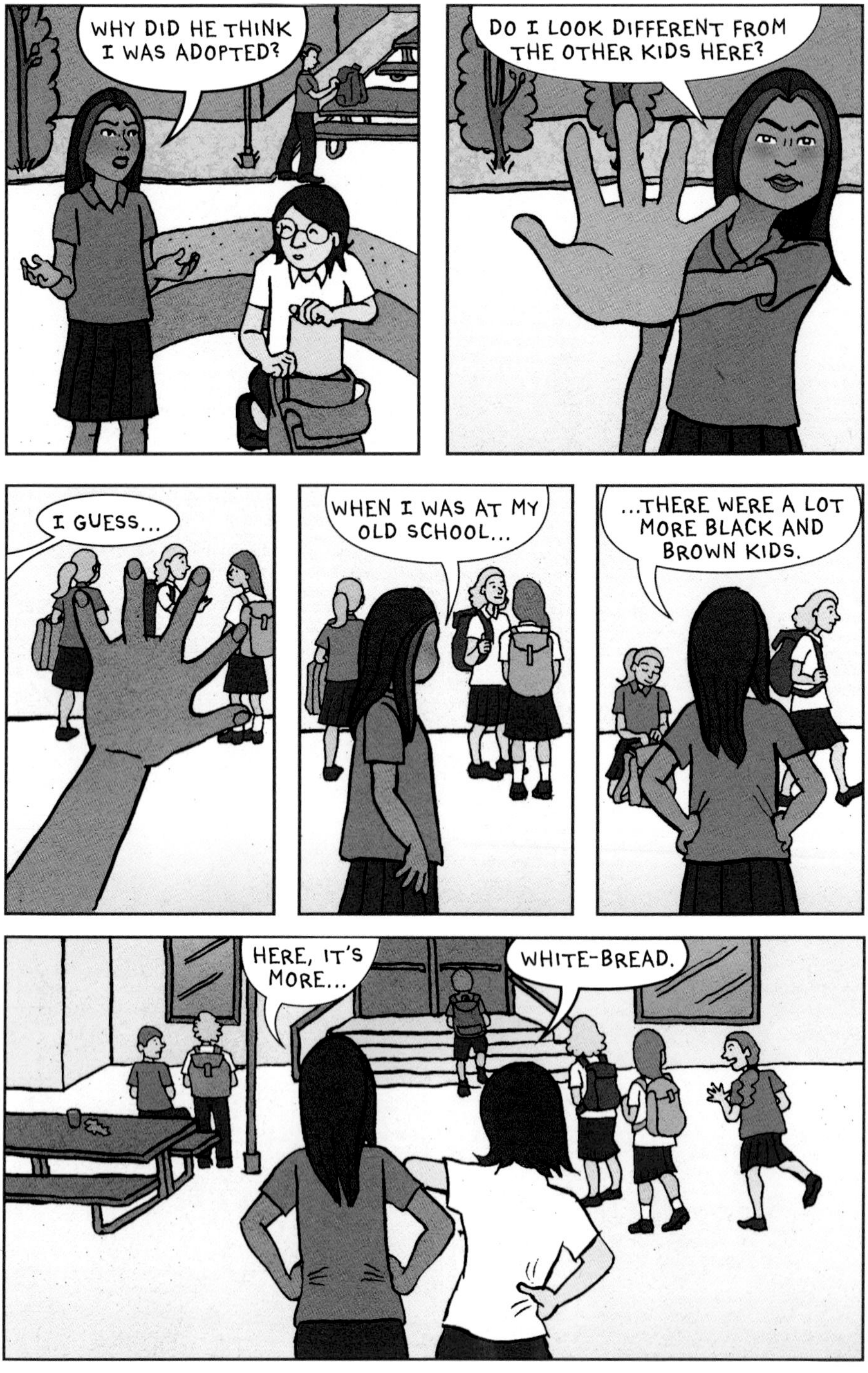
WHY DID HE THINK I WAS ADOPTED?
DO I LOOK DIFFERENT FROM THE OTHER KIDS HERE?
I GUESS...
WHEN I WAS AT MY OLD SCHOOL...
...THERE WERE A LOT MORE BLACK AND BROWN KIDS.
HERE, IT'S MORE...
WHITE-BREAD.

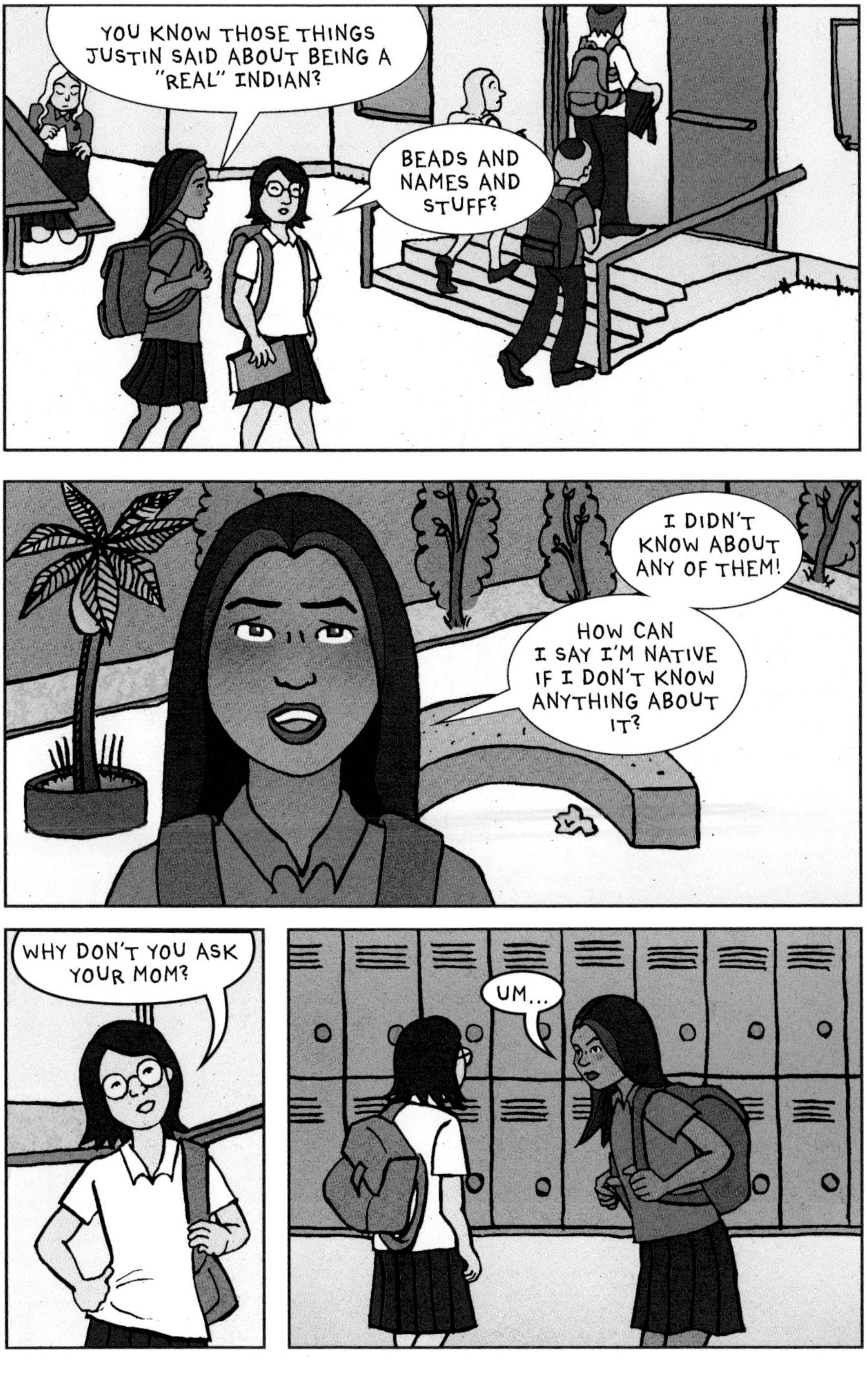
YOU KNOW THOSE THINGS JUSTIN SAID ABOUT BEING A "REAL" INDIAN?
BEADS AND NAMES AND STUFF?
I DIDN'T KNOW ABOUT ANY OF THEM!
HOW CAN I SAY I'M NATIVE IF I DON'T KNOW ANYTHING ABOUT IT?
WHY DON'T YOU ASK YOUR MOM?
UM...

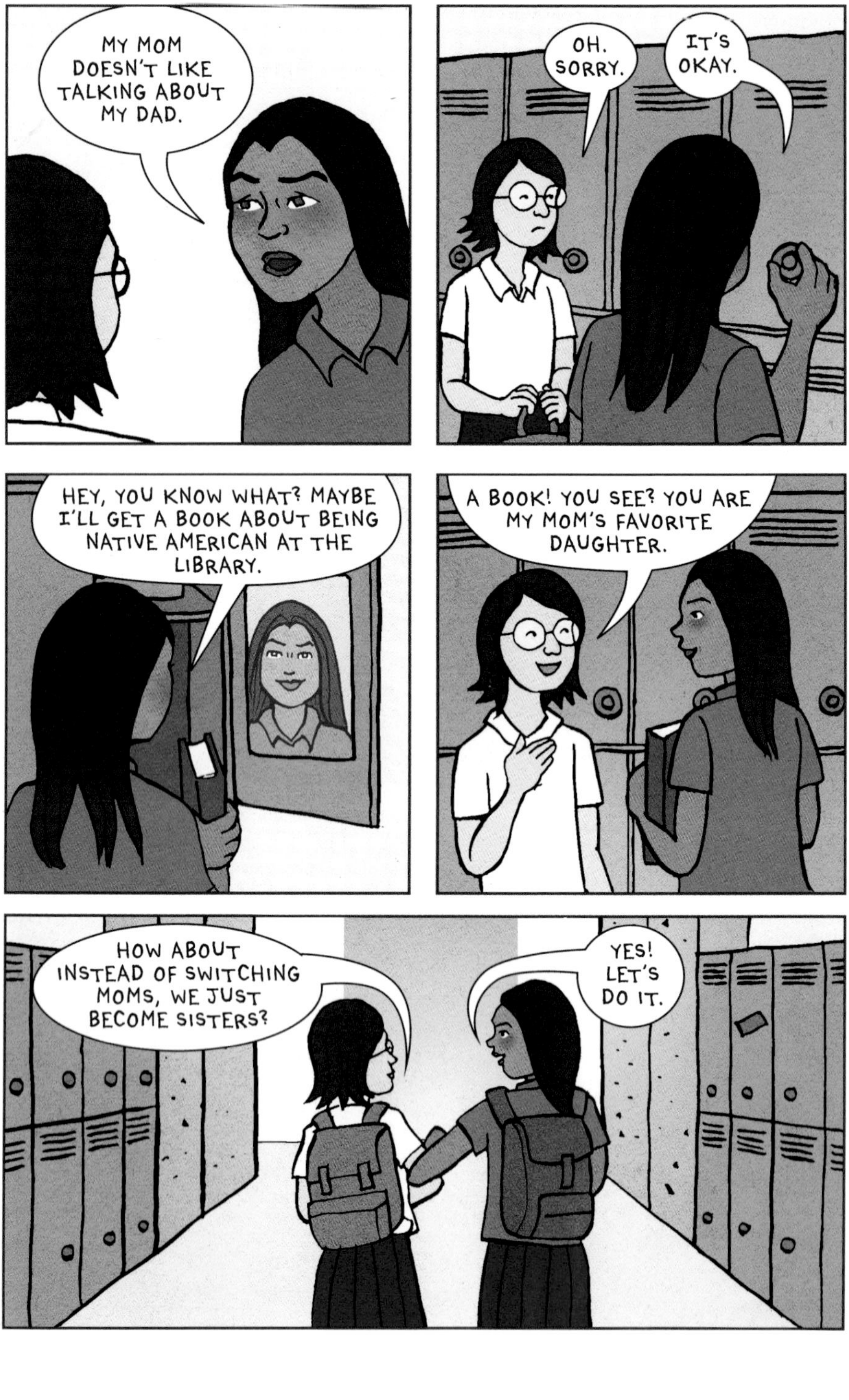
MY MOM DOESN'T LIKE TALKING ABOUT MY DAD.
OH. SORRY.
IT'S OKAY.
HEY, YOU KNOW WHAT? MAYBE I'LL GET A BOOK ABOUT BEING NATIVE AMERICAN AT THE LIBRARY.
A BOOK! YOU SEE? YOU ARE MY MOM'S FAVORITE DAUGHTER.
HOW ABOUT INSTEAD OF SWITCHING MOMS, WE JUST BECOME SISTERS?
YES! LET'S DO IT.

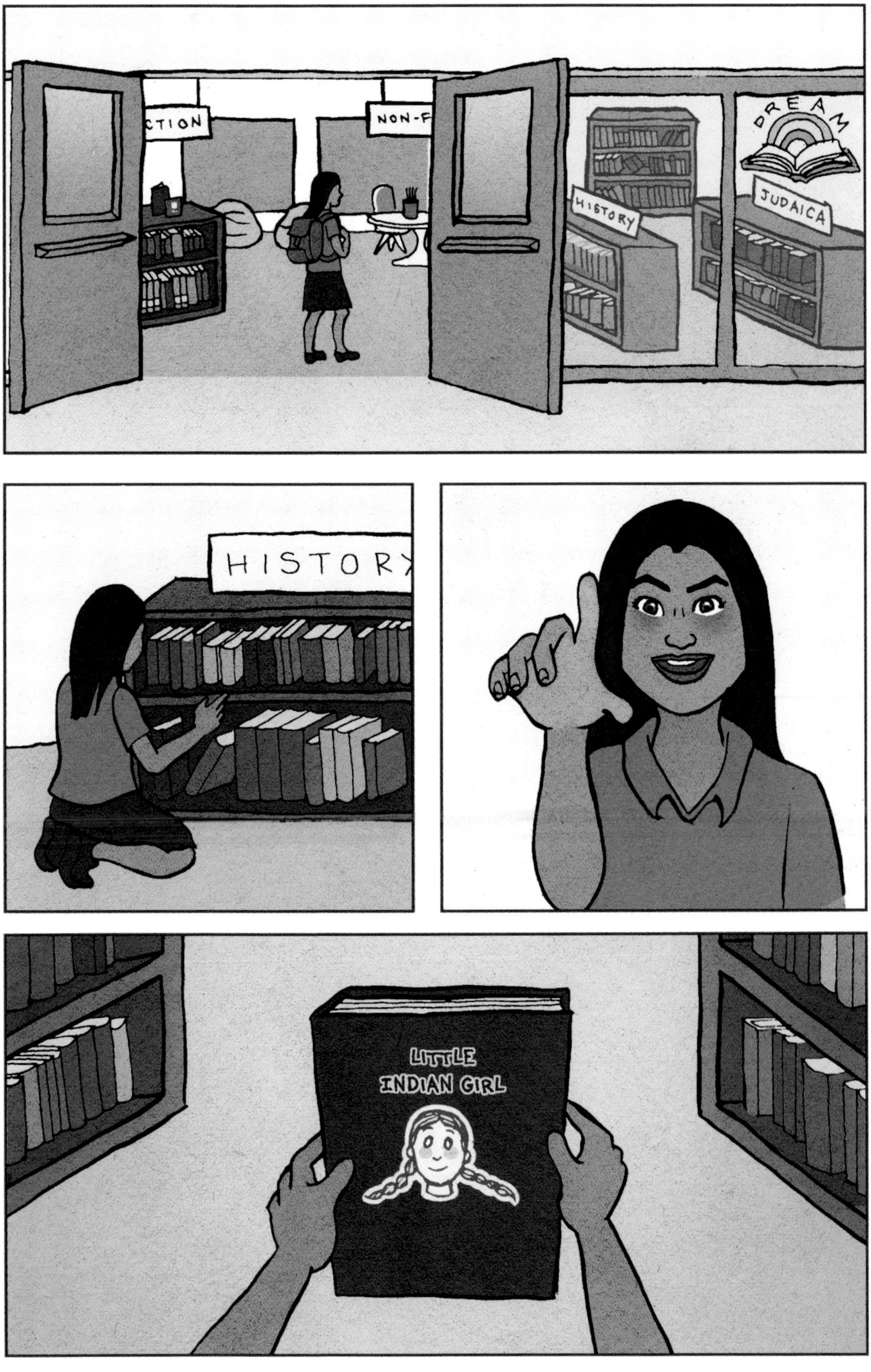
CTION
NON-F
HISTORY
DREAM
JUDAICA
HISTOR
LITTLE
INDIAN GIRL

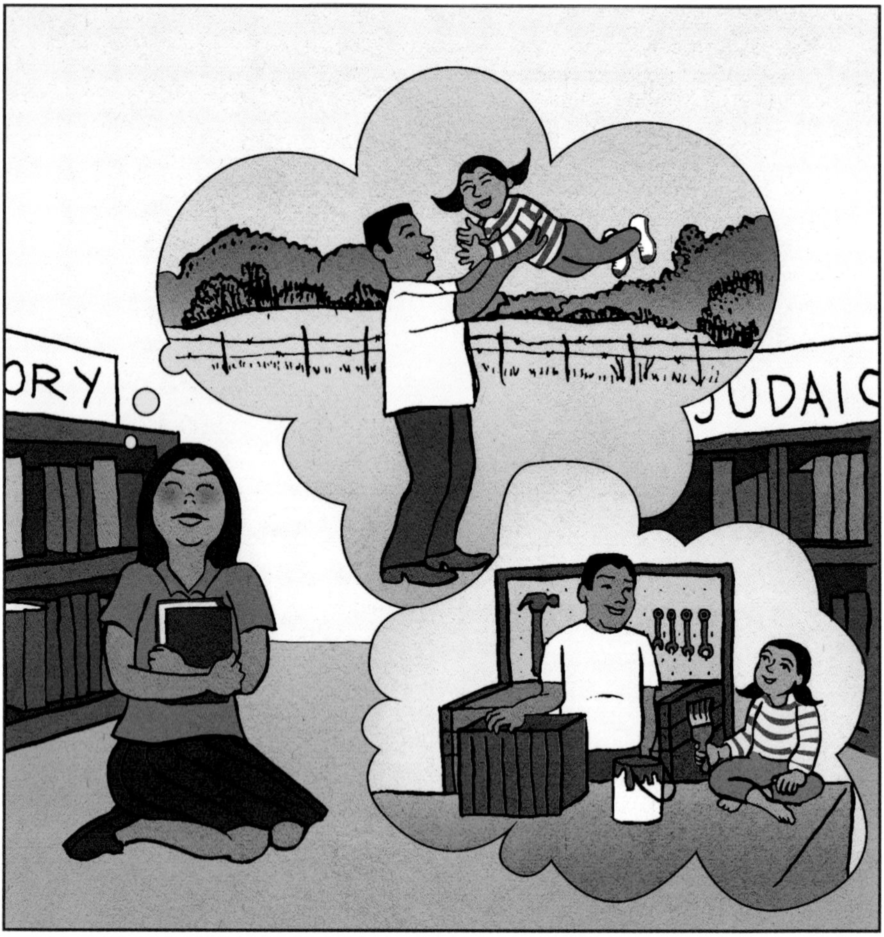
ORY
JUDAIC

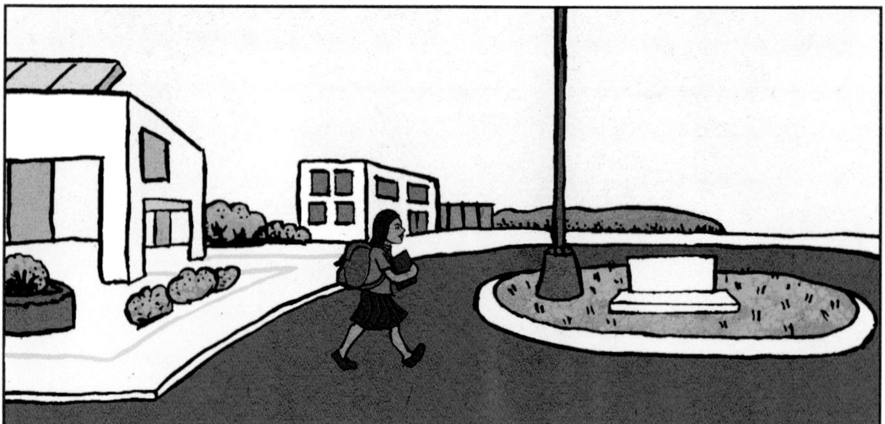

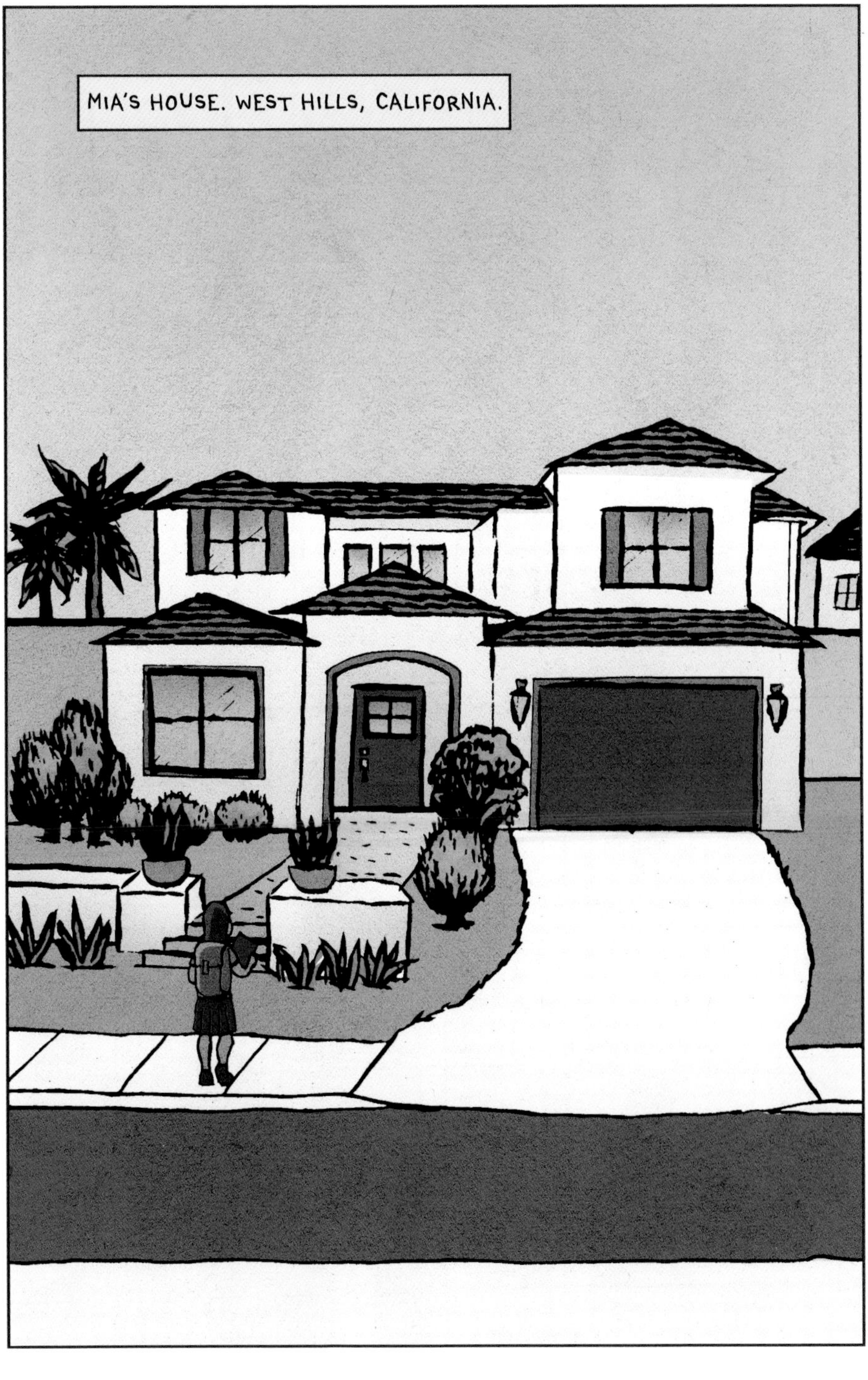
MIA'S HOUSE. WEST HILLS, CALIFORNIA.

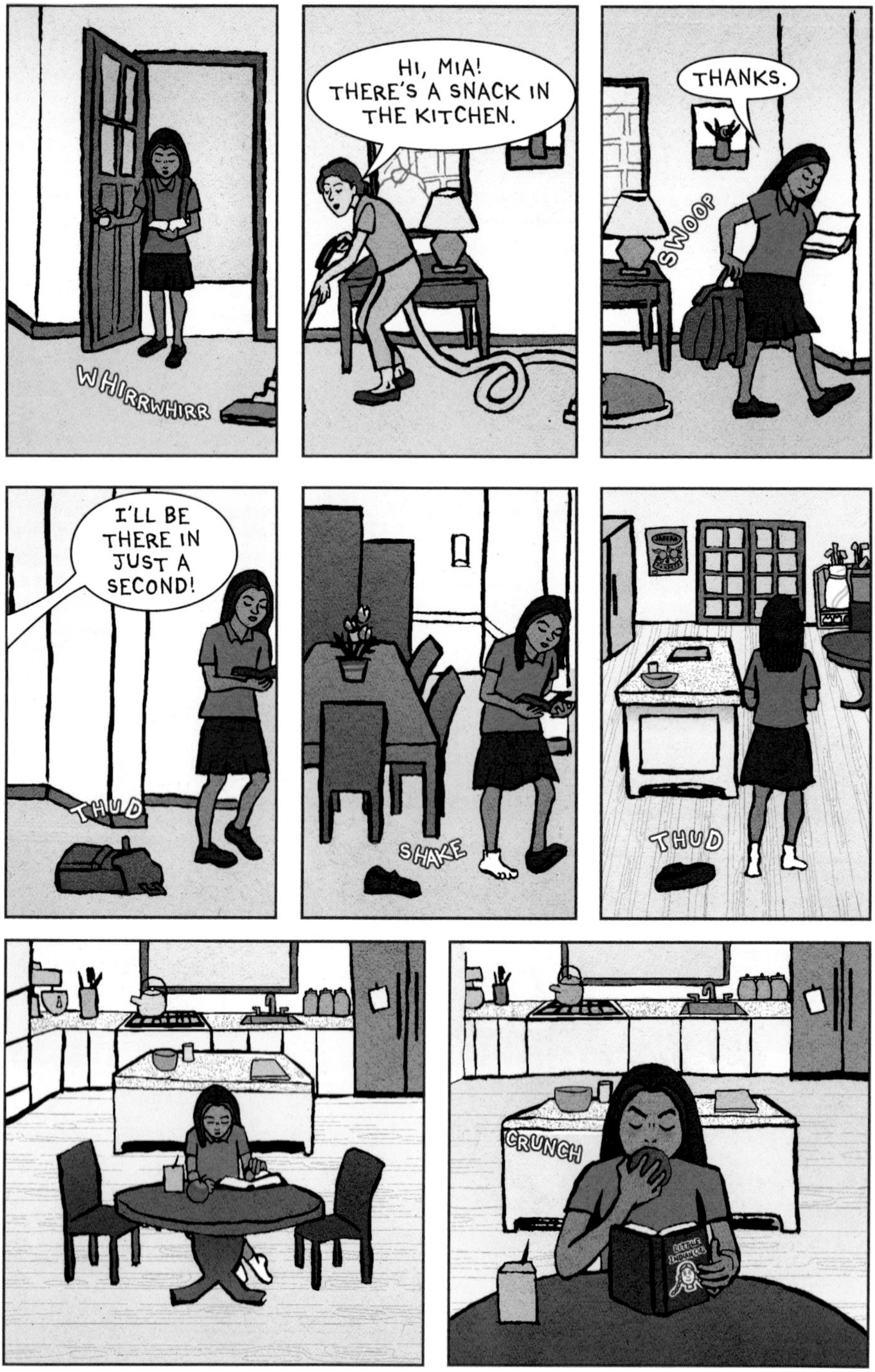
WHIRRWHIRR
HI, MIA! THERE'S A SNACK IN THE KITCHEN.
THANKS.
SWOOP
I'LL BE THERE IN JUST A SECOND!
THUD
SHAKE
THUD
CRUNCH

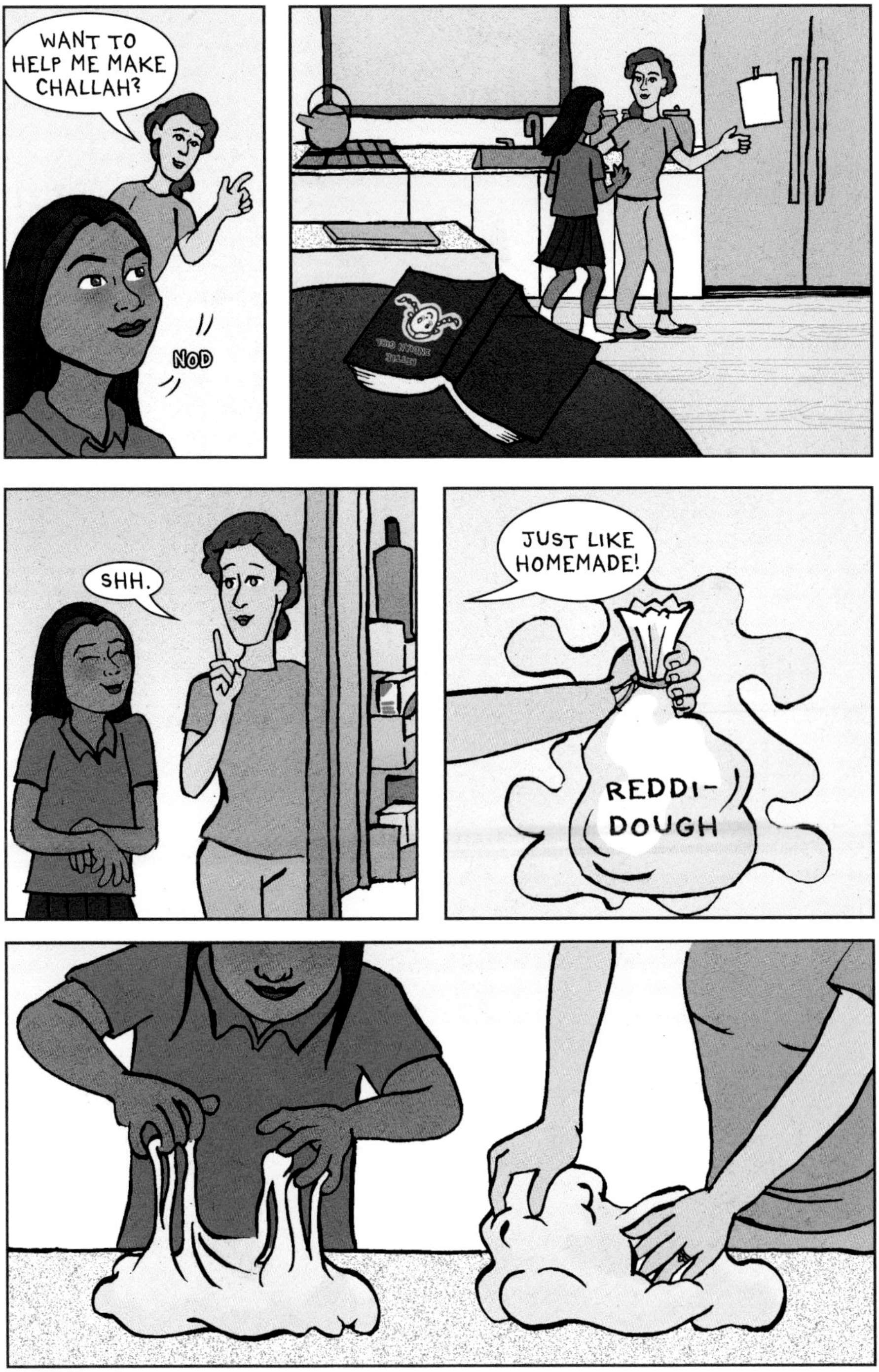
WANT TO HELP ME MAKE CHALLAH?
NOD
SHH.
JUST LIKE HOMEMADE!
REDDI-DOUGH

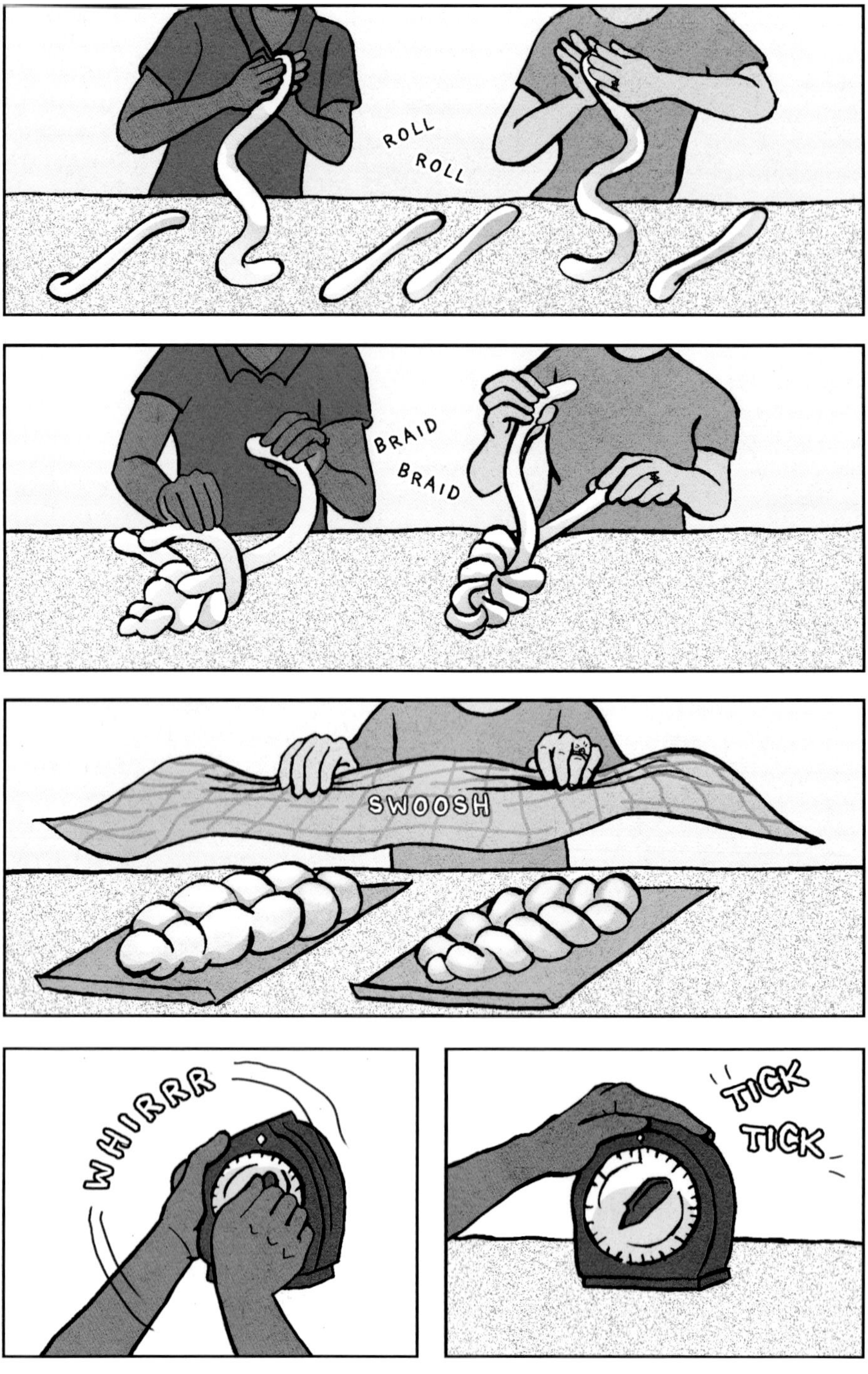
ROLL
ROLL
BRAID
BRAID
SWOOSH
WHIRRR
TICK
TICK

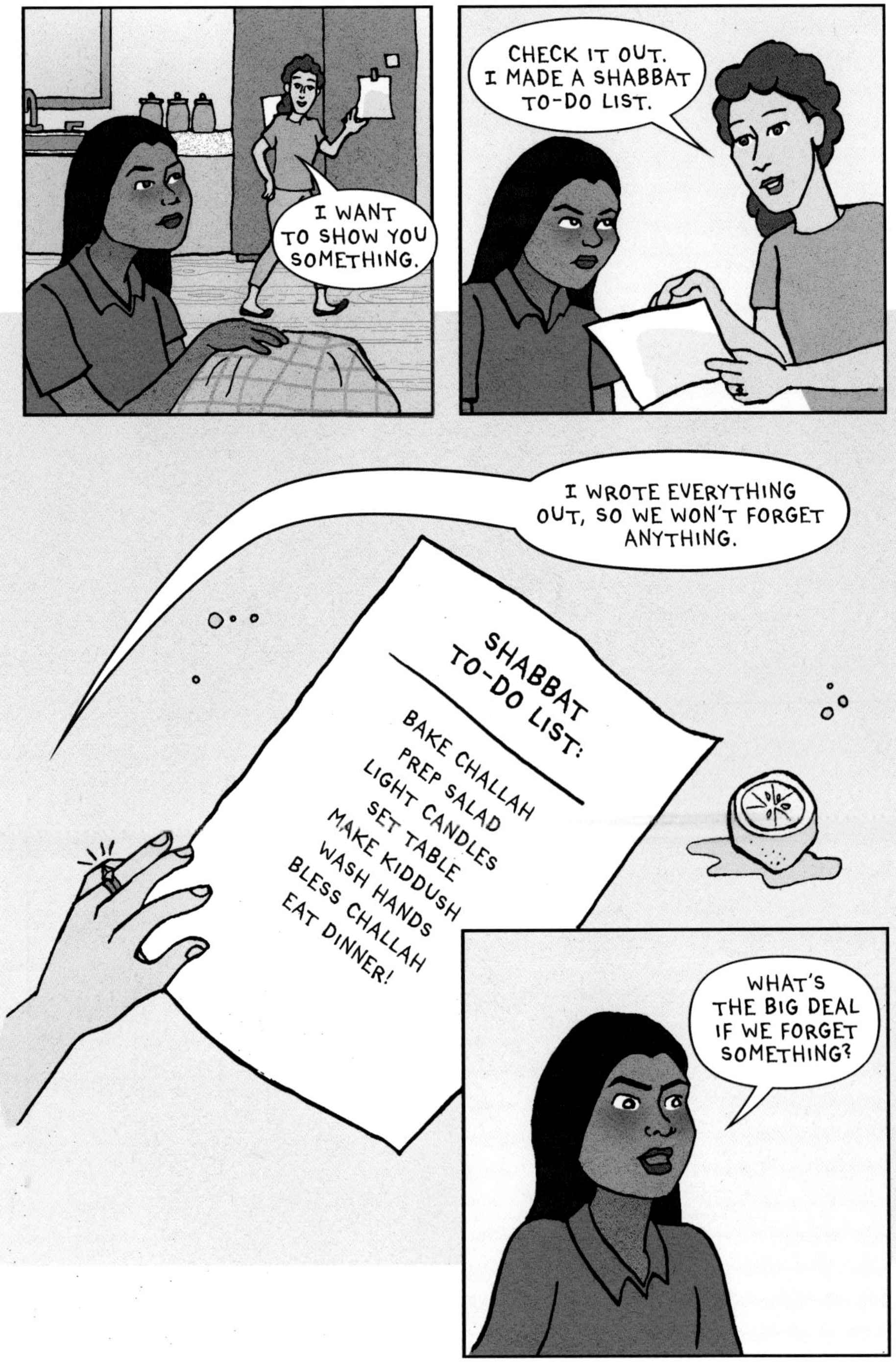
I WANT TO SHOW YOU SOMETHING.
CHECK IT OUT. I MADE A SHABBAT TO-DO LIST.
I WROTE EVERYTHING OUT, SO WE WON'T FORGET ANYTHING.
SHABBAT TO-DO LIST:
BAKE CHALLAH
PREP SALAD
LIGHT CANDLES
SET TABLE
MAKE KIDDUSH
WASH HANDS
BLESS CHALLAH
EAT DINNER!
WHAT'S THE BIG DEAL IF WE FORGET SOMETHING?

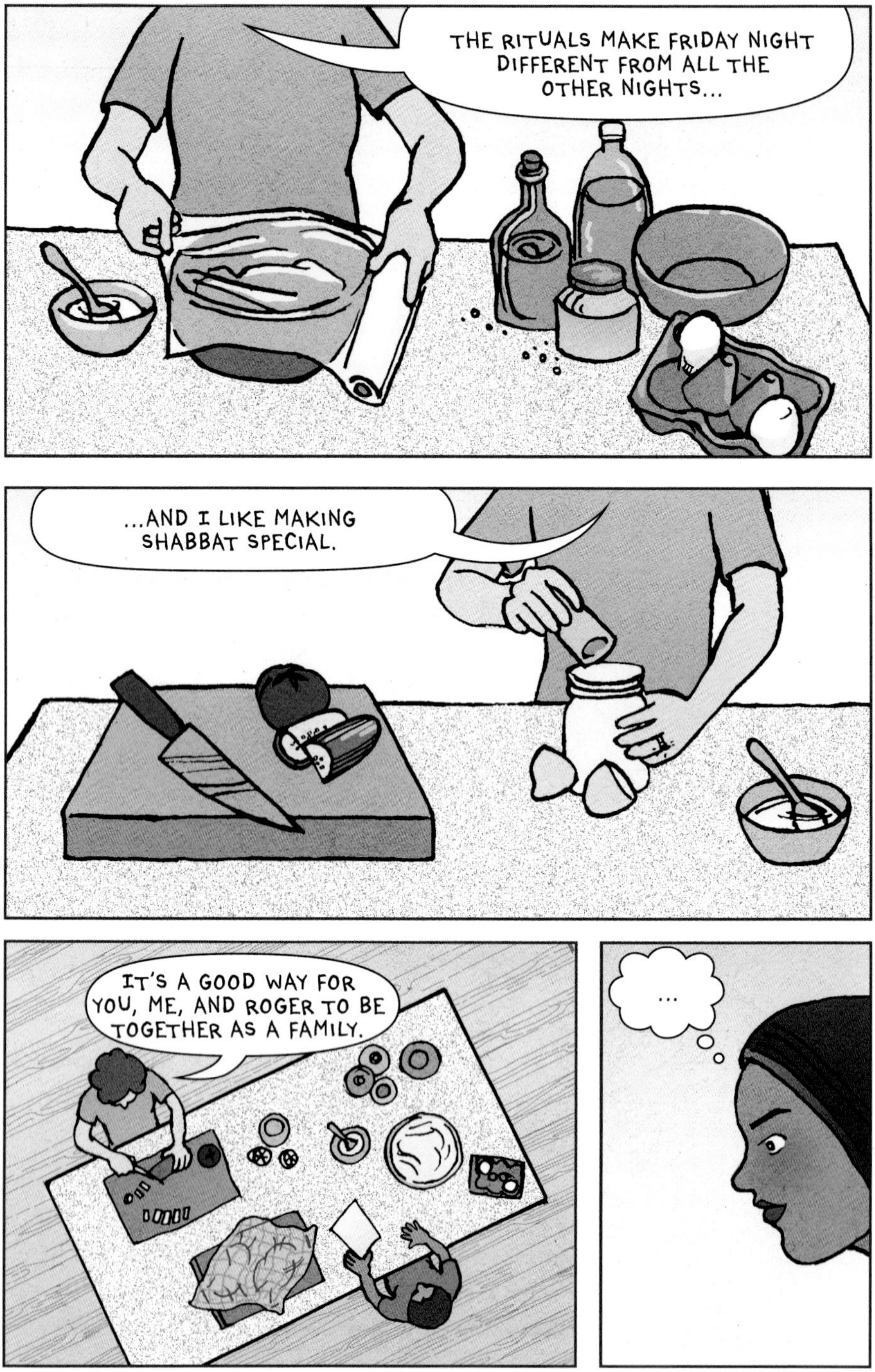
THE RITUALS MAKE FRIDAY NIGHT DIFFERENT FROM ALL THE OTHER NIGHTS...
...AND I LIKE MAKING SHABBAT SPECIAL.
IT'S A GOOD WAY FOR YOU, ME, AND ROGER TO BE TOGETHER AS A FAMILY.
...

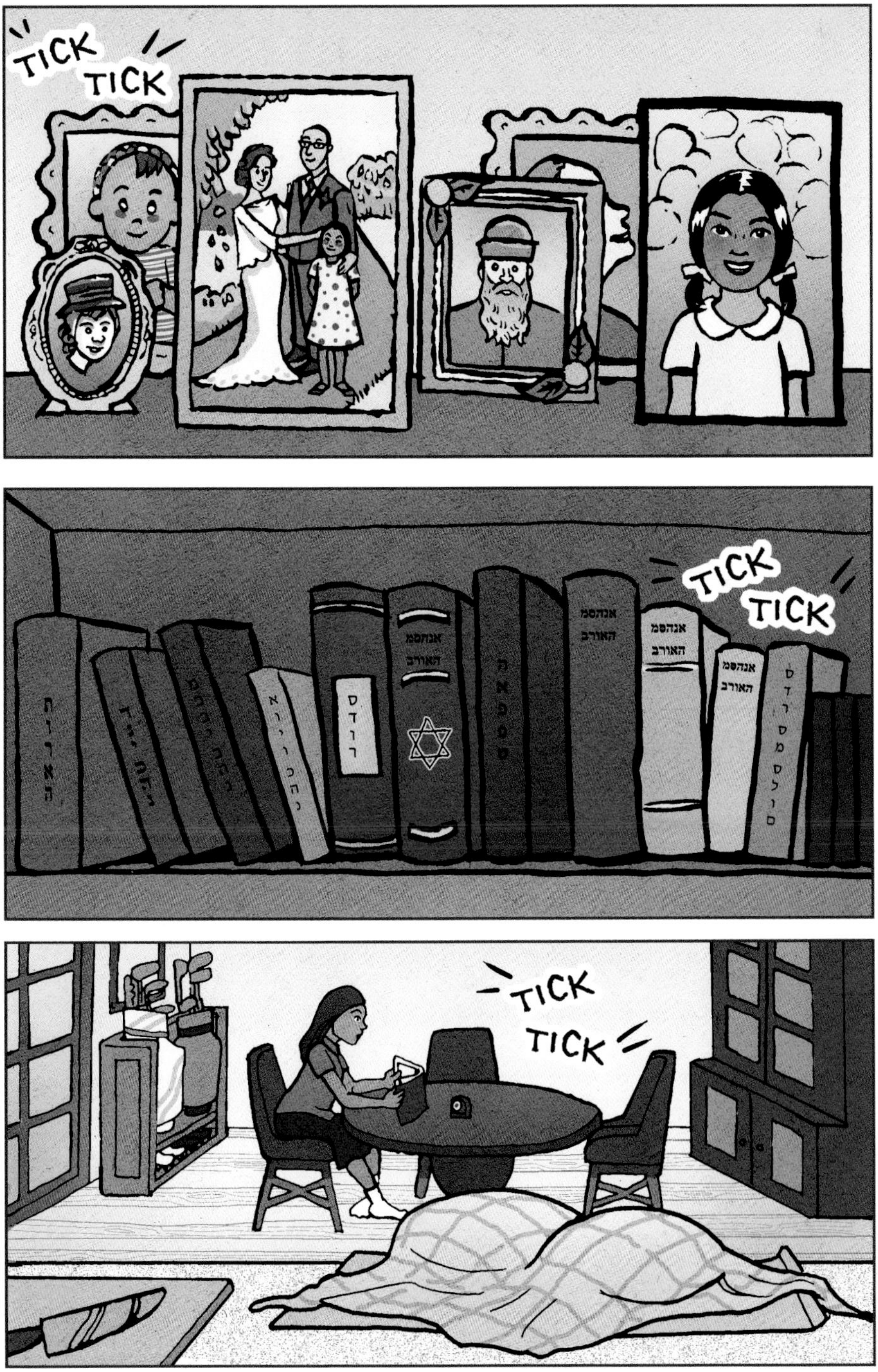
TICK
TICK
TICK
TICK
TICK
TICK

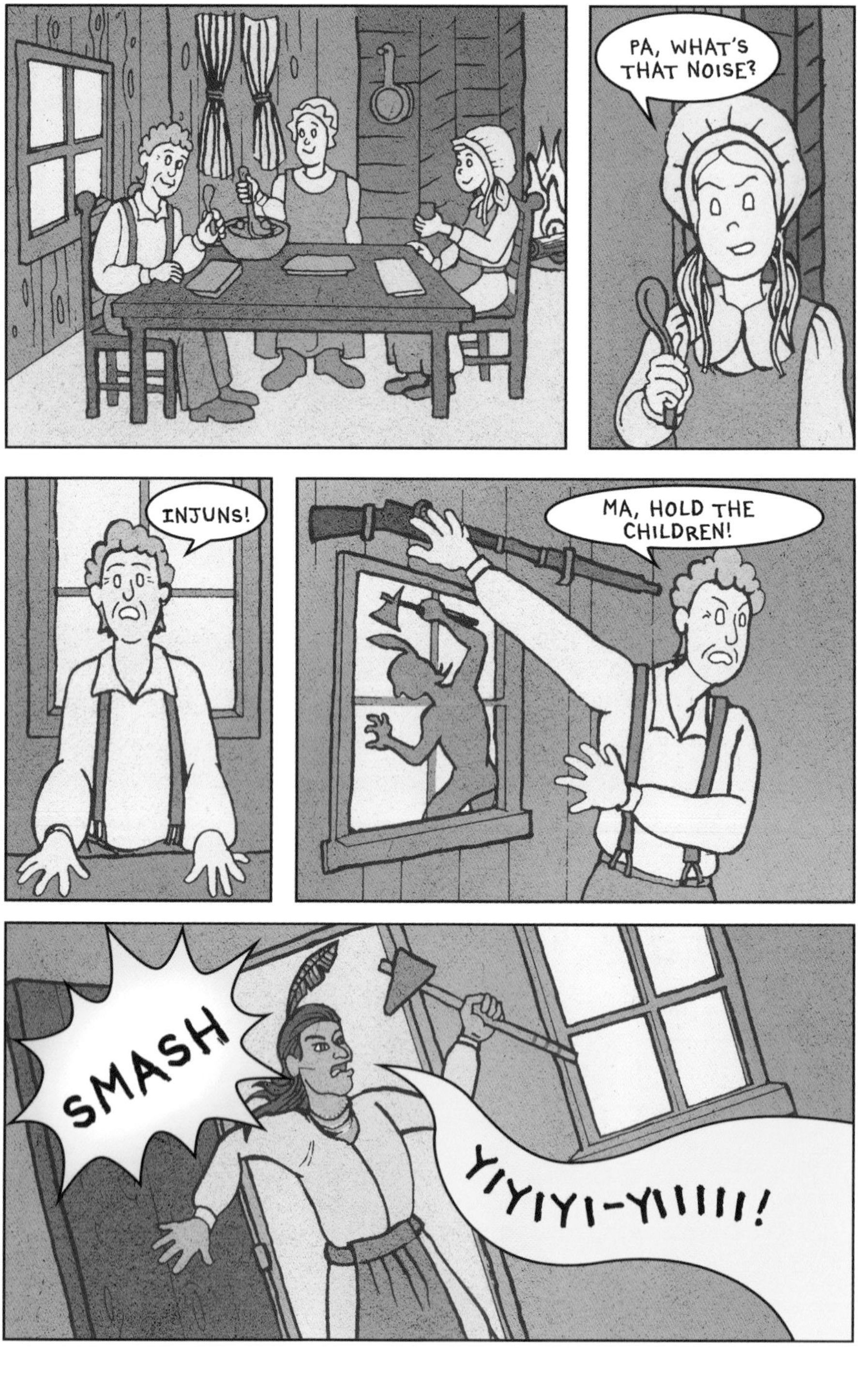
PA, WHAT'S THAT NOISE?
INJUNS!
MA, HOLD THE CHILDREN!
SMASH
YIYIYI-YIIIII!

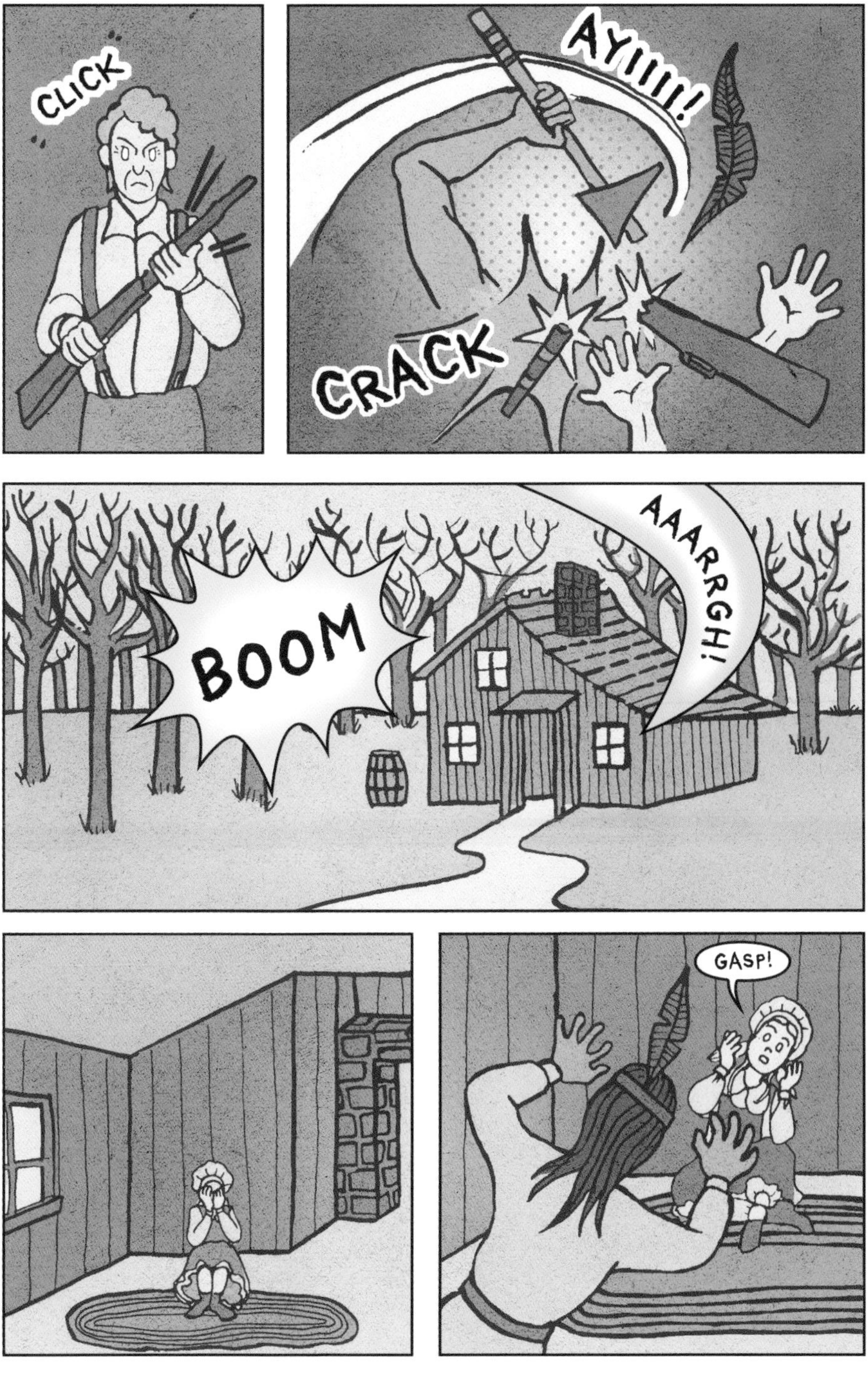
CLICK
AYIIIII!
CRACK
BOOM
AAARRGH!
GASP!

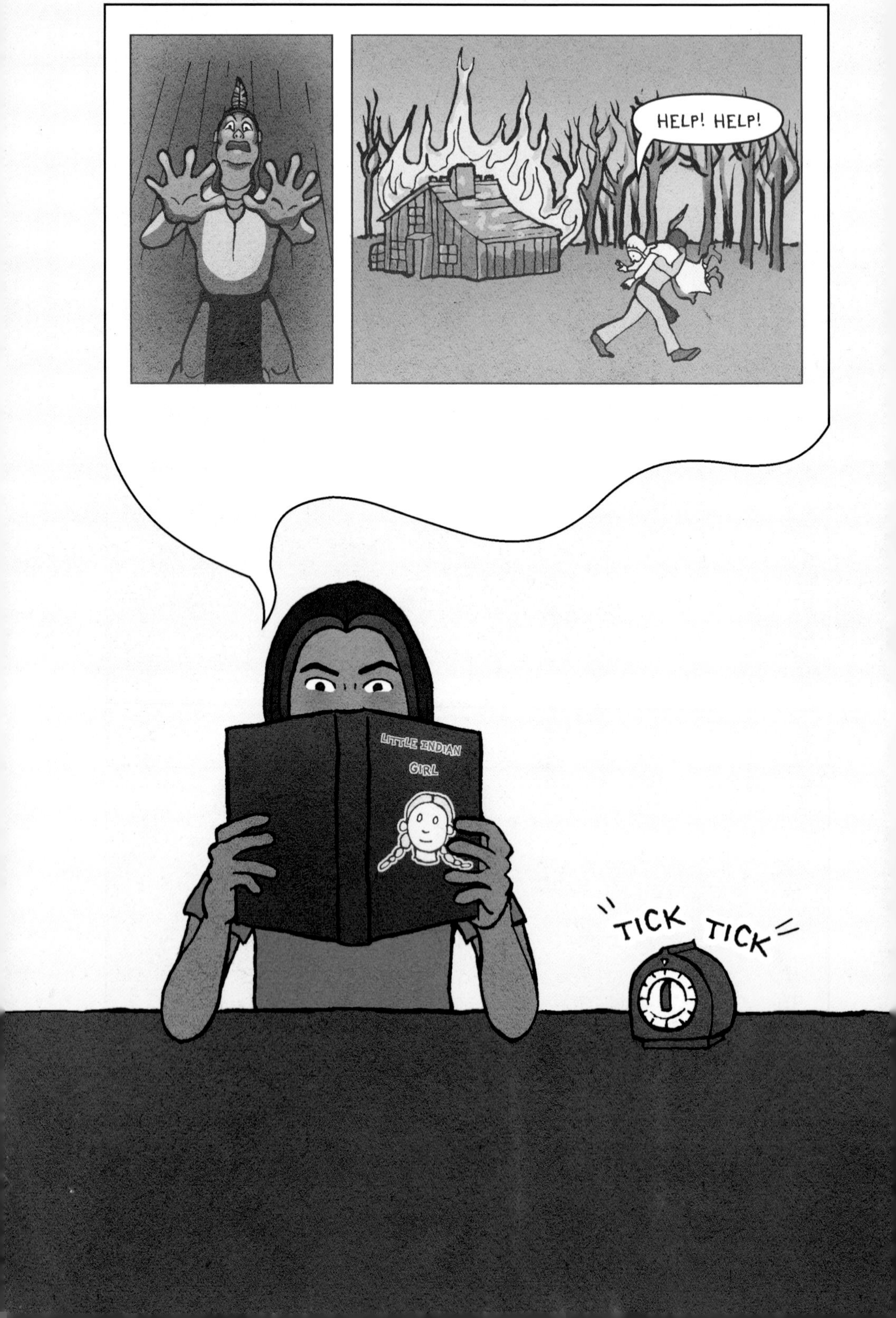
HELP! HELP!
LITTLE INDIAN GIRL
TICK TICK

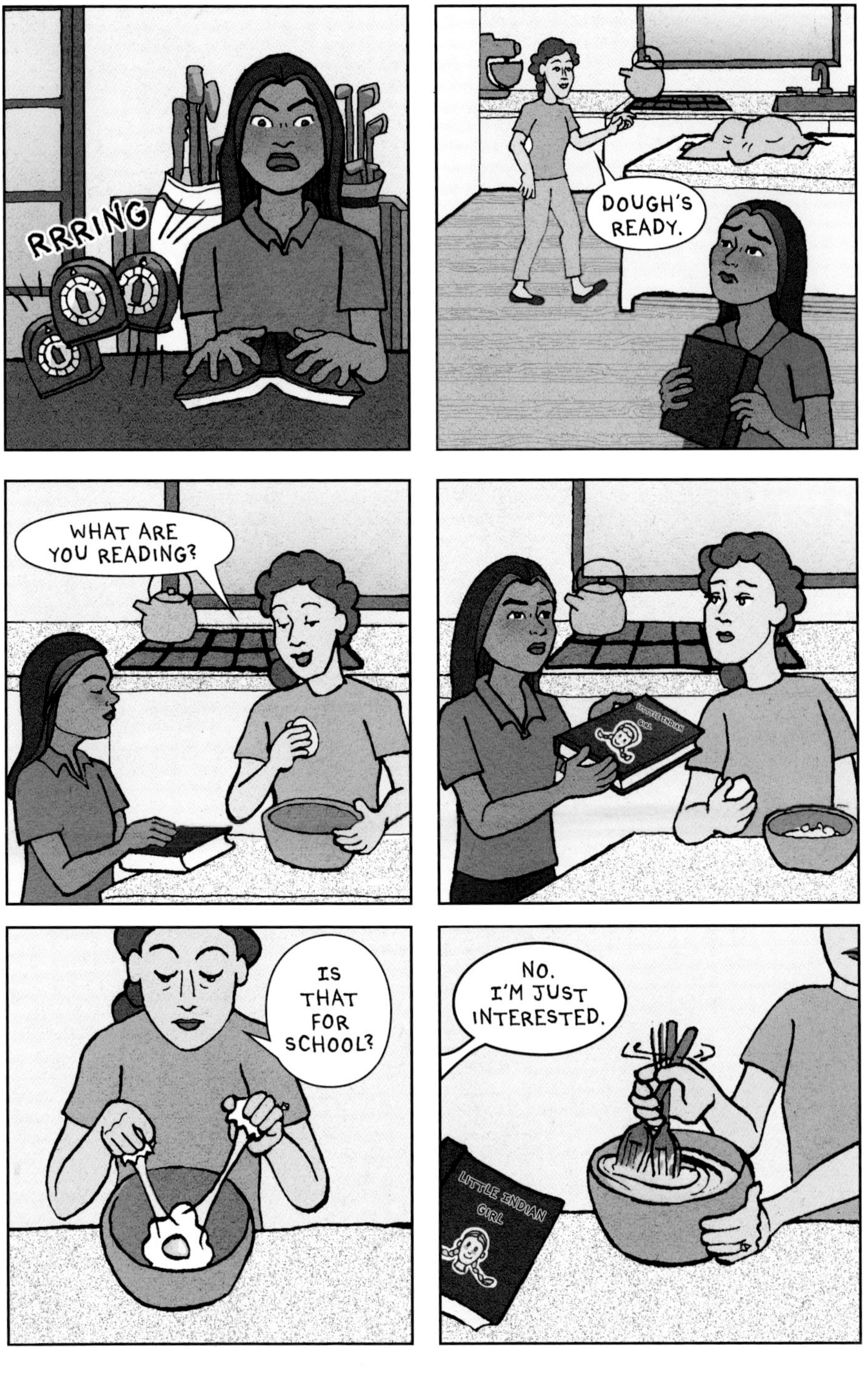
RRRING
DOUGH'S READY.
WHAT ARE YOU READING?
LITTLE INDIAN GIRL
IS THAT FOR SCHOOL?
NO. I'M JUST INTERESTED.
LITTLE INDIAN GIRL

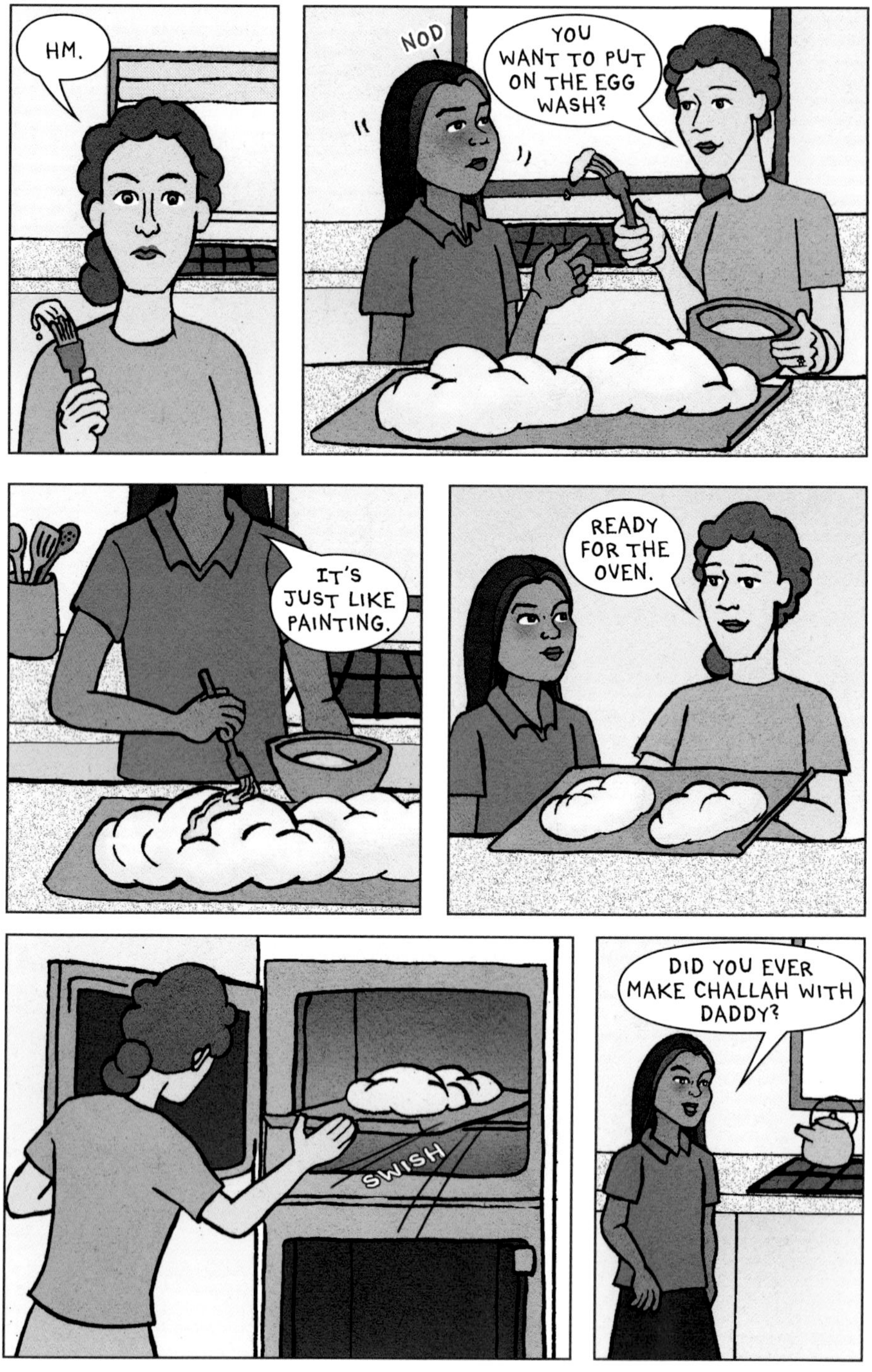
HM.
NOD
YOU WANT TO PUT ON THE EGG WASH?
IT'S JUST LIKE PAINTING.
READY FOR THE OVEN.
SWISH
DID YOU EVER MAKE CHALLAH WITH DADDY?

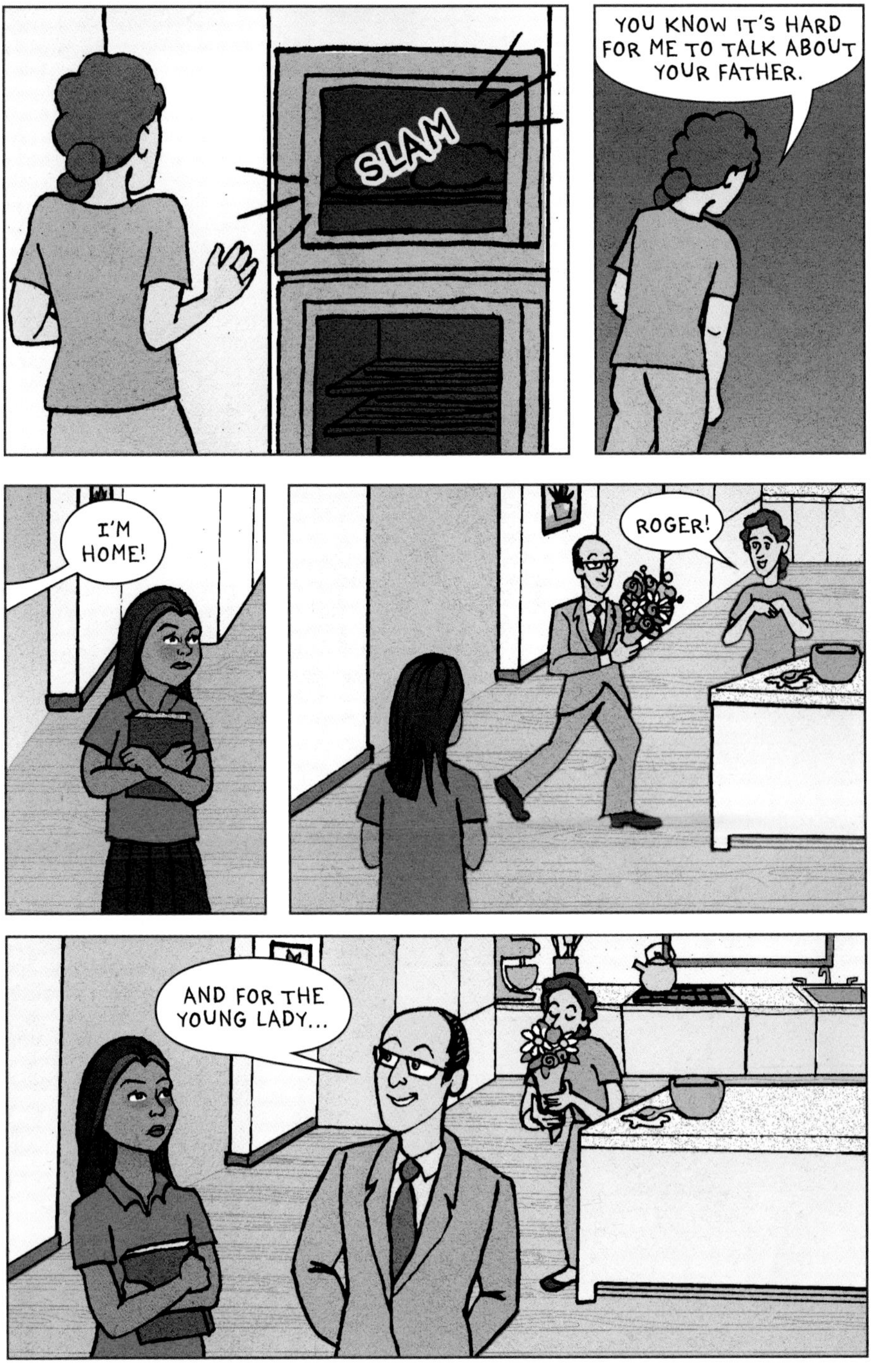
SLAM
YOU KNOW IT'S HARD FOR ME TO TALK ABOUT YOUR FATHER.
I'M HOME!
ROGER!
AND FOR THE YOUNG LADY...

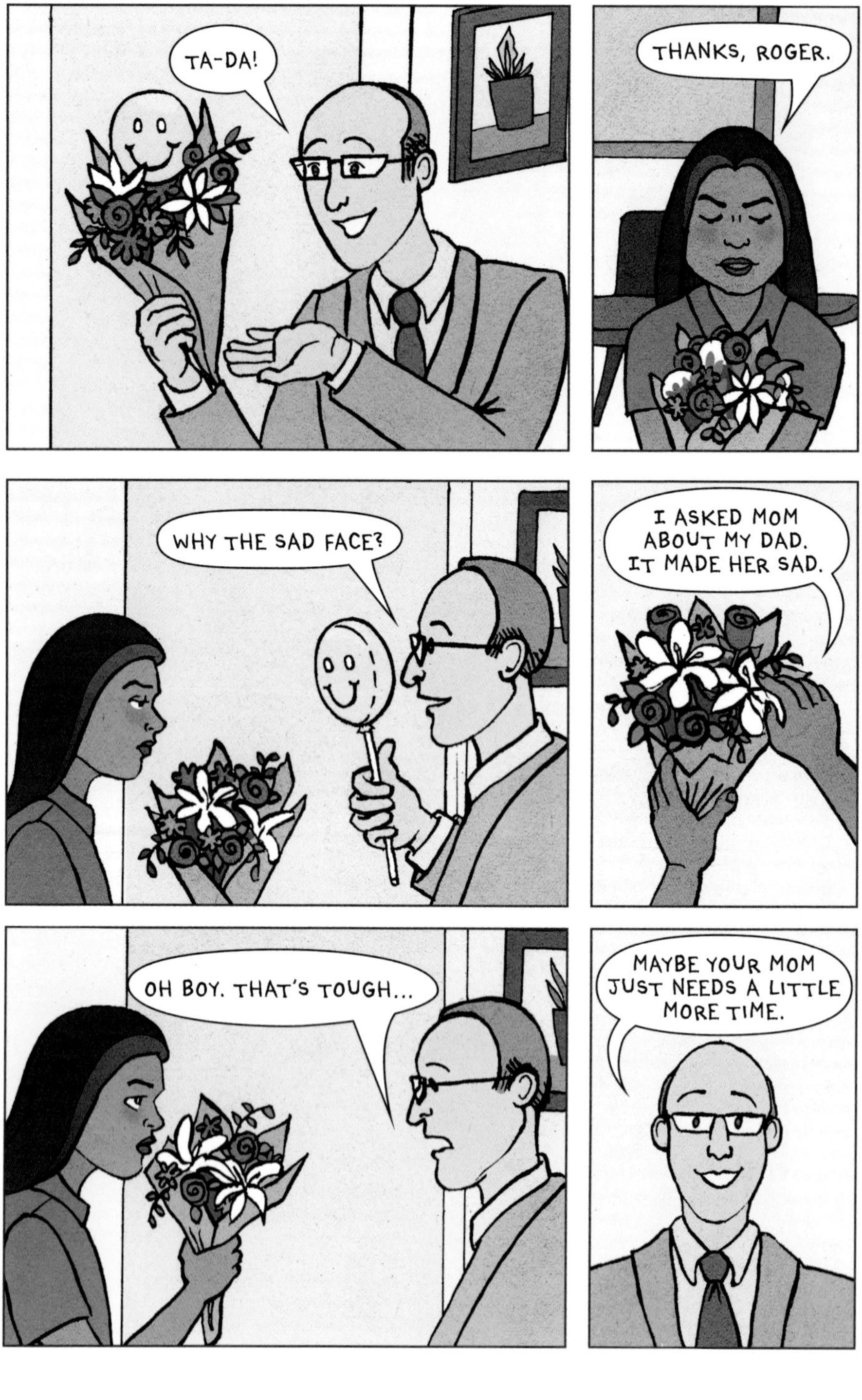
TA-DA!
THANKS, ROGER.
WHY THE SAD FACE?
I ASKED MOM ABOUT MY DAD. IT MADE HER SAD.
OH BOY. THAT'S TOUGH...
MAYBE YOUR MOM JUST NEEDS A LITTLE MORE TIME.

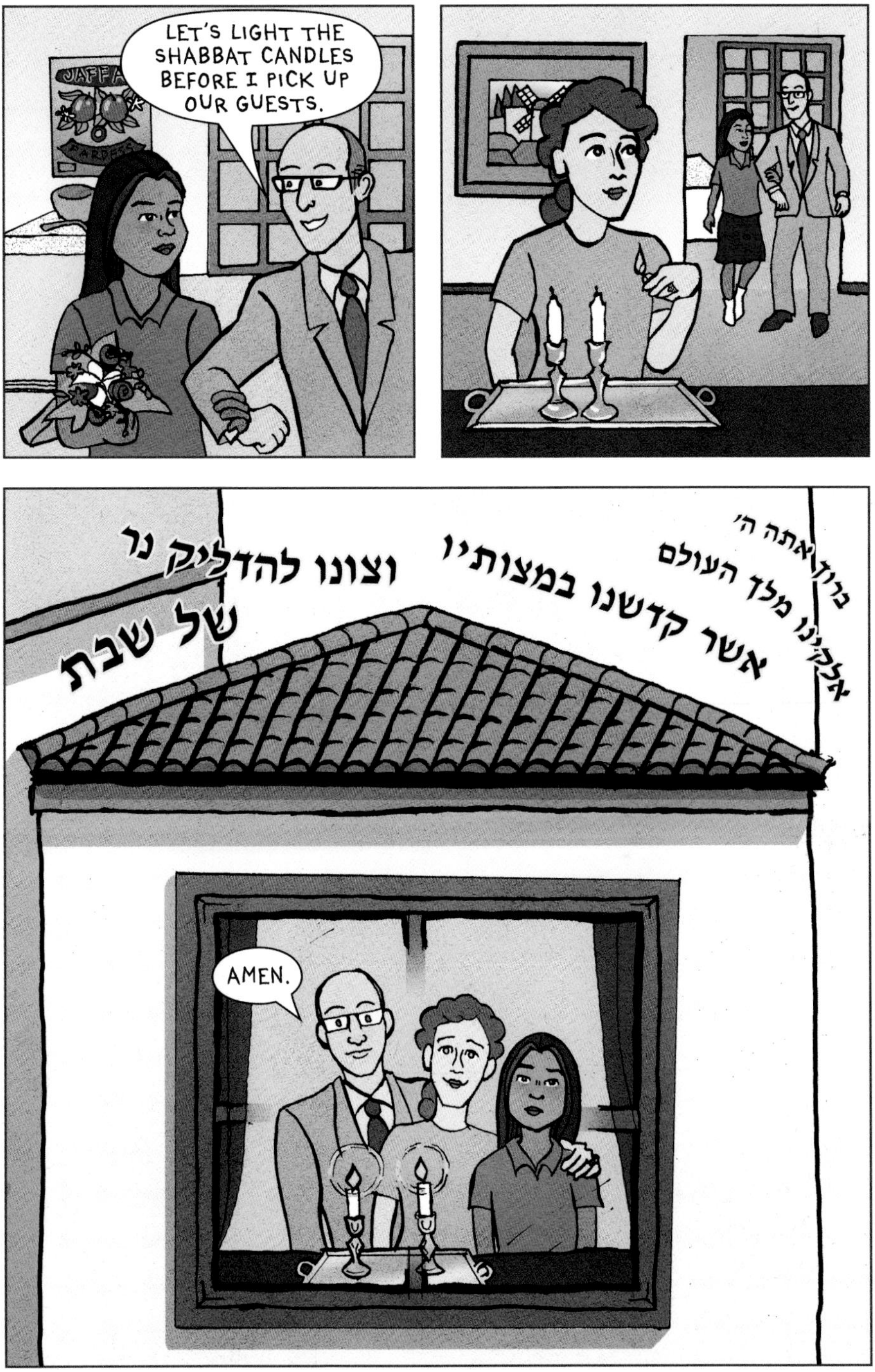
LET'S LIGHT THE SHABBAT CANDLES BEFORE I PICK UP OUR GUESTS.
JAFFA
ברוך אתה ה׳
אלקינו מלך העולם
אשר קדשנו במצותיו
וצונו להדליק נר
של שבת
AMEN.

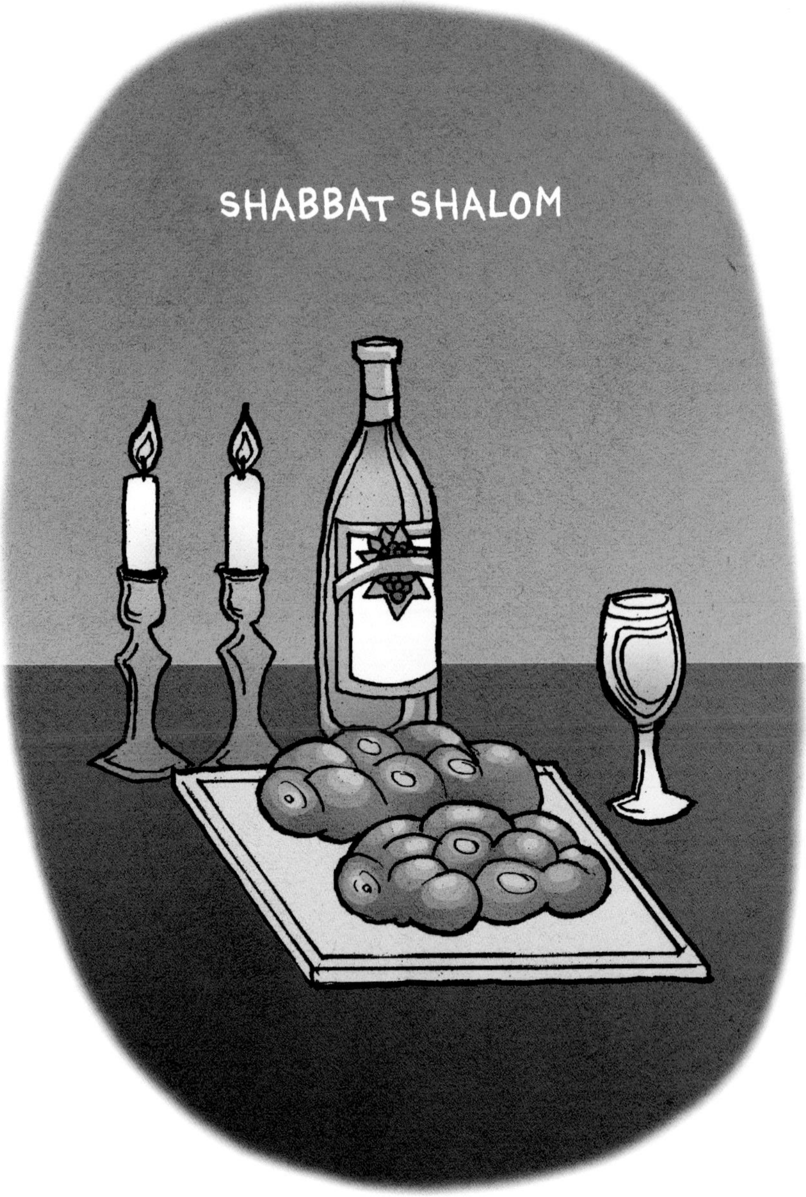
SHABBAT SHALOM

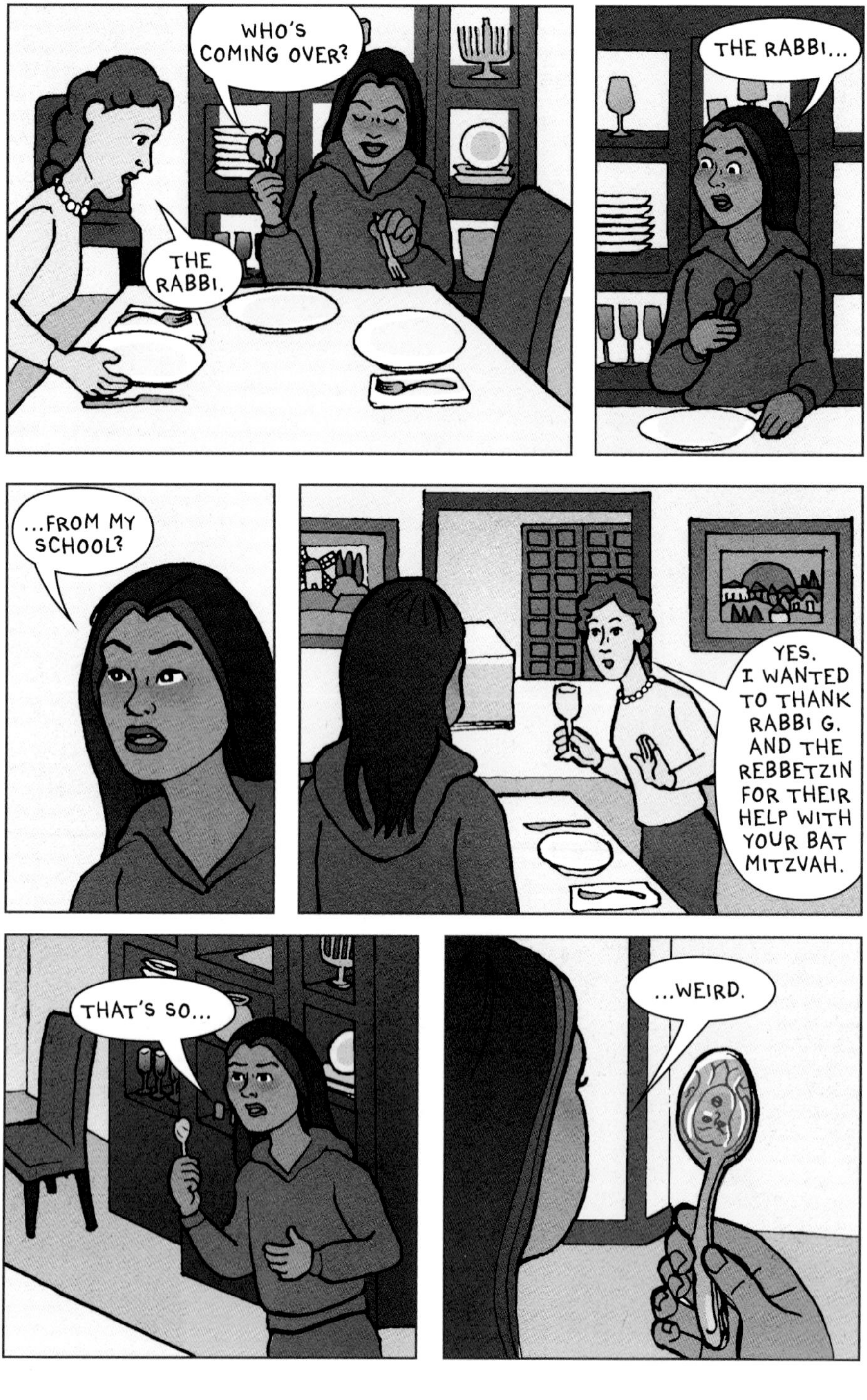
WHO'S COMING OVER?
THE RABBI.
THE RABBI...
...FROM MY SCHOOL?
YES. I WANTED TO THANK RABBI G. AND THE REBBETZIN FOR THEIR HELP WITH YOUR BAT MITZVAH.
THAT'S SO...
...WEIRD.

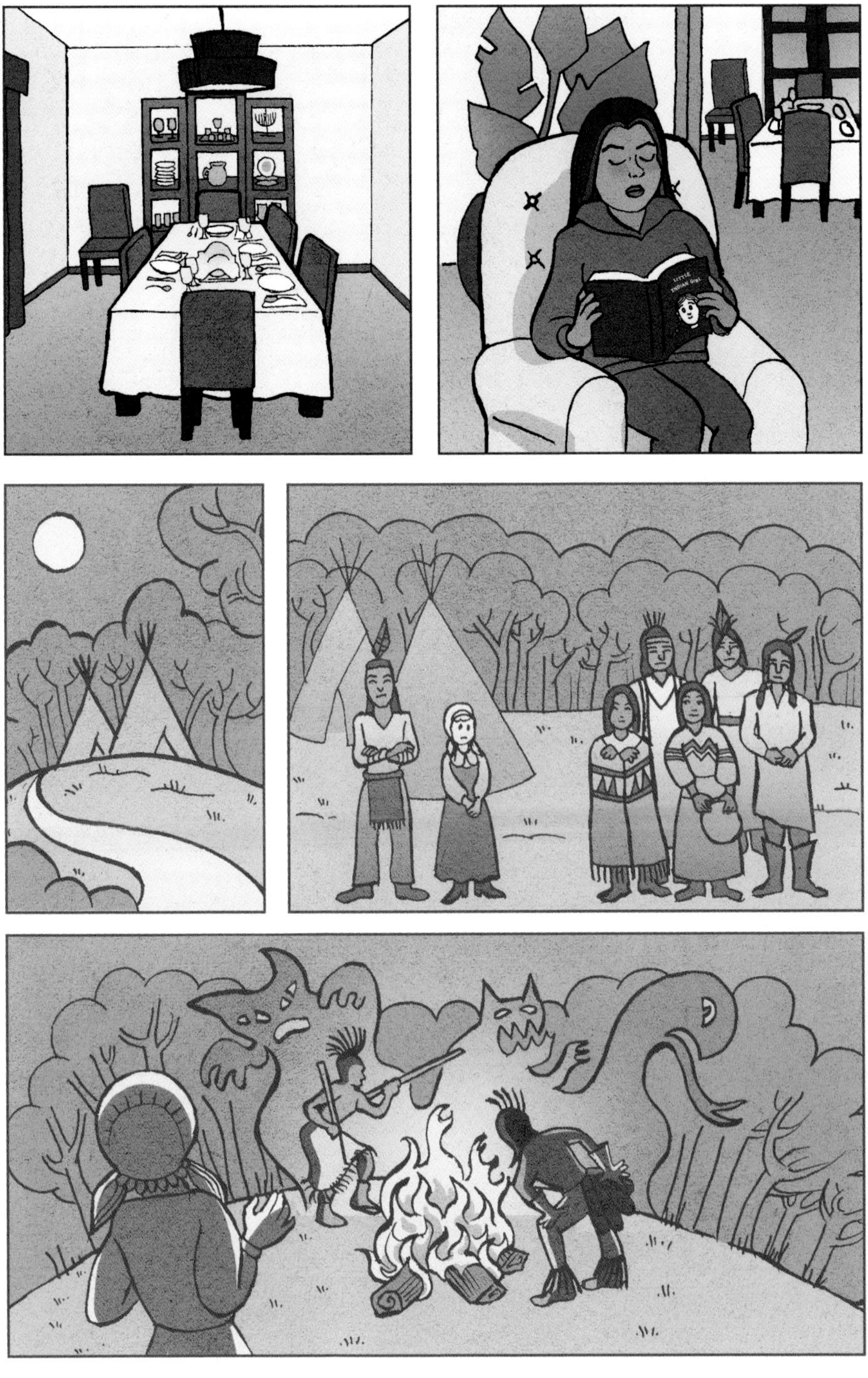
LITTLE INDIAN GIRL

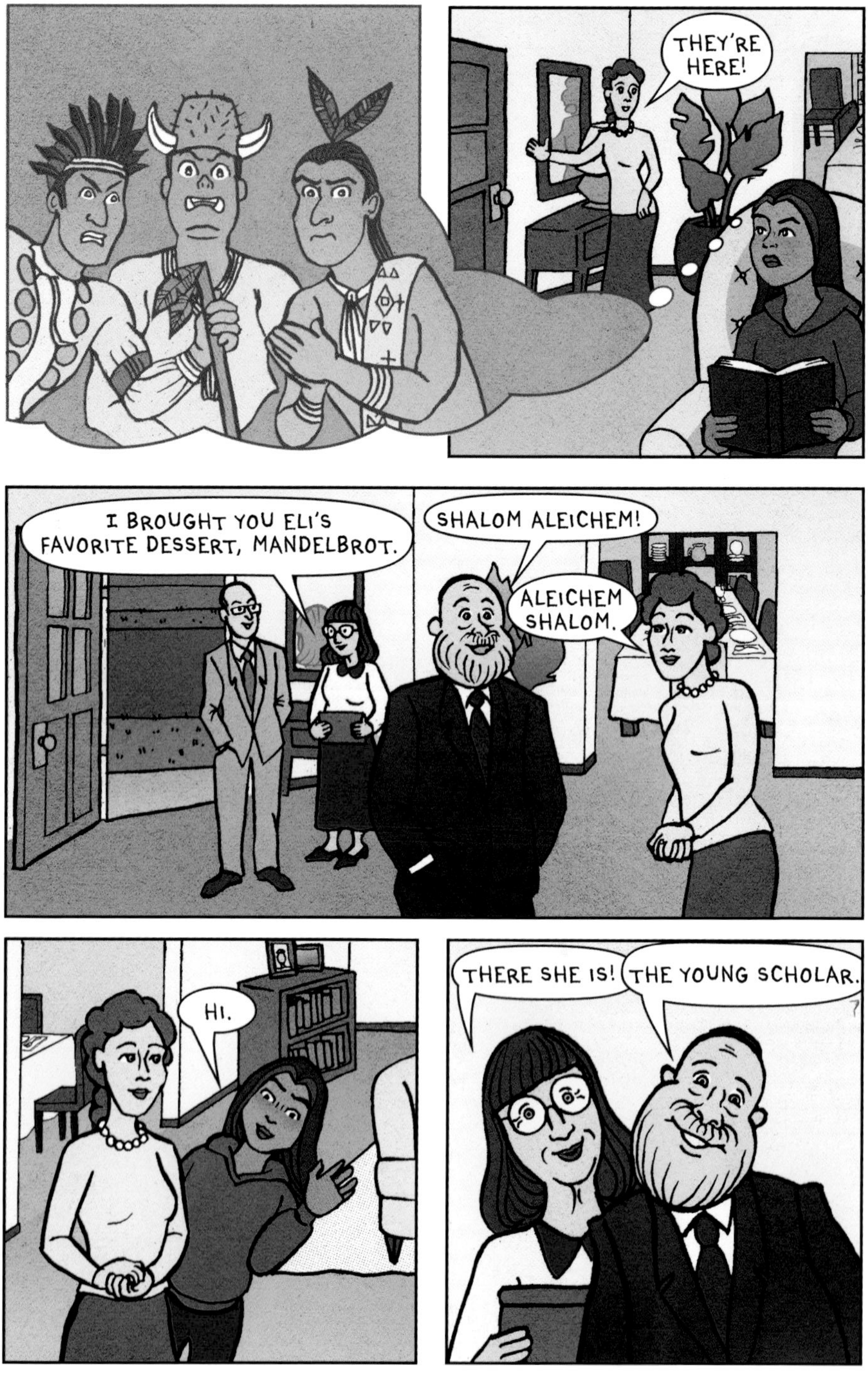
THEY'RE HERE!
I BROUGHT YOU ELI'S FAVORITE DESSERT, MANDELBROT.
SHALOM ALEICHEM!
ALEICHEM SHALOM.
HI.
THERE SHE IS!
THE YOUNG SCHOLAR.

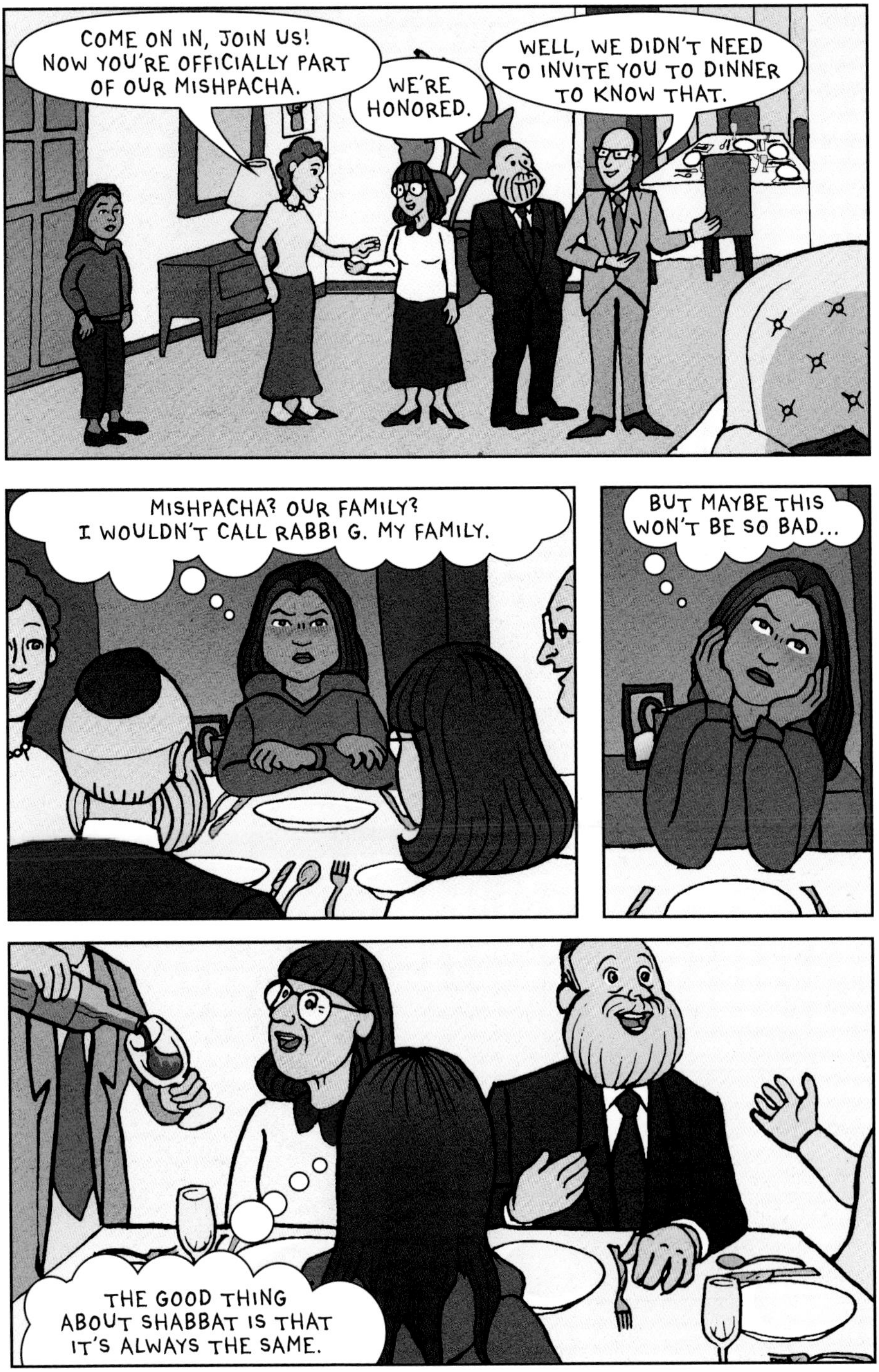
COME ON IN, JOIN US! NOW YOU'RE OFFICIALLY PART OF OUR MISHPACHA.
WE'RE HONORED.
WELL, WE DIDN'T NEED TO INVITE YOU TO DINNER TO KNOW THAT.
MISHPACHA? OUR FAMILY? I WOULDN'T CALL RABBI G. MY FAMILY.
BUT MAYBE THIS WON'T BE SO BAD...
THE GOOD THING ABOUT SHABBAT IS THAT IT'S ALWAYS THE SAME.

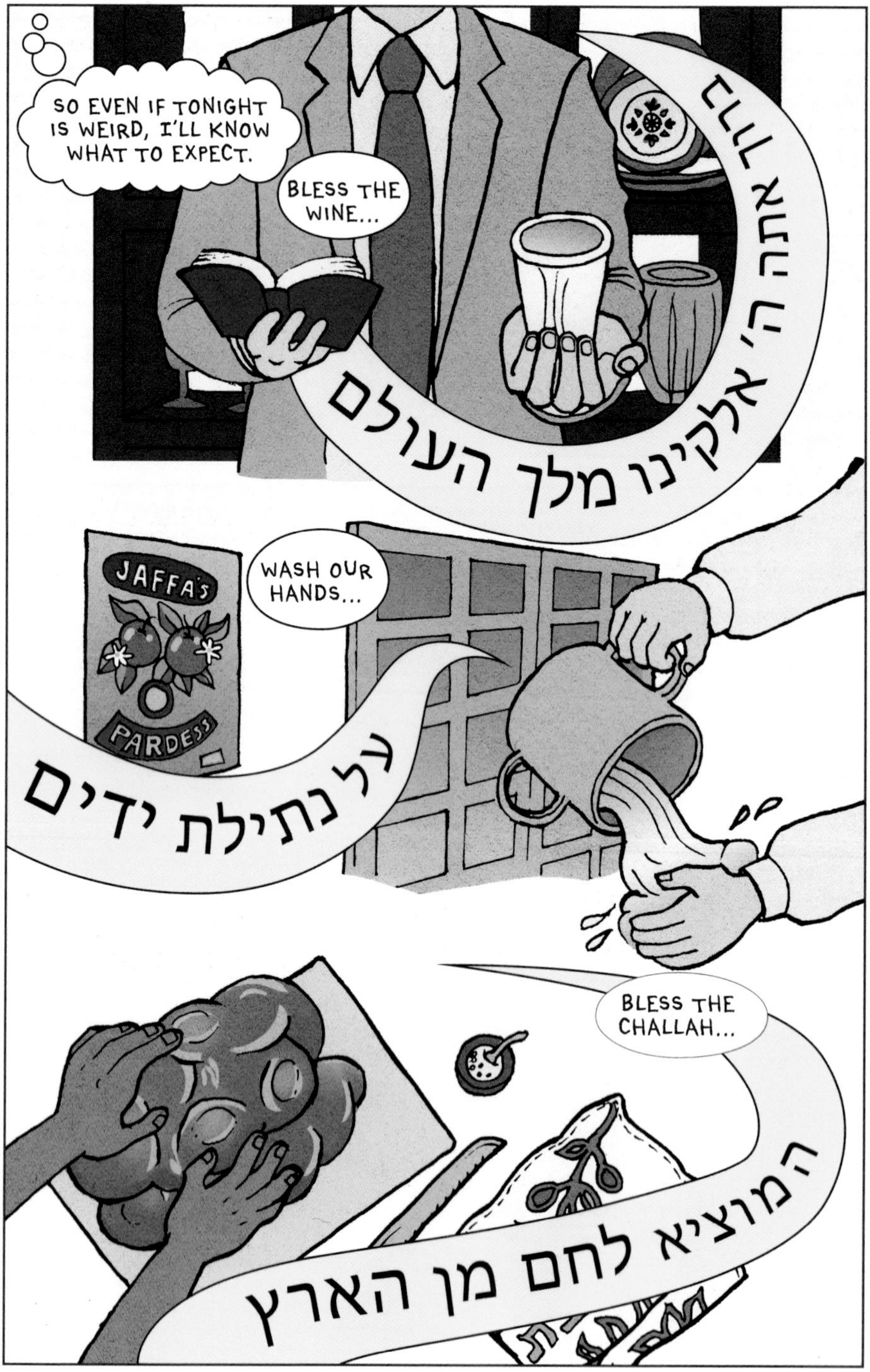
SO EVEN IF TONIGHT IS WEIRD, I'LL KNOW WHAT TO EXPECT.
BLESS THE WINE...
ברוך אתה ה׳ אלקינו מלך העולם
JAFFA'S
PARDESS
WASH OUR HANDS...
על נתילת ידים
BLESS THE CHALLAH...
המוציא לחם מן הארץ

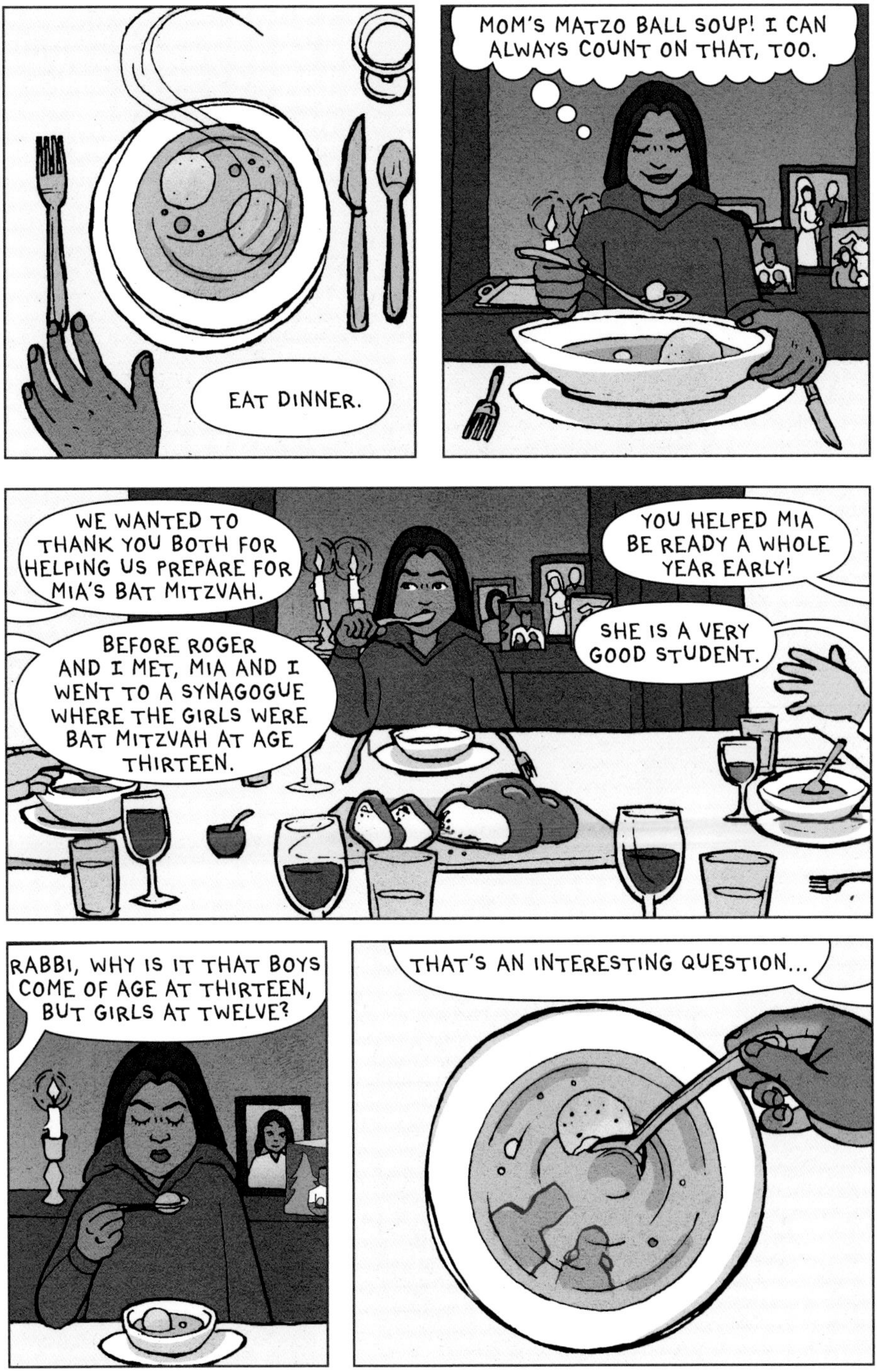
EAT DINNER.
MOM'S MATZO BALL SOUP! I CAN ALWAYS COUNT ON THAT, TOO.
WE WANTED TO THANK YOU BOTH FOR HELPING US PREPARE FOR MIA'S BAT MITZVAH.
BEFORE ROGER AND I MET, MIA AND I WENT TO A SYNAGOGUE WHERE THE GIRLS WERE BAT MITZVAH AT AGE THIRTEEN.
YOU HELPED MIA BE READY A WHOLE YEAR EARLY!
SHE IS A VERY GOOD STUDENT.
RABBI, WHY IS IT THAT BOYS COME OF AGE AT THIRTEEN, BUT GIRLS AT TWELVE?
THAT'S AN INTERESTING QUESTION...

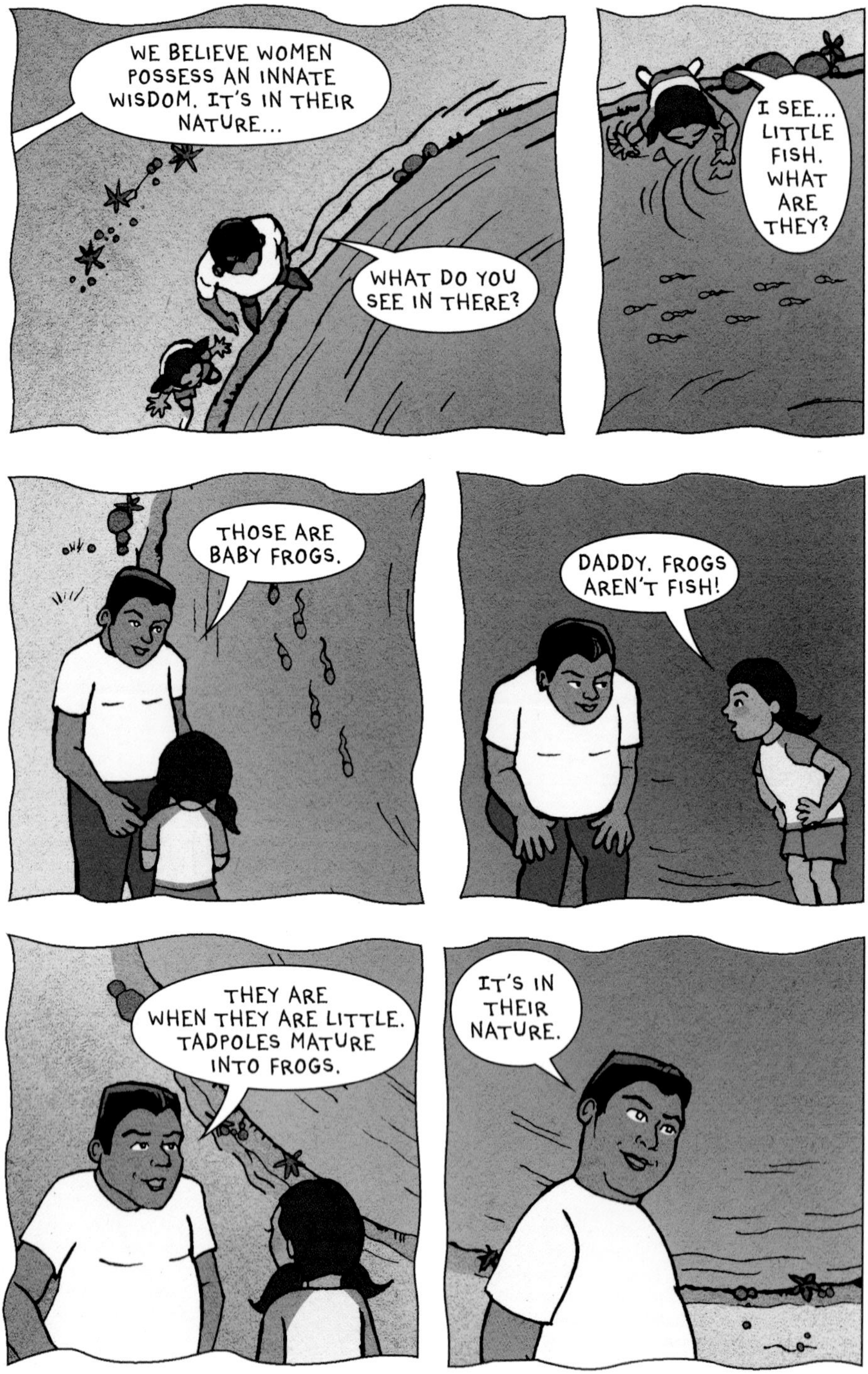
WE BELIEVE WOMEN POSSESS AN INNATE WISDOM. IT'S IN THEIR NATURE...
WHAT DO YOU SEE IN THERE?
I SEE... LITTLE FISH. WHAT ARE THEY?
THOSE ARE BABY FROGS.
DADDY. FROGS AREN'T FISH!
THEY ARE WHEN THEY ARE LITTLE. TADPOLES MATURE INTO FROGS.
IT'S IN THEIR NATURE.

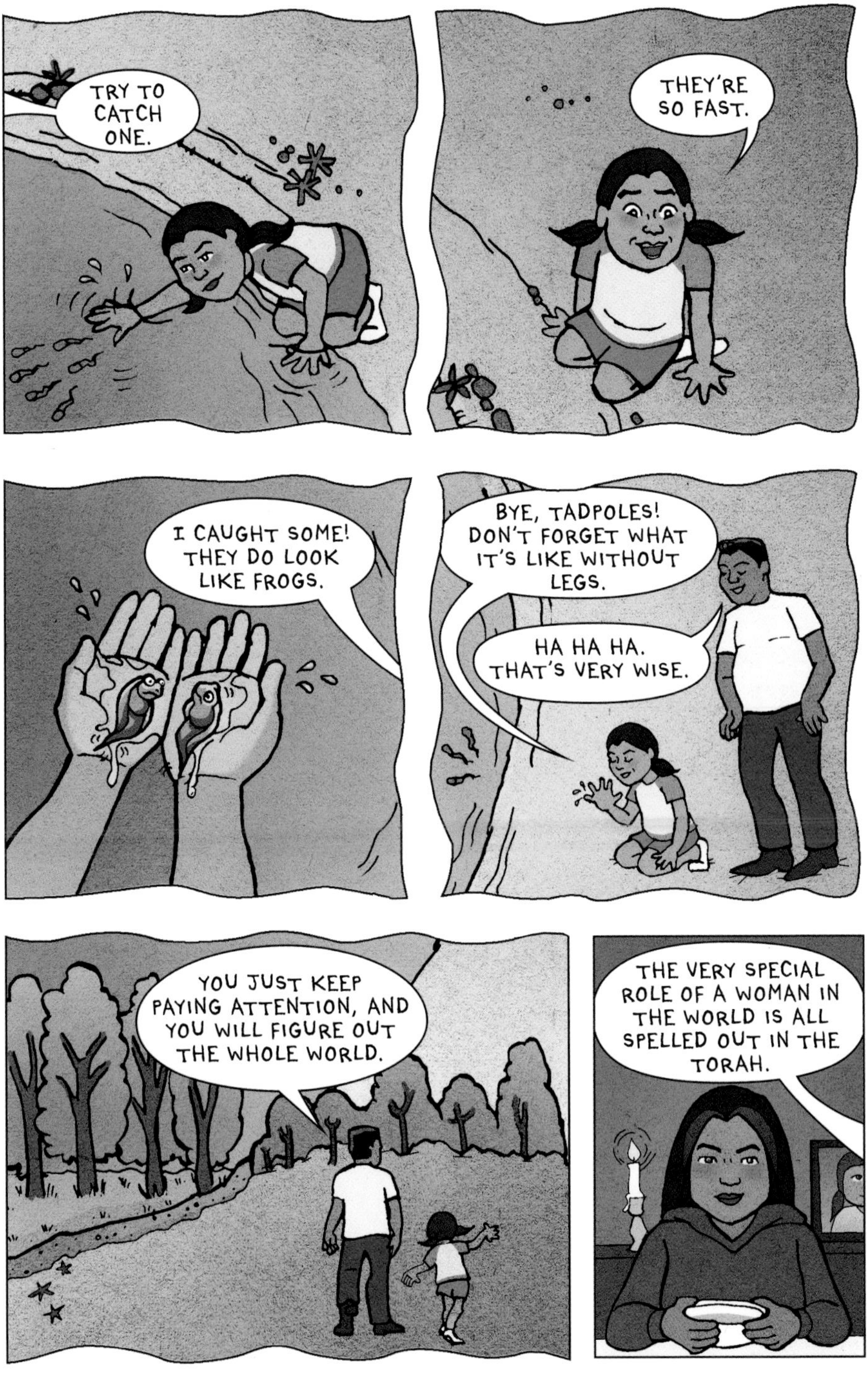
TRY TO CATCH ONE.
THEY'RE SO FAST.
I CAUGHT SOME! THEY DO LOOK LIKE FROGS.
BYE, TADPOLES! DON'T FORGET WHAT IT'S LIKE WITHOUT LEGS.
HA HA HA. THAT'S VERY WISE.
YOU JUST KEEP PAYING ATTENTION, AND YOU WILL FIGURE OUT THE WHOLE WORLD.
THE VERY SPECIAL ROLE OF A WOMAN IN THE WORLD IS ALL SPELLED OUT IN THE TORAH.

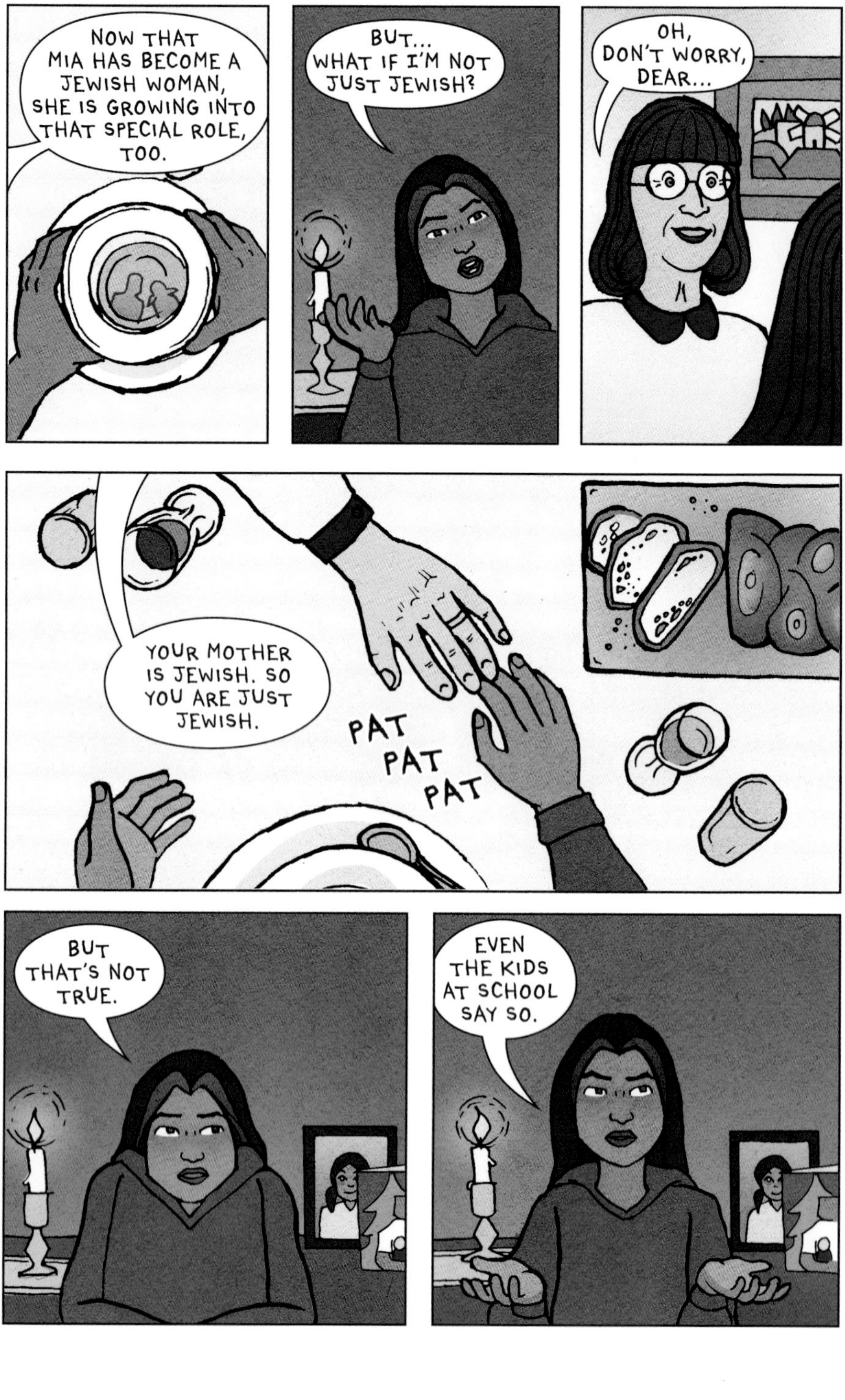
NOW THAT MIA HAS BECOME A JEWISH WOMAN, SHE IS GROWING INTO THAT SPECIAL ROLE, TOO.
BUT... WHAT IF I'M NOT JUST JEWISH?
OH, DON'T WORRY, DEAR...
YOUR MOTHER IS JEWISH. SO YOU ARE JUST JEWISH.
PAT PAT PAT
BUT THAT'S NOT TRUE.
EVEN THE KIDS AT SCHOOL SAY SO.

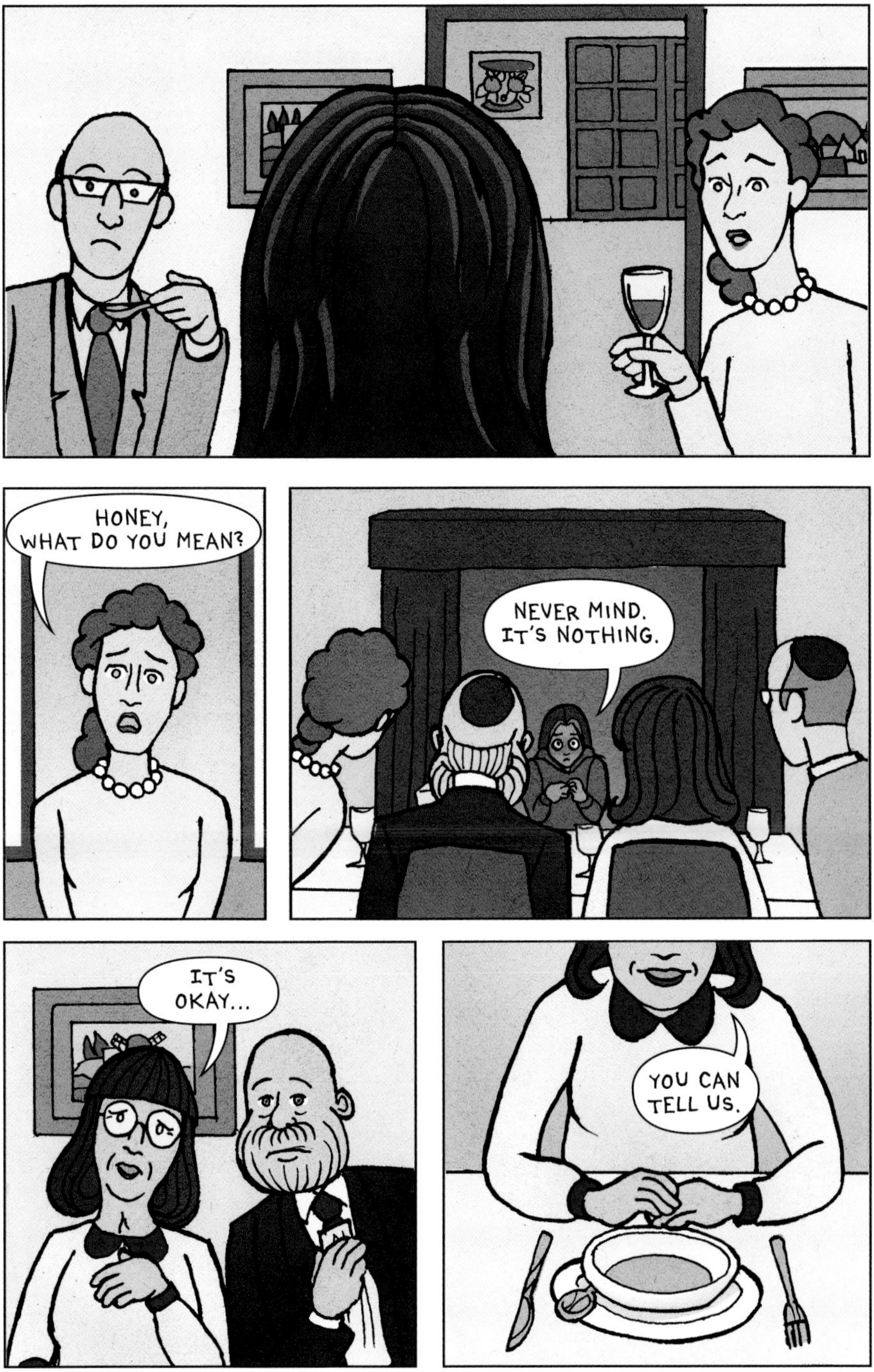
HONEY, WHAT DO YOU MEAN?
NEVER MIND. IT'S NOTHING.
IT'S OKAY...
YOU CAN TELL US.

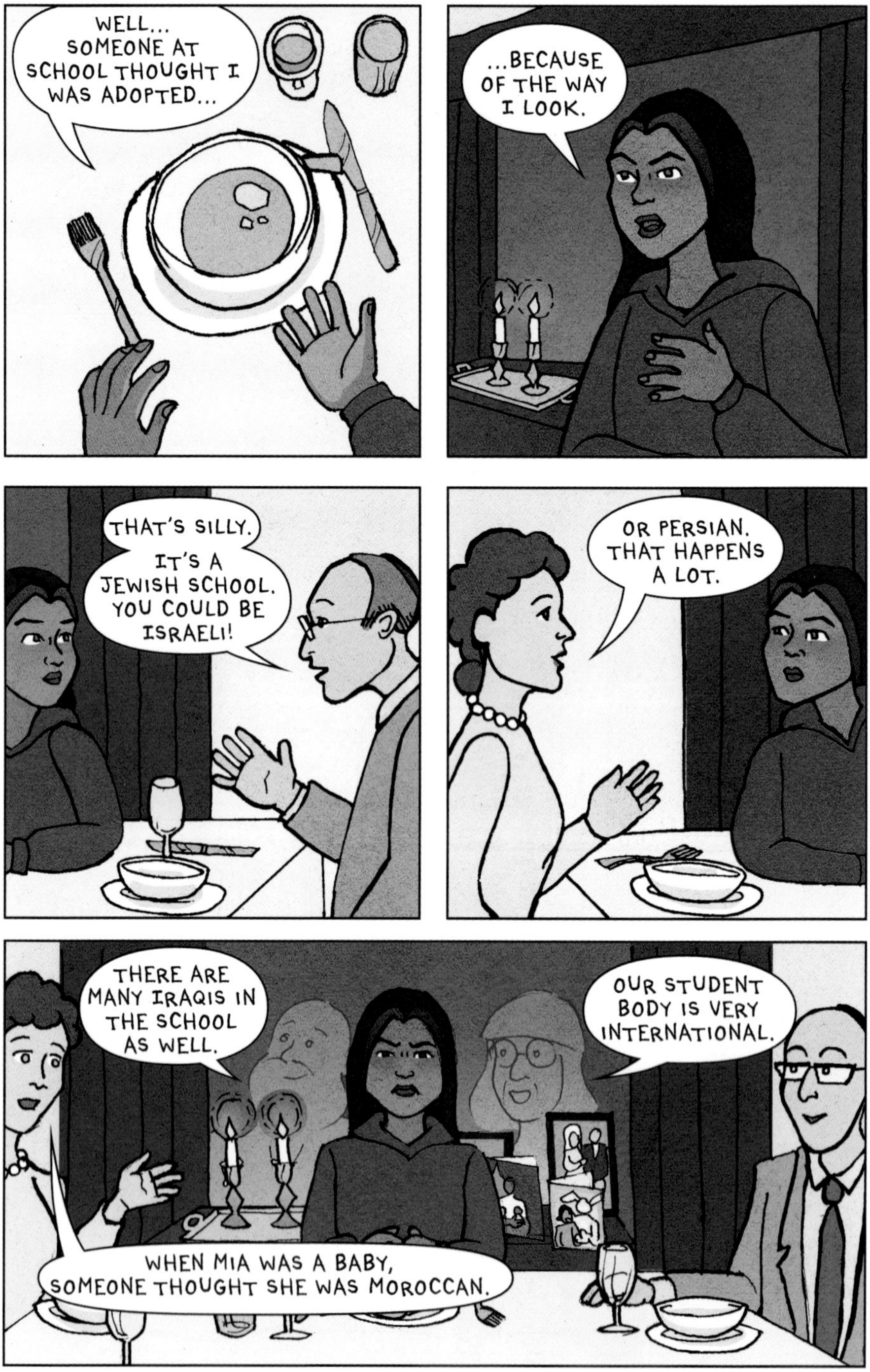
WELL... SOMEONE AT SCHOOL THOUGHT I WAS ADOPTED...
...BECAUSE OF THE WAY I LOOK.
THAT'S SILLY.
IT'S A JEWISH SCHOOL. YOU COULD BE ISRAELI!
OR PERSIAN. THAT HAPPENS A LOT.
THERE ARE MANY IRAQIS IN THE SCHOOL AS WELL.
OUR STUDENT BODY IS VERY INTERNATIONAL.
WHEN MIA WAS A BABY, SOMEONE THOUGHT SHE WAS MOROCCAN.

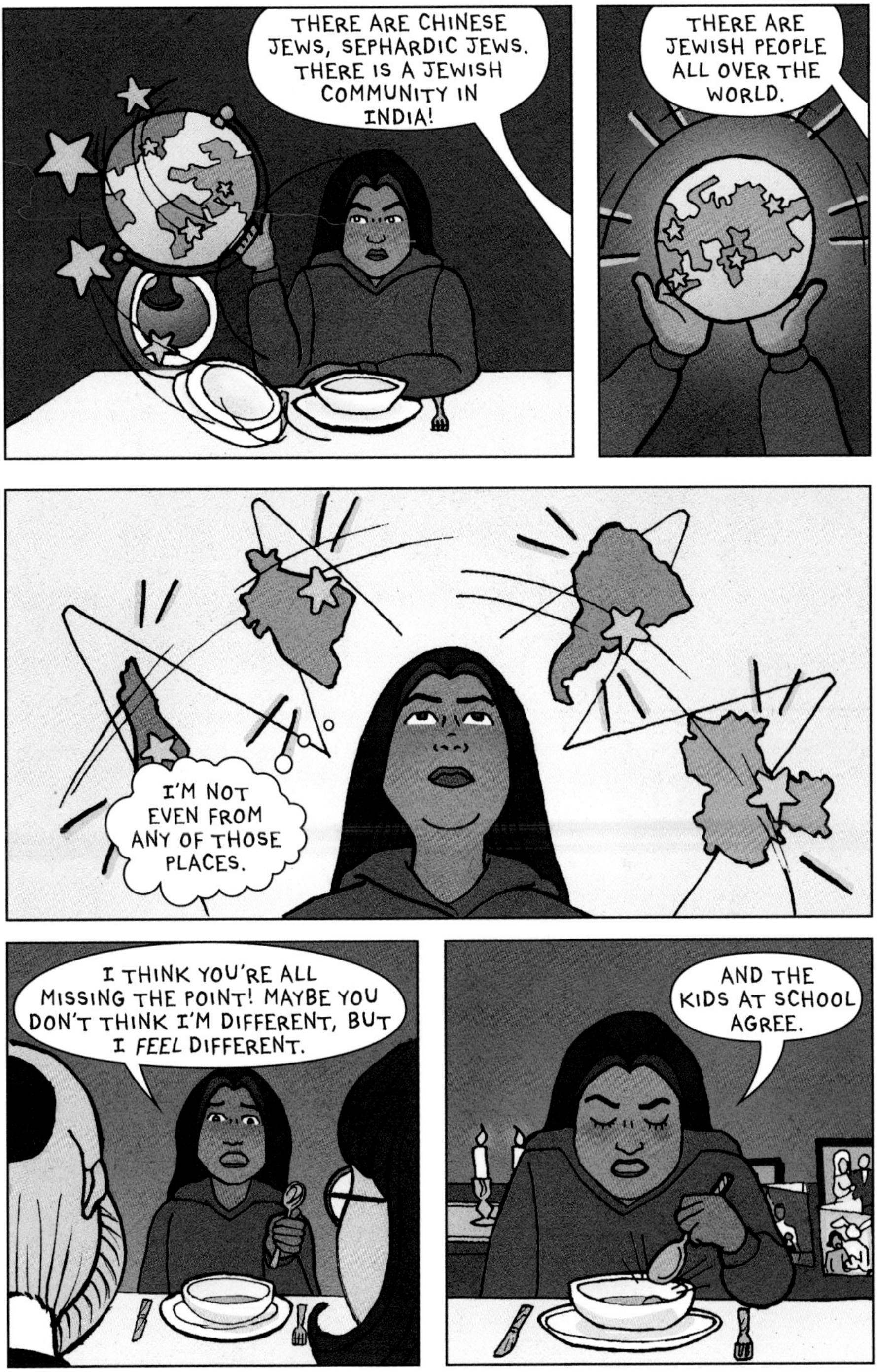
THERE ARE CHINESE JEWS, SEPHARDIC JEWS. THERE IS A JEWISH COMMUNITY IN INDIA!
THERE ARE JEWISH PEOPLE ALL OVER THE WORLD.
I'M NOT EVEN FROM ANY OF THOSE PLACES.
I THINK YOU'RE ALL MISSING THE POINT! MAYBE YOU DON'T THINK I'M DIFFERENT, BUT I *FEEL* DIFFERENT.
AND THE KIDS AT SCHOOL AGREE.

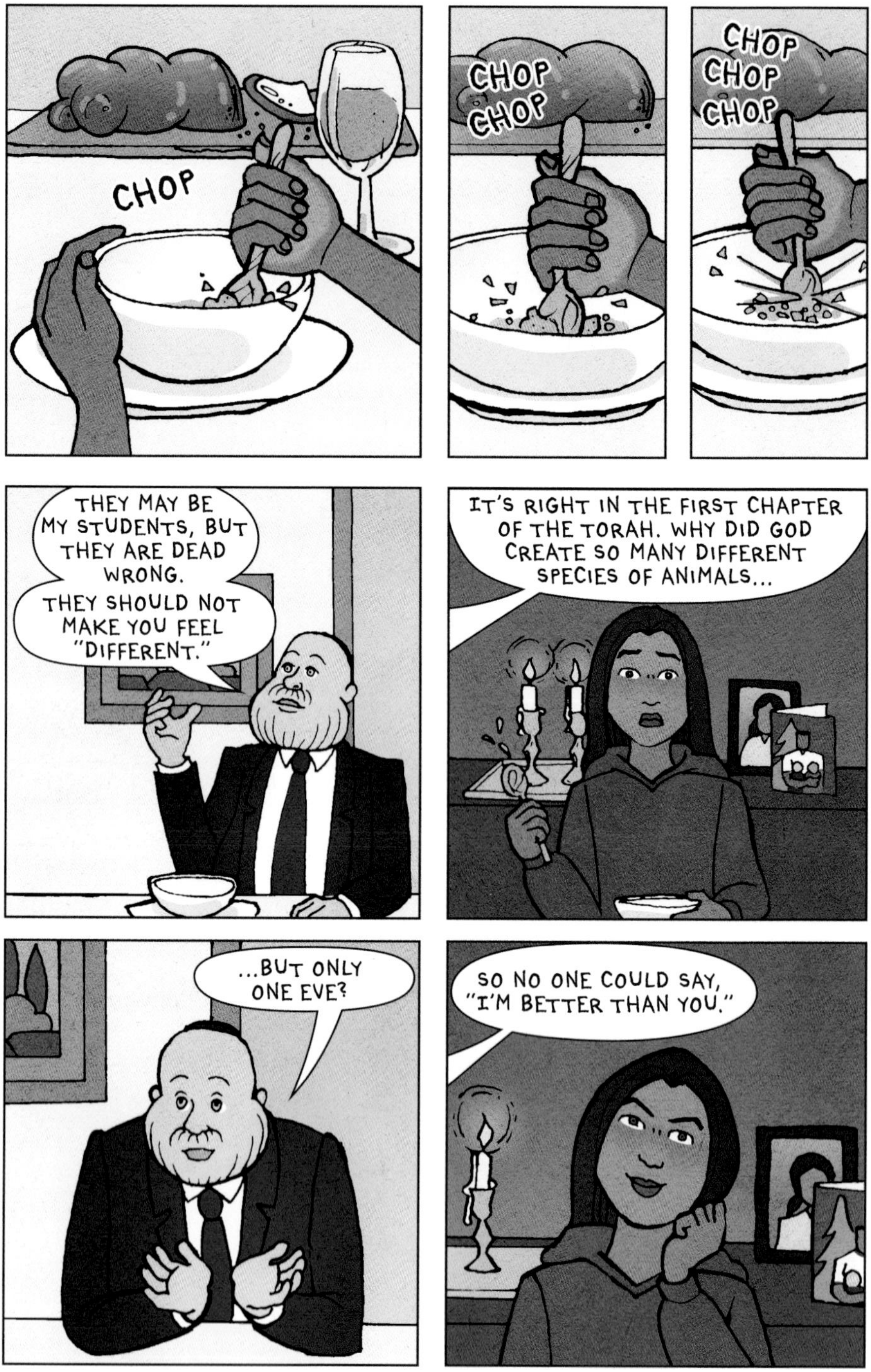
CHOP
CHOP CHOP
CHOP CHOP CHOP
THEY MAY BE MY STUDENTS, BUT THEY ARE DEAD WRONG.
THEY SHOULD NOT MAKE YOU FEEL "DIFFERENT."
IT'S RIGHT IN THE FIRST CHAPTER OF THE TORAH. WHY DID GOD CREATE SO MANY DIFFERENT SPECIES OF ANIMALS...
...BUT ONLY ONE EVE?
SO NO ONE COULD SAY, "I'M BETTER THAN YOU."

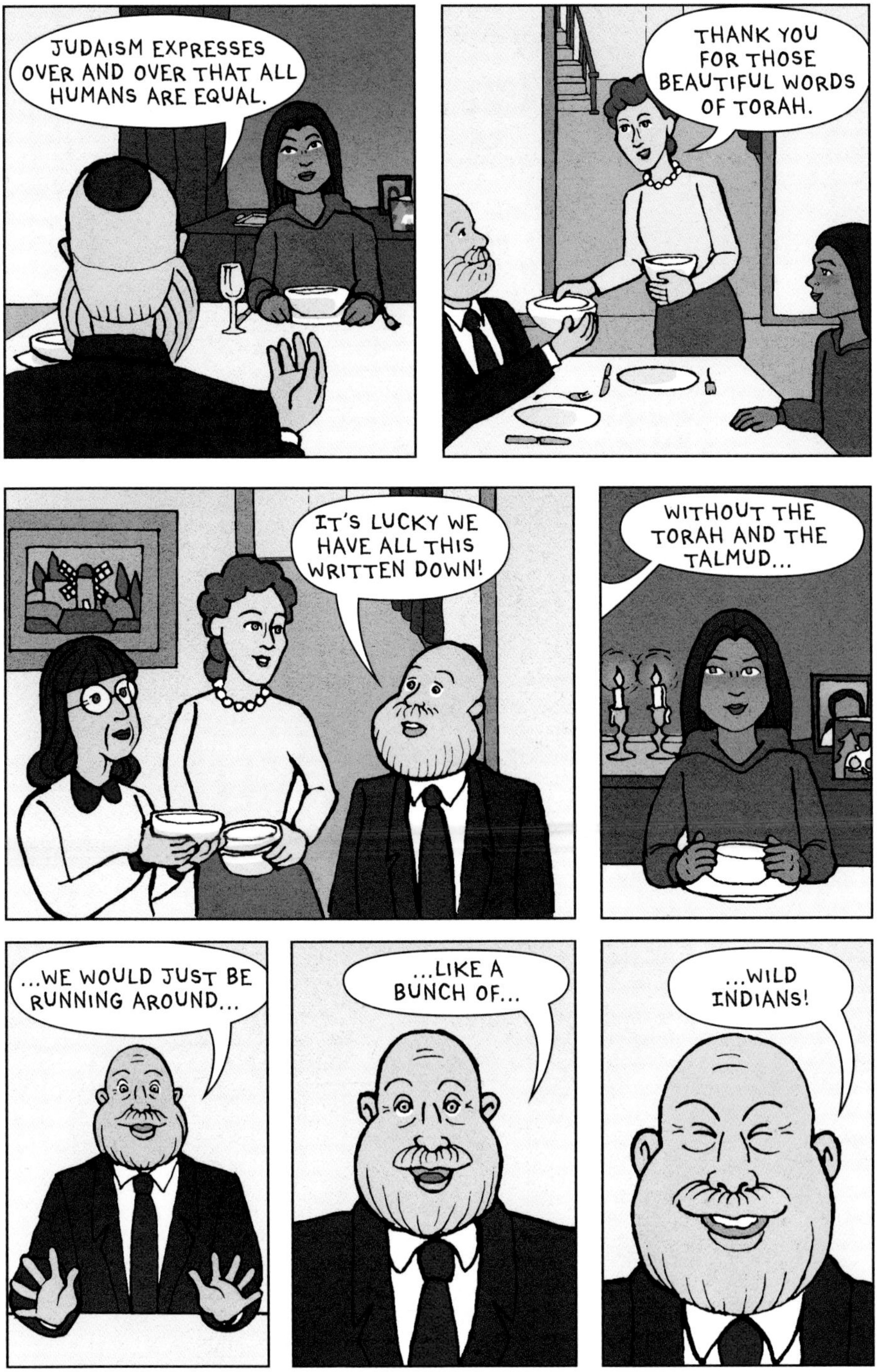
JUDAISM EXPRESSES OVER AND OVER THAT ALL HUMANS ARE EQUAL.
THANK YOU FOR THOSE BEAUTIFUL WORDS OF TORAH.
IT'S LUCKY WE HAVE ALL THIS WRITTEN DOWN!
WITHOUT THE TORAH AND THE TALMUD...
...WE WOULD JUST BE RUNNING AROUND...
...LIKE A BUNCH OF...
...WILD INDIANS!

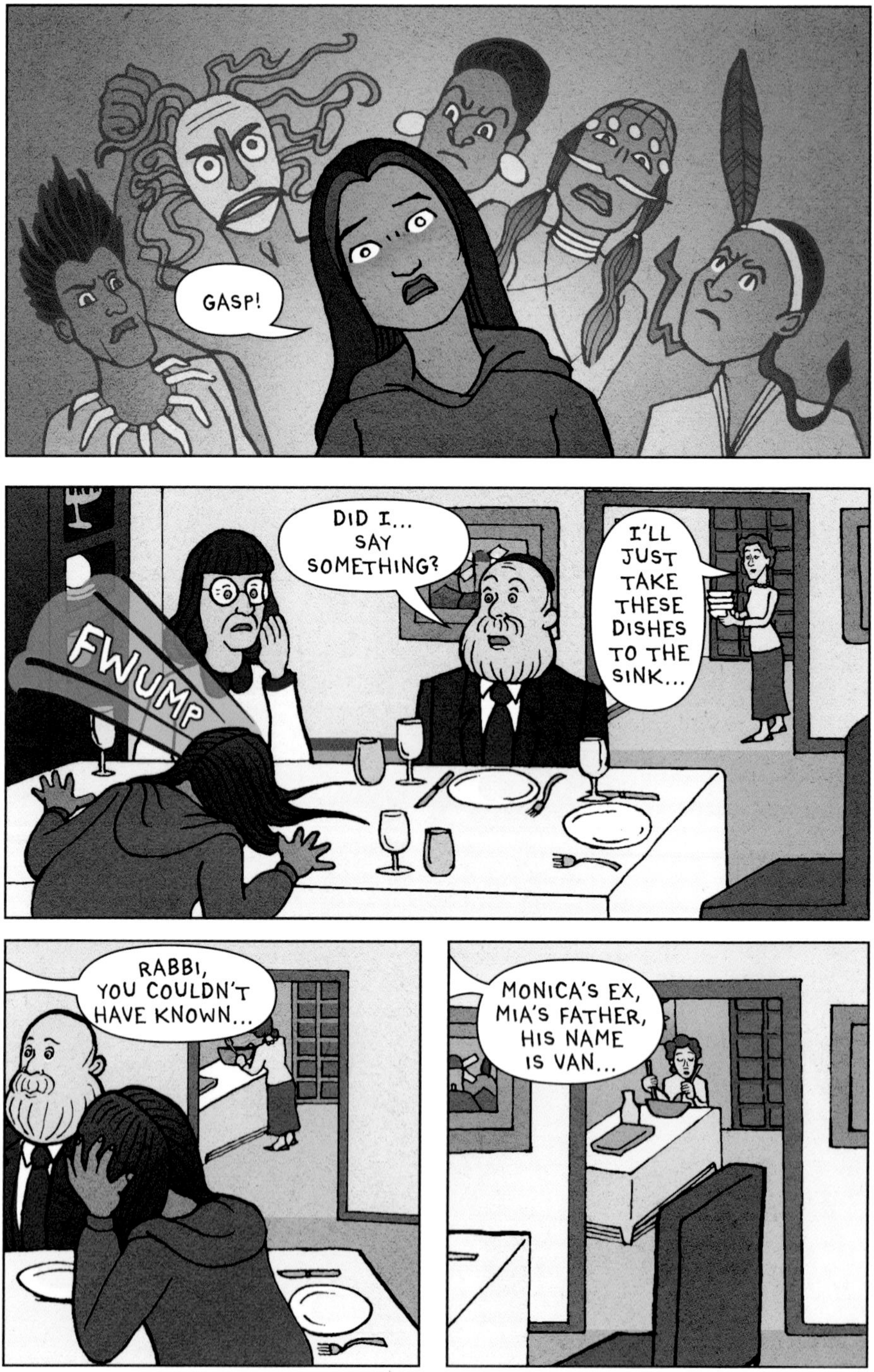
GASP!
DID I... SAY SOMETHING?
I'LL JUST TAKE THESE DISHES TO THE SINK...
FWUMP
RABBI, YOU COULDN'T HAVE KNOWN...
MONICA'S EX, MIA'S FATHER, HIS NAME IS VAN...

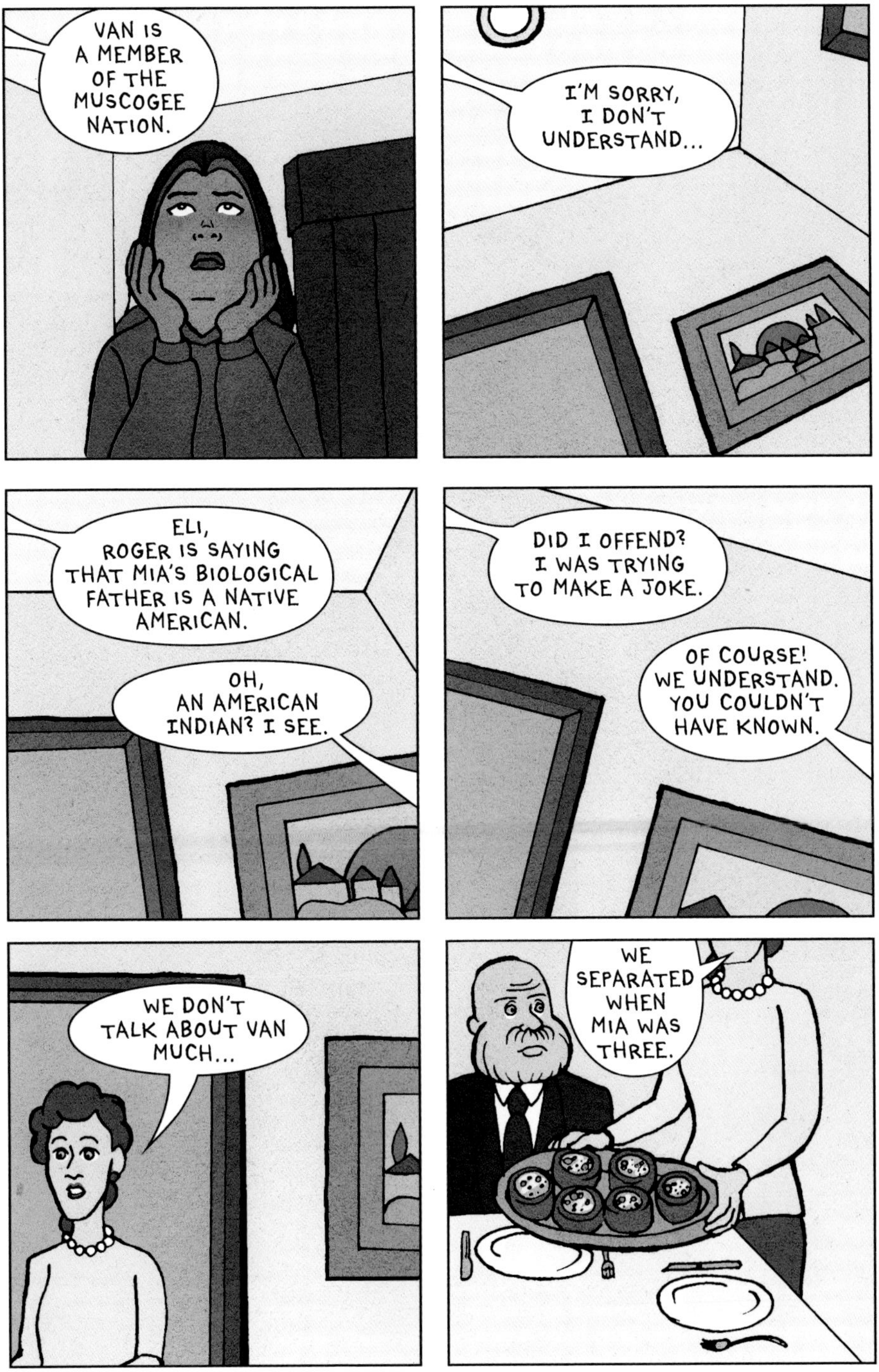
VAN IS A MEMBER OF THE MUSCOGEE NATION.
I'M SORRY, I DON'T UNDERSTAND...
ELI, ROGER IS SAYING THAT MIA'S BIOLOGICAL FATHER IS A NATIVE AMERICAN.
OH, AN AMERICAN INDIAN? I SEE.
DID I OFFEND? I WAS TRYING TO MAKE A JOKE.
OF COURSE! WE UNDERSTAND. YOU COULDN'T HAVE KNOWN.
WE DON'T TALK ABOUT VAN MUCH...
WE SEPARATED WHEN MIA WAS THREE.

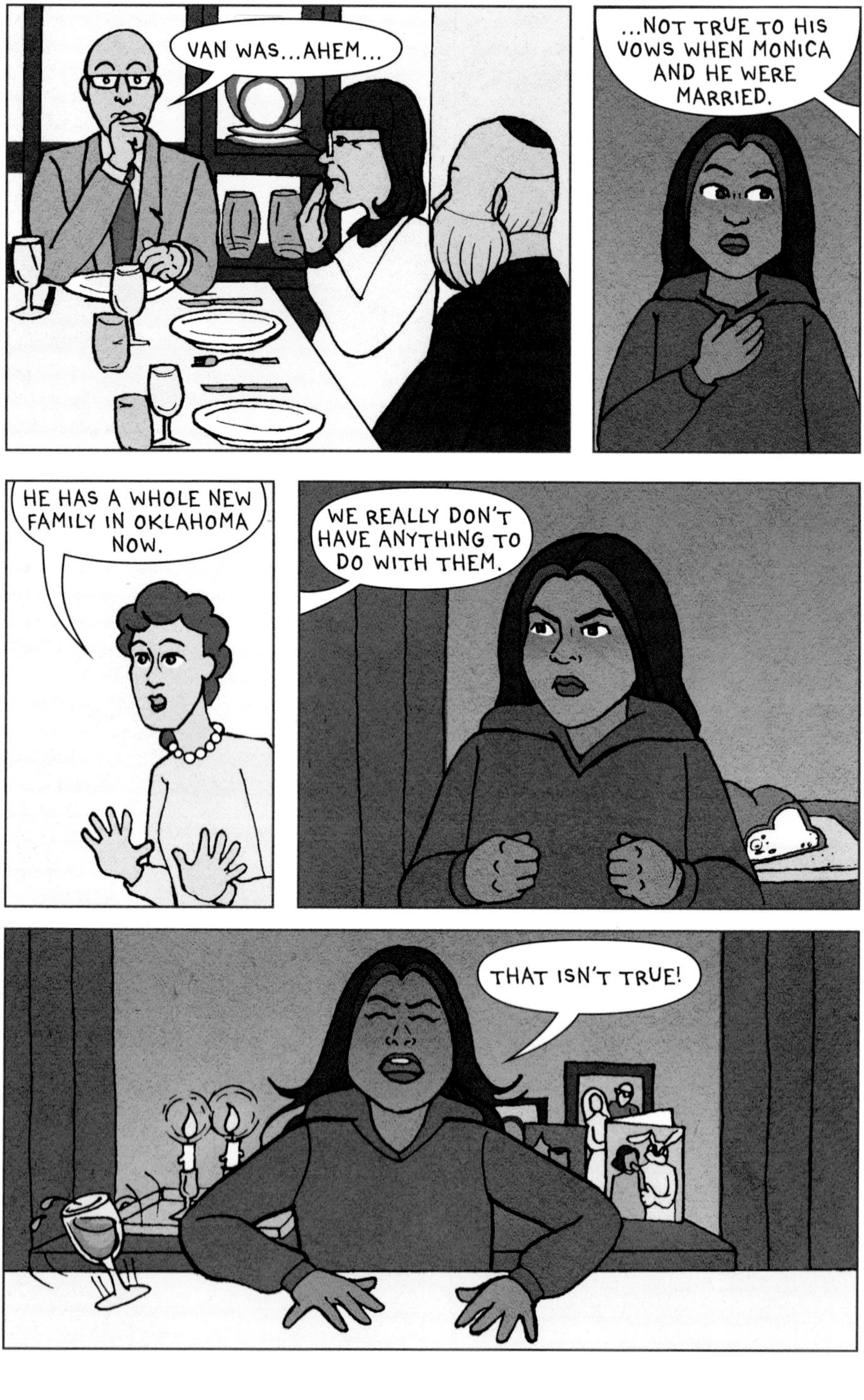
VAN WAS...AHEM...
...NOT TRUE TO HIS VOWS WHEN MONICA AND HE WERE MARRIED.
HE HAS A WHOLE NEW FAMILY IN OKLAHOMA NOW.
WE REALLY DON'T HAVE ANYTHING TO DO WITH THEM.
THAT ISN'T TRUE!

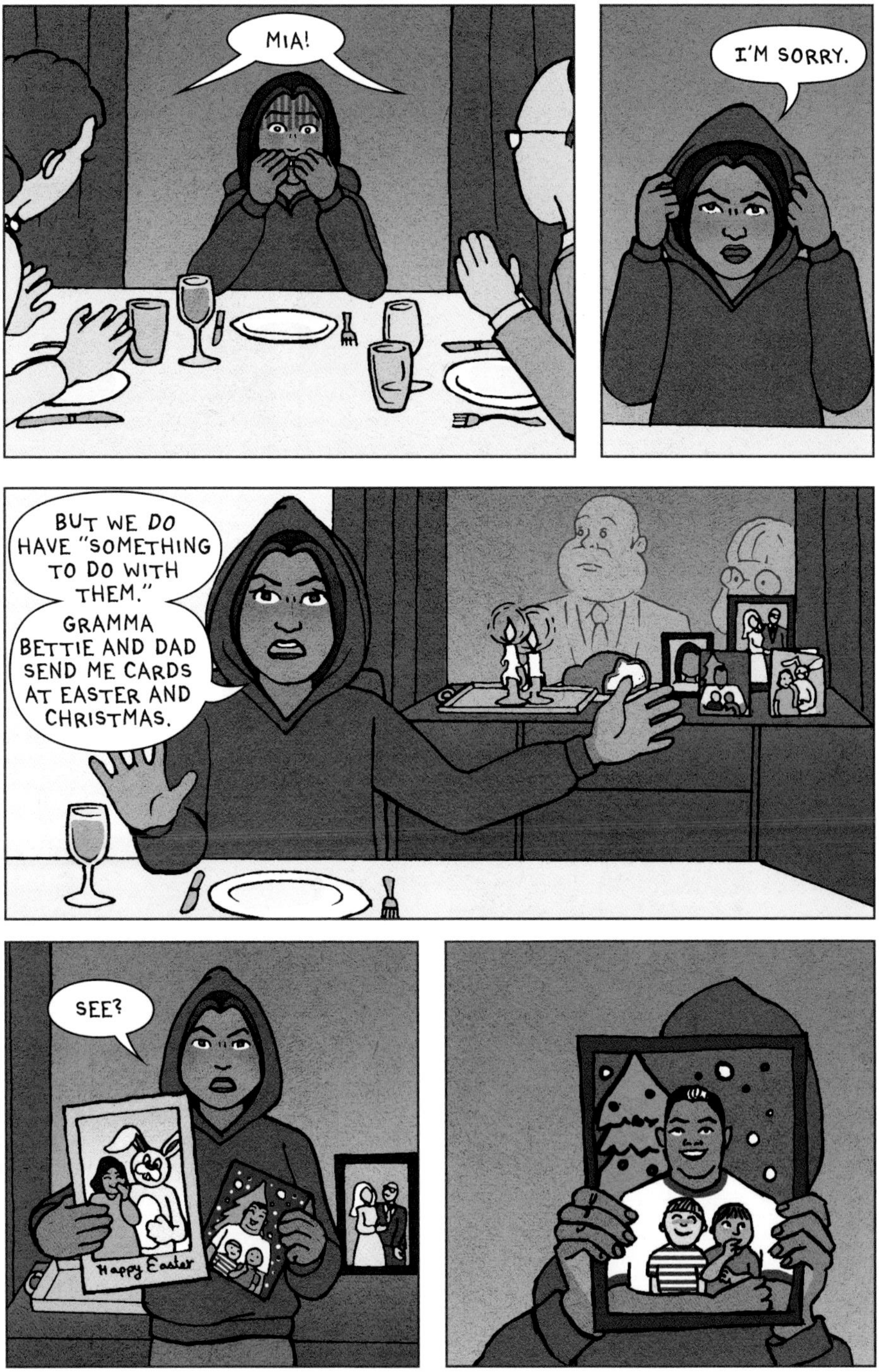
MIA!
I'M SORRY.
BUT WE *DO* HAVE "SOMETHING TO DO WITH THEM."
GRAMMA BETTIE AND DAD SEND ME CARDS AT EASTER AND CHRISTMAS.
SEE?
Happy Easter

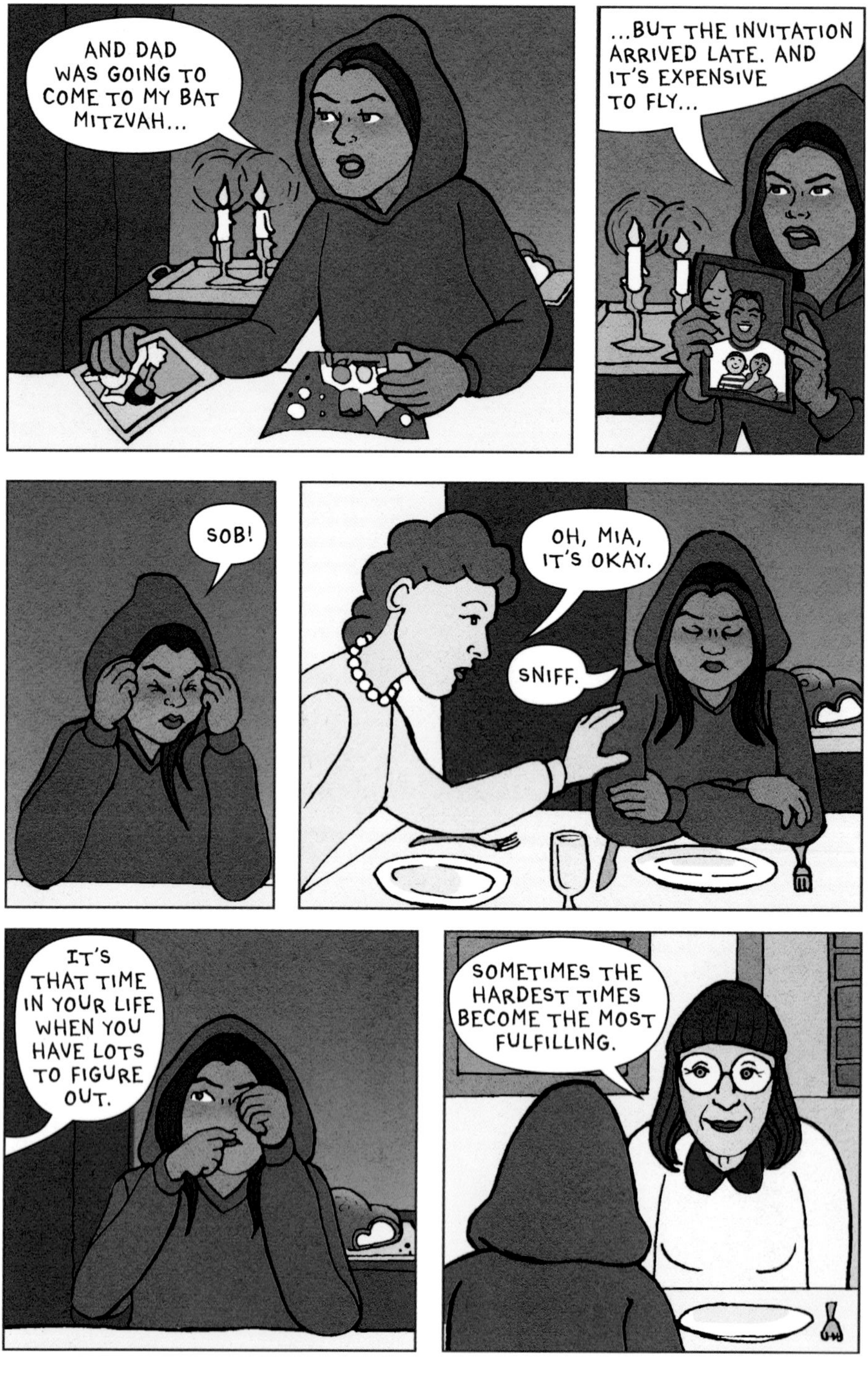
AND DAD WAS GOING TO COME TO MY BAT MITZVAH...
...BUT THE INVITATION ARRIVED LATE. AND IT'S EXPENSIVE TO FLY...
SOB!
OH, MIA, IT'S OKAY.
SNIFF.
IT'S THAT TIME IN YOUR LIFE WHEN YOU HAVE LOTS TO FIGURE OUT.
SOMETIMES THE HARDEST TIMES BECOME THE MOST FULFILLING.

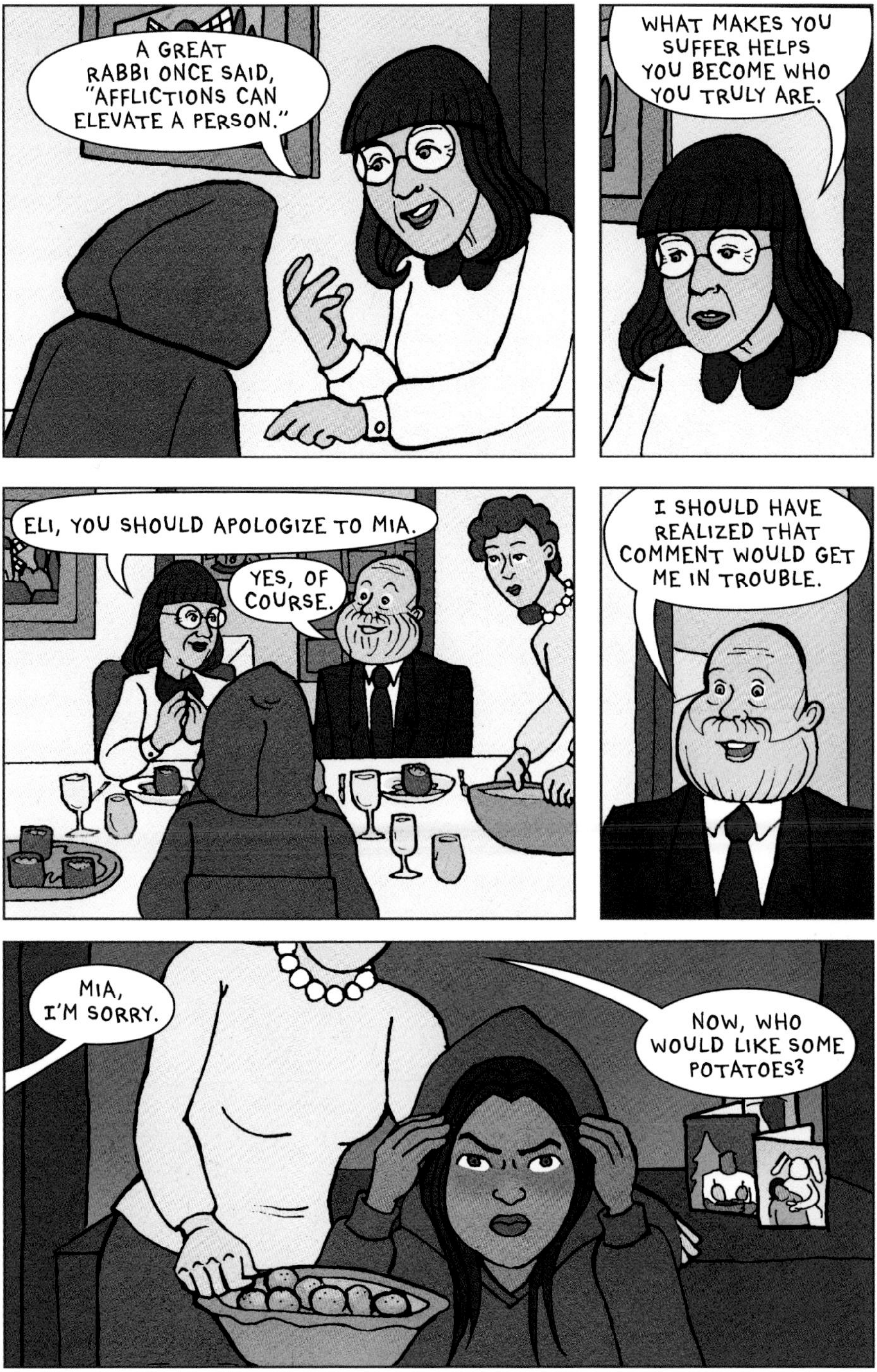
A GREAT RABBI ONCE SAID, "AFFLICTIONS CAN ELEVATE A PERSON."
WHAT MAKES YOU SUFFER HELPS YOU BECOME WHO YOU TRULY ARE.
ELI, YOU SHOULD APOLOGIZE TO MIA.
YES, OF COURSE.
I SHOULD HAVE REALIZED THAT COMMENT WOULD GET ME IN TROUBLE.
MIA, I'M SORRY.
NOW, WHO WOULD LIKE SOME POTATOES?

THE PLAN

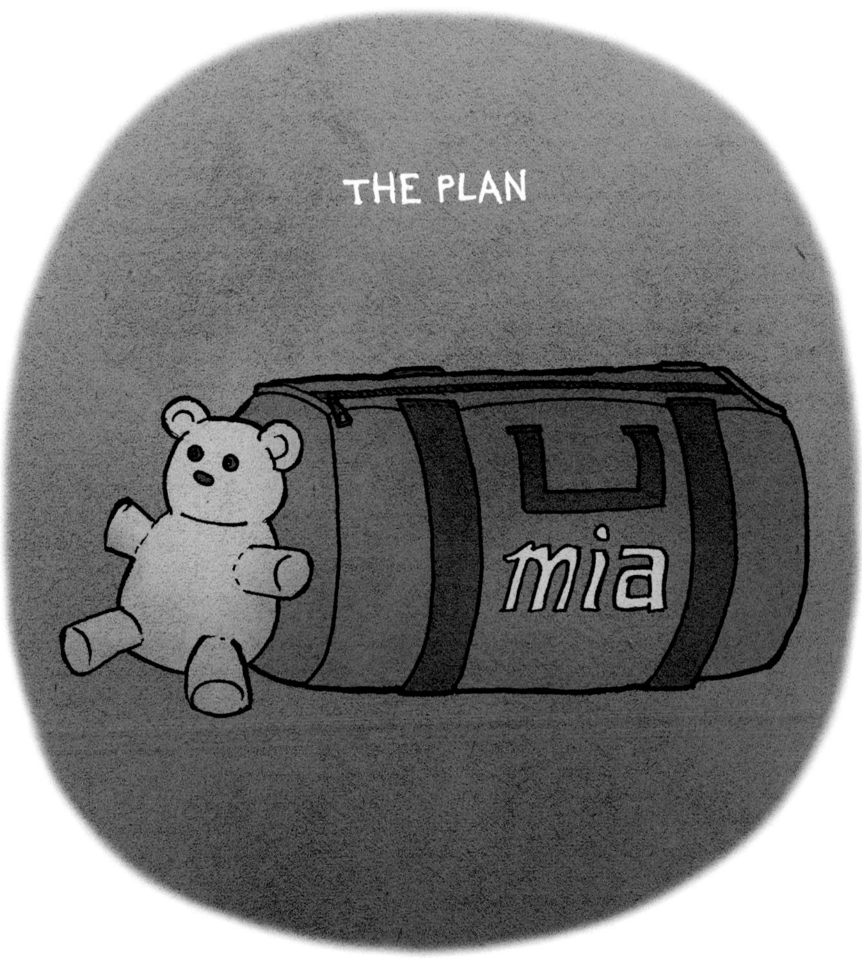
mia

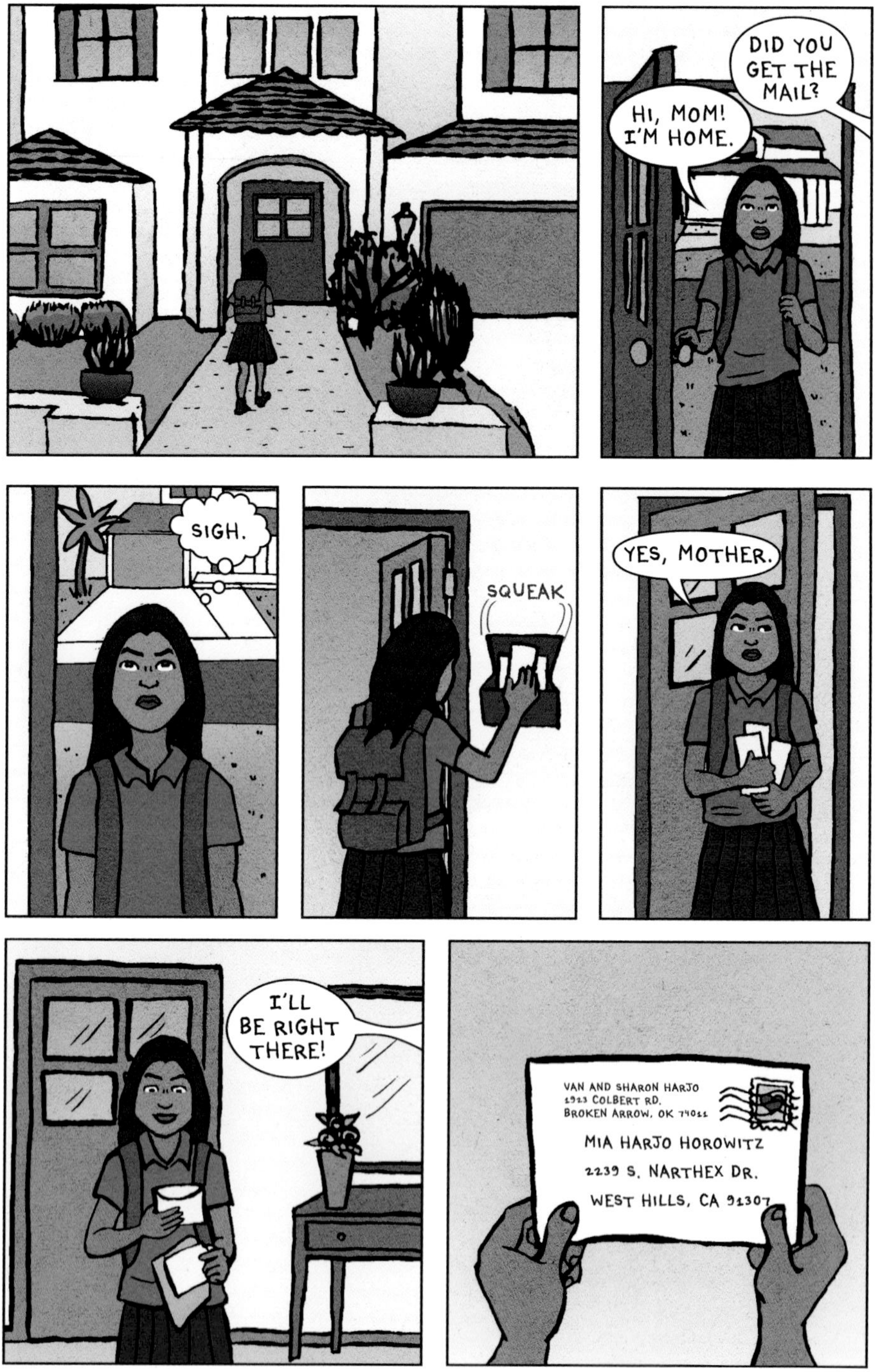
HI, MOM! I'M HOME.
DID YOU GET THE MAIL?
SIGH.
SQUEAK
YES, MOTHER.
I'LL BE RIGHT THERE!
VAN AND SHARON HARJO
1923 COLBERT RD.
BROKEN ARROW, OK 74011
MIA HARJO HOROWITZ
2239 S. NARTHEX DR.
WEST HILLS, CA 91307

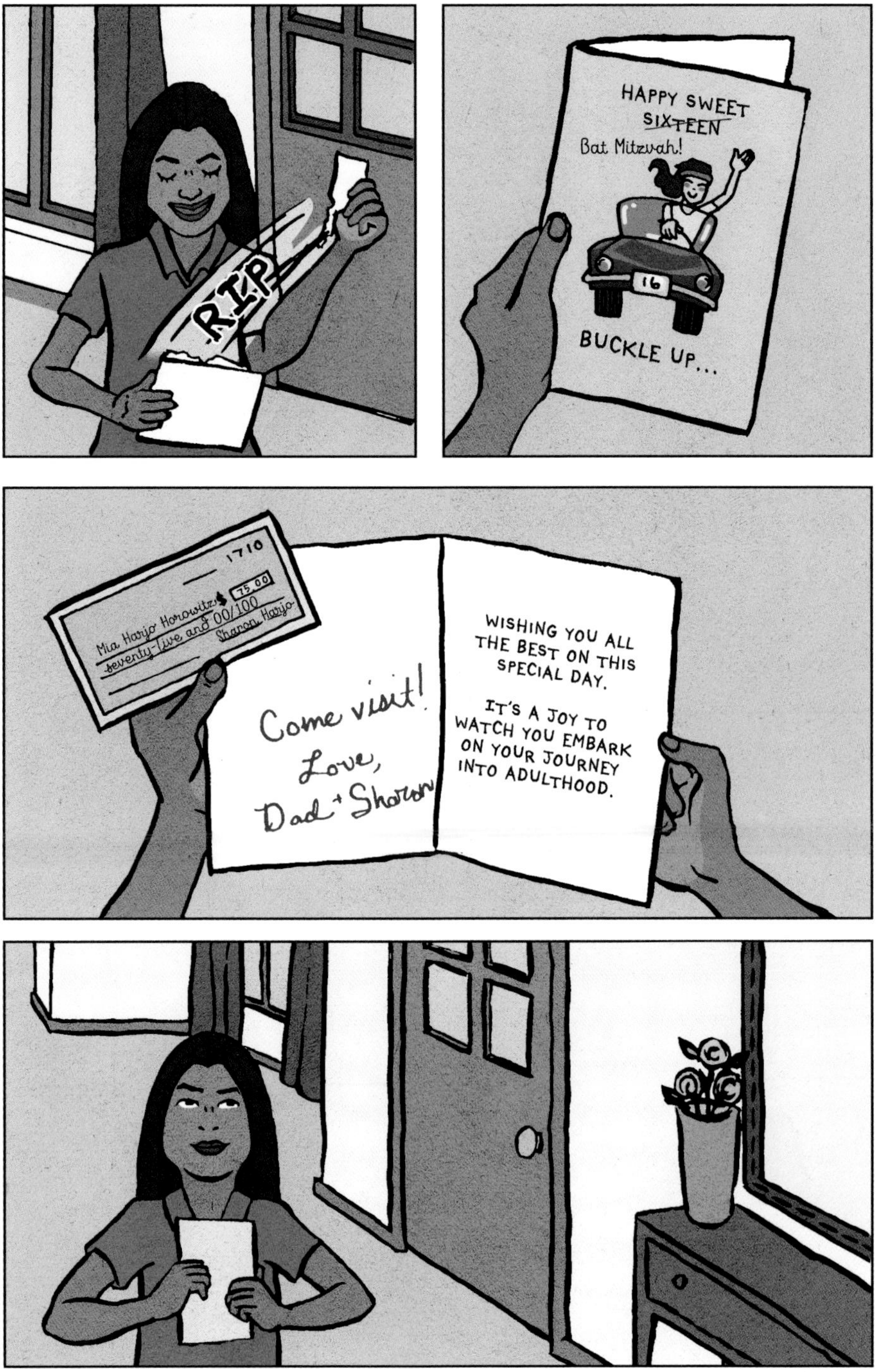
RIP
HAPPY SWEET SIXTEEN
Bat Mitzvah!
16
BUCKLE UP...
1710
75.00
Mia Harjo Horowitz
seventy-five and 00/100
Sharon Harjo
Come visit!
Love,
Dad + Sharon
WISHING YOU ALL THE BEST ON THIS SPECIAL DAY.
IT'S A JOY TO WATCH YOU EMBARK ON YOUR JOURNEY INTO ADULTHOOD.

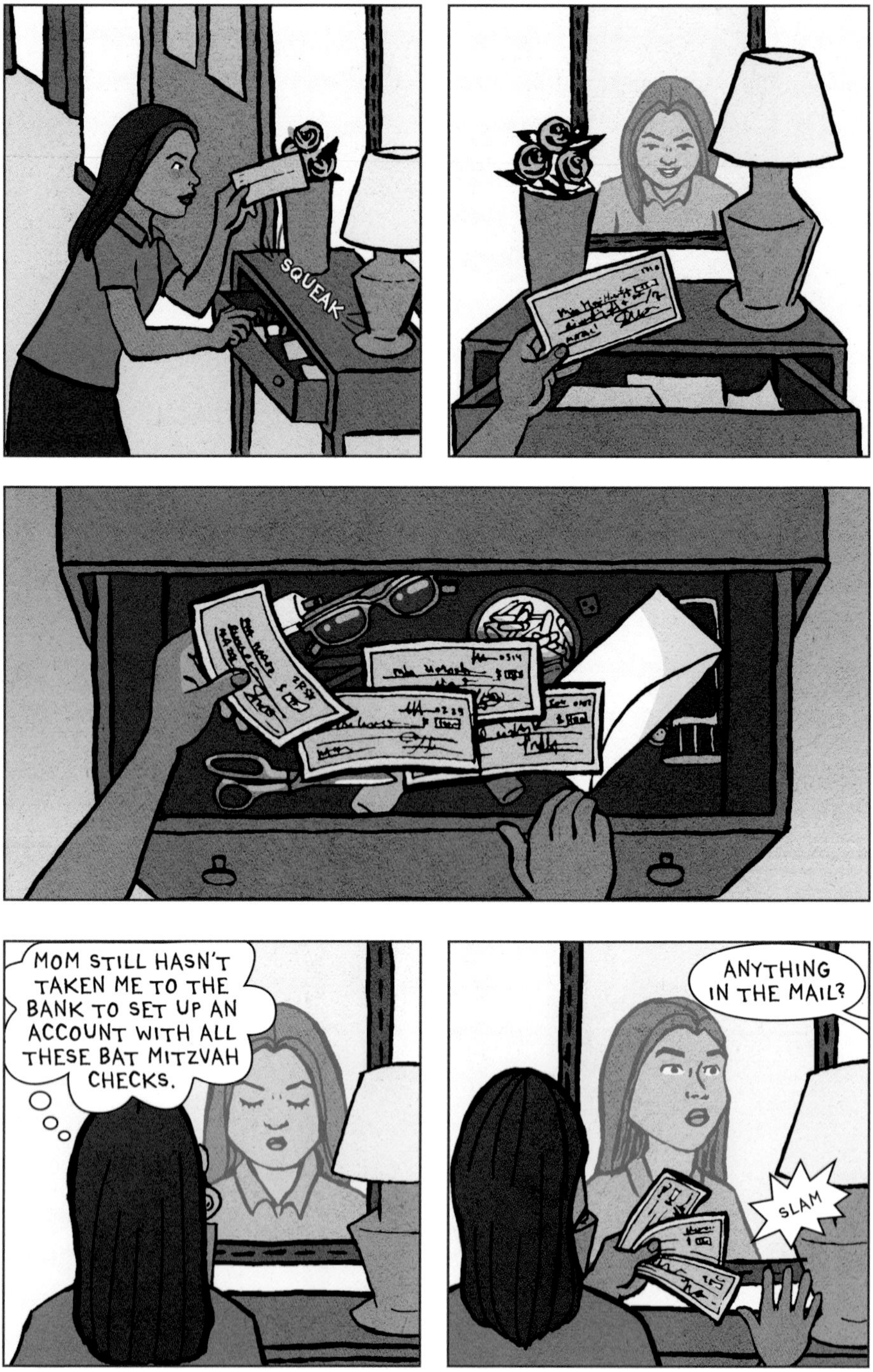
SQUEAK
MOM STILL HASN'T TAKEN ME TO THE BANK TO SET UP AN ACCOUNT WITH ALL THESE BAT MITZVAH CHECKS.
ANYTHING IN THE MAIL?
SLAM

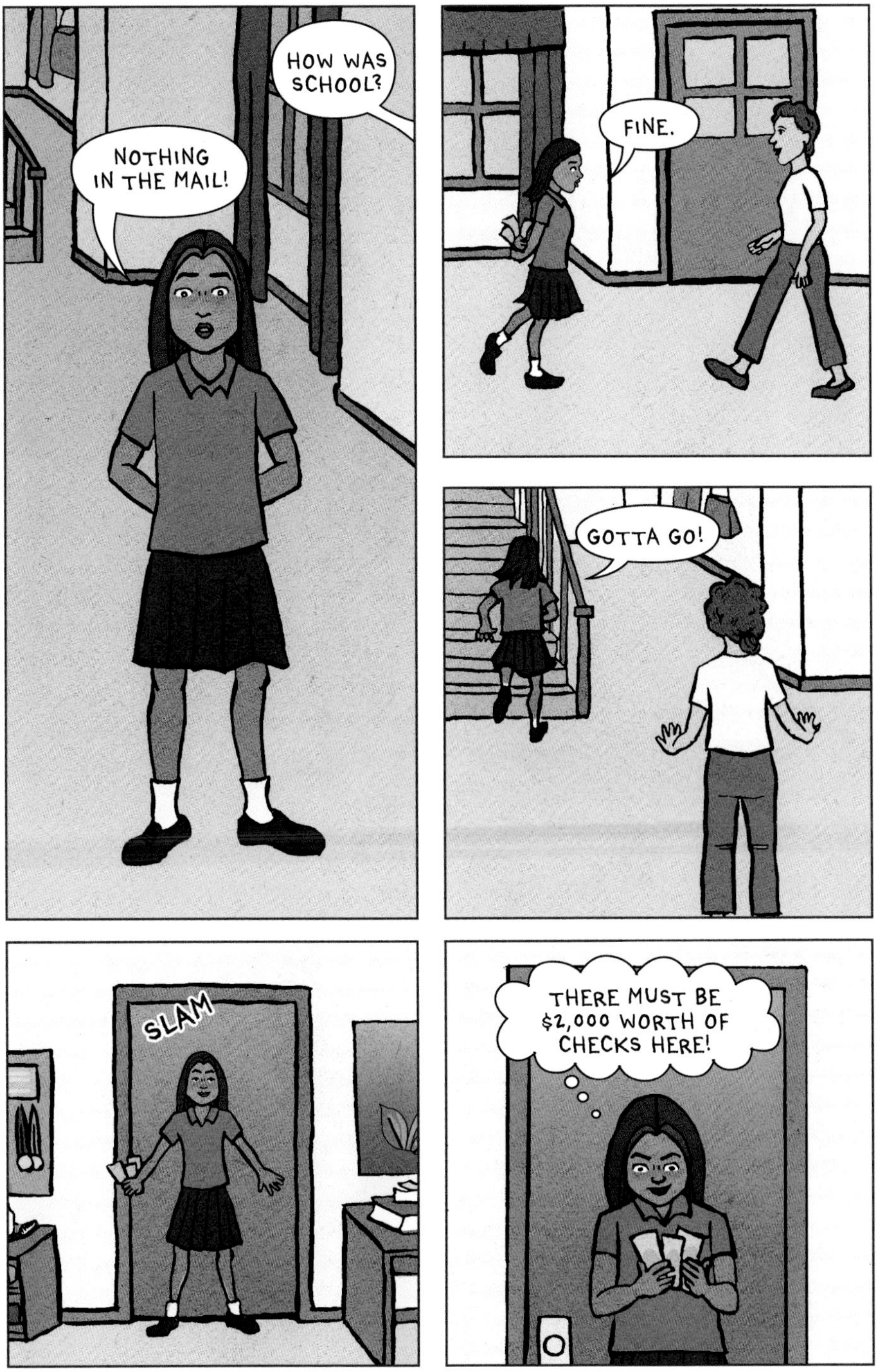
HOW WAS SCHOOL?
NOTHING IN THE MAIL!
FINE.
GOTTA GO!
SLAM
THERE MUST BE $2,000 WORTH OF CHECKS HERE!

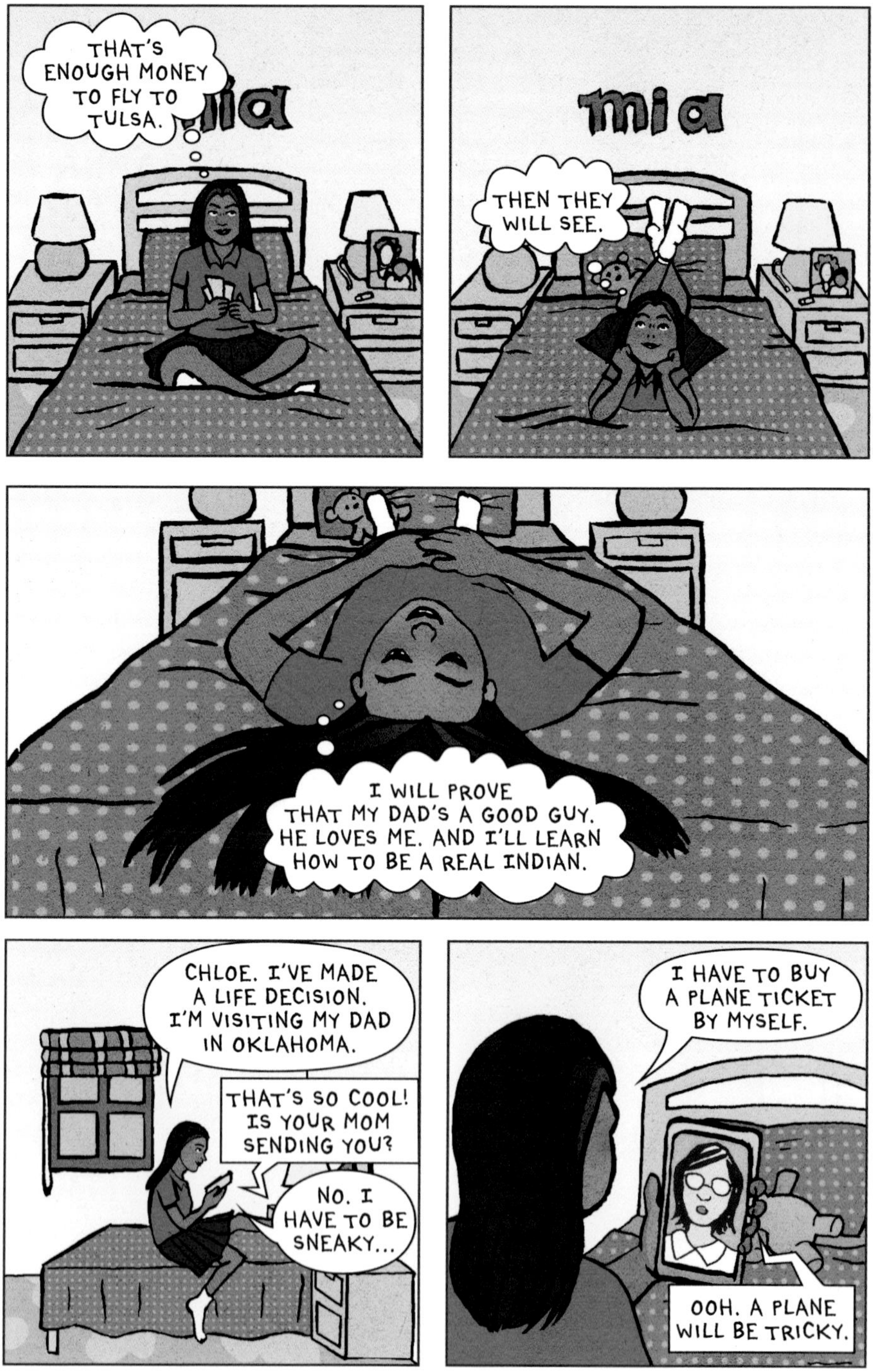
THAT'S ENOUGH MONEY TO FLY TO TULSA.
mia
THEN THEY WILL SEE.
I WILL PROVE THAT MY DAD'S A GOOD GUY. HE LOVES ME. AND I'LL LEARN HOW TO BE A REAL INDIAN.
CHLOE. I'VE MADE A LIFE DECISION. I'M VISITING MY DAD IN OKLAHOMA.
THAT'S SO COOL! IS YOUR MOM SENDING YOU?
NO. I HAVE TO BE SNEAKY...
I HAVE TO BUY A PLANE TICKET BY MYSELF.
OOH. A PLANE WILL BE TRICKY.

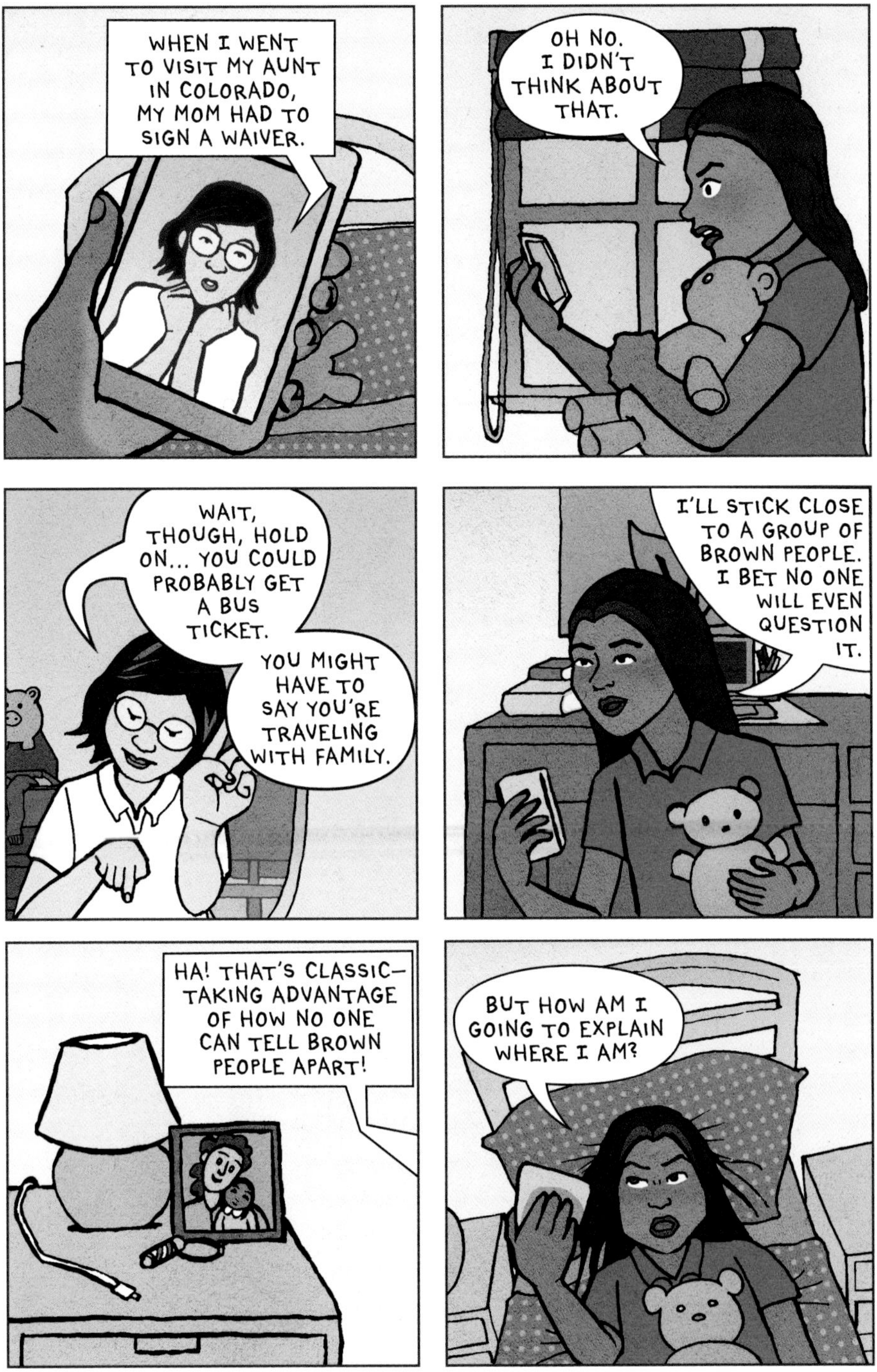
WHEN I WENT TO VISIT MY AUNT IN COLORADO, MY MOM HAD TO SIGN A WAIVER.
OH NO. I DIDN'T THINK ABOUT THAT.
WAIT, THOUGH, HOLD ON... YOU COULD PROBABLY GET A BUS TICKET.
YOU MIGHT HAVE TO SAY YOU'RE TRAVELING WITH FAMILY.
I'LL STICK CLOSE TO A GROUP OF BROWN PEOPLE. I BET NO ONE WILL EVEN QUESTION IT.
HA! THAT'S CLASSIC— TAKING ADVANTAGE OF HOW NO ONE CAN TELL BROWN PEOPLE APART!
BUT HOW AM I GOING TO EXPLAIN WHERE I AM?

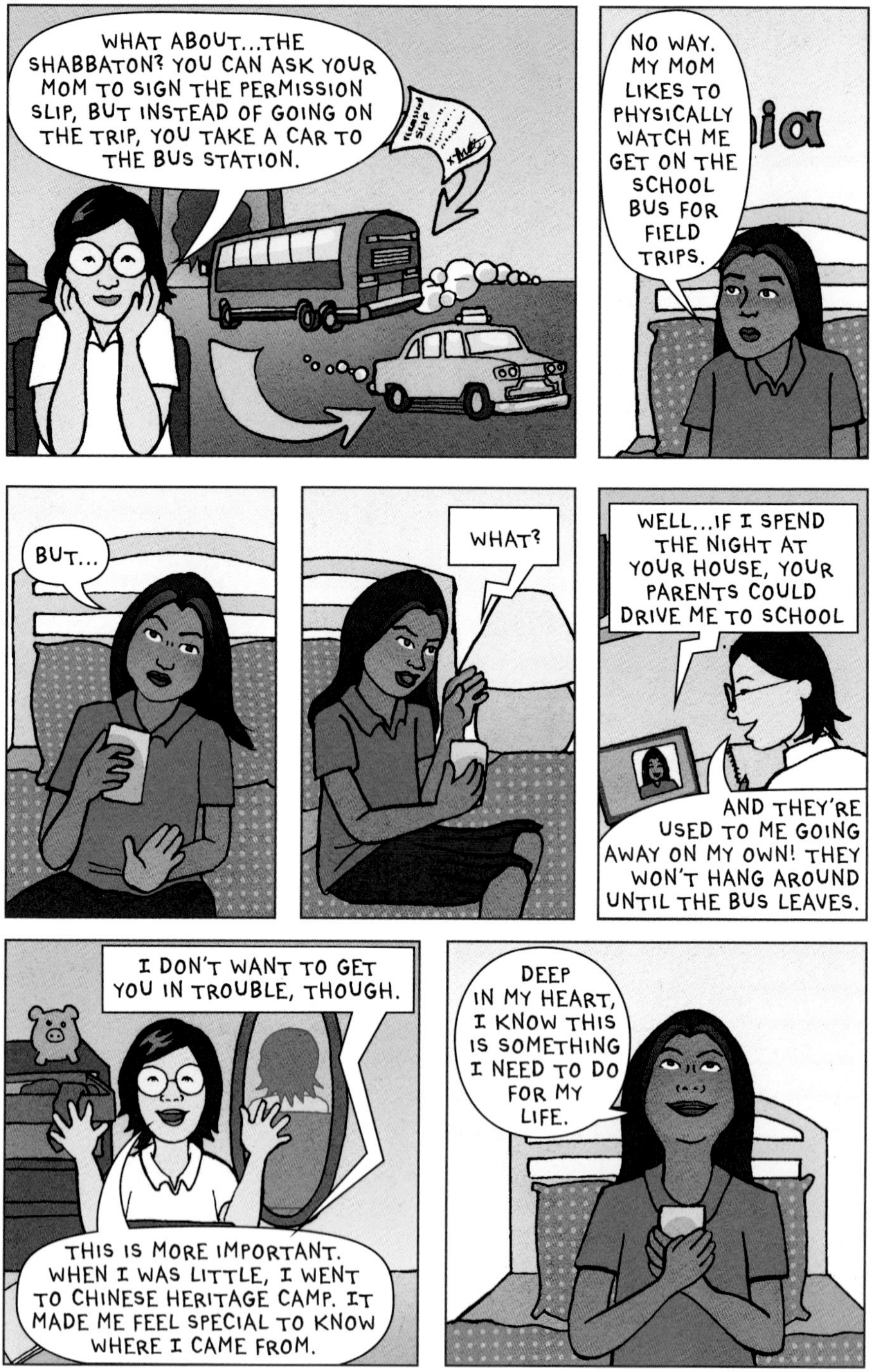
WHAT ABOUT...THE SHABBATON? YOU CAN ASK YOUR MOM TO SIGN THE PERMISSION SLIP, BUT INSTEAD OF GOING ON THE TRIP, YOU TAKE A CAR TO THE BUS STATION.
NO WAY. MY MOM LIKES TO PHYSICALLY WATCH ME GET ON THE SCHOOL BUS FOR FIELD TRIPS.
BUT...
WHAT?
WELL...IF I SPEND THE NIGHT AT YOUR HOUSE, YOUR PARENTS COULD DRIVE ME TO SCHOOL
AND THEY'RE USED TO ME GOING AWAY ON MY OWN! THEY WON'T HANG AROUND UNTIL THE BUS LEAVES.
I DON'T WANT TO GET YOU IN TROUBLE, THOUGH.
THIS IS MORE IMPORTANT. WHEN I WAS LITTLE, I WENT TO CHINESE HERITAGE CAMP. IT MADE ME FEEL SPECIAL TO KNOW WHERE I CAME FROM.
DEEP IN MY HEART, I KNOW THIS IS SOMETHING I NEED TO DO FOR MY LIFE.

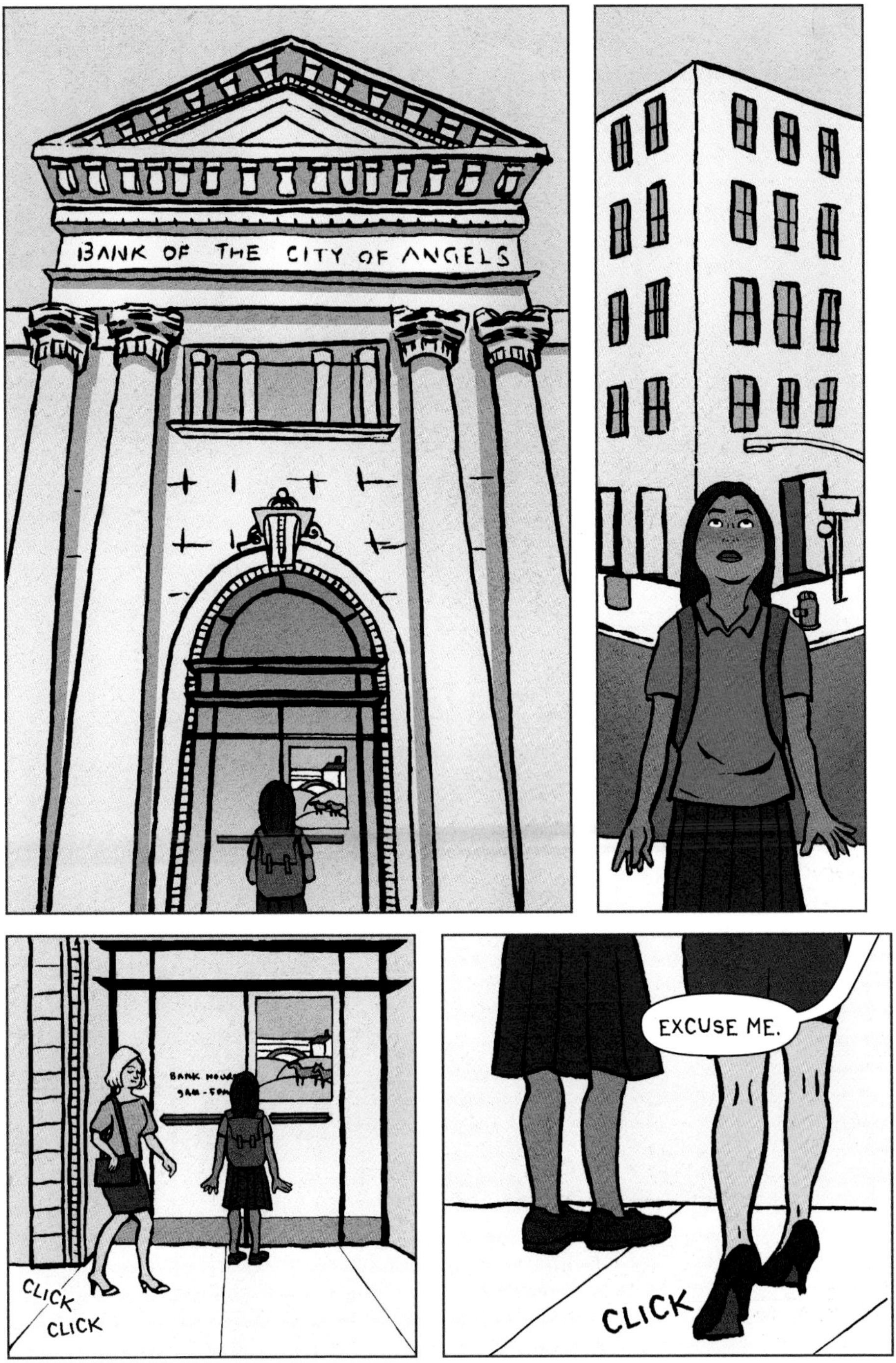
BANK OF THE CITY OF ANGELS
CLICK
CLICK
EXCUSE ME.
CLICK

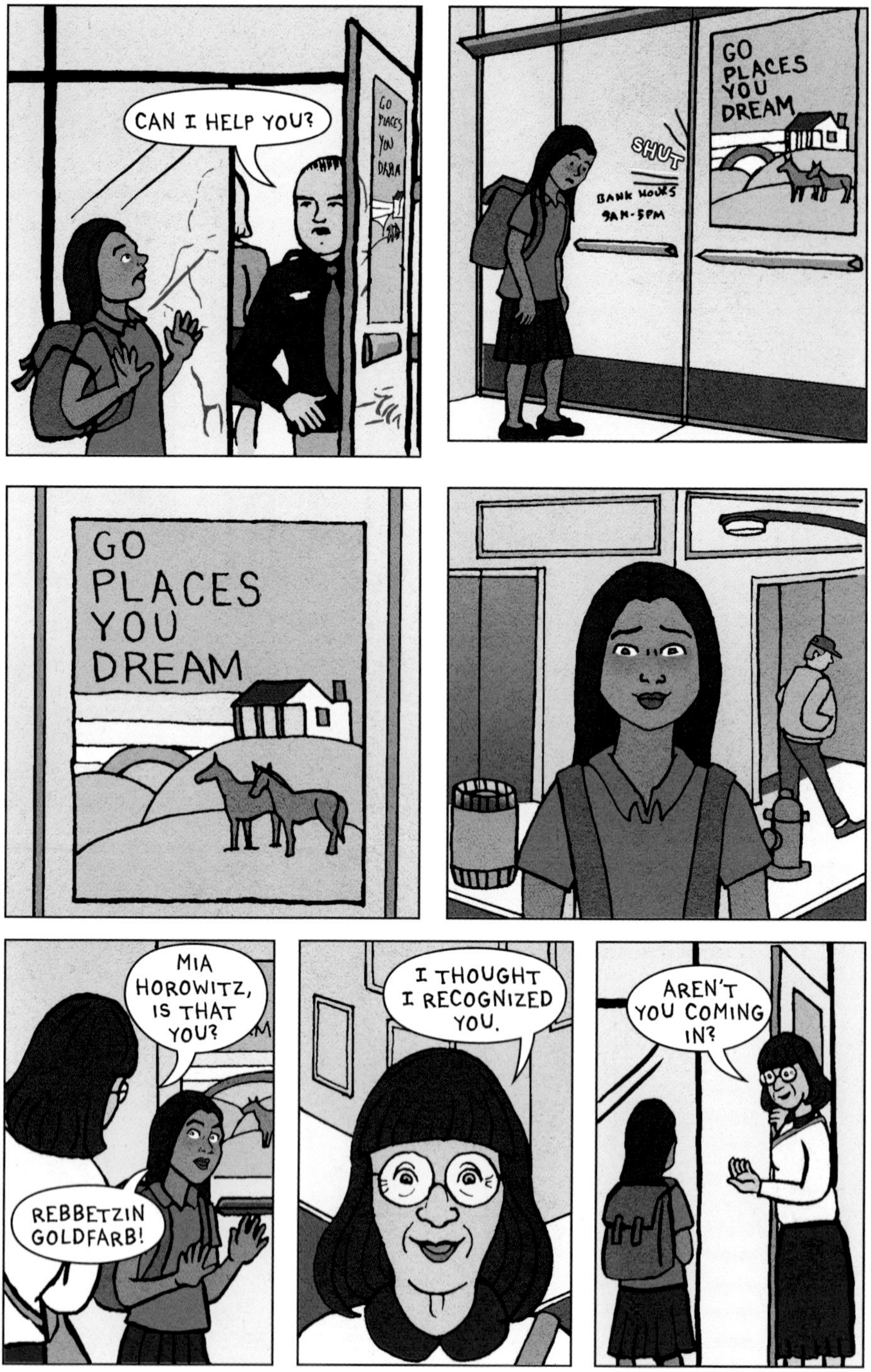
CAN I HELP YOU?
GO PLACES YOU DREAM
SHUT
BANK HOURS 9AM-5PM
GO PLACES YOU DREAM
GO PLACES YOU DREAM
MIA HOROWITZ, IS THAT YOU?
REBBETZIN GOLDFARB!
I THOUGHT I RECOGNIZED YOU.
AREN'T YOU COMING IN?

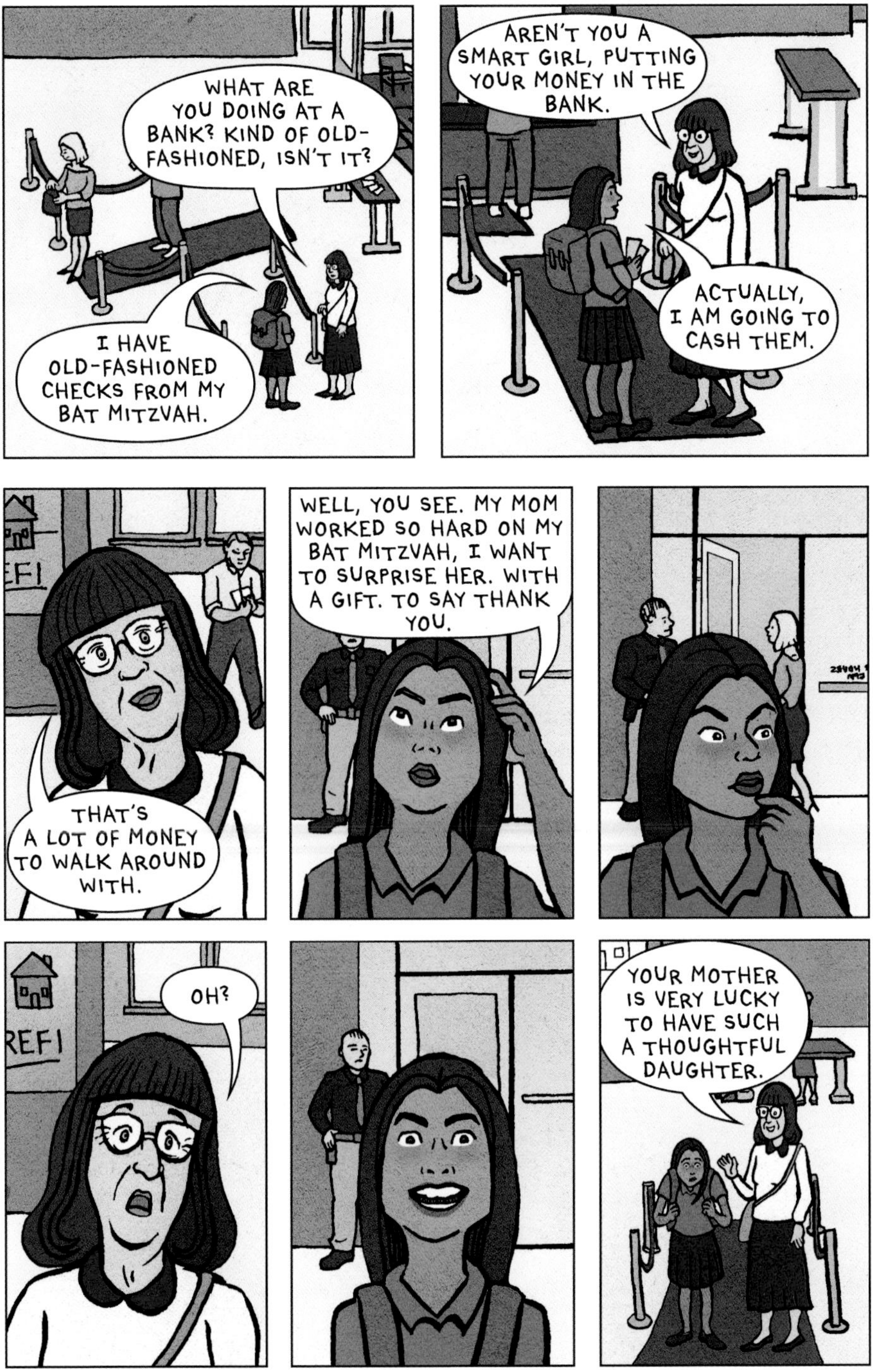
WHAT ARE YOU DOING AT A BANK? KIND OF OLD-FASHIONED, ISN'T IT?
I HAVE OLD-FASHIONED CHECKS FROM MY BAT MITZVAH.
AREN'T YOU A SMART GIRL, PUTTING YOUR MONEY IN THE BANK.
ACTUALLY, I AM GOING TO CASH THEM.
REFI
THAT'S A LOT OF MONEY TO WALK AROUND WITH.
WELL, YOU SEE. MY MOM WORKED SO HARD ON MY BAT MITZVAH, I WANT TO SURPRISE HER. WITH A GIFT. TO SAY THANK YOU.
REFI
OH?
YOUR MOTHER IS VERY LUCKY TO HAVE SUCH A THOUGHTFUL DAUGHTER.

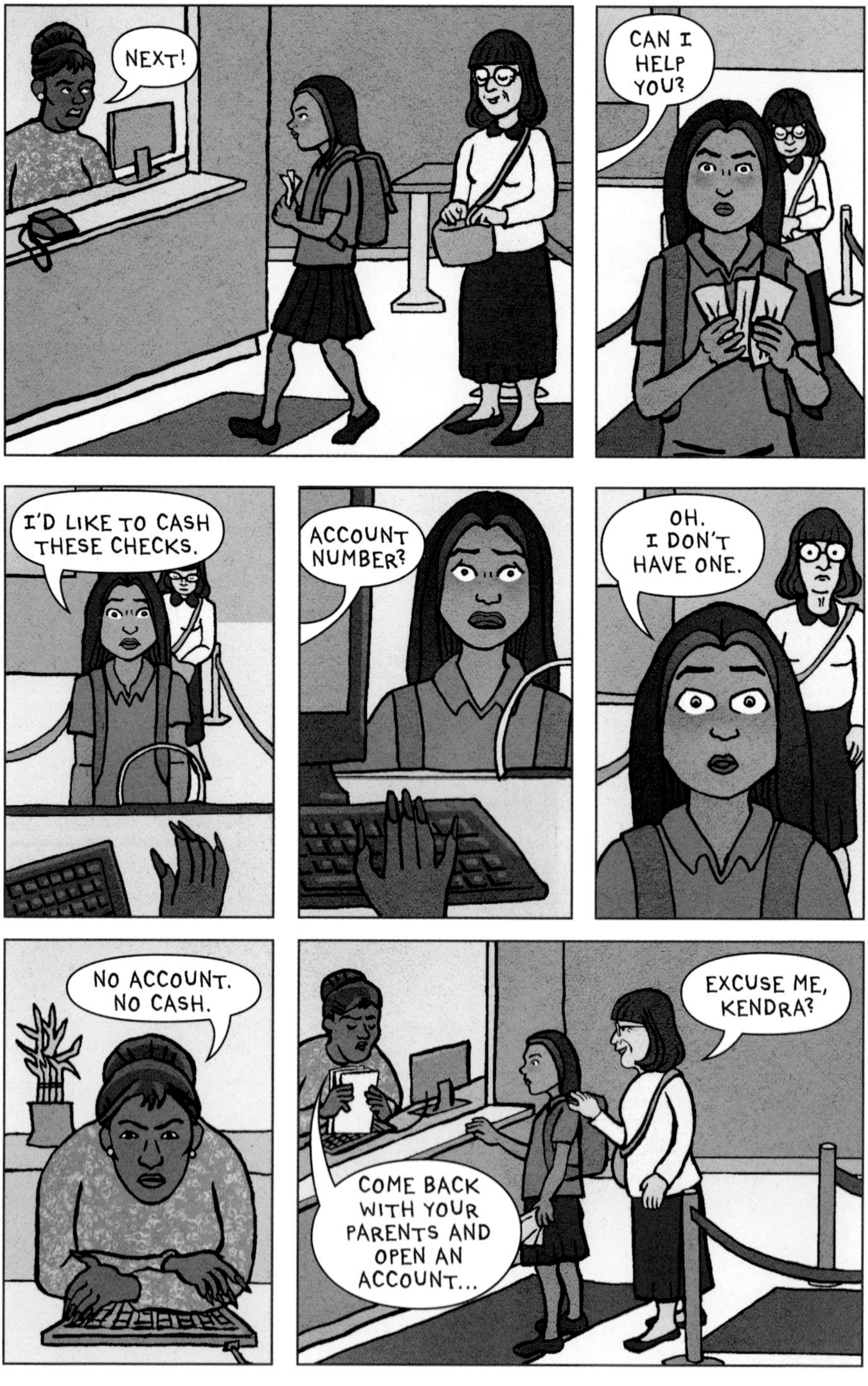
NEXT!
CAN I HELP YOU?
I'D LIKE TO CASH THESE CHECKS.
ACCOUNT NUMBER?
OH. I DON'T HAVE ONE.
NO ACCOUNT. NO CASH.
COME BACK WITH YOUR PARENTS AND OPEN AN ACCOUNT...
EXCUSE ME, KENDRA?

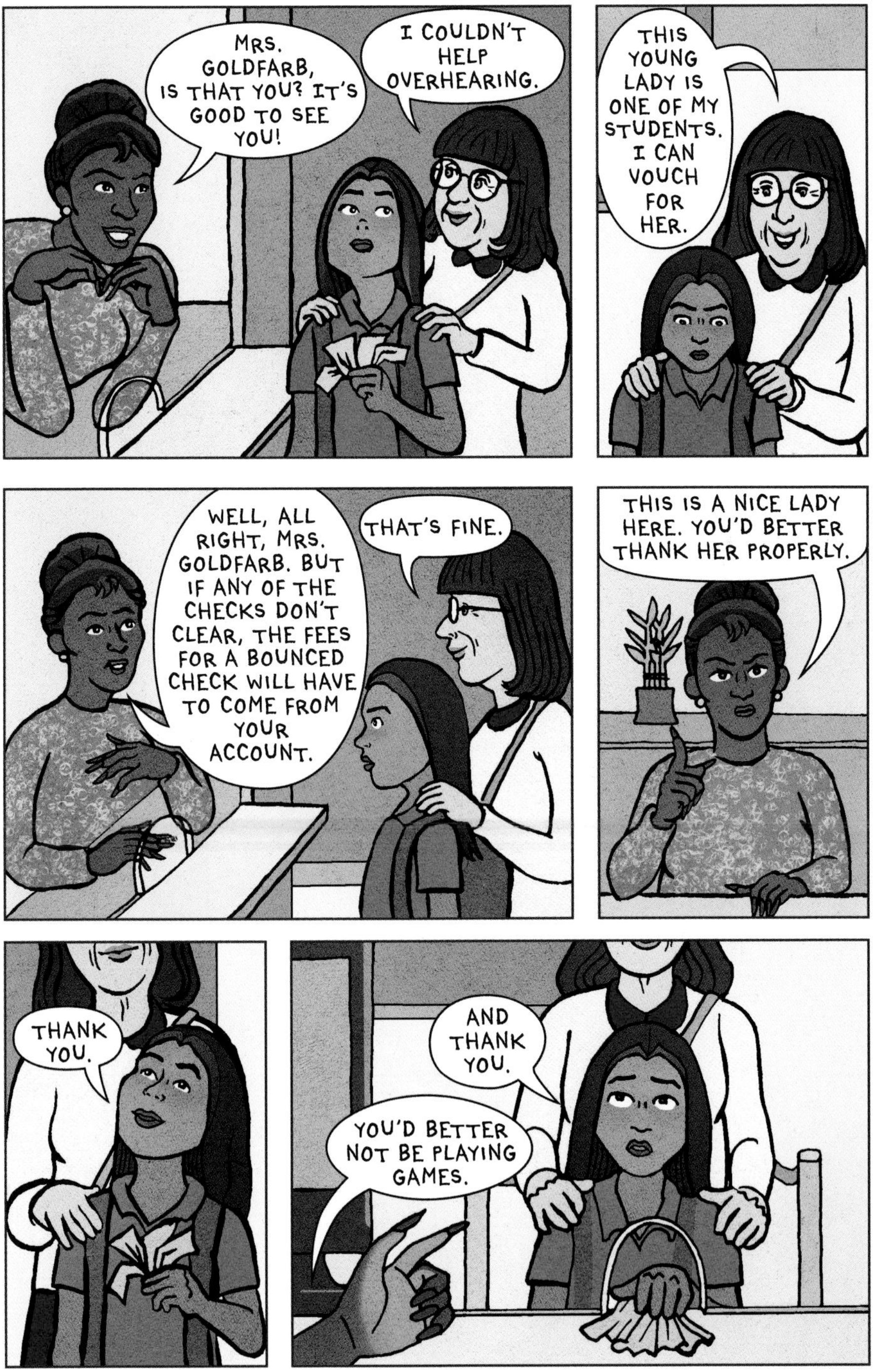
MRS. GOLDFARB, IS THAT YOU? IT'S GOOD TO SEE YOU!
I COULDN'T HELP OVERHEARING.
THIS YOUNG LADY IS ONE OF MY STUDENTS. I CAN VOUCH FOR HER.
WELL, ALL RIGHT, MRS. GOLDFARB. BUT IF ANY OF THE CHECKS DON'T CLEAR, THE FEES FOR A BOUNCED CHECK WILL HAVE TO COME FROM YOUR ACCOUNT.
THAT'S FINE.
THIS IS A NICE LADY HERE. YOU'D BETTER THANK HER PROPERLY.
THANK YOU.
AND THANK YOU.
YOU'D BETTER NOT BE PLAYING GAMES.

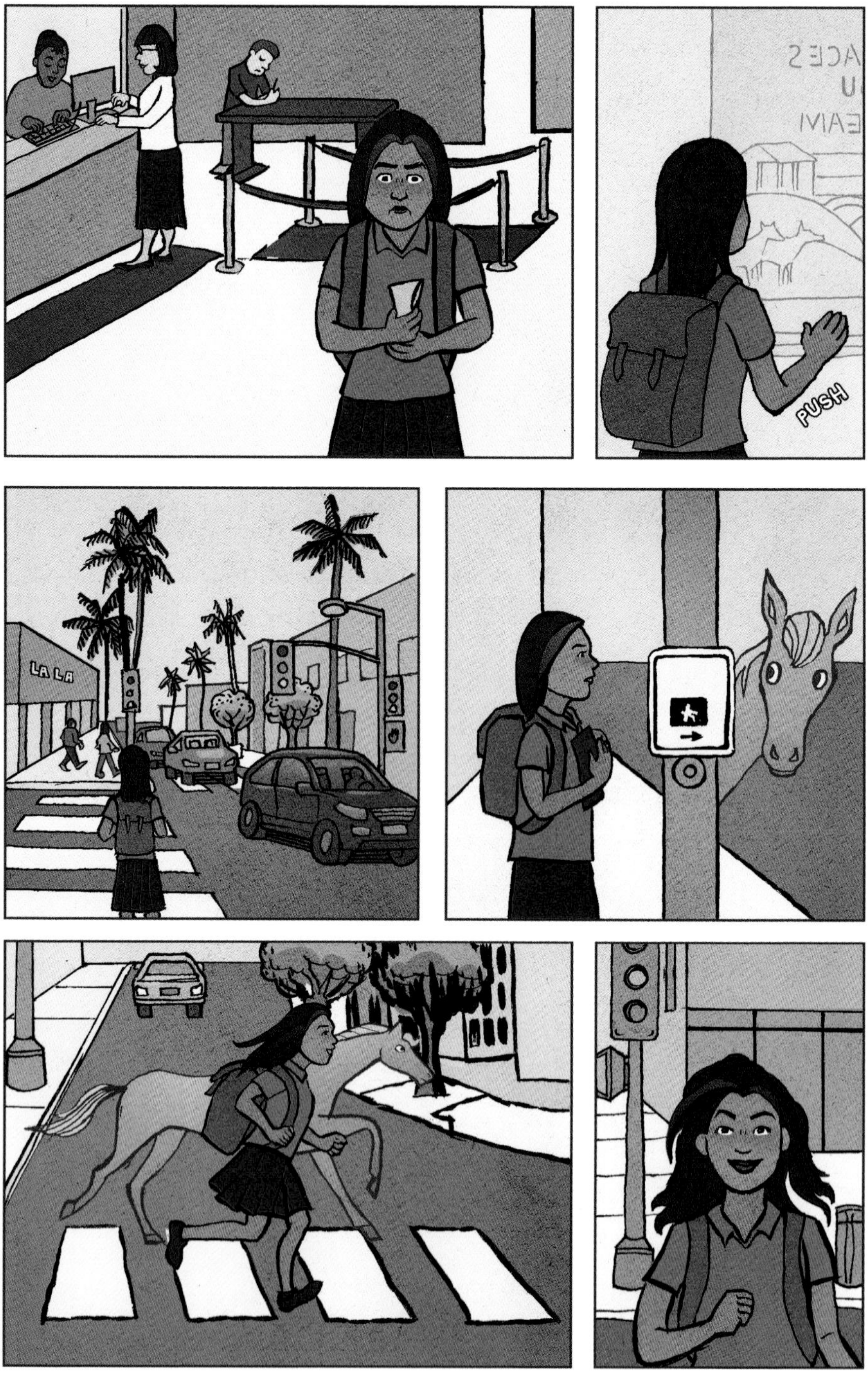
PUSH
LA LA

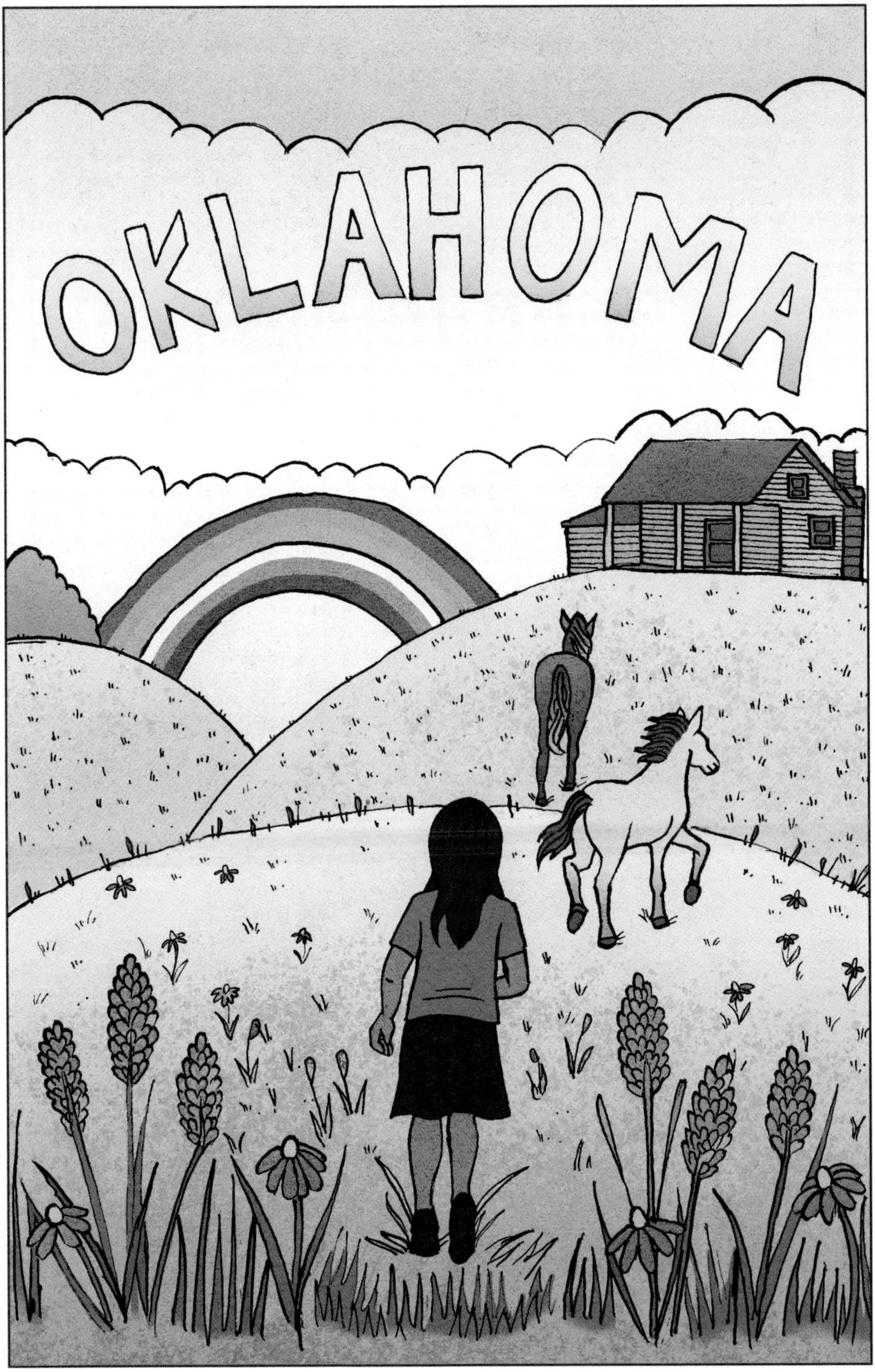
OKLAHOMA

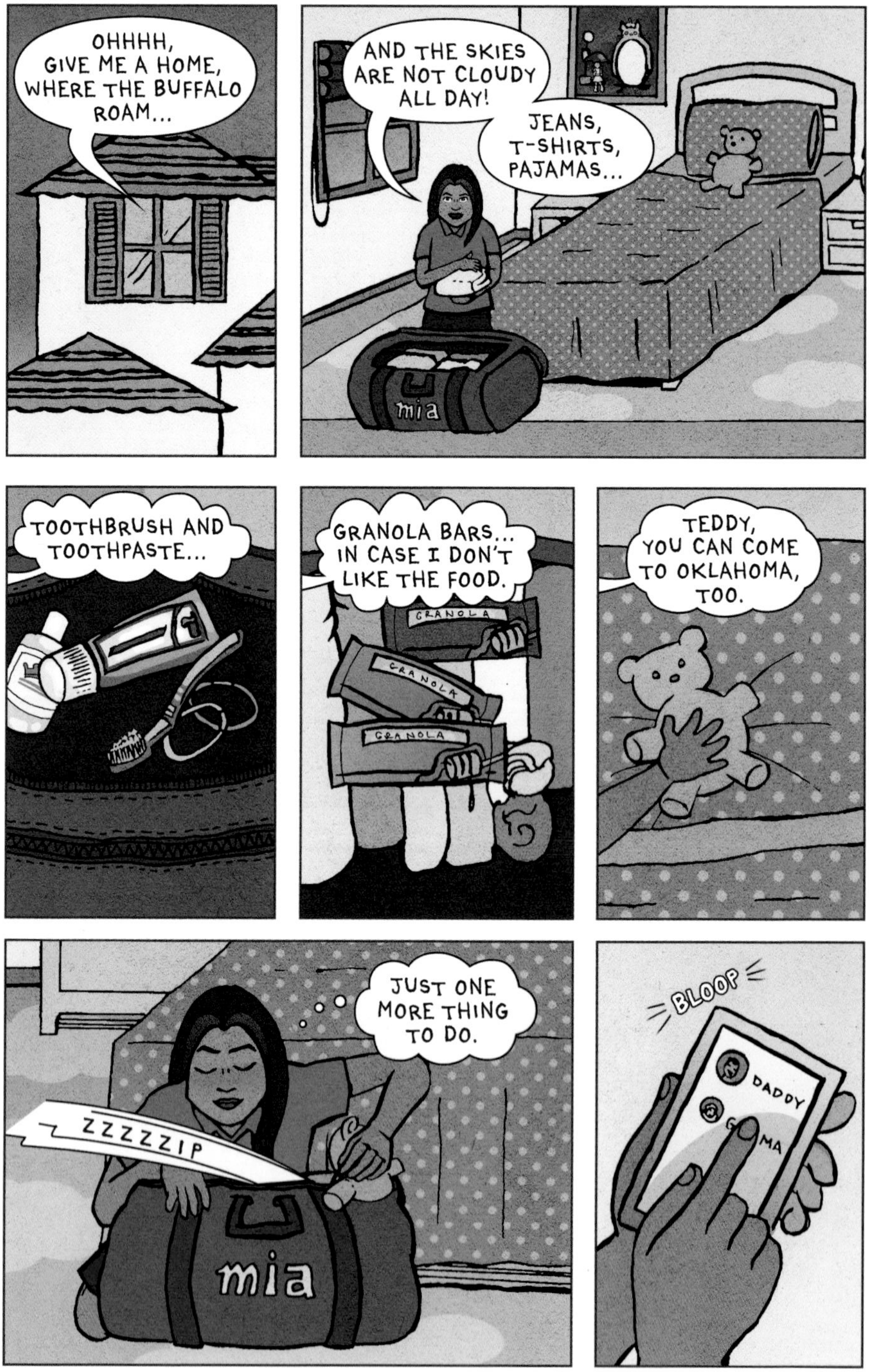
OHHHH, GIVE ME A HOME, WHERE THE BUFFALO ROAM...
AND THE SKIES ARE NOT CLOUDY ALL DAY!
JEANS, T-SHIRTS, PAJAMAS...
mia
TOOTHBRUSH AND TOOTHPASTE...
GRANOLA BARS... IN CASE I DON'T LIKE THE FOOD.
GRANOLA
GRANOLA
GRANOLA
TEDDY, YOU CAN COME TO OKLAHOMA, TOO.
JUST ONE MORE THING TO DO.
ZZZZZIP
mia
BLOOP
DADDY

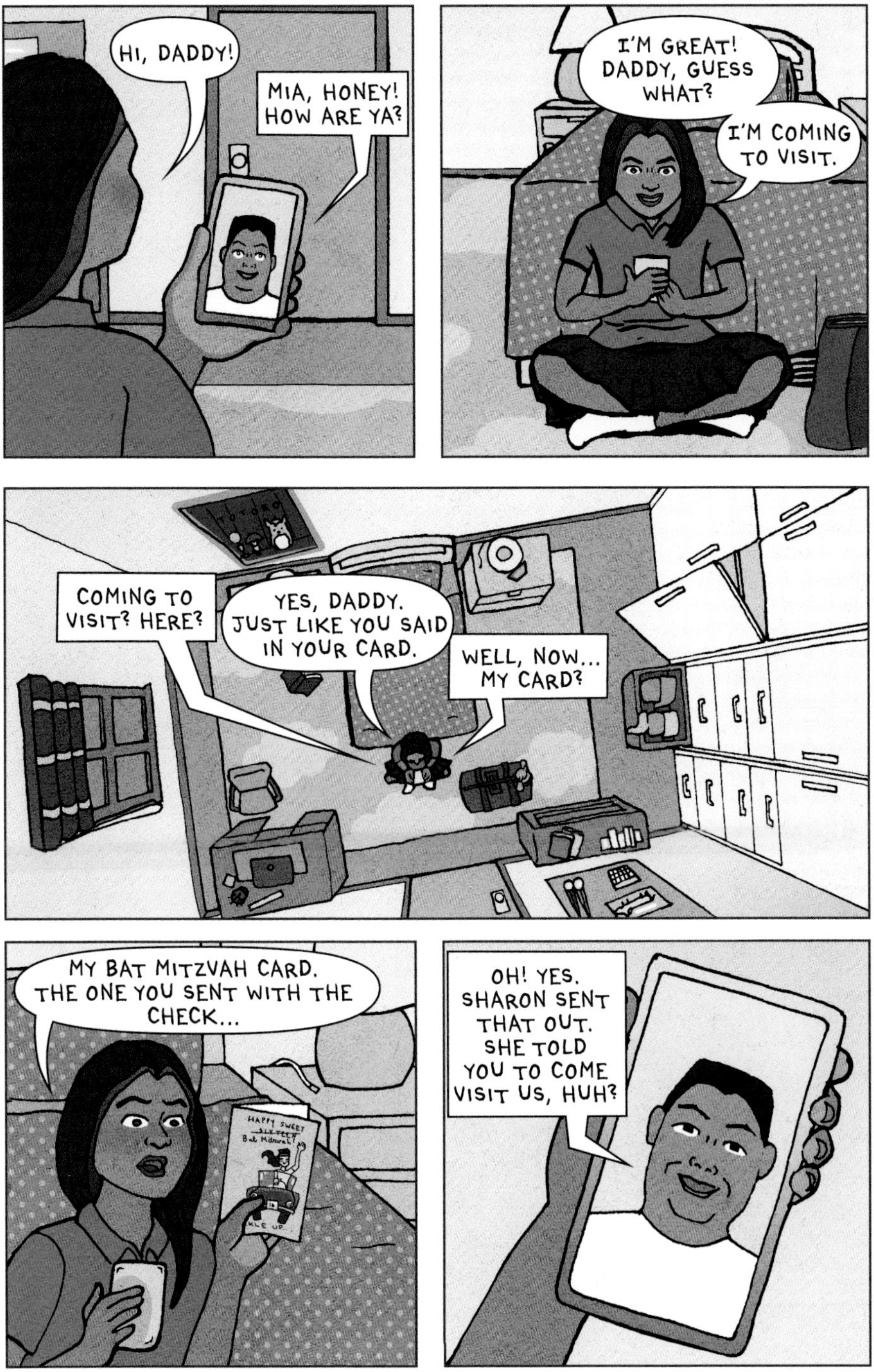
HI, DADDY!
MIA, HONEY! HOW ARE YA?
I'M GREAT! DADDY, GUESS WHAT?
I'M COMING TO VISIT.
COMING TO VISIT? HERE?
YES, DADDY. JUST LIKE YOU SAID IN YOUR CARD.
WELL, NOW... MY CARD?
MY BAT MITZVAH CARD. THE ONE YOU SENT WITH THE CHECK...
OH! YES. SHARON SENT THAT OUT. SHE TOLD YOU TO COME VISIT US, HUH?

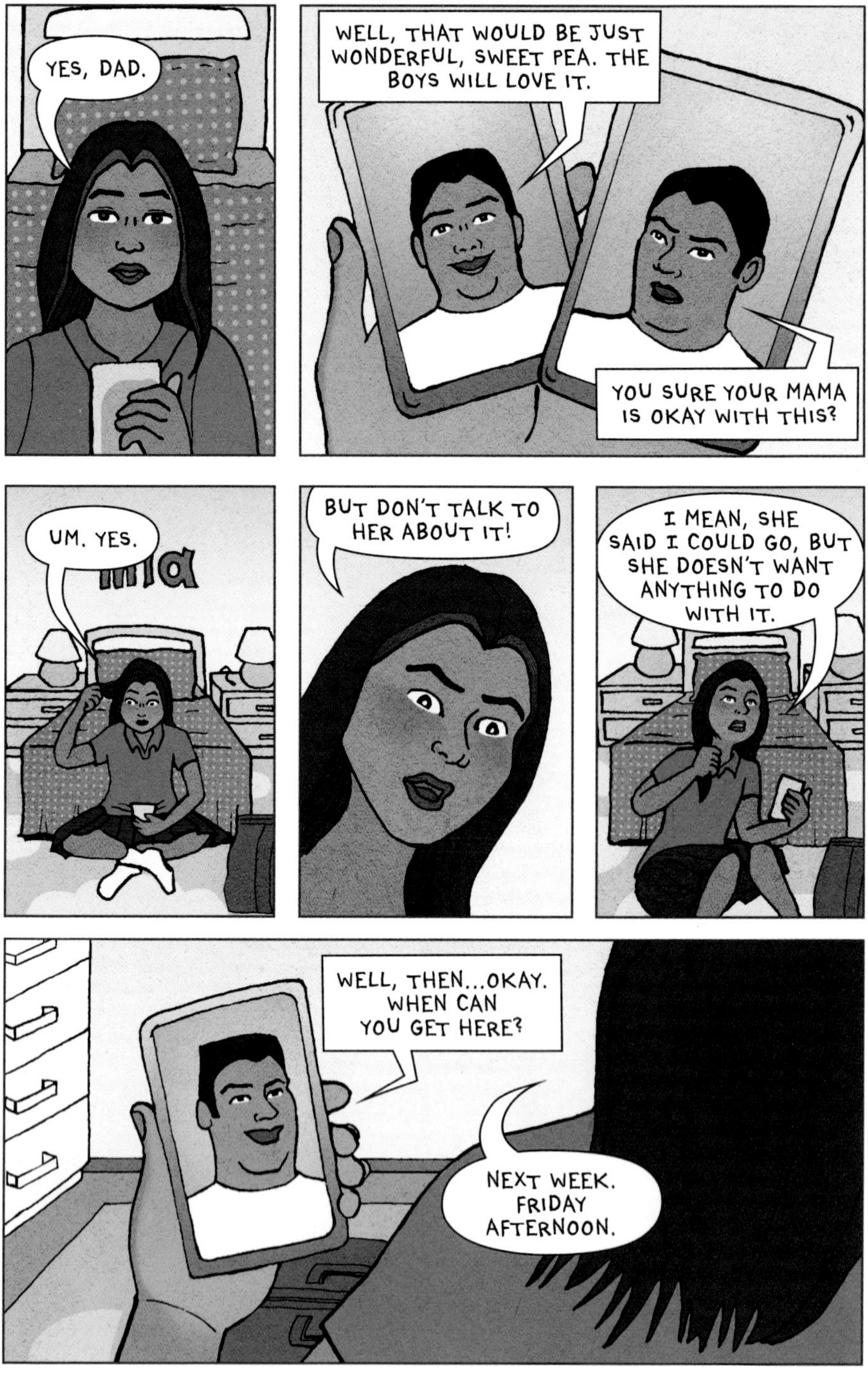
YES, DAD.
WELL, THAT WOULD BE JUST WONDERFUL, SWEET PEA. THE BOYS WILL LOVE IT.
YOU SURE YOUR MAMA IS OKAY WITH THIS?
UM. YES.
mia
BUT DON'T TALK TO HER ABOUT IT!
I MEAN, SHE SAID I COULD GO, BUT SHE DOESN'T WANT ANYTHING TO DO WITH IT.
WELL, THEN...OKAY. WHEN CAN YOU GET HERE?
NEXT WEEK. FRIDAY AFTERNOON.

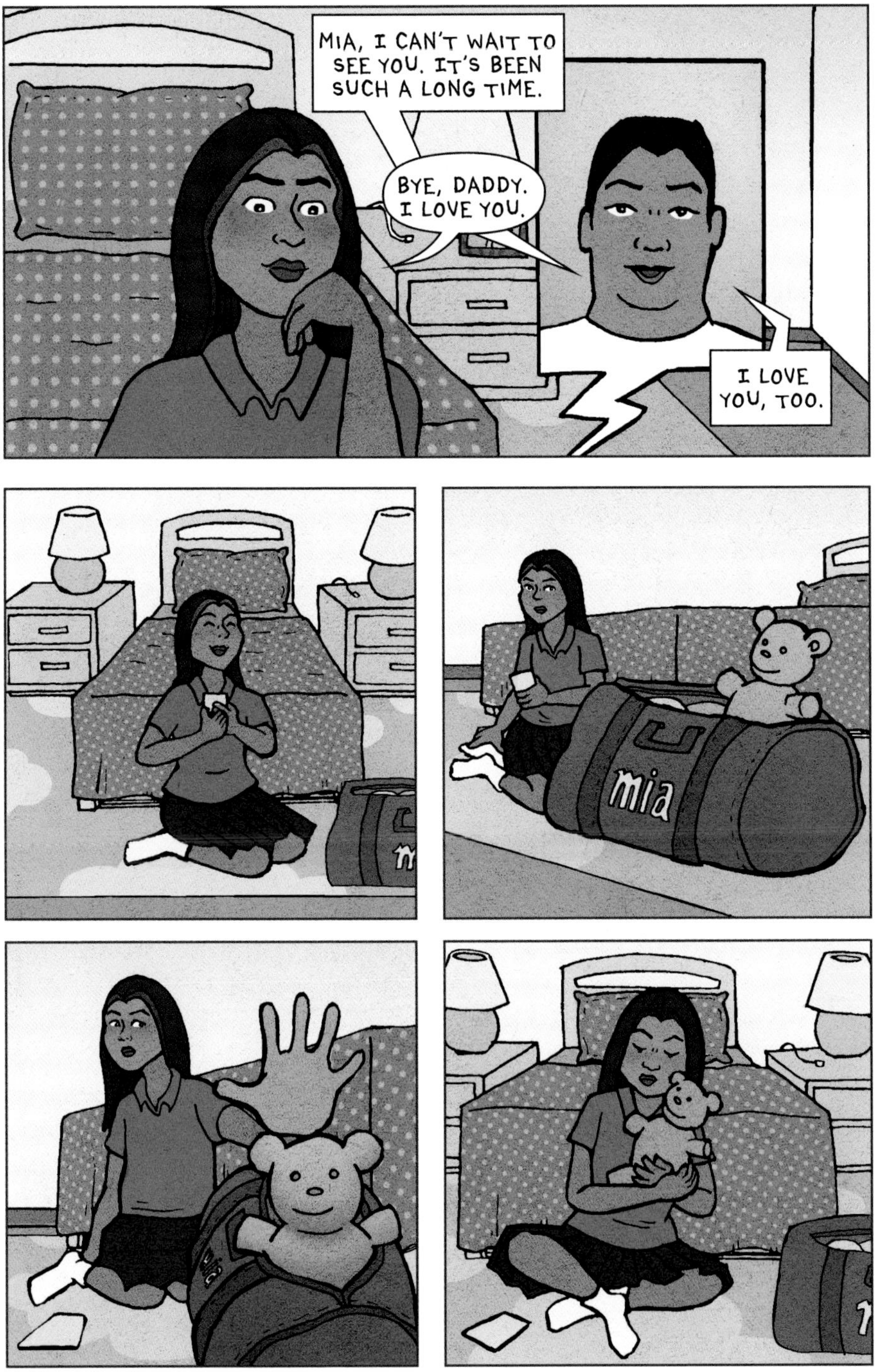
MIA, I CAN'T WAIT TO SEE YOU. IT'S BEEN SUCH A LONG TIME.
BYE, DADDY. I LOVE YOU.
I LOVE YOU, TOO.
mia

THE JOURNEY

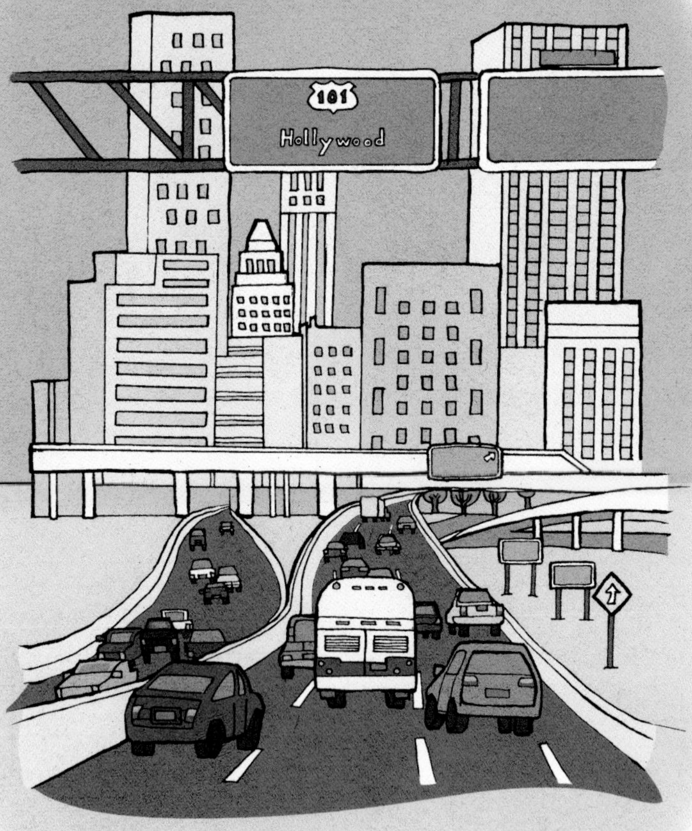
101
Hollywood

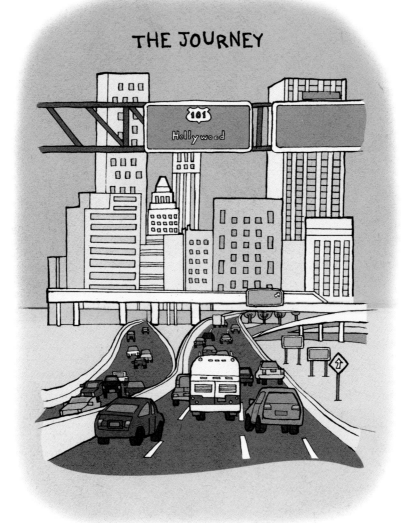

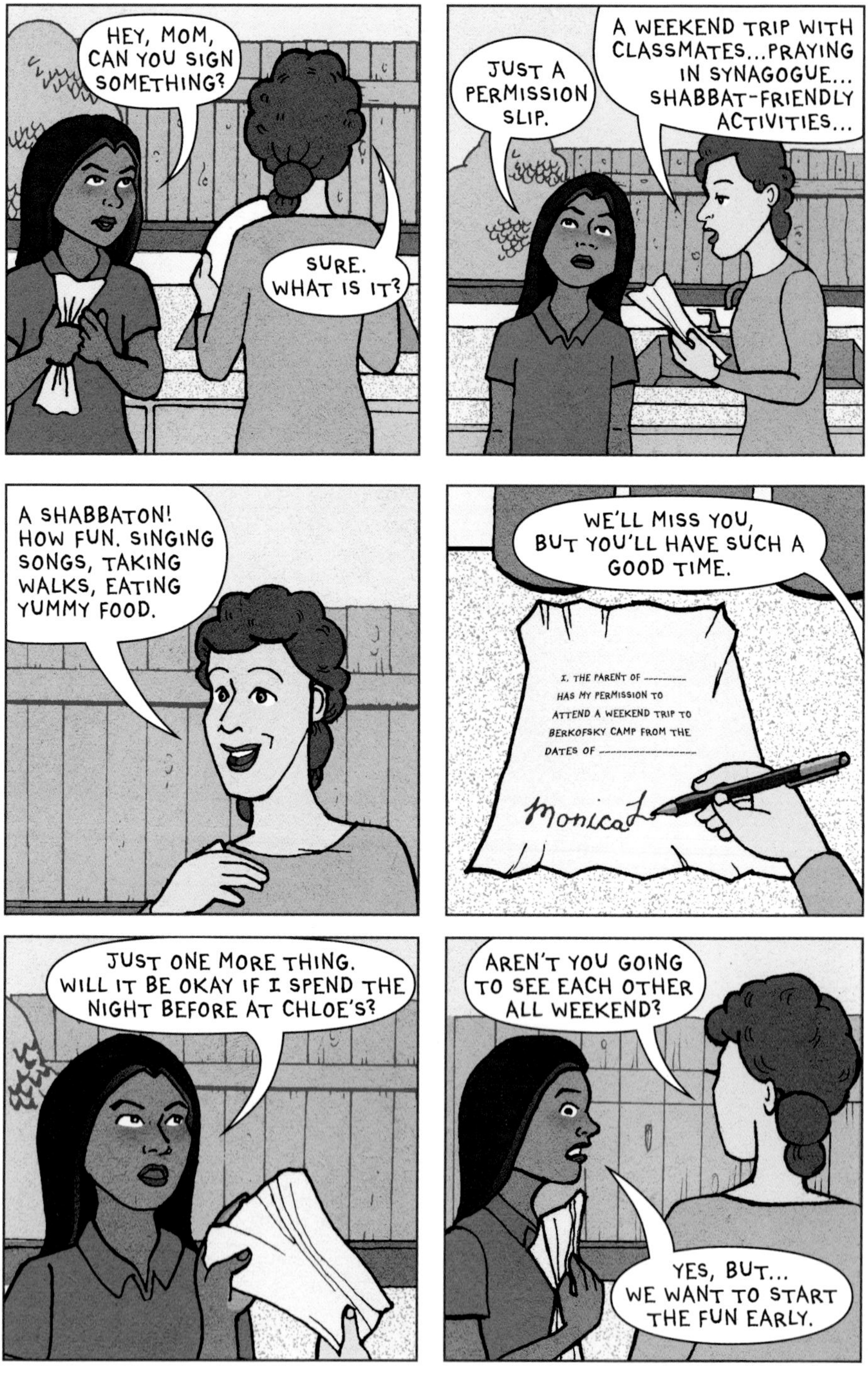
HEY, MOM, CAN YOU SIGN SOMETHING?
SURE. WHAT IS IT?
JUST A PERMISSION SLIP.
A WEEKEND TRIP WITH CLASSMATES...PRAYING IN SYNAGOGUE... SHABBAT-FRIENDLY ACTIVITIES...
A SHABBATON! HOW FUN. SINGING SONGS, TAKING WALKS, EATING YUMMY FOOD.
WE'LL MISS YOU, BUT YOU'LL HAVE SUCH A GOOD TIME.
I, THE PARENT OF
HAS MY PERMISSION TO
ATTEND A WEEKEND TRIP TO
BERKOFSKY CAMP FROM THE
DATES OF
JUST ONE MORE THING. WILL IT BE OKAY IF I SPEND THE NIGHT BEFORE AT CHLOE'S?
AREN'T YOU GOING TO SEE EACH OTHER ALL WEEKEND?
YES, BUT... WE WANT TO START THE FUN EARLY.

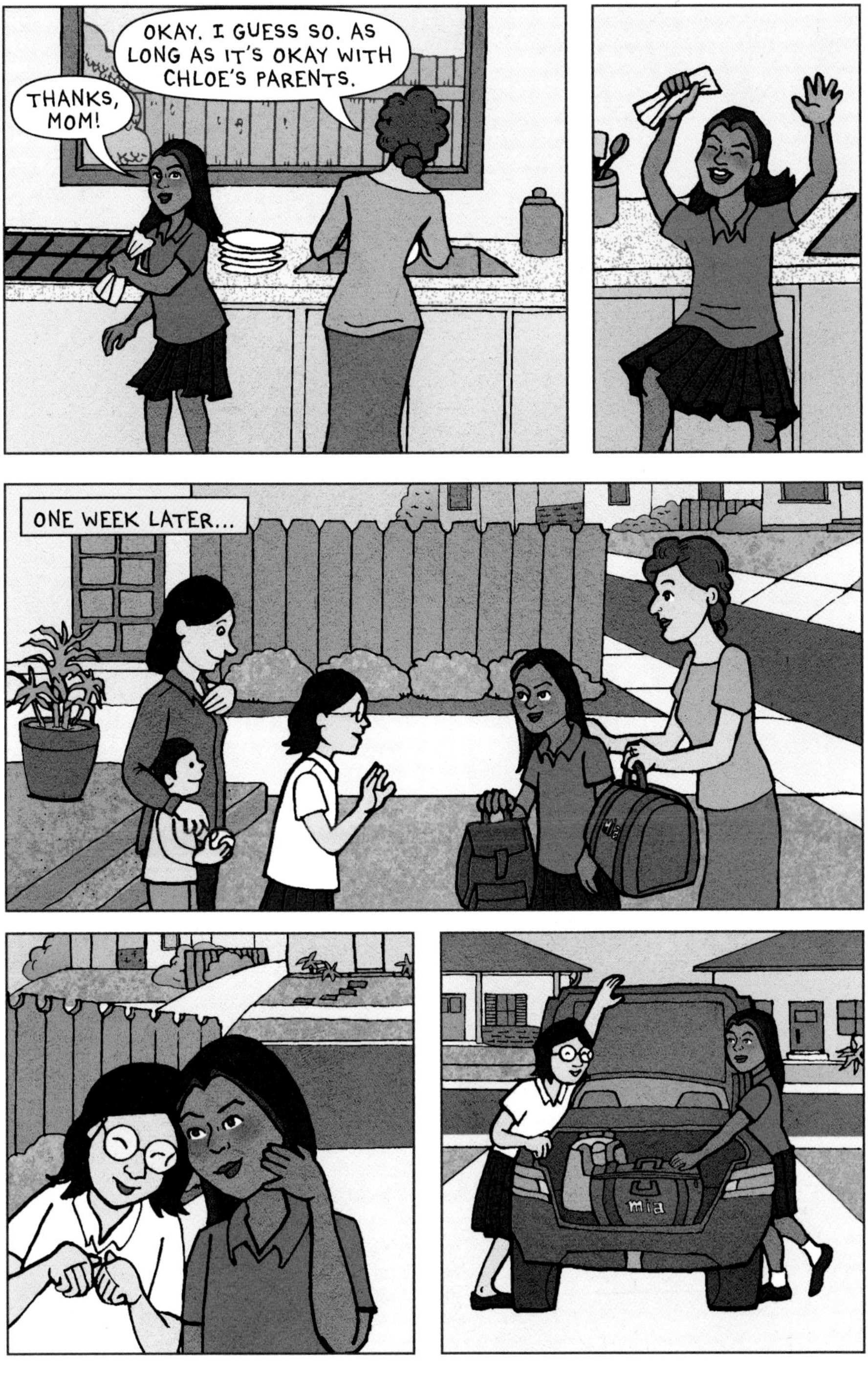
OKAY. I GUESS SO. AS LONG AS IT'S OKAY WITH CHLOE'S PARENTS.
THANKS, MOM!
ONE WEEK LATER...
mia

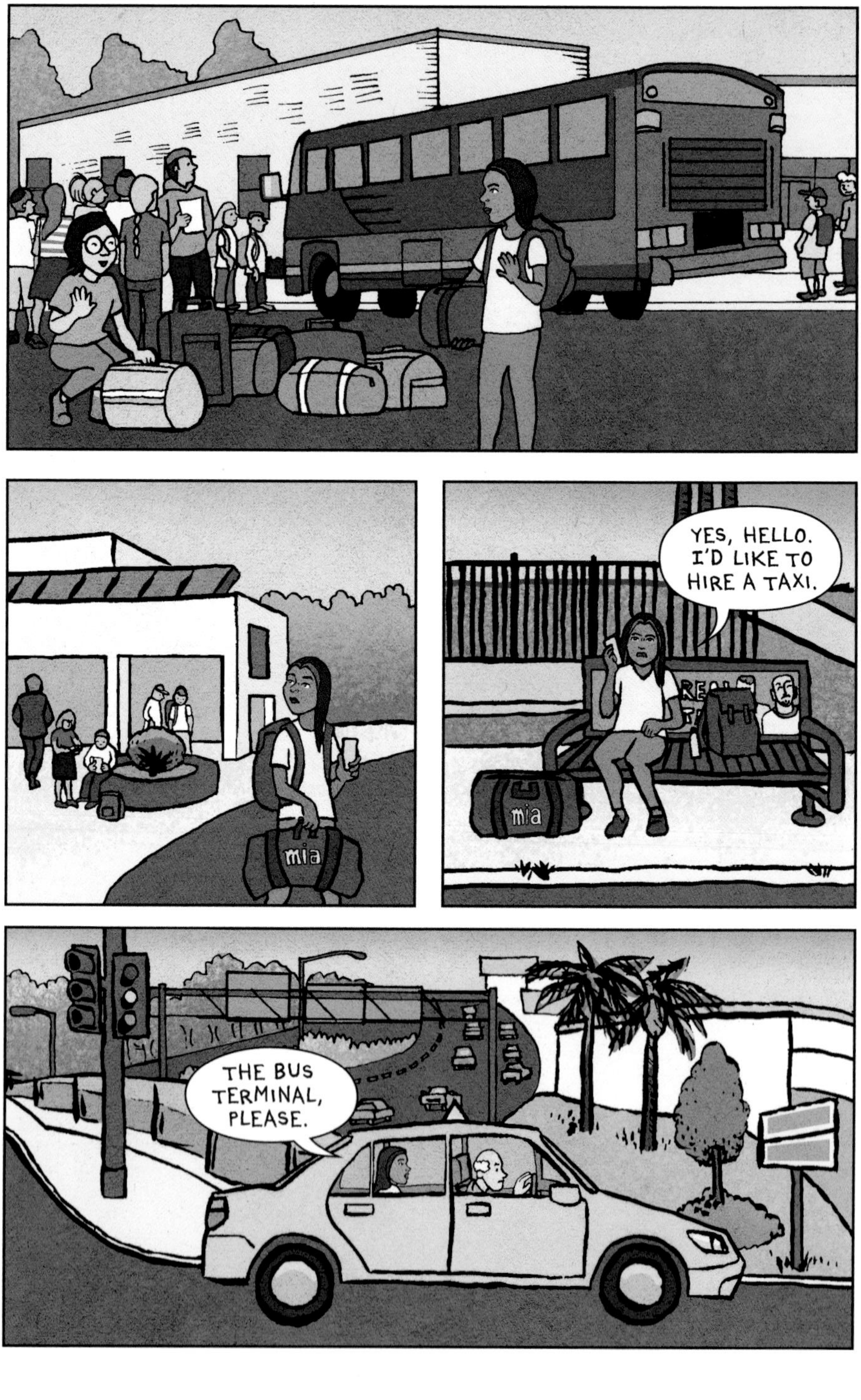
mia
YES, HELLO. I'D LIKE TO HIRE A TAXI.
mia
THE BUS TERMINAL, PLEASE.

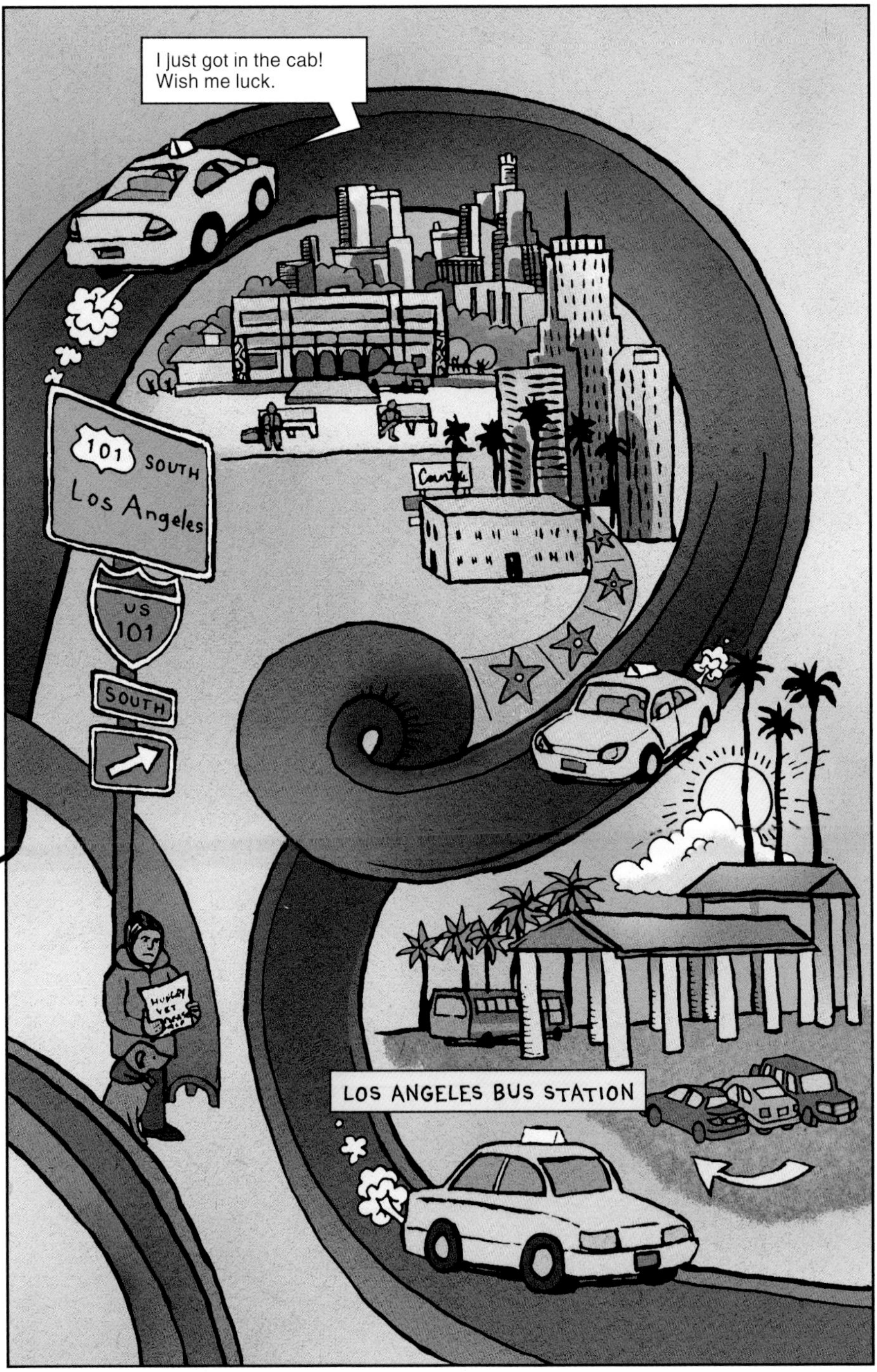
I just got in the cab!
Wish me luck.
101 SOUTH
Los Angeles
US 101
SOUTH
LOS ANGELES BUS STATION

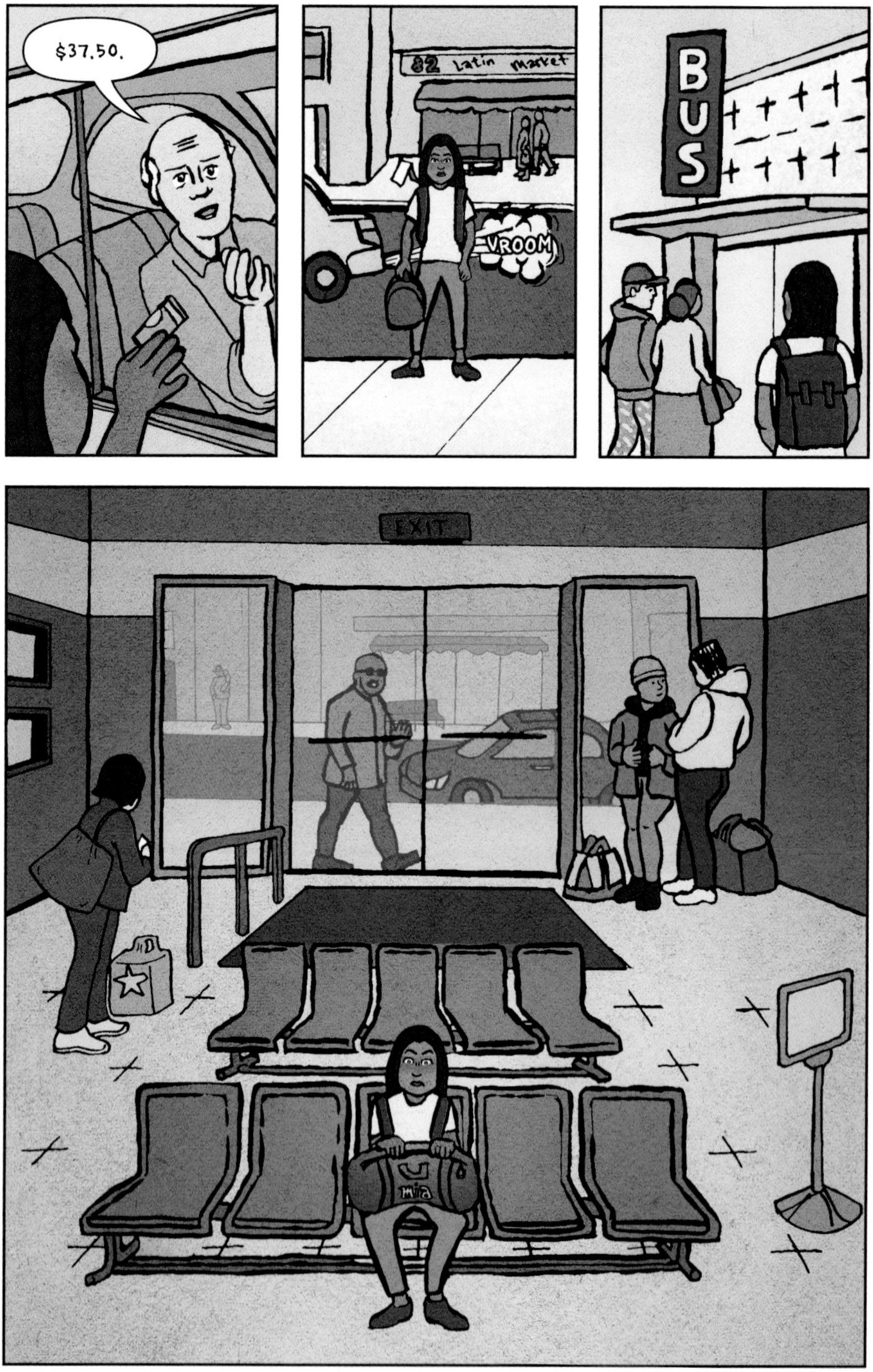
$37.50.
82 Latin market
VROOM
BUS
EXIT
mia

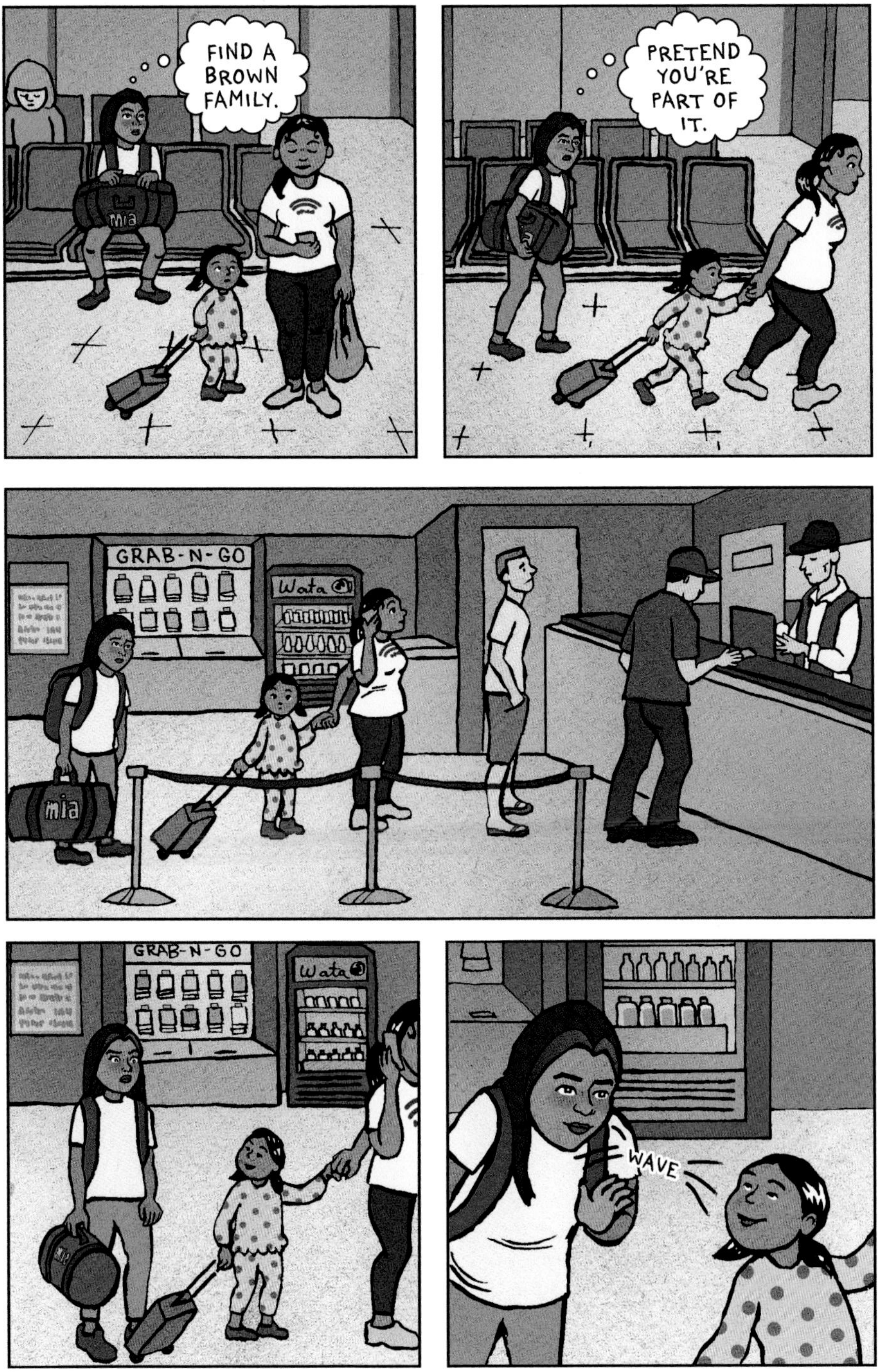
FIND A BROWN FAMILY.
mia
PRETEND YOU'RE PART OF IT.
GRAB-N-GO
Wata
mia
GRAB-N-GO
Wata
WAVE

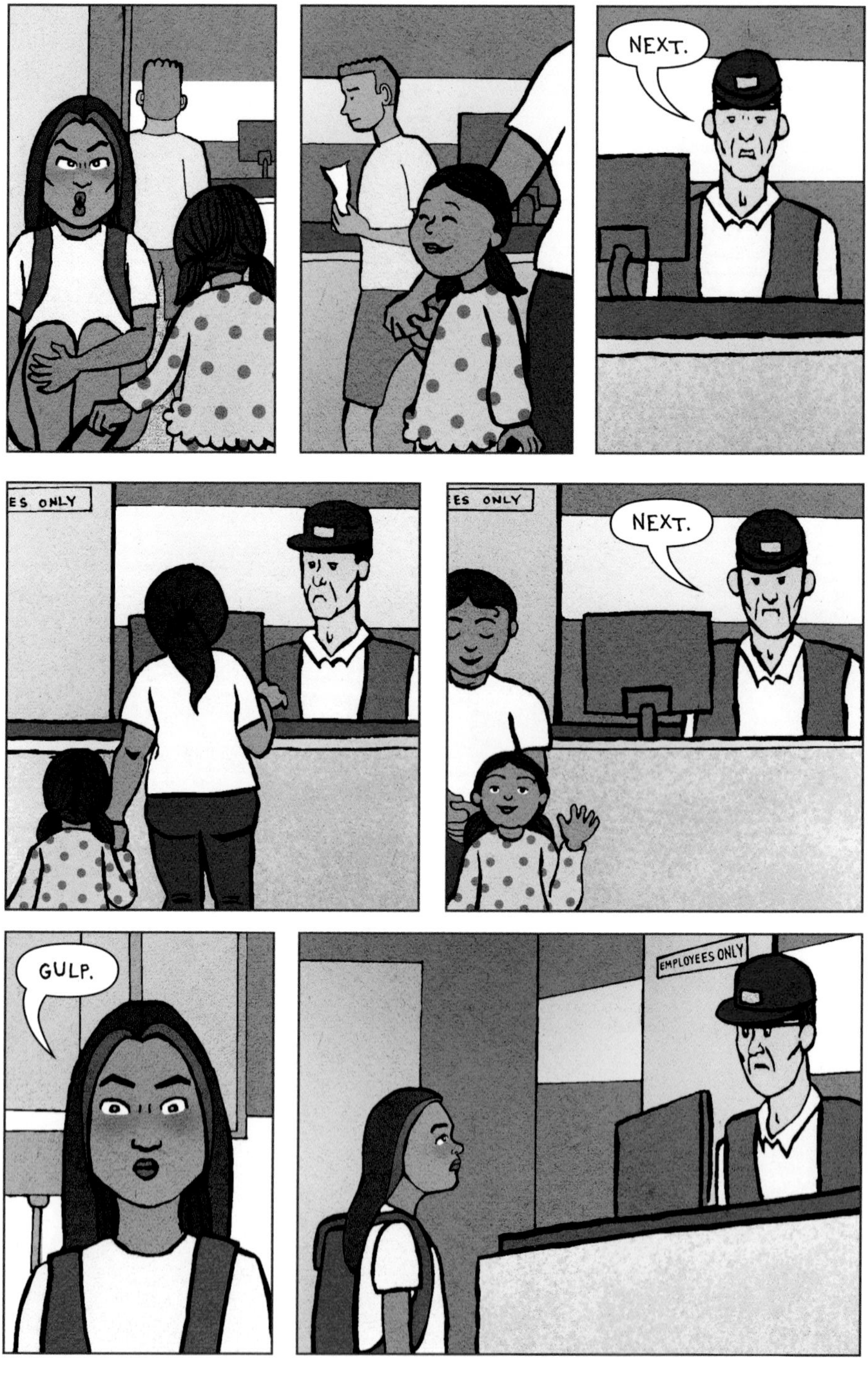
NEXT.
ES ONLY
ES ONLY
NEXT.
GULP.
EMPLOYEES ONLY

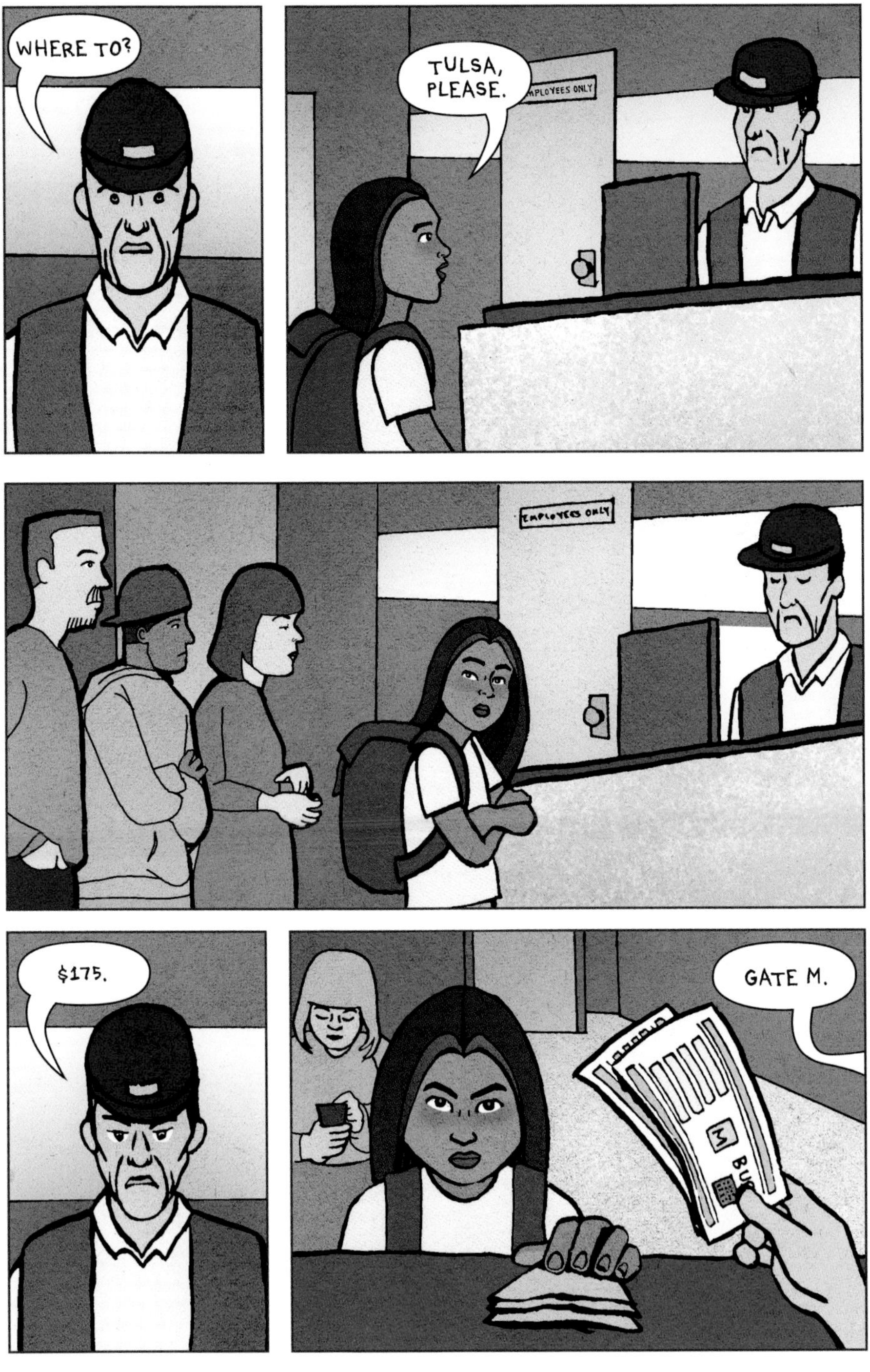
WHERE TO?
TULSA, PLEASE.
EMPLOYEES ONLY
EMPLOYEES ONLY
$175.
GATE M.

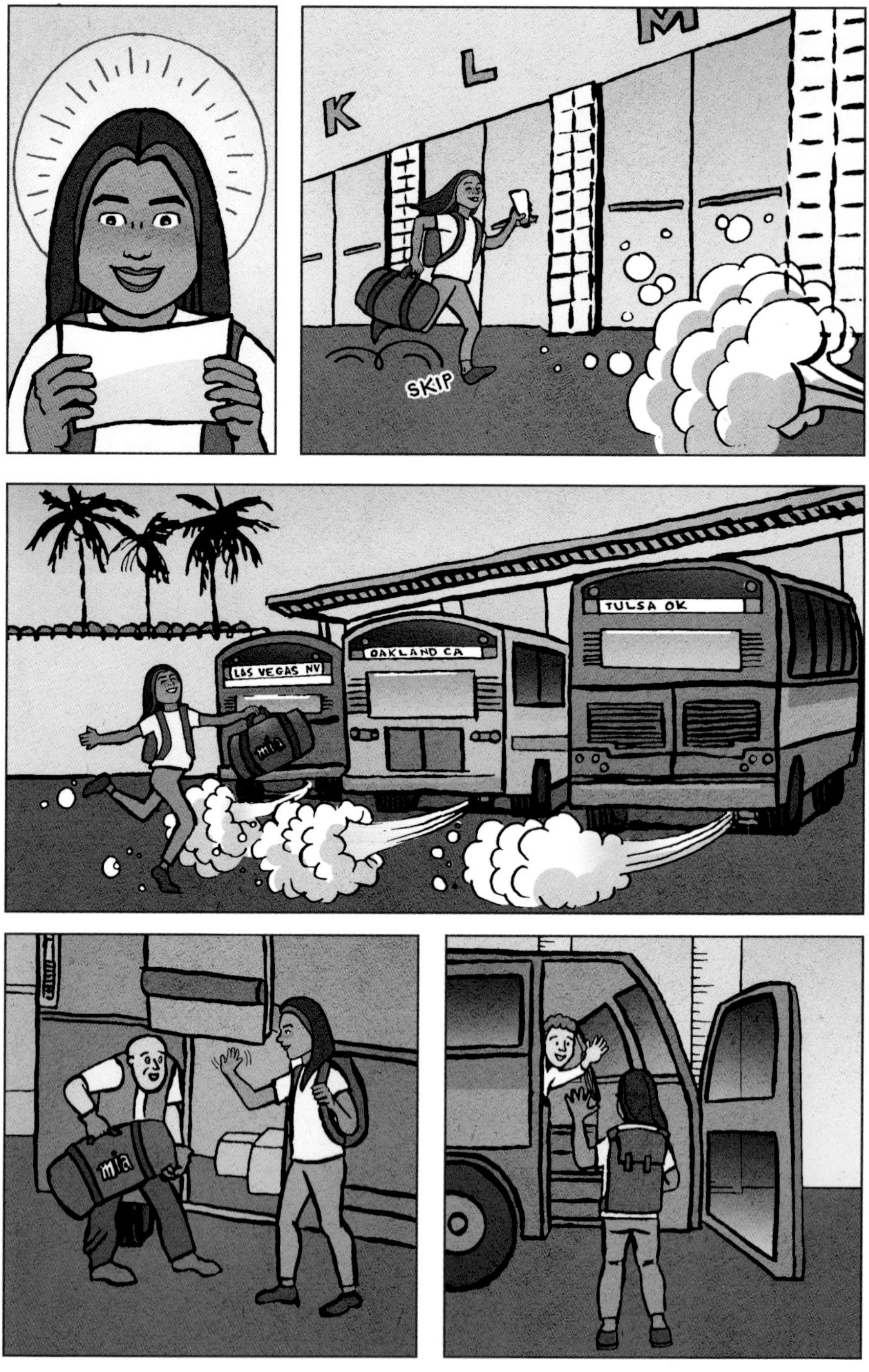
K
L
M
SKIP
LAS VEGAS NV
OAKLAND CA
TULSA OK
mia
mia

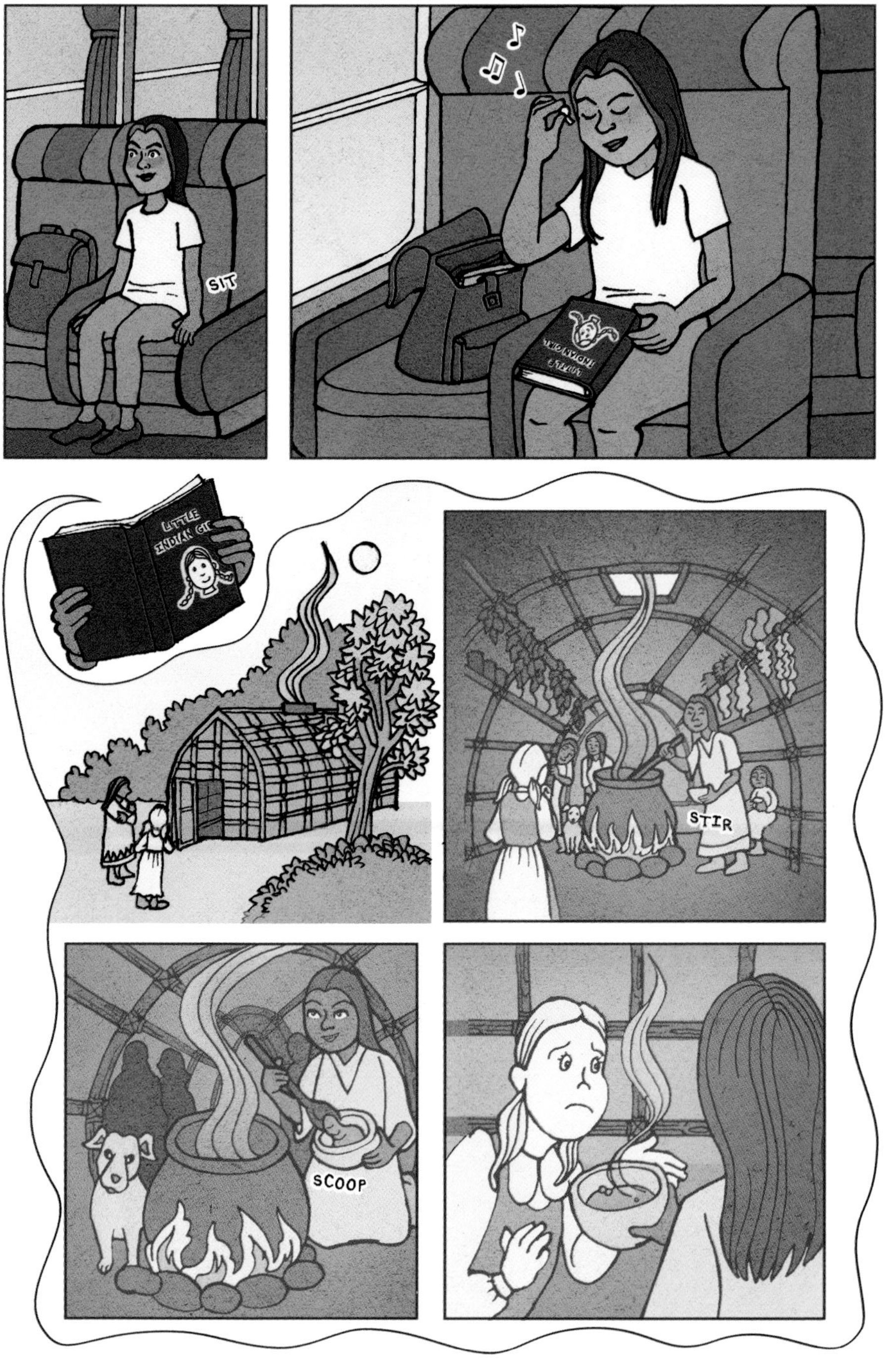
SIT
LITTLE
INDIAN GI
STIR
SCOOP

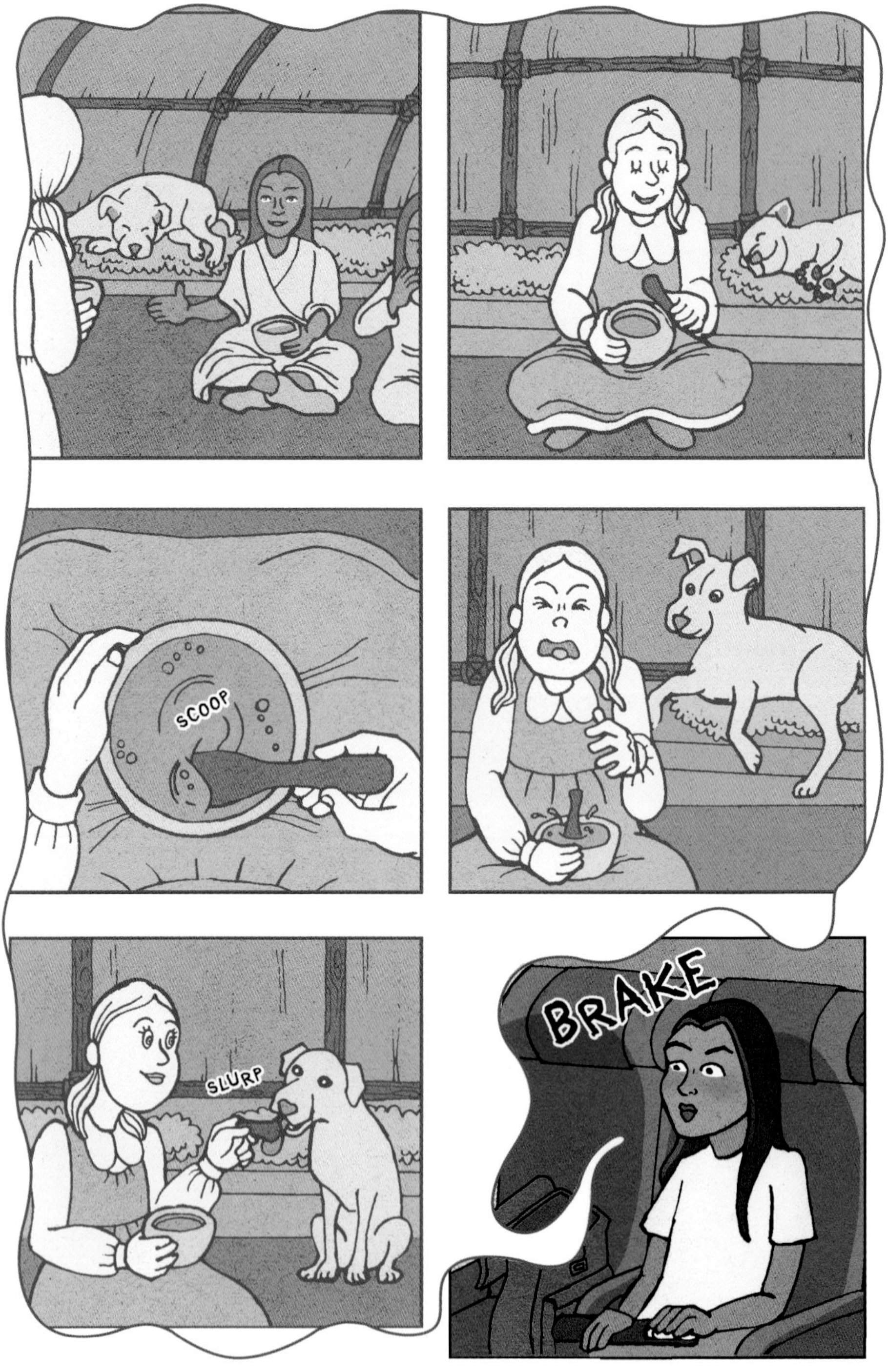
SCOOP
SLURP
BRAKE

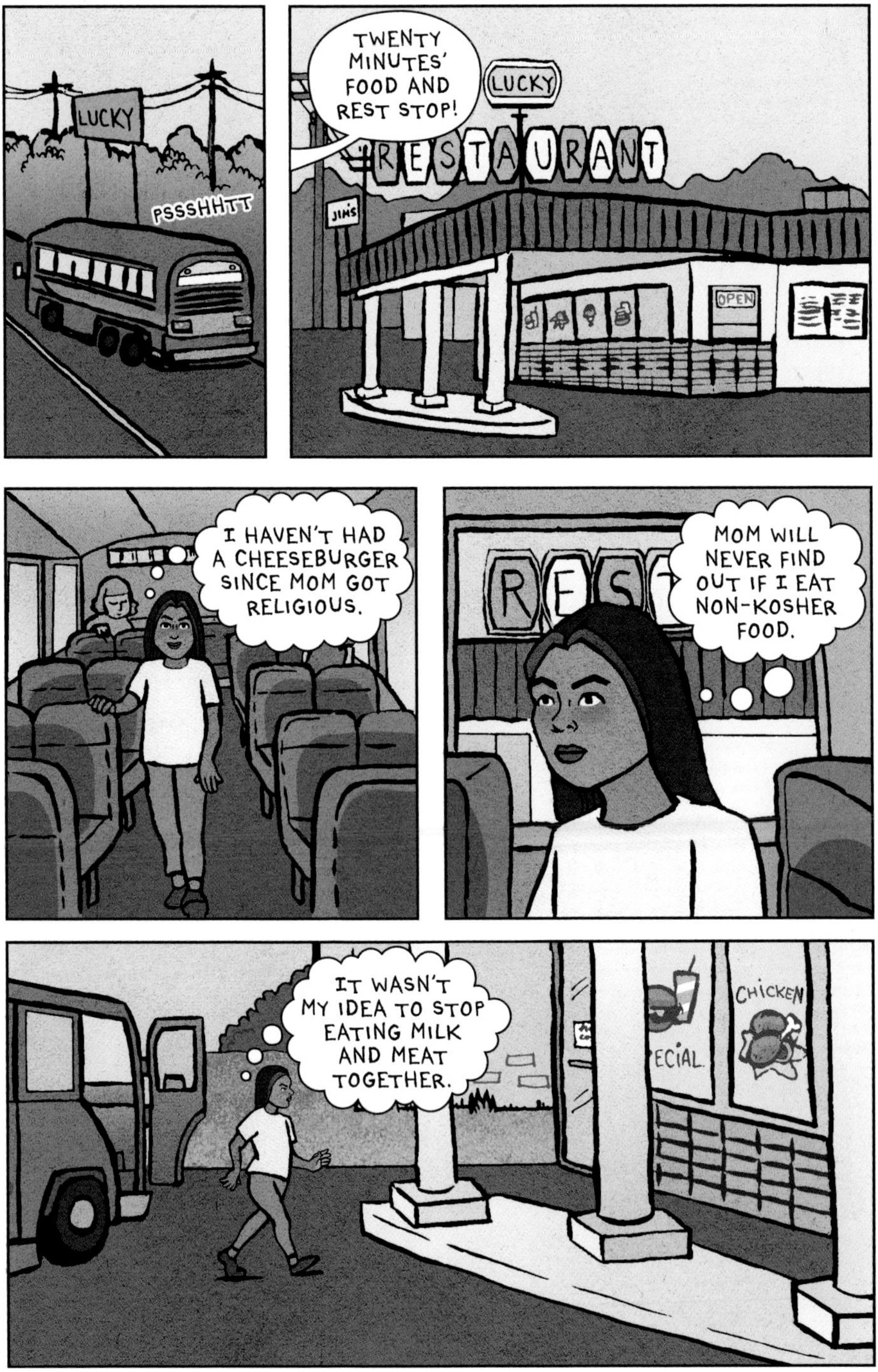
LUCKY
PSSSHHTT
TWENTY MINUTES' FOOD AND REST STOP!
LUCKY
RESTAURANT
JIM'S
OPEN
I HAVEN'T HAD A CHEESEBURGER SINCE MOM GOT RELIGIOUS.
MOM WILL NEVER FIND OUT IF I EAT NON-KOSHER FOOD.
IT WASN'T MY IDEA TO STOP EATING MILK AND MEAT TOGETHER.
CHICKEN
ECIAL

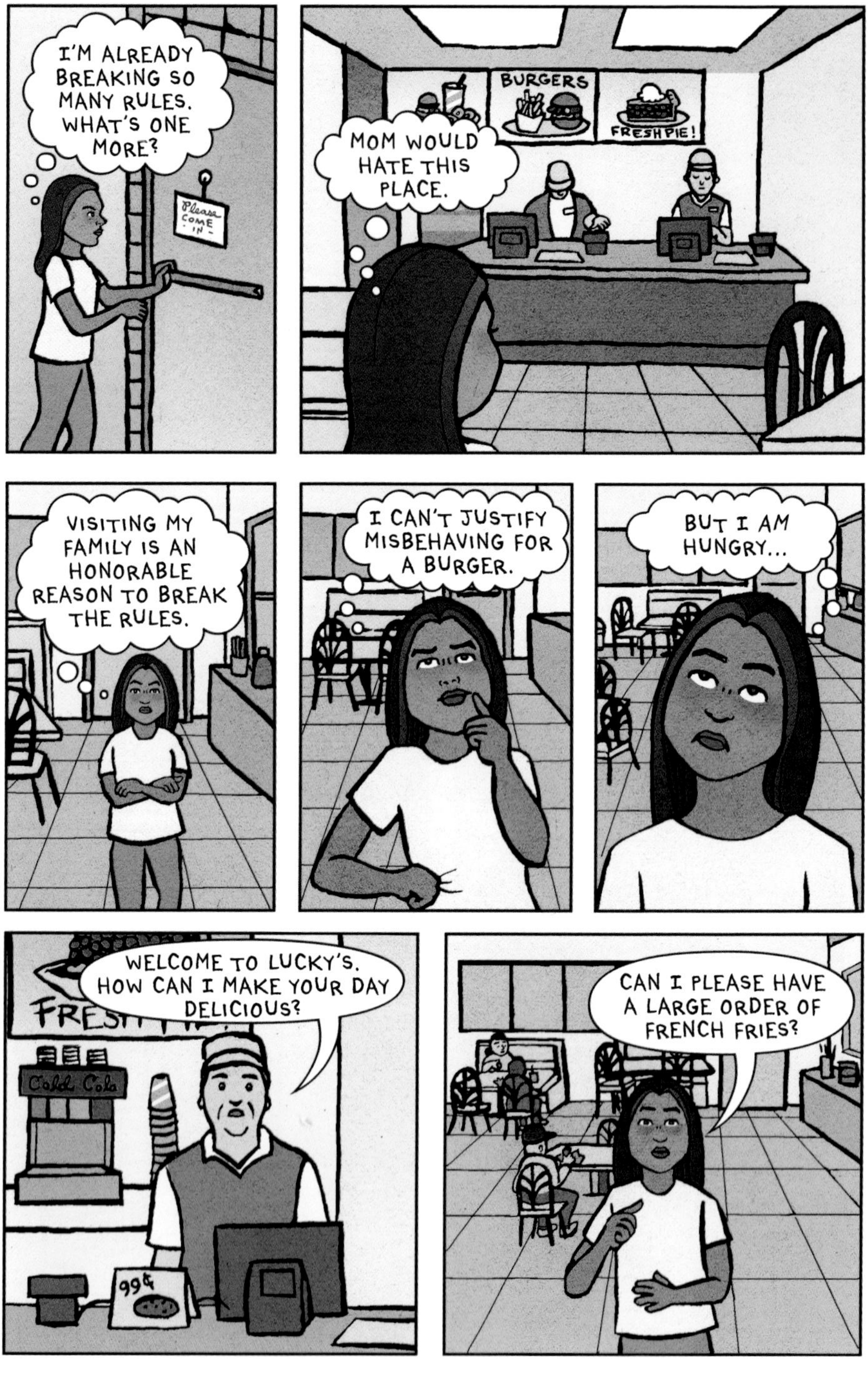
I'M ALREADY BREAKING SO MANY RULES. WHAT'S ONE MORE?
Please COME IN
BURGERS
FRESH PIE!
MOM WOULD HATE THIS PLACE.
VISITING MY FAMILY IS AN HONORABLE REASON TO BREAK THE RULES.
I CAN'T JUSTIFY MISBEHAVING FOR A BURGER.
BUT I AM HUNGRY...
WELCOME TO LUCKY'S. HOW CAN I MAKE YOUR DAY DELICIOUS?
Cold Cola
99¢
CAN I PLEASE HAVE A LARGE ORDER OF FRENCH FRIES?

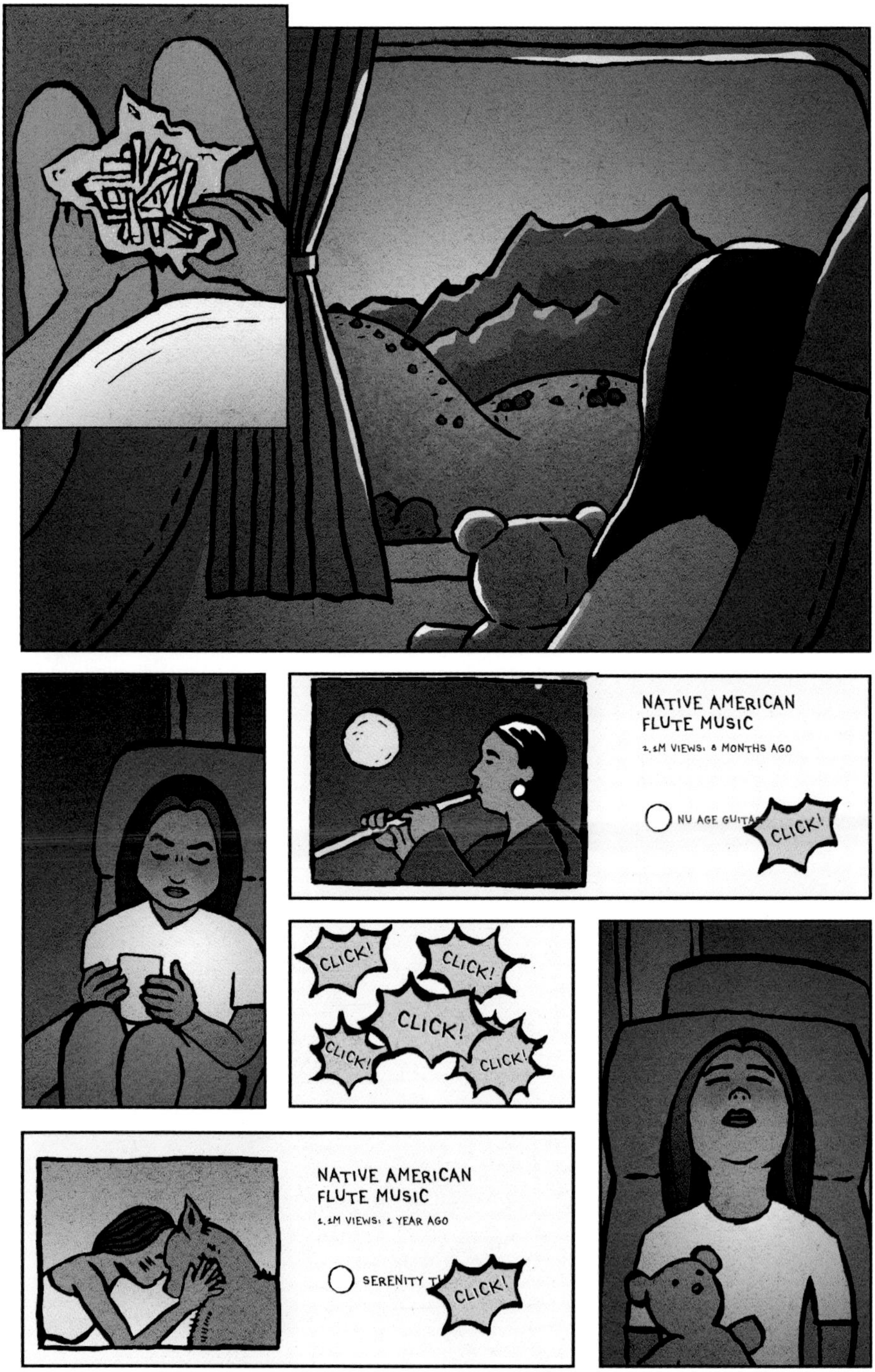

NATIVE AMERICAN FLUTE MUSIC
1.1M VIEWS: 8 MONTHS AGO
NU AGE GUITA
CLICK!
CLICK!
CLICK!
CLICK!
CLICK!
CLICK!
NATIVE AMERICAN FLUTE MUSIC
1.1M VIEWS: 1 YEAR AGO
SERENITY
CLICK!

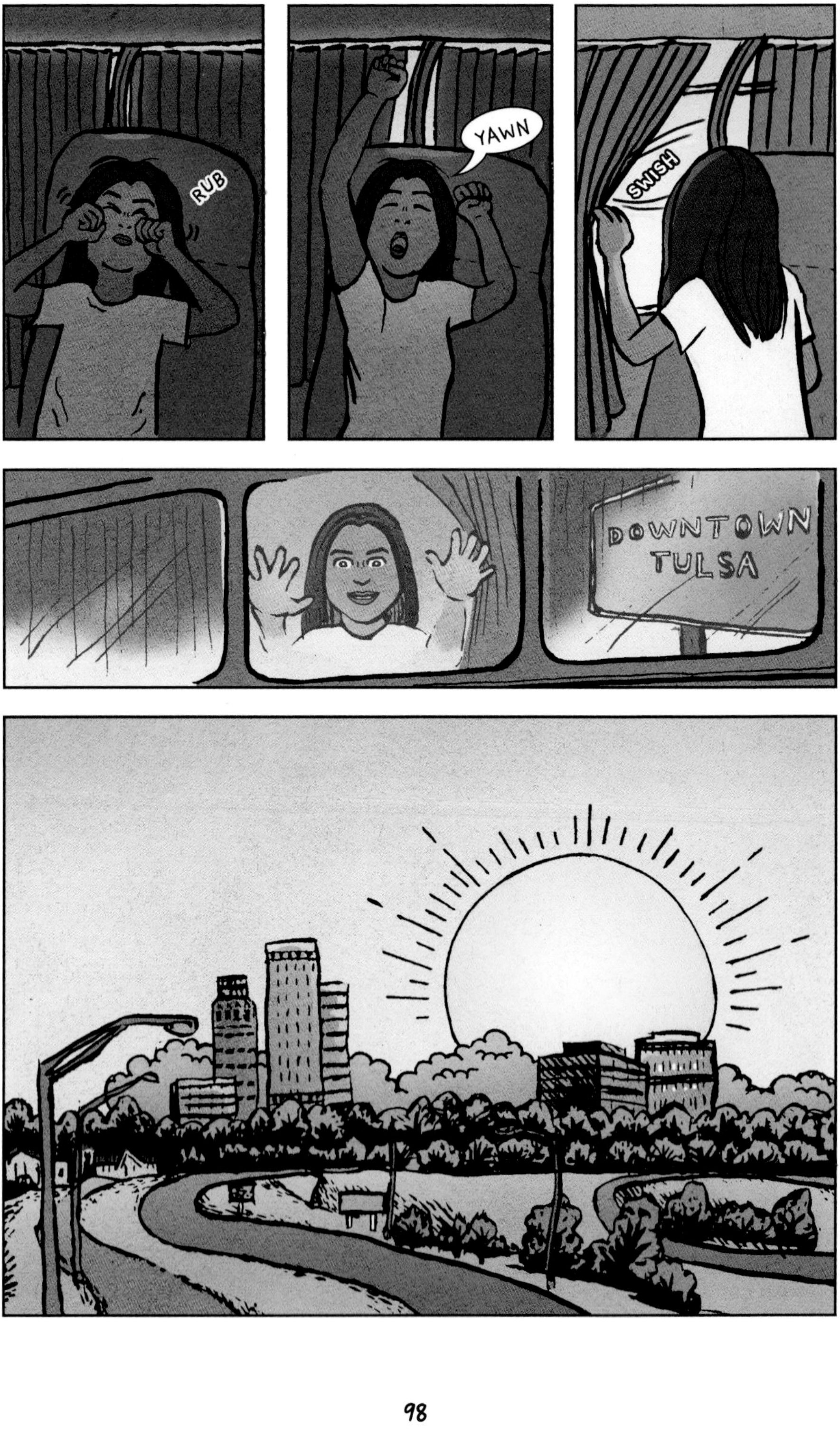
RUB
YAWN
SWISH
DOWNTOWN TULSA

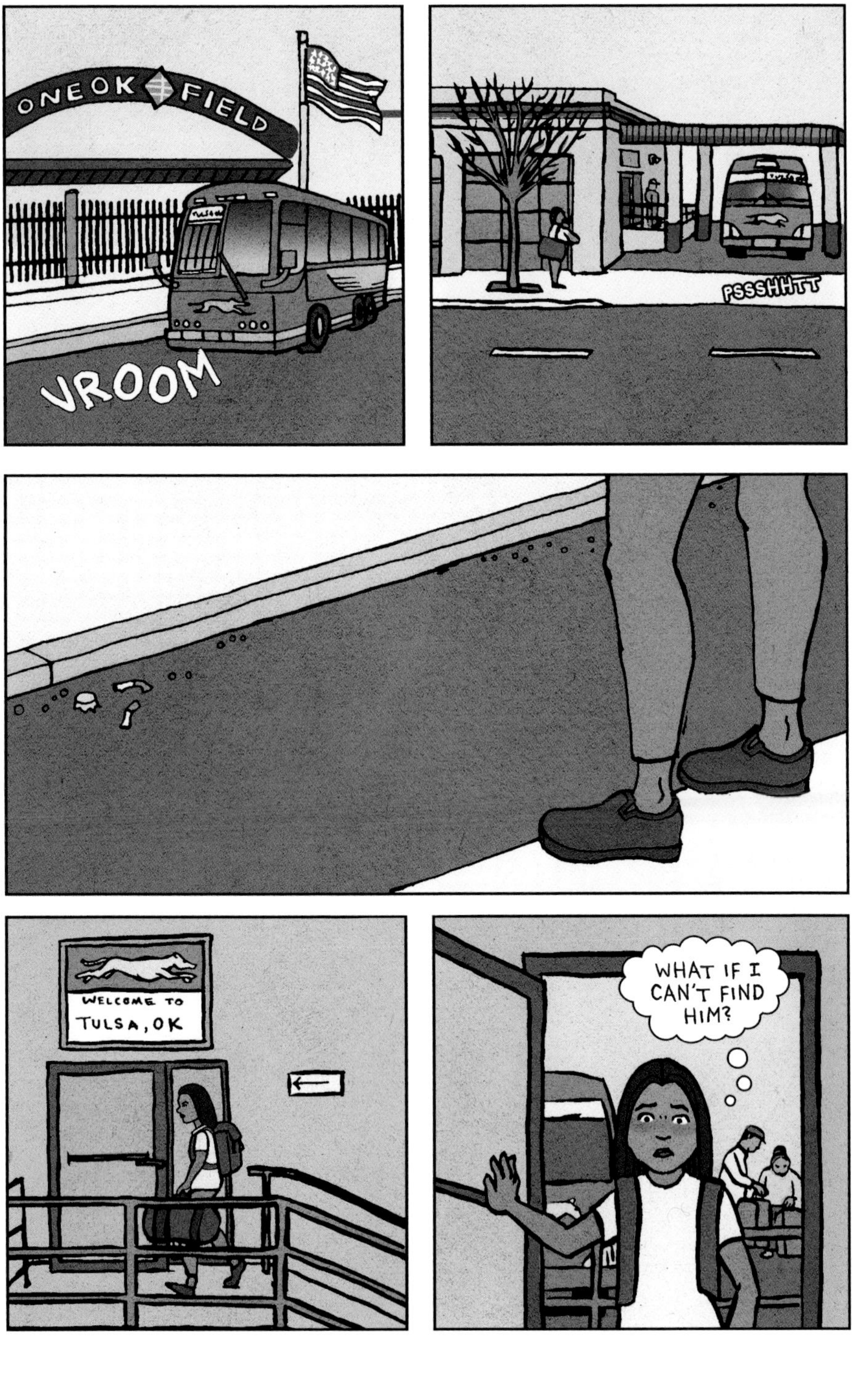
ONEOK FIELD
VROOM
PSSSHHTT
WELCOME TO
TULSA, OK
WHAT IF I CAN'T FIND HIM?

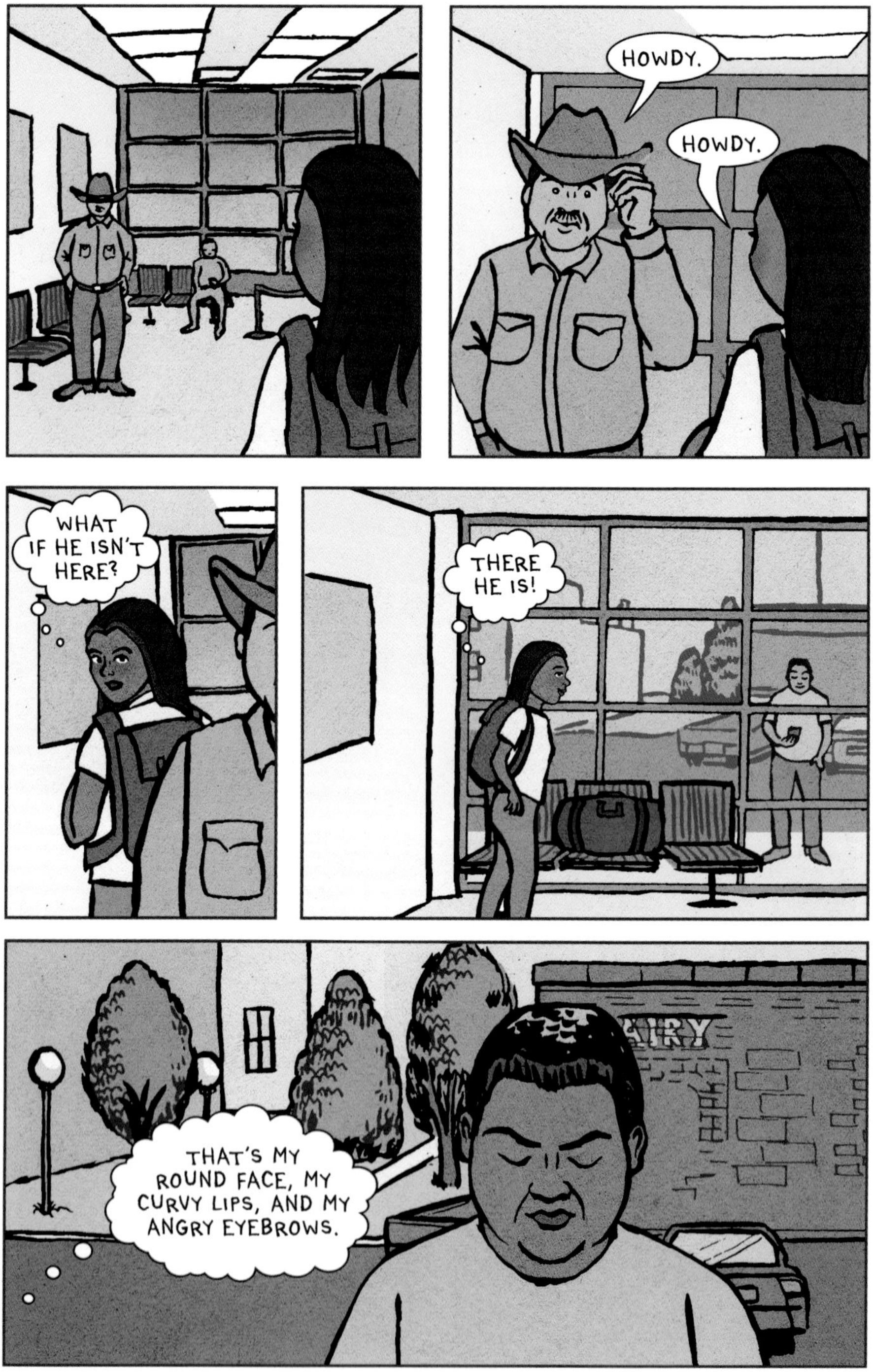
HOWDY.
HOWDY.
WHAT IF HE ISN'T HERE?
THERE HE IS!
THAT'S MY ROUND FACE, MY CURVY LIPS, AND MY ANGRY EYEBROWS.

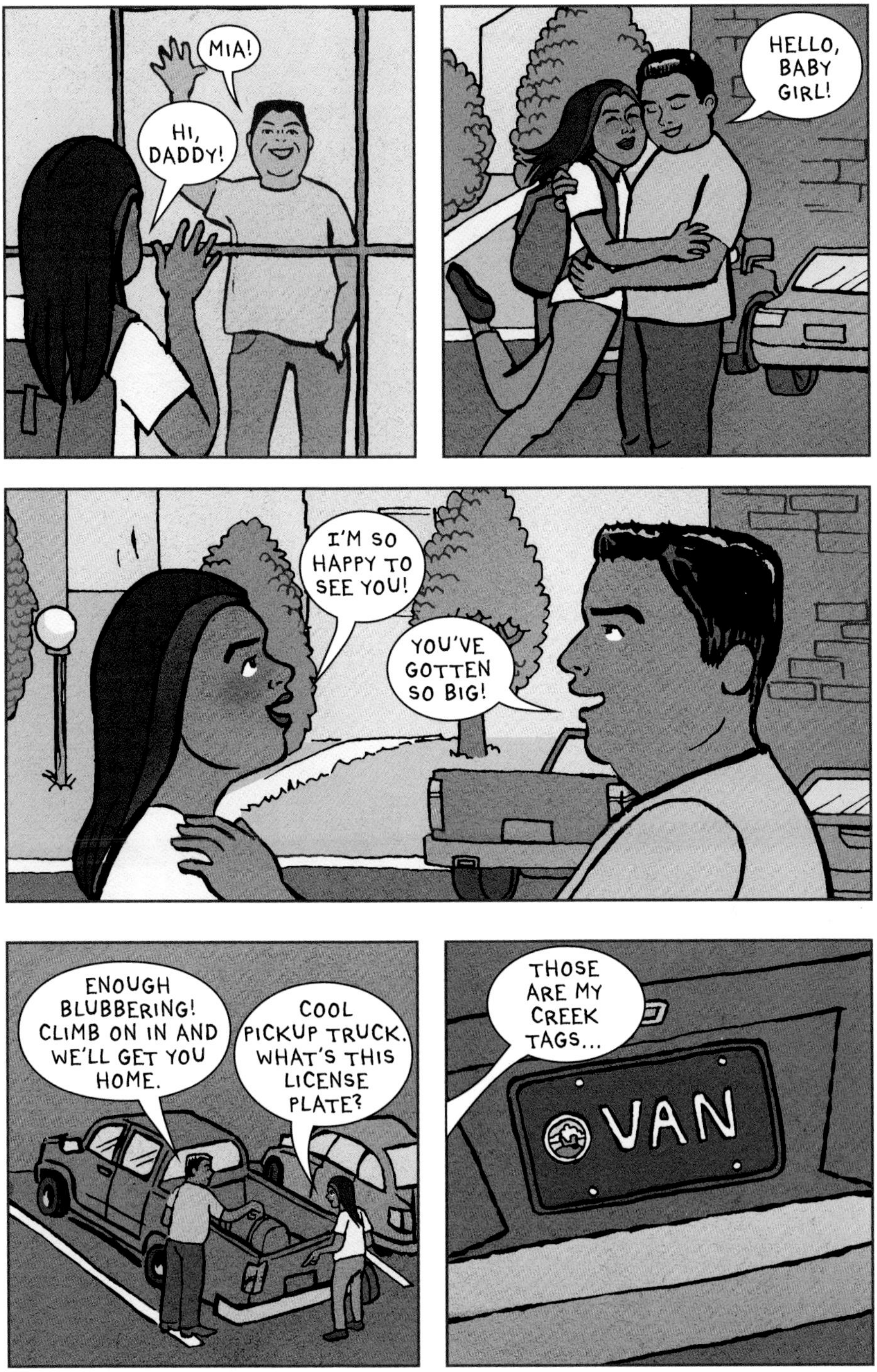
MIA!
HI, DADDY!
HELLO, BABY GIRL!
I'M SO HAPPY TO SEE YOU!
YOU'VE GOTTEN SO BIG!
ENOUGH BLUBBERING! CLIMB ON IN AND WE'LL GET YOU HOME.
COOL PICKUP TRUCK. WHAT'S THIS LICENSE PLATE?
THOSE ARE MY CREEK TAGS...
VAN

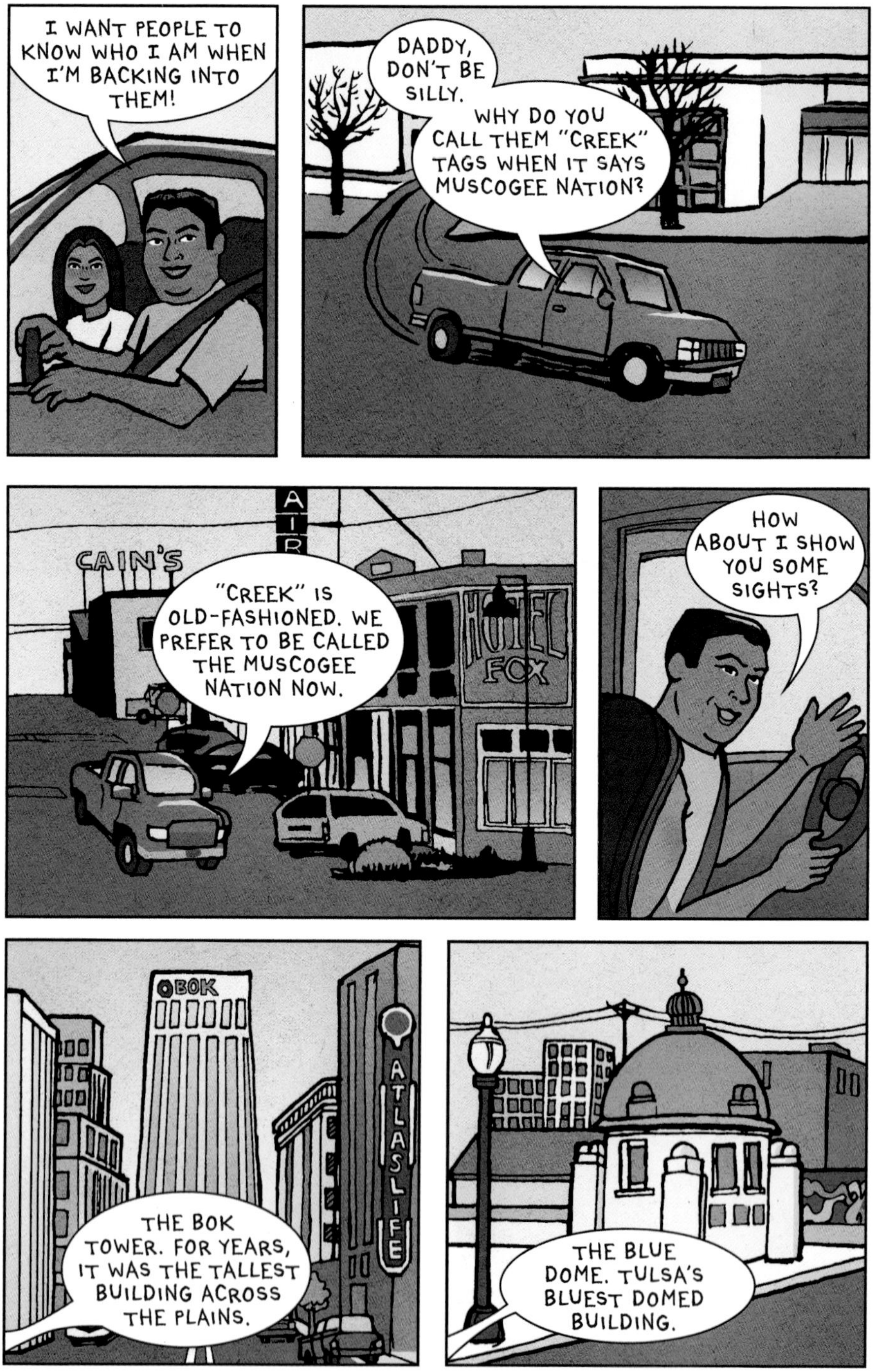
I WANT PEOPLE TO KNOW WHO I AM WHEN I'M BACKING INTO THEM!
DADDY, DON'T BE SILLY.
WHY DO YOU CALL THEM "CREEK" TAGS WHEN IT SAYS MUSCOGEE NATION?
CAIN'S
AIR
HOTEL FOX
"CREEK" IS OLD-FASHIONED. WE PREFER TO BE CALLED THE MUSCOGEE NATION NOW.
HOW ABOUT I SHOW YOU SOME SIGHTS?
BOK
ATLAS LIFE
THE BOK TOWER. FOR YEARS, IT WAS THE TALLEST BUILDING ACROSS THE PLAINS.
THE BLUE DOME. TULSA'S BLUEST DOMED BUILDING.

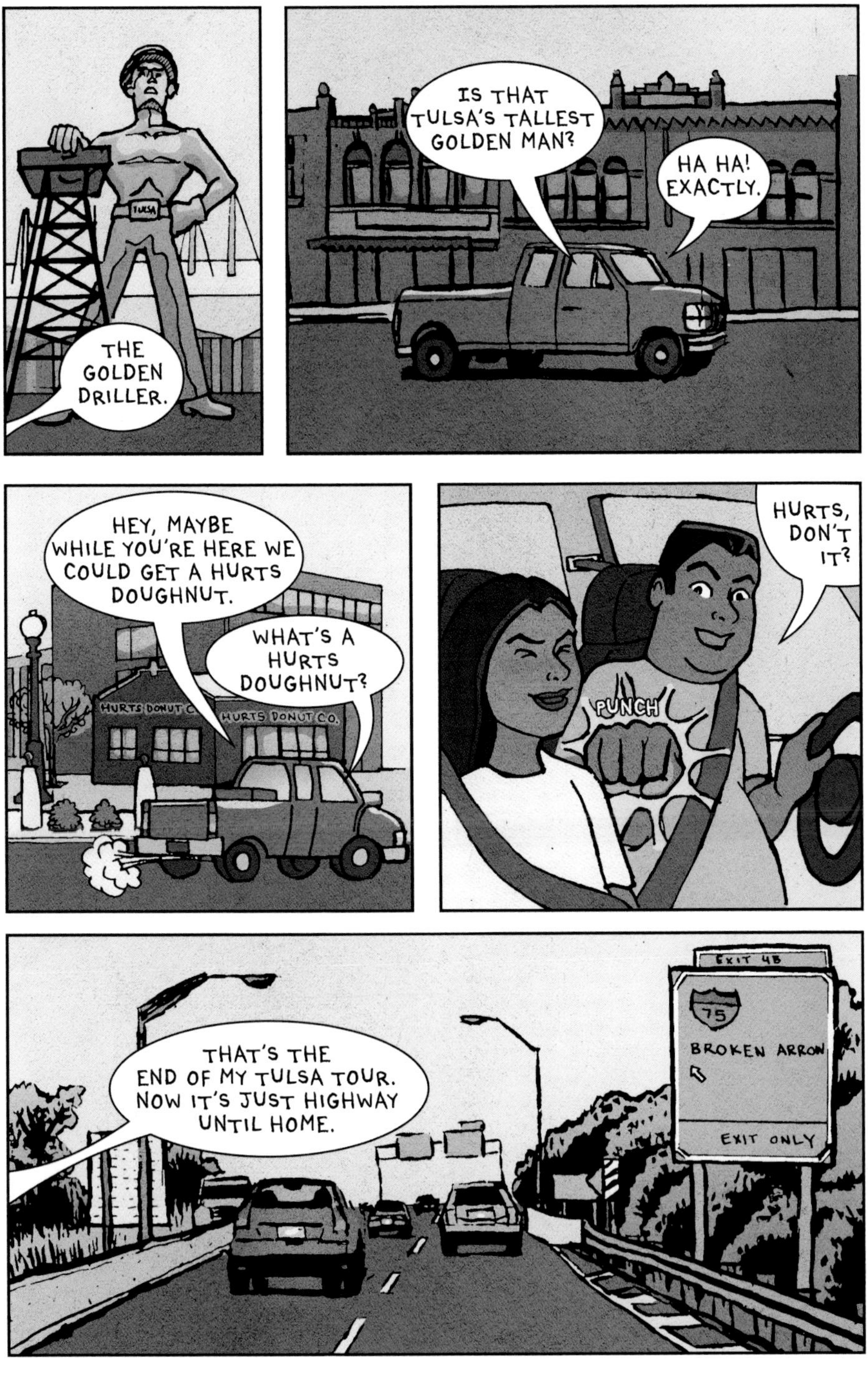
TULSA
THE GOLDEN DRILLER.
IS THAT TULSA'S TALLEST GOLDEN MAN?
HA HA! EXACTLY.
HEY, MAYBE WHILE YOU'RE HERE WE COULD GET A HURTS DOUGHNUT.
HURTS DONUT CO.
HURTS DONUT CO.
WHAT'S A HURTS DOUGHNUT?
HURTS, DON'T IT?
PUNCH
THAT'S THE END OF MY TULSA TOUR. NOW IT'S JUST HIGHWAY UNTIL HOME.
EXIT 4B
75
BROKEN ARROW
EXIT ONLY

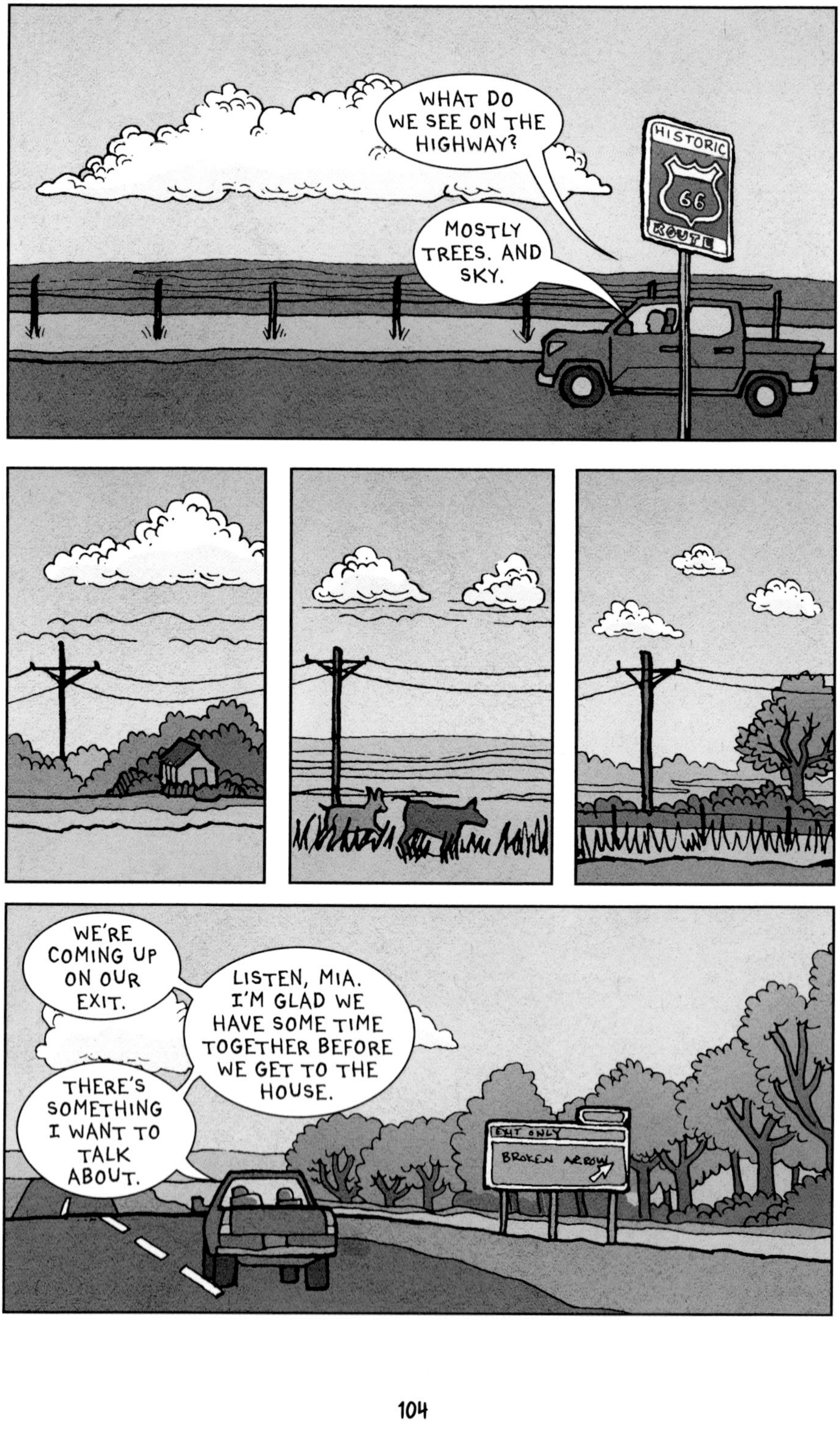

WHAT DO WE SEE ON THE HIGHWAY?
MOSTLY TREES. AND SKY.
HISTORIC 66 ROUTE
WE'RE COMING UP ON OUR EXIT.
LISTEN, MIA. I'M GLAD WE HAVE SOME TIME TOGETHER BEFORE WE GET TO THE HOUSE.
THERE'S SOMETHING I WANT TO TALK ABOUT.
EXIT ONLY
BROKEN ARROW

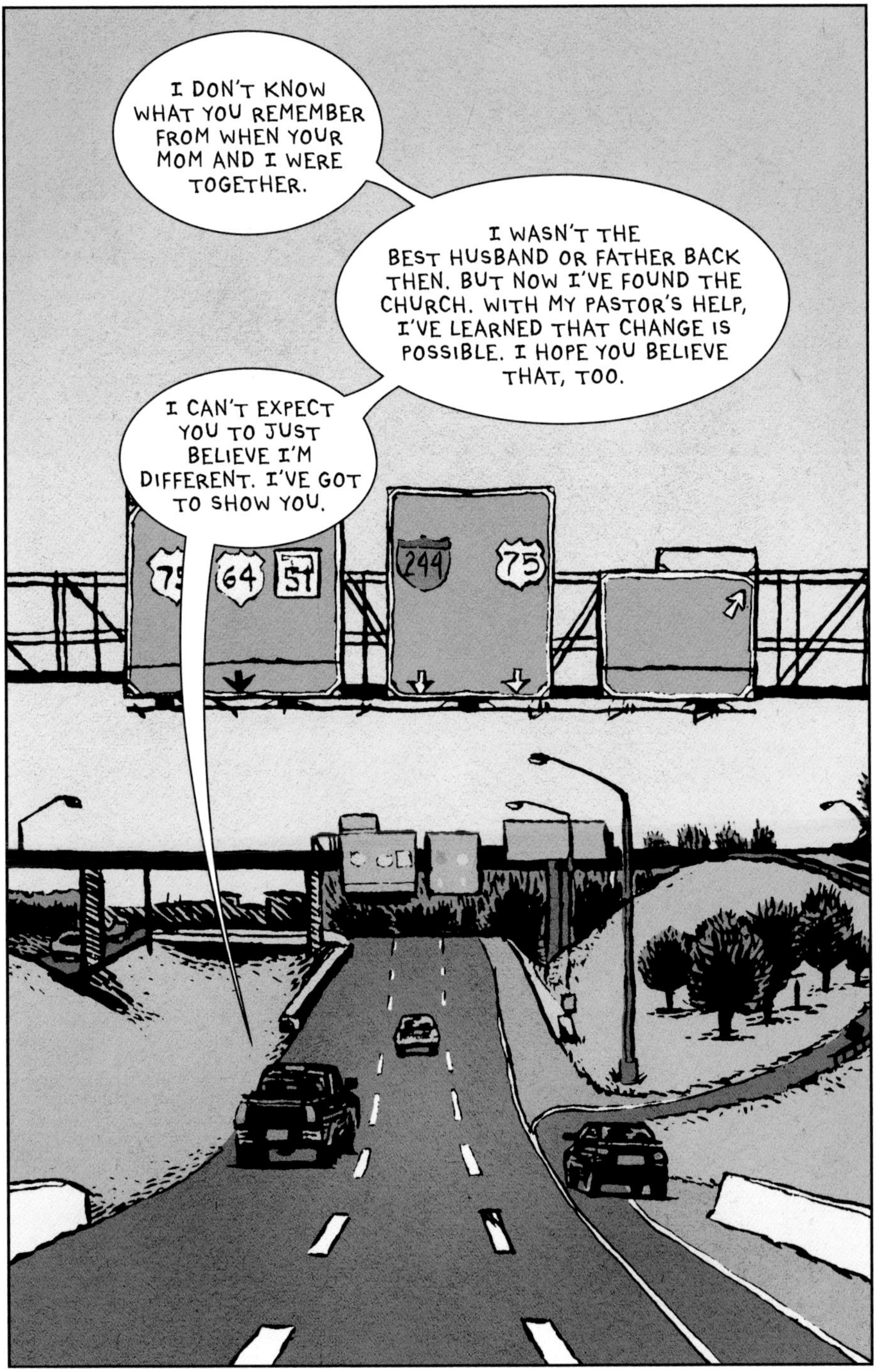
I DON'T KNOW WHAT YOU REMEMBER FROM WHEN YOUR MOM AND I WERE TOGETHER.
I WASN'T THE BEST HUSBAND OR FATHER BACK THEN. BUT NOW I'VE FOUND THE CHURCH. WITH MY PASTOR'S HELP, I'VE LEARNED THAT CHANGE IS POSSIBLE. I HOPE YOU BELIEVE THAT, TOO.
I CAN'T EXPECT YOU TO JUST BELIEVE I'M DIFFERENT. I'VE GOT TO SHOW YOU.
75
64
51
244
75

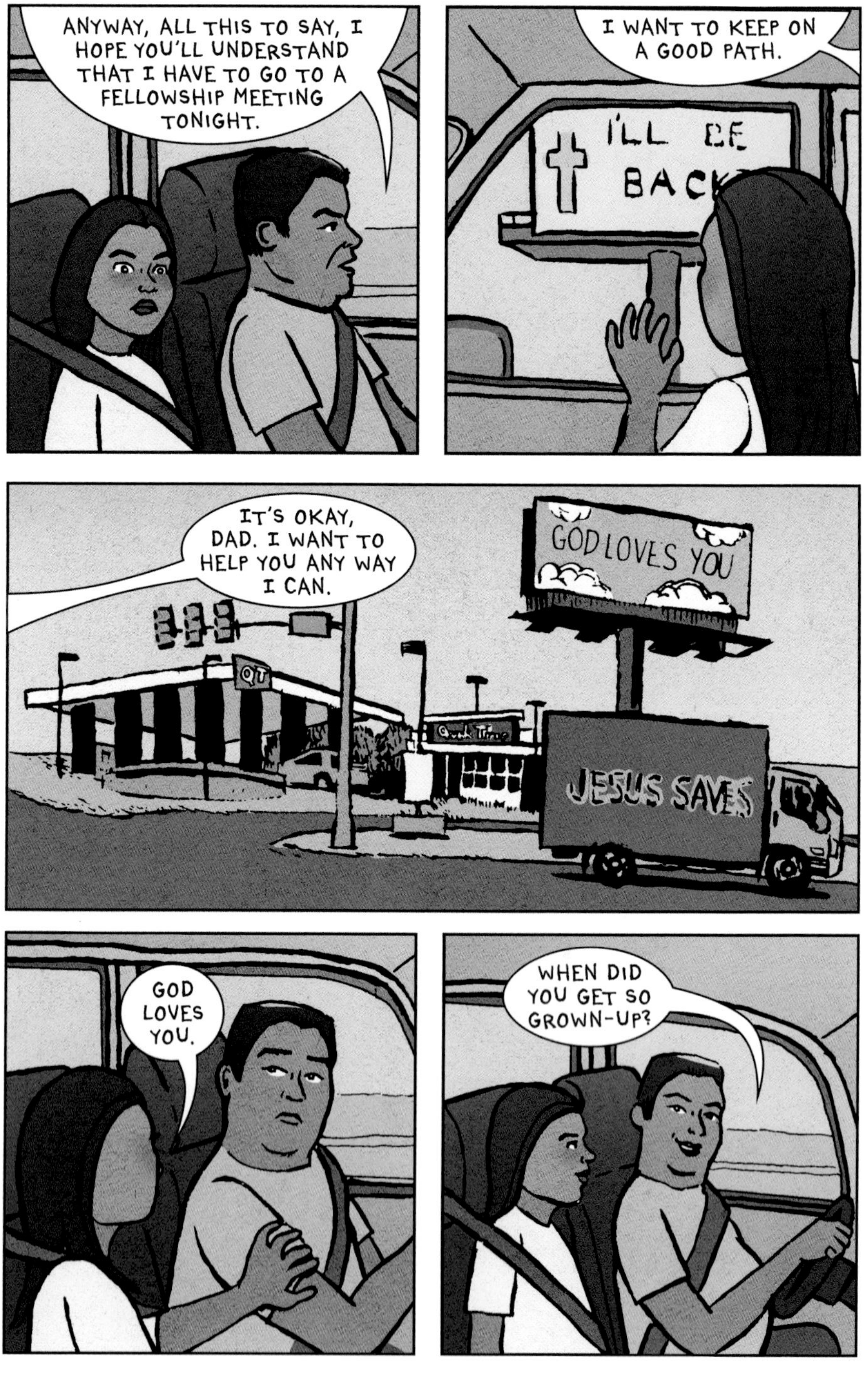

ANYWAY, ALL THIS TO SAY, I HOPE YOU'LL UNDERSTAND THAT I HAVE TO GO TO A FELLOWSHIP MEETING TONIGHT.
I WANT TO KEEP ON A GOOD PATH.
I'LL BE
BAC
IT'S OKAY, DAD. I WANT TO HELP YOU ANY WAY I CAN.
GOD LOVES YOU
QT
JESUS SAVES
GOD LOVES YOU.
WHEN DID YOU GET SO GROWN-UP?

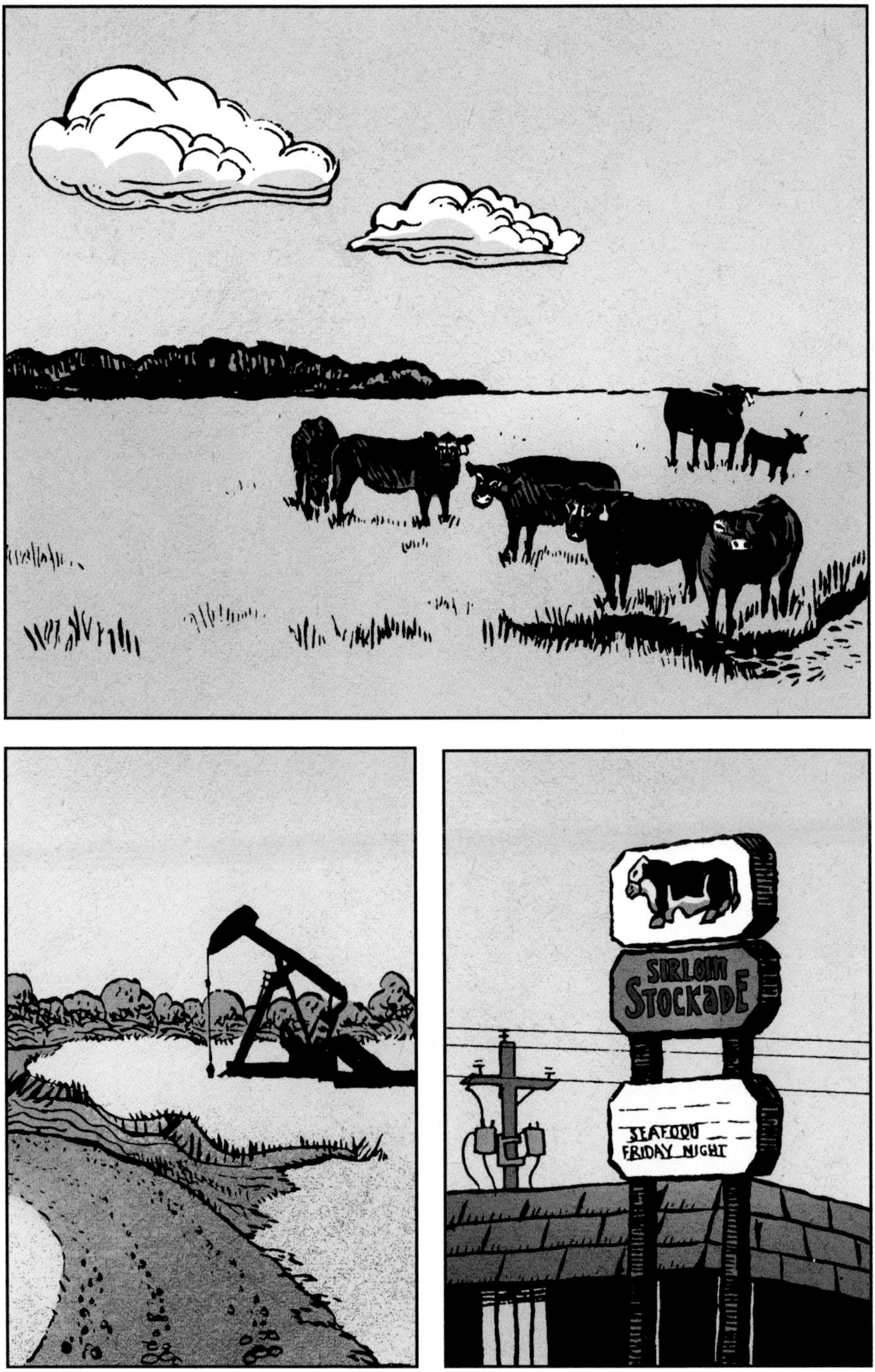
SIRLOIN STOCKADE
SEAFOOD
FRIDAY NIGHT

HOME ON THE RANGE

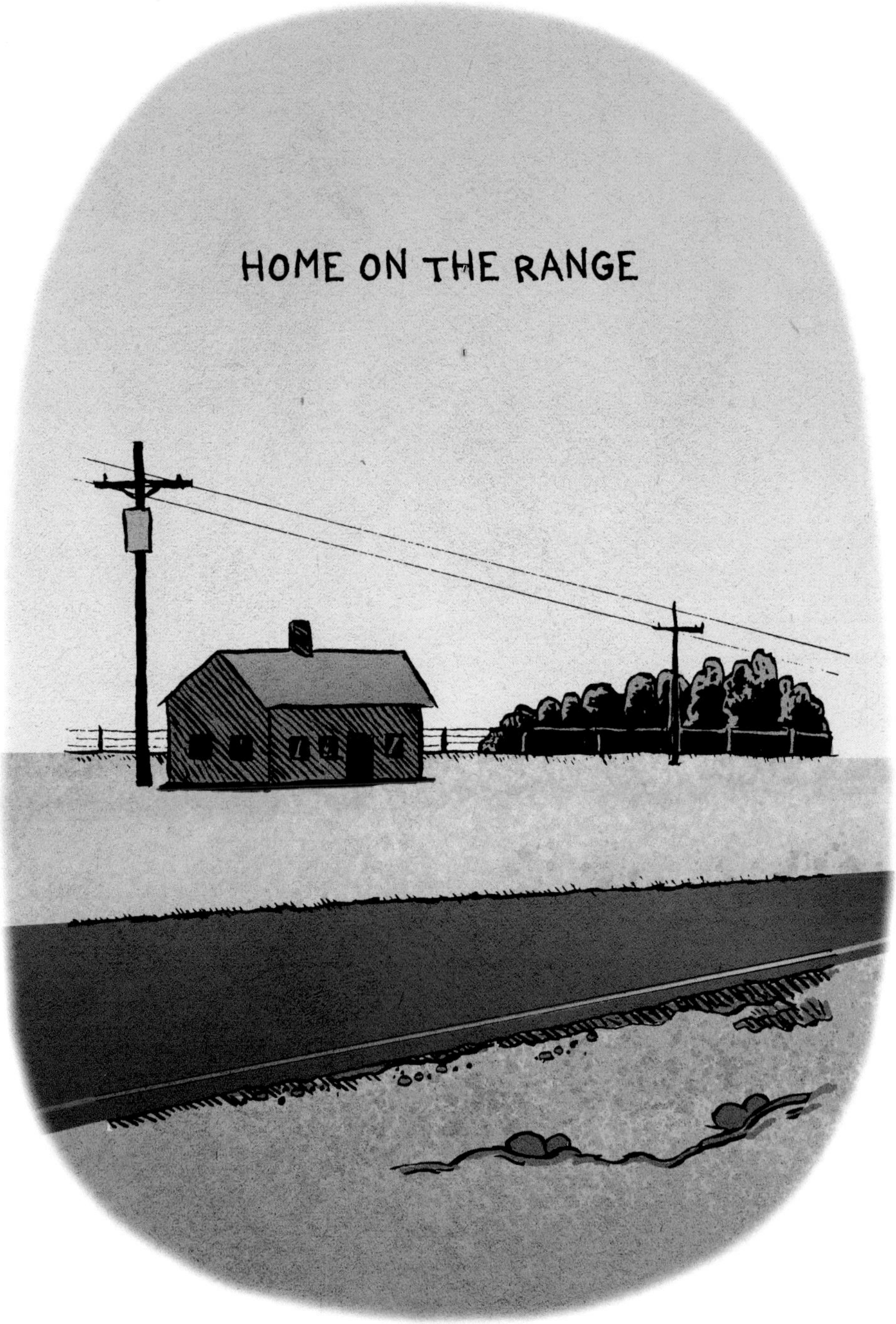

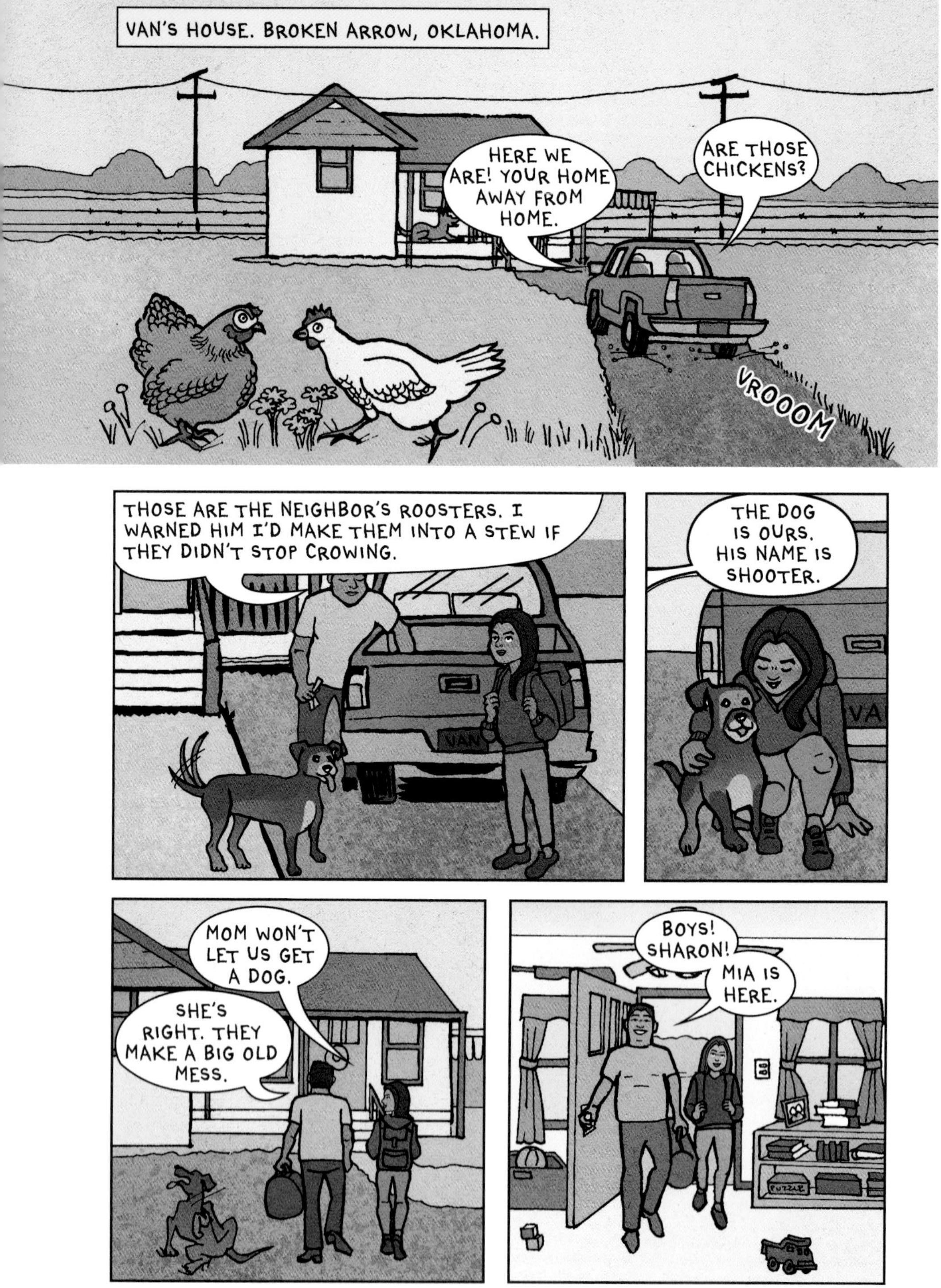
VAN'S HOUSE. BROKEN ARROW, OKLAHOMA.
HERE WE ARE! YOUR HOME AWAY FROM HOME.
ARE THOSE CHICKENS?
VROOOM
THOSE ARE THE NEIGHBOR'S ROOSTERS. I WARNED HIM I'D MAKE THEM INTO A STEW IF THEY DIDN'T STOP CROWING.
VAN
THE DOG IS OURS. HIS NAME IS SHOOTER.
MOM WON'T LET US GET A DOG.
SHE'S RIGHT. THEY MAKE A BIG OLD MESS.
BOYS! SHARON!
MIA IS HERE.
PUZZLE

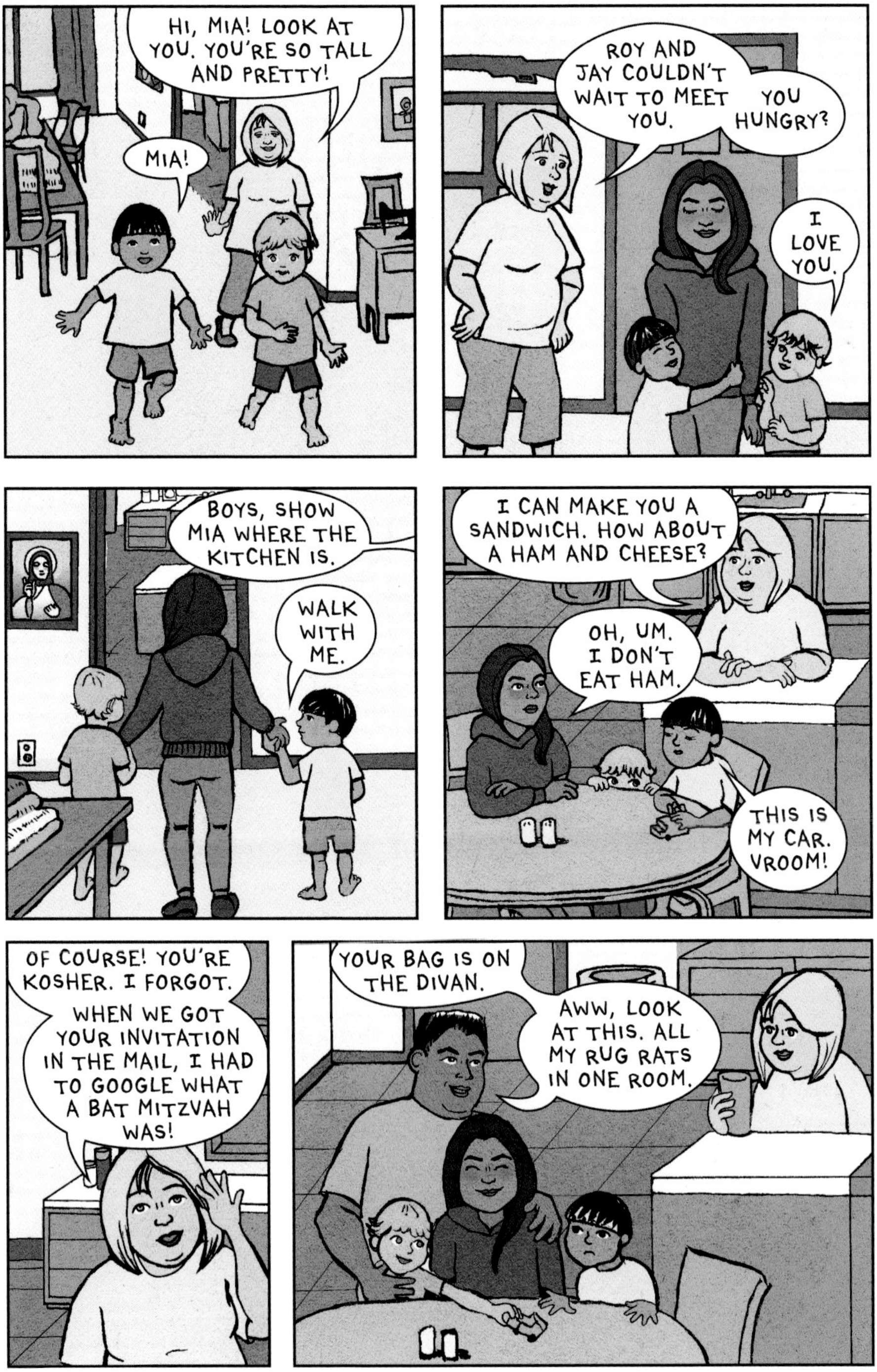
HI, MIA! LOOK AT YOU. YOU'RE SO TALL AND PRETTY!
MIA!
ROY AND JAY COULDN'T WAIT TO MEET YOU.
YOU HUNGRY?
I LOVE YOU.
BOYS, SHOW MIA WHERE THE KITCHEN IS.
WALK WITH ME.
I CAN MAKE YOU A SANDWICH. HOW ABOUT A HAM AND CHEESE?
OH, UM. I DON'T EAT HAM.
THIS IS MY CAR. VROOM!
OF COURSE! YOU'RE KOSHER. I FORGOT.
WHEN WE GOT YOUR INVITATION IN THE MAIL, I HAD TO GOOGLE WHAT A BAT MITZVAH WAS!
YOUR BAG IS ON THE DIVAN.
AWW, LOOK AT THIS. ALL MY RUG RATS IN ONE ROOM.

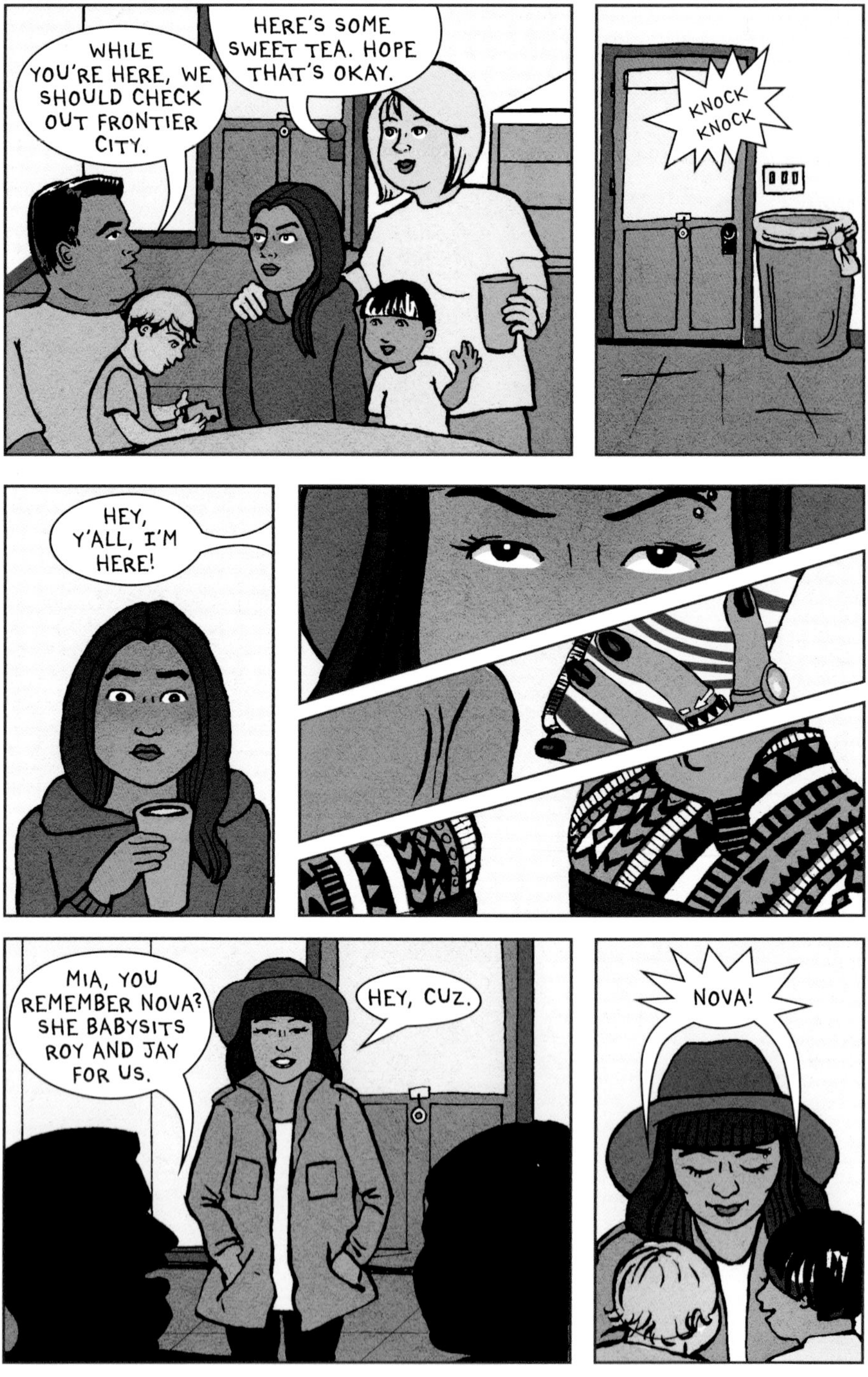
WHILE YOU'RE HERE, WE SHOULD CHECK OUT FRONTIER CITY.
HERE'S SOME SWEET TEA. HOPE THAT'S OKAY.
KNOCK KNOCK
HEY, Y'ALL, I'M HERE!
MIA, YOU REMEMBER NOVA? SHE BABYSITS ROY AND JAY FOR US.
HEY, CUZ.
NOVA!

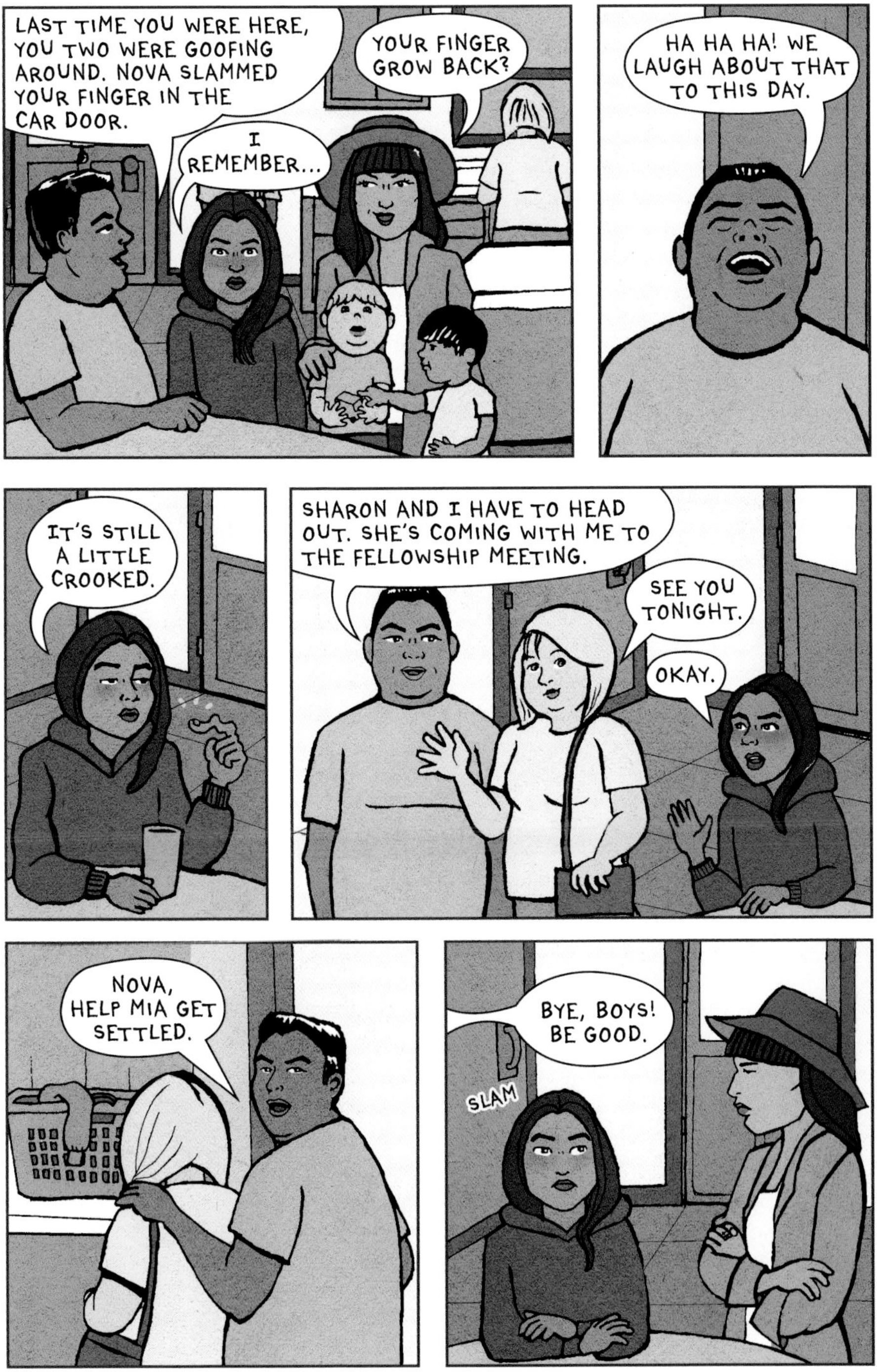
LAST TIME YOU WERE HERE, YOU TWO WERE GOOFING AROUND. NOVA SLAMMED YOUR FINGER IN THE CAR DOOR.
I REMEMBER...
YOUR FINGER GROW BACK?
HA HA HA! WE LAUGH ABOUT THAT TO THIS DAY.
IT'S STILL A LITTLE CROOKED.
SHARON AND I HAVE TO HEAD OUT. SHE'S COMING WITH ME TO THE FELLOWSHIP MEETING.
SEE YOU TONIGHT.
OKAY.
NOVA, HELP MIA GET SETTLED.
BYE, BOYS! BE GOOD.
SLAM

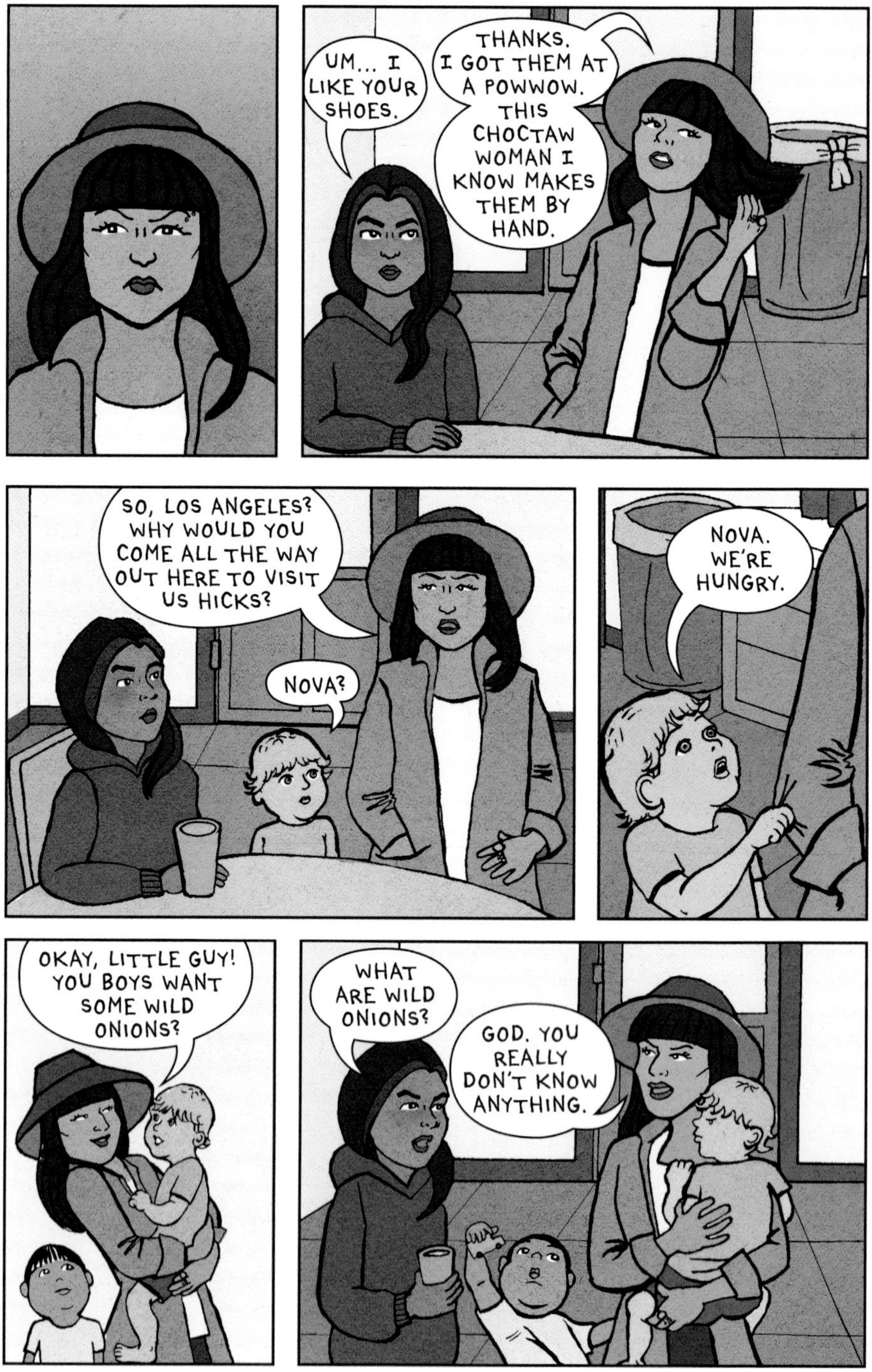
UM... I LIKE YOUR SHOES.
THANKS. I GOT THEM AT A POWWOW. THIS CHOCTAW WOMAN I KNOW MAKES THEM BY HAND.
SO, LOS ANGELES? WHY WOULD YOU COME ALL THE WAY OUT HERE TO VISIT US HICKS?
NOVA?
NOVA. WE'RE HUNGRY.
OKAY, LITTLE GUY! YOU BOYS WANT SOME WILD ONIONS?
WHAT ARE WILD ONIONS?
GOD. YOU REALLY DON'T KNOW ANYTHING.

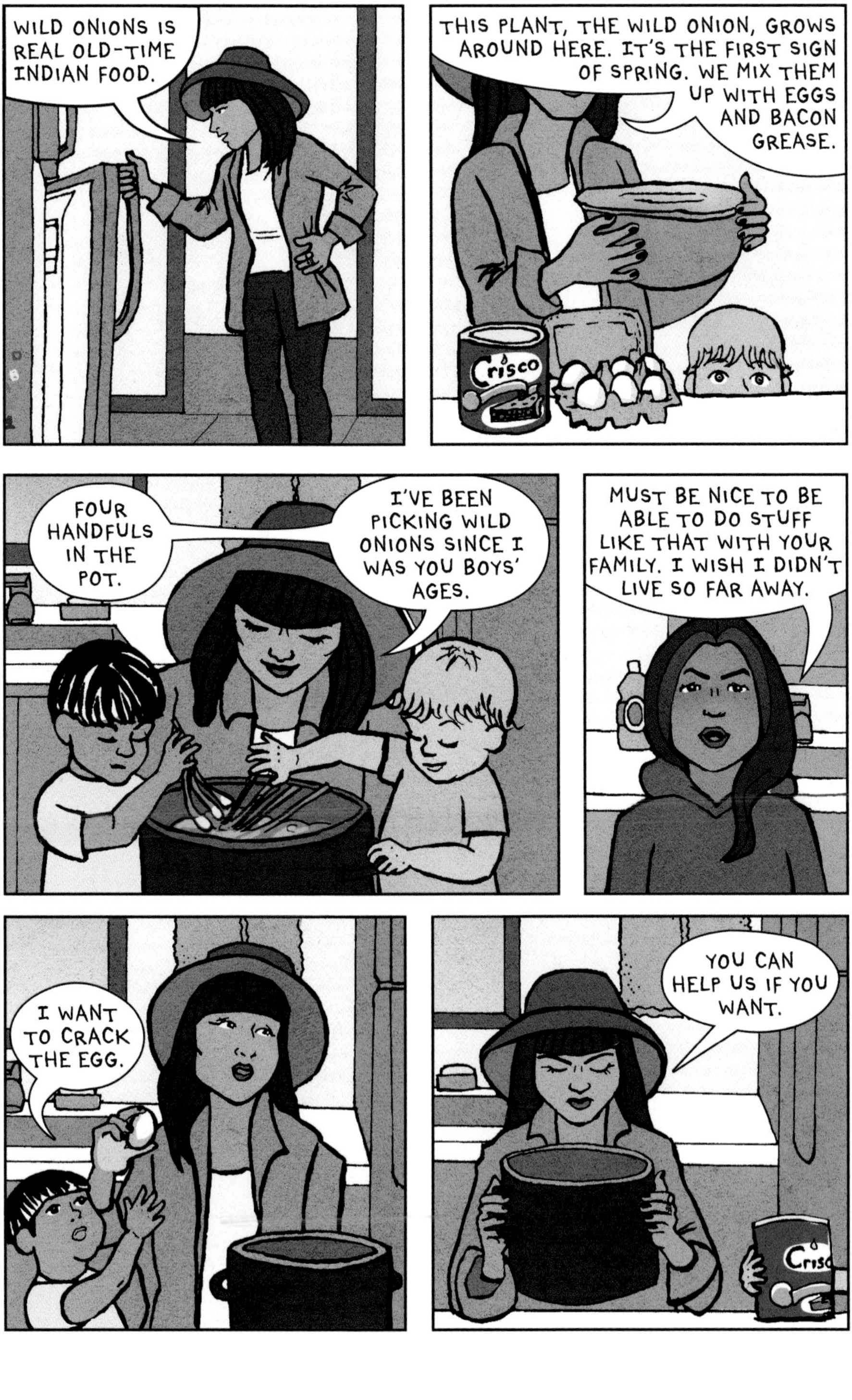
WILD ONIONS IS REAL OLD-TIME INDIAN FOOD.
THIS PLANT, THE WILD ONION, GROWS AROUND HERE. IT'S THE FIRST SIGN OF SPRING. WE MIX THEM UP WITH EGGS AND BACON GREASE.
Crisco
FOUR HANDFULS IN THE POT.
I'VE BEEN PICKING WILD ONIONS SINCE I WAS YOU BOYS' AGES.
MUST BE NICE TO BE ABLE TO DO STUFF LIKE THAT WITH YOUR FAMILY. I WISH I DIDN'T LIVE SO FAR AWAY.
I WANT TO CRACK THE EGG.
YOU CAN HELP US IF YOU WANT.

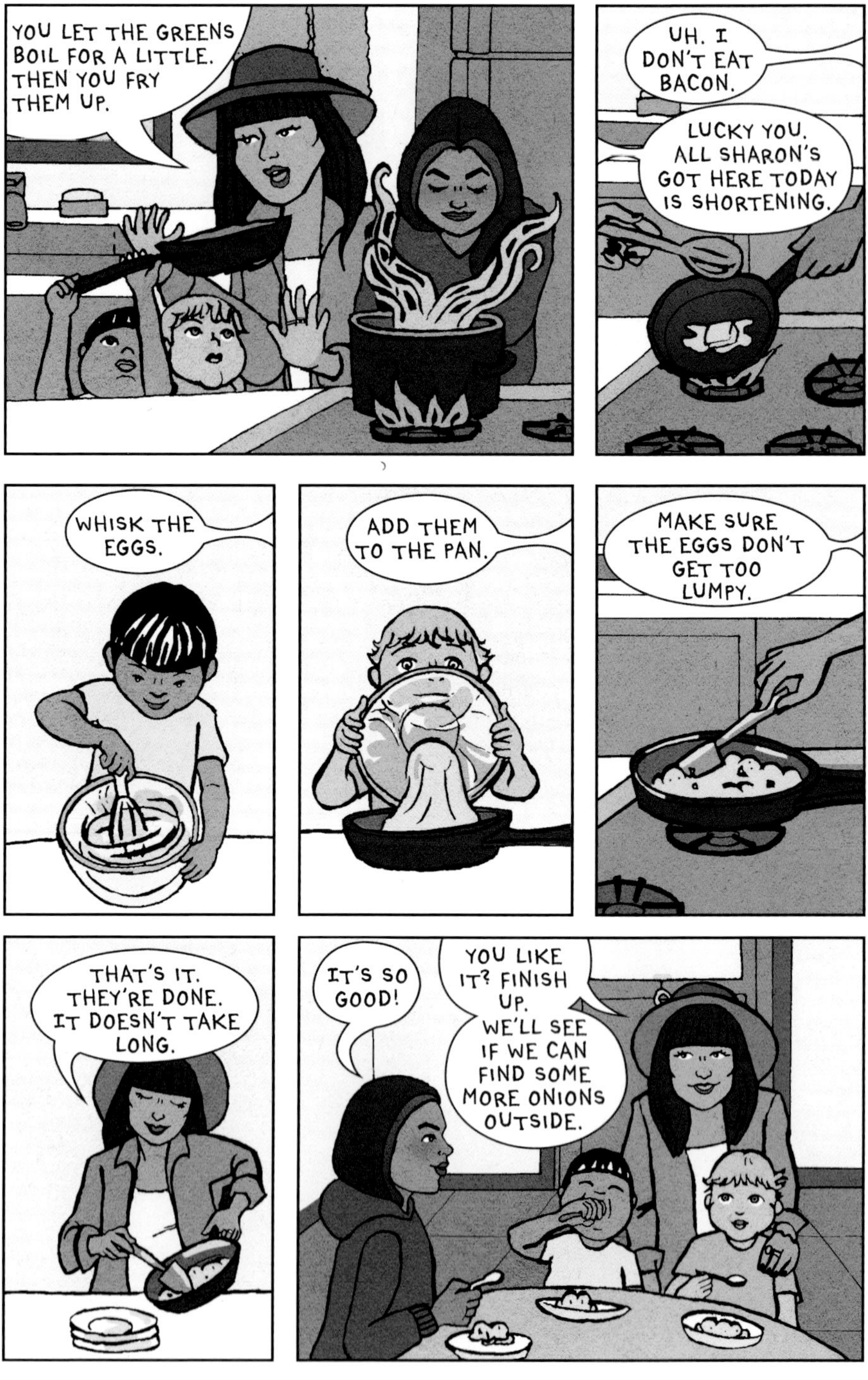
YOU LET THE GREENS BOIL FOR A LITTLE. THEN YOU FRY THEM UP.
UH. I DON'T EAT BACON.
LUCKY YOU. ALL SHARON'S GOT HERE TODAY IS SHORTENING.
WHISK THE EGGS.
ADD THEM TO THE PAN.
MAKE SURE THE EGGS DON'T GET TOO LUMPY.
THAT'S IT. THEY'RE DONE. IT DOESN'T TAKE LONG.
IT'S SO GOOD!
YOU LIKE IT? FINISH UP.
WE'LL SEE IF WE CAN FIND SOME MORE ONIONS OUTSIDE.

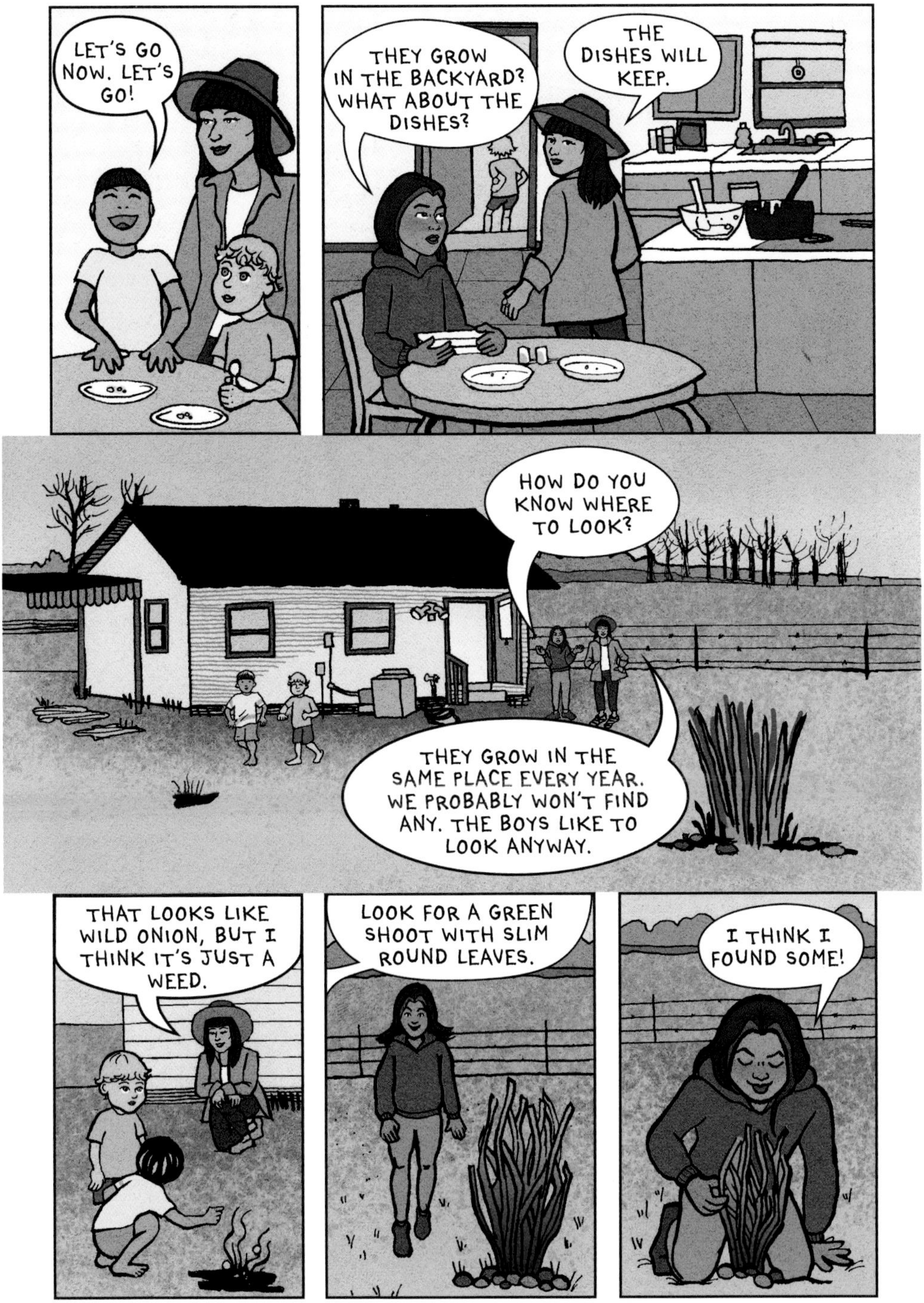
LET'S GO NOW. LET'S GO!
THEY GROW IN THE BACKYARD? WHAT ABOUT THE DISHES?
THE DISHES WILL KEEP.
HOW DO YOU KNOW WHERE TO LOOK?
THEY GROW IN THE SAME PLACE EVERY YEAR. WE PROBABLY WON'T FIND ANY. THE BOYS LIKE TO LOOK ANYWAY.
THAT LOOKS LIKE WILD ONION, BUT I THINK IT'S JUST A WEED.
LOOK FOR A GREEN SHOOT WITH SLIM ROUND LEAVES.
I THINK I FOUND SOME!

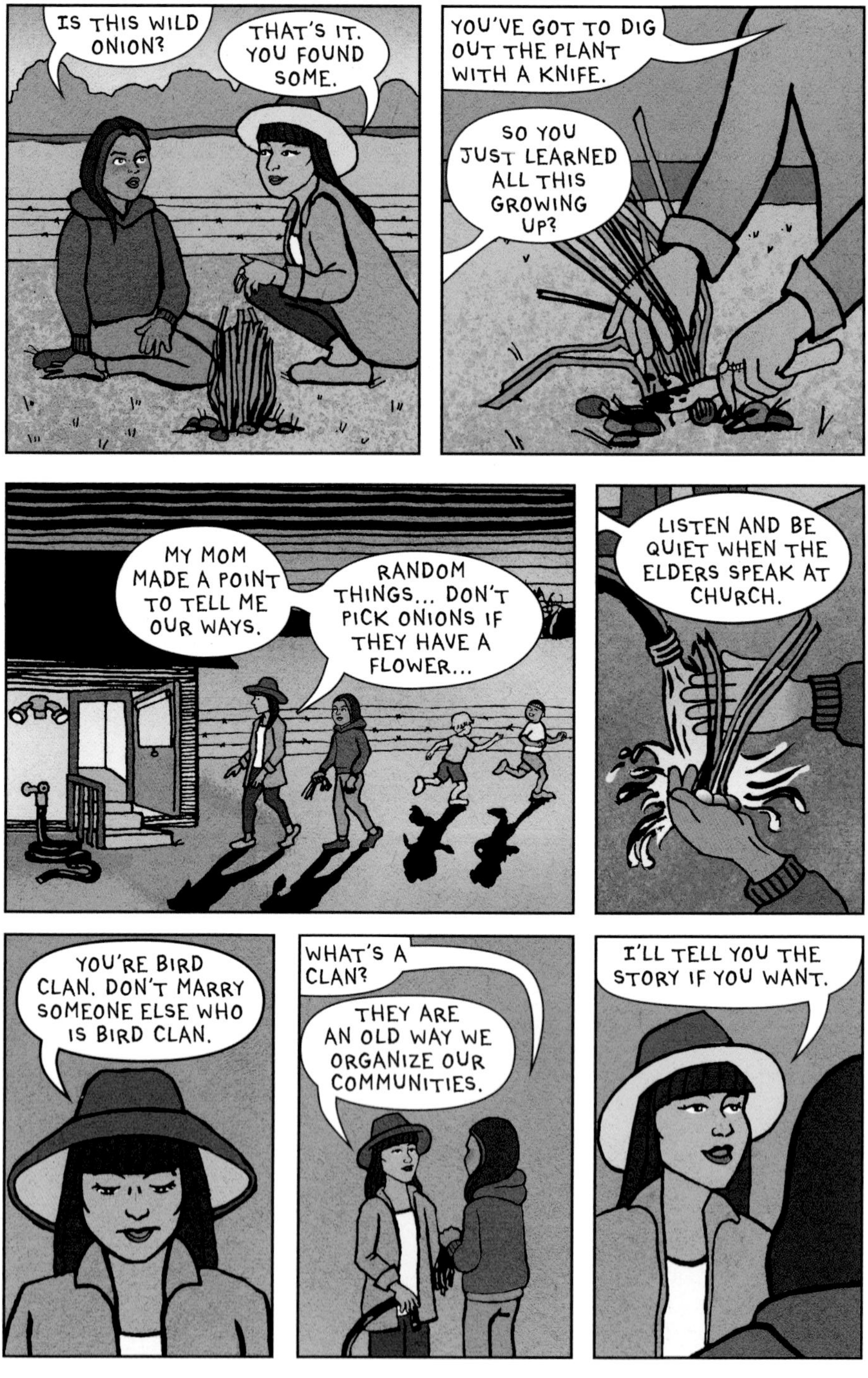
IS THIS WILD ONION?
THAT'S IT. YOU FOUND SOME.
YOU'VE GOT TO DIG OUT THE PLANT WITH A KNIFE.
SO YOU JUST LEARNED ALL THIS GROWING UP?
MY MOM MADE A POINT TO TELL ME OUR WAYS.
RANDOM THINGS... DON'T PICK ONIONS IF THEY HAVE A FLOWER...
LISTEN AND BE QUIET WHEN THE ELDERS SPEAK AT CHURCH.
YOU'RE BIRD CLAN. DON'T MARRY SOMEONE ELSE WHO IS BIRD CLAN.
WHAT'S A CLAN?
THEY ARE AN OLD WAY WE ORGANIZE OUR COMMUNITIES.
I'LL TELL YOU THE STORY IF YOU WANT.

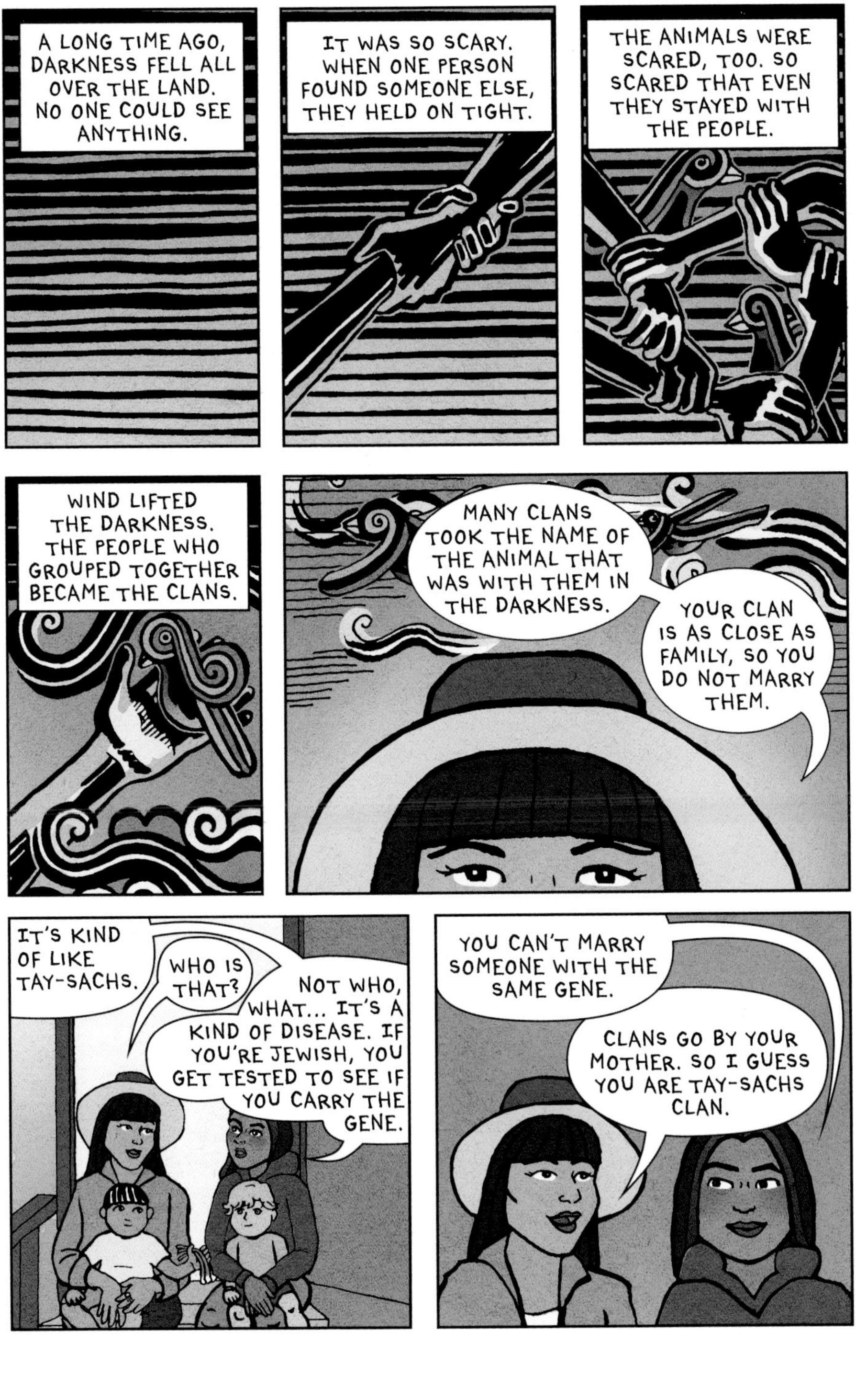

A LONG TIME AGO, DARKNESS FELL ALL OVER THE LAND. NO ONE COULD SEE ANYTHING.
IT WAS SO SCARY. WHEN ONE PERSON FOUND SOMEONE ELSE, THEY HELD ON TIGHT.
THE ANIMALS WERE SCARED, TOO. SO SCARED THAT EVEN THEY STAYED WITH THE PEOPLE.
WIND LIFTED THE DARKNESS. THE PEOPLE WHO GROUPED TOGETHER BECAME THE CLANS.
MANY CLANS TOOK THE NAME OF THE ANIMAL THAT WAS WITH THEM IN THE DARKNESS.
YOUR CLAN IS AS CLOSE AS FAMILY, SO YOU DO NOT MARRY THEM.
IT'S KIND OF LIKE TAY-SACHS.
WHO IS THAT?
NOT WHO, WHAT... IT'S A KIND OF DISEASE. IF YOU'RE JEWISH, YOU GET TESTED TO SEE IF YOU CARRY THE GENE.
YOU CAN'T MARRY SOMEONE WITH THE SAME GENE.
CLANS GO BY YOUR MOTHER. SO I GUESS YOU ARE TAY-SACHS CLAN.

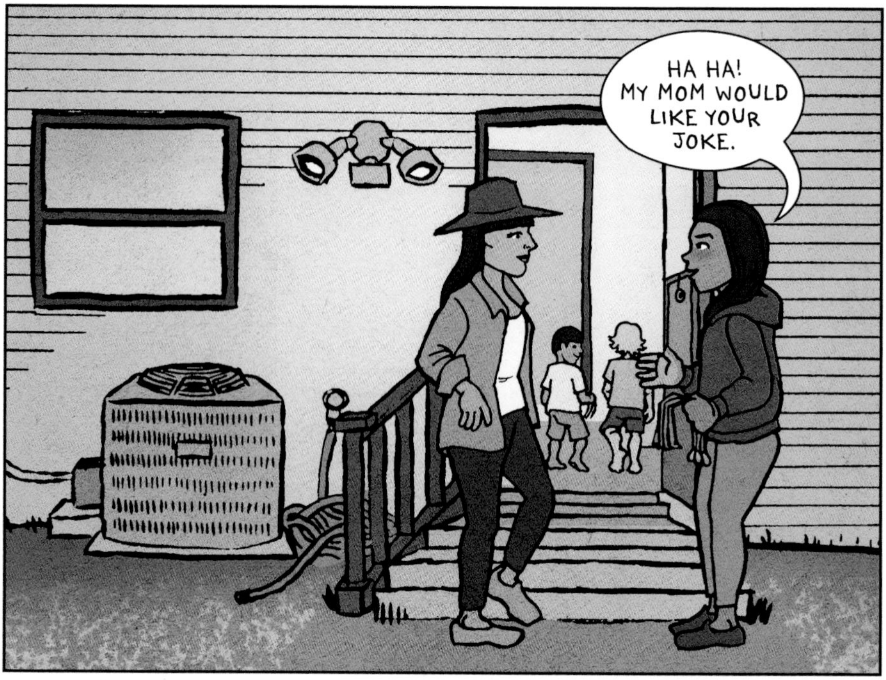
HA HA! MY MOM WOULD LIKE YOUR JOKE.

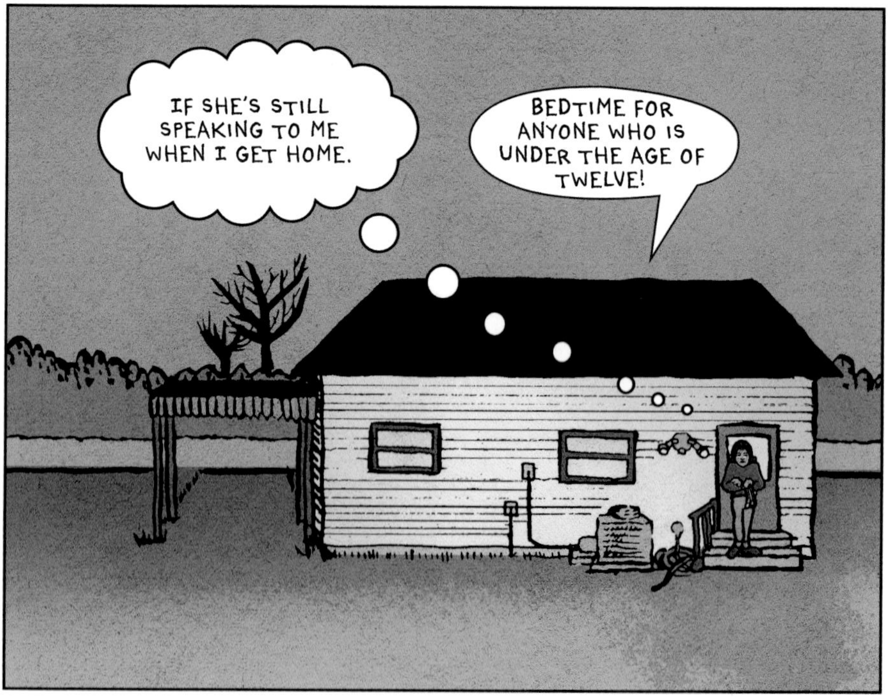
IF SHE'S STILL SPEAKING TO ME WHEN I GET HOME.
BEDTIME FOR ANYONE WHO IS UNDER THE AGE OF TWELVE!

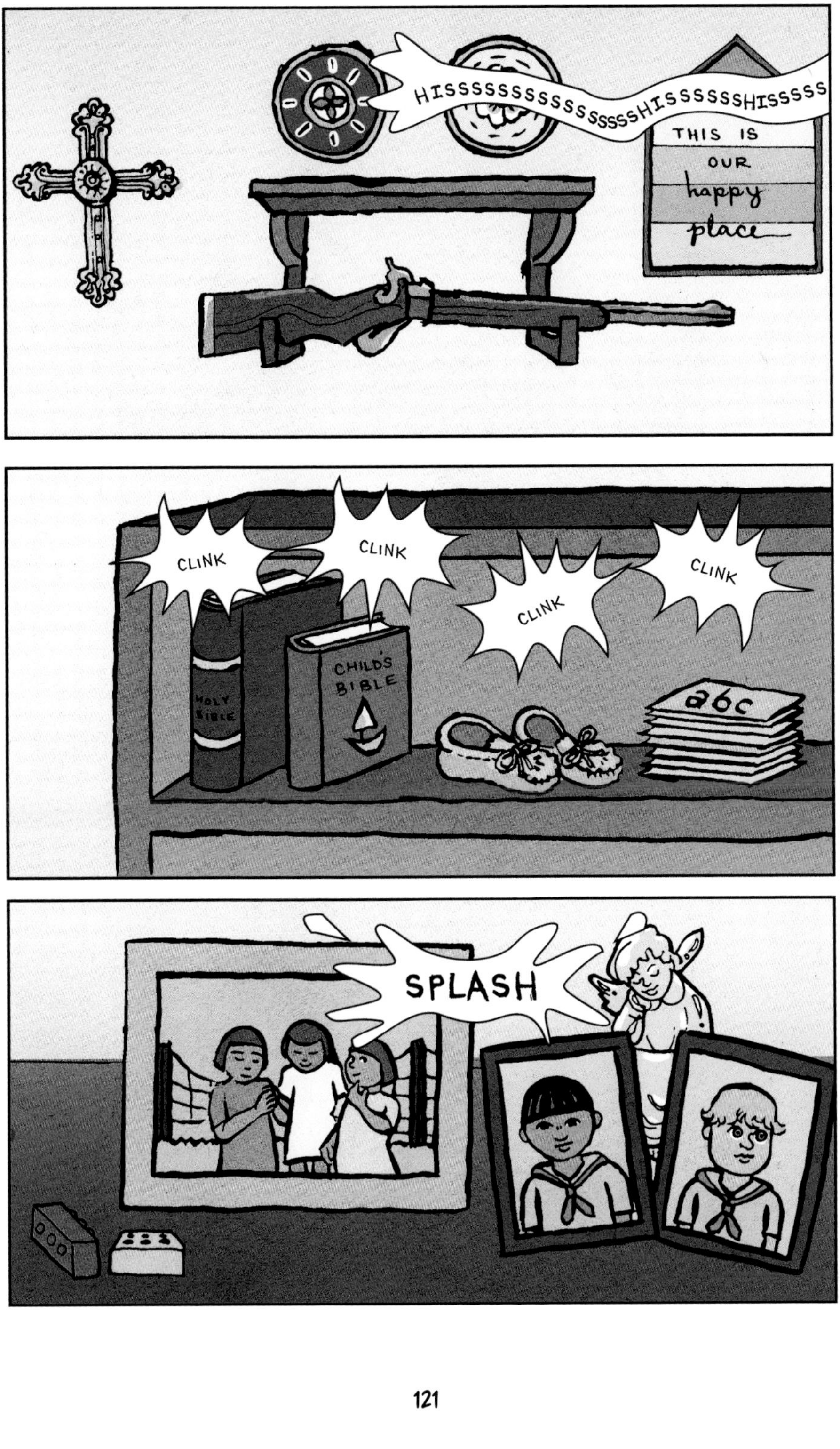
HISSSSSSSSSSSSSSSSSSHISSSSSSHISSSSS
THIS IS OUR happy place
CLINK
CLINK
CLINK
CLINK
HOLY BIBLE
CHILD'S BIBLE
abc
SPLASH

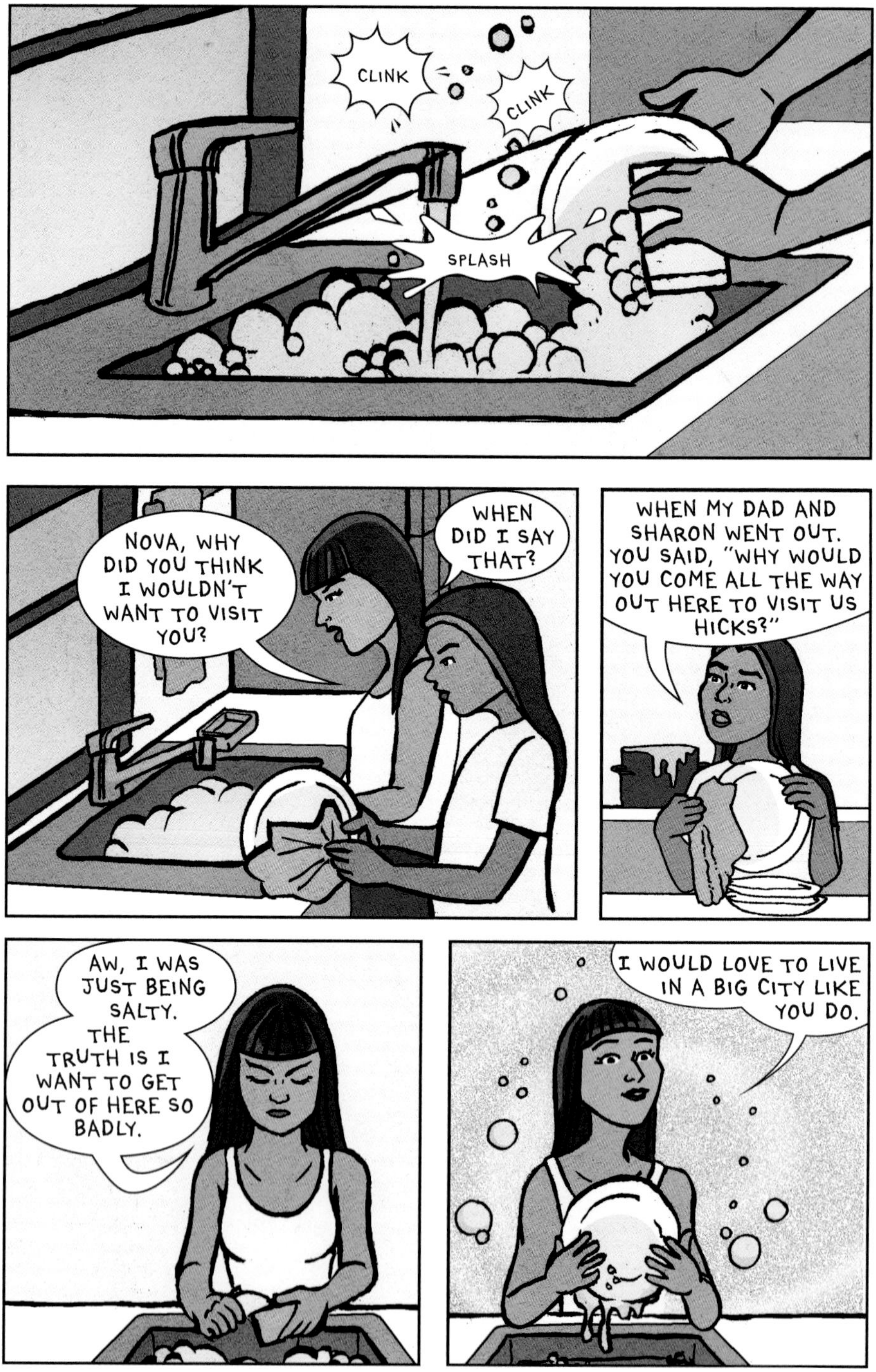
CLINK
CLINK
SPLASH
NOVA, WHY DID YOU THINK I WOULDN'T WANT TO VISIT YOU?
WHEN DID I SAY THAT?
WHEN MY DAD AND SHARON WENT OUT. YOU SAID, "WHY WOULD YOU COME ALL THE WAY OUT HERE TO VISIT US HICKS?"
AW, I WAS JUST BEING SALTY.
THE TRUTH IS I WANT TO GET OUT OF HERE SO BADLY.
I WOULD LOVE TO LIVE IN A BIG CITY LIKE YOU DO.

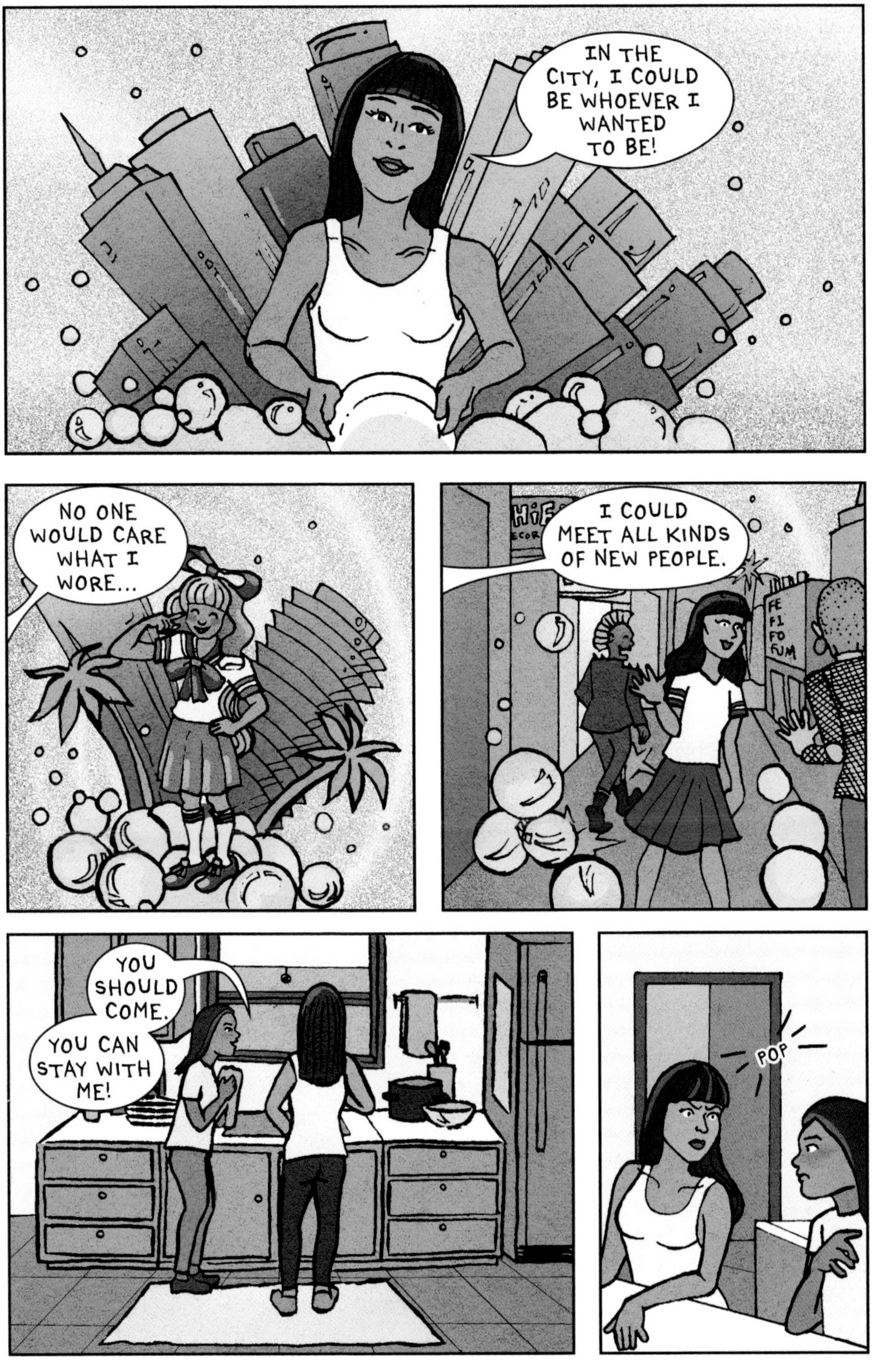
IN THE CITY, I COULD BE WHOEVER I WANTED TO BE!
NO ONE WOULD CARE WHAT I WORE...
I COULD MEET ALL KINDS OF NEW PEOPLE.
FE FI FO FUM
YOU SHOULD COME.
YOU CAN STAY WITH ME!
POP

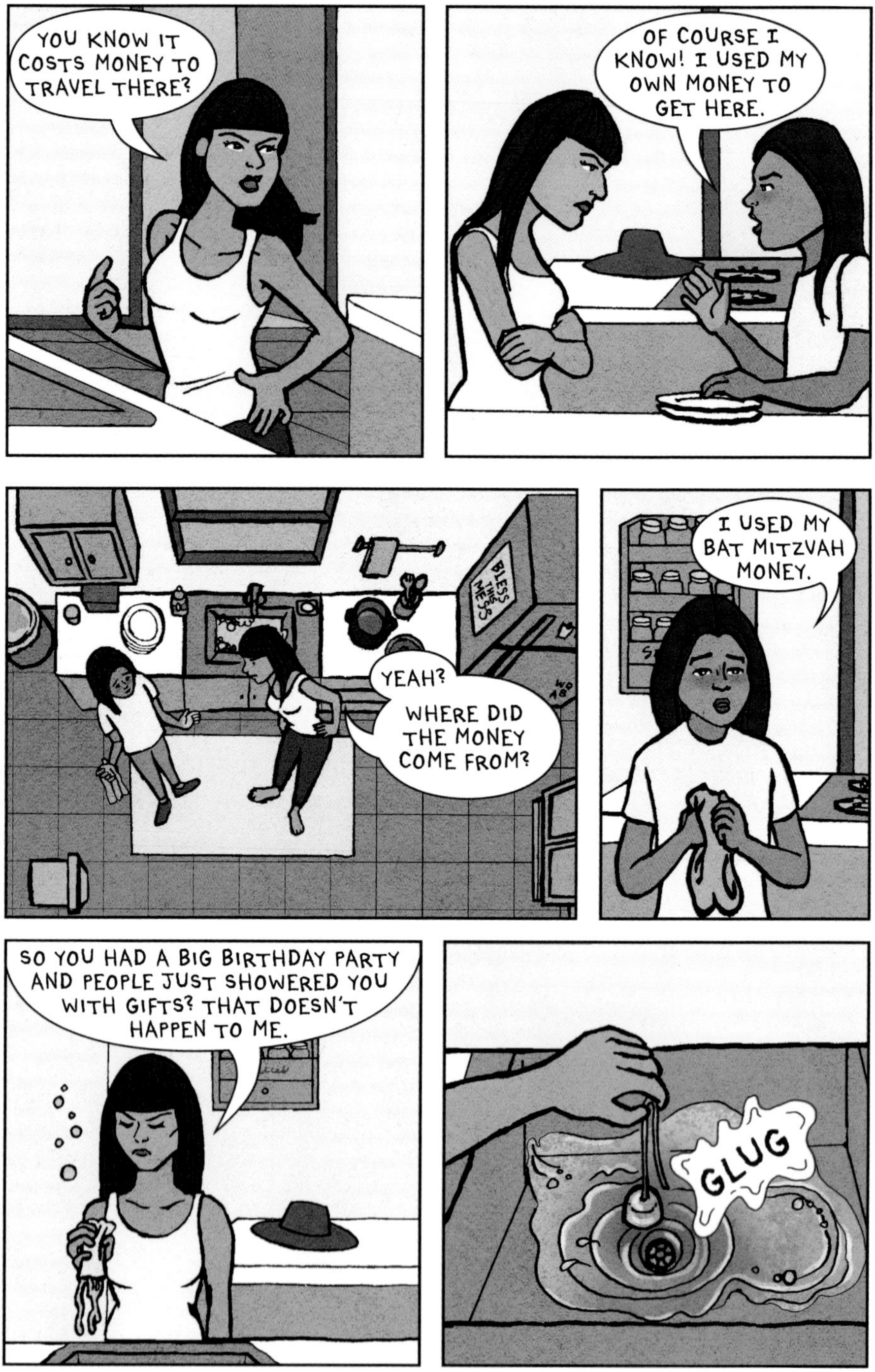
YOU KNOW IT COSTS MONEY TO TRAVEL THERE?
OF COURSE I KNOW! I USED MY OWN MONEY TO GET HERE.
BLESS THIS MESS
YEAH?
WHERE DID THE MONEY COME FROM?
I USED MY BAT MITZVAH MONEY.
SO YOU HAD A BIG BIRTHDAY PARTY AND PEOPLE JUST SHOWERED YOU WITH GIFTS? THAT DOESN'T HAPPEN TO ME.
GLUG

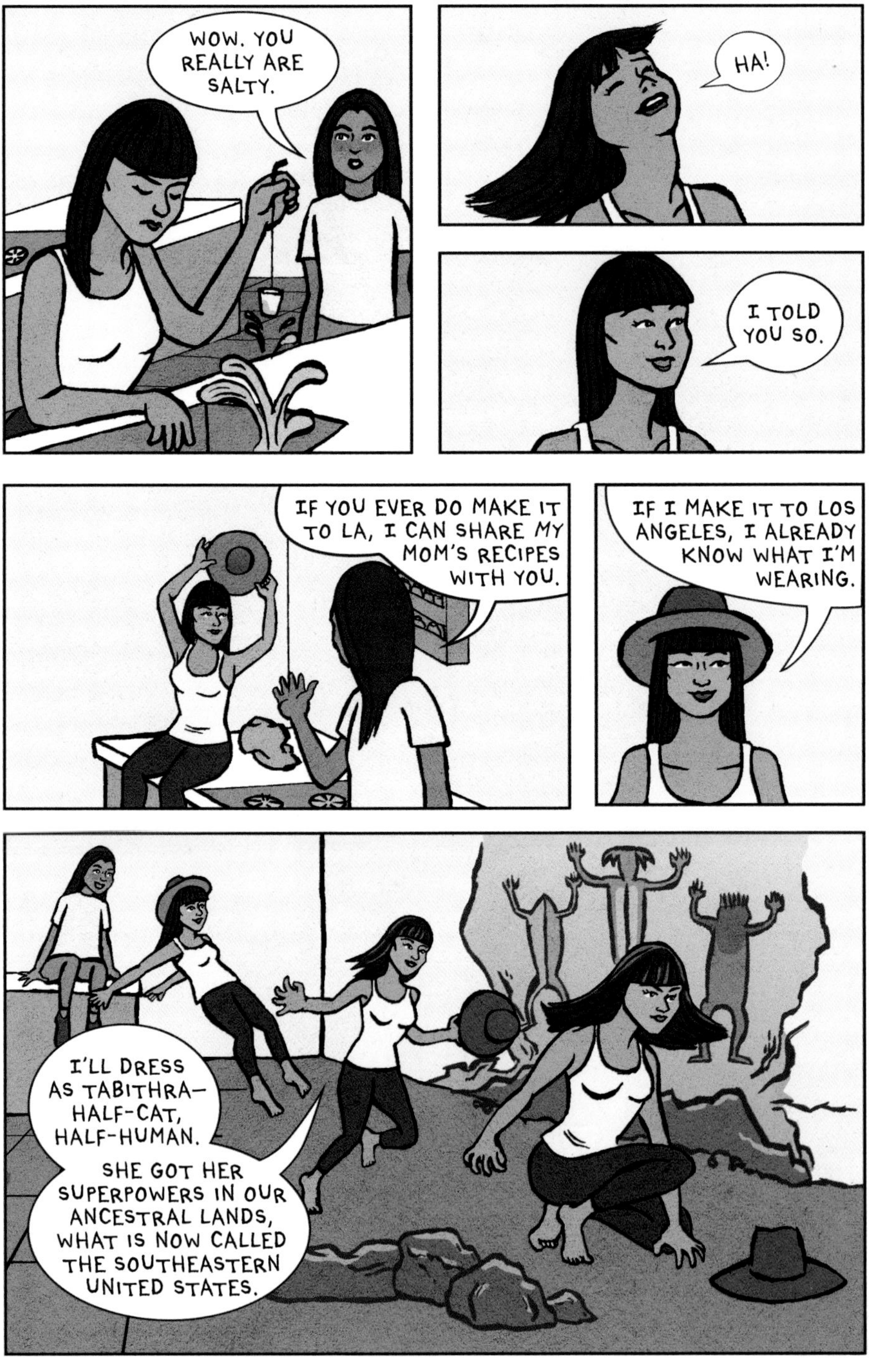
WOW. YOU REALLY ARE SALTY.
HA!
I TOLD YOU SO.
IF YOU EVER DO MAKE IT TO LA, I CAN SHARE MY MOM'S RECIPES WITH YOU.
IF I MAKE IT TO LOS ANGELES, I ALREADY KNOW WHAT I'M WEARING.
I'LL DRESS AS TABITHRA– HALF-CAT, HALF-HUMAN.
SHE GOT HER SUPERPOWERS IN OUR ANCESTRAL LANDS, WHAT IS NOW CALLED THE SOUTHEASTERN UNITED STATES.

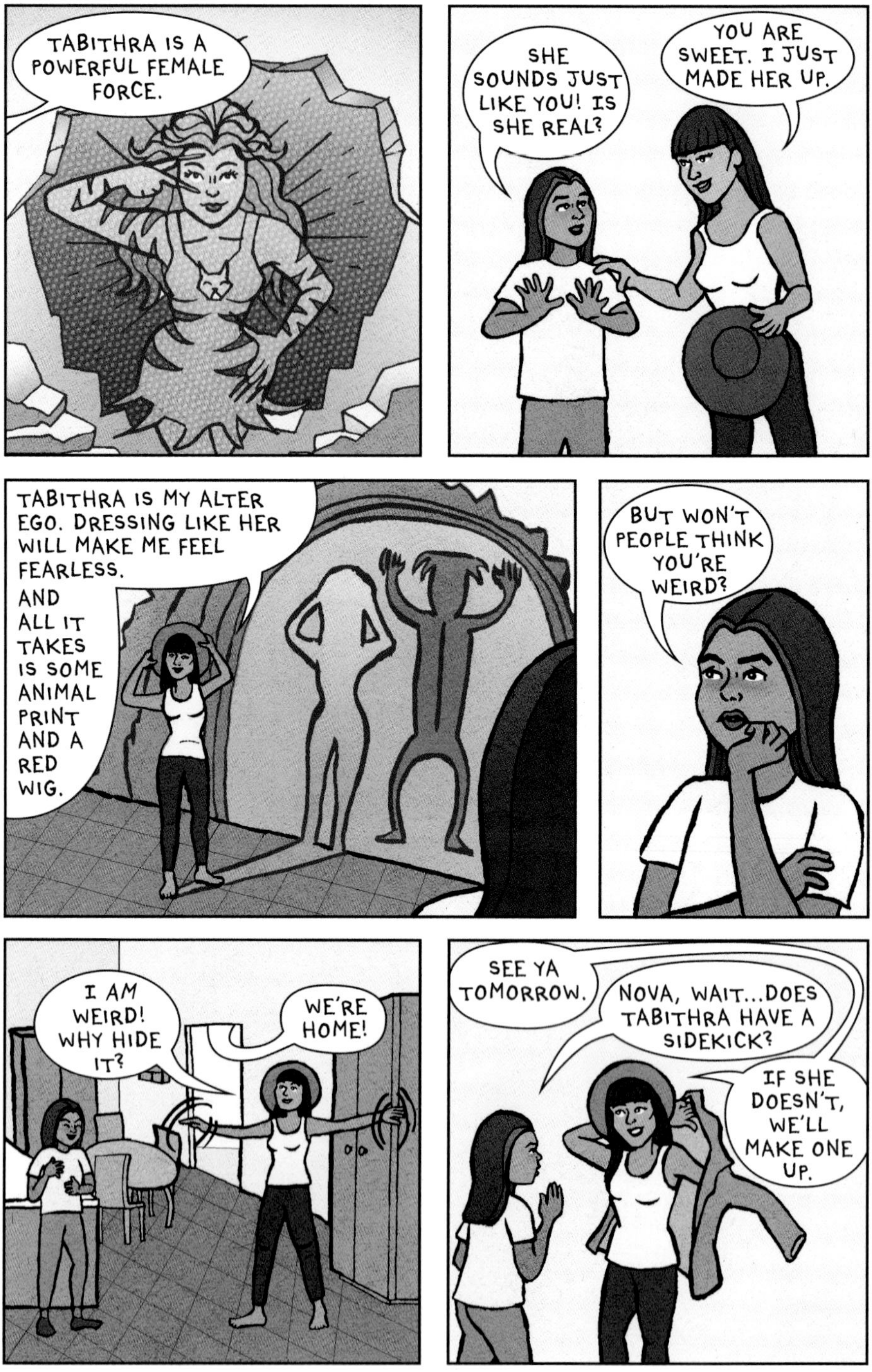
TABITHRA IS A POWERFUL FEMALE FORCE.
SHE SOUNDS JUST LIKE YOU! IS SHE REAL?
YOU ARE SWEET. I JUST MADE HER UP.
TABITHRA IS MY ALTER EGO. DRESSING LIKE HER WILL MAKE ME FEEL FEARLESS.
AND ALL IT TAKES IS SOME ANIMAL PRINT AND A RED WIG.
BUT WON'T PEOPLE THINK YOU'RE WEIRD?
I AM WEIRD! WHY HIDE IT?
WE'RE HOME!
SEE YA TOMORROW.
NOVA, WAIT...DOES TABITHRA HAVE A SIDEKICK?
IF SHE DOESN'T, WE'LL MAKE ONE UP.

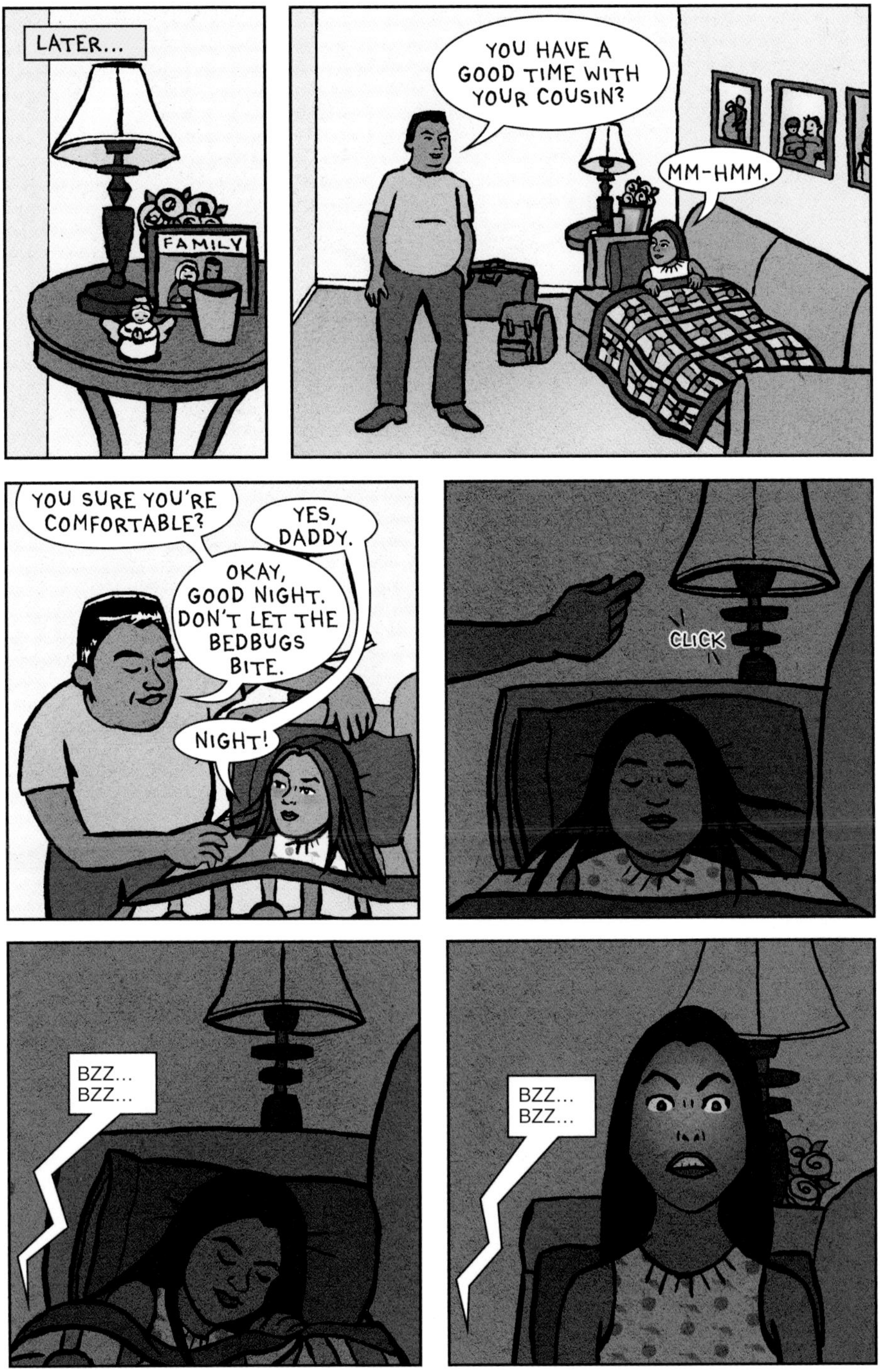
LATER...
FAMILY
YOU HAVE A GOOD TIME WITH YOUR COUSIN?
MM-HMM.
YOU SURE YOU'RE COMFORTABLE?
YES, DADDY.
OKAY, GOOD NIGHT. DON'T LET THE BEDBUGS BITE.
NIGHT!
CLICK
BZZ... BZZ...
BZZ... BZZ...

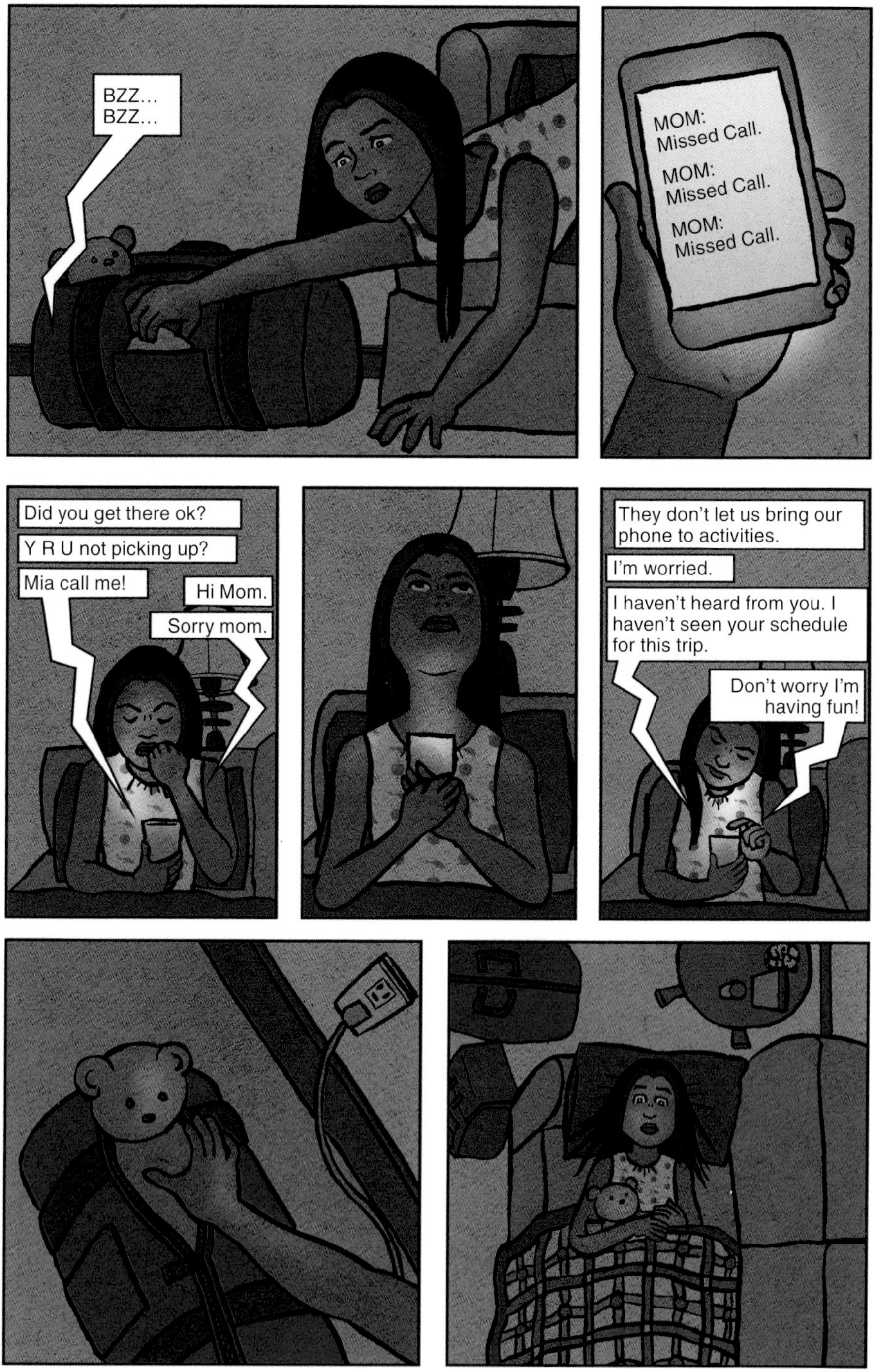
BZZ...
BZZ...
MOM:
Missed Call.
MOM:
Missed Call.
MOM:
Missed Call.
Did you get there ok?
Y R U not picking up?
Mia call me!
Hi Mom.
Sorry mom.
They don't let us bring our phone to activities.
I'm worried.
I haven't heard from you. I haven't seen your schedule for this trip.
Don't worry I'm having fun!

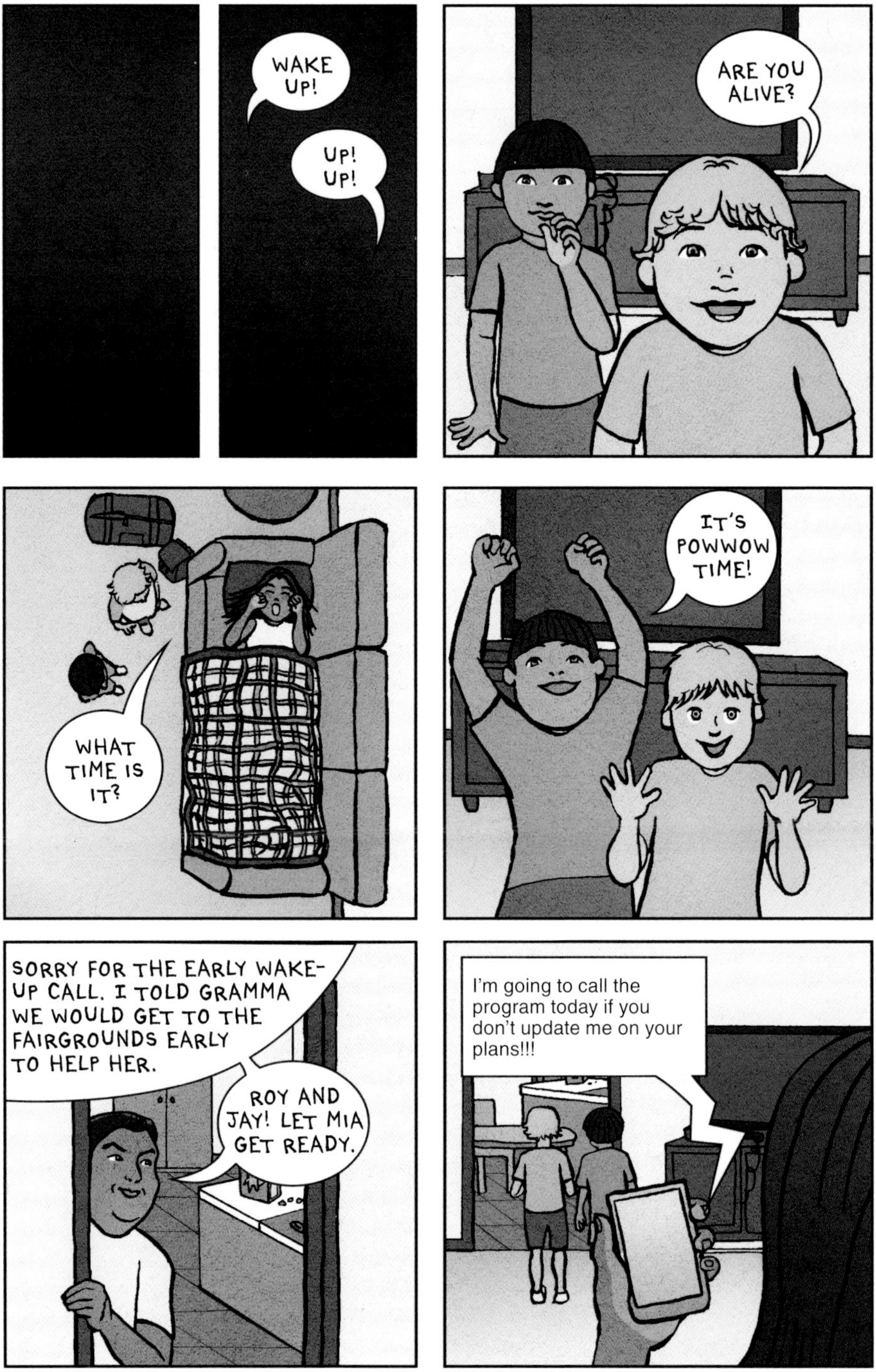
WAKE UP!
UP! UP!
ARE YOU ALIVE?
WHAT TIME IS IT?
IT'S POWWOW TIME!
SORRY FOR THE EARLY WAKE-UP CALL. I TOLD GRAMMA WE WOULD GET TO THE FAIRGROUNDS EARLY TO HELP HER.
ROY AND JAY! LET MIA GET READY.
I'm going to call the program today if you don't update me on your plans!!!

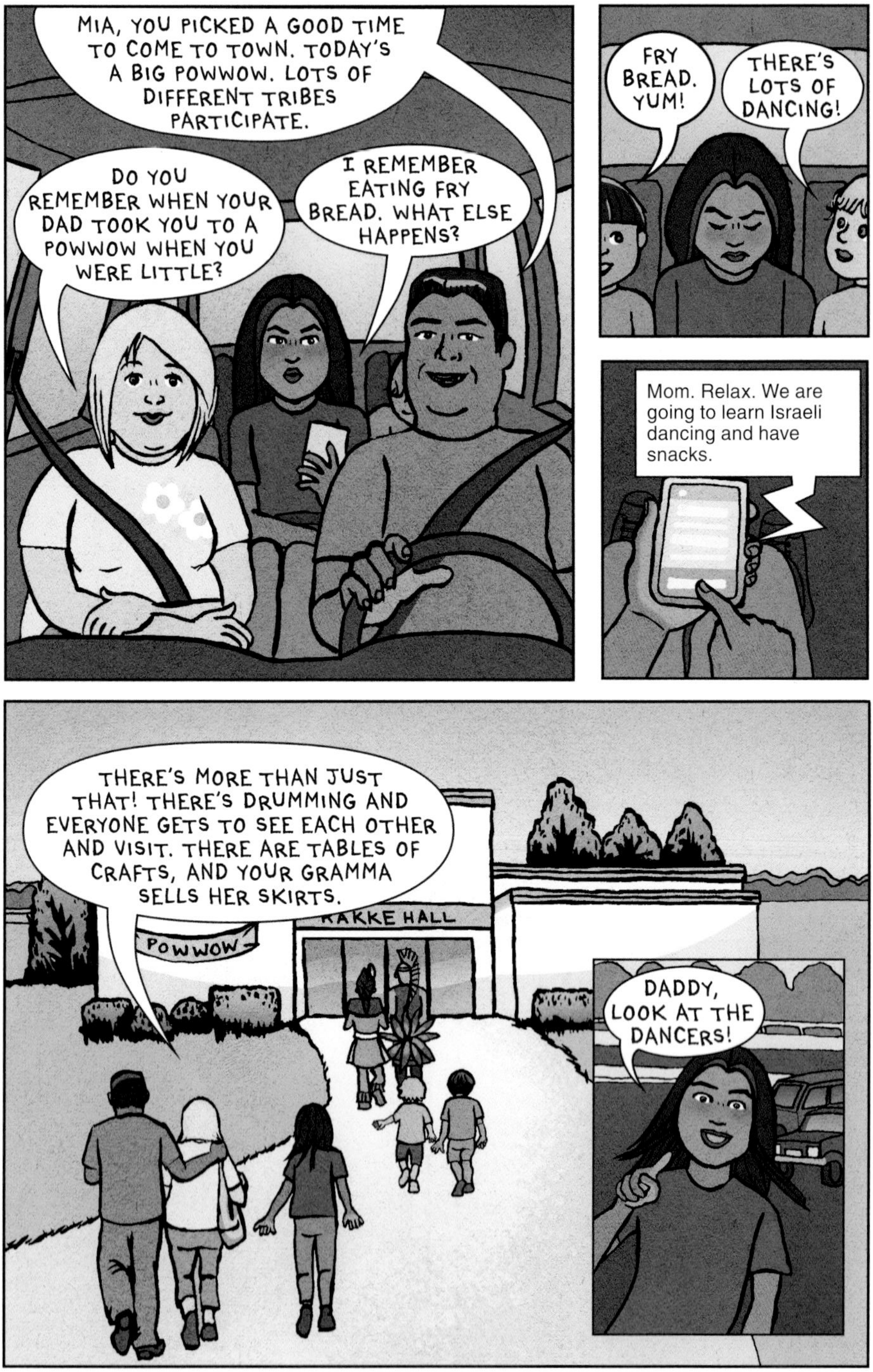
MIA, YOU PICKED A GOOD TIME TO COME TO TOWN. TODAY'S A BIG POWWOW. LOTS OF DIFFERENT TRIBES PARTICIPATE.
DO YOU REMEMBER WHEN YOUR DAD TOOK YOU TO A POWWOW WHEN YOU WERE LITTLE?
I REMEMBER EATING FRY BREAD. WHAT ELSE HAPPENS?
FRY BREAD. YUM!
THERE'S LOTS OF DANCING!
Mom. Relax. We are going to learn Israeli dancing and have snacks.
THERE'S MORE THAN JUST THAT! THERE'S DRUMMING AND EVERYONE GETS TO SEE EACH OTHER AND VISIT. THERE ARE TABLES OF CRAFTS, AND YOUR GRAMMA SELLS HER SKIRTS.
POWWOW
DADDY, LOOK AT THE DANCERS!

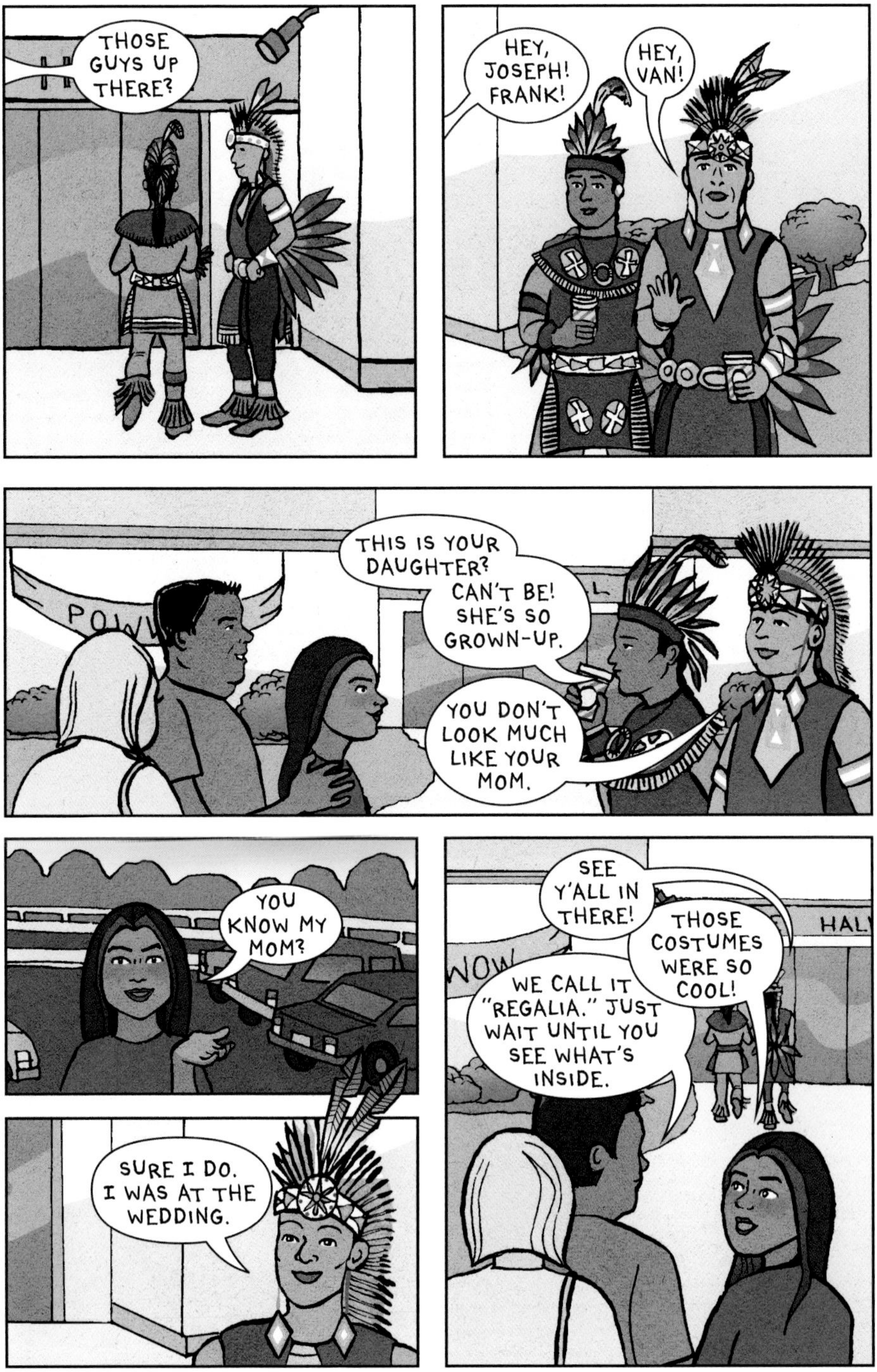
THOSE GUYS UP THERE?
HEY, JOSEPH! FRANK!
HEY, VAN!
THIS IS YOUR DAUGHTER?
CAN'T BE! SHE'S SO GROWN-UP.
YOU DON'T LOOK MUCH LIKE YOUR MOM.
YOU KNOW MY MOM?
SURE I DO. I WAS AT THE WEDDING.
SEE Y'ALL IN THERE!
THOSE COSTUMES WERE SO COOL!
WE CALL IT "REGALIA." JUST WAIT UNTIL YOU SEE WHAT'S INSIDE.

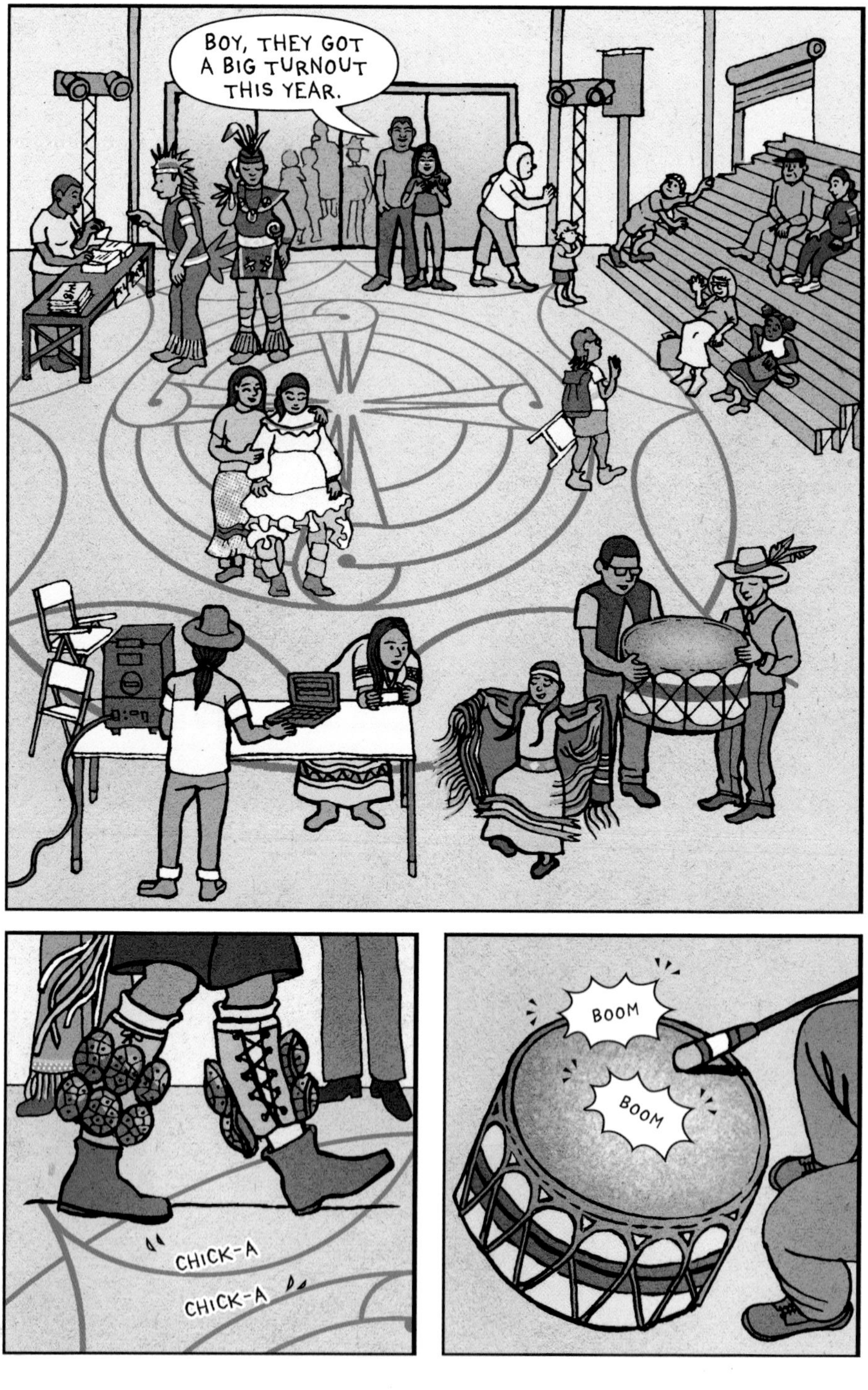
BOY, THEY GOT A BIG TURNOUT THIS YEAR.
CHICK-A
CHICK-A
BOOM
BOOM

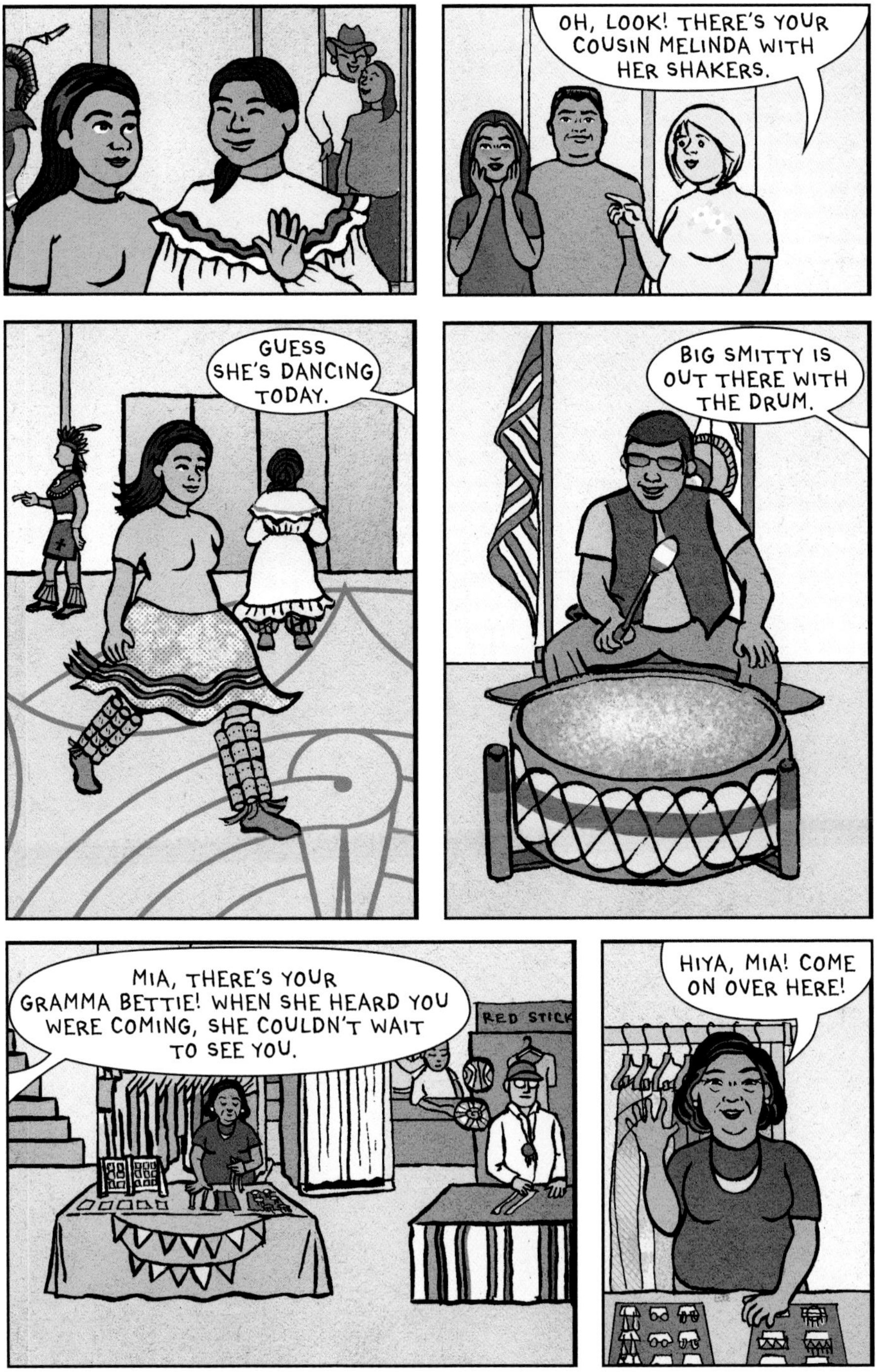
OH, LOOK! THERE'S YOUR COUSIN MELINDA WITH HER SHAKERS.
GUESS SHE'S DANCING TODAY.
BIG SMITTY IS OUT THERE WITH THE DRUM.
MIA, THERE'S YOUR GRAMMA BETTIE! WHEN SHE HEARD YOU WERE COMING, SHE COULDN'T WAIT TO SEE YOU.
RED STICK
HIYA, MIA! COME ON OVER HERE!

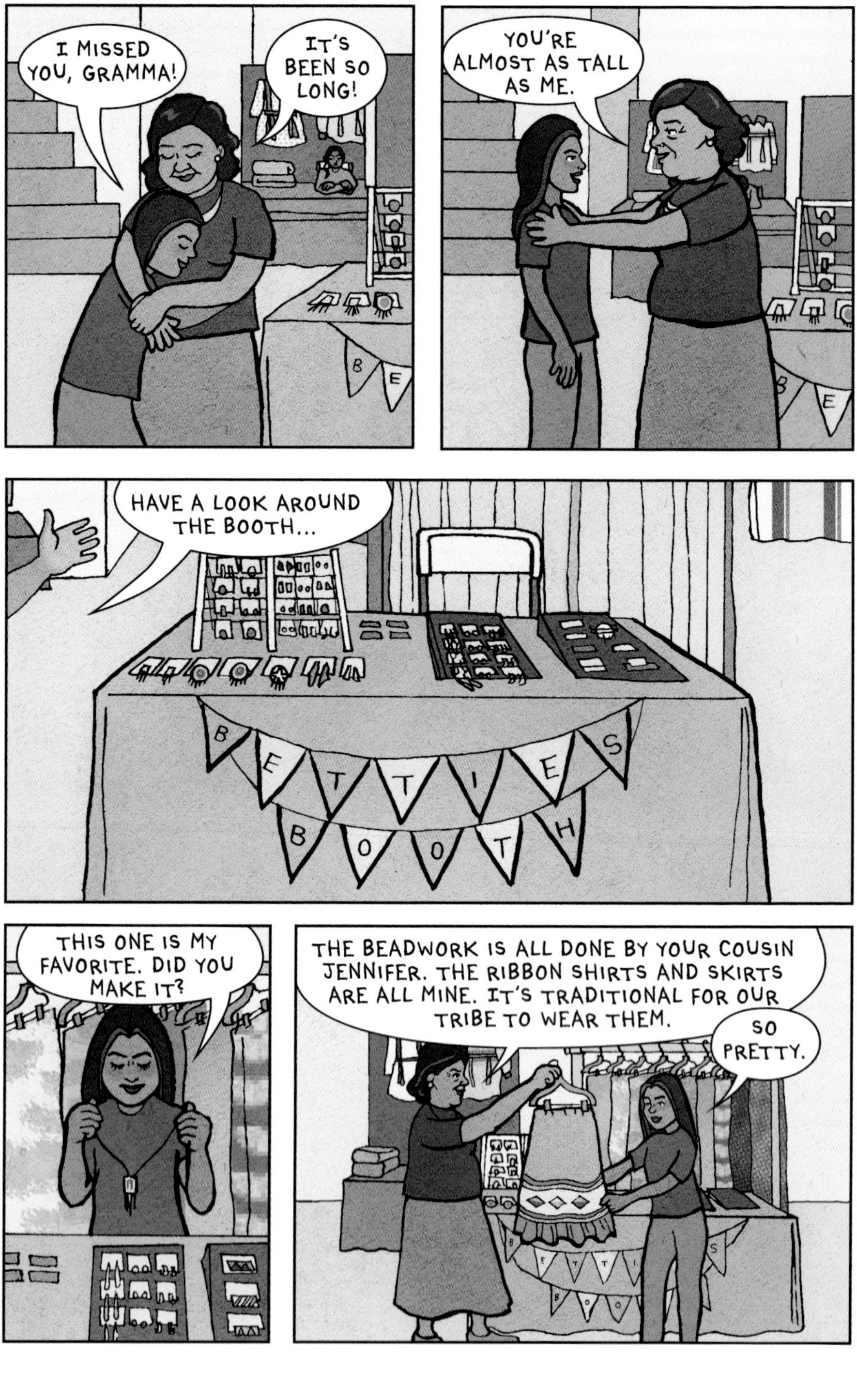
I MISSED YOU, GRAMMA!
IT'S BEEN SO LONG!
YOU'RE ALMOST AS TALL AS ME.
HAVE A LOOK AROUND THE BOOTH...
BETTIES BOOTH
THIS ONE IS MY FAVORITE. DID YOU MAKE IT?
THE BEADWORK IS ALL DONE BY YOUR COUSIN JENNIFER. THE RIBBON SHIRTS AND SKIRTS ARE ALL MINE. IT'S TRADITIONAL FOR OUR TRIBE TO WEAR THEM.
SO PRETTY.

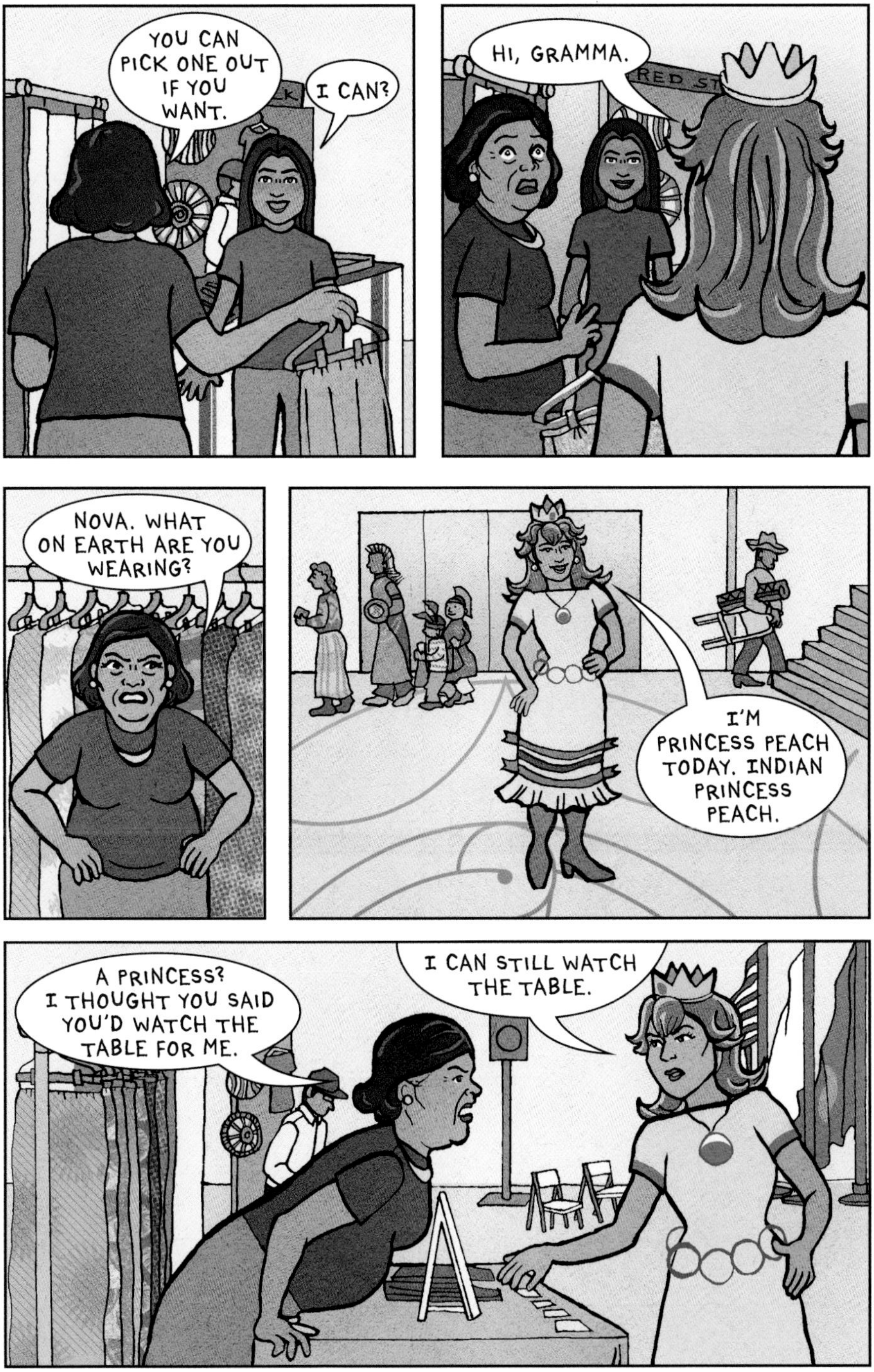
YOU CAN PICK ONE OUT IF YOU WANT.
I CAN?
HI, GRAMMA.
NOVA. WHAT ON EARTH ARE YOU WEARING?
I'M PRINCESS PEACH TODAY. INDIAN PRINCESS PEACH.
A PRINCESS? I THOUGHT YOU SAID YOU'D WATCH THE TABLE FOR ME.
I CAN STILL WATCH THE TABLE.

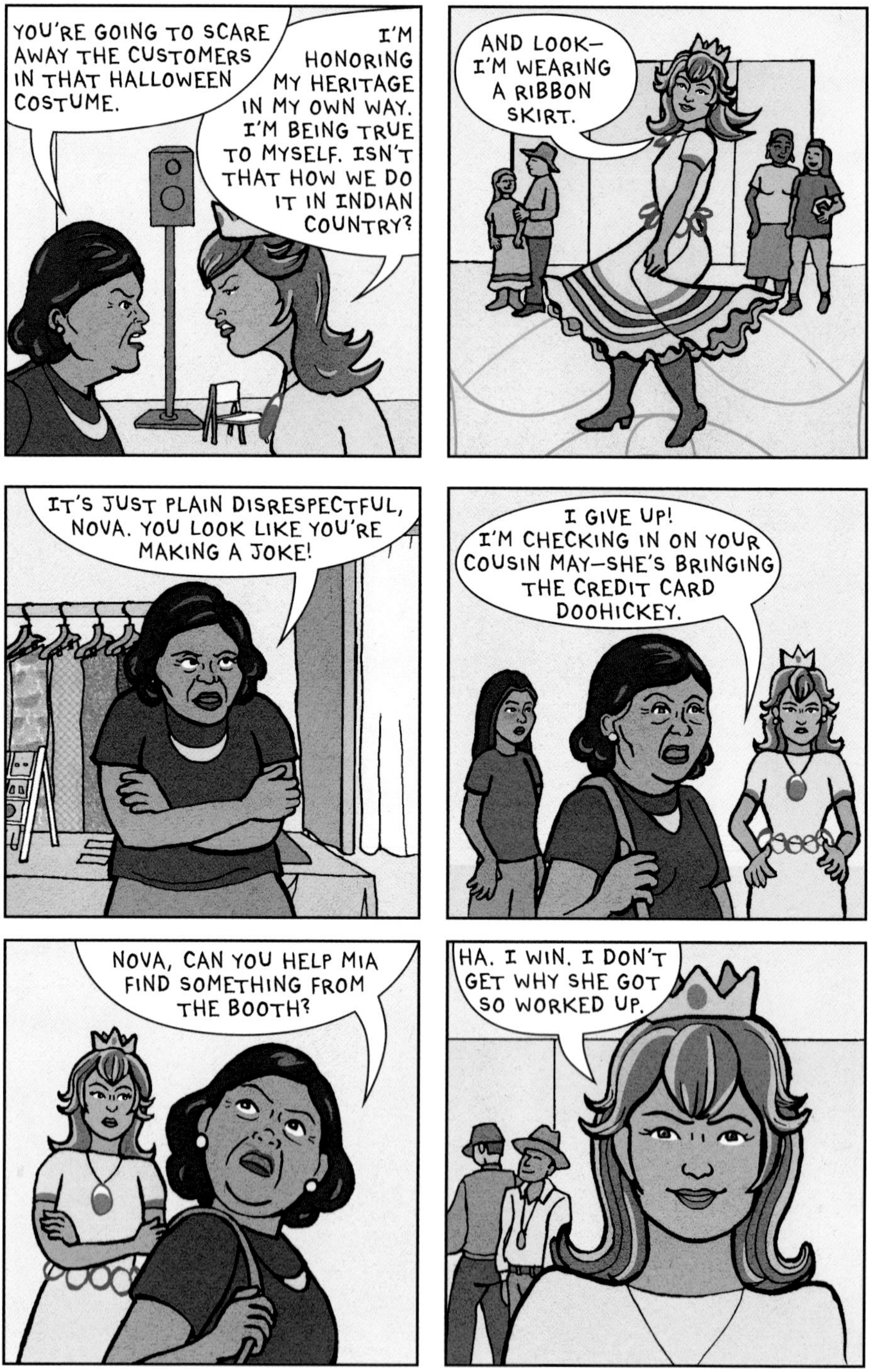
YOU'RE GOING TO SCARE AWAY THE CUSTOMERS IN THAT HALLOWEEN COSTUME.
I'M HONORING MY HERITAGE IN MY OWN WAY. I'M BEING TRUE TO MYSELF. ISN'T THAT HOW WE DO IT IN INDIAN COUNTRY?
AND LOOK— I'M WEARING A RIBBON SKIRT.
IT'S JUST PLAIN DISRESPECTFUL, NOVA. YOU LOOK LIKE YOU'RE MAKING A JOKE!
I GIVE UP! I'M CHECKING IN ON YOUR COUSIN MAY—SHE'S BRINGING THE CREDIT CARD DOOHICKEY.
NOVA, CAN YOU HELP MIA FIND SOMETHING FROM THE BOOTH?
HA. I WIN. I DON'T GET WHY SHE GOT SO WORKED UP.

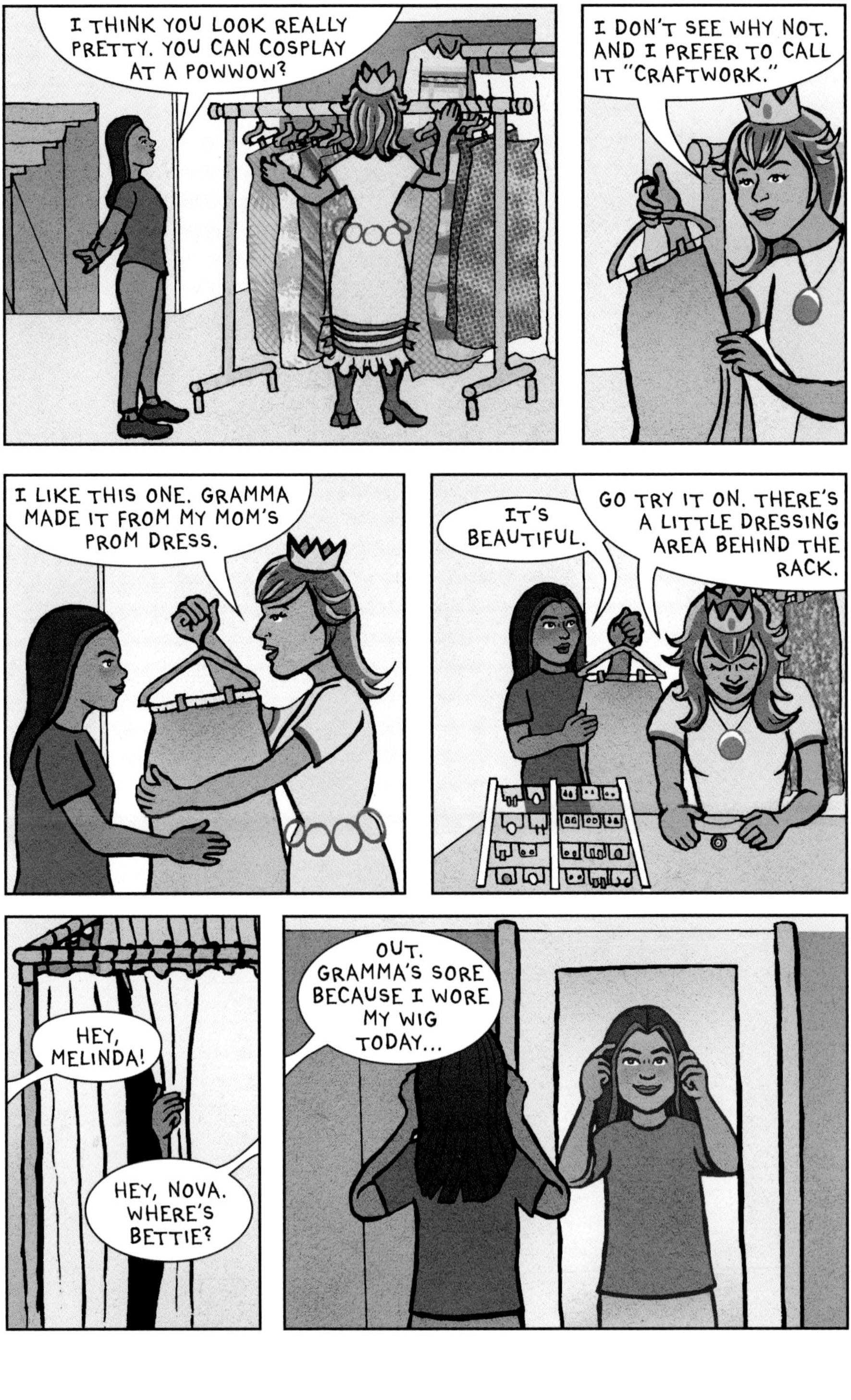
I THINK YOU LOOK REALLY PRETTY. YOU CAN COSPLAY AT A POWWOW?
I DON'T SEE WHY NOT. AND I PREFER TO CALL IT "CRAFTWORK."
I LIKE THIS ONE. GRAMMA MADE IT FROM MY MOM'S PROM DRESS.
IT'S BEAUTIFUL.
GO TRY IT ON. THERE'S A LITTLE DRESSING AREA BEHIND THE RACK.
HEY, MELINDA!
HEY, NOVA. WHERE'S BETTIE?
OUT. GRAMMA'S SORE BECAUSE I WORE MY WIG TODAY...

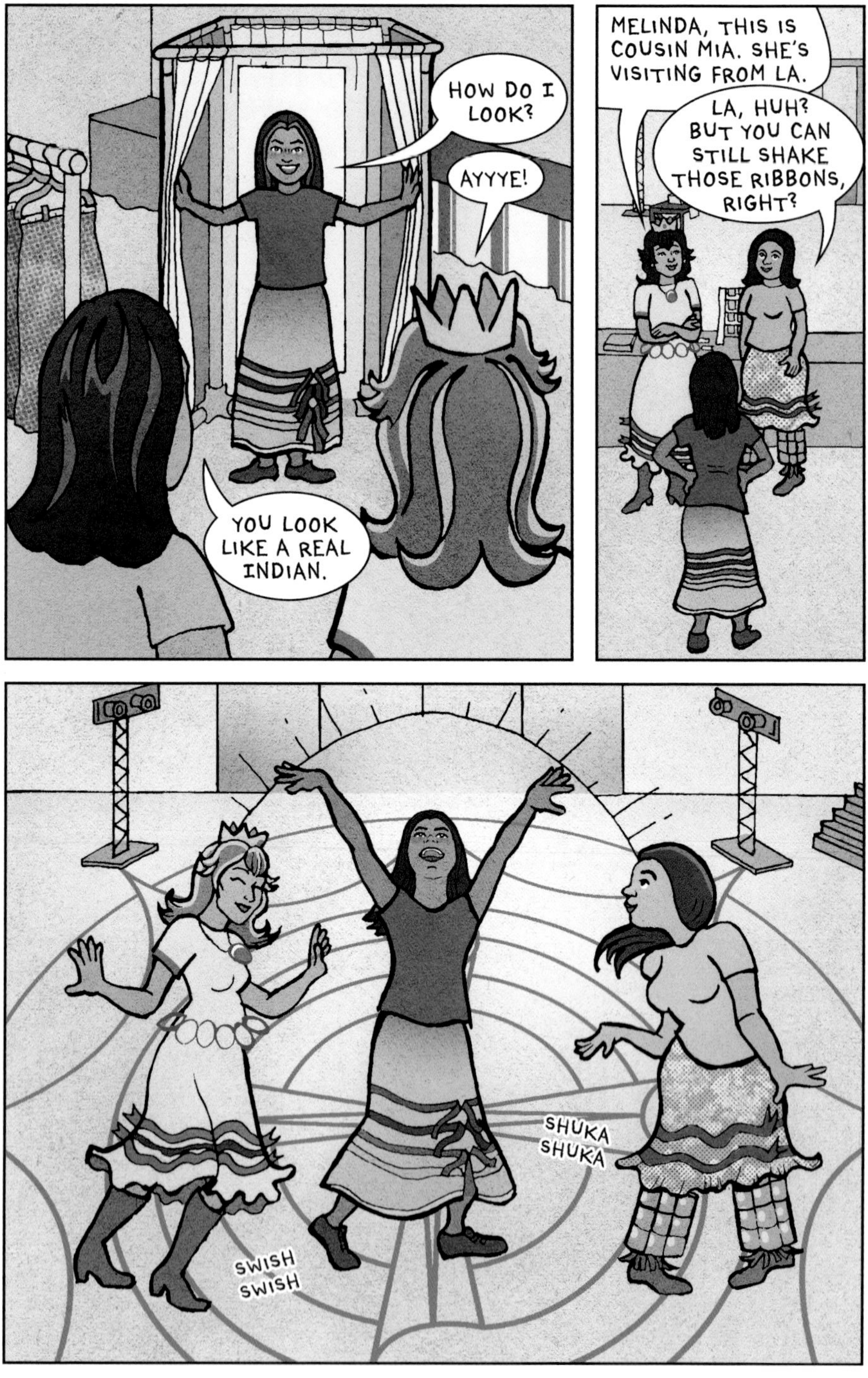
HOW DO I LOOK?
AYYYE!
YOU LOOK LIKE A REAL INDIAN.
MELINDA, THIS IS COUSIN MIA. SHE'S VISITING FROM LA.
LA, HUH? BUT YOU CAN STILL SHAKE THOSE RIBBONS, RIGHT?
SHUKA SHUKA
SWISH SWISH

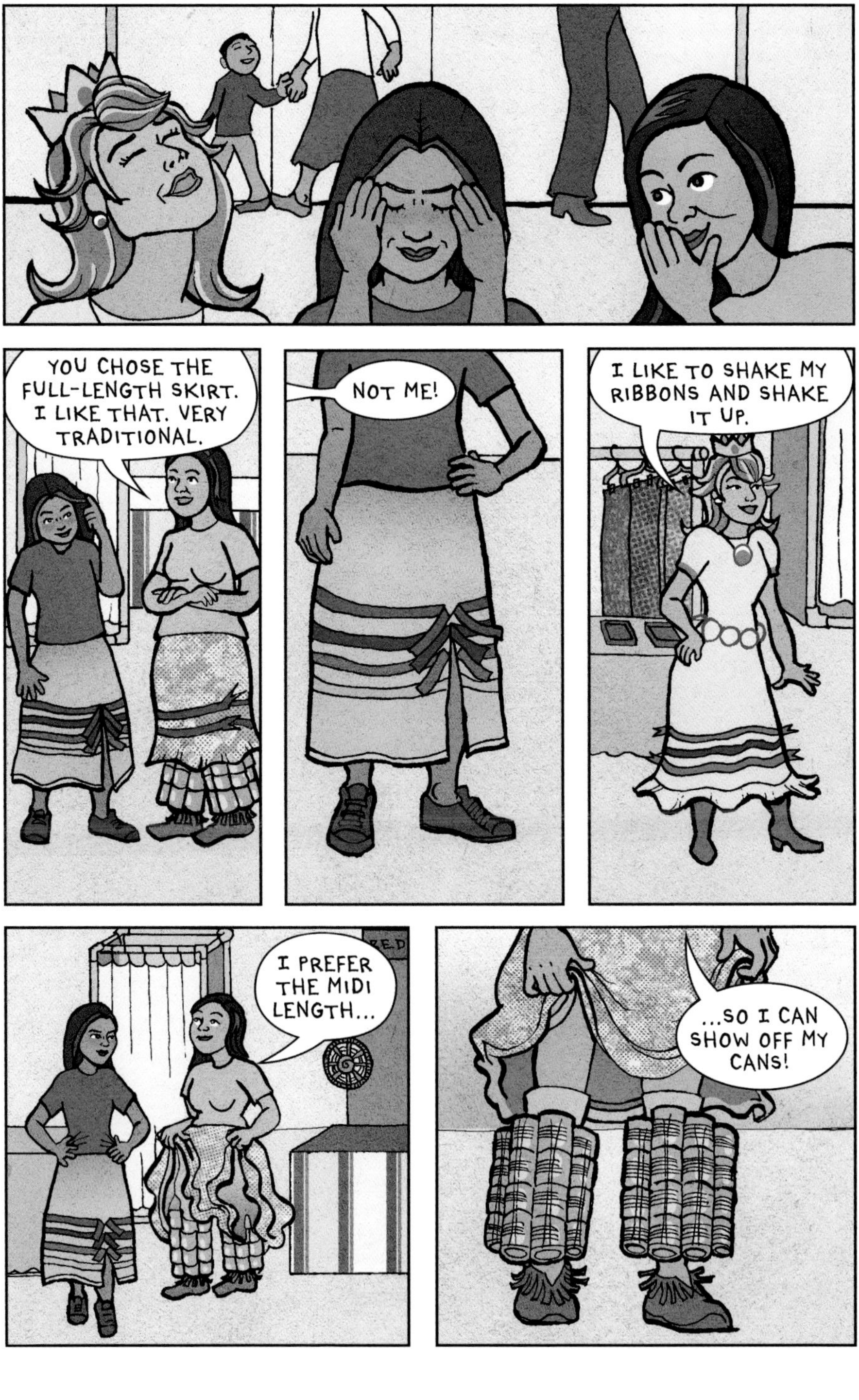
YOU CHOSE THE FULL-LENGTH SKIRT. I LIKE THAT. VERY TRADITIONAL.
NOT ME!
I LIKE TO SHAKE MY RIBBONS AND SHAKE IT UP.
I PREFER THE MIDI LENGTH...
...SO I CAN SHOW OFF MY CANS!

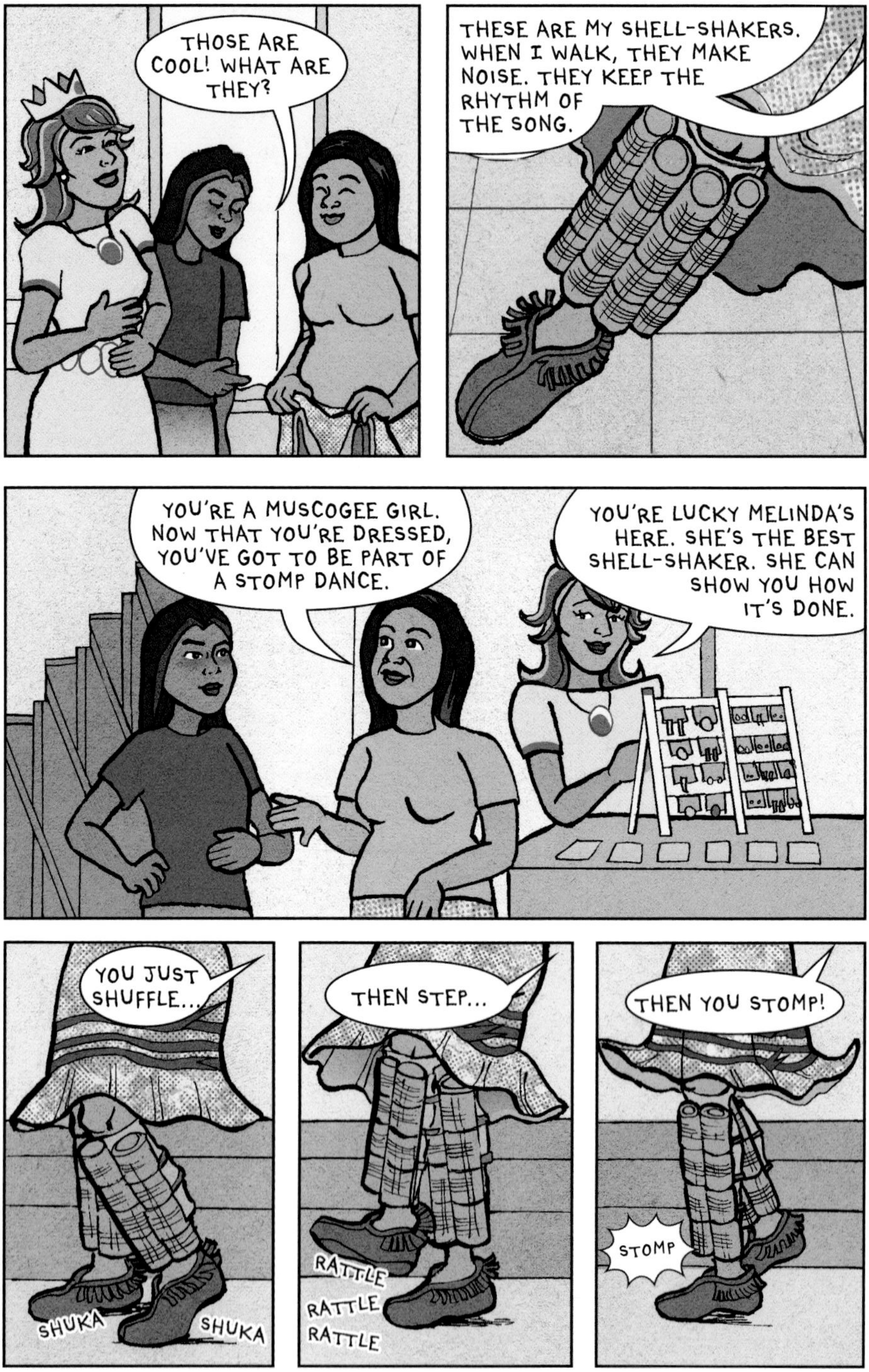
THOSE ARE COOL! WHAT ARE THEY?
THESE ARE MY SHELL-SHAKERS. WHEN I WALK, THEY MAKE NOISE. THEY KEEP THE RHYTHM OF THE SONG.
YOU'RE A MUSCOGEE GIRL. NOW THAT YOU'RE DRESSED, YOU'VE GOT TO BE PART OF A STOMP DANCE.
YOU'RE LUCKY MELINDA'S HERE. SHE'S THE BEST SHELL-SHAKER. SHE CAN SHOW YOU HOW IT'S DONE.
YOU JUST SHUFFLE...
SHUKA
SHUKA
THEN STEP...
RATTLE
RATTLE
RATTLE
THEN YOU STOMP!
STOMP

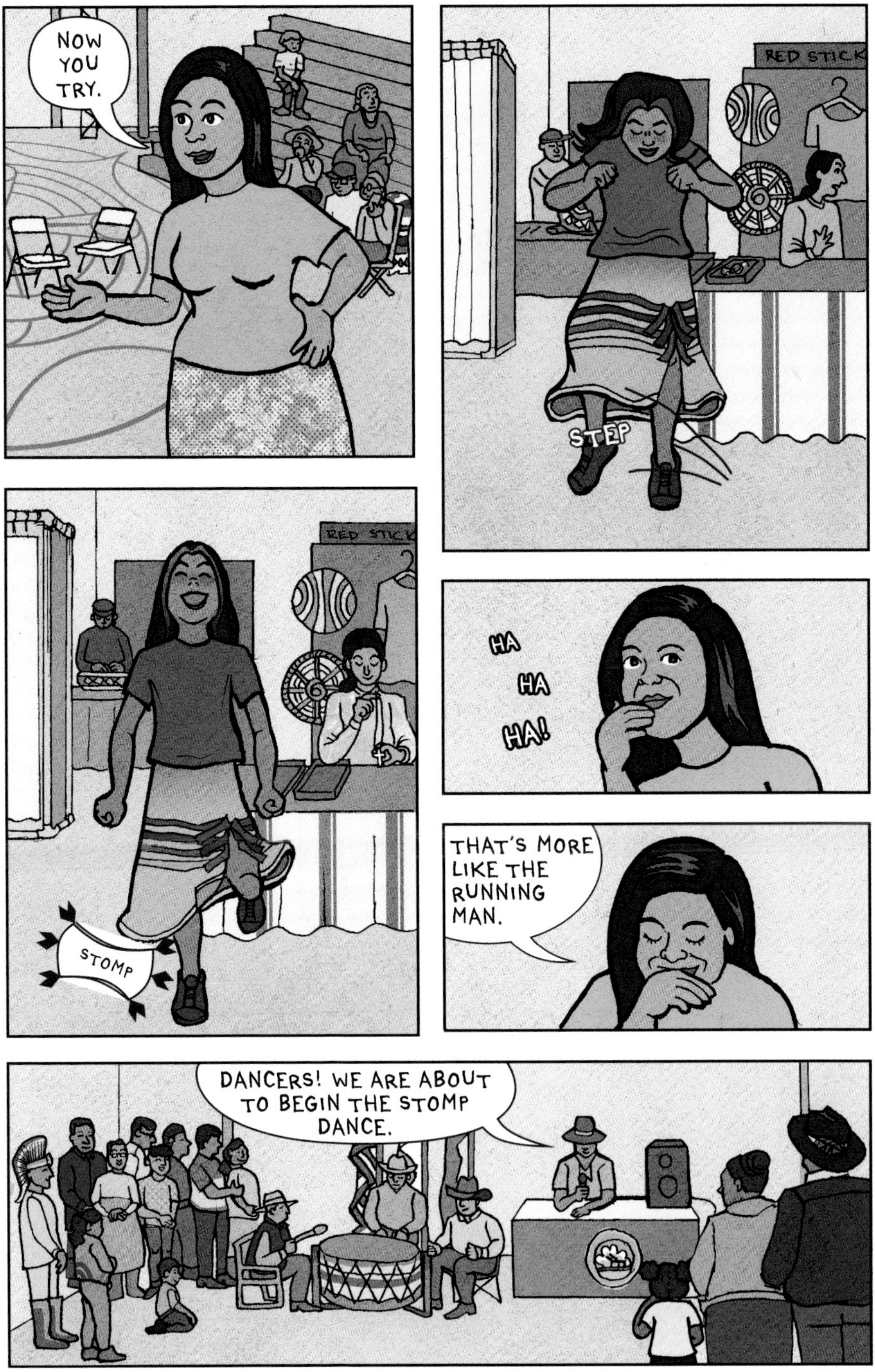
NOW YOU TRY.
RED STICK
STEP
RED STICK
STOMP
HA
HA
HA!
THAT'S MORE LIKE THE RUNNING MAN.
DANCERS! WE ARE ABOUT TO BEGIN THE STOMP DANCE.

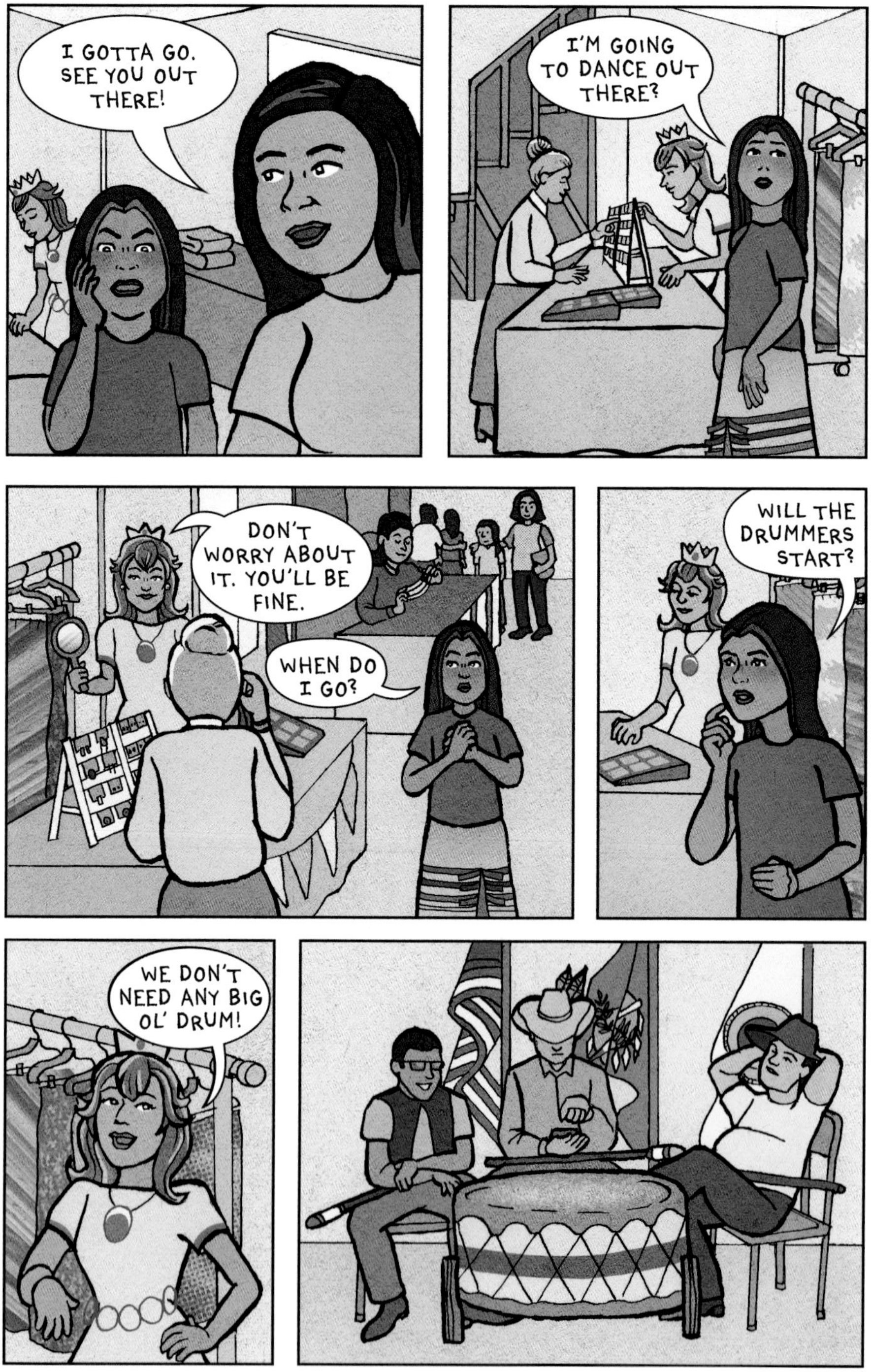
I GOTTA GO. SEE YOU OUT THERE!
I'M GOING TO DANCE OUT THERE?
DON'T WORRY ABOUT IT. YOU'LL BE FINE.
WHEN DO I GO?
WILL THE DRUMMERS START?
WE DON'T NEED ANY BIG OL' DRUM!

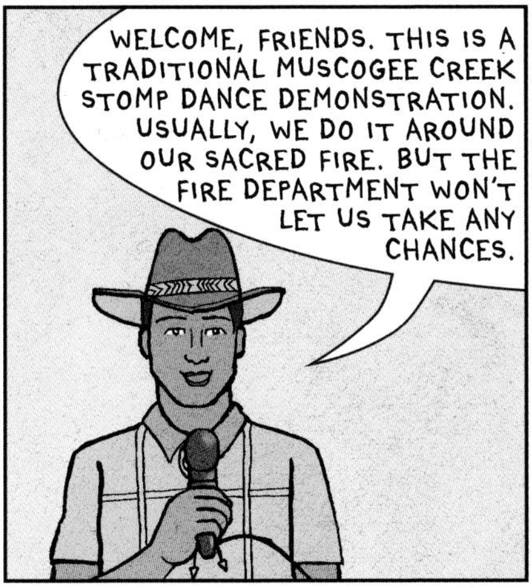
WELCOME, FRIENDS. THIS IS A TRADITIONAL MUSCOGEE CREEK STOMP DANCE DEMONSTRATION. USUALLY, WE DO IT AROUND OUR SACRED FIRE. BUT THE FIRE DEPARTMENT WON'T LET US TAKE ANY CHANCES.

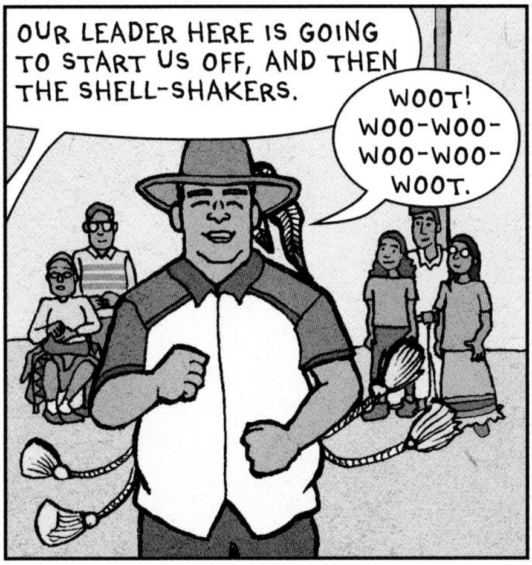
OUR LEADER HERE IS GOING TO START US OFF, AND THEN THE SHELL-SHAKERS.
WOOT! WOO-WOO-WOO-WOO-WOOT.

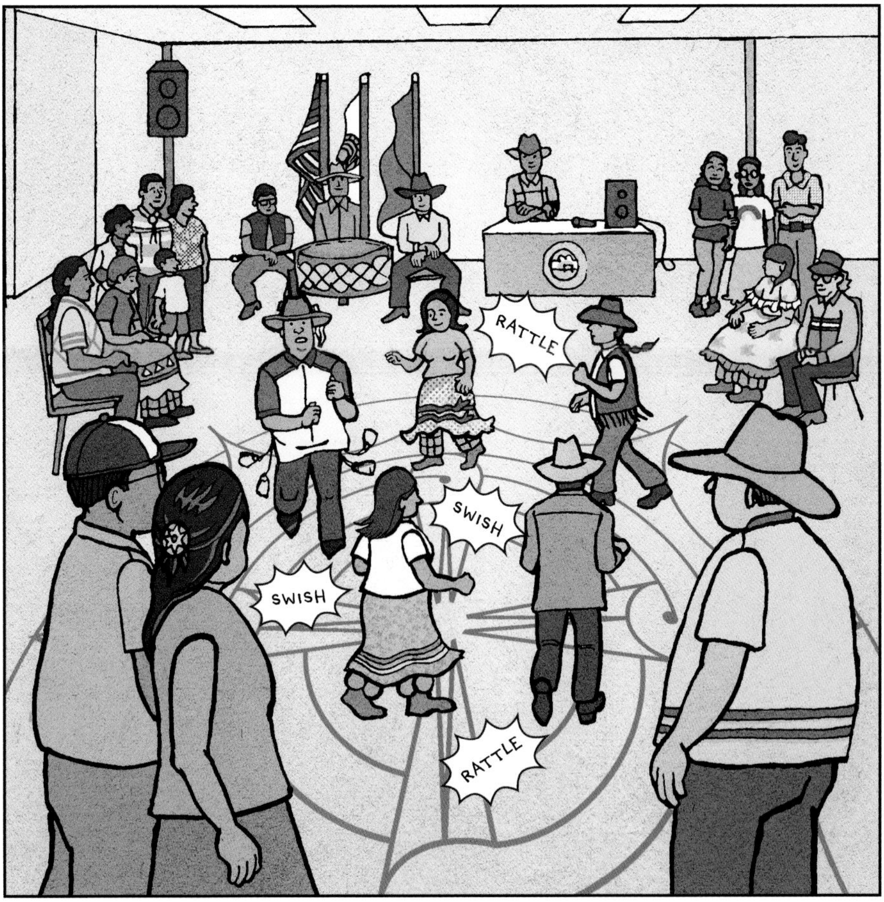
RATTLE
SWISH
SWISH
RATTLE

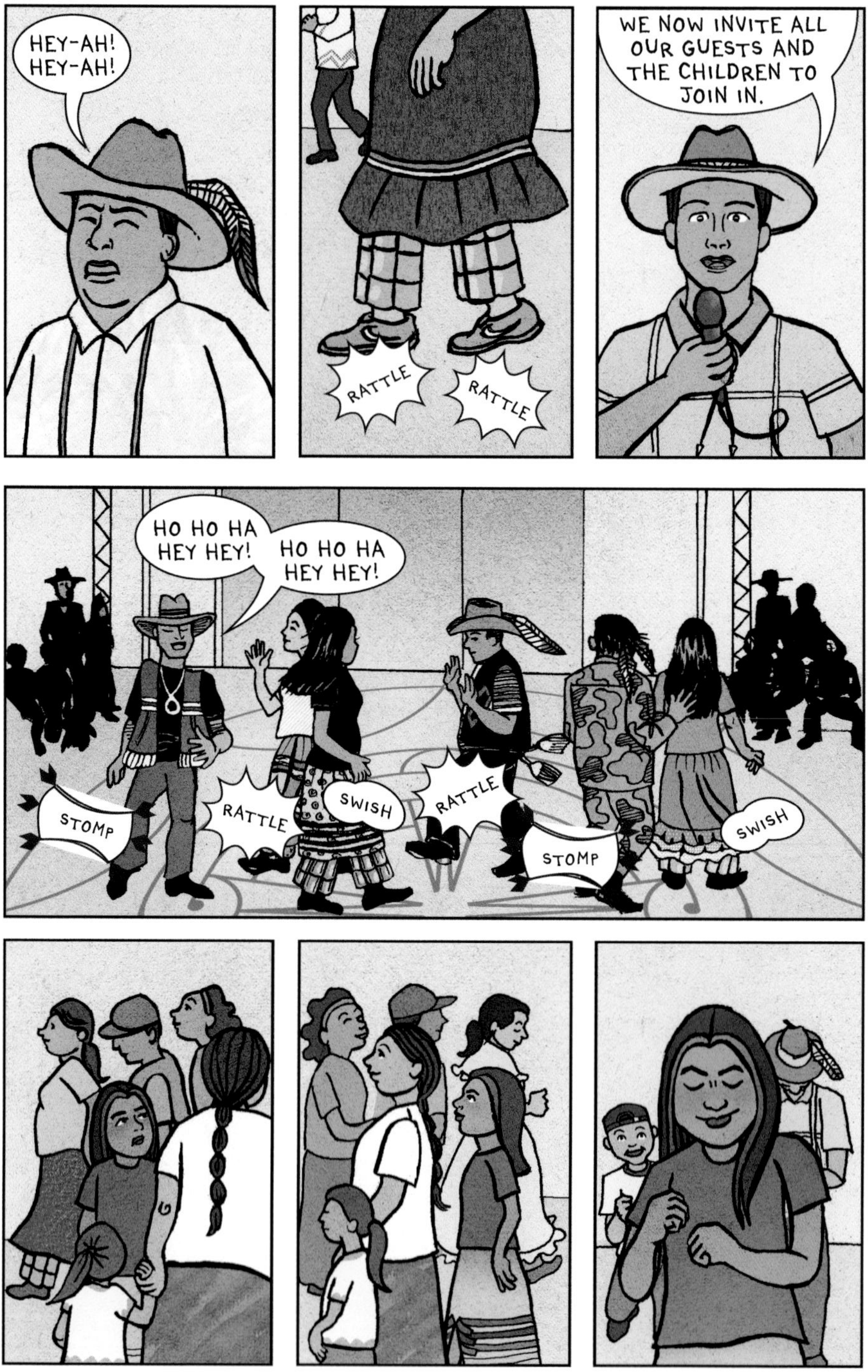
HEY-AH!
HEY-AH!
RATTLE
RATTLE
WE NOW INVITE ALL OUR GUESTS AND THE CHILDREN TO JOIN IN.
HO HO HA HEY HEY!
HO HO HA HEY HEY!
STOMP
RATTLE
SWISH
RATTLE
STOMP
SWISH

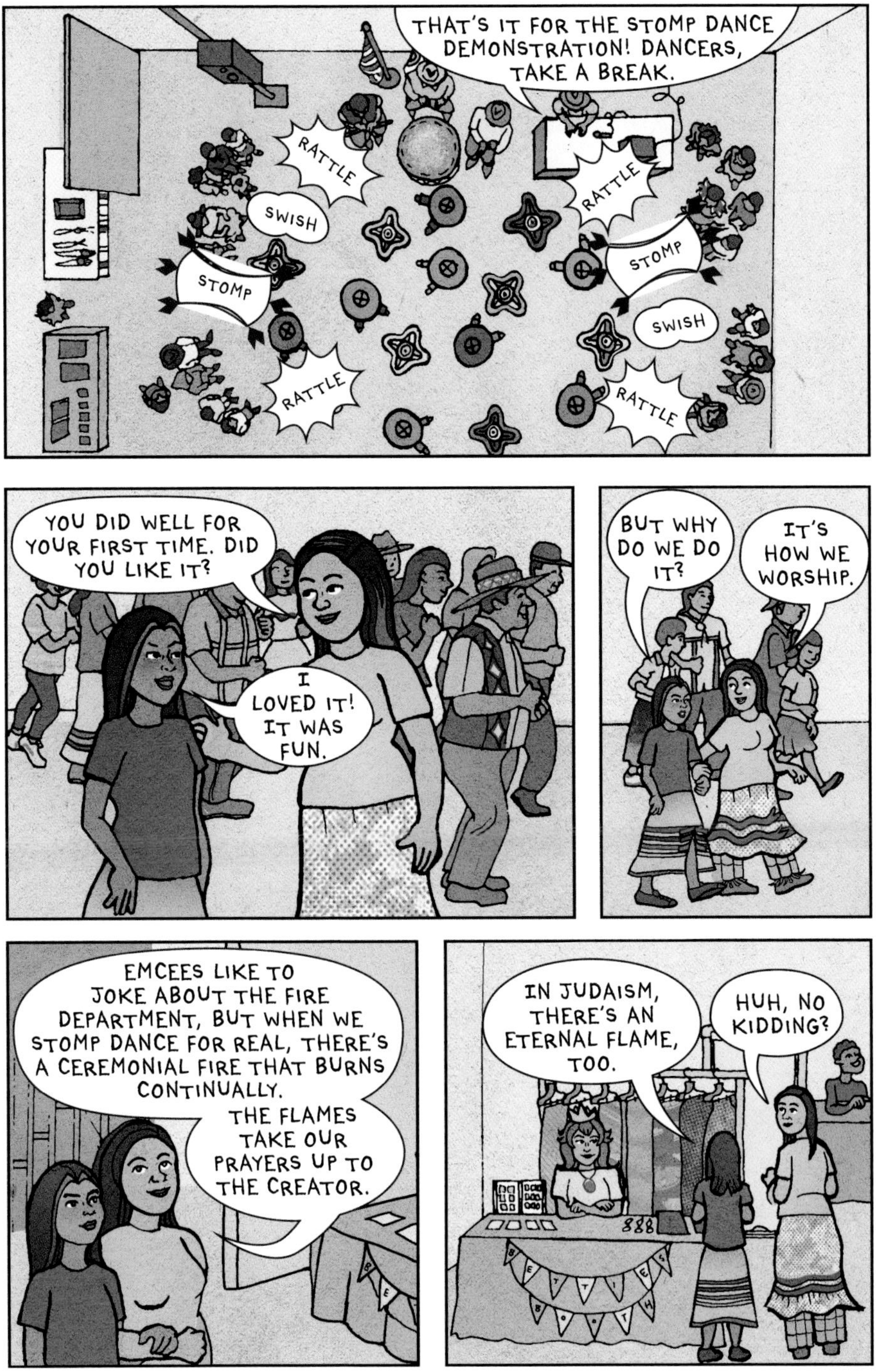
THAT'S IT FOR THE STOMP DANCE DEMONSTRATION! DANCERS, TAKE A BREAK.
RATTLE
SWISH
STOMP
RATTLE
RATTLE
STOMP
SWISH
RATTLE
YOU DID WELL FOR YOUR FIRST TIME. DID YOU LIKE IT?
I LOVED IT! IT WAS FUN.
BUT WHY DO WE DO IT?
IT'S HOW WE WORSHIP.
EMCEES LIKE TO JOKE ABOUT THE FIRE DEPARTMENT, BUT WHEN WE STOMP DANCE FOR REAL, THERE'S A CEREMONIAL FIRE THAT BURNS CONTINUALLY.
THE FLAMES TAKE OUR PRAYERS UP TO THE CREATOR.
IN JUDAISM, THERE'S AN ETERNAL FLAME, TOO.
HUH, NO KIDDING?
BETTIES BOOTH

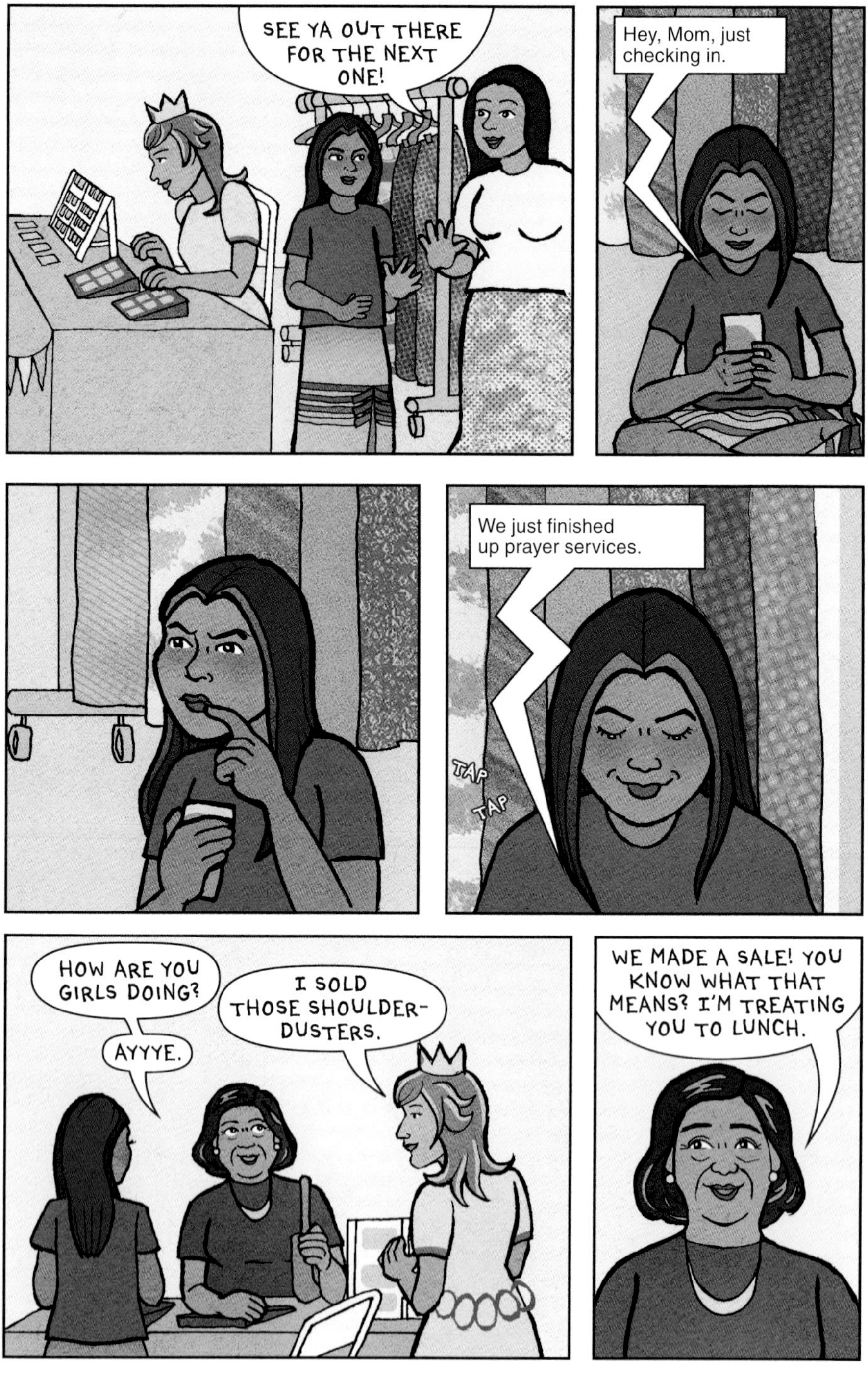
SEE YA OUT THERE FOR THE NEXT ONE!
Hey, Mom, just checking in.
We just finished up prayer services.
TAP
TAP
HOW ARE YOU GIRLS DOING?
AYYYE.
I SOLD THOSE SHOULDER-DUSTERS.
WE MADE A SALE! YOU KNOW WHAT THAT MEANS? I'M TREATING YOU TO LUNCH.

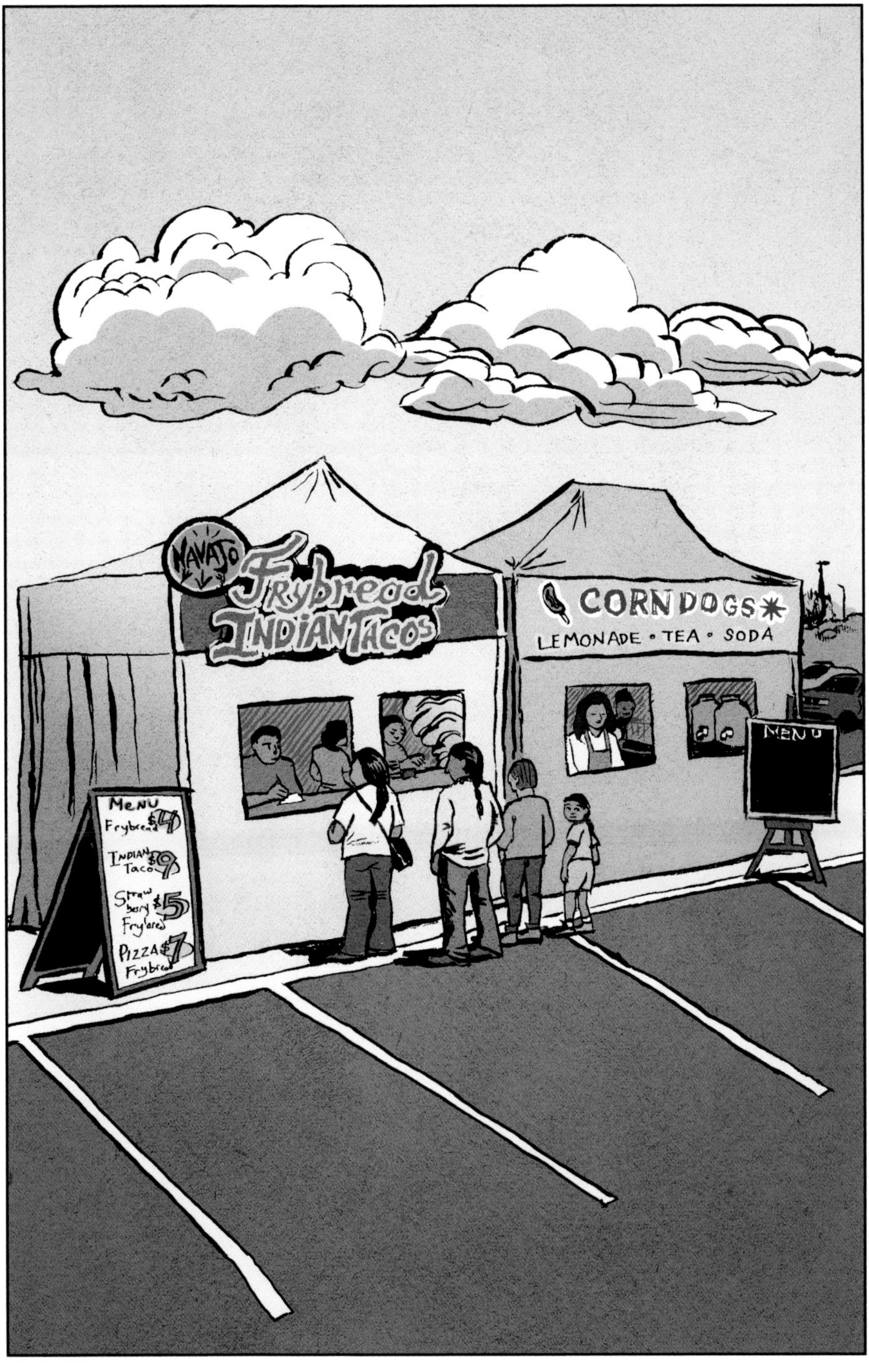
NAVAJO
Frybread
INDIAN TACOS
CORN DOGS
LEMONADE • TEA • SODA
MENU
MeNU
Frybread $4
INDIAN Taco $9
Straw berry $5
PIZZA $7

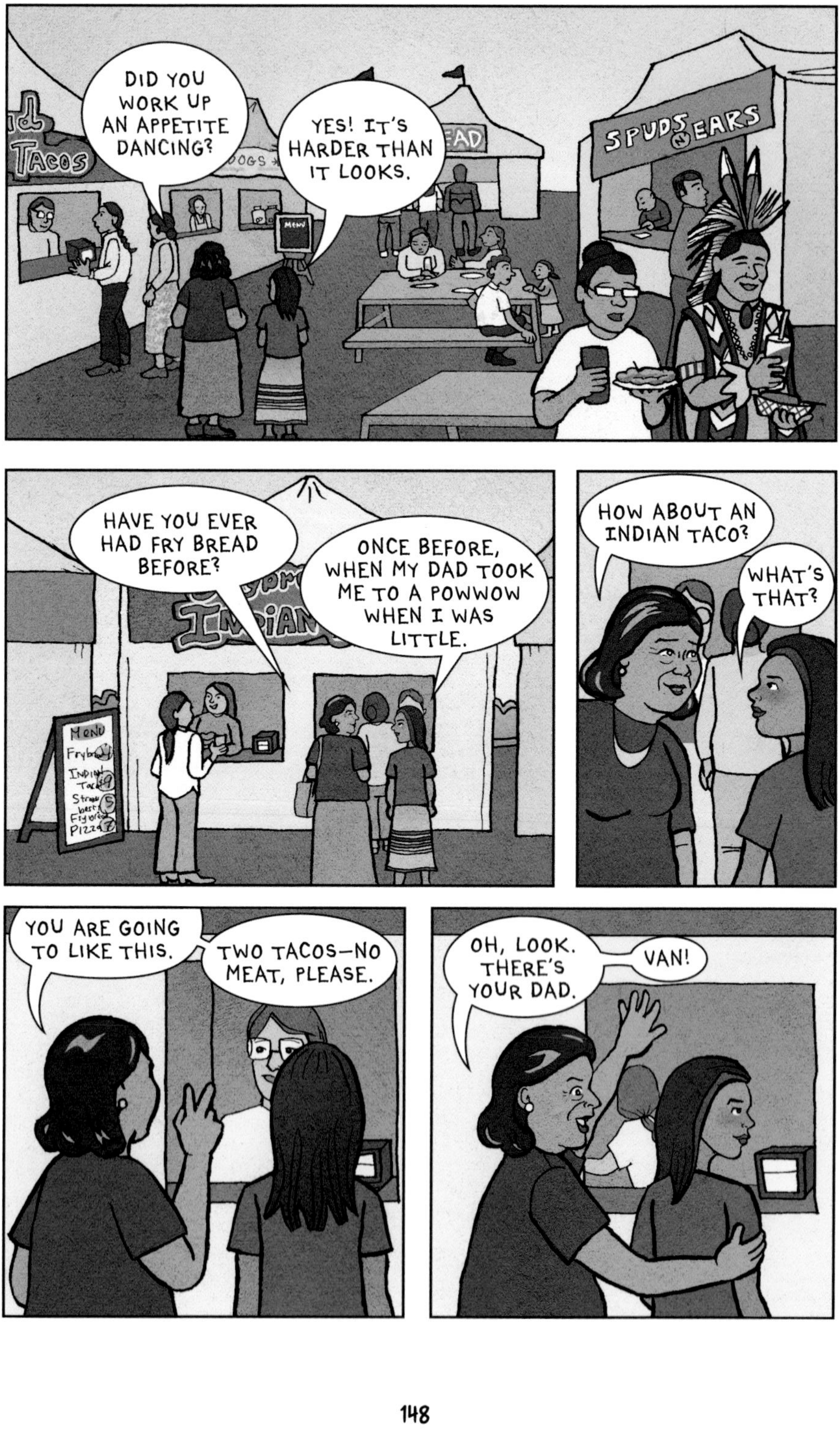
DID YOU WORK UP AN APPETITE DANCING?
YES! IT'S HARDER THAN IT LOOKS.
HAVE YOU EVER HAD FRY BREAD BEFORE?
ONCE BEFORE, WHEN MY DAD TOOK ME TO A POWWOW WHEN I WAS LITTLE.
HOW ABOUT AN INDIAN TACO?
WHAT'S THAT?
YOU ARE GOING TO LIKE THIS.
TWO TACOS—NO MEAT, PLEASE.
OH, LOOK. THERE'S YOUR DAD.
VAN!

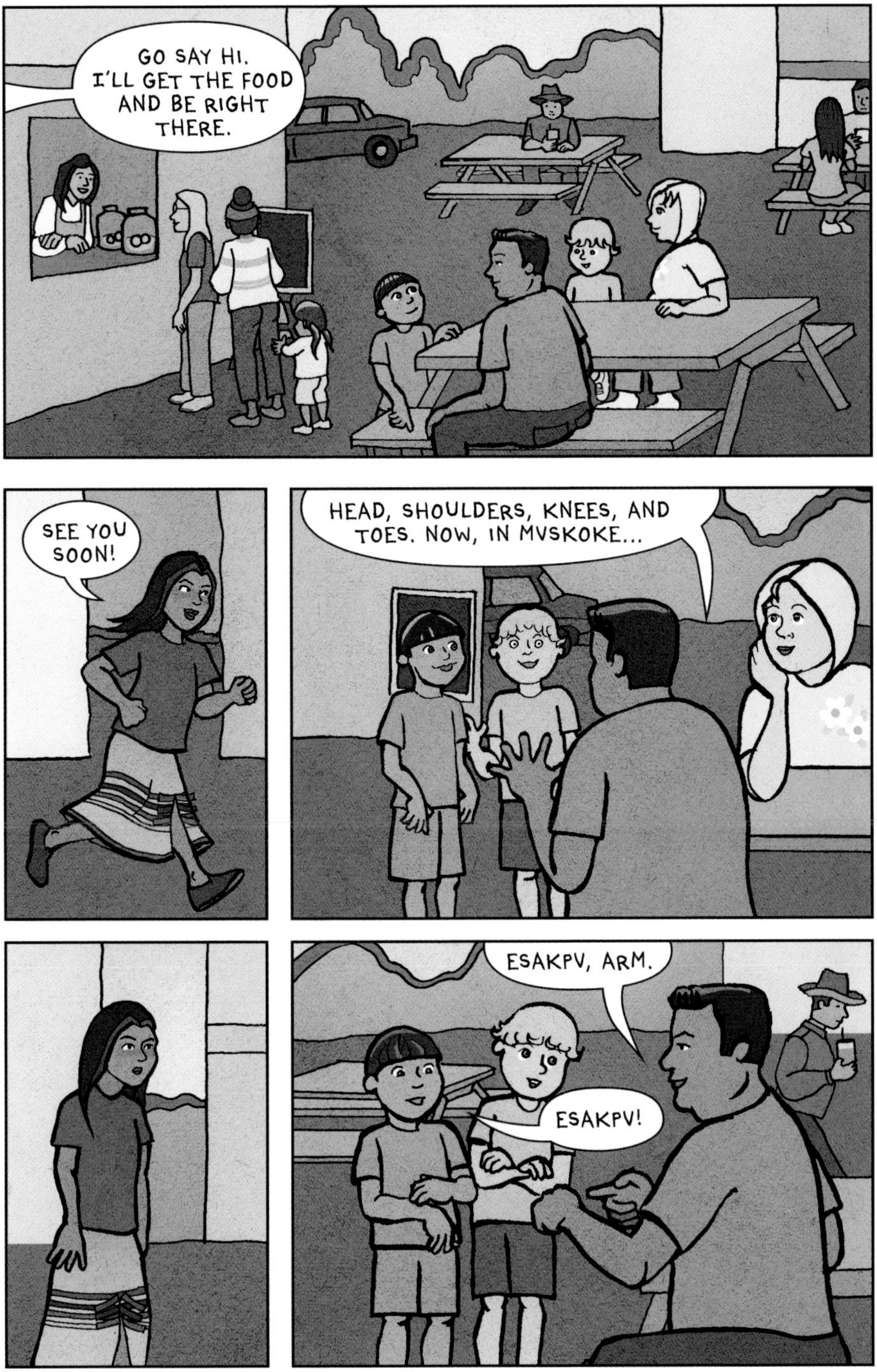
GO SAY HI. I'LL GET THE FOOD AND BE RIGHT THERE.
SEE YOU SOON!
HEAD, SHOULDERS, KNEES, AND TOES. NOW, IN MVSKOKE...
ESAKPV, ARM.
ESAKPV!

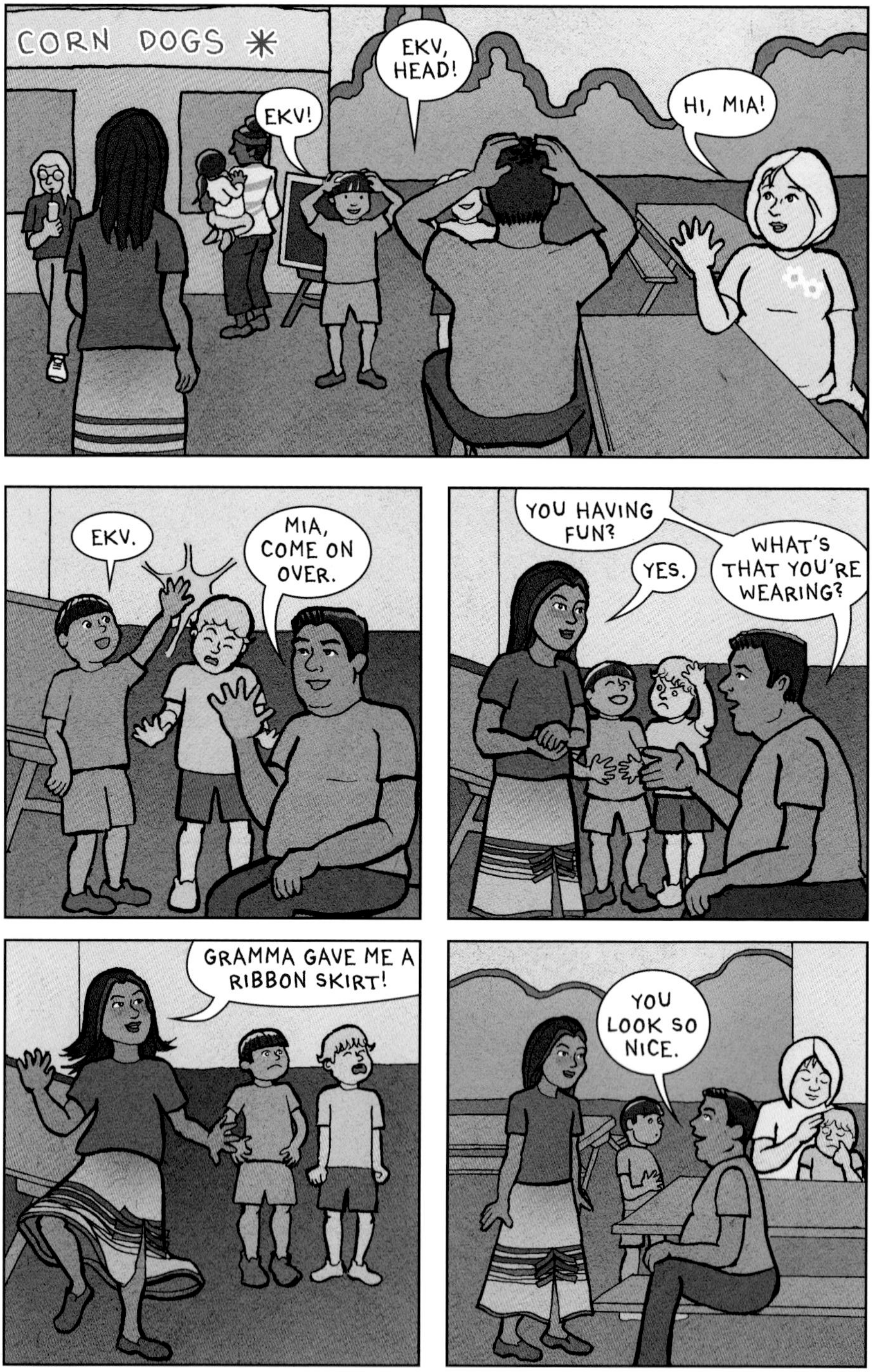
CORN DOGS
EKV!
EKV, HEAD!
HI, MIA!
EKV.
MIA, COME ON OVER.
YOU HAVING FUN?
YES.
WHAT'S THAT YOU'RE WEARING?
GRAMMA GAVE ME A RIBBON SKIRT!
YOU LOOK SO NICE.

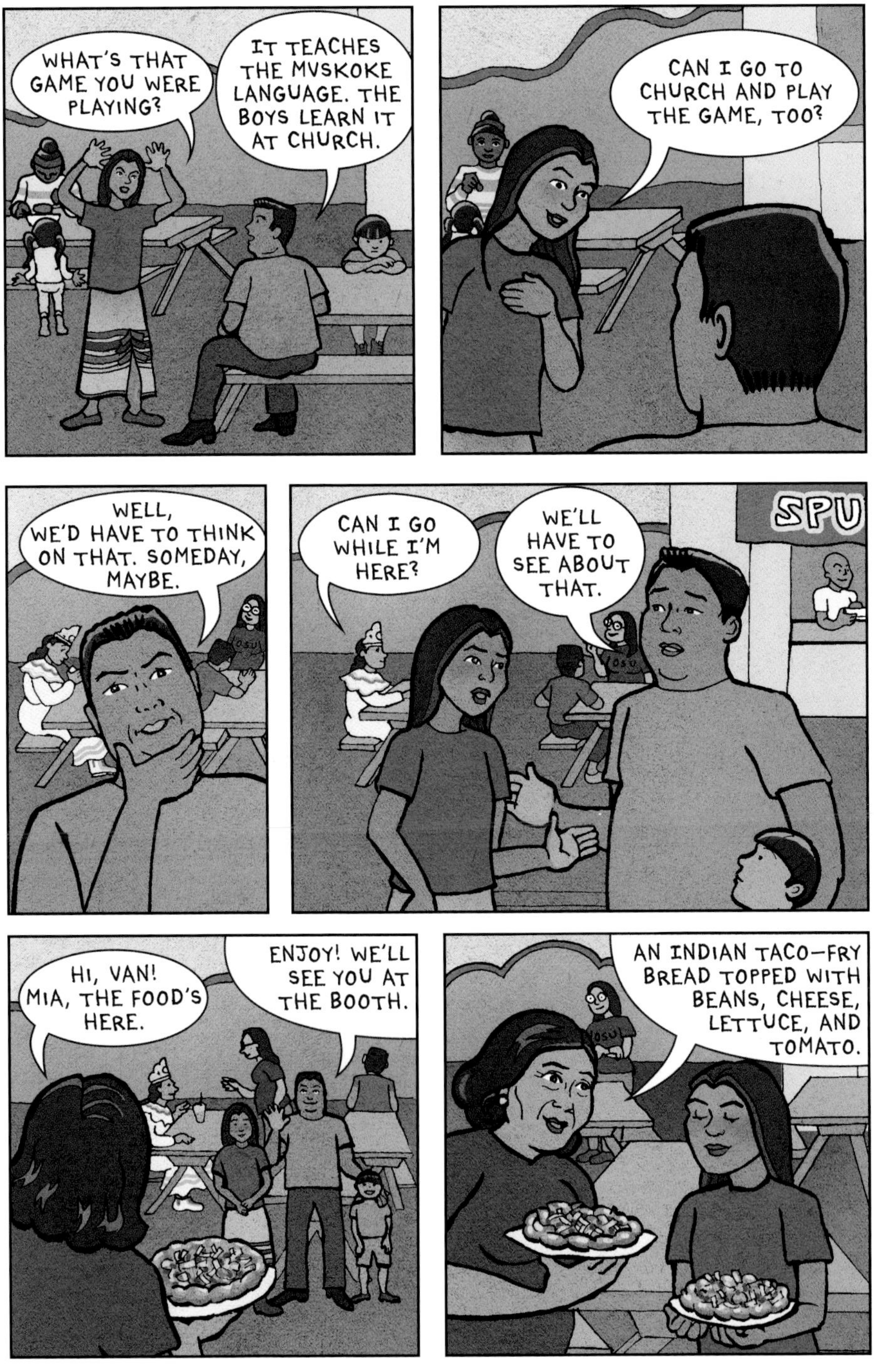
WHAT'S THAT GAME YOU WERE PLAYING?
IT TEACHES THE MVSKOKE LANGUAGE. THE BOYS LEARN IT AT CHURCH.
CAN I GO TO CHURCH AND PLAY THE GAME, TOO?
WELL, WE'D HAVE TO THINK ON THAT. SOMEDAY, MAYBE.
CAN I GO WHILE I'M HERE?
WE'LL HAVE TO SEE ABOUT THAT.
SPU
HI, VAN! MIA, THE FOOD'S HERE.
ENJOY! WE'LL SEE YOU AT THE BOOTH.
AN INDIAN TACO—FRY BREAD TOPPED WITH BEANS, CHEESE, LETTUCE, AND TOMATO.

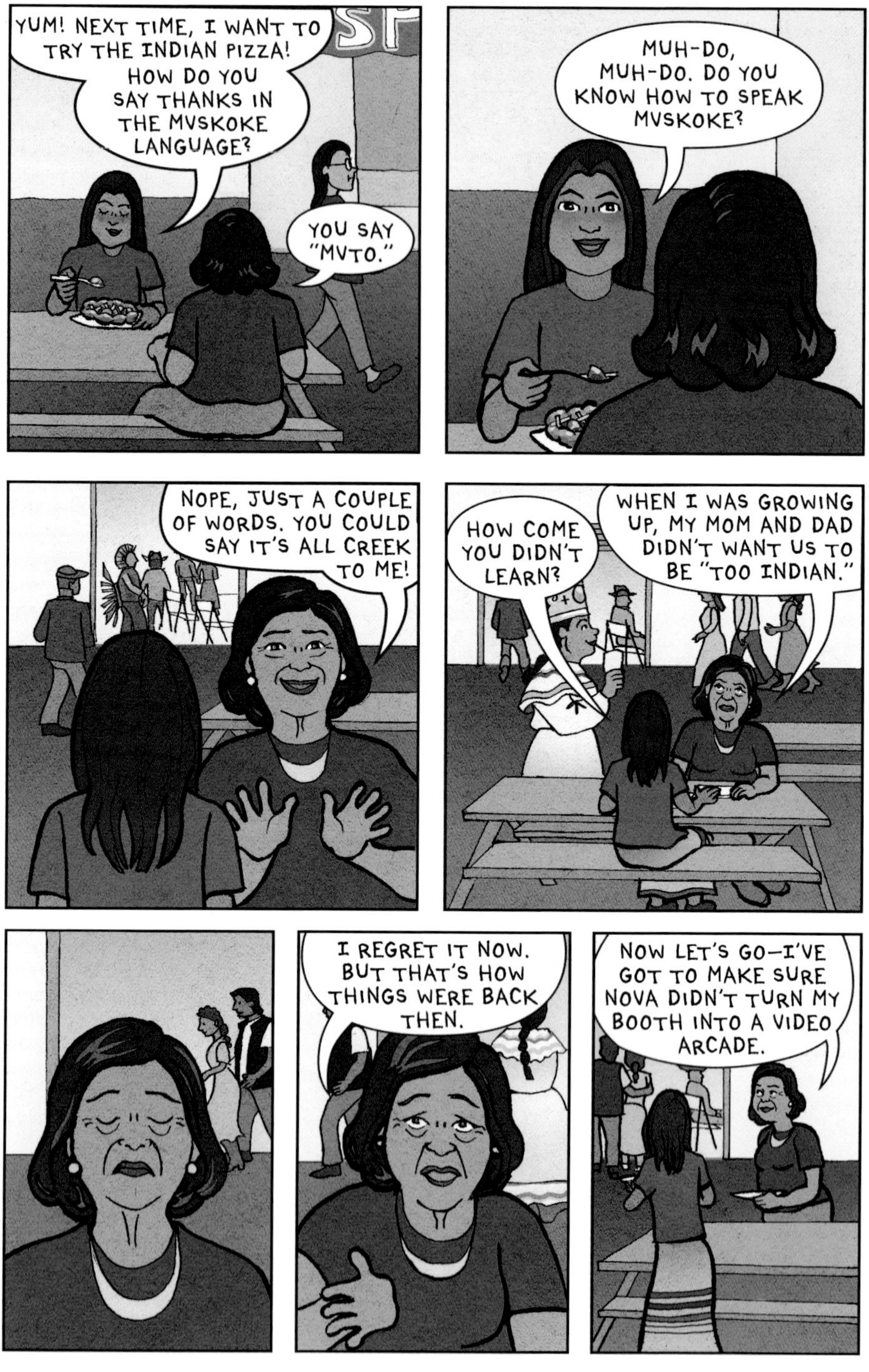
YUM! NEXT TIME, I WANT TO TRY THE INDIAN PIZZA!
HOW DO YOU SAY THANKS IN THE MVSKOKE LANGUAGE?
YOU SAY "MVTO."
MUH-DO, MUH-DO. DO YOU KNOW HOW TO SPEAK MVSKOKE?
NOPE, JUST A COUPLE OF WORDS. YOU COULD SAY IT'S ALL CREEK TO ME!
HOW COME YOU DIDN'T LEARN?
WHEN I WAS GROWING UP, MY MOM AND DAD DIDN'T WANT US TO BE "TOO INDIAN."
I REGRET IT NOW. BUT THAT'S HOW THINGS WERE BACK THEN.
NOW LET'S GO—I'VE GOT TO MAKE SURE NOVA DIDN'T TURN MY BOOTH INTO A VIDEO ARCADE.

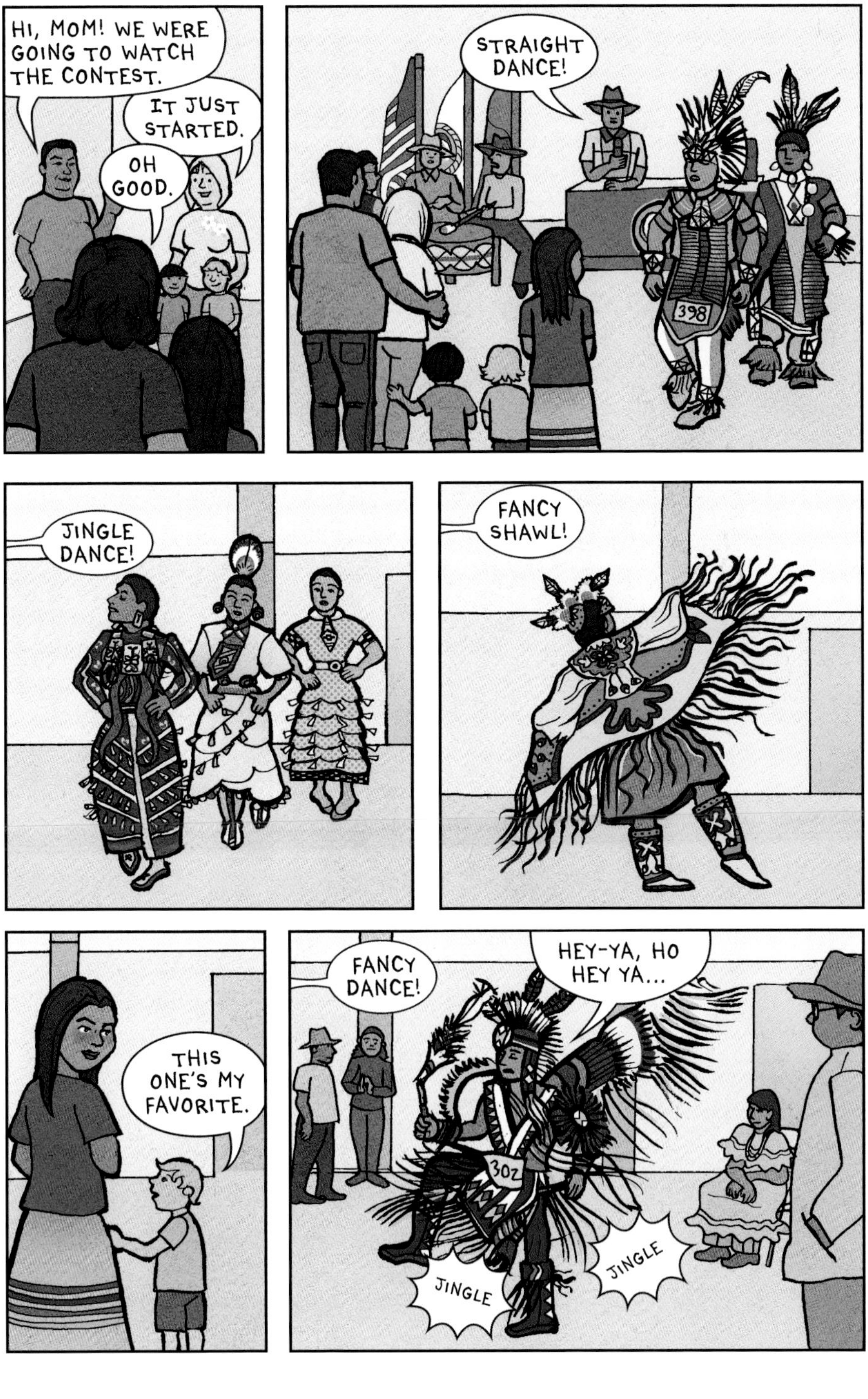
HI, MOM! WE WERE GOING TO WATCH THE CONTEST.
IT JUST STARTED.
OH GOOD.
STRAIGHT DANCE!
398
JINGLE DANCE!
FANCY SHAWL!
THIS ONE'S MY FAVORITE.
FANCY DANCE!
HEY-YA, HO HEY YA...
302
JINGLE
JINGLE

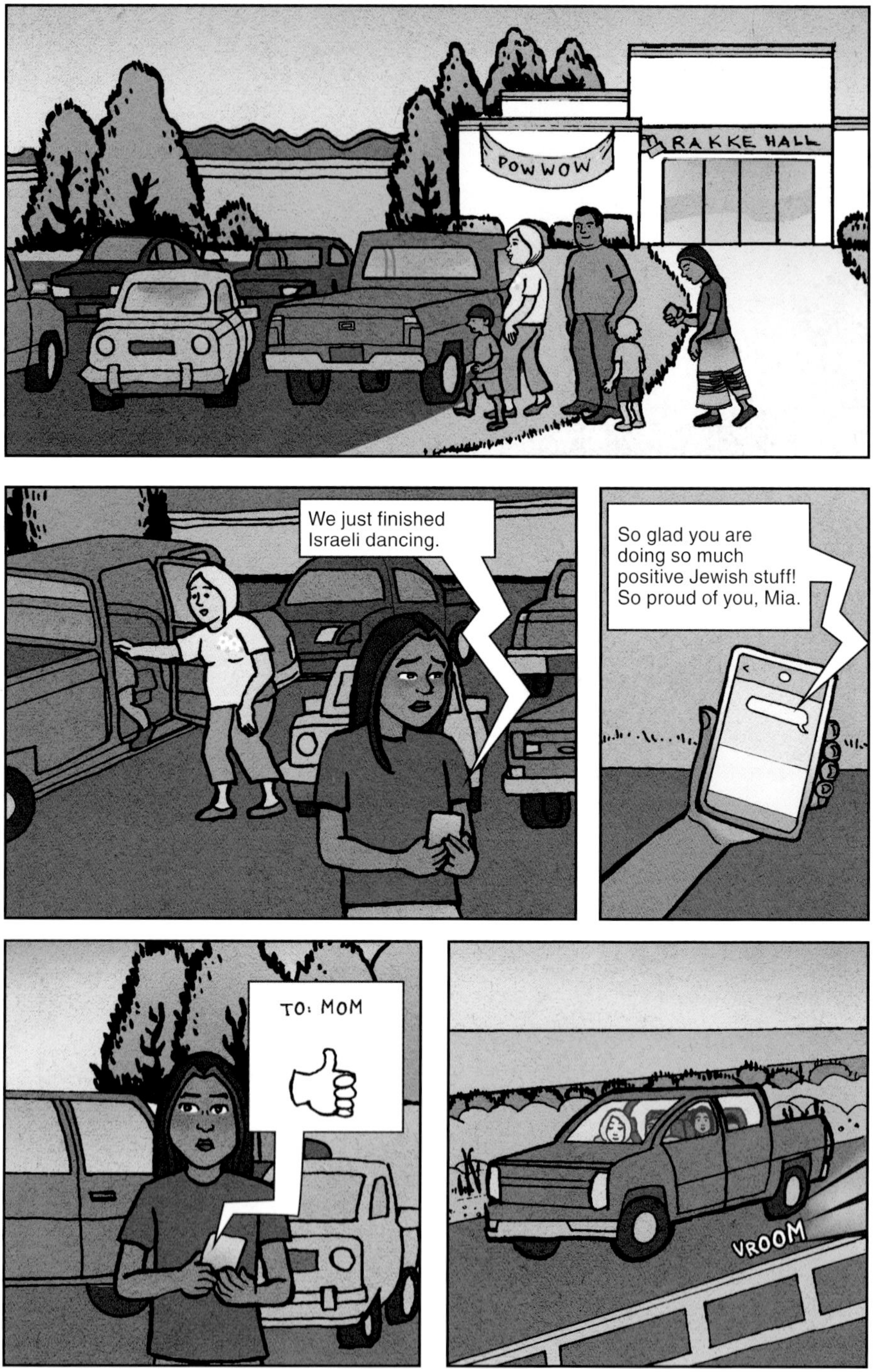
POW WOW
RAKKE HALL
We just finished Israeli dancing.
So glad you are doing so much positive Jewish stuff! So proud of you, Mia.
TO: MOM
VROOM

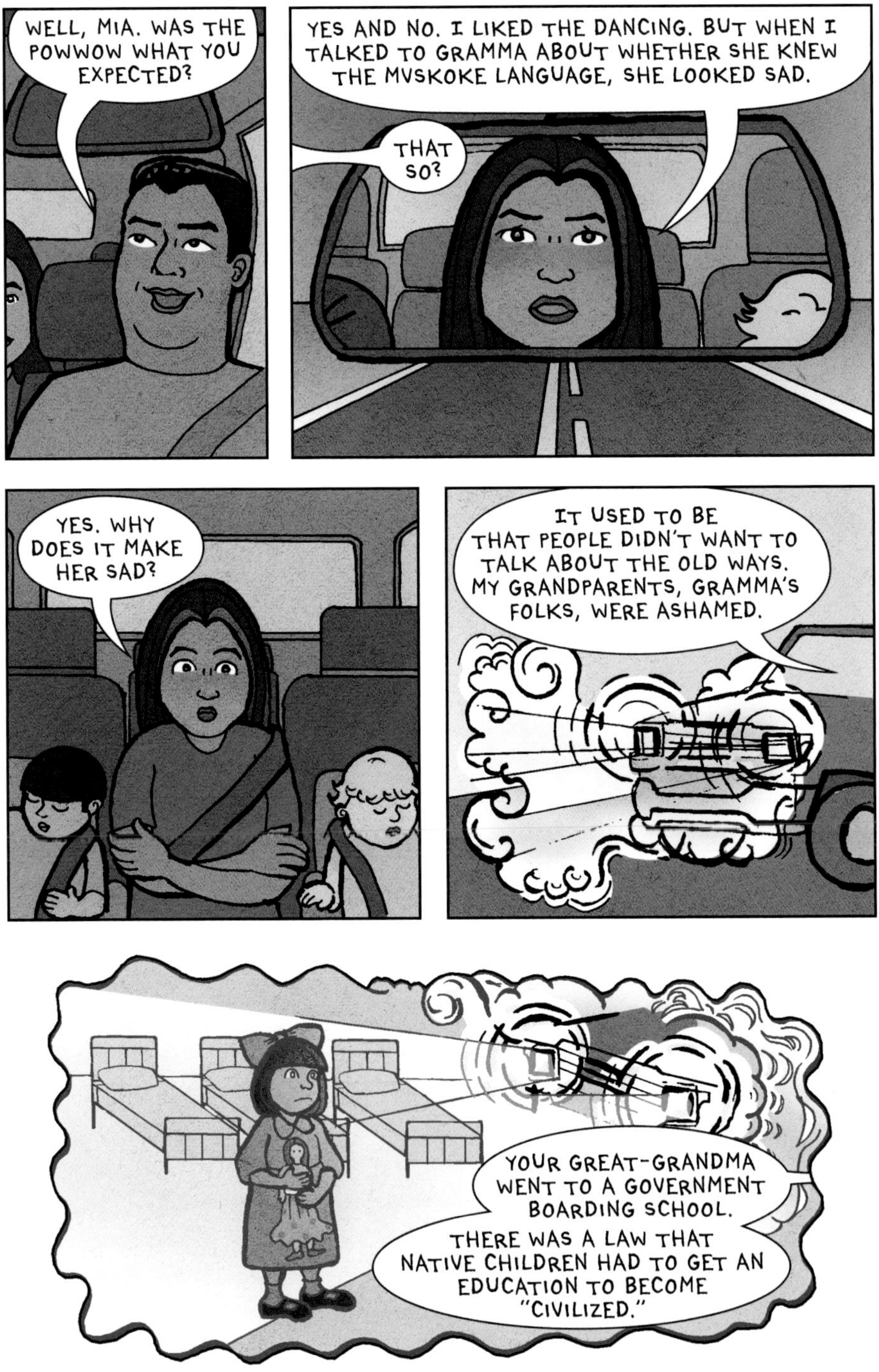
WELL, MIA. WAS THE POWWOW WHAT YOU EXPECTED?
YES AND NO. I LIKED THE DANCING. BUT WHEN I TALKED TO GRAMMA ABOUT WHETHER SHE KNEW THE MVSKOKE LANGUAGE, SHE LOOKED SAD.
THAT SO?
YES. WHY DOES IT MAKE HER SAD?
IT USED TO BE THAT PEOPLE DIDN'T WANT TO TALK ABOUT THE OLD WAYS. MY GRANDPARENTS, GRAMMA'S FOLKS, WERE ASHAMED.
YOUR GREAT-GRANDMA WENT TO A GOVERNMENT BOARDING SCHOOL.
THERE WAS A LAW THAT NATIVE CHILDREN HAD TO GET AN EDUCATION TO BECOME "CIVILIZED."

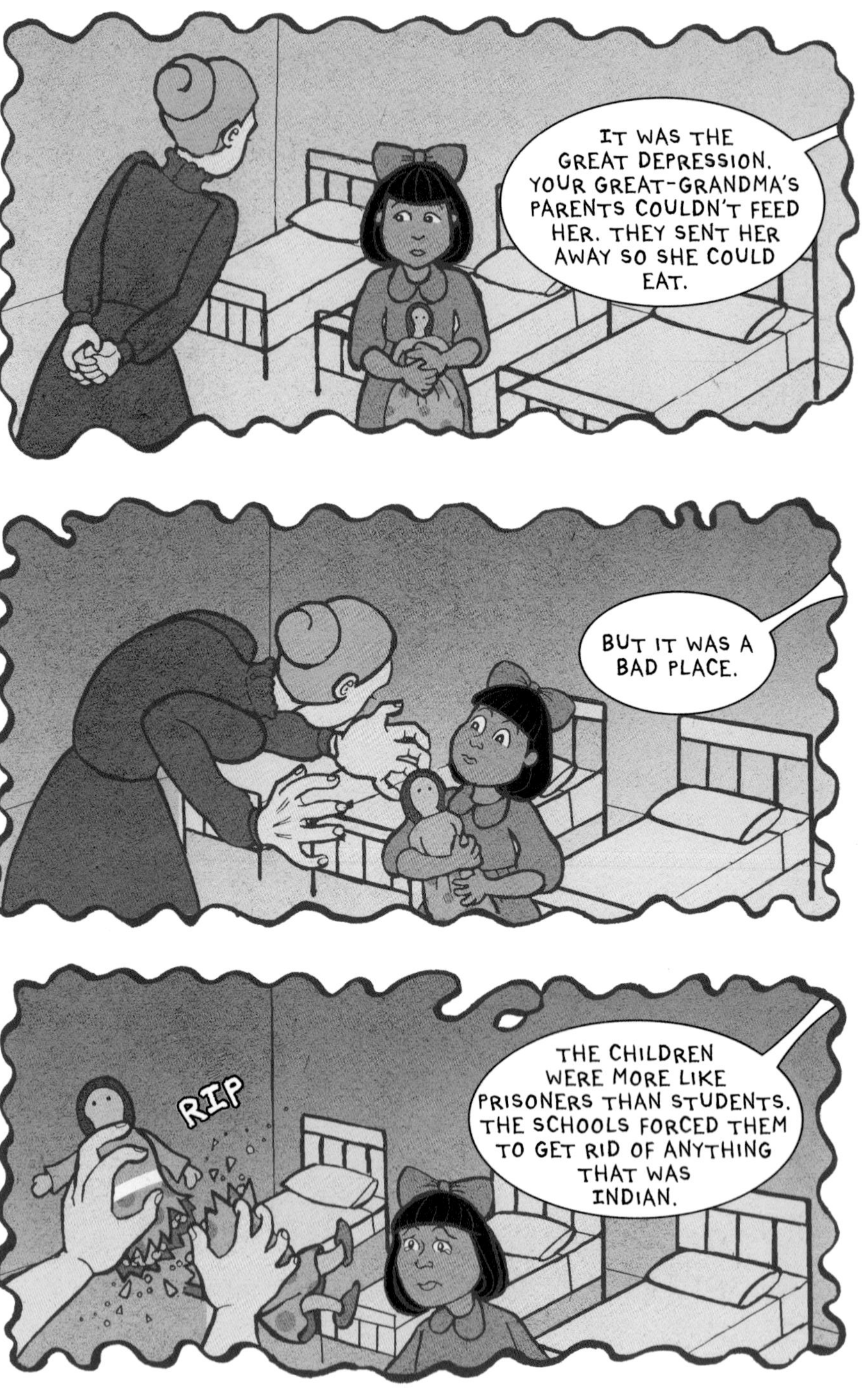
IT WAS THE GREAT DEPRESSION. YOUR GREAT-GRANDMA'S PARENTS COULDN'T FEED HER. THEY SENT HER AWAY SO SHE COULD EAT.
BUT IT WAS A BAD PLACE.
RIP
THE CHILDREN WERE MORE LIKE PRISONERS THAN STUDENTS. THE SCHOOLS FORCED THEM TO GET RID OF ANYTHING THAT WAS INDIAN.

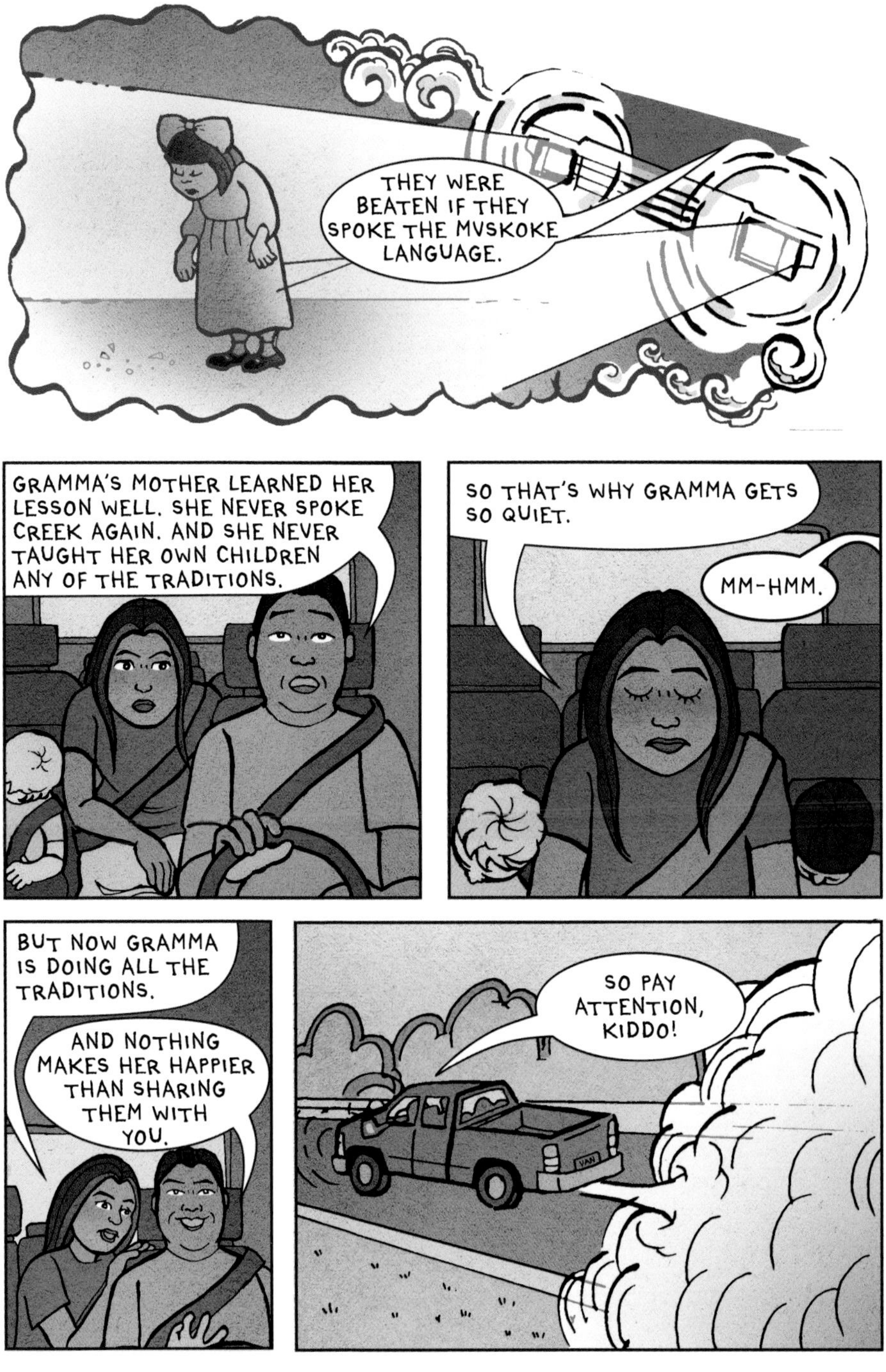
THEY WERE BEATEN IF THEY SPOKE THE MVSKOKE LANGUAGE.
GRAMMA'S MOTHER LEARNED HER LESSON WELL. SHE NEVER SPOKE CREEK AGAIN. AND SHE NEVER TAUGHT HER OWN CHILDREN ANY OF THE TRADITIONS.
SO THAT'S WHY GRAMMA GETS SO QUIET.
MM-HMM.
BUT NOW GRAMMA IS DOING ALL THE TRADITIONS.
AND NOTHING MAKES HER HAPPIER THAN SHARING THEM WITH YOU.
SO PAY ATTENTION, KIDDO!
VAN

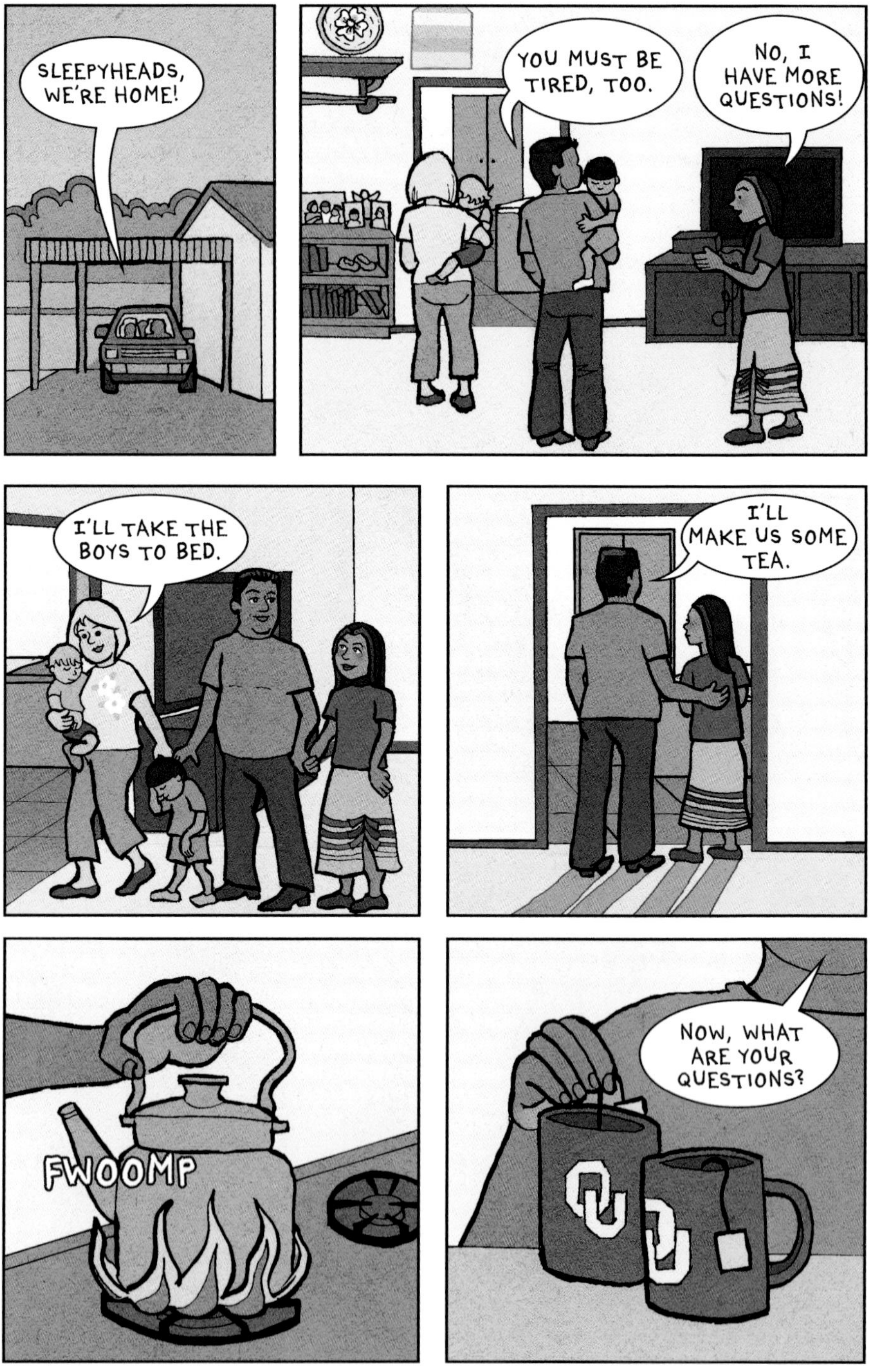
SLEEPYHEADS, WE'RE HOME!
YOU MUST BE TIRED, TOO.
NO, I HAVE MORE QUESTIONS!
I'LL TAKE THE BOYS TO BED.
I'LL MAKE US SOME TEA.
FWOOMP
NOW, WHAT ARE YOUR QUESTIONS?

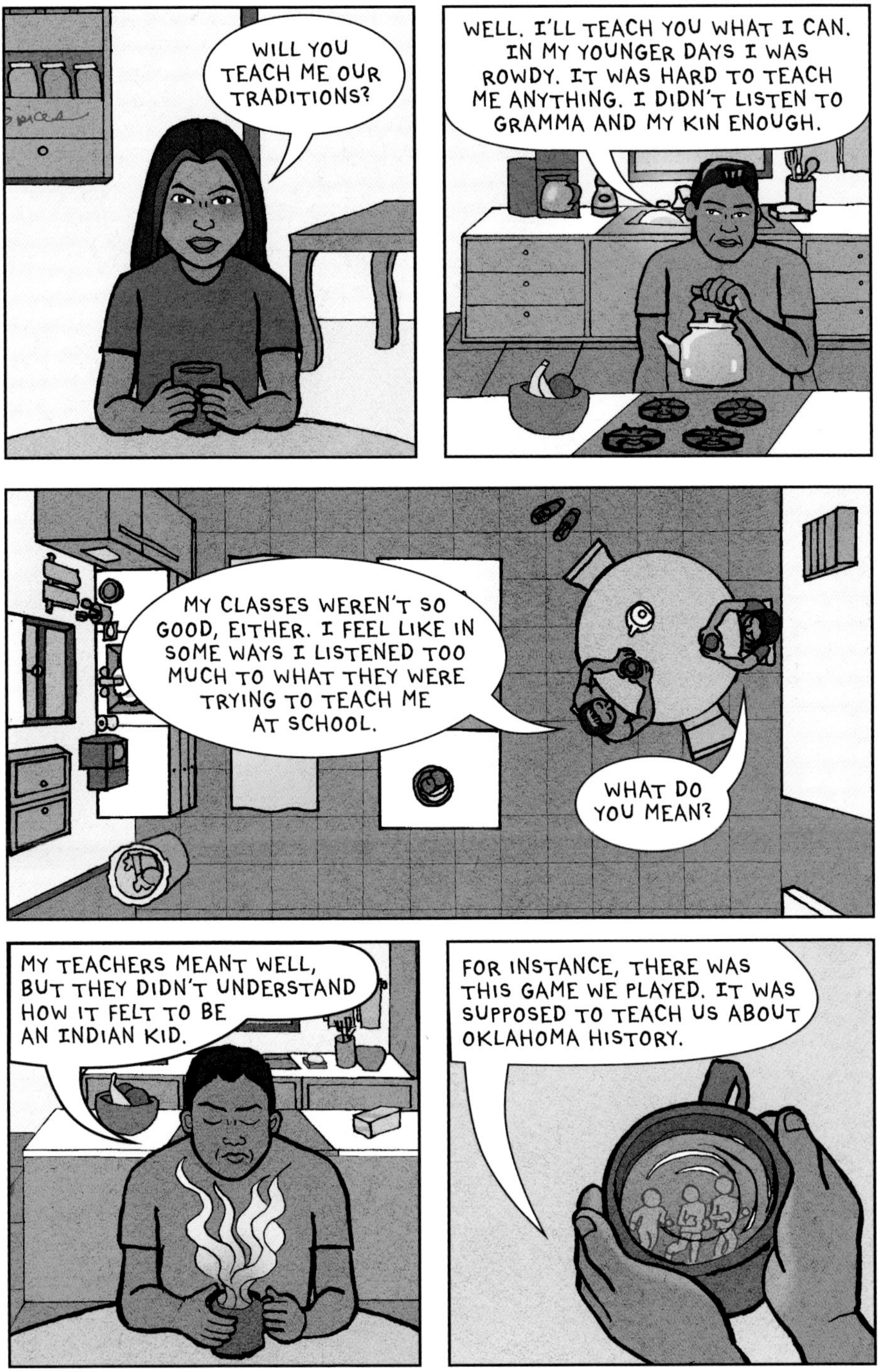
WILL YOU TEACH ME OUR TRADITIONS?
WELL. I'LL TEACH YOU WHAT I CAN. IN MY YOUNGER DAYS I WAS ROWDY. IT WAS HARD TO TEACH ME ANYTHING. I DIDN'T LISTEN TO GRAMMA AND MY KIN ENOUGH.
MY CLASSES WEREN'T SO GOOD, EITHER. I FEEL LIKE IN SOME WAYS I LISTENED TOO MUCH TO WHAT THEY WERE TRYING TO TEACH ME AT SCHOOL.
WHAT DO YOU MEAN?
MY TEACHERS MEANT WELL, BUT THEY DIDN'T UNDERSTAND HOW IT FELT TO BE AN INDIAN KID.
FOR INSTANCE, THERE WAS THIS GAME WE PLAYED. IT WAS SUPPOSED TO TEACH US ABOUT OKLAHOMA HISTORY.

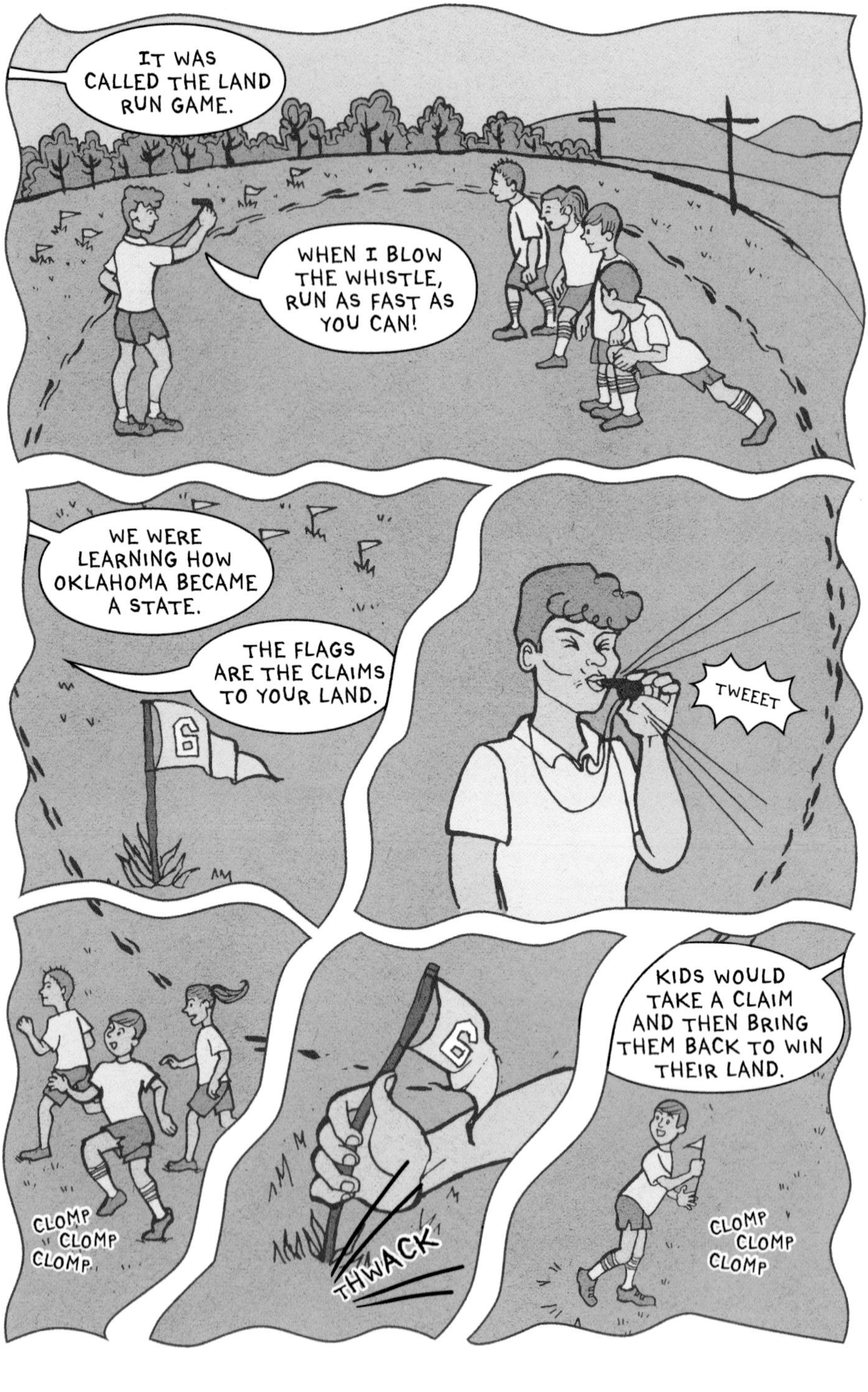
IT WAS CALLED THE LAND RUN GAME.
WHEN I BLOW THE WHISTLE, RUN AS FAST AS YOU CAN!
WE WERE LEARNING HOW OKLAHOMA BECAME A STATE.
THE FLAGS ARE THE CLAIMS TO YOUR LAND.
TWEEET
CLOMP CLOMP CLOMP
THWACK
KIDS WOULD TAKE A CLAIM AND THEN BRING THEM BACK TO WIN THEIR LAND.
CLOMP CLOMP CLOMP

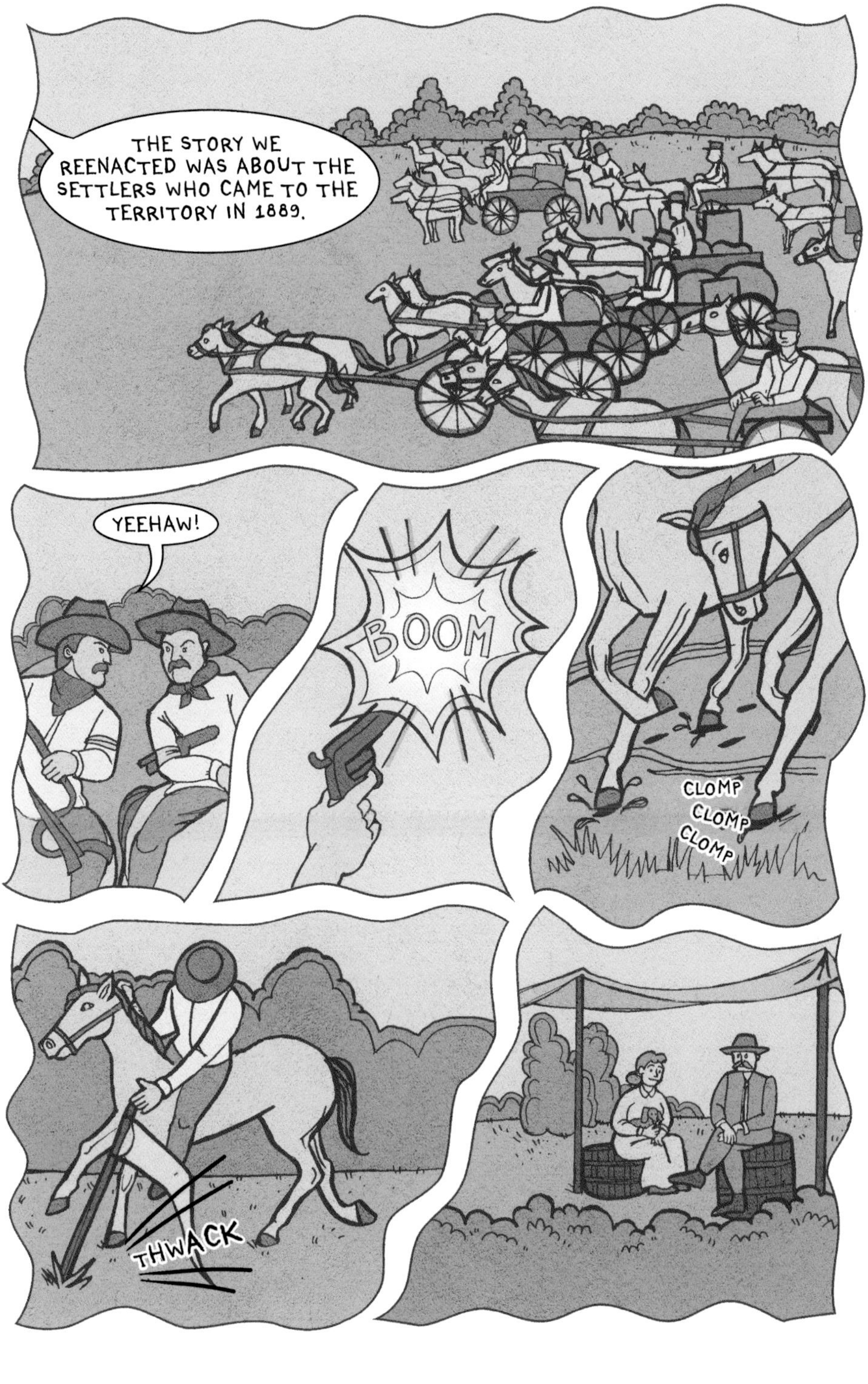
THE STORY WE REENACTED WAS ABOUT THE SETTLERS WHO CAME TO THE TERRITORY IN 1889.
YEEHAW!
BOOM
CLOMP
CLOMP
CLOMP
THWACK

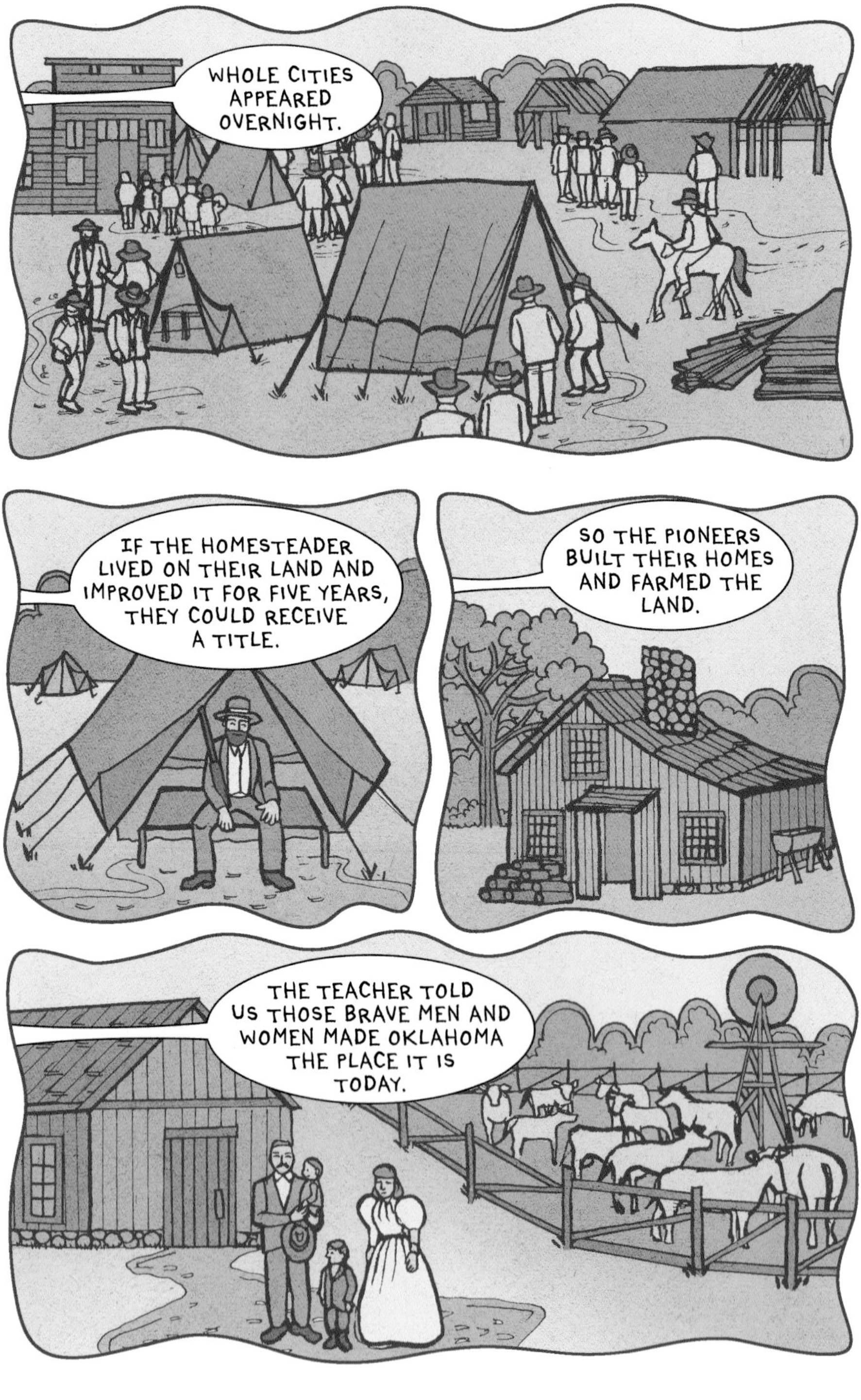
WHOLE CITIES APPEARED OVERNIGHT.
IF THE HOMESTEADER LIVED ON THEIR LAND AND IMPROVED IT FOR FIVE YEARS, THEY COULD RECEIVE A TITLE.
SO THE PIONEERS BUILT THEIR HOMES AND FARMED THE LAND.
THE TEACHER TOLD US THOSE BRAVE MEN AND WOMEN MADE OKLAHOMA THE PLACE IT IS TODAY.

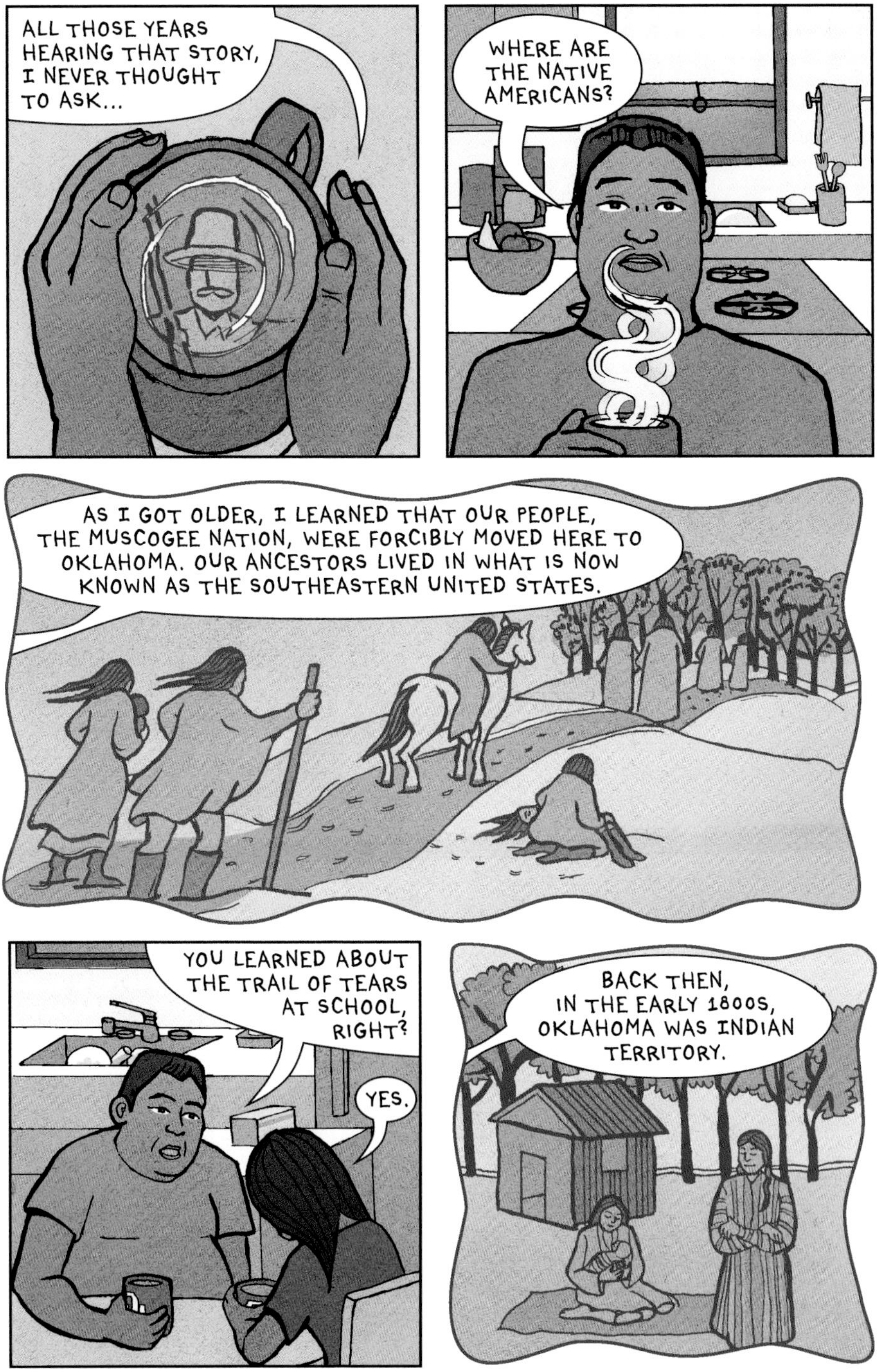
ALL THOSE YEARS HEARING THAT STORY, I NEVER THOUGHT TO ASK...
WHERE ARE THE NATIVE AMERICANS?
AS I GOT OLDER, I LEARNED THAT OUR PEOPLE, THE MUSCOGEE NATION, WERE FORCIBLY MOVED HERE TO OKLAHOMA. OUR ANCESTORS LIVED IN WHAT IS NOW KNOWN AS THE SOUTHEASTERN UNITED STATES.
YOU LEARNED ABOUT THE TRAIL OF TEARS AT SCHOOL, RIGHT?
YES.
BACK THEN, IN THE EARLY 1800S, OKLAHOMA WAS INDIAN TERRITORY.

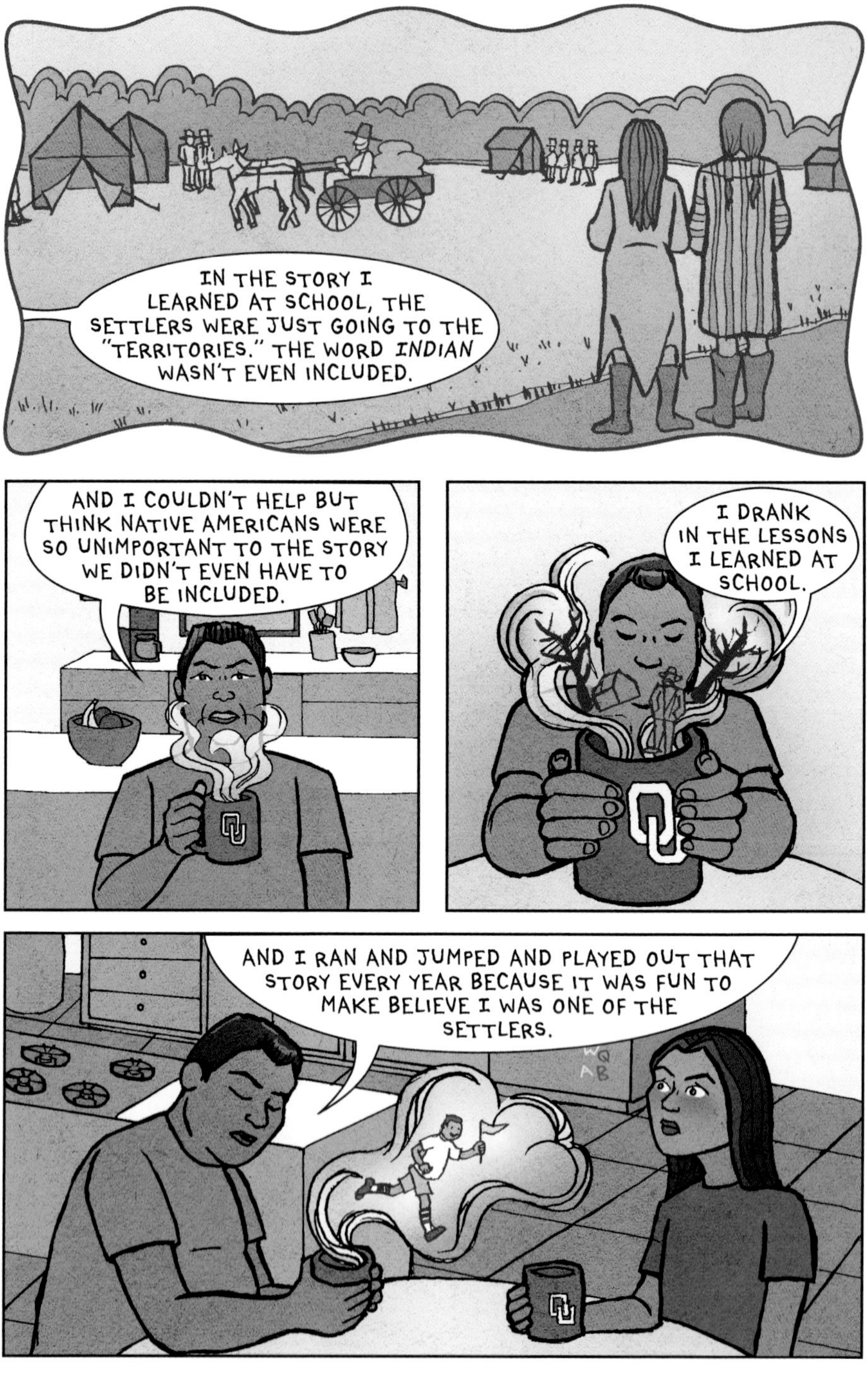
IN THE STORY I LEARNED AT SCHOOL, THE SETTLERS WERE JUST GOING TO THE "TERRITORIES." THE WORD *INDIAN* WASN'T EVEN INCLUDED.
AND I COULDN'T HELP BUT THINK NATIVE AMERICANS WERE SO UNIMPORTANT TO THE STORY WE DIDN'T EVEN HAVE TO BE INCLUDED.
I DRANK IN THE LESSONS I LEARNED AT SCHOOL.
AND I RAN AND JUMPED AND PLAYED OUT THAT STORY EVERY YEAR BECAUSE IT WAS FUN TO MAKE BELIEVE I WAS ONE OF THE SETTLERS.

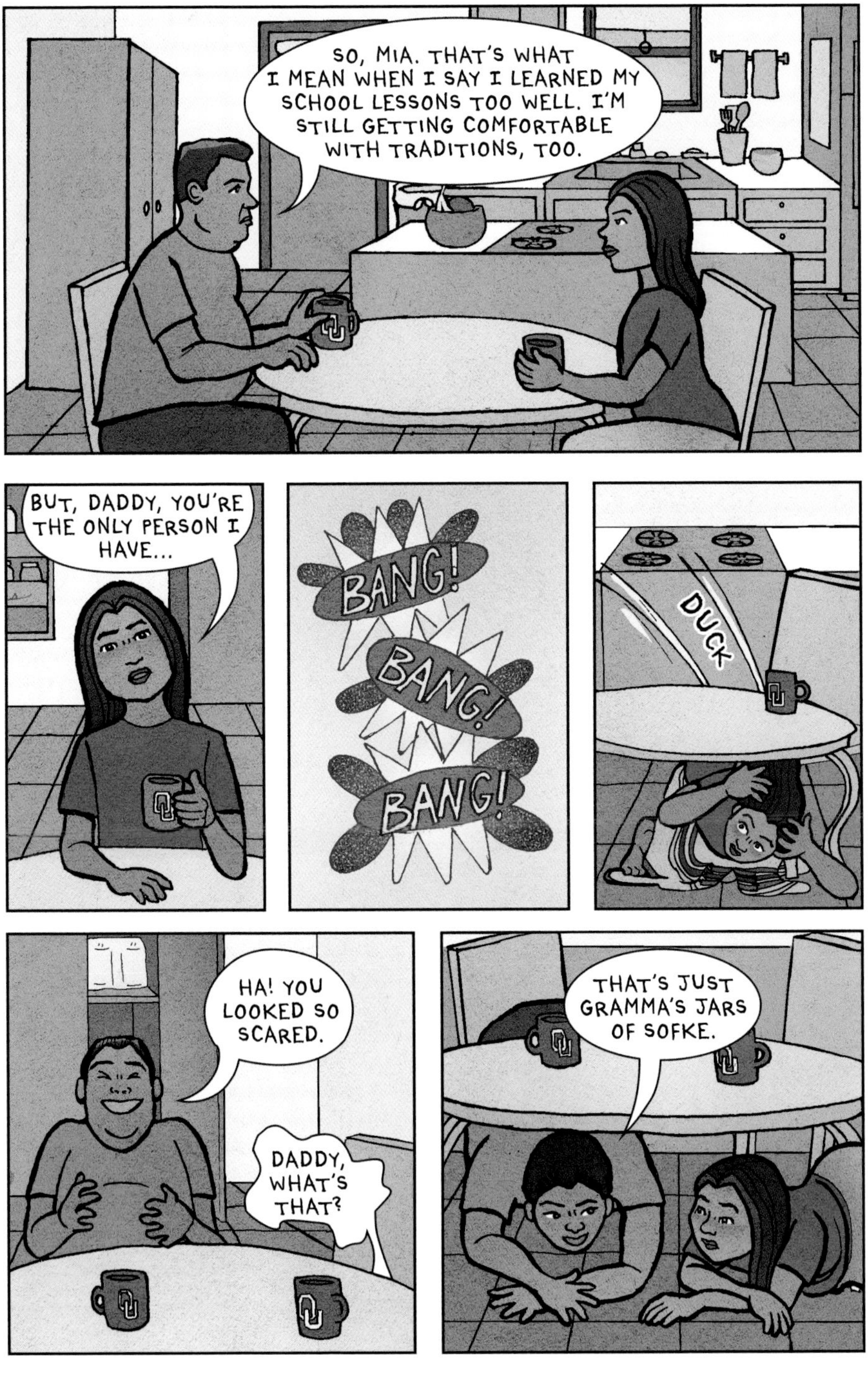
SO, MIA. THAT'S WHAT I MEAN WHEN I SAY I LEARNED MY SCHOOL LESSONS TOO WELL. I'M STILL GETTING COMFORTABLE WITH TRADITIONS, TOO.
BUT, DADDY, YOU'RE THE ONLY PERSON I HAVE...
BANG!
BANG!
BANG!
DUCK
HA! YOU LOOKED SO SCARED.
DADDY, WHAT'S THAT?
THAT'S JUST GRAMMA'S JARS OF SOFKE.

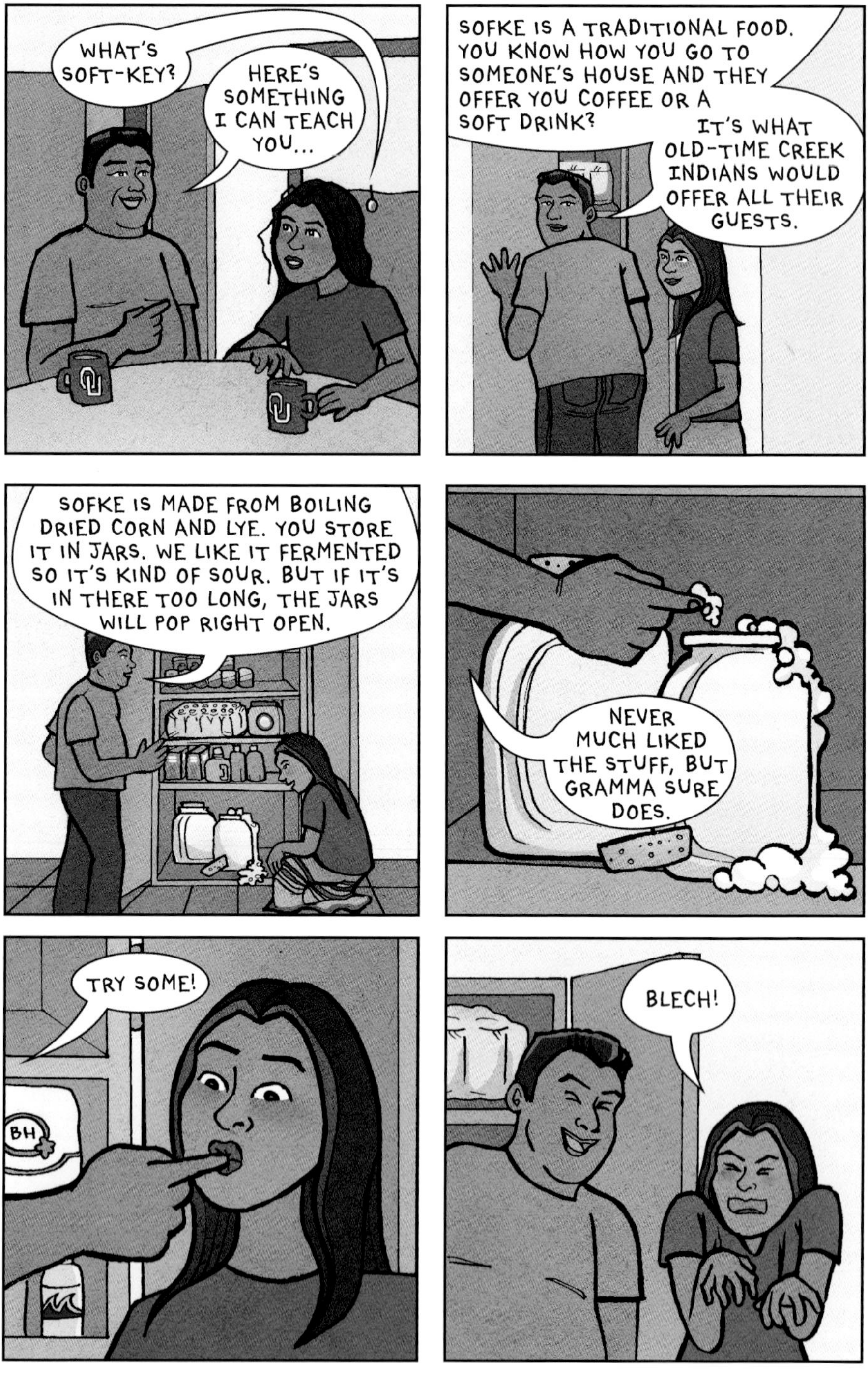
WHAT'S SOFT-KEY?
HERE'S SOMETHING I CAN TEACH YOU...
SOFKE IS A TRADITIONAL FOOD. YOU KNOW HOW YOU GO TO SOMEONE'S HOUSE AND THEY OFFER YOU COFFEE OR A SOFT DRINK?
IT'S WHAT OLD-TIME CREEK INDIANS WOULD OFFER ALL THEIR GUESTS.
SOFKE IS MADE FROM BOILING DRIED CORN AND LYE. YOU STORE IT IN JARS. WE LIKE IT FERMENTED SO IT'S KIND OF SOUR. BUT IF IT'S IN THERE TOO LONG, THE JARS WILL POP RIGHT OPEN.
NEVER MUCH LIKED THE STUFF, BUT GRAMMA SURE DOES.
TRY SOME!
BH
BLECH!

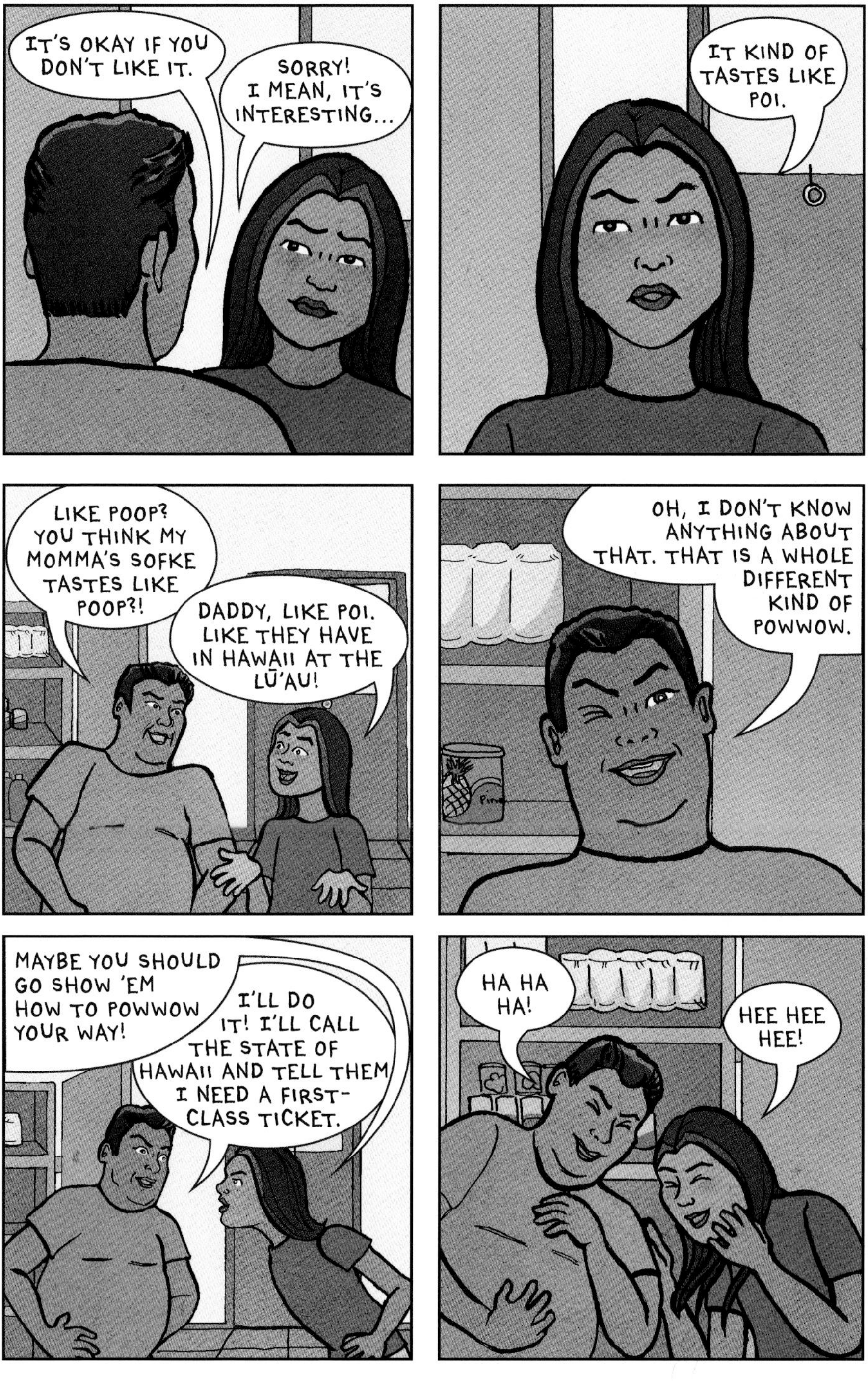
IT'S OKAY IF YOU DON'T LIKE IT.
SORRY! I MEAN, IT'S INTERESTING...
IT KIND OF TASTES LIKE POI.
LIKE POOP? YOU THINK MY MOMMA'S SOFKE TASTES LIKE POOP?!
DADDY, LIKE POI. LIKE THEY HAVE IN HAWAII AT THE LŪ'AU!
OH, I DON'T KNOW ANYTHING ABOUT THAT. THAT IS A WHOLE DIFFERENT KIND OF POWWOW.
MAYBE YOU SHOULD GO SHOW 'EM HOW TO POWWOW YOUR WAY!
I'LL DO IT! I'LL CALL THE STATE OF HAWAII AND TELL THEM I NEED A FIRST-CLASS TICKET.
HA HA HA!
HEE HEE HEE!

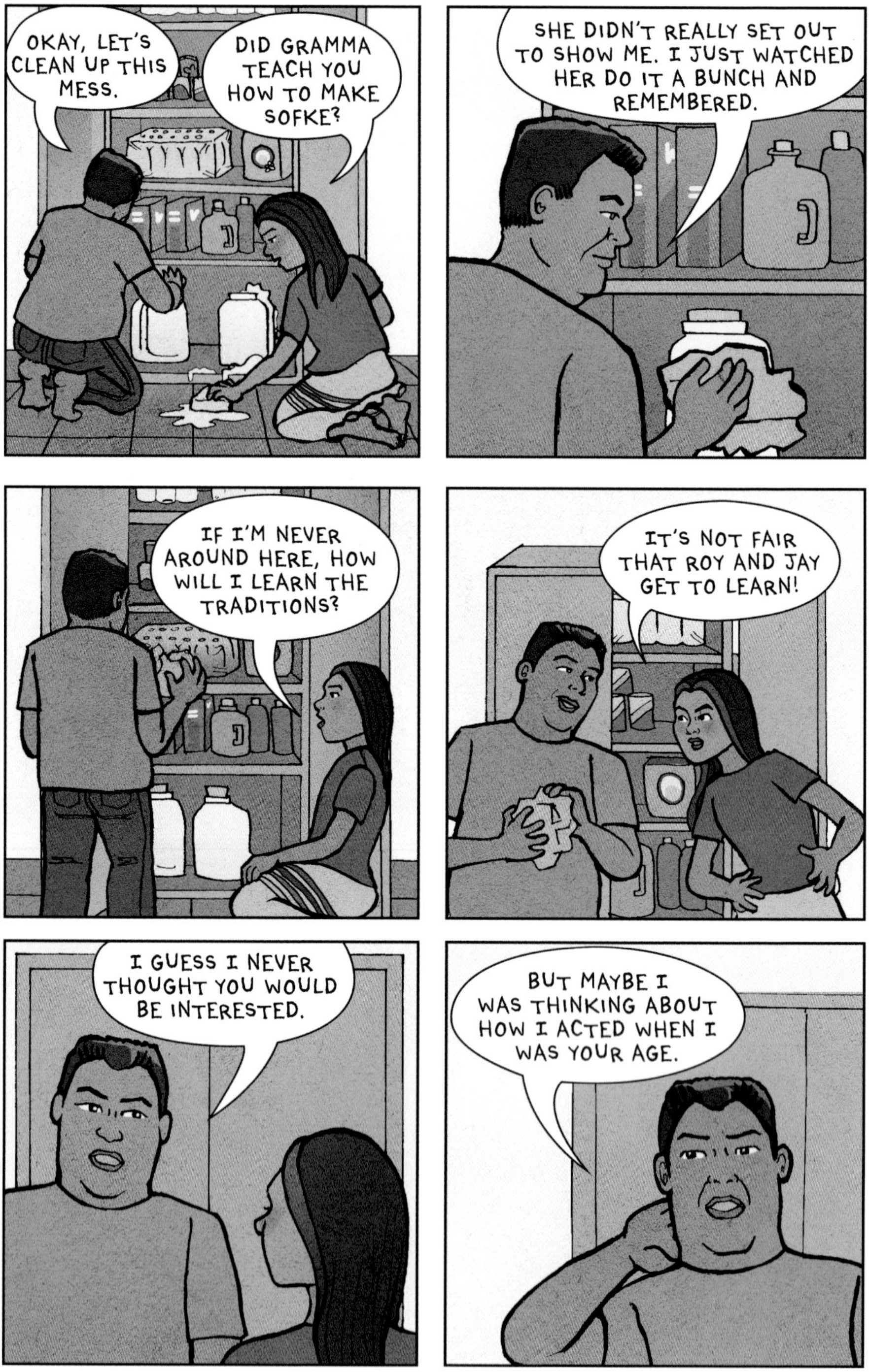
OKAY, LET'S CLEAN UP THIS MESS.
DID GRAMMA TEACH YOU HOW TO MAKE SOFKE?
SHE DIDN'T REALLY SET OUT TO SHOW ME. I JUST WATCHED HER DO IT A BUNCH AND REMEMBERED.
IF I'M NEVER AROUND HERE, HOW WILL I LEARN THE TRADITIONS?
IT'S NOT FAIR THAT ROY AND JAY GET TO LEARN!
I GUESS I NEVER THOUGHT YOU WOULD BE INTERESTED.
BUT MAYBE I WAS THINKING ABOUT HOW I ACTED WHEN I WAS YOUR AGE.

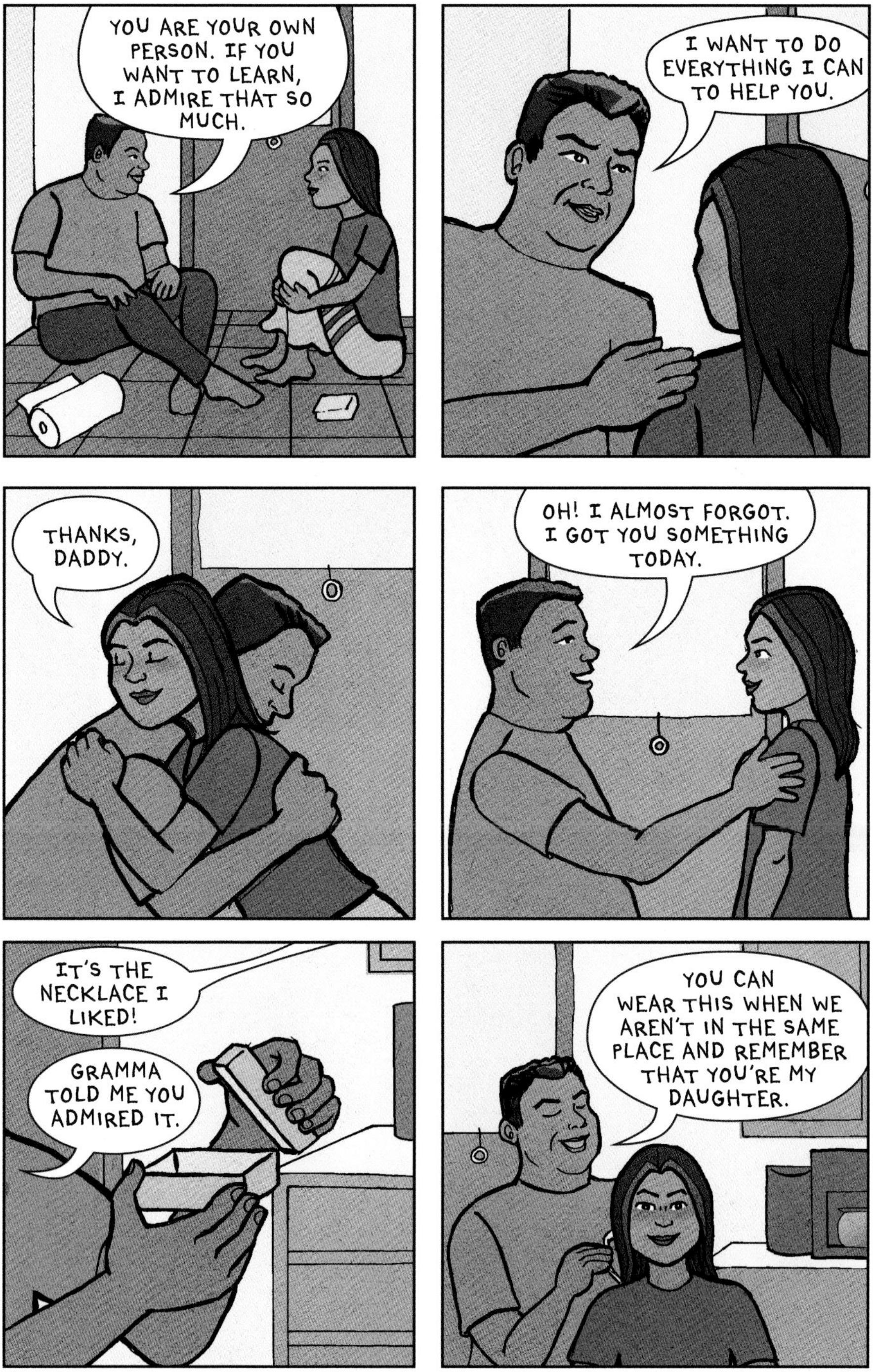
YOU ARE YOUR OWN PERSON. IF YOU WANT TO LEARN, I ADMIRE THAT SO MUCH.
I WANT TO DO EVERYTHING I CAN TO HELP YOU.
THANKS, DADDY.
OH! I ALMOST FORGOT. I GOT YOU SOMETHING TODAY.
IT'S THE NECKLACE I LIKED!
GRAMMA TOLD ME YOU ADMIRED IT.
YOU CAN WEAR THIS WHEN WE AREN'T IN THE SAME PLACE AND REMEMBER THAT YOU'RE MY DAUGHTER.

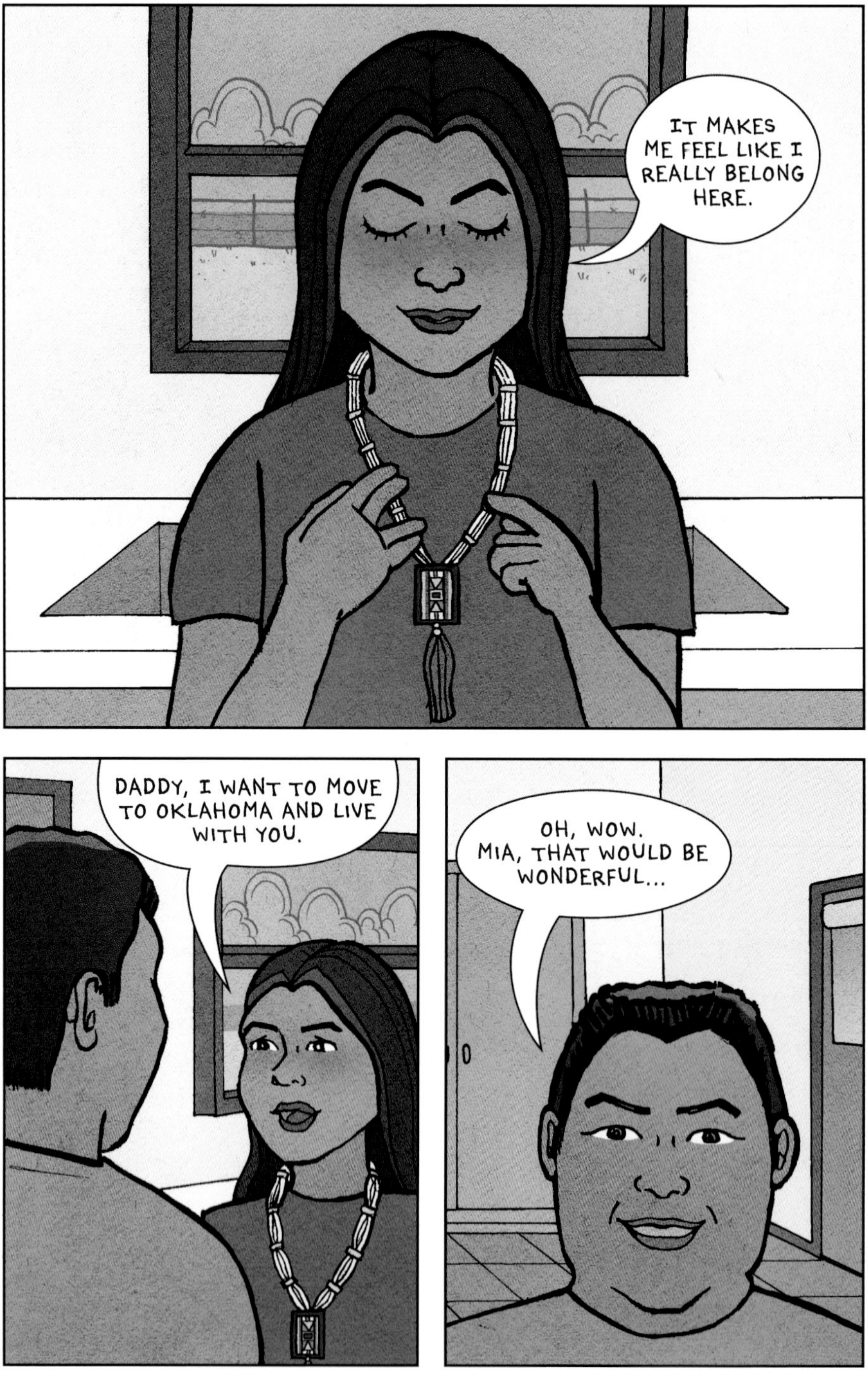
IT MAKES ME FEEL LIKE I REALLY BELONG HERE.
DADDY, I WANT TO MOVE TO OKLAHOMA AND LIVE WITH YOU.
OH, WOW. MIA, THAT WOULD BE WONDERFUL...

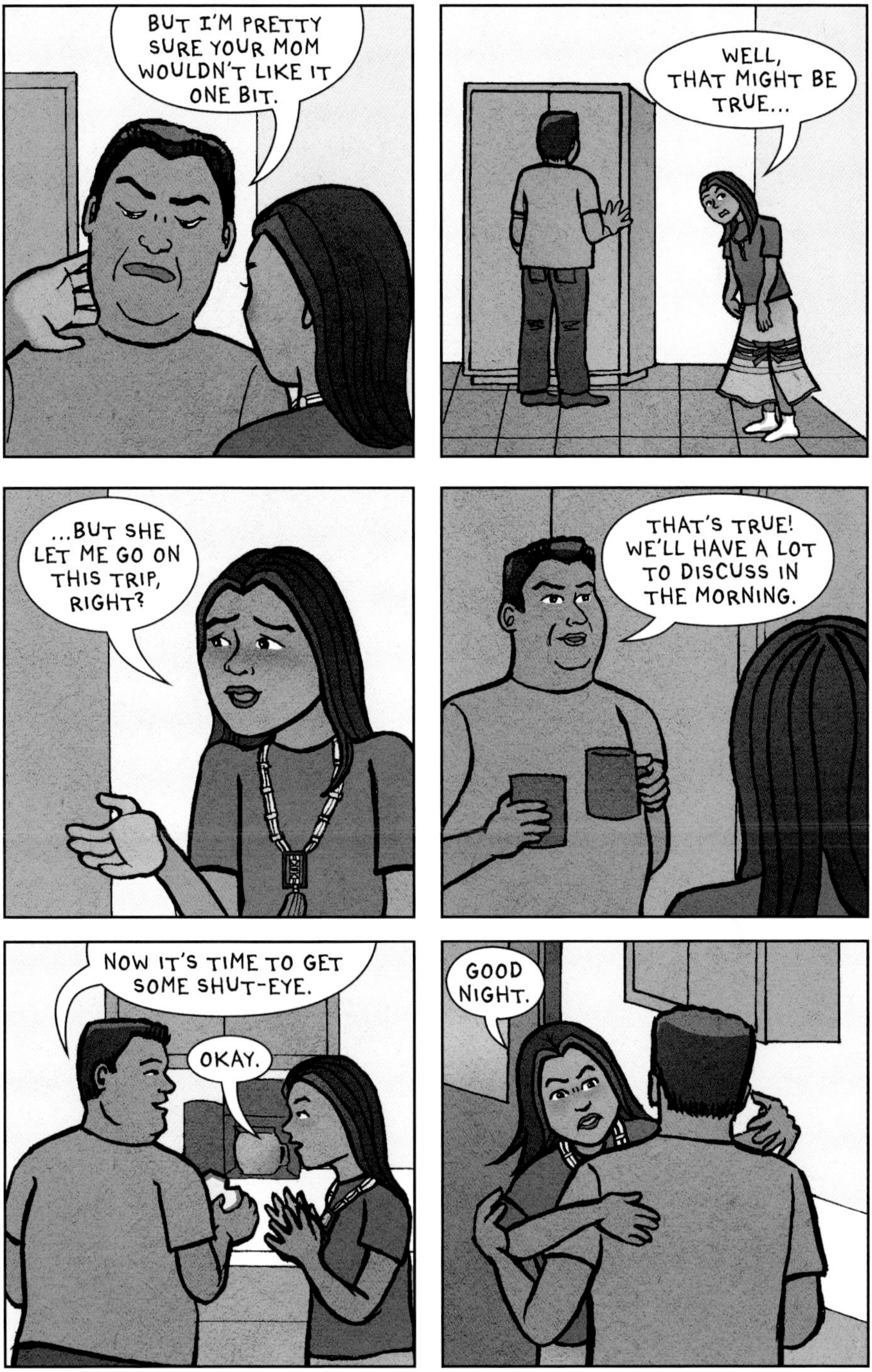
BUT I'M PRETTY SURE YOUR MOM WOULDN'T LIKE IT ONE BIT.
WELL, THAT MIGHT BE TRUE...
...BUT SHE LET ME GO ON THIS TRIP, RIGHT?
THAT'S TRUE! WE'LL HAVE A LOT TO DISCUSS IN THE MORNING.
NOW IT'S TIME TO GET SOME SHUT-EYE.
OKAY.
GOOD NIGHT.

CHICKENS COME HOME

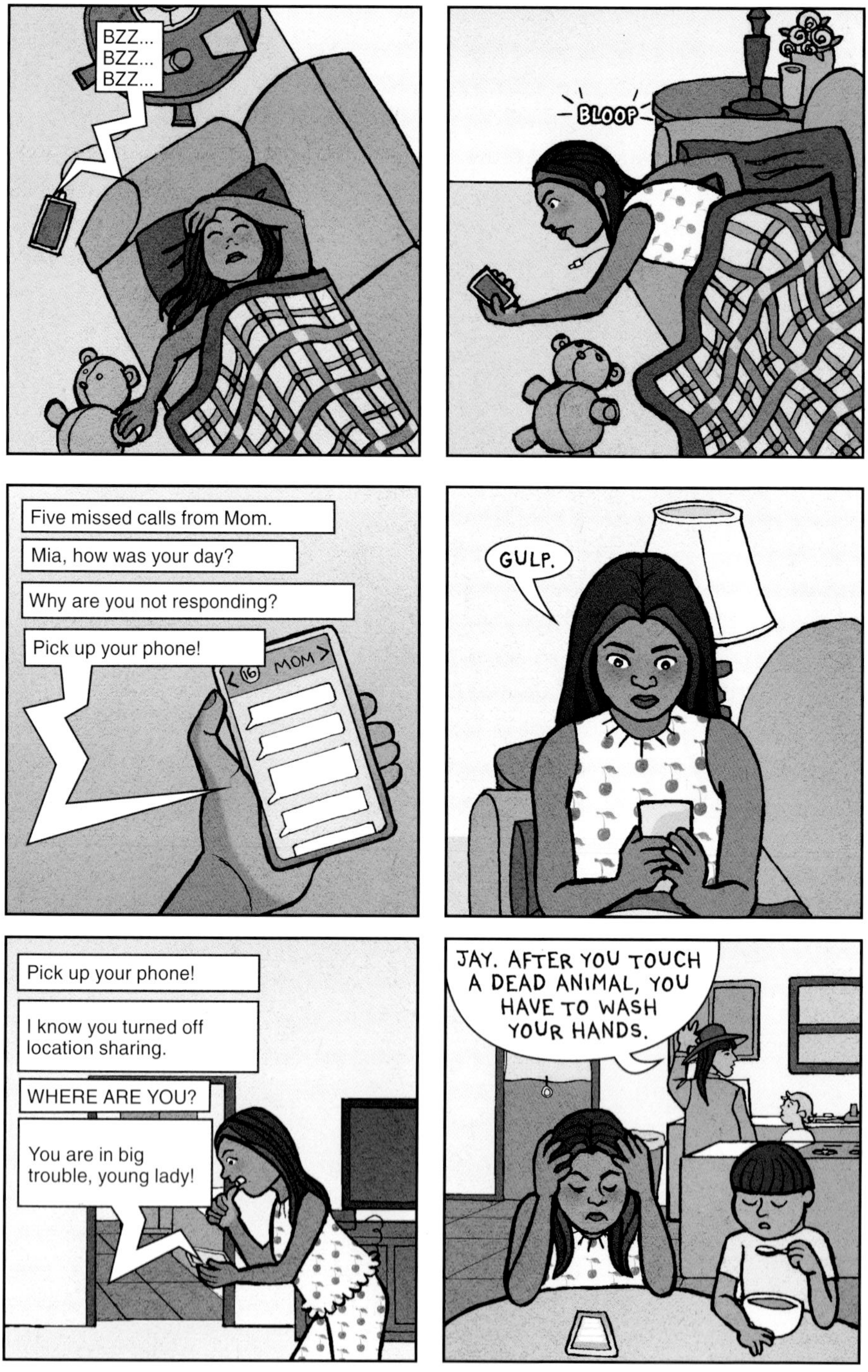
BZZ... BZZ... BZZ...
BLOOP
Five missed calls from Mom.
Mia, how was your day?
Why are you not responding?
Pick up your phone!
(16) MOM
GULP.
Pick up your phone!
I know you turned off location sharing.
WHERE ARE YOU?
You are in big trouble, young lady!
JAY. AFTER YOU TOUCH A DEAD ANIMAL, YOU HAVE TO WASH YOUR HANDS.

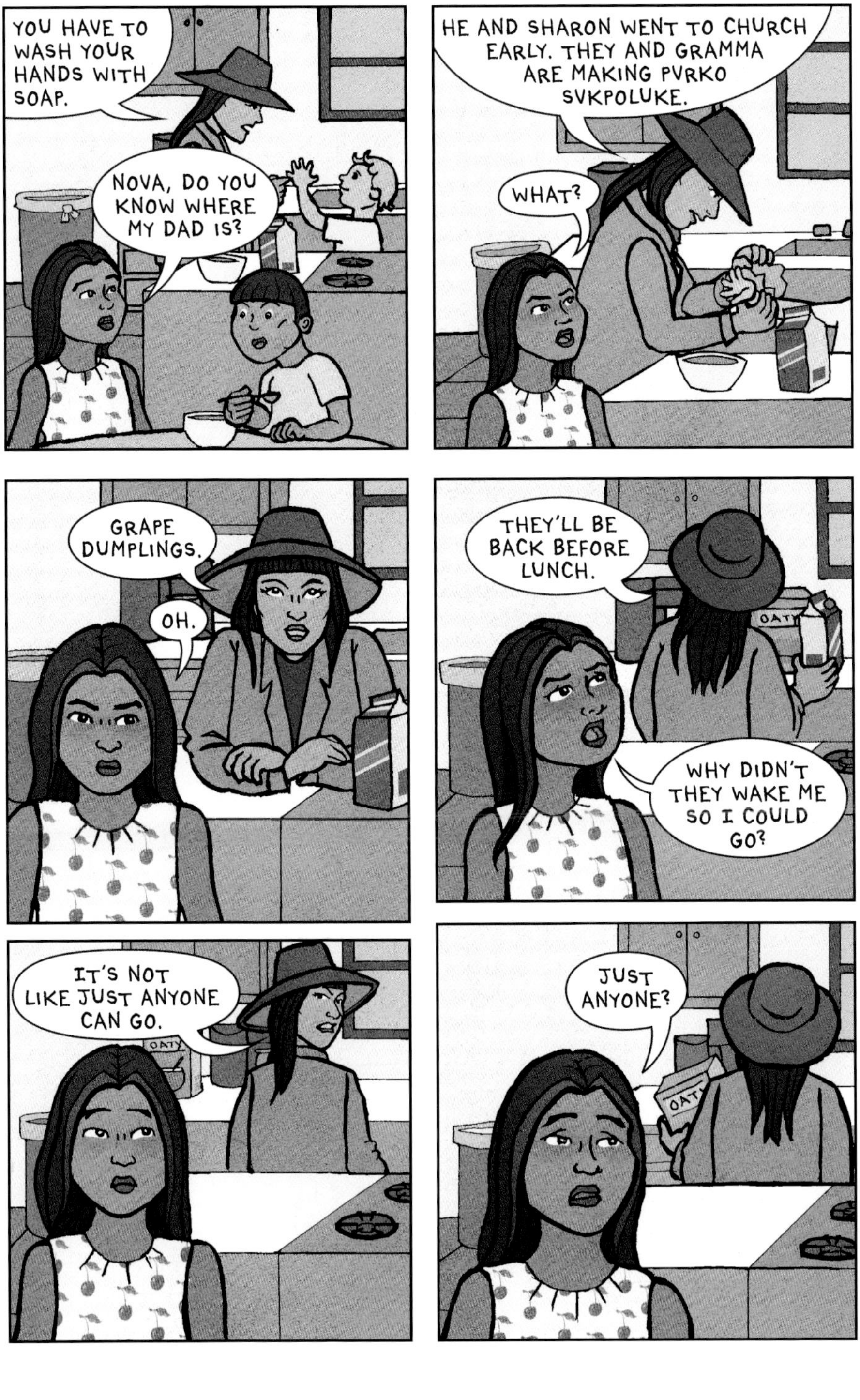
YOU HAVE TO WASH YOUR HANDS WITH SOAP.
NOVA, DO YOU KNOW WHERE MY DAD IS?
HE AND SHARON WENT TO CHURCH EARLY. THEY AND GRAMMA ARE MAKING PVRKO SVKPOLUKE.
WHAT?
GRAPE DUMPLINGS.
OH.
THEY'LL BE BACK BEFORE LUNCH.
WHY DIDN'T THEY WAKE ME SO I COULD GO?
IT'S NOT LIKE JUST ANYONE CAN GO.
JUST ANYONE?

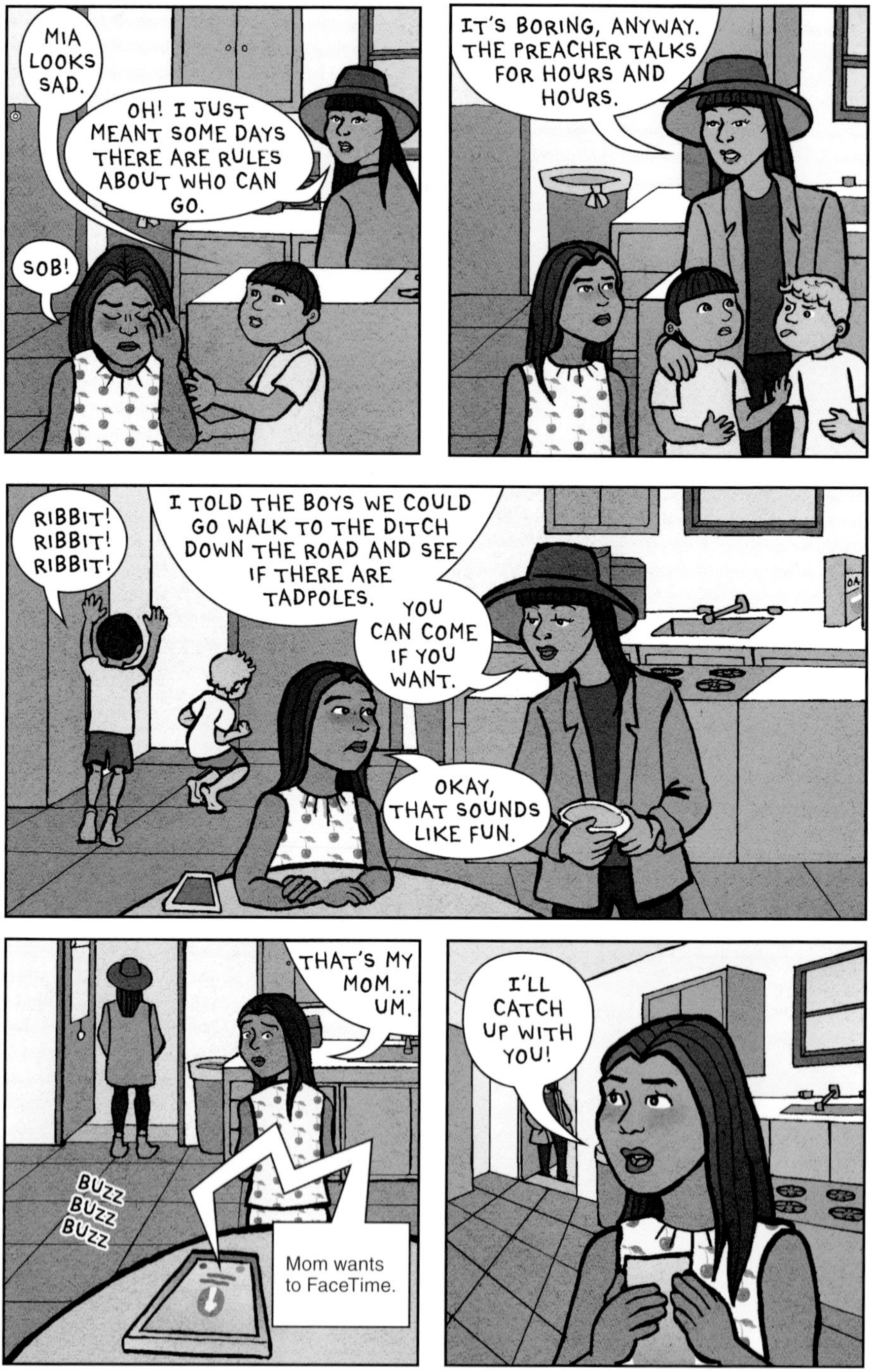
MIA LOOKS SAD.
OH! I JUST MEANT SOME DAYS THERE ARE RULES ABOUT WHO CAN GO.
SOB!
IT'S BORING, ANYWAY. THE PREACHER TALKS FOR HOURS AND HOURS.
RIBBIT! RIBBIT! RIBBIT!
I TOLD THE BOYS WE COULD GO WALK TO THE DITCH DOWN THE ROAD AND SEE IF THERE ARE TADPOLES.
YOU CAN COME IF YOU WANT.
OKAY, THAT SOUNDS LIKE FUN.
THAT'S MY MOM... UM.
BUZZ BUZZ BUZZ
Mom wants to FaceTime.
I'LL CATCH UP WITH YOU!

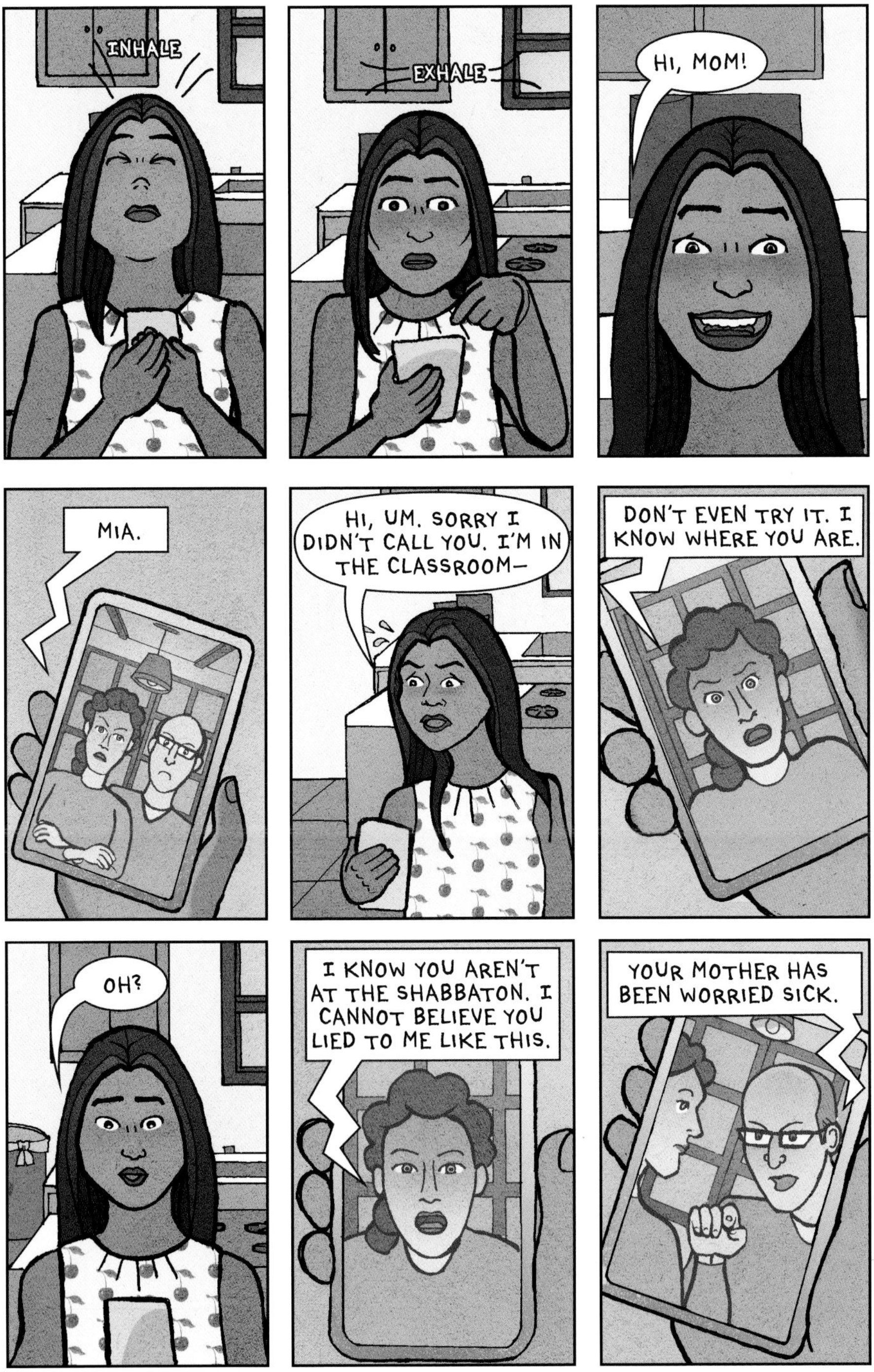
INHALE
EXHALE
HI, MOM!
MIA.
HI, UM. SORRY I DIDN'T CALL YOU. I'M IN THE CLASSROOM—
DON'T EVEN TRY IT. I KNOW WHERE YOU ARE.
OH?
I KNOW YOU AREN'T AT THE SHABBATON. I CANNOT BELIEVE YOU LIED TO ME LIKE THIS.
YOUR MOTHER HAS BEEN WORRIED SICK.

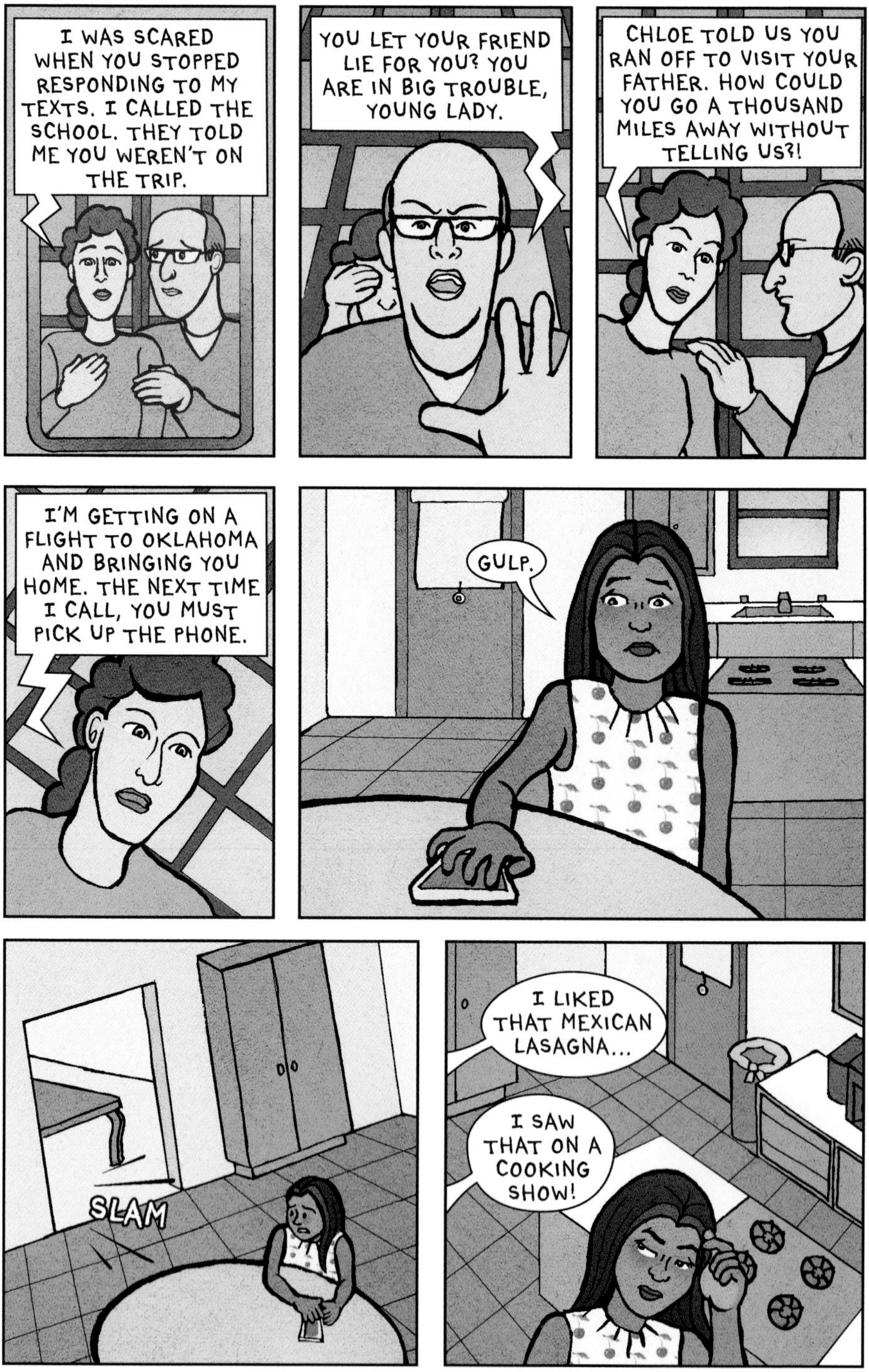
I WAS SCARED WHEN YOU STOPPED RESPONDING TO MY TEXTS. I CALLED THE SCHOOL. THEY TOLD ME YOU WEREN'T ON THE TRIP.
YOU LET YOUR FRIEND LIE FOR YOU? YOU ARE IN BIG TROUBLE, YOUNG LADY.
CHLOE TOLD US YOU RAN OFF TO VISIT YOUR FATHER. HOW COULD YOU GO A THOUSAND MILES AWAY WITHOUT TELLING US?!
I'M GETTING ON A FLIGHT TO OKLAHOMA AND BRINGING YOU HOME. THE NEXT TIME I CALL, YOU MUST PICK UP THE PHONE.
GULP.
SLAM
I LIKED THAT MEXICAN LASAGNA...
I SAW THAT ON A COOKING SHOW!

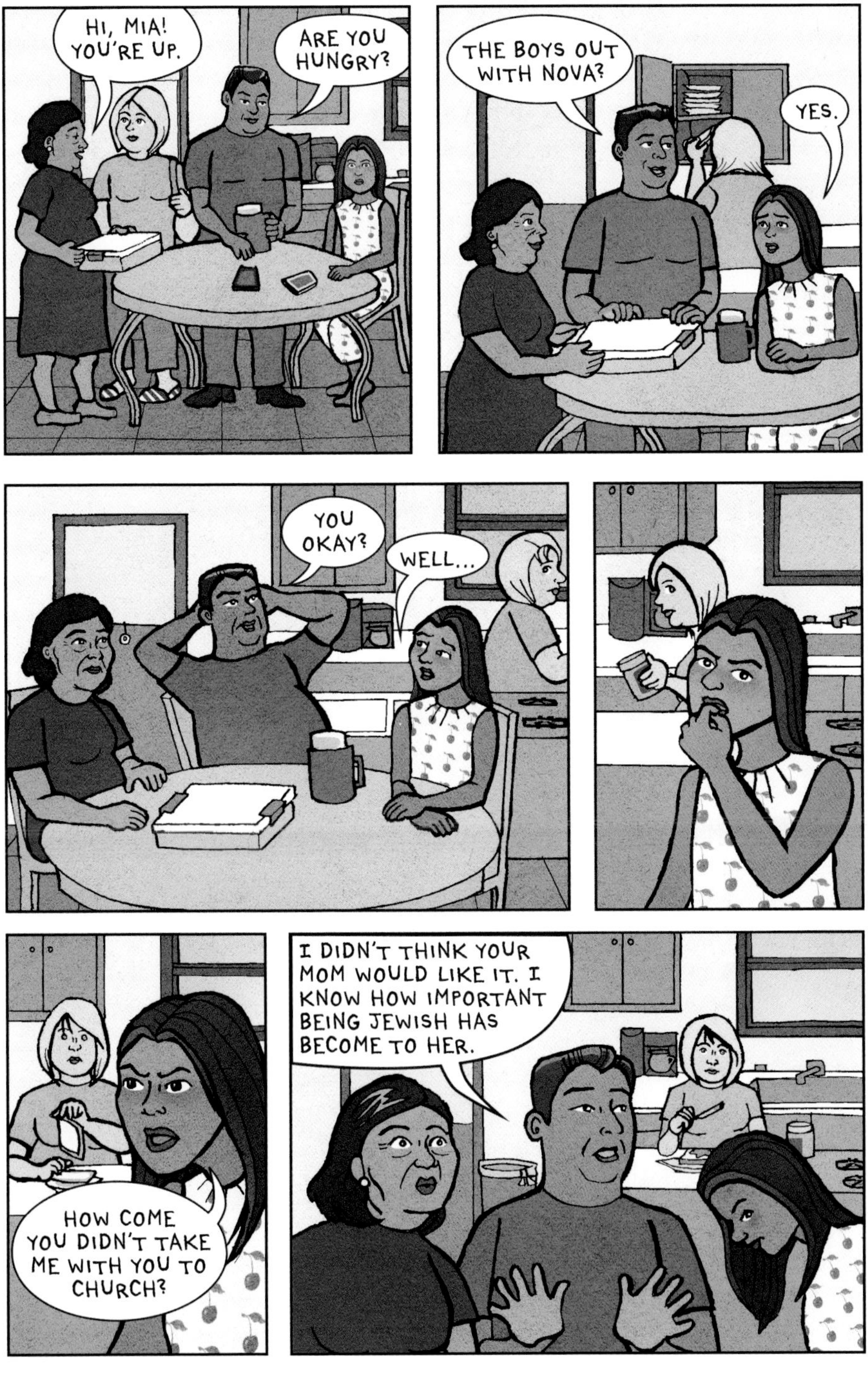
HI, MIA! YOU'RE UP.
ARE YOU HUNGRY?
THE BOYS OUT WITH NOVA?
YES.
YOU OKAY?
WELL...
HOW COME YOU DIDN'T TAKE ME WITH YOU TO CHURCH?
I DIDN'T THINK YOUR MOM WOULD LIKE IT. I KNOW HOW IMPORTANT BEING JEWISH HAS BECOME TO HER.

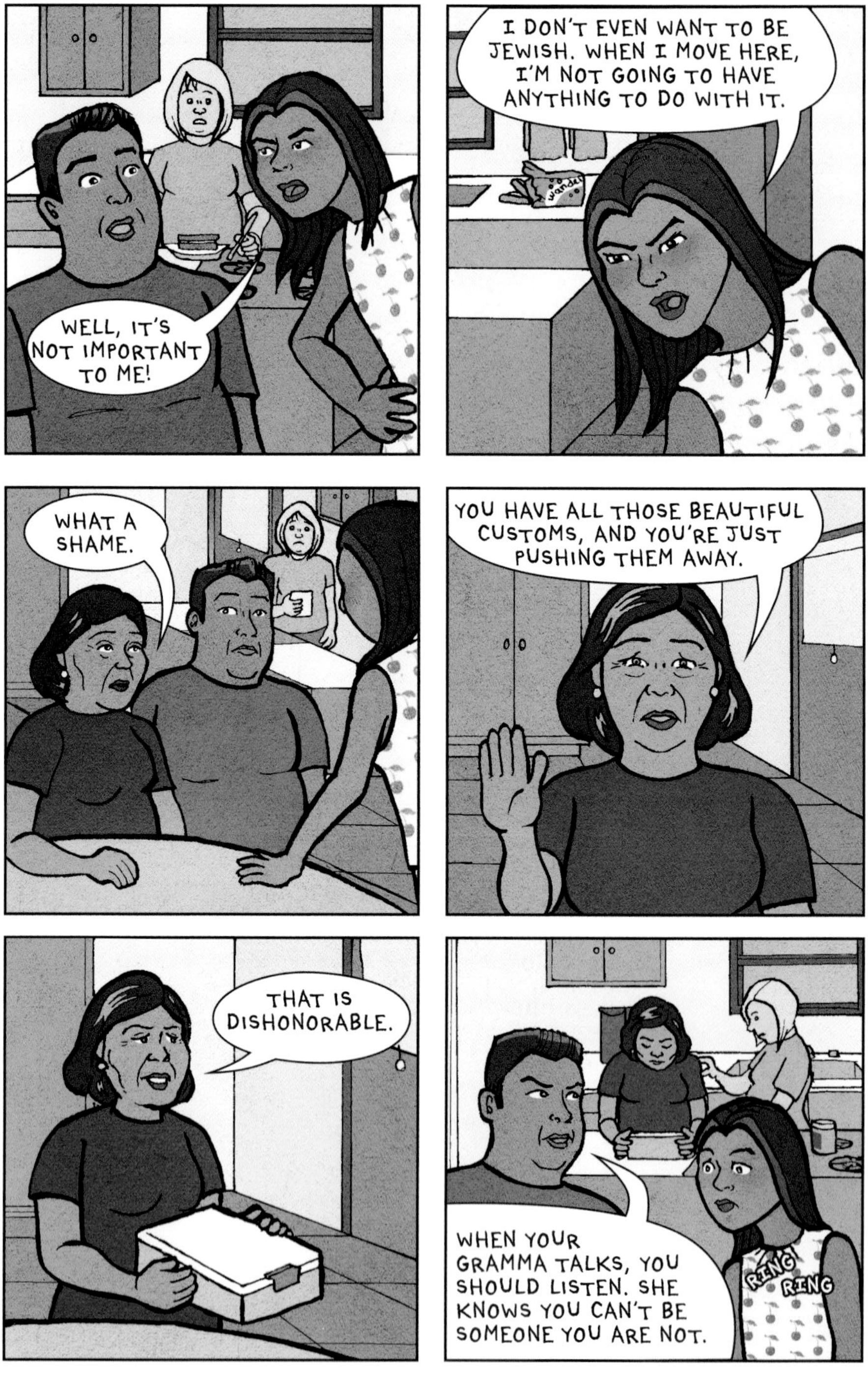
WELL, IT'S NOT IMPORTANT TO ME!
I DON'T EVEN WANT TO BE JEWISH. WHEN I MOVE HERE, I'M NOT GOING TO HAVE ANYTHING TO DO WITH IT.
WHAT A SHAME.
YOU HAVE ALL THOSE BEAUTIFUL CUSTOMS, AND YOU'RE JUST PUSHING THEM AWAY.
THAT IS DISHONORABLE.
WHEN YOUR GRAMMA TALKS, YOU SHOULD LISTEN. SHE KNOWS YOU CAN'T BE SOMEONE YOU ARE NOT.
RING
RING

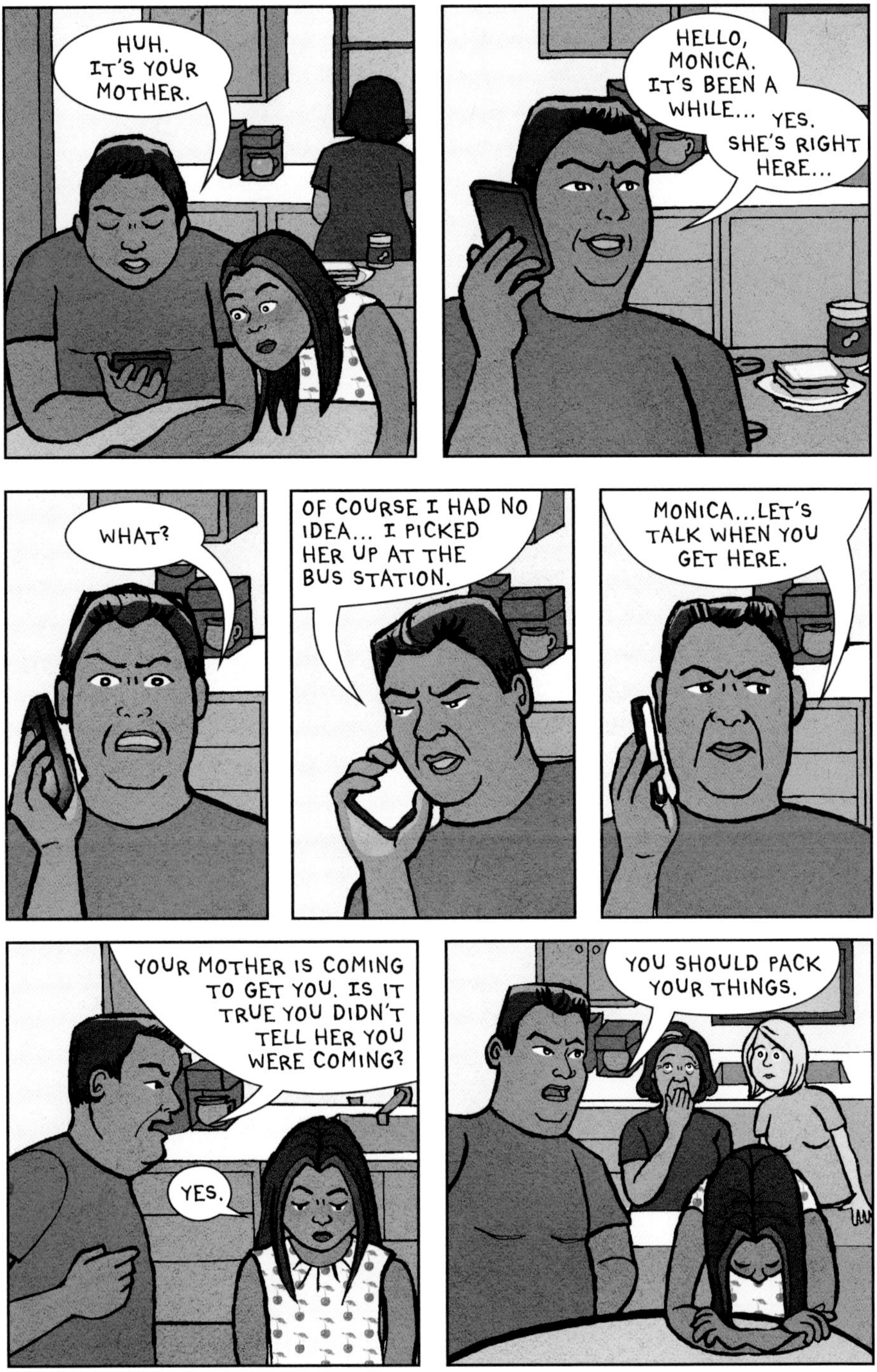
HUH. IT'S YOUR MOTHER.
HELLO, MONICA. IT'S BEEN A WHILE...
YES. SHE'S RIGHT HERE...
WHAT?
OF COURSE I HAD NO IDEA... I PICKED HER UP AT THE BUS STATION.
MONICA...LET'S TALK WHEN YOU GET HERE.
YOUR MOTHER IS COMING TO GET YOU. IS IT TRUE YOU DIDN'T TELL HER YOU WERE COMING?
YES.
YOU SHOULD PACK YOUR THINGS.

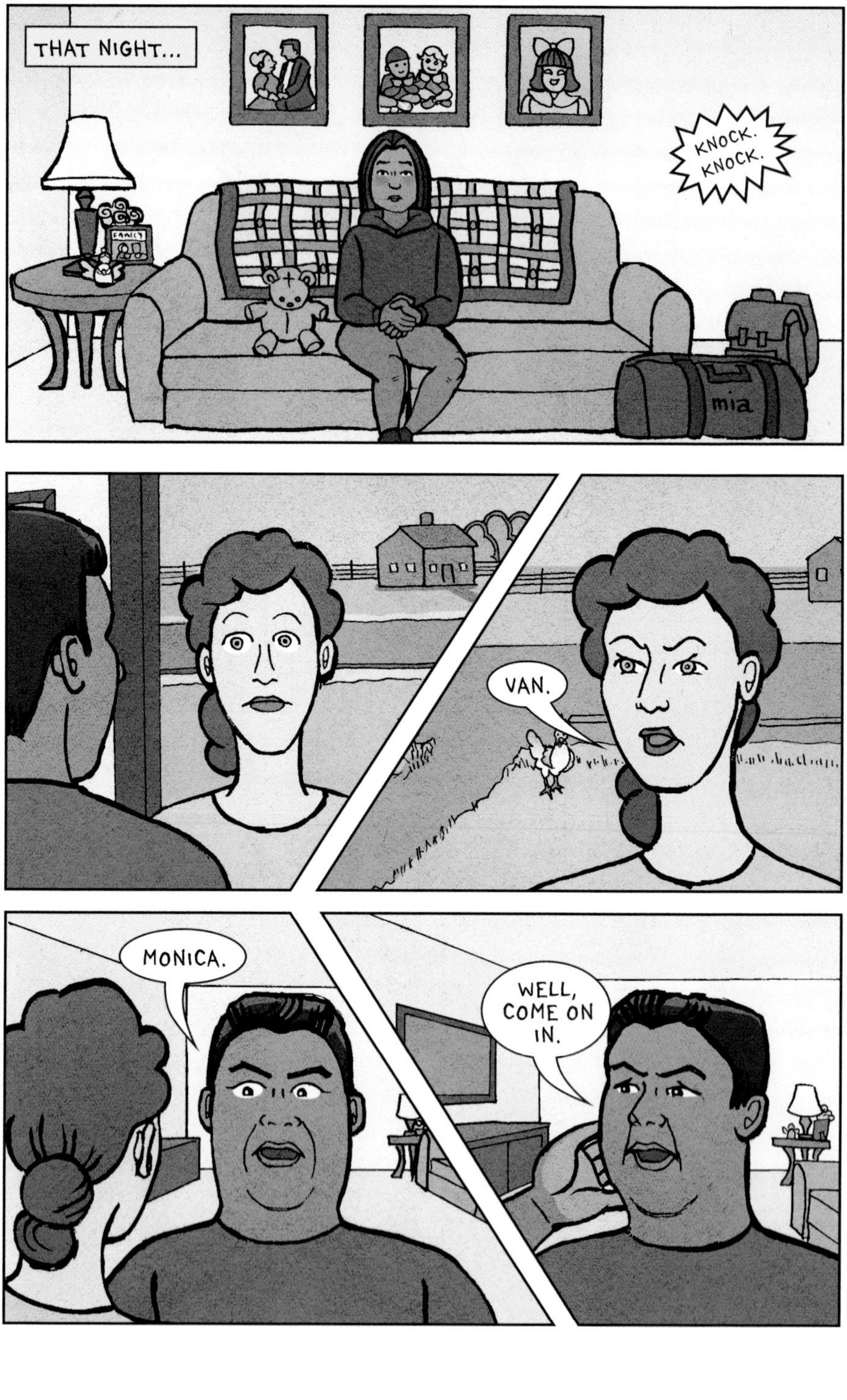

THAT NIGHT...
FAMILY
KNOCK. KNOCK.
mia
VAN.
MONICA.
WELL, COME ON IN.

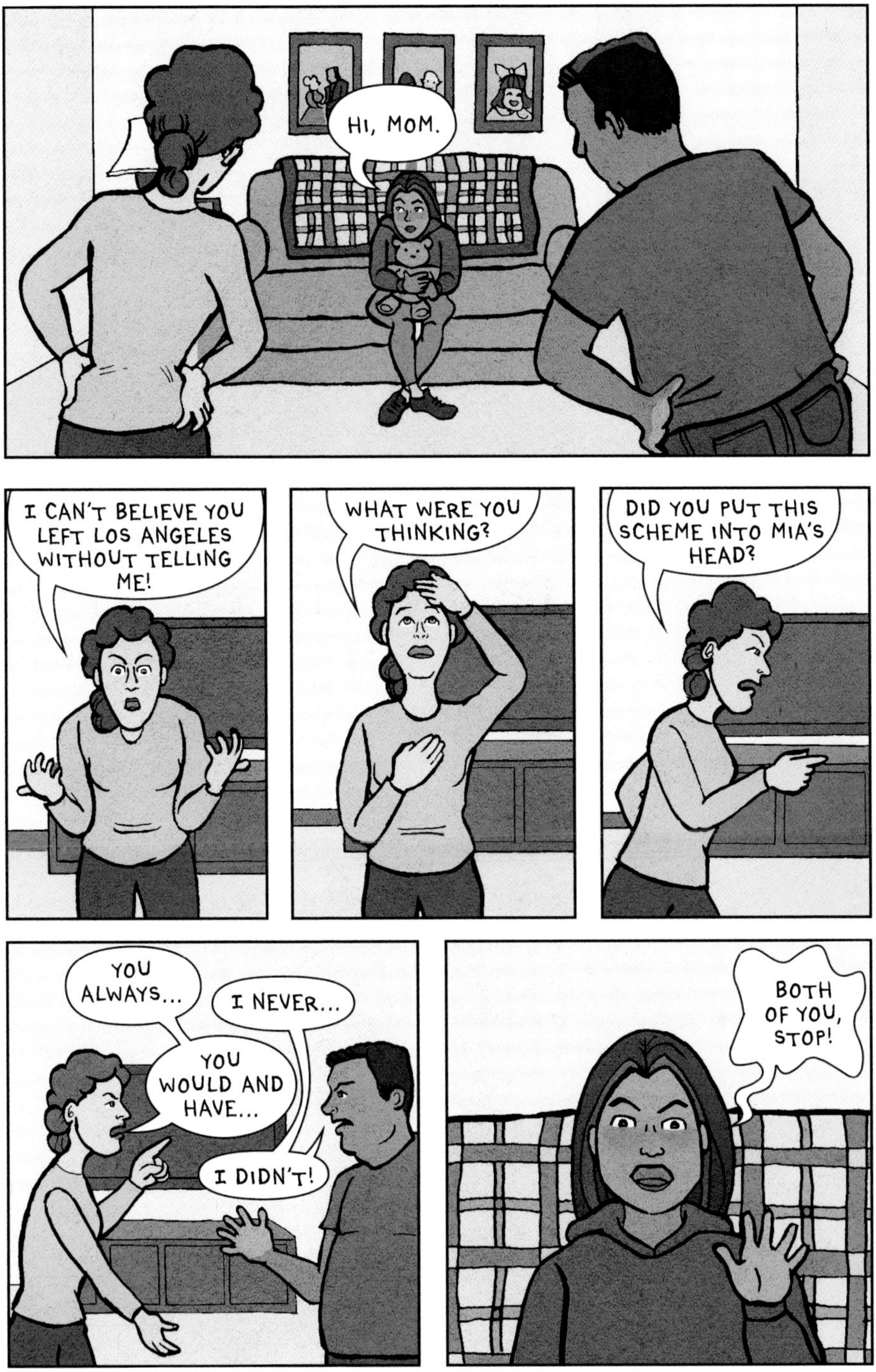
HI, MOM.
I CAN'T BELIEVE YOU LEFT LOS ANGELES WITHOUT TELLING ME!
WHAT WERE YOU THINKING?
DID YOU PUT THIS SCHEME INTO MIA'S HEAD?
YOU ALWAYS...
I NEVER...
YOU WOULD AND HAVE...
I DIDN'T!
BOTH OF YOU, STOP!

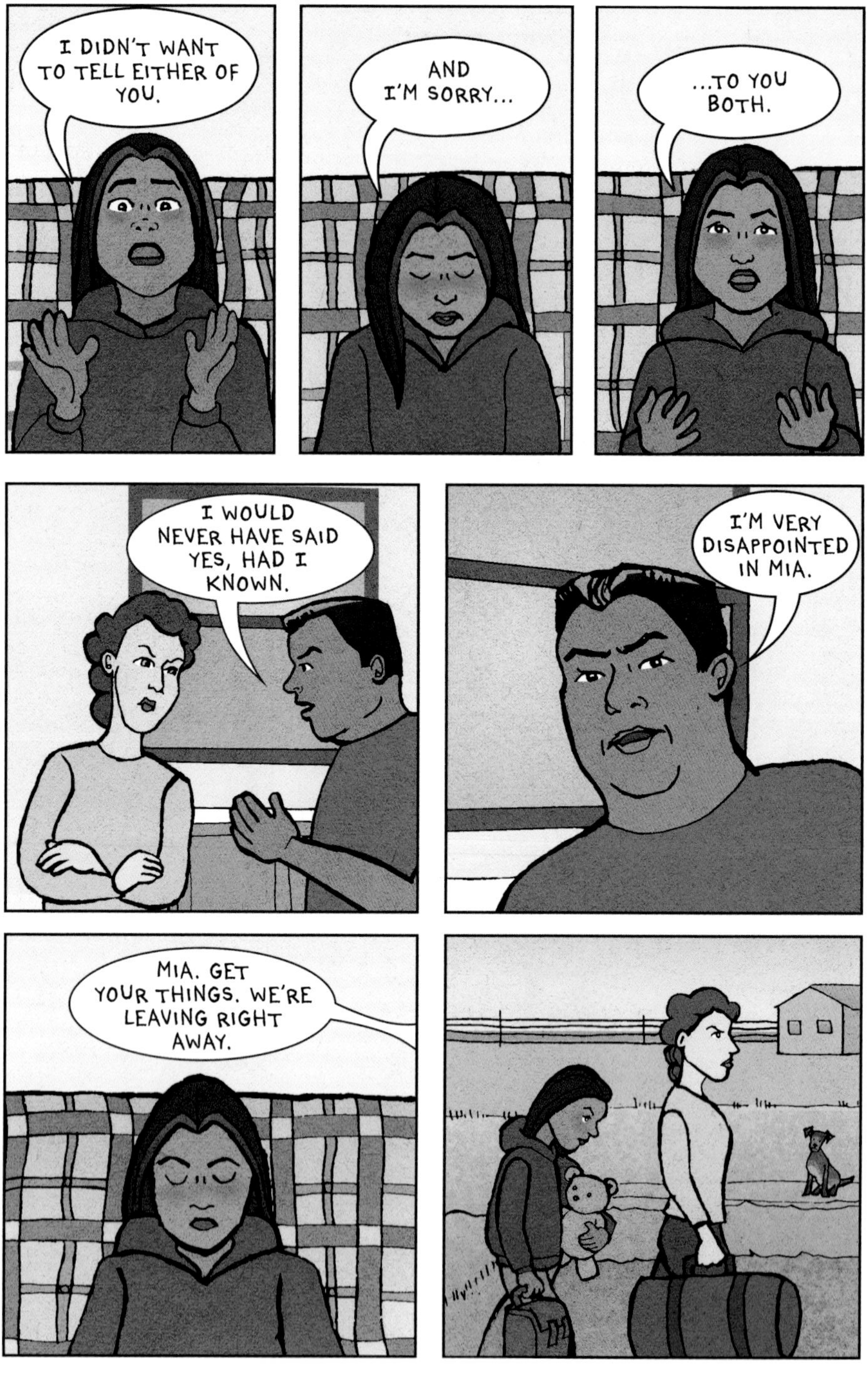
I DIDN'T WANT TO TELL EITHER OF YOU.
AND I'M SORRY...
...TO YOU BOTH.
I WOULD NEVER HAVE SAID YES, HAD I KNOWN.
I'M VERY DISAPPOINTED IN MIA.
MIA. GET YOUR THINGS. WE'RE LEAVING RIGHT AWAY.

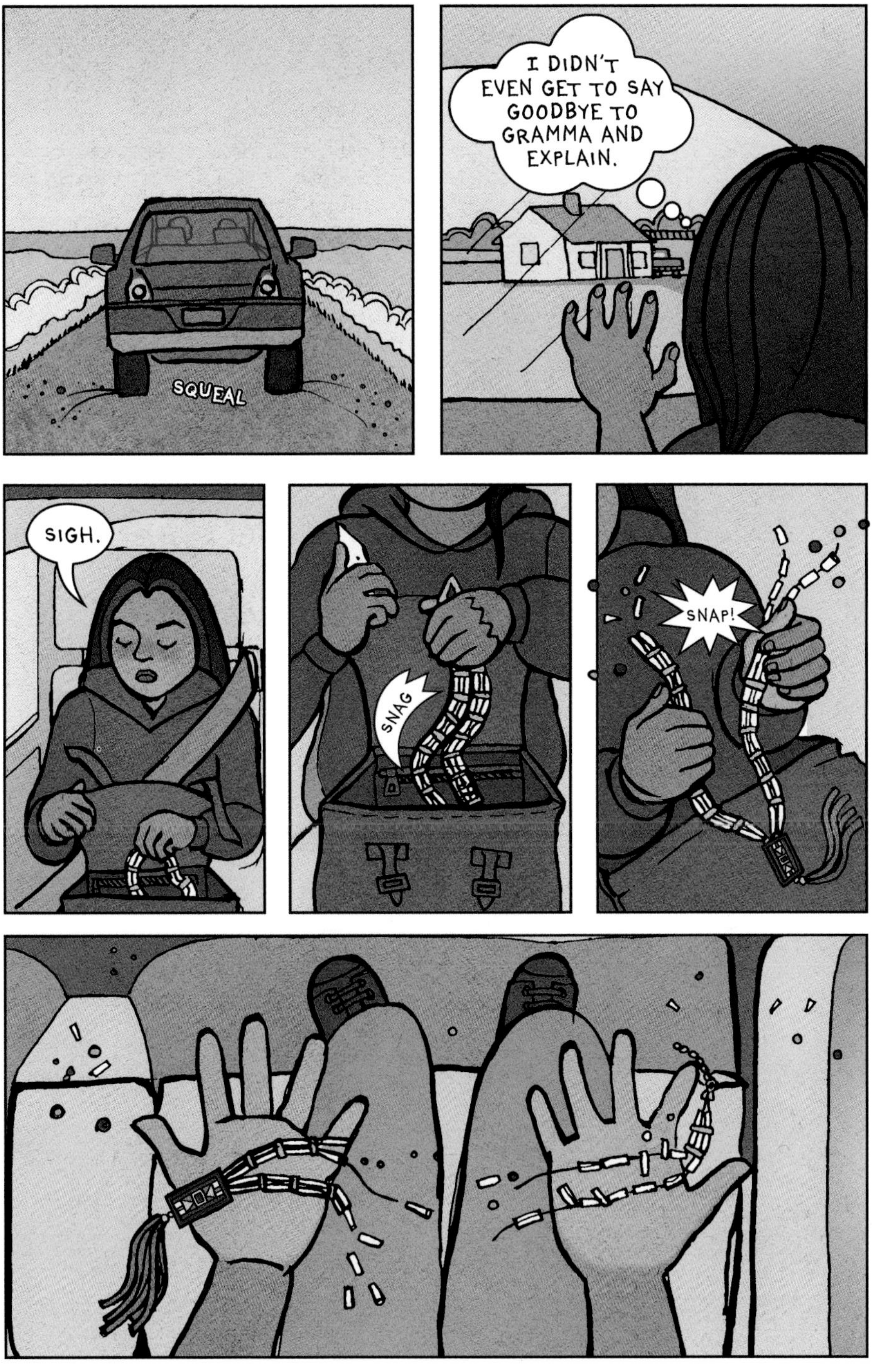
SQUEAL
I DIDN'T EVEN GET TO SAY GOODBYE TO GRAMMA AND EXPLAIN.
SIGH.
SNAG
SNAP!

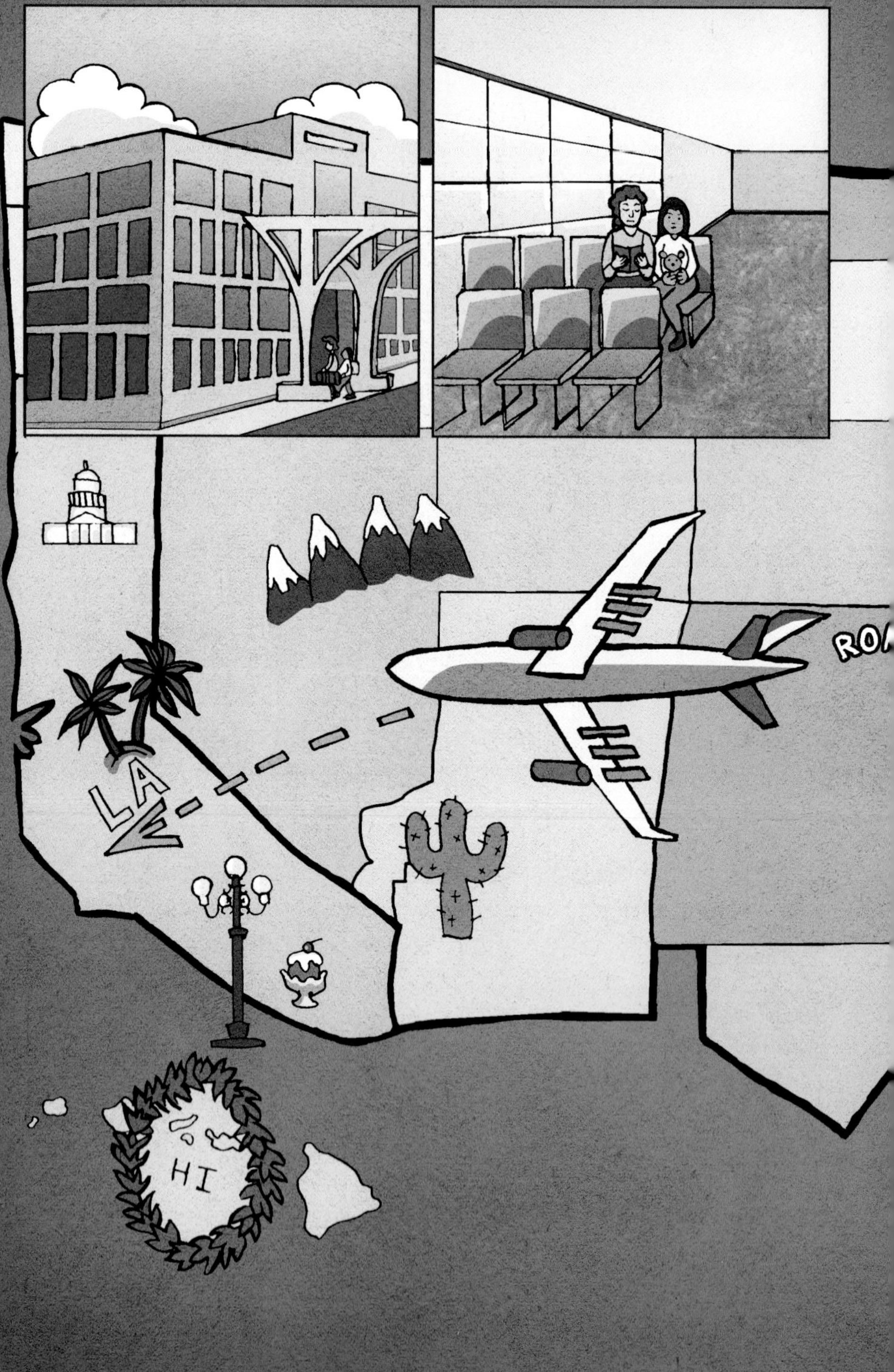
LA
HI

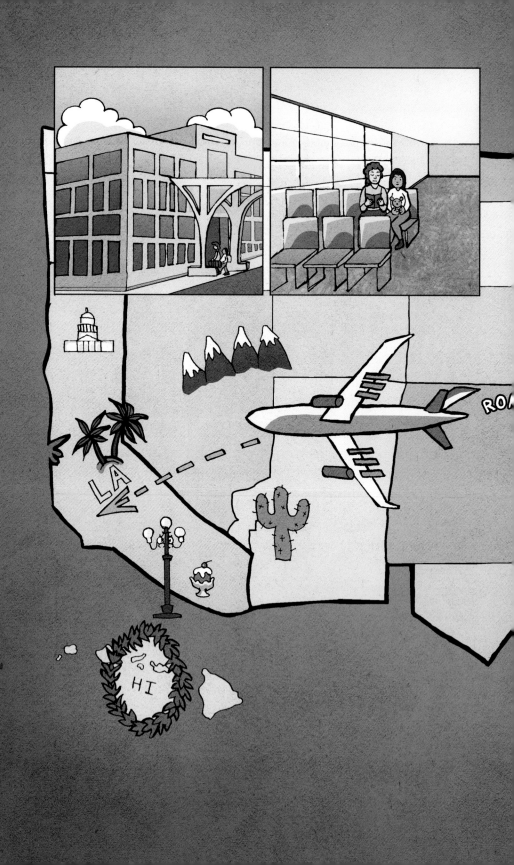

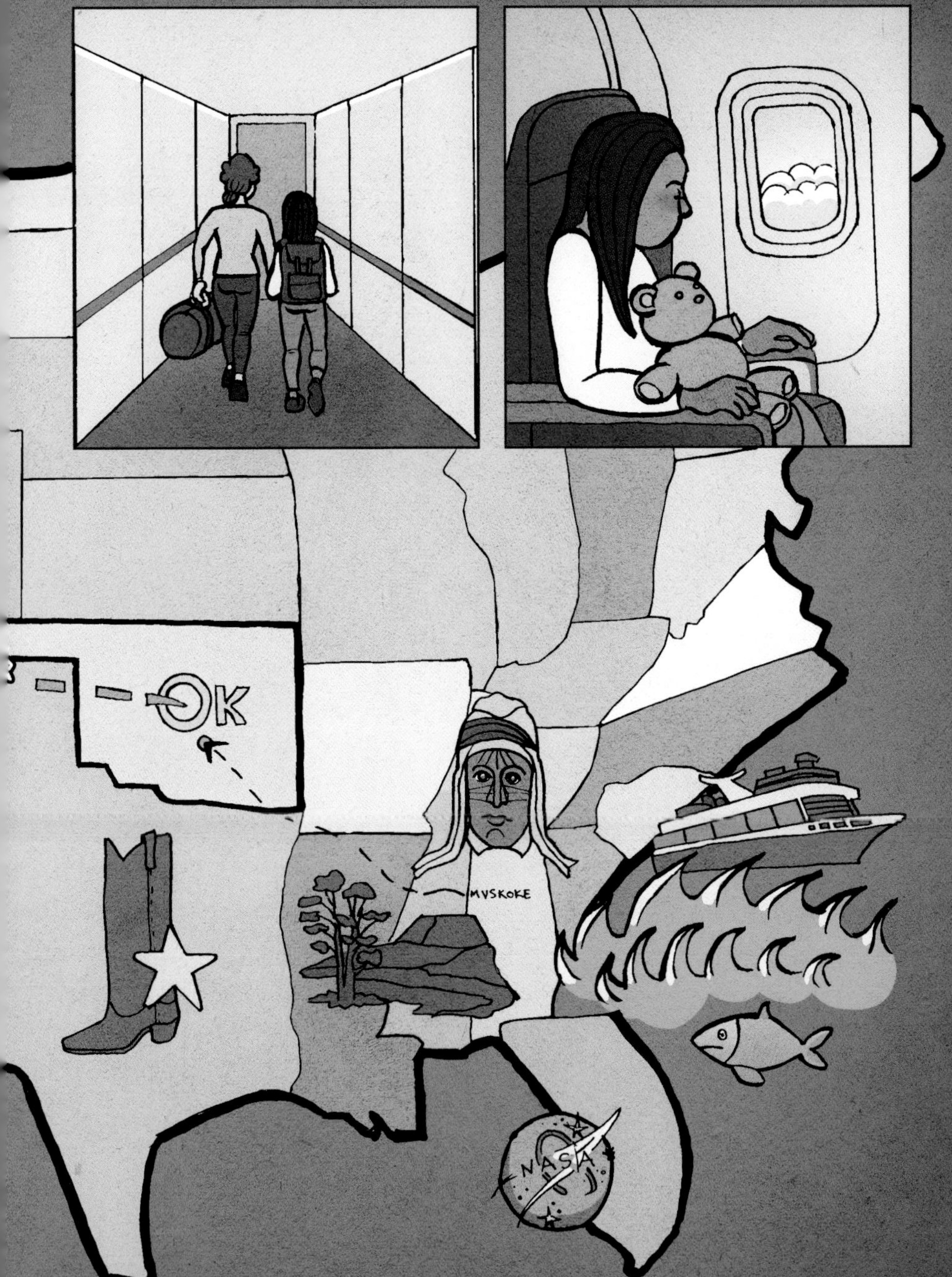
OK
MVSKOKE
NASA

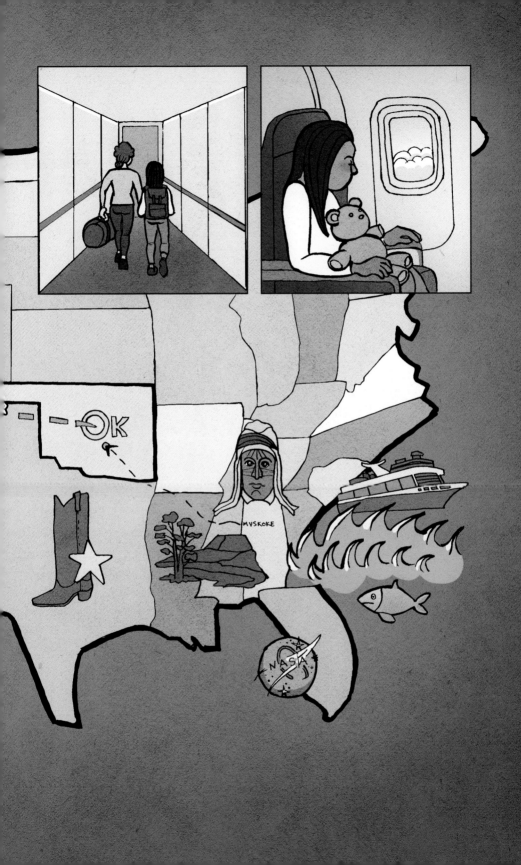

MISSING OKLAHOMA

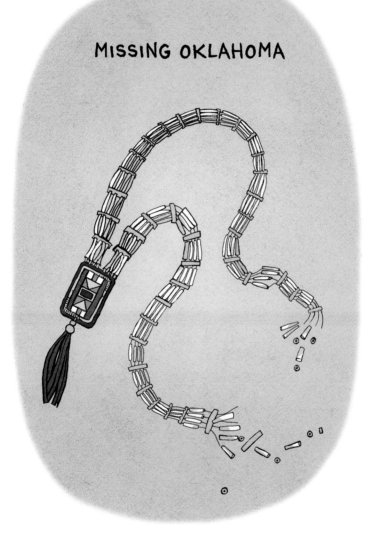

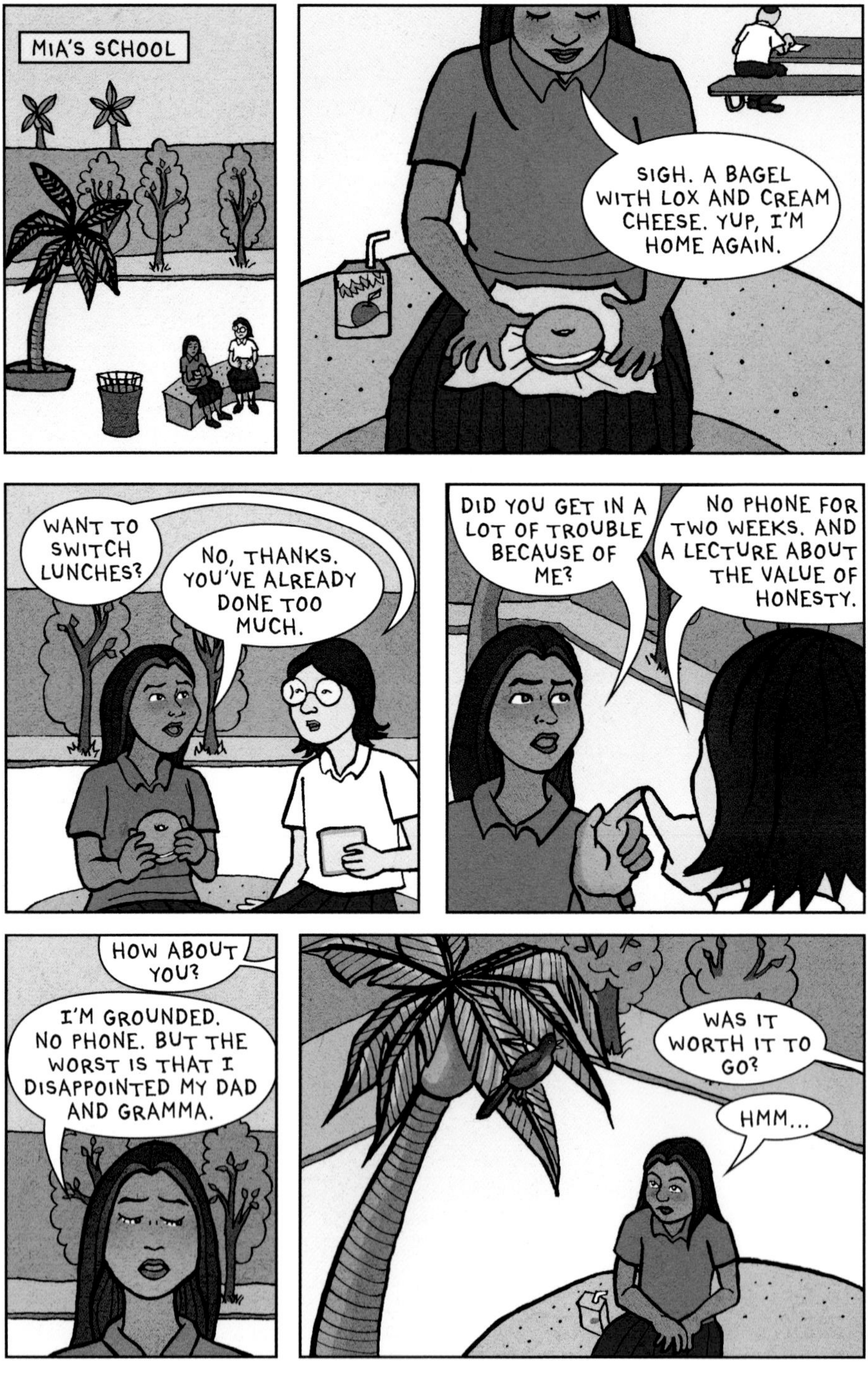
MIA'S SCHOOL
SIGH. A BAGEL WITH LOX AND CREAM CHEESE. YUP, I'M HOME AGAIN.
WANT TO SWITCH LUNCHES?
NO, THANKS. YOU'VE ALREADY DONE TOO MUCH.
DID YOU GET IN A LOT OF TROUBLE BECAUSE OF ME?
NO PHONE FOR TWO WEEKS. AND A LECTURE ABOUT THE VALUE OF HONESTY.
HOW ABOUT YOU?
I'M GROUNDED. NO PHONE. BUT THE WORST IS THAT I DISAPPOINTED MY DAD AND GRAMMA.
WAS IT WORTH IT TO GO?
HMM...

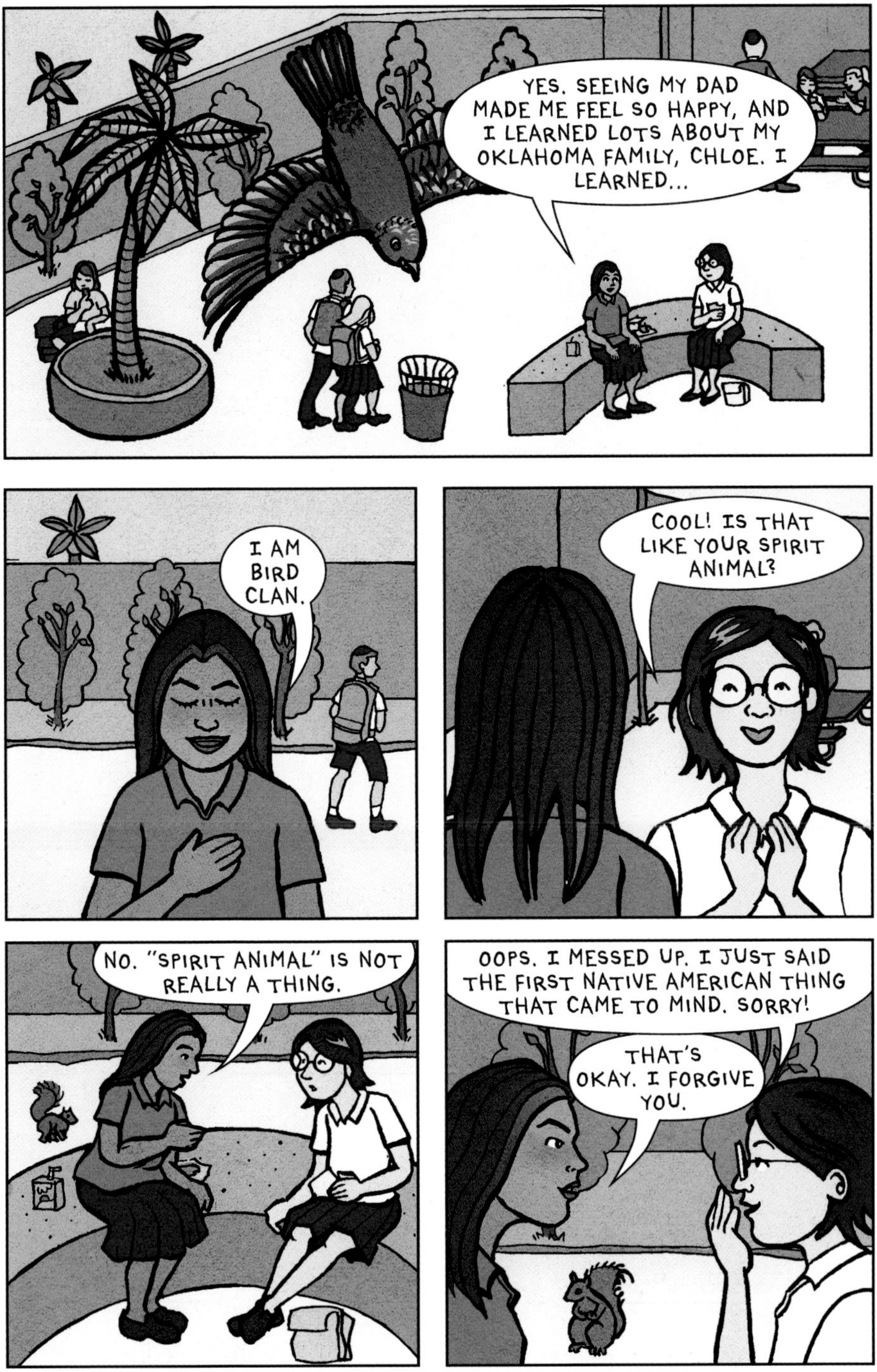
YES. SEEING MY DAD MADE ME FEEL SO HAPPY, AND I LEARNED LOTS ABOUT MY OKLAHOMA FAMILY, CHLOE. I LEARNED...
I AM BIRD CLAN.
COOL! IS THAT LIKE YOUR SPIRIT ANIMAL?
NO. "SPIRIT ANIMAL" IS NOT REALLY A THING.
OOPS. I MESSED UP. I JUST SAID THE FIRST NATIVE AMERICAN THING THAT CAME TO MIND. SORRY!
THAT'S OKAY. I FORGIVE YOU.

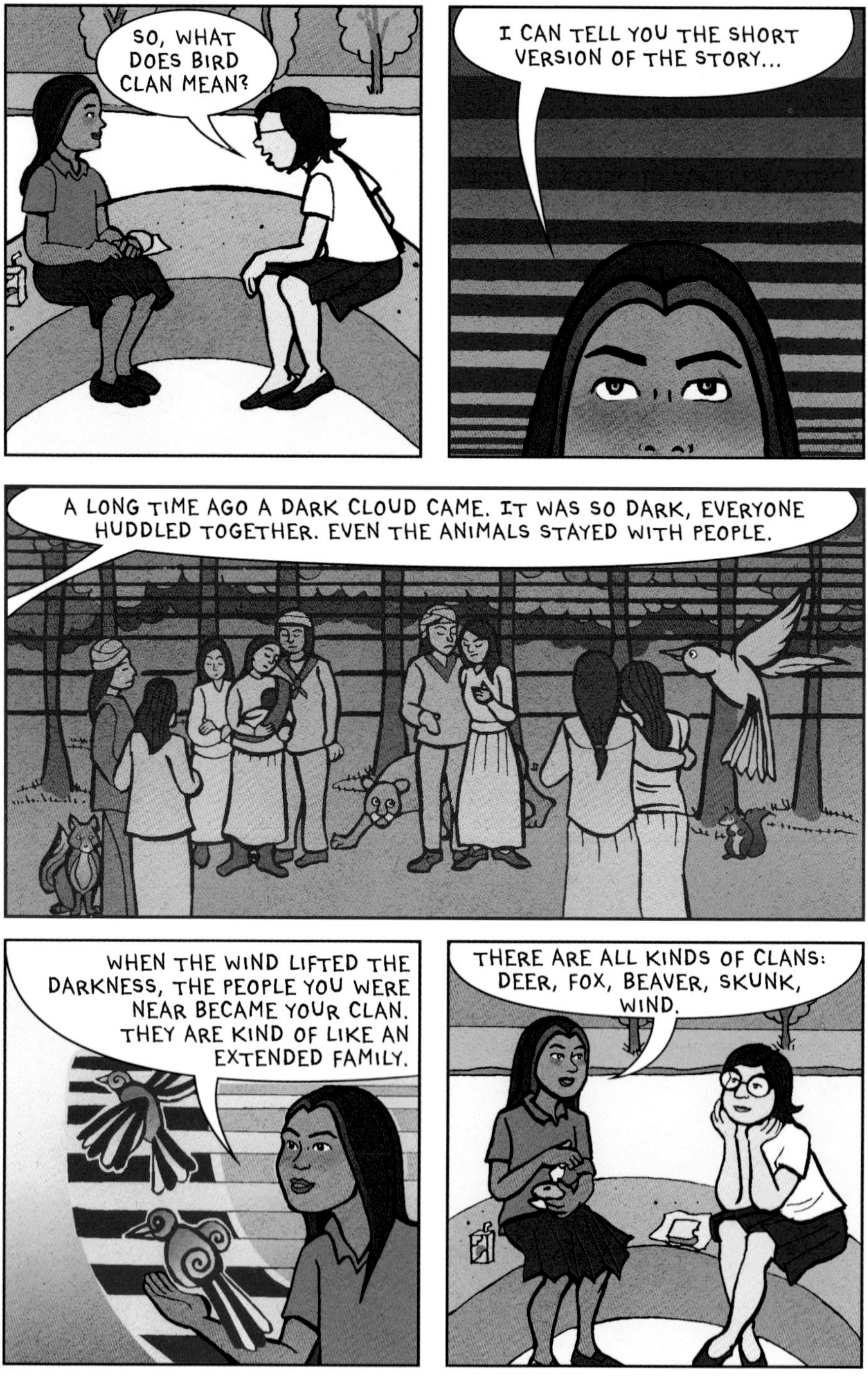
SO, WHAT DOES BIRD CLAN MEAN?
I CAN TELL YOU THE SHORT VERSION OF THE STORY...
A LONG TIME AGO A DARK CLOUD CAME. IT WAS SO DARK, EVERYONE HUDDLED TOGETHER. EVEN THE ANIMALS STAYED WITH PEOPLE.
WHEN THE WIND LIFTED THE DARKNESS, THE PEOPLE YOU WERE NEAR BECAME YOUR CLAN. THEY ARE KIND OF LIKE AN EXTENDED FAMILY.
THERE ARE ALL KINDS OF CLANS: DEER, FOX, BEAVER, SKUNK, WIND.

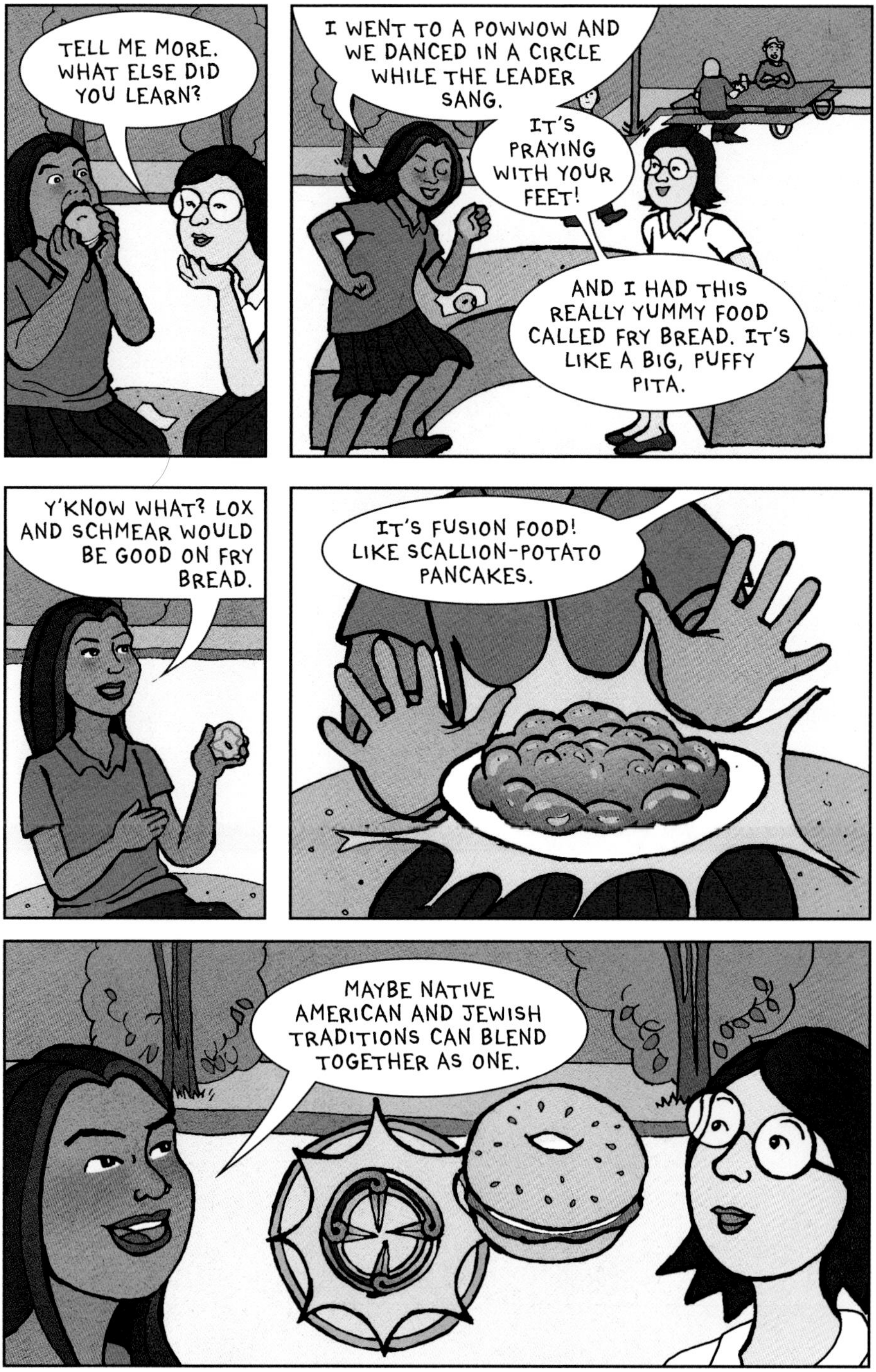
TELL ME MORE. WHAT ELSE DID YOU LEARN?
I WENT TO A POWWOW AND WE DANCED IN A CIRCLE WHILE THE LEADER SANG.
IT'S PRAYING WITH YOUR FEET!
AND I HAD THIS REALLY YUMMY FOOD CALLED FRY BREAD. IT'S LIKE A BIG, PUFFY PITA.
Y'KNOW WHAT? LOX AND SCHMEAR WOULD BE GOOD ON FRY BREAD.
IT'S FUSION FOOD! LIKE SCALLION-POTATO PANCAKES.
MAYBE NATIVE AMERICAN AND JEWISH TRADITIONS CAN BLEND TOGETHER AS ONE.

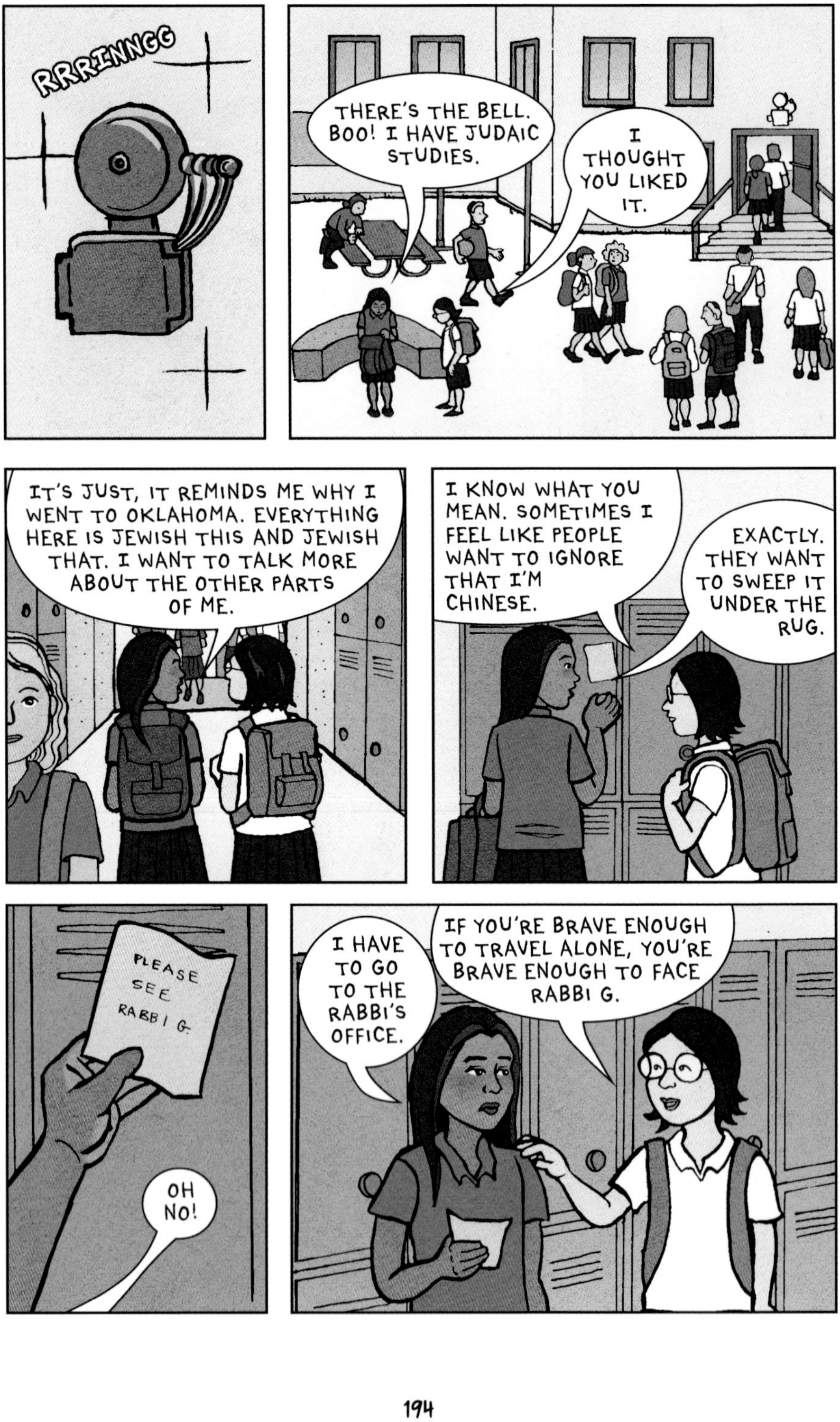
RRRINNGG
THERE'S THE BELL. BOO! I HAVE JUDAIC STUDIES.
I THOUGHT YOU LIKED IT.
IT'S JUST, IT REMINDS ME WHY I WENT TO OKLAHOMA. EVERYTHING HERE IS JEWISH THIS AND JEWISH THAT. I WANT TO TALK MORE ABOUT THE OTHER PARTS OF ME.
I KNOW WHAT YOU MEAN. SOMETIMES I FEEL LIKE PEOPLE WANT TO IGNORE THAT I'M CHINESE.
EXACTLY. THEY WANT TO SWEEP IT UNDER THE RUG.
PLEASE SEE RABBI G.
OH NO!
I HAVE TO GO TO THE RABBI'S OFFICE.
IF YOU'RE BRAVE ENOUGH TO TRAVEL ALONE, YOU'RE BRAVE ENOUGH TO FACE RABBI G.

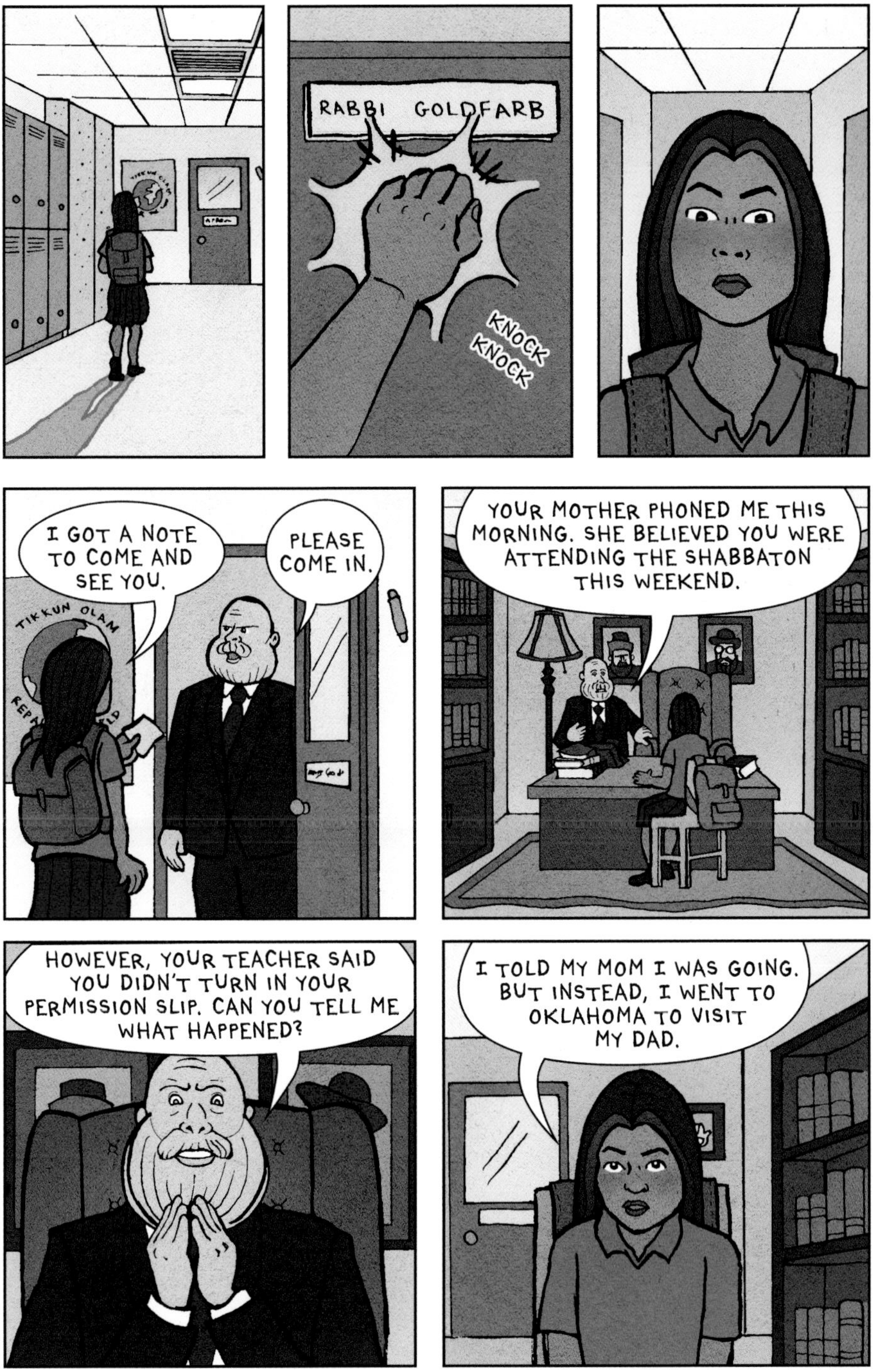
RABBI GOLDFARB
KNOCK KNOCK
I GOT A NOTE TO COME AND SEE YOU.
PLEASE COME IN.
TIKKUN OLAM
YOUR MOTHER PHONED ME THIS MORNING. SHE BELIEVED YOU WERE ATTENDING THE SHABBATON THIS WEEKEND.
HOWEVER, YOUR TEACHER SAID YOU DIDN'T TURN IN YOUR PERMISSION SLIP. CAN YOU TELL ME WHAT HAPPENED?
I TOLD MY MOM I WAS GOING. BUT INSTEAD, I WENT TO OKLAHOMA TO VISIT MY DAD.

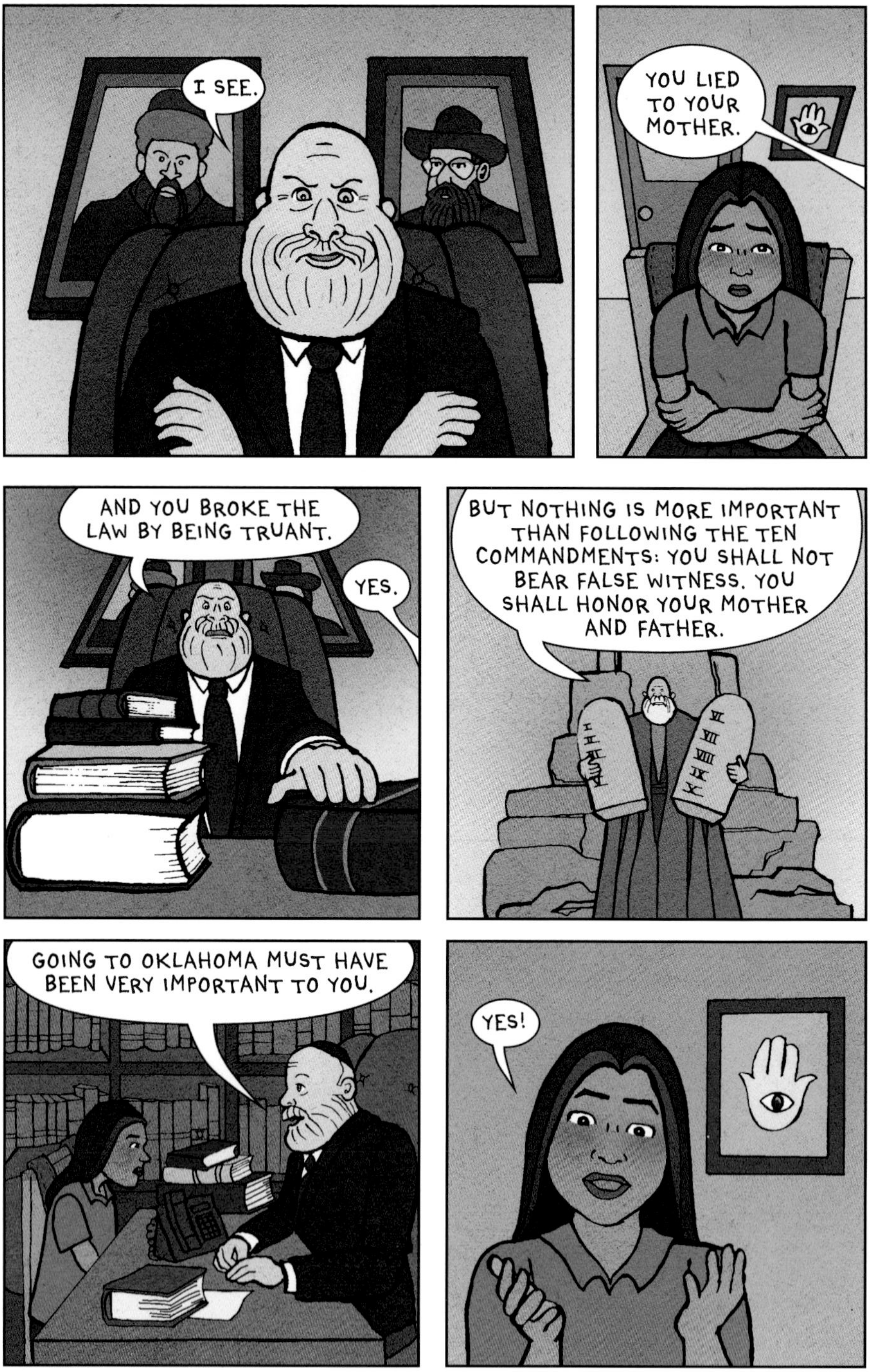
I SEE.
YOU LIED TO YOUR MOTHER.
AND YOU BROKE THE LAW BY BEING TRUANT.
YES.
BUT NOTHING IS MORE IMPORTANT THAN FOLLOWING THE TEN COMMANDMENTS: YOU SHALL NOT BEAR FALSE WITNESS. YOU SHALL HONOR YOUR MOTHER AND FATHER.
GOING TO OKLAHOMA MUST HAVE BEEN VERY IMPORTANT TO YOU.
YES!

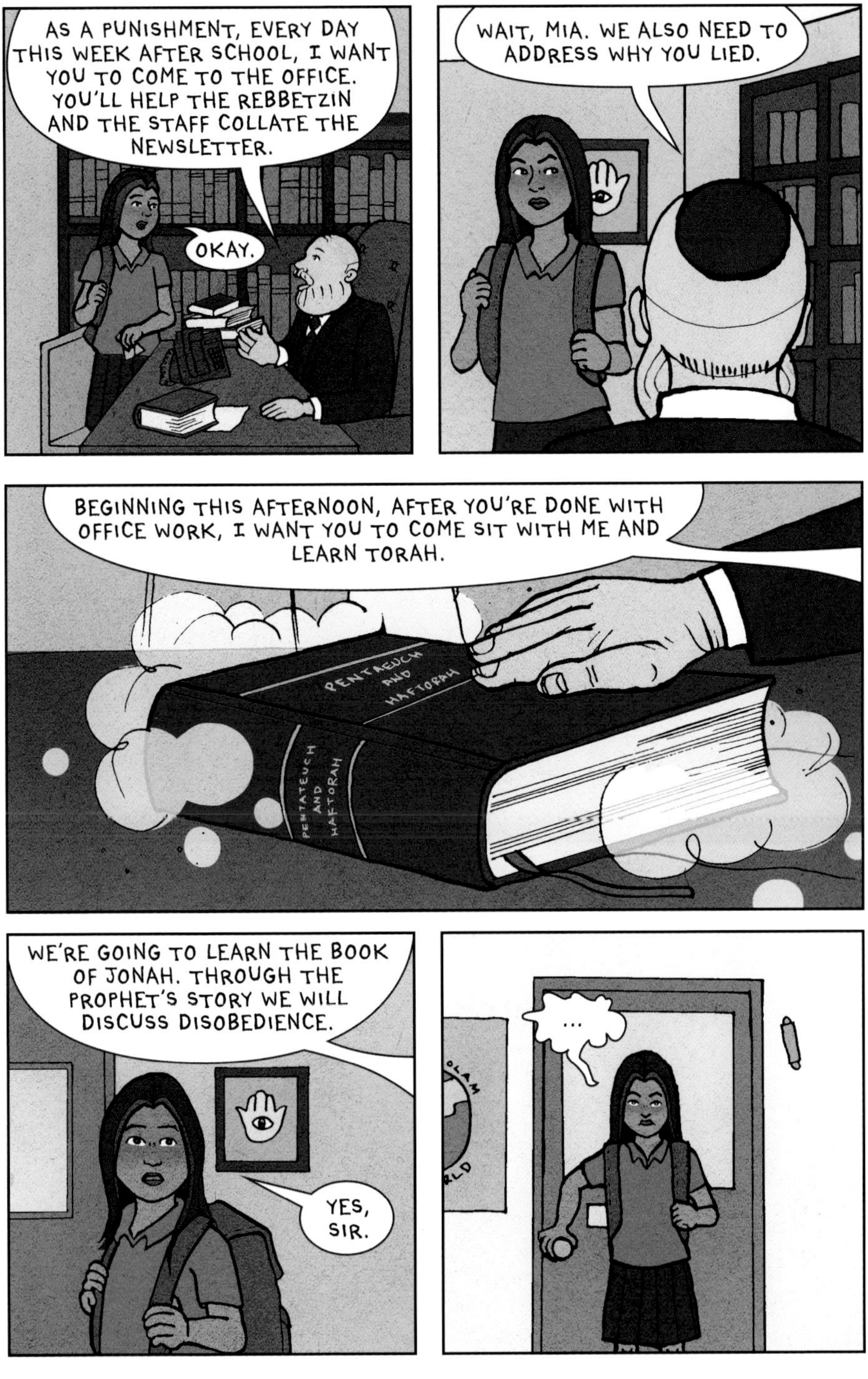
AS A PUNISHMENT, EVERY DAY THIS WEEK AFTER SCHOOL, I WANT YOU TO COME TO THE OFFICE. YOU'LL HELP THE REBBETZIN AND THE STAFF COLLATE THE NEWSLETTER.
OKAY.
WAIT, MIA. WE ALSO NEED TO ADDRESS WHY YOU LIED.
BEGINNING THIS AFTERNOON, AFTER YOU'RE DONE WITH OFFICE WORK, I WANT YOU TO COME SIT WITH ME AND LEARN TORAH.
PENTATEUCH AND HAFTORAH
PENTATEUCH AND HAFTORAH
WE'RE GOING TO LEARN THE BOOK OF JONAH. THROUGH THE PROPHET'S STORY WE WILL DISCUSS DISOBEDIENCE.
YES, SIR.
...

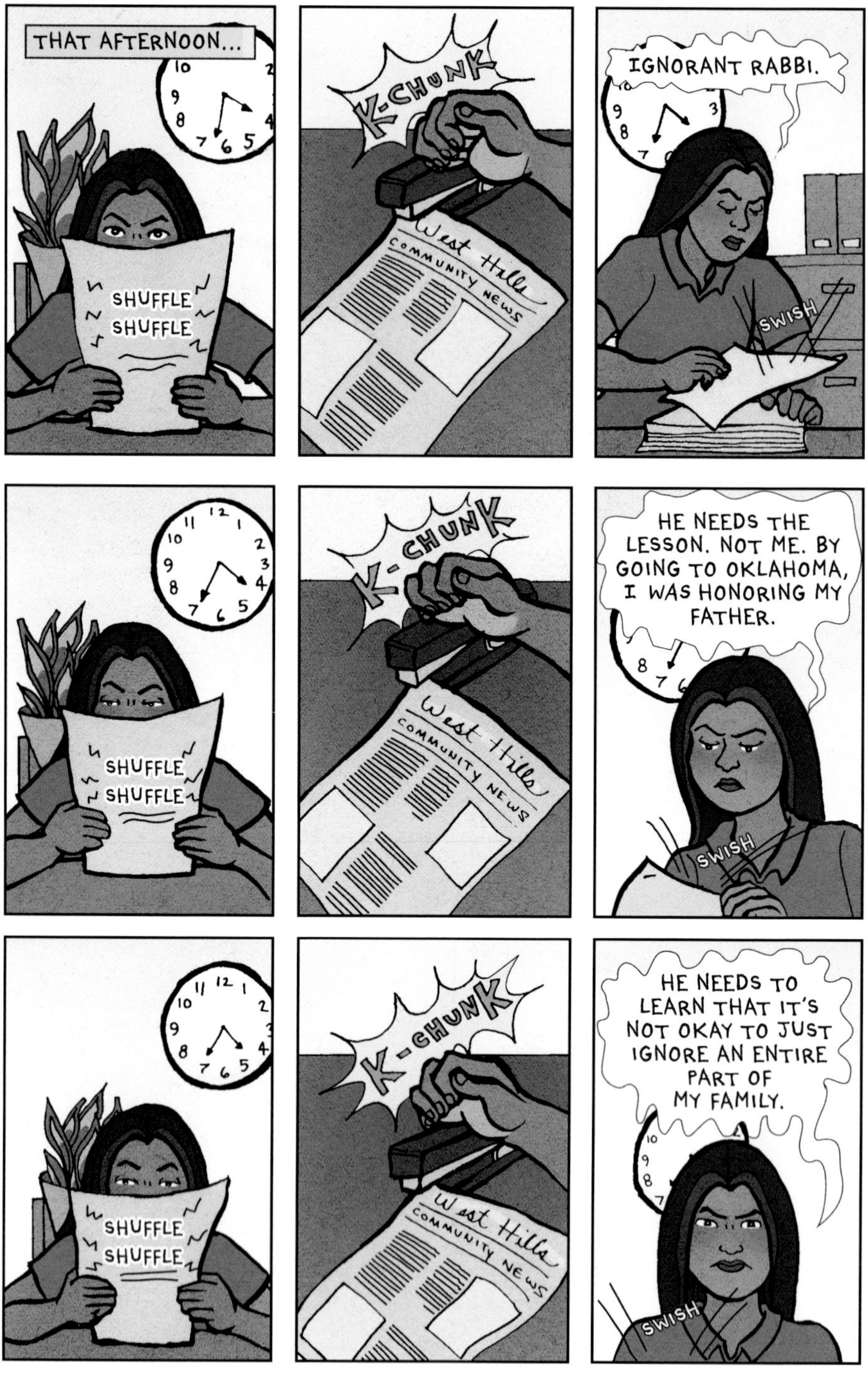
THAT AFTERNOON...
SHUFFLE SHUFFLE
K-CHUNK
West Hills COMMUNITY NEWS
IGNORANT RABBI.
SWISH
SHUFFLE SHUFFLE
K-CHUNK
West Hills COMMUNITY NEWS
HE NEEDS THE LESSON. NOT ME. BY GOING TO OKLAHOMA, I WAS HONORING MY FATHER.
SWISH
SHUFFLE SHUFFLE
K-CHUNK
West Hills COMMUNITY NEWS
HE NEEDS TO LEARN THAT IT'S NOT OKAY TO JUST IGNORE AN ENTIRE PART OF MY FAMILY.
SWISH

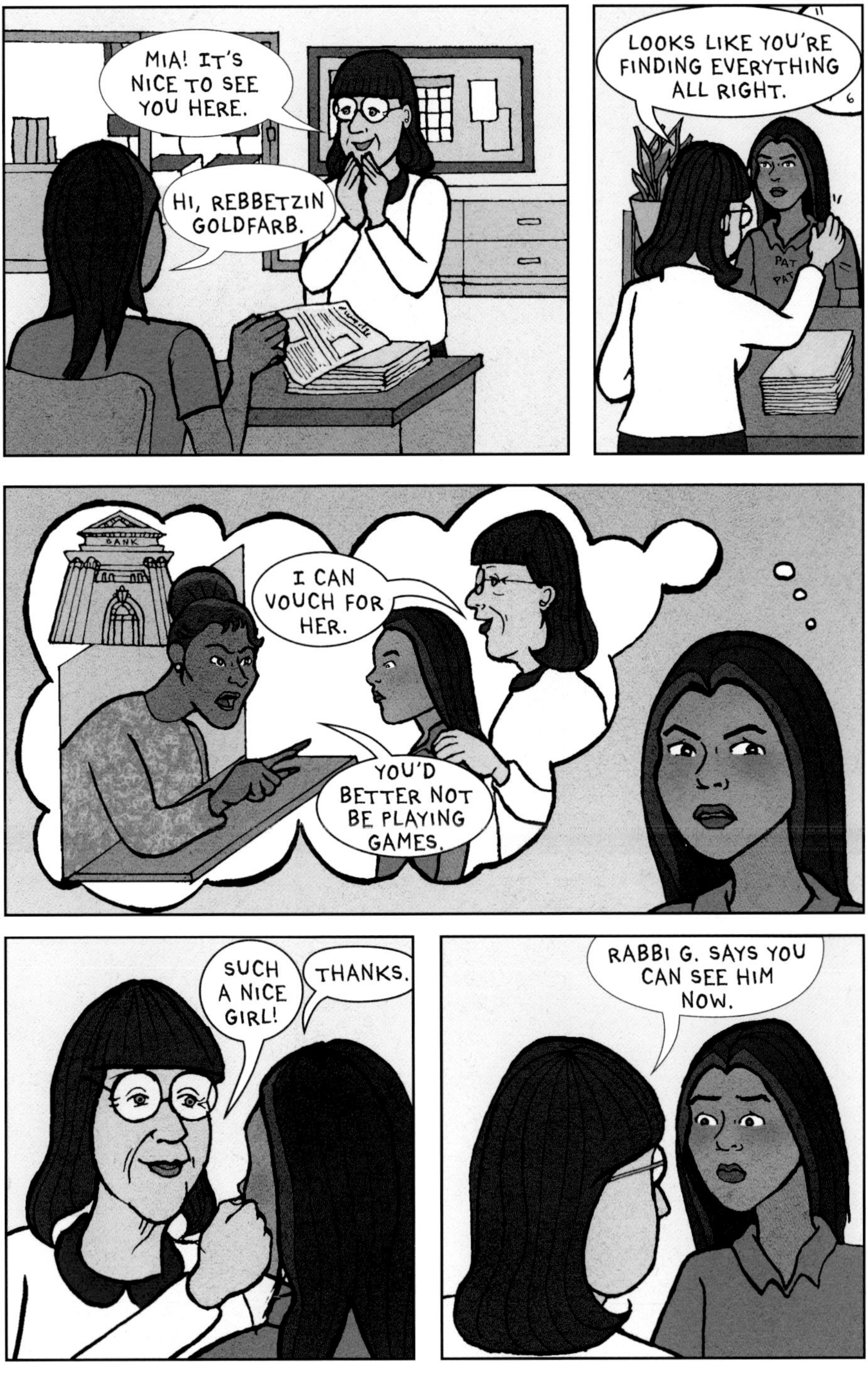
MIA! IT'S NICE TO SEE YOU HERE.
HI, REBBETZIN GOLDFARB.
LOOKS LIKE YOU'RE FINDING EVERYTHING ALL RIGHT.
PAT PAT
BANK
I CAN VOUCH FOR HER.
YOU'D BETTER NOT BE PLAYING GAMES.
SUCH A NICE GIRL!
THANKS.
RABBI G. SAYS YOU CAN SEE HIM NOW.

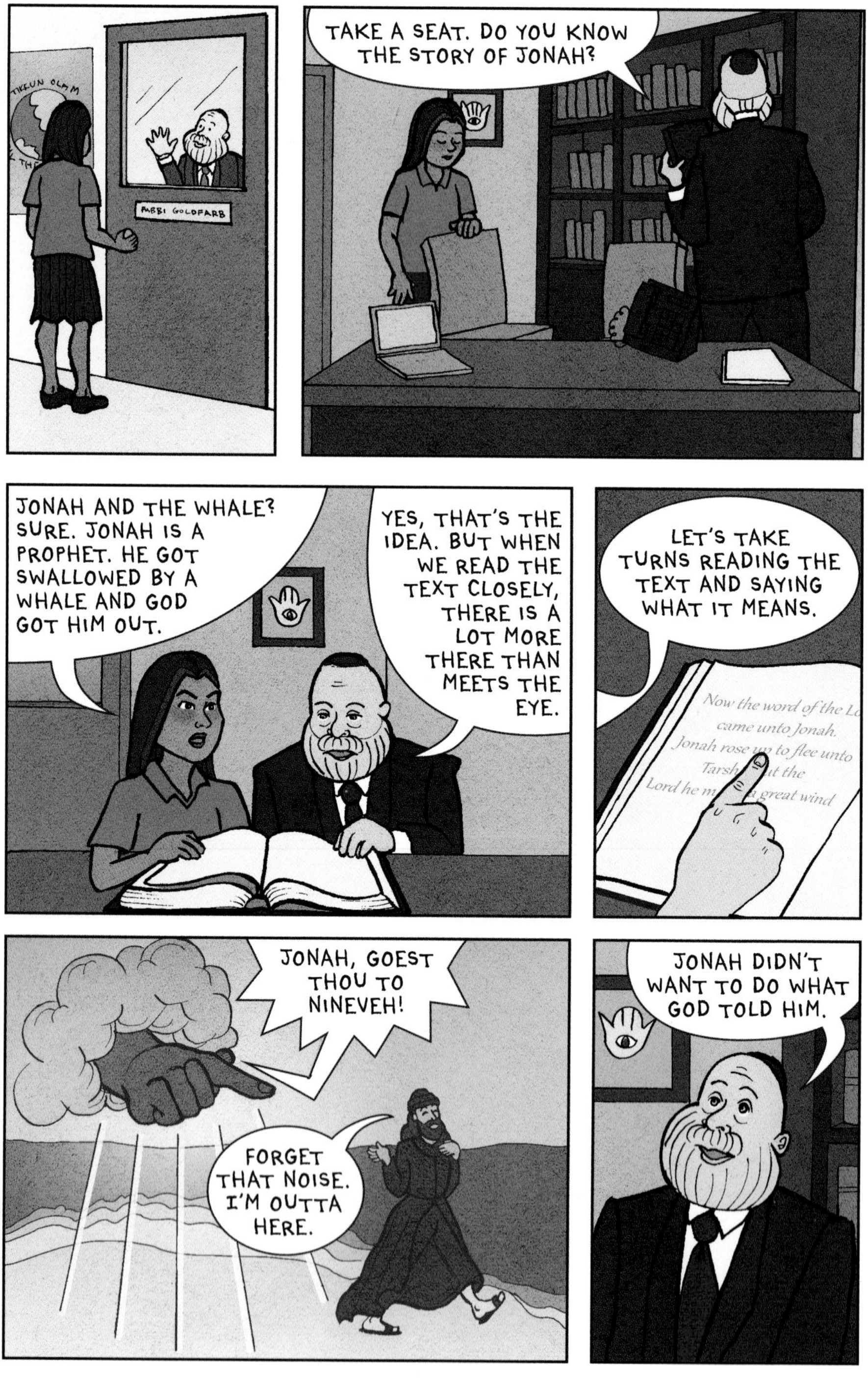
TIKKUN OLAM
RABBI GOLDFARB
TAKE A SEAT. DO YOU KNOW THE STORY OF JONAH?
JONAH AND THE WHALE? SURE. JONAH IS A PROPHET. HE GOT SWALLOWED BY A WHALE AND GOD GOT HIM OUT.
YES, THAT'S THE IDEA. BUT WHEN WE READ THE TEXT CLOSELY, THERE IS A LOT MORE THERE THAN MEETS THE EYE.
LET'S TAKE TURNS READING THE TEXT AND SAYING WHAT IT MEANS.
came unto Jonah.
JONAH, GOEST THOU TO NINEVEH!
FORGET THAT NOISE. I'M OUTTA HERE.
JONAH DIDN'T WANT TO DO WHAT GOD TOLD HIM.

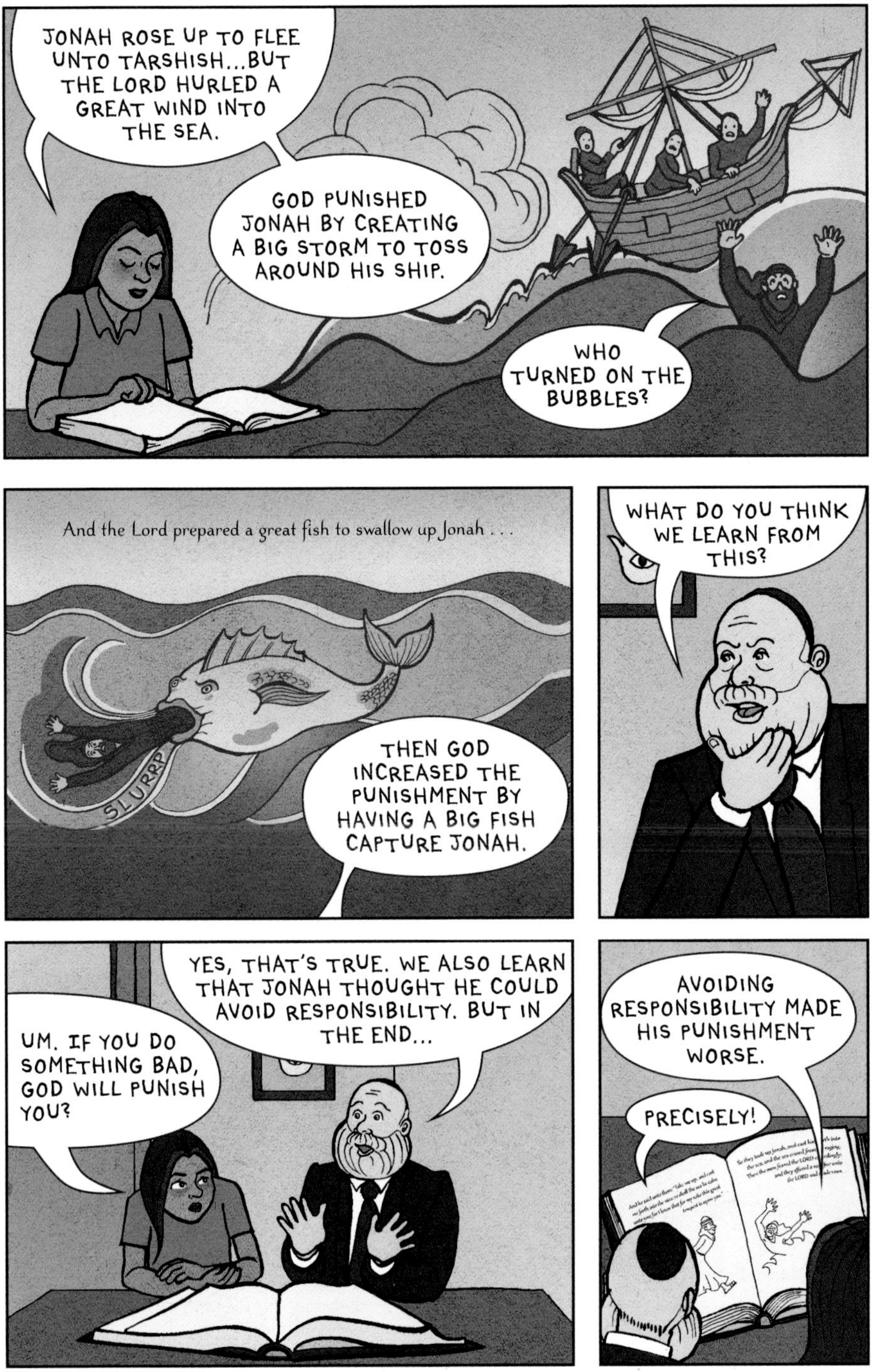
JONAH ROSE UP TO FLEE UNTO TARSHISH...BUT THE LORD HURLED A GREAT WIND INTO THE SEA.
GOD PUNISHED JONAH BY CREATING A BIG STORM TO TOSS AROUND HIS SHIP.
WHO TURNED ON THE BUBBLES?
And the Lord prepared a great fish to swallow up Jonah . . .
SLURRP
THEN GOD INCREASED THE PUNISHMENT BY HAVING A BIG FISH CAPTURE JONAH.
WHAT DO YOU THINK WE LEARN FROM THIS?
UM. IF YOU DO SOMETHING BAD, GOD WILL PUNISH YOU?
YES, THAT'S TRUE. WE ALSO LEARN THAT JONAH THOUGHT HE COULD AVOID RESPONSIBILITY. BUT IN THE END...
AVOIDING RESPONSIBILITY MADE HIS PUNISHMENT WORSE.
PRECISELY!

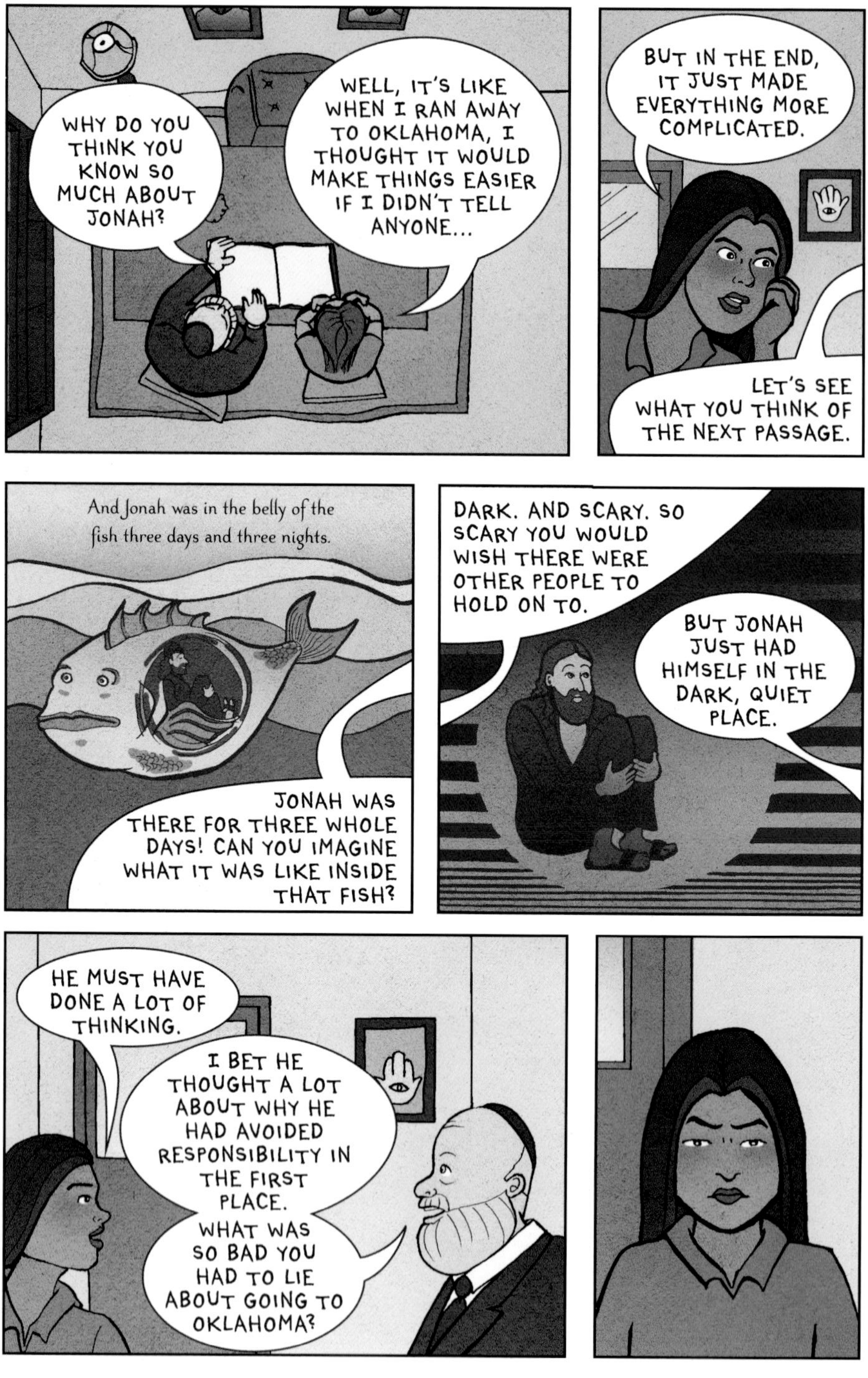
WHY DO YOU THINK YOU KNOW SO MUCH ABOUT JONAH?
WELL, IT'S LIKE WHEN I RAN AWAY TO OKLAHOMA, I THOUGHT IT WOULD MAKE THINGS EASIER IF I DIDN'T TELL ANYONE...
BUT IN THE END, IT JUST MADE EVERYTHING MORE COMPLICATED.
LET'S SEE WHAT YOU THINK OF THE NEXT PASSAGE.
And Jonah was in the belly of the fish three days and three nights.
JONAH WAS THERE FOR THREE WHOLE DAYS! CAN YOU IMAGINE WHAT IT WAS LIKE INSIDE THAT FISH?
DARK. AND SCARY. SO SCARY YOU WOULD WISH THERE WERE OTHER PEOPLE TO HOLD ON TO.
BUT JONAH JUST HAD HIMSELF IN THE DARK, QUIET PLACE.
HE MUST HAVE DONE A LOT OF THINKING.
I BET HE THOUGHT A LOT ABOUT WHY HE HAD AVOIDED RESPONSIBILITY IN THE FIRST PLACE.
WHAT WAS SO BAD YOU HAD TO LIE ABOUT GOING TO OKLAHOMA?

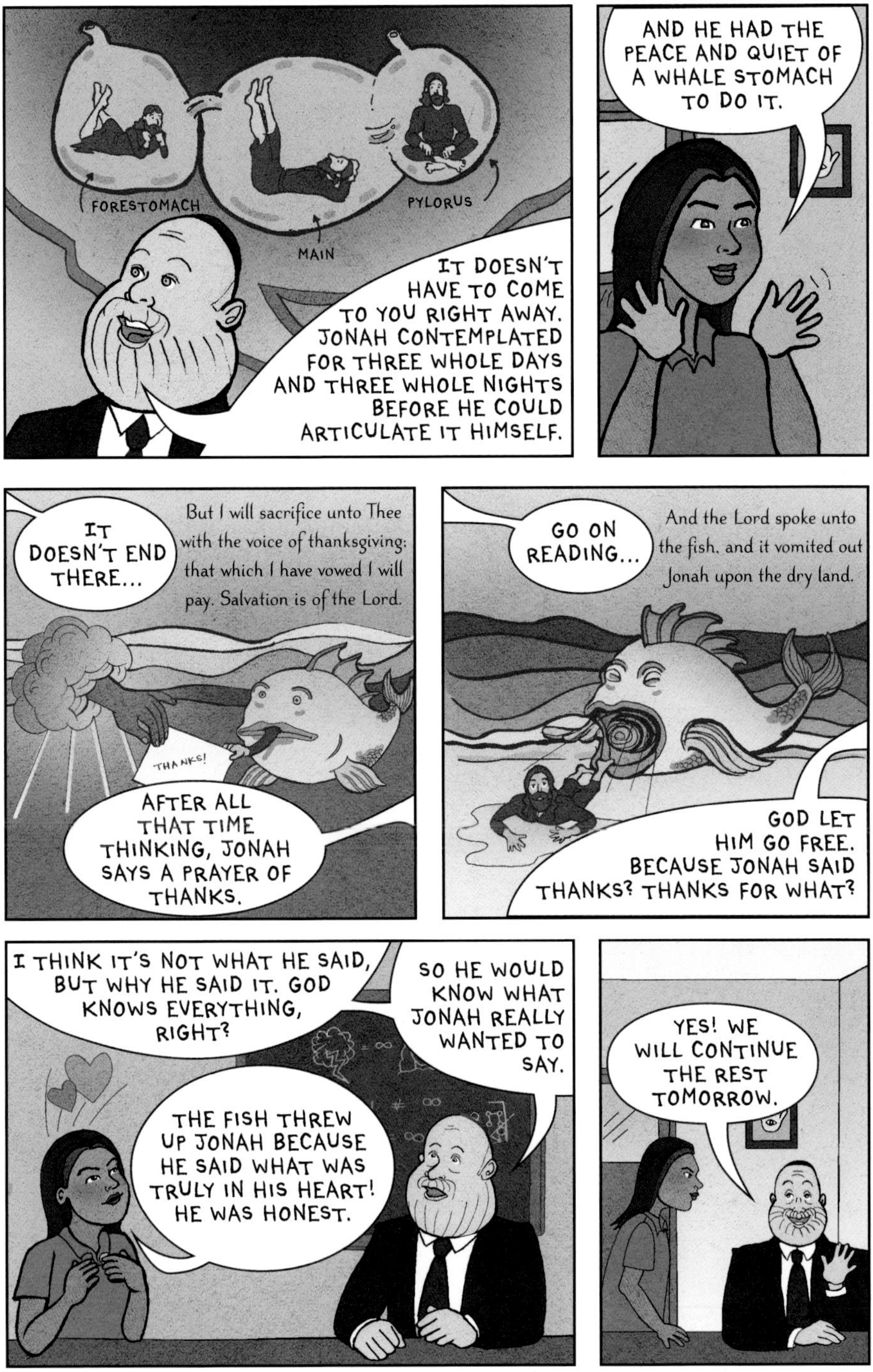
FORESTOMACH
MAIN
PYLORUS
IT DOESN'T HAVE TO COME TO YOU RIGHT AWAY. JONAH CONTEMPLATED FOR THREE WHOLE DAYS AND THREE WHOLE NIGHTS BEFORE HE COULD ARTICULATE IT HIMSELF.
AND HE HAD THE PEACE AND QUIET OF A WHALE STOMACH TO DO IT.
IT DOESN'T END THERE...
But I will sacrifice unto Thee with the voice of thanksgiving; that which I have vowed I will pay. Salvation is of the Lord.
THANKS!
AFTER ALL THAT TIME THINKING, JONAH SAYS A PRAYER OF THANKS.
GO ON READING...
And the Lord spoke unto the fish, and it vomited out Jonah upon the dry land.
GOD LET HIM GO FREE. BECAUSE JONAH SAID THANKS? THANKS FOR WHAT?
I THINK IT'S NOT WHAT HE SAID, BUT WHY HE SAID IT. GOD KNOWS EVERYTHING, RIGHT?
SO HE WOULD KNOW WHAT JONAH REALLY WANTED TO SAY.
THE FISH THREW UP JONAH BECAUSE HE SAID WHAT WAS TRULY IN HIS HEART! HE WAS HONEST.
YES! WE WILL CONTINUE THE REST TOMORROW.

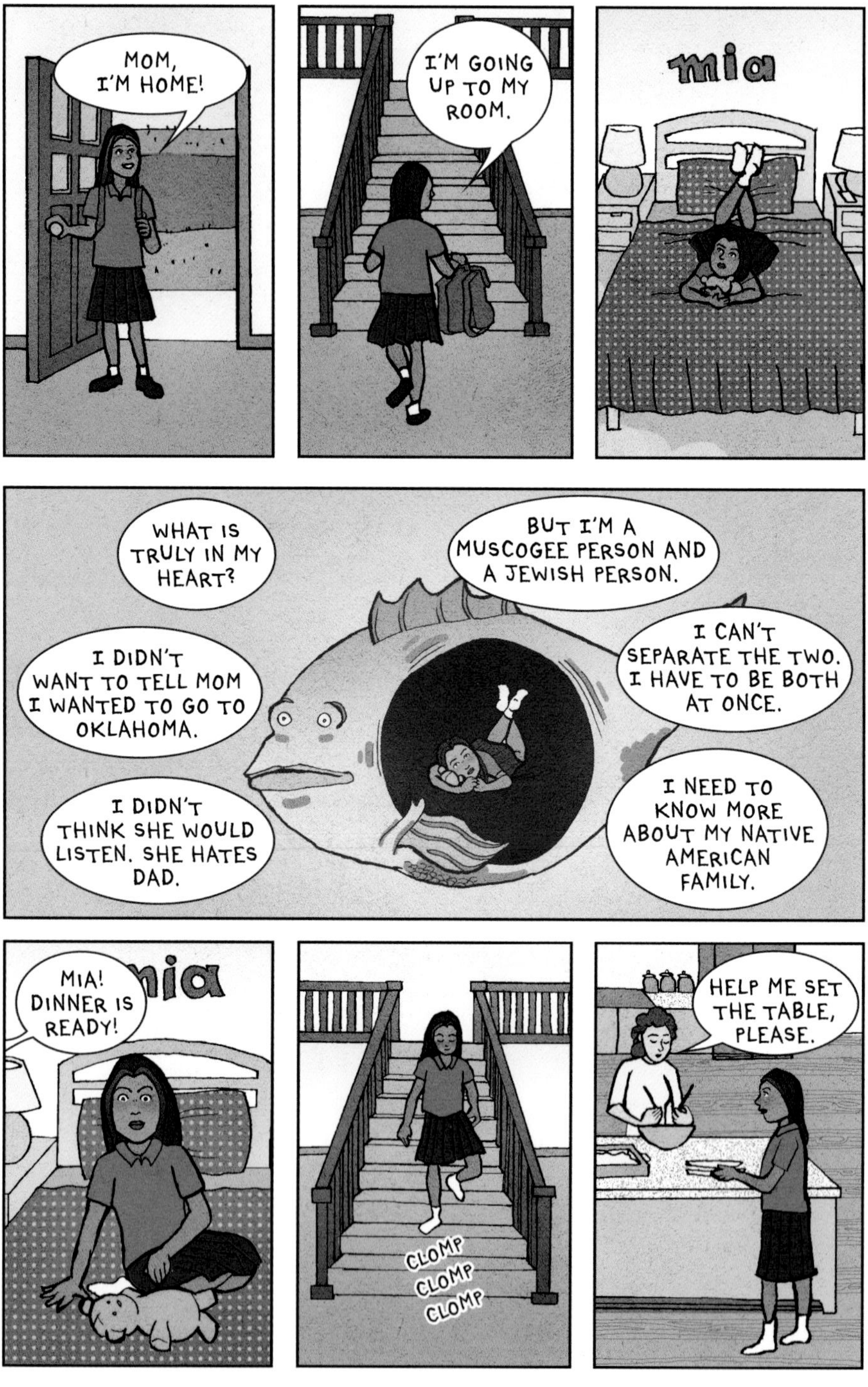
MOM, I'M HOME!
I'M GOING UP TO MY ROOM.
mia
WHAT IS TRULY IN MY HEART?
BUT I'M A MUSCOGEE PERSON AND A JEWISH PERSON.
I DIDN'T WANT TO TELL MOM I WANTED TO GO TO OKLAHOMA.
I CAN'T SEPARATE THE TWO. I HAVE TO BE BOTH AT ONCE.
I DIDN'T THINK SHE WOULD LISTEN. SHE HATES DAD.
I NEED TO KNOW MORE ABOUT MY NATIVE AMERICAN FAMILY.
MIA! DINNER IS READY!
CLOMP
CLOMP
CLOMP
HELP ME SET THE TABLE, PLEASE.

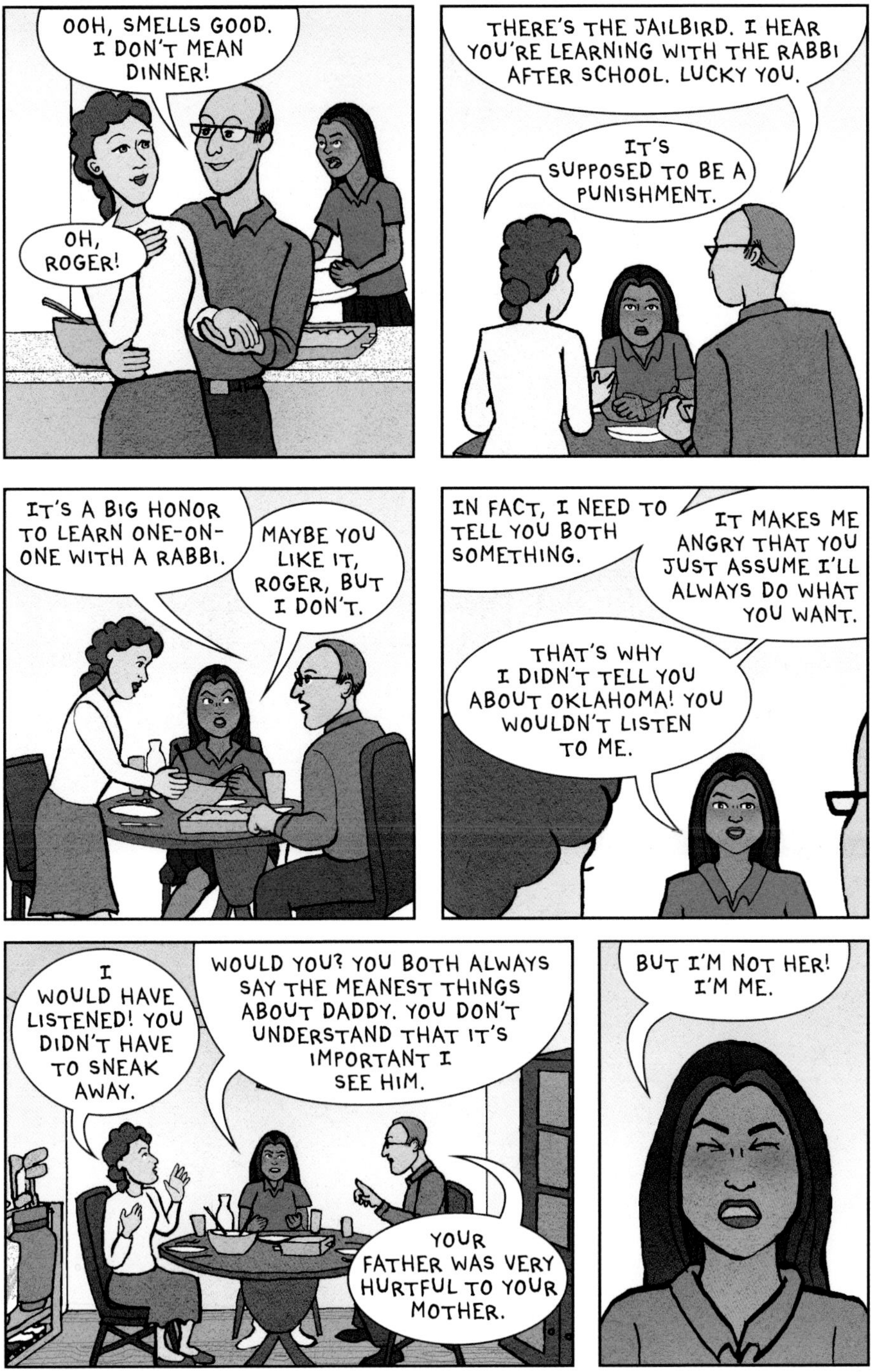
OOH, SMELLS GOOD. I DON'T MEAN DINNER!
OH, ROGER!
THERE'S THE JAILBIRD. I HEAR YOU'RE LEARNING WITH THE RABBI AFTER SCHOOL. LUCKY YOU.
IT'S SUPPOSED TO BE A PUNISHMENT.
IT'S A BIG HONOR TO LEARN ONE-ON-ONE WITH A RABBI.
MAYBE YOU LIKE IT, ROGER, BUT I DON'T.
IN FACT, I NEED TO TELL YOU BOTH SOMETHING.
IT MAKES ME ANGRY THAT YOU JUST ASSUME I'LL ALWAYS DO WHAT YOU WANT.
THAT'S WHY I DIDN'T TELL YOU ABOUT OKLAHOMA! YOU WOULDN'T LISTEN TO ME.
I WOULD HAVE LISTENED! YOU DIDN'T HAVE TO SNEAK AWAY.
WOULD YOU? YOU BOTH ALWAYS SAY THE MEANEST THINGS ABOUT DADDY. YOU DON'T UNDERSTAND THAT IT'S IMPORTANT I SEE HIM.
YOUR FATHER WAS VERY HURTFUL TO YOUR MOTHER.
BUT I'M NOT HER! I'M ME.

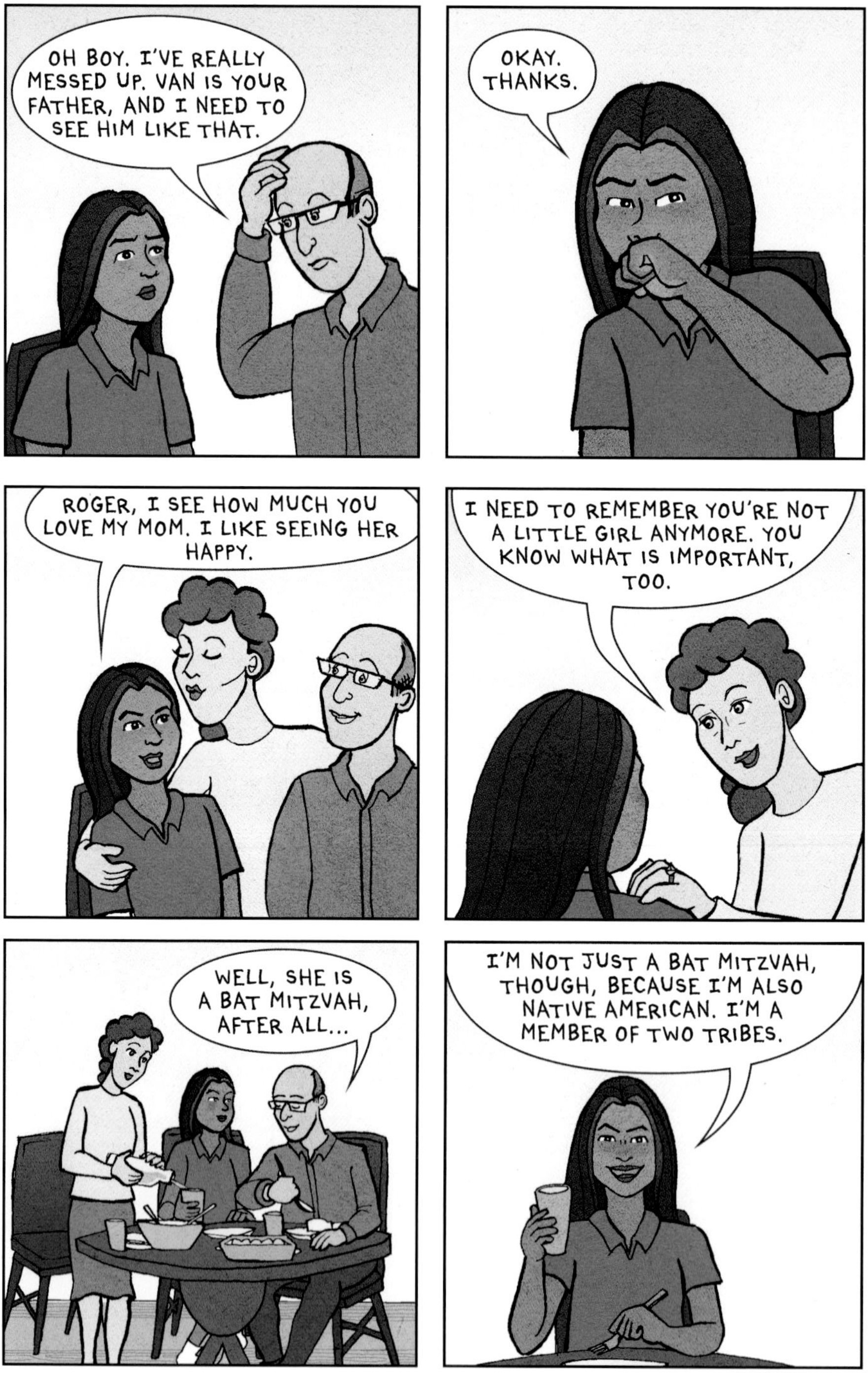
OH BOY. I'VE REALLY MESSED UP. VAN IS YOUR FATHER, AND I NEED TO SEE HIM LIKE THAT.
OKAY. THANKS.
ROGER, I SEE HOW MUCH YOU LOVE MY MOM. I LIKE SEEING HER HAPPY.
I NEED TO REMEMBER YOU'RE NOT A LITTLE GIRL ANYMORE. YOU KNOW WHAT IS IMPORTANT, TOO.
WELL, SHE IS A BAT MITZVAH, AFTER ALL...
I'M NOT JUST A BAT MITZVAH, THOUGH, BECAUSE I'M ALSO NATIVE AMERICAN. I'M A MEMBER OF TWO TRIBES.

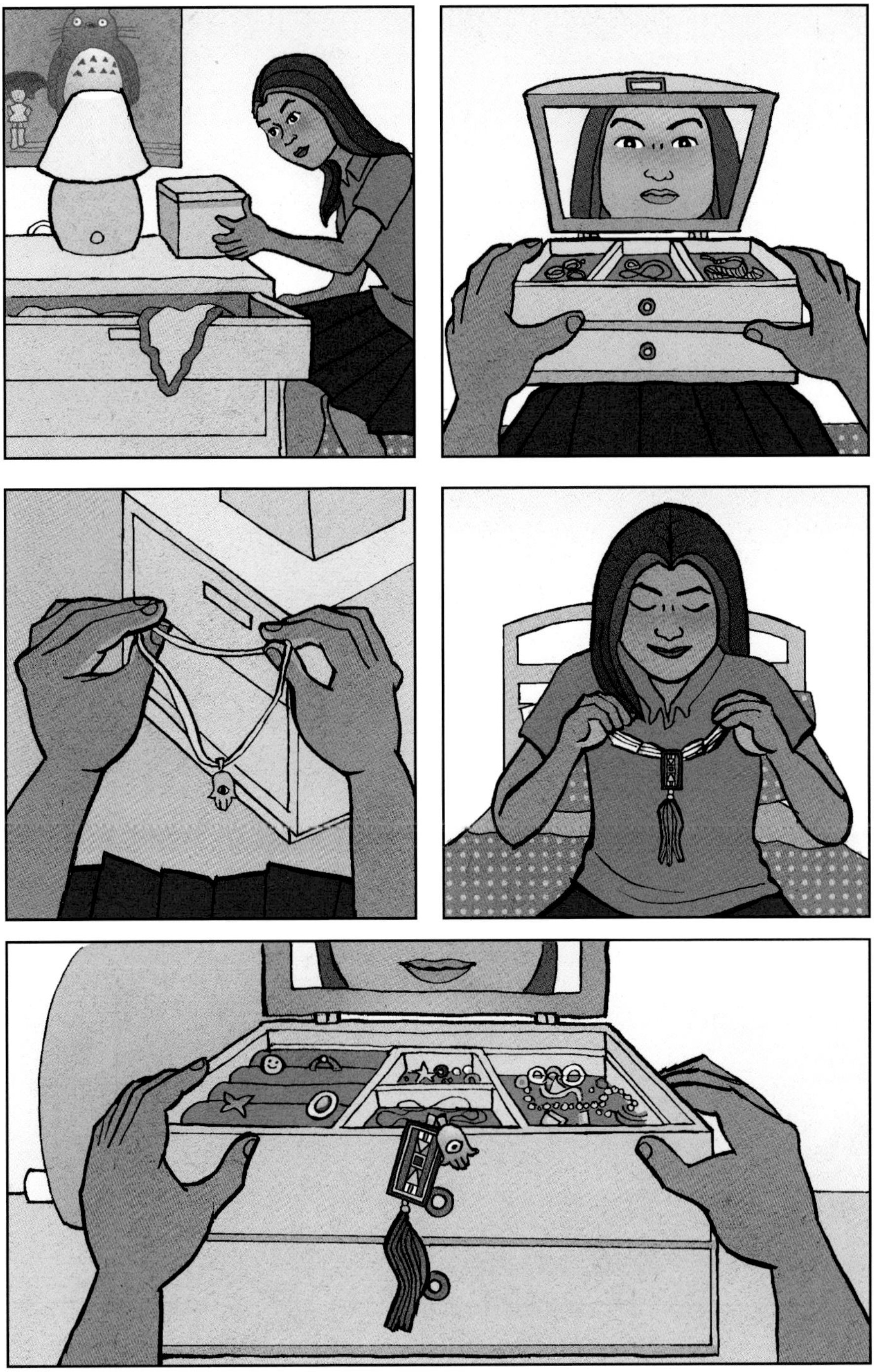

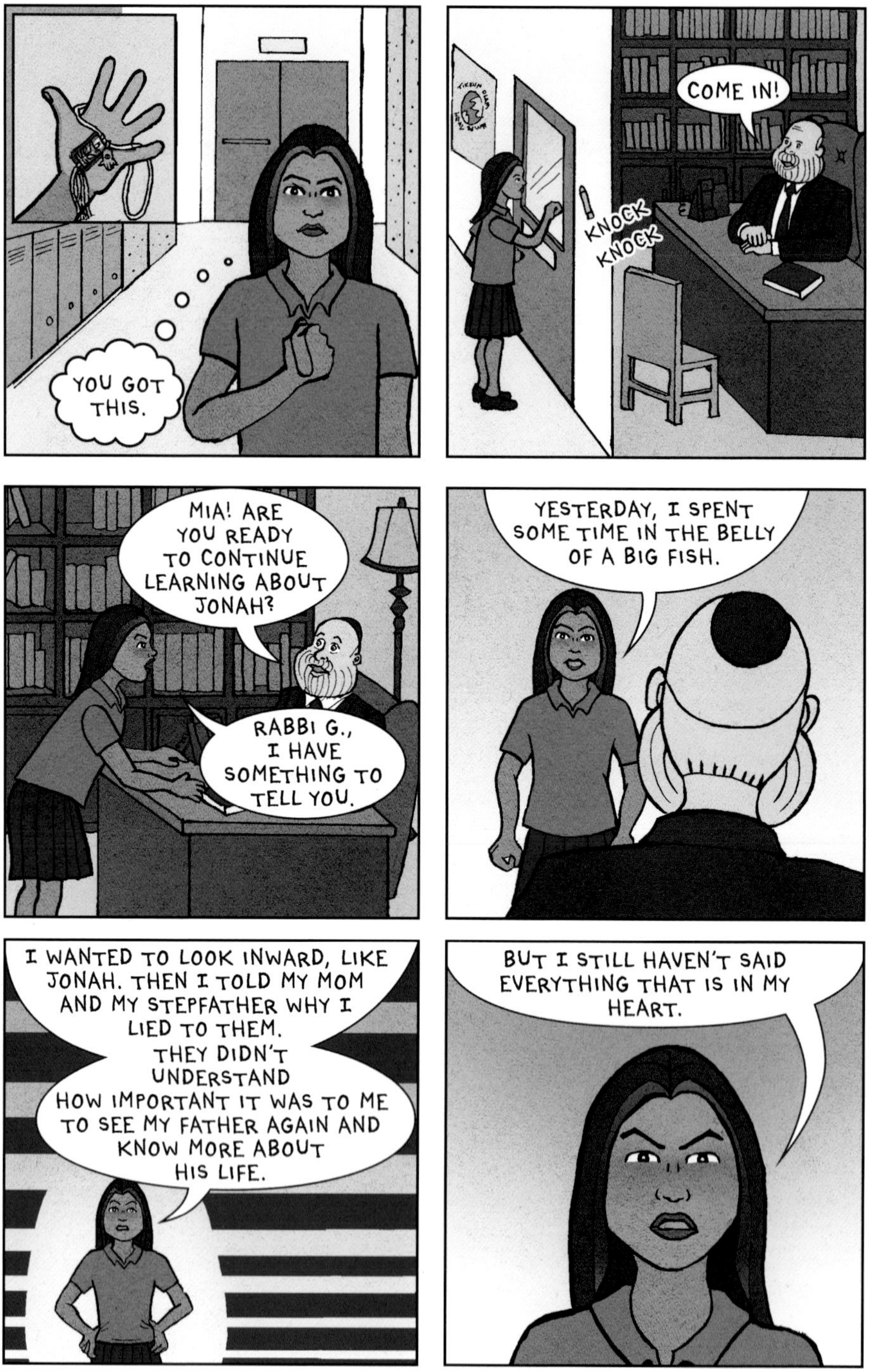
YOU GOT THIS.
COME IN!
KNOCK KNOCK
MIA! ARE YOU READY TO CONTINUE LEARNING ABOUT JONAH?
RABBI G., I HAVE SOMETHING TO TELL YOU.
YESTERDAY, I SPENT SOME TIME IN THE BELLY OF A BIG FISH.
I WANTED TO LOOK INWARD, LIKE JONAH. THEN I TOLD MY MOM AND MY STEPFATHER WHY I LIED TO THEM. THEY DIDN'T UNDERSTAND HOW IMPORTANT IT WAS TO ME TO SEE MY FATHER AGAIN AND KNOW MORE ABOUT HIS LIFE.
BUT I STILL HAVEN'T SAID EVERYTHING THAT IS IN MY HEART.

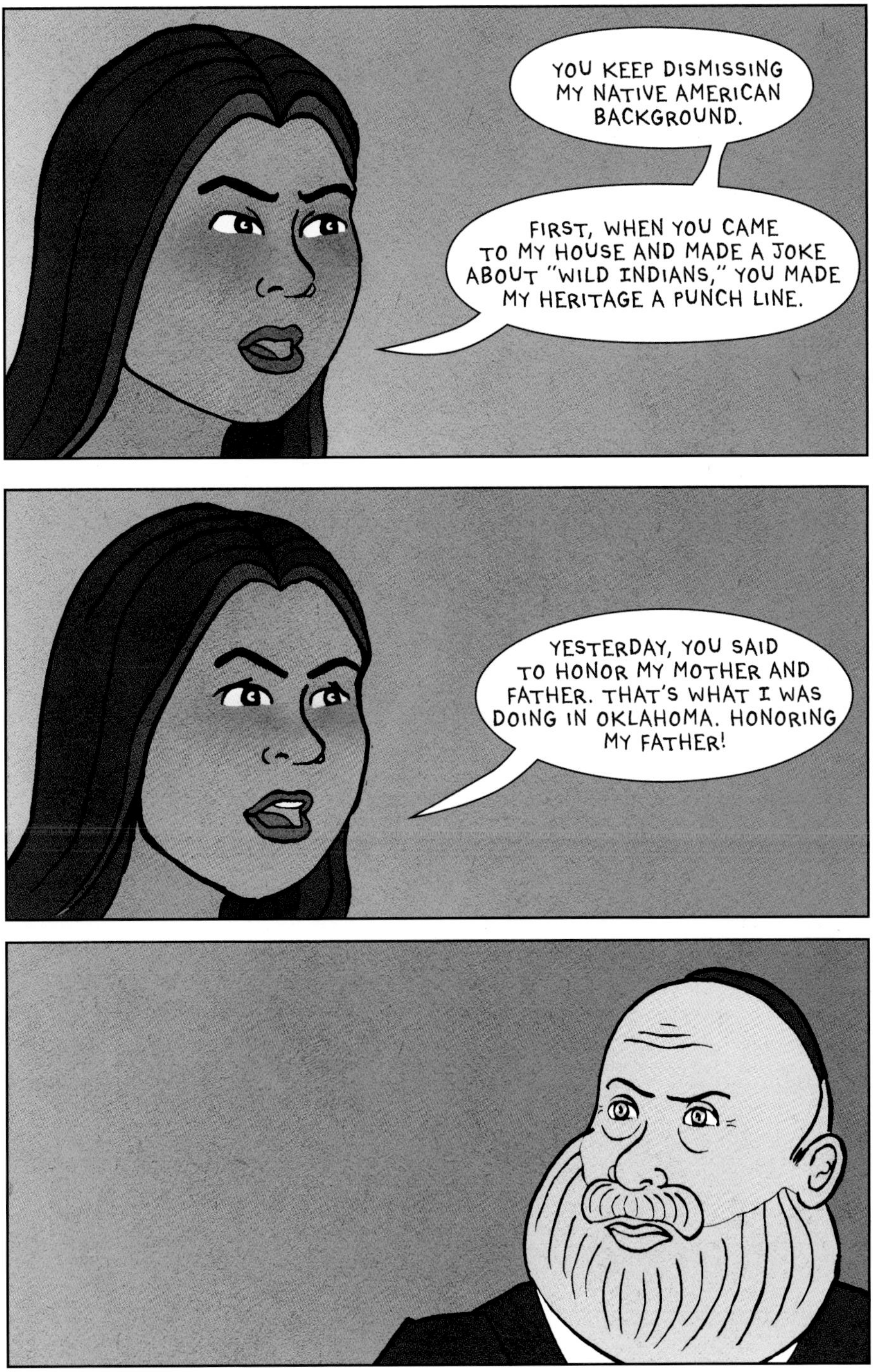
YOU KEEP DISMISSING MY NATIVE AMERICAN BACKGROUND.
FIRST, WHEN YOU CAME TO MY HOUSE AND MADE A JOKE ABOUT "WILD INDIANS," YOU MADE MY HERITAGE A PUNCH LINE.
YESTERDAY, YOU SAID TO HONOR MY MOTHER AND FATHER. THAT'S WHAT I WAS DOING IN OKLAHOMA. HONORING MY FATHER!

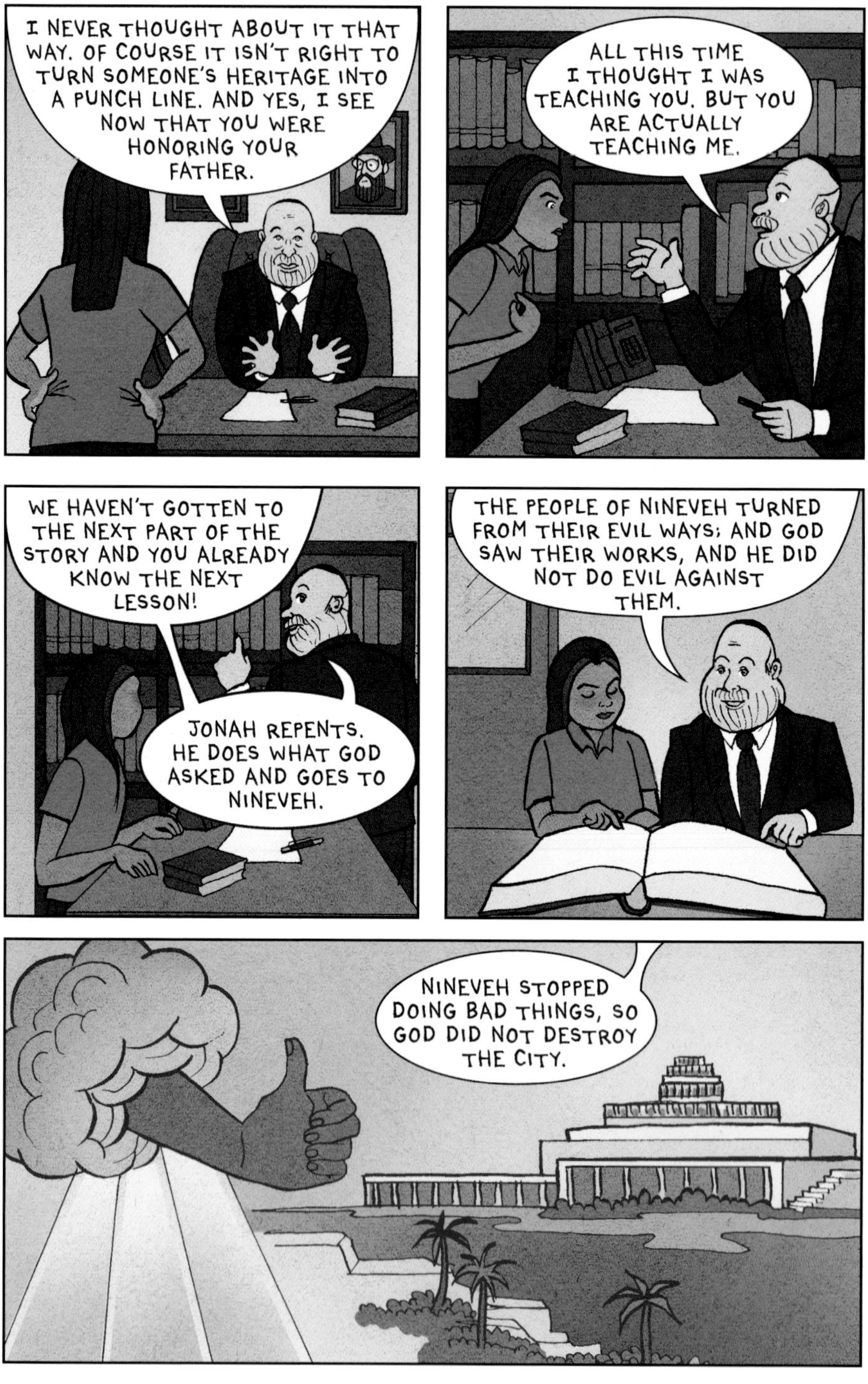
I NEVER THOUGHT ABOUT IT THAT WAY. OF COURSE IT ISN'T RIGHT TO TURN SOMEONE'S HERITAGE INTO A PUNCH LINE. AND YES, I SEE NOW THAT YOU WERE HONORING YOUR FATHER.
ALL THIS TIME I THOUGHT I WAS TEACHING YOU. BUT YOU ARE ACTUALLY TEACHING ME.
WE HAVEN'T GOTTEN TO THE NEXT PART OF THE STORY AND YOU ALREADY KNOW THE NEXT LESSON!
JONAH REPENTS. HE DOES WHAT GOD ASKED AND GOES TO NINEVEH.
THE PEOPLE OF NINEVEH TURNED FROM THEIR EVIL WAYS; AND GOD SAW THEIR WORKS, AND HE DID NOT DO EVIL AGAINST THEM.
NINEVEH STOPPED DOING BAD THINGS, SO GOD DID NOT DESTROY THE CITY.

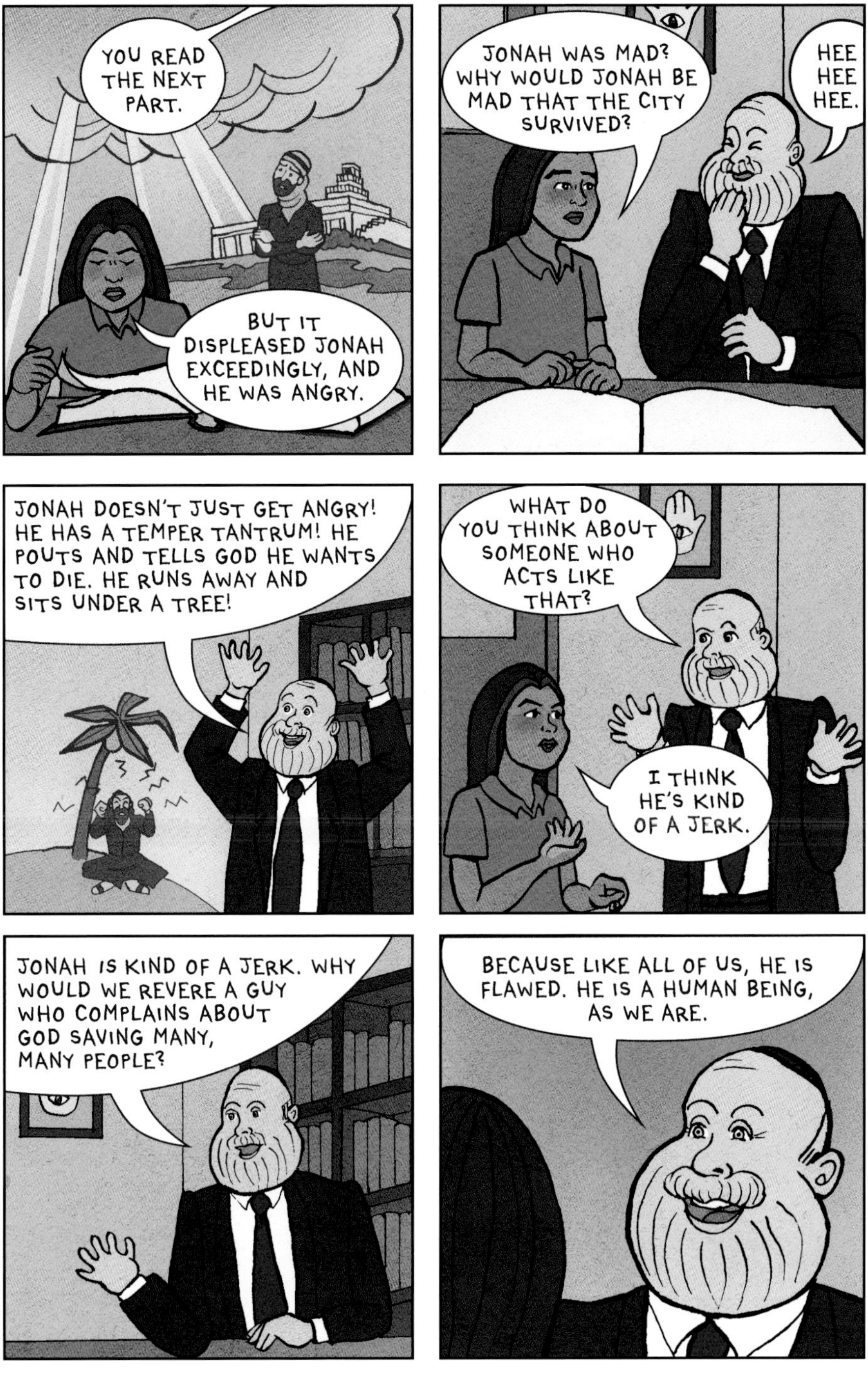
YOU READ THE NEXT PART.
BUT IT DISPLEASED JONAH EXCEEDINGLY, AND HE WAS ANGRY.
JONAH WAS MAD? WHY WOULD JONAH BE MAD THAT THE CITY SURVIVED?
HEE HEE HEE.
JONAH DOESN'T JUST GET ANGRY! HE HAS A TEMPER TANTRUM! HE POUTS AND TELLS GOD HE WANTS TO DIE. HE RUNS AWAY AND SITS UNDER A TREE!
WHAT DO YOU THINK ABOUT SOMEONE WHO ACTS LIKE THAT?
I THINK HE'S KIND OF A JERK.
JONAH IS KIND OF A JERK. WHY WOULD WE REVERE A GUY WHO COMPLAINS ABOUT GOD SAVING MANY, MANY PEOPLE?
BECAUSE LIKE ALL OF US, HE IS FLAWED. HE IS A HUMAN BEING, AS WE ARE.

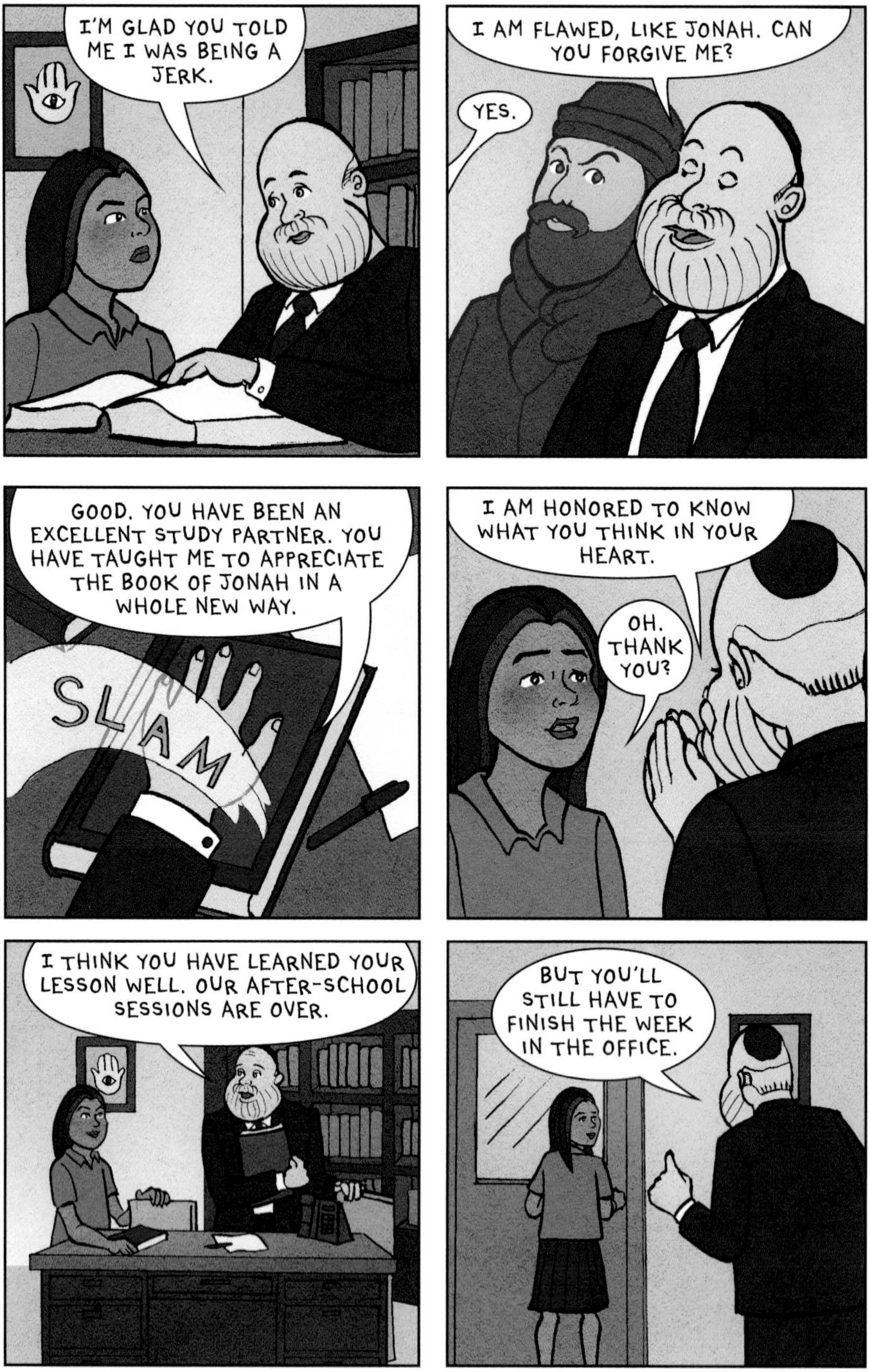
I'M GLAD YOU TOLD ME I WAS BEING A JERK.
I AM FLAWED, LIKE JONAH. CAN YOU FORGIVE ME?
YES.
GOOD. YOU HAVE BEEN AN EXCELLENT STUDY PARTNER. YOU HAVE TAUGHT ME TO APPRECIATE THE BOOK OF JONAH IN A WHOLE NEW WAY.
SLAM
I AM HONORED TO KNOW WHAT YOU THINK IN YOUR HEART.
OH. THANK YOU?
I THINK YOU HAVE LEARNED YOUR LESSON WELL. OUR AFTER-SCHOOL SESSIONS ARE OVER.
BUT YOU'LL STILL HAVE TO FINISH THE WEEK IN THE OFFICE.

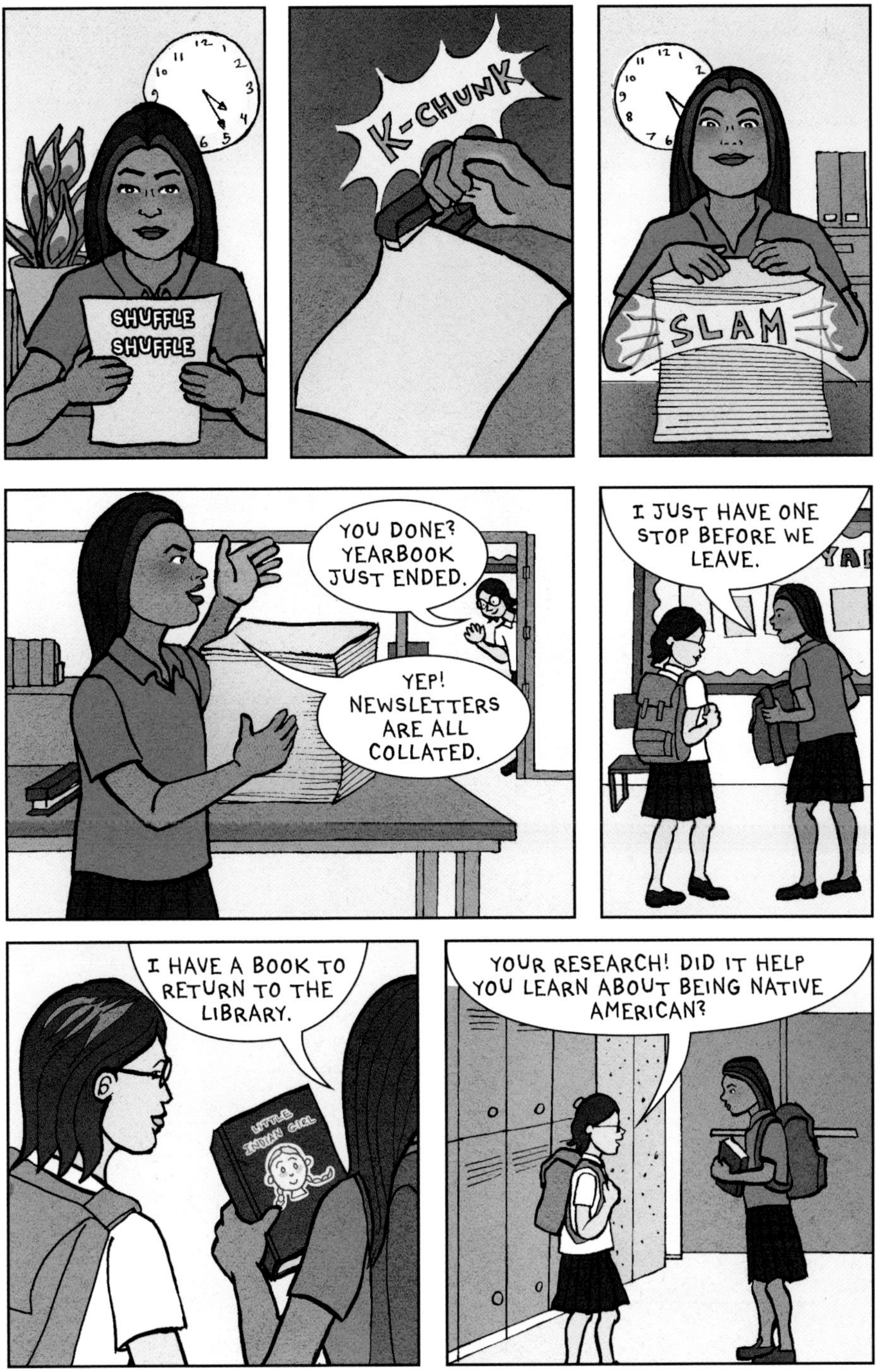
SHUFFLE SHUFFLE
K-CHUNK
SLAM
YOU DONE? YEARBOOK JUST ENDED.
YEP! NEWSLETTERS ARE ALL COLLATED.
I JUST HAVE ONE STOP BEFORE WE LEAVE.
I HAVE A BOOK TO RETURN TO THE LIBRARY.
LITTLE INDIAN GIRL
YOUR RESEARCH! DID IT HELP YOU LEARN ABOUT BEING NATIVE AMERICAN?

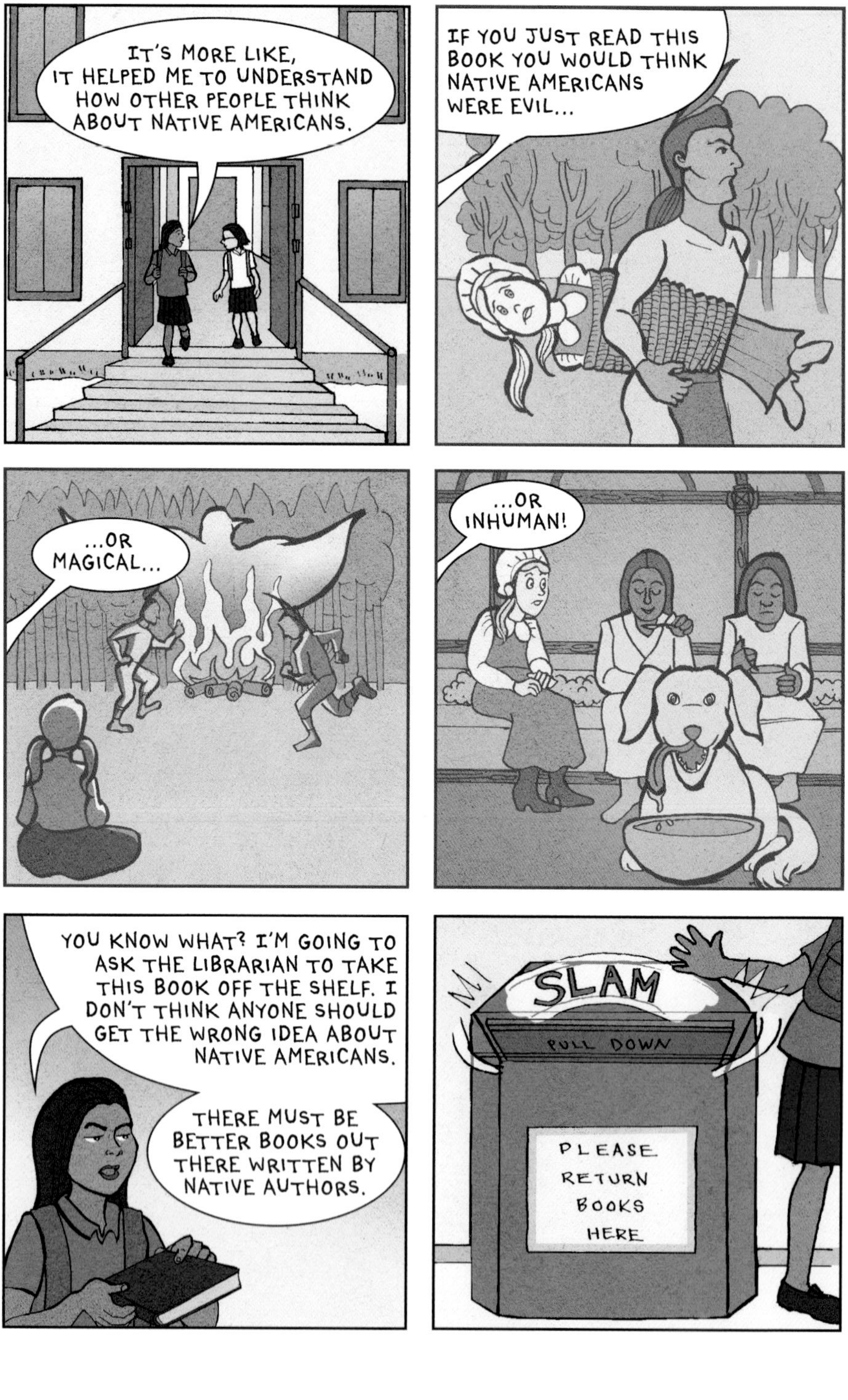
IT'S MORE LIKE, IT HELPED ME TO UNDERSTAND HOW OTHER PEOPLE THINK ABOUT NATIVE AMERICANS.
IF YOU JUST READ THIS BOOK YOU WOULD THINK NATIVE AMERICANS WERE EVIL...
...OR MAGICAL...
...OR INHUMAN!
YOU KNOW WHAT? I'M GOING TO ASK THE LIBRARIAN TO TAKE THIS BOOK OFF THE SHELF. I DON'T THINK ANYONE SHOULD GET THE WRONG IDEA ABOUT NATIVE AMERICANS.
THERE MUST BE BETTER BOOKS OUT THERE WRITTEN BY NATIVE AUTHORS.
SLAM
PULL DOWN
PLEASE RETURN BOOKS HERE

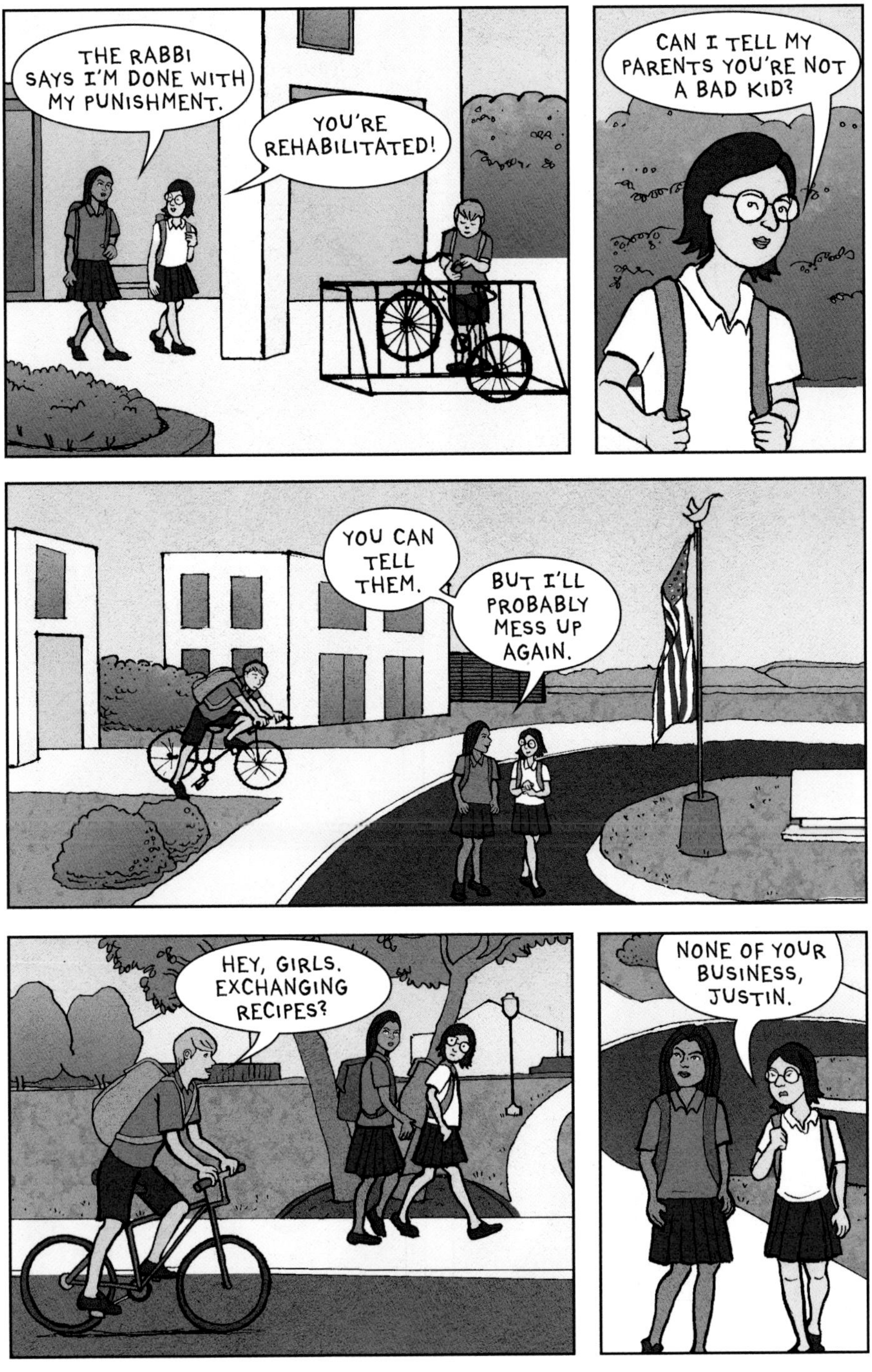
THE RABBI SAYS I'M DONE WITH MY PUNISHMENT.
YOU'RE REHABILITATED!
CAN I TELL MY PARENTS YOU'RE NOT A BAD KID?
YOU CAN TELL THEM.
BUT I'LL PROBABLY MESS UP AGAIN.
HEY, GIRLS. EXCHANGING RECIPES?
NONE OF YOUR BUSINESS, JUSTIN.

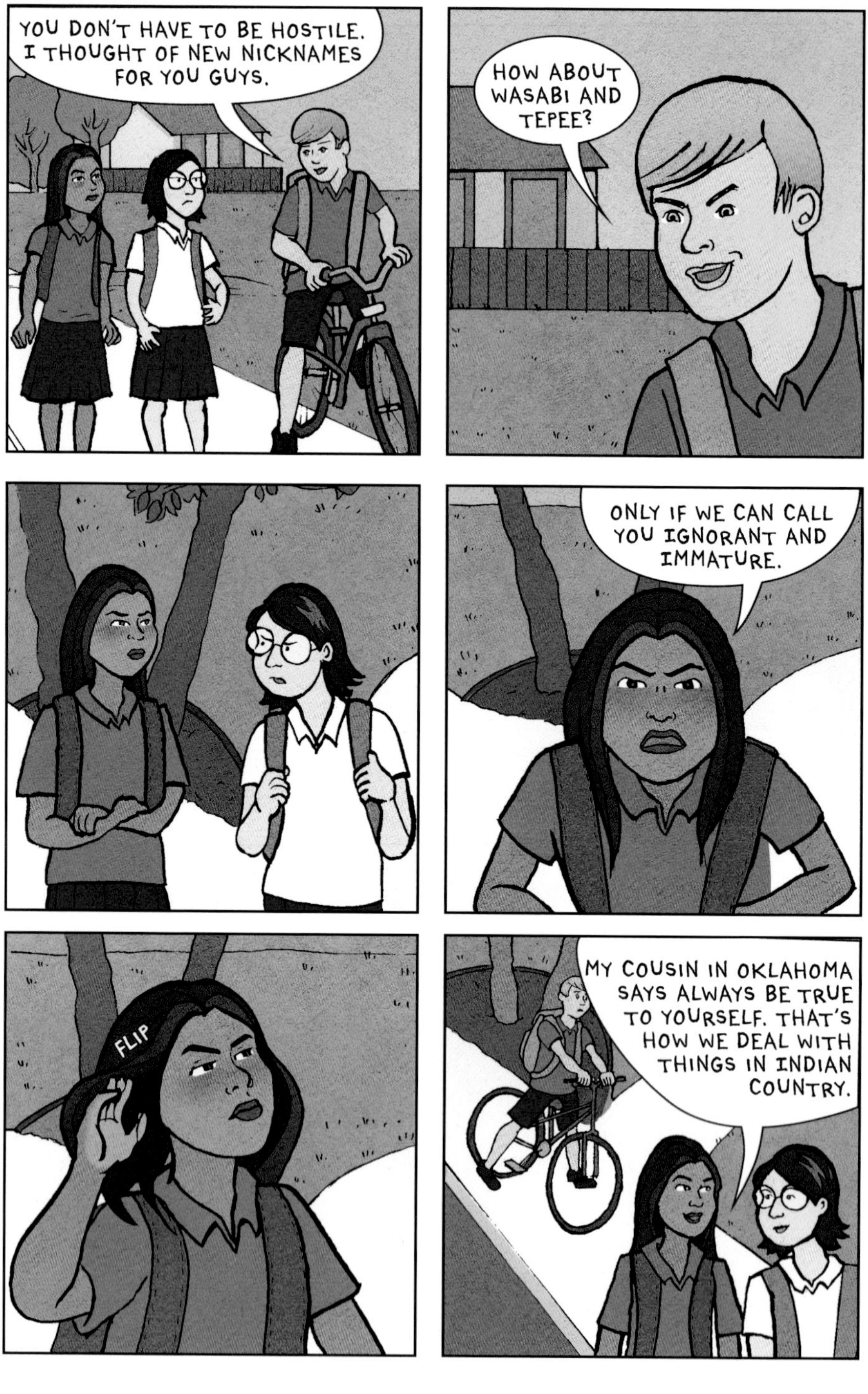
YOU DON'T HAVE TO BE HOSTILE. I THOUGHT OF NEW NICKNAMES FOR YOU GUYS.
HOW ABOUT WASABI AND TEPEE?
ONLY IF WE CAN CALL YOU IGNORANT AND IMMATURE.
FLIP
MY COUSIN IN OKLAHOMA SAYS ALWAYS BE TRUE TO YOURSELF. THAT'S HOW WE DEAL WITH THINGS IN INDIAN COUNTRY.

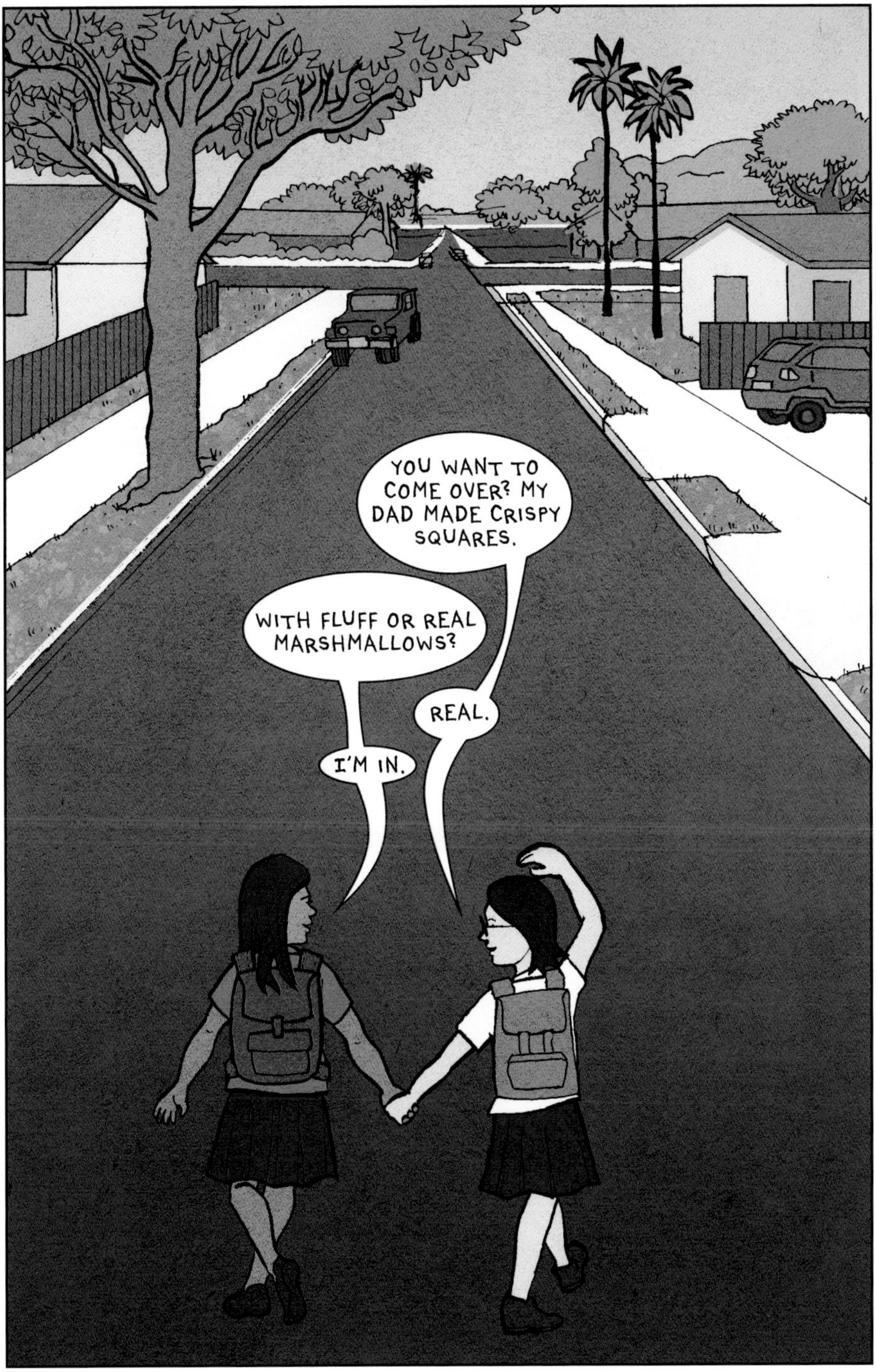
YOU WANT TO COME OVER? MY DAD MADE CRISPY SQUARES.
WITH FLUFF OR REAL MARSHMALLOWS?
REAL.
I'M IN.

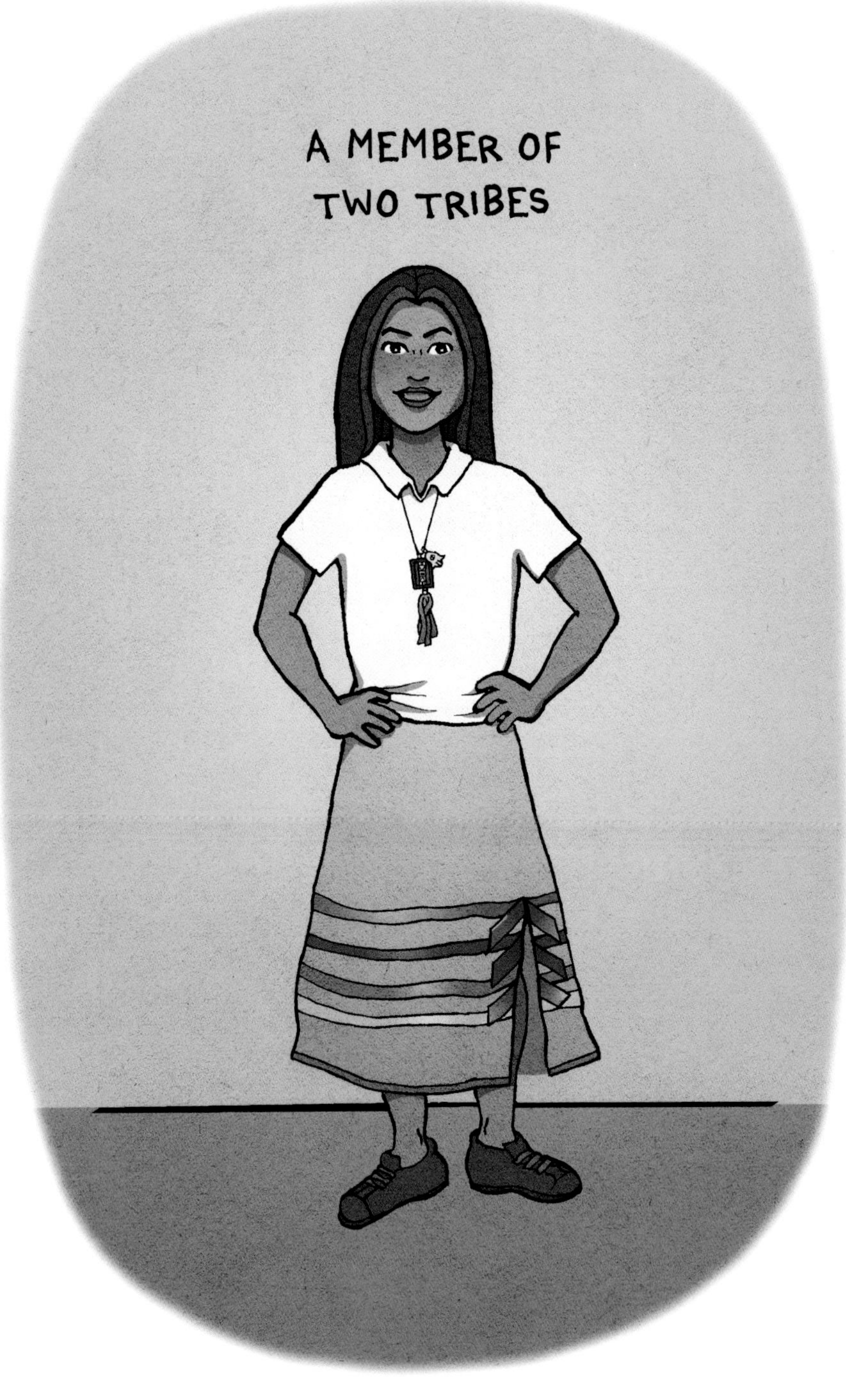
A MEMBER OF
TWO TRIBES

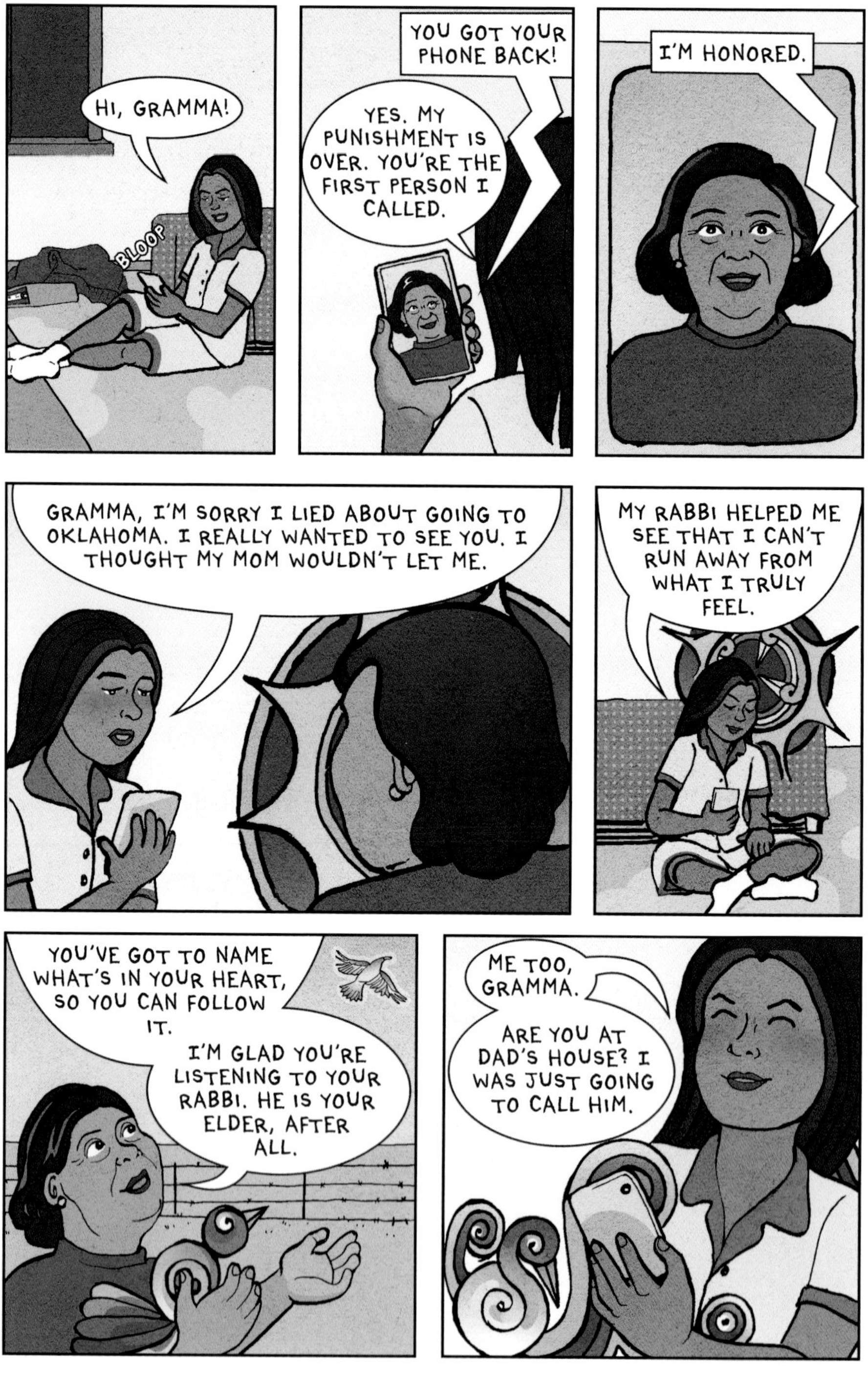
HI, GRAMMA!
BLOOP
YOU GOT YOUR PHONE BACK!
YES. MY PUNISHMENT IS OVER. YOU'RE THE FIRST PERSON I CALLED.
I'M HONORED.
GRAMMA, I'M SORRY I LIED ABOUT GOING TO OKLAHOMA. I REALLY WANTED TO SEE YOU. I THOUGHT MY MOM WOULDN'T LET ME.
MY RABBI HELPED ME SEE THAT I CAN'T RUN AWAY FROM WHAT I TRULY FEEL.
YOU'VE GOT TO NAME WHAT'S IN YOUR HEART, SO YOU CAN FOLLOW IT.
I'M GLAD YOU'RE LISTENING TO YOUR RABBI. HE IS YOUR ELDER, AFTER ALL.
ME TOO, GRAMMA.
ARE YOU AT DAD'S HOUSE? I WAS JUST GOING TO CALL HIM.

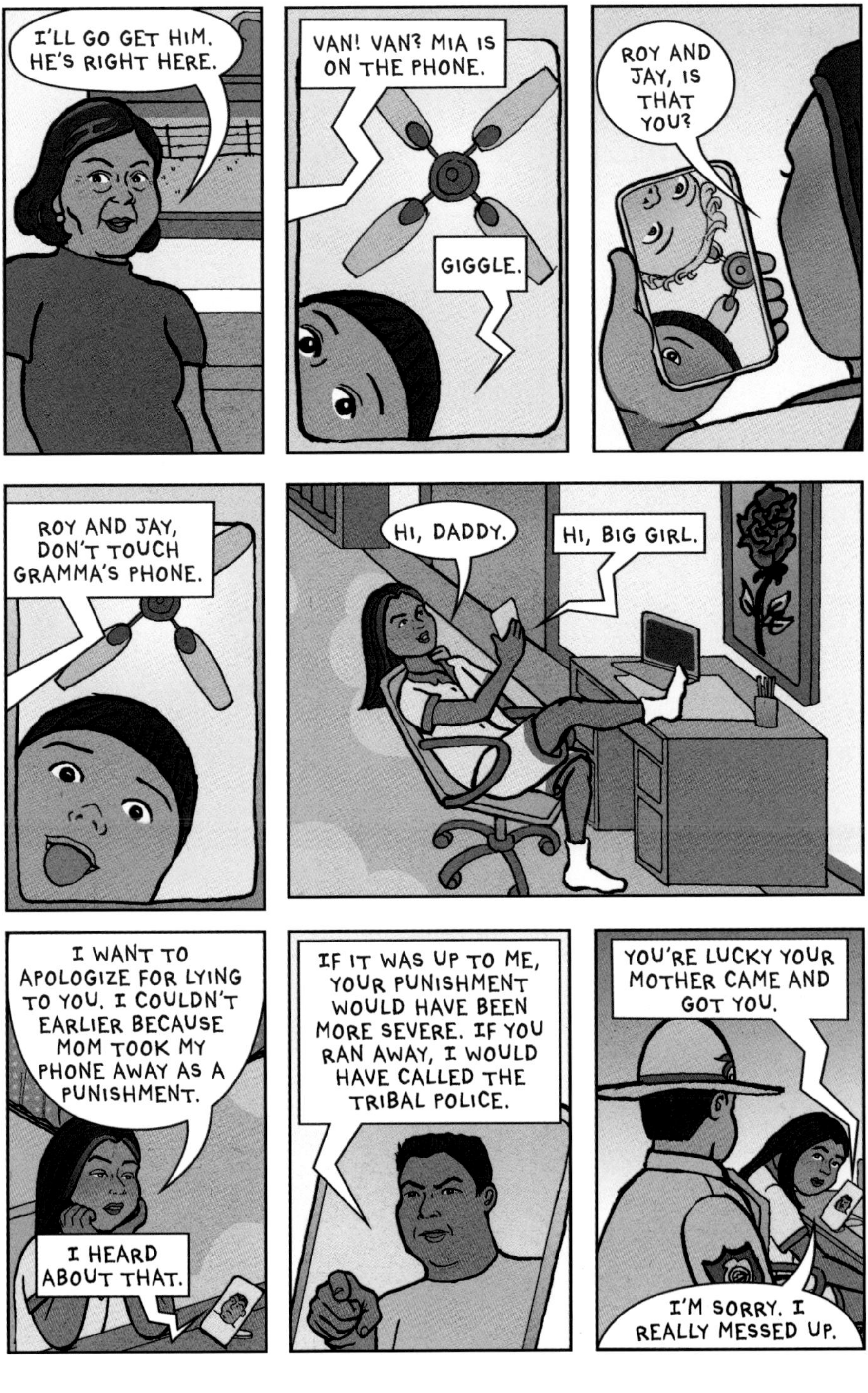
I'LL GO GET HIM. HE'S RIGHT HERE.
VAN! VAN? MIA IS ON THE PHONE.
GIGGLE.
ROY AND JAY, IS THAT YOU?
ROY AND JAY, DON'T TOUCH GRAMMA'S PHONE.
HI, DADDY.
HI, BIG GIRL.
I WANT TO APOLOGIZE FOR LYING TO YOU. I COULDN'T EARLIER BECAUSE MOM TOOK MY PHONE AWAY AS A PUNISHMENT.
I HEARD ABOUT THAT.
IF IT WAS UP TO ME, YOUR PUNISHMENT WOULD HAVE BEEN MORE SEVERE. IF YOU RAN AWAY, I WOULD HAVE CALLED THE TRIBAL POLICE.
YOU'RE LUCKY YOUR MOTHER CAME AND GOT YOU.
I'M SORRY. I REALLY MESSED UP.

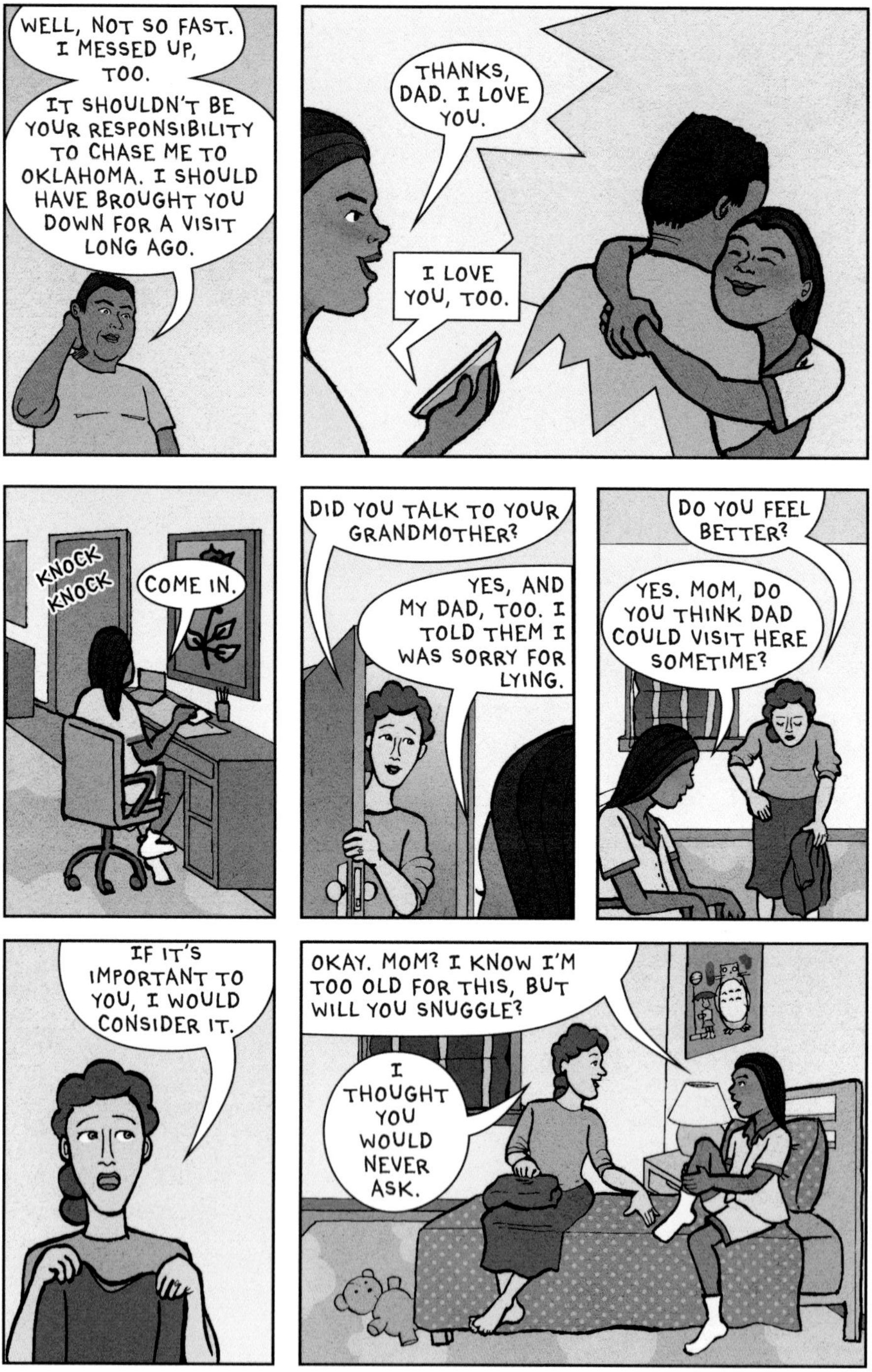
WELL, NOT SO FAST. I MESSED UP, TOO.
IT SHOULDN'T BE YOUR RESPONSIBILITY TO CHASE ME TO OKLAHOMA. I SHOULD HAVE BROUGHT YOU DOWN FOR A VISIT LONG AGO.
THANKS, DAD. I LOVE YOU.
I LOVE YOU, TOO.
KNOCK KNOCK
COME IN.
DID YOU TALK TO YOUR GRANDMOTHER?
YES, AND MY DAD, TOO. I TOLD THEM I WAS SORRY FOR LYING.
DO YOU FEEL BETTER?
YES. MOM, DO YOU THINK DAD COULD VISIT HERE SOMETIME?
IF IT'S IMPORTANT TO YOU, I WOULD CONSIDER IT.
OKAY. MOM? I KNOW I'M TOO OLD FOR THIS, BUT WILL YOU SNUGGLE?
I THOUGHT YOU WOULD NEVER ASK.

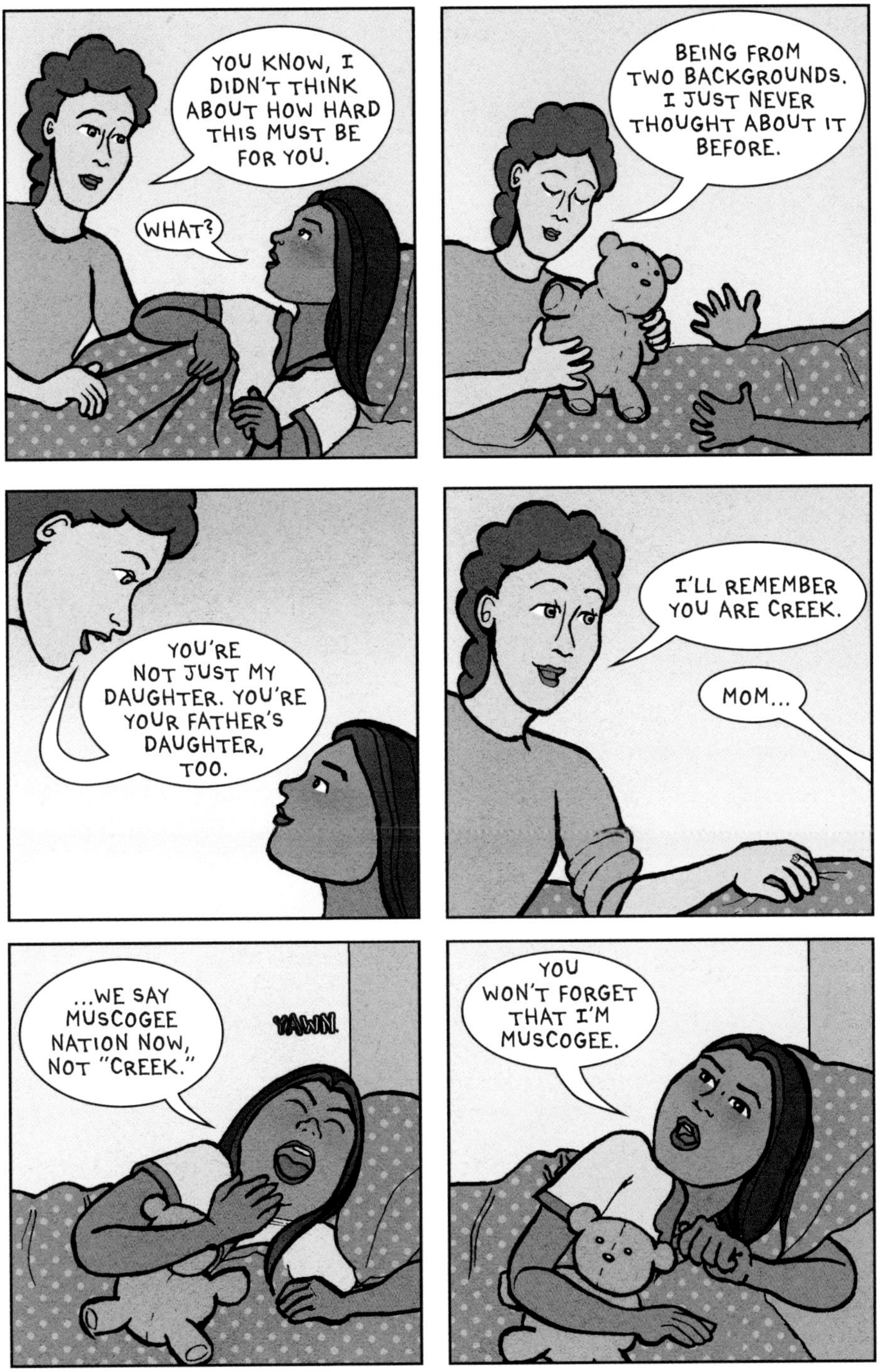
YOU KNOW, I DIDN'T THINK ABOUT HOW HARD THIS MUST BE FOR YOU.
WHAT?
BEING FROM TWO BACKGROUNDS. I JUST NEVER THOUGHT ABOUT IT BEFORE.
YOU'RE NOT JUST MY DAUGHTER. YOU'RE YOUR FATHER'S DAUGHTER, TOO.
I'LL REMEMBER YOU ARE CREEK.
MOM...
...WE SAY MUSCOGEE NATION NOW, NOT "CREEK."
YAWN.
YOU WON'T FORGET THAT I'M MUSCOGEE.

ALEICHEM SHALOM

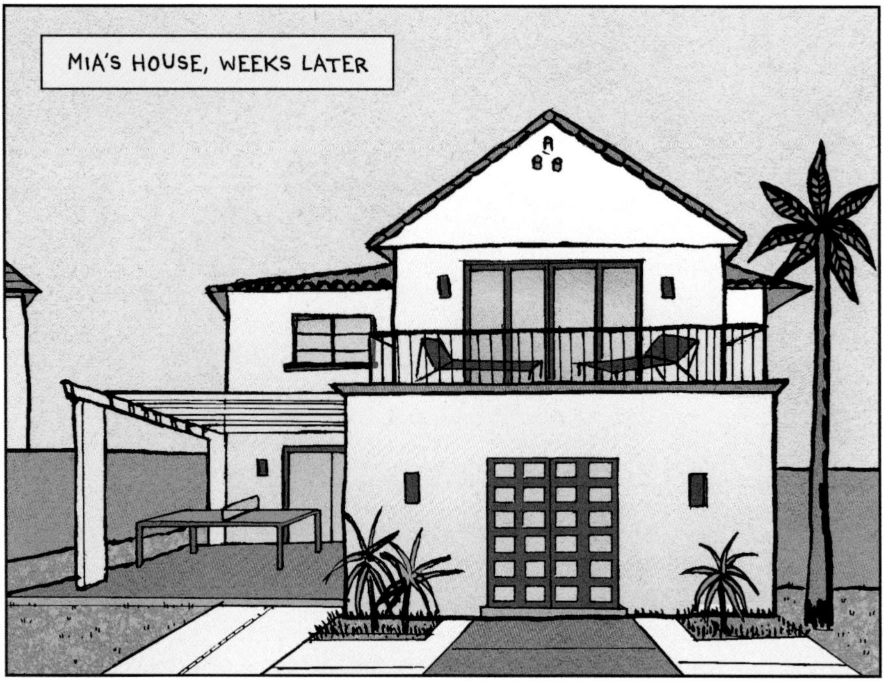
MIA'S HOUSE, WEEKS LATER

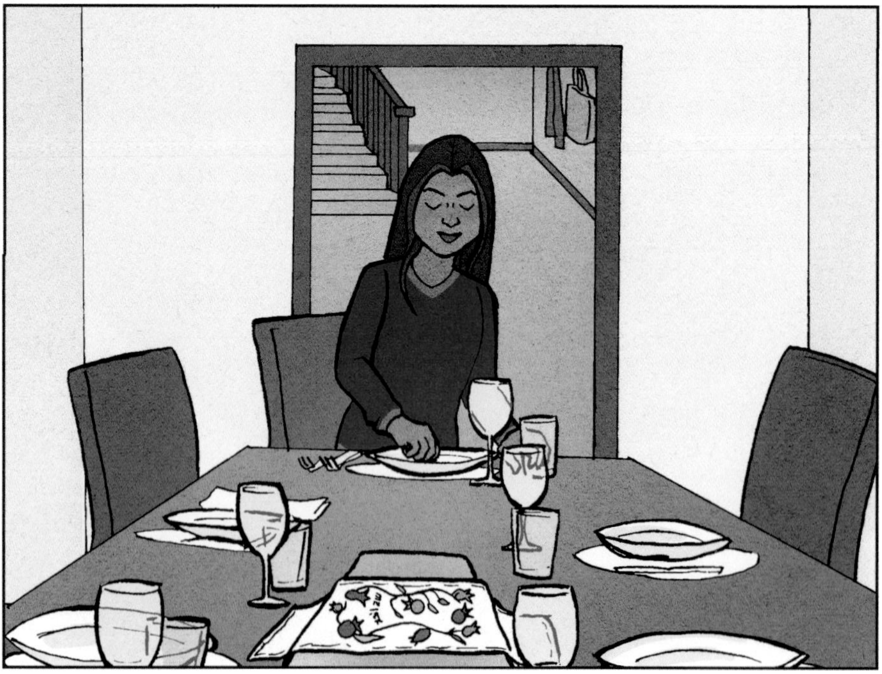

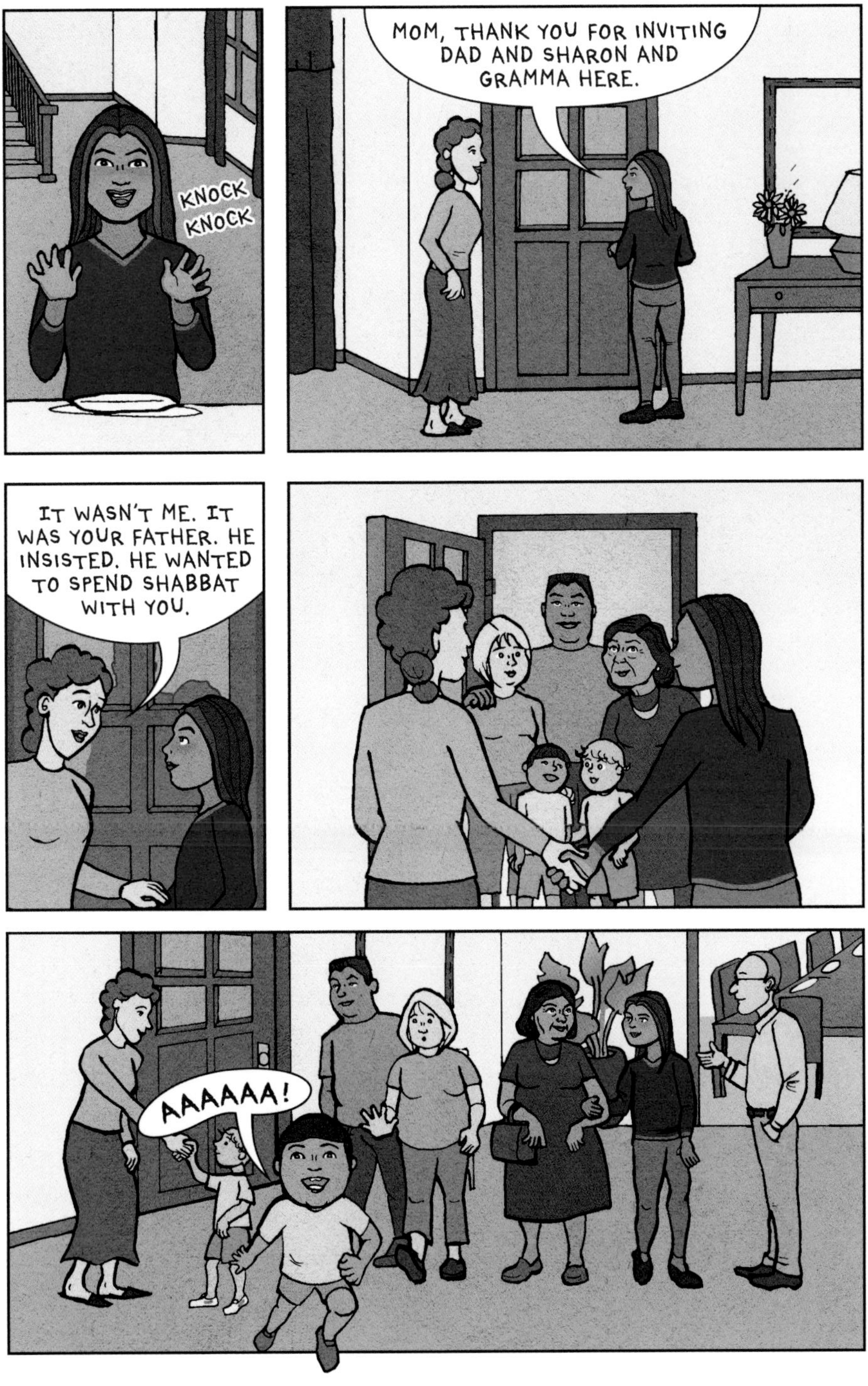
KNOCK KNOCK
MOM, THANK YOU FOR INVITING DAD AND SHARON AND GRAMMA HERE.
IT WASN'T ME. IT WAS YOUR FATHER. HE INSISTED. HE WANTED TO SPEND SHABBAT WITH YOU.
AAAAAA!

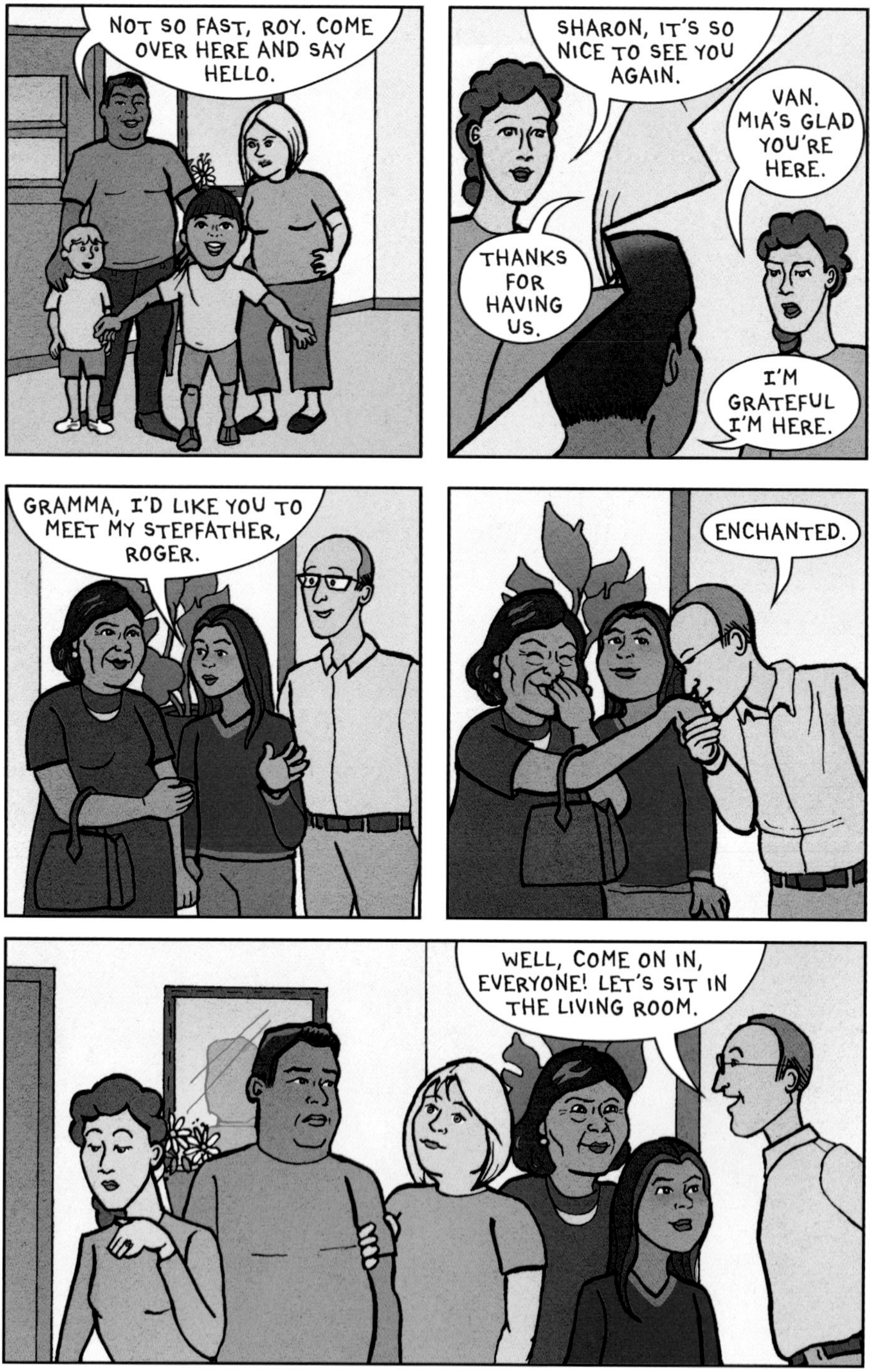
NOT SO FAST, ROY. COME OVER HERE AND SAY HELLO.
SHARON, IT'S SO NICE TO SEE YOU AGAIN.
VAN. MIA'S GLAD YOU'RE HERE.
THANKS FOR HAVING US.
I'M GRATEFUL I'M HERE.
GRAMMA, I'D LIKE YOU TO MEET MY STEPFATHER, ROGER.
ENCHANTED.
WELL, COME ON IN, EVERYONE! LET'S SIT IN THE LIVING ROOM.

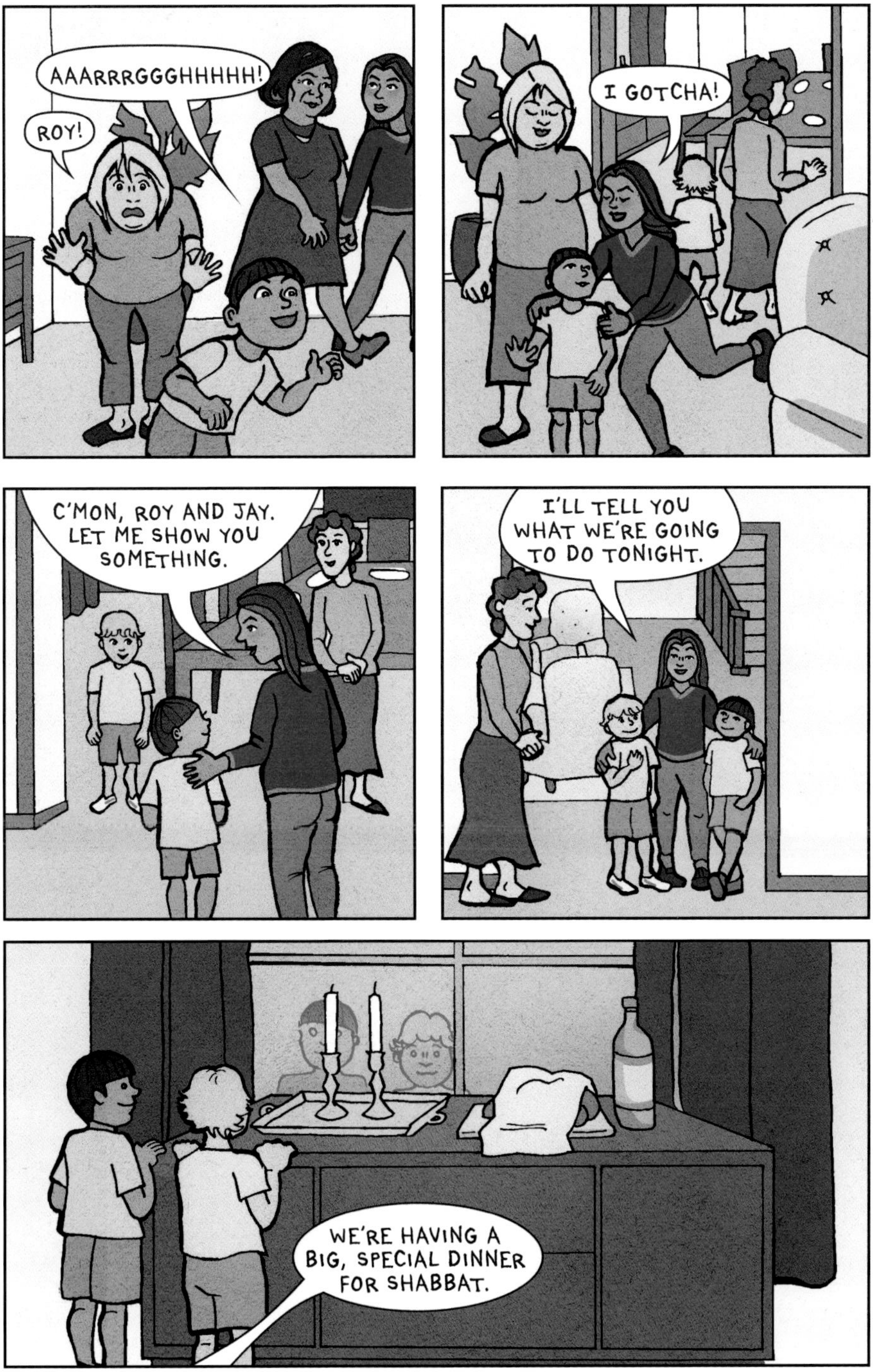
AAARRRGGGHHHHH!
ROY!
I GOTCHA!
C'MON, ROY AND JAY. LET ME SHOW YOU SOMETHING.
I'LL TELL YOU WHAT WE'RE GOING TO DO TONIGHT.
WE'RE HAVING A BIG, SPECIAL DINNER FOR SHABBAT.

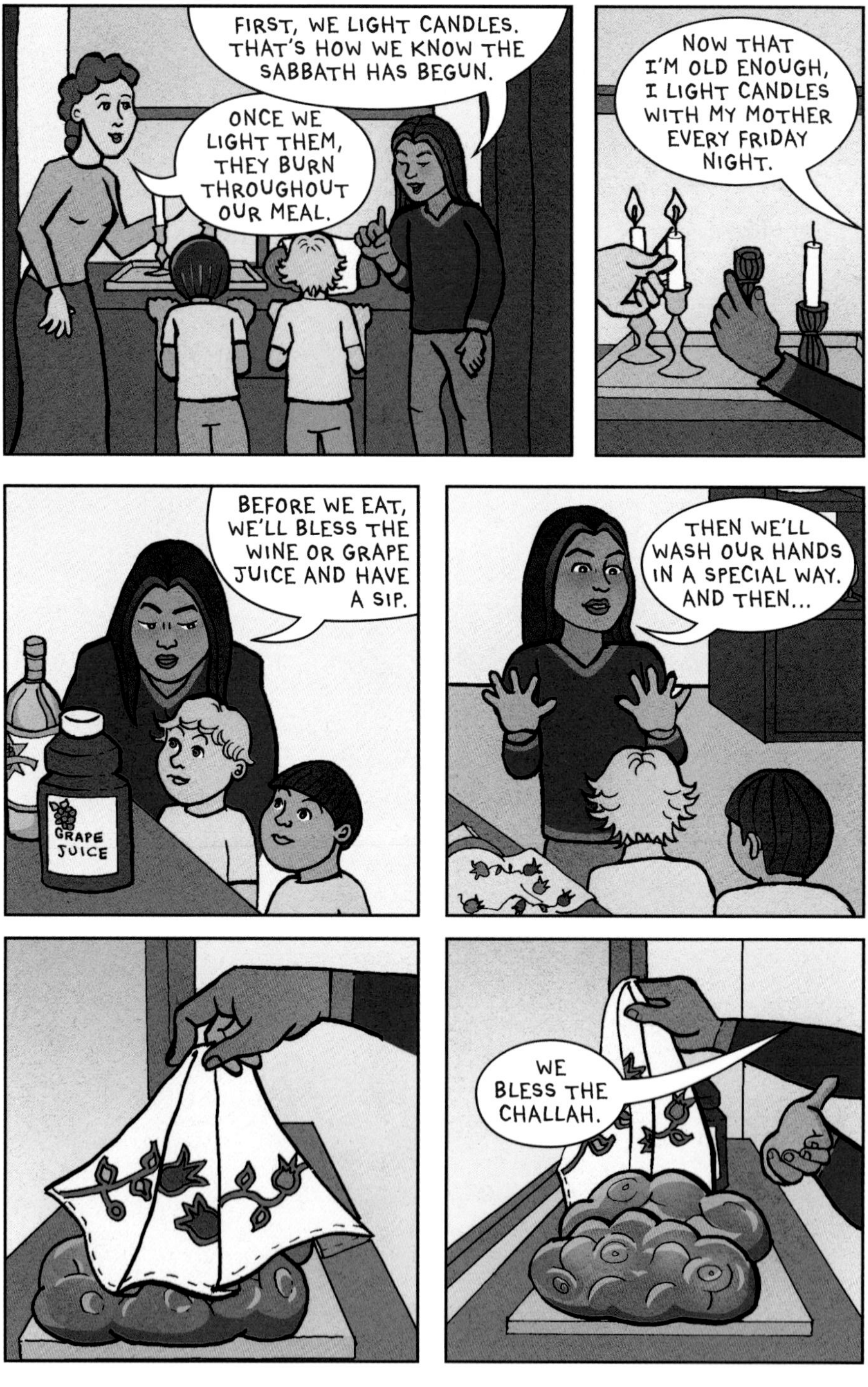
FIRST, WE LIGHT CANDLES. THAT'S HOW WE KNOW THE SABBATH HAS BEGUN.
ONCE WE LIGHT THEM, THEY BURN THROUGHOUT OUR MEAL.
NOW THAT I'M OLD ENOUGH, I LIGHT CANDLES WITH MY MOTHER EVERY FRIDAY NIGHT.
BEFORE WE EAT, WE'LL BLESS THE WINE OR GRAPE JUICE AND HAVE A SIP.
GRAPE JUICE
THEN WE'LL WASH OUR HANDS IN A SPECIAL WAY. AND THEN...
WE BLESS THE CHALLAH.

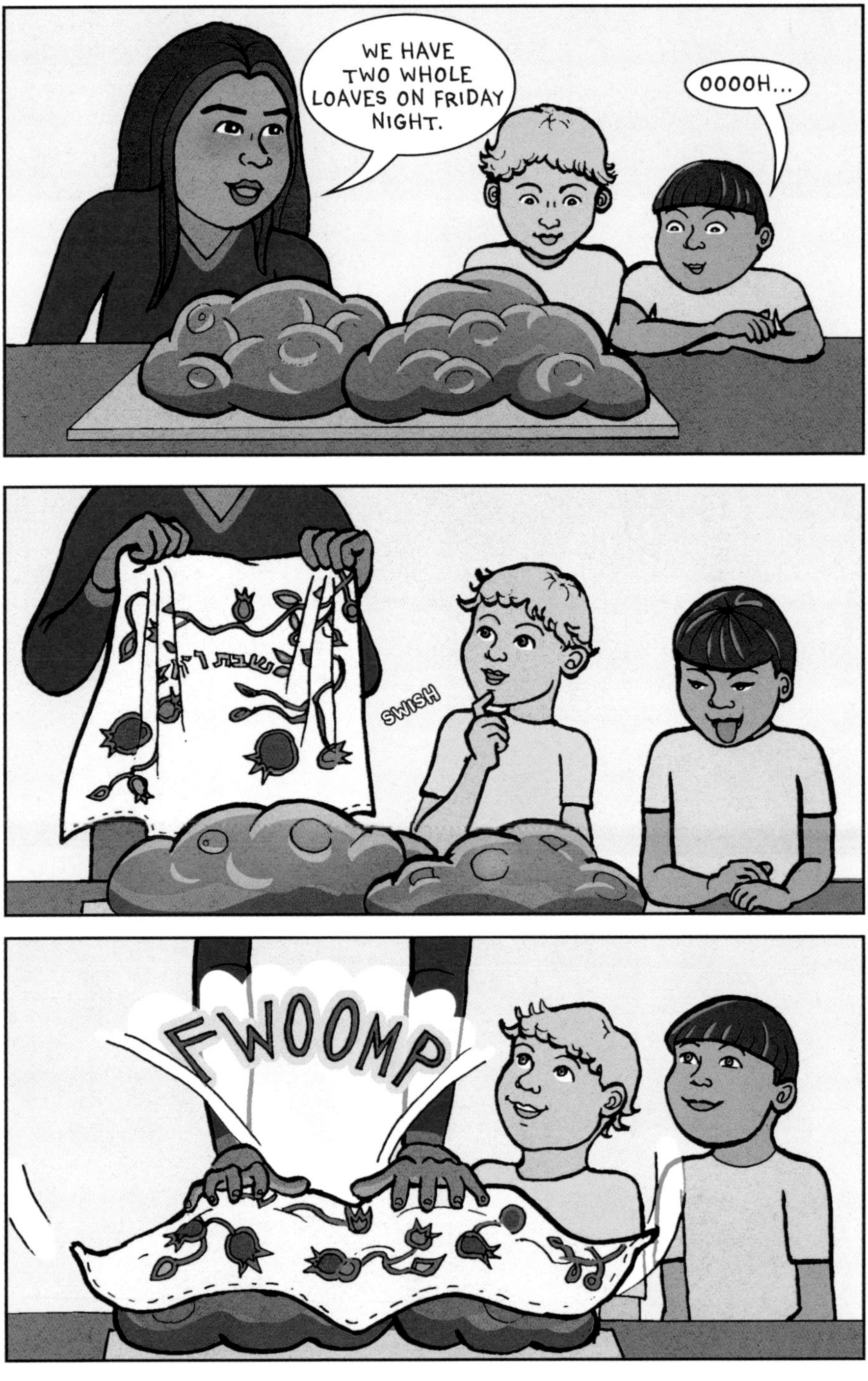
WE HAVE TWO WHOLE LOAVES ON FRIDAY NIGHT.
OOOOH...
שבת
SWISH
FWOOMP

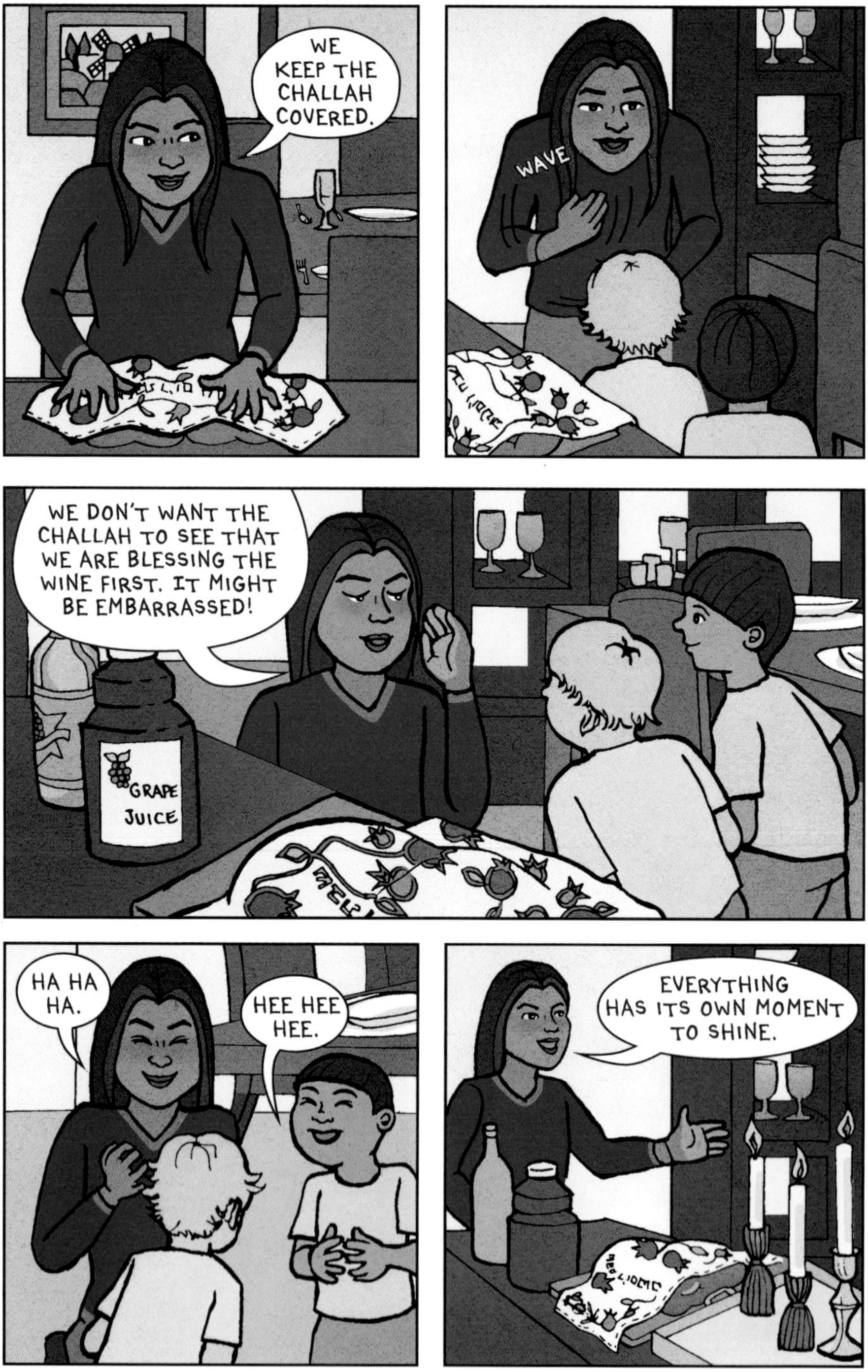
WE KEEP THE CHALLAH COVERED.
WAVE
WE DON'T WANT THE CHALLAH TO SEE THAT WE ARE BLESSING THE WINE FIRST. IT MIGHT BE EMBARRASSED!
GRAPE JUICE
HA HA HA.
HEE HEE HEE.
EVERYTHING HAS ITS OWN MOMENT TO SHINE.

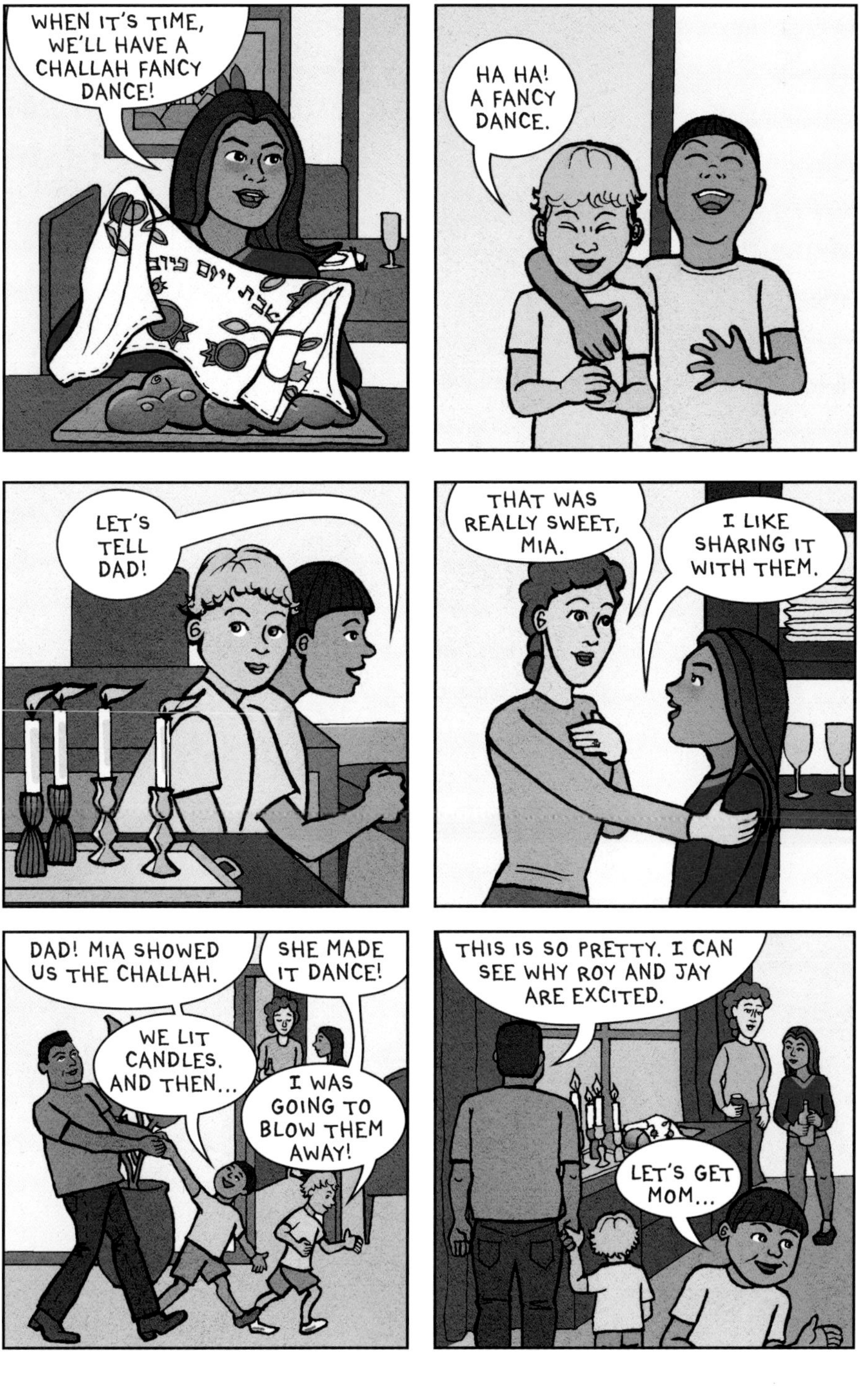
WHEN IT'S TIME, WE'LL HAVE A CHALLAH FANCY DANCE!
HA HA! A FANCY DANCE.
LET'S TELL DAD!
THAT WAS REALLY SWEET, MIA.
I LIKE SHARING IT WITH THEM.
DAD! MIA SHOWED US THE CHALLAH.
SHE MADE IT DANCE!
WE LIT CANDLES. AND THEN...
I WAS GOING TO BLOW THEM AWAY!
THIS IS SO PRETTY. I CAN SEE WHY ROY AND JAY ARE EXCITED.
LET'S GET MOM...

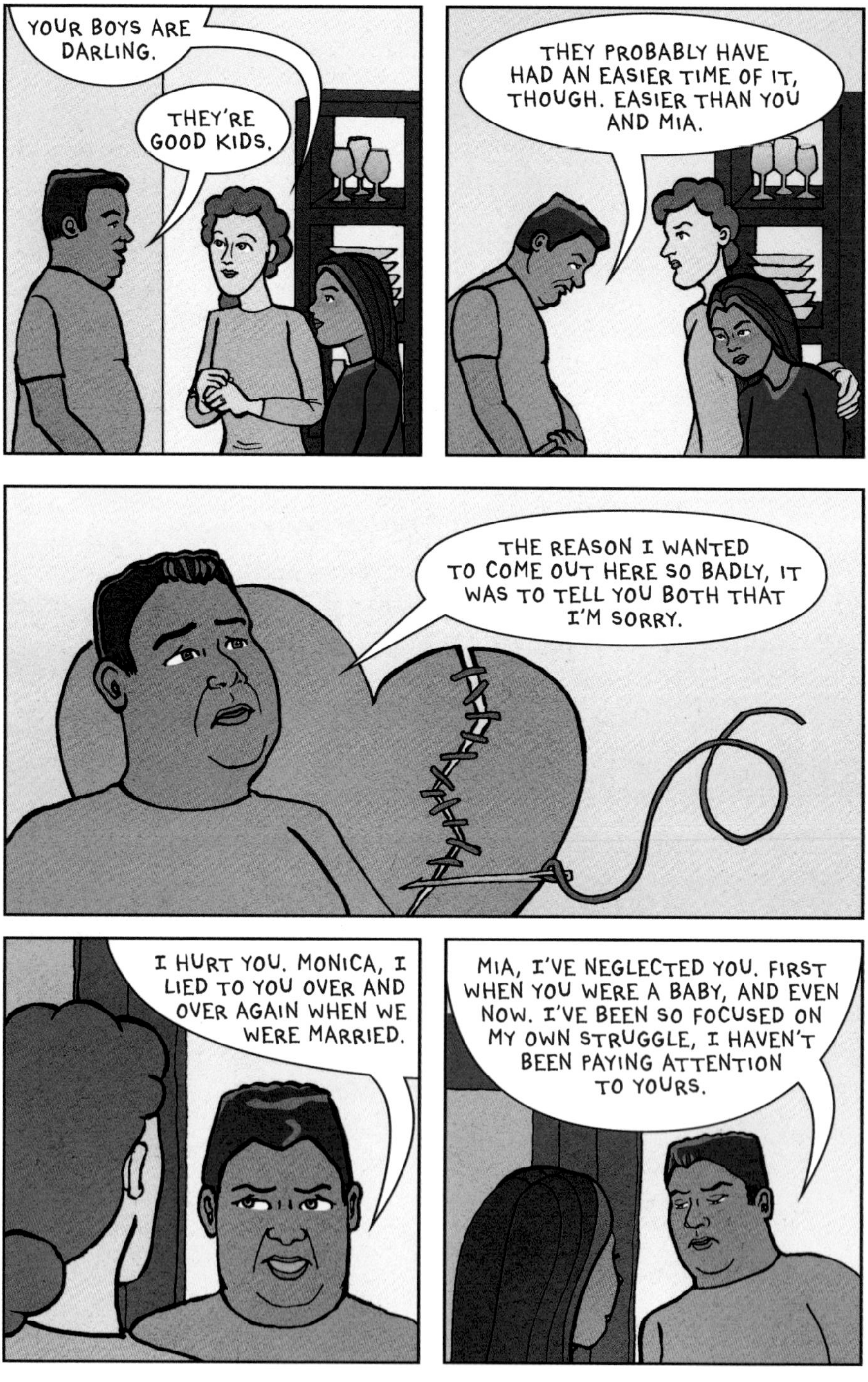
YOUR BOYS ARE DARLING.
THEY'RE GOOD KIDS.
THEY PROBABLY HAVE HAD AN EASIER TIME OF IT, THOUGH. EASIER THAN YOU AND MIA.
THE REASON I WANTED TO COME OUT HERE SO BADLY, IT WAS TO TELL YOU BOTH THAT I'M SORRY.
I HURT YOU. MONICA, I LIED TO YOU OVER AND OVER AGAIN WHEN WE WERE MARRIED.
MIA, I'VE NEGLECTED YOU. FIRST WHEN YOU WERE A BABY, AND EVEN NOW. I'VE BEEN SO FOCUSED ON MY OWN STRUGGLE, I HAVEN'T BEEN PAYING ATTENTION TO YOURS.

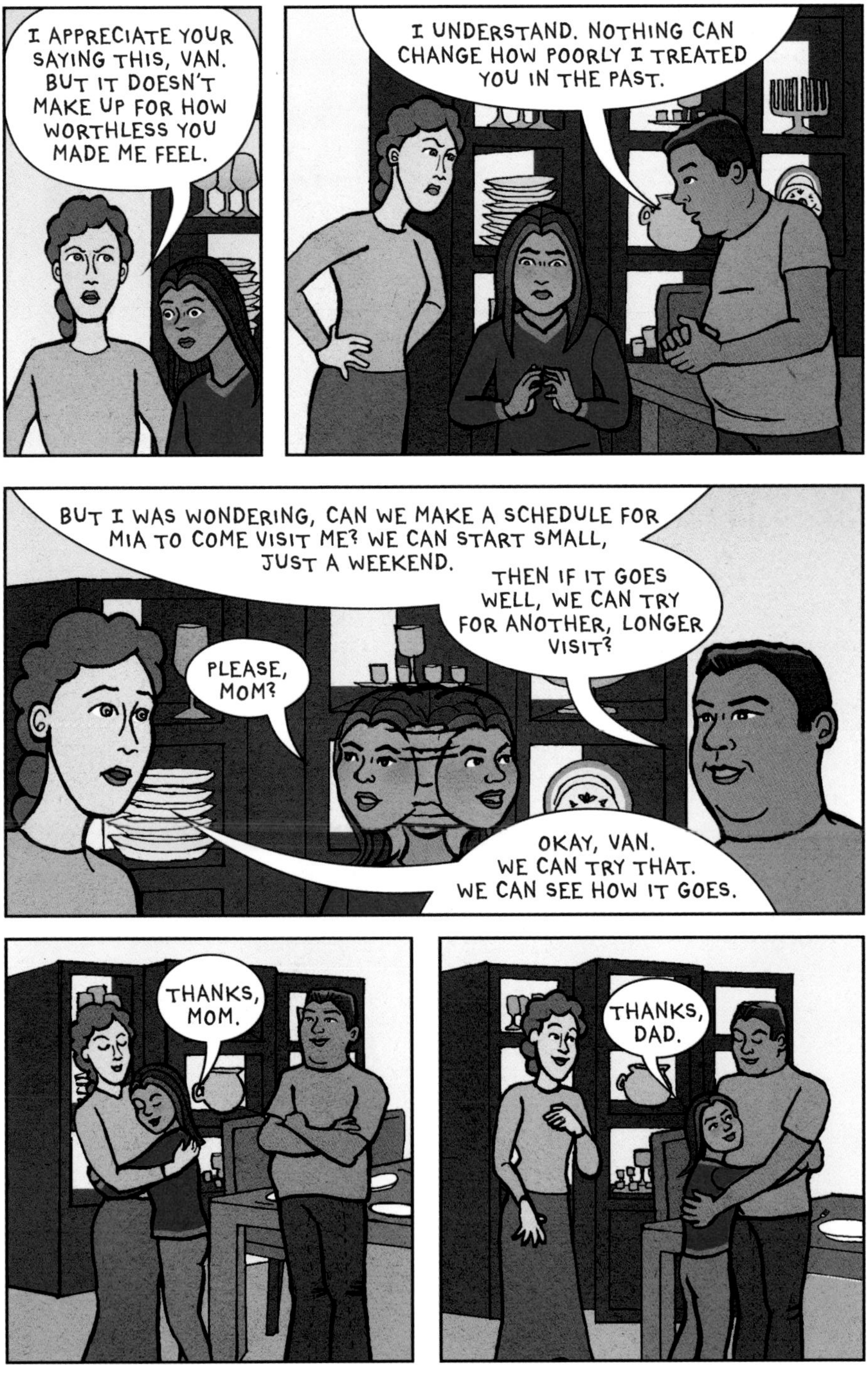
I APPRECIATE YOUR SAYING THIS, VAN. BUT IT DOESN'T MAKE UP FOR HOW WORTHLESS YOU MADE ME FEEL.
I UNDERSTAND. NOTHING CAN CHANGE HOW POORLY I TREATED YOU IN THE PAST.
BUT I WAS WONDERING, CAN WE MAKE A SCHEDULE FOR MIA TO COME VISIT ME? WE CAN START SMALL, JUST A WEEKEND.
THEN IF IT GOES WELL, WE CAN TRY FOR ANOTHER, LONGER VISIT?
PLEASE, MOM?
OKAY, VAN. WE CAN TRY THAT. WE CAN SEE HOW IT GOES.
THANKS, MOM.
THANKS, DAD.

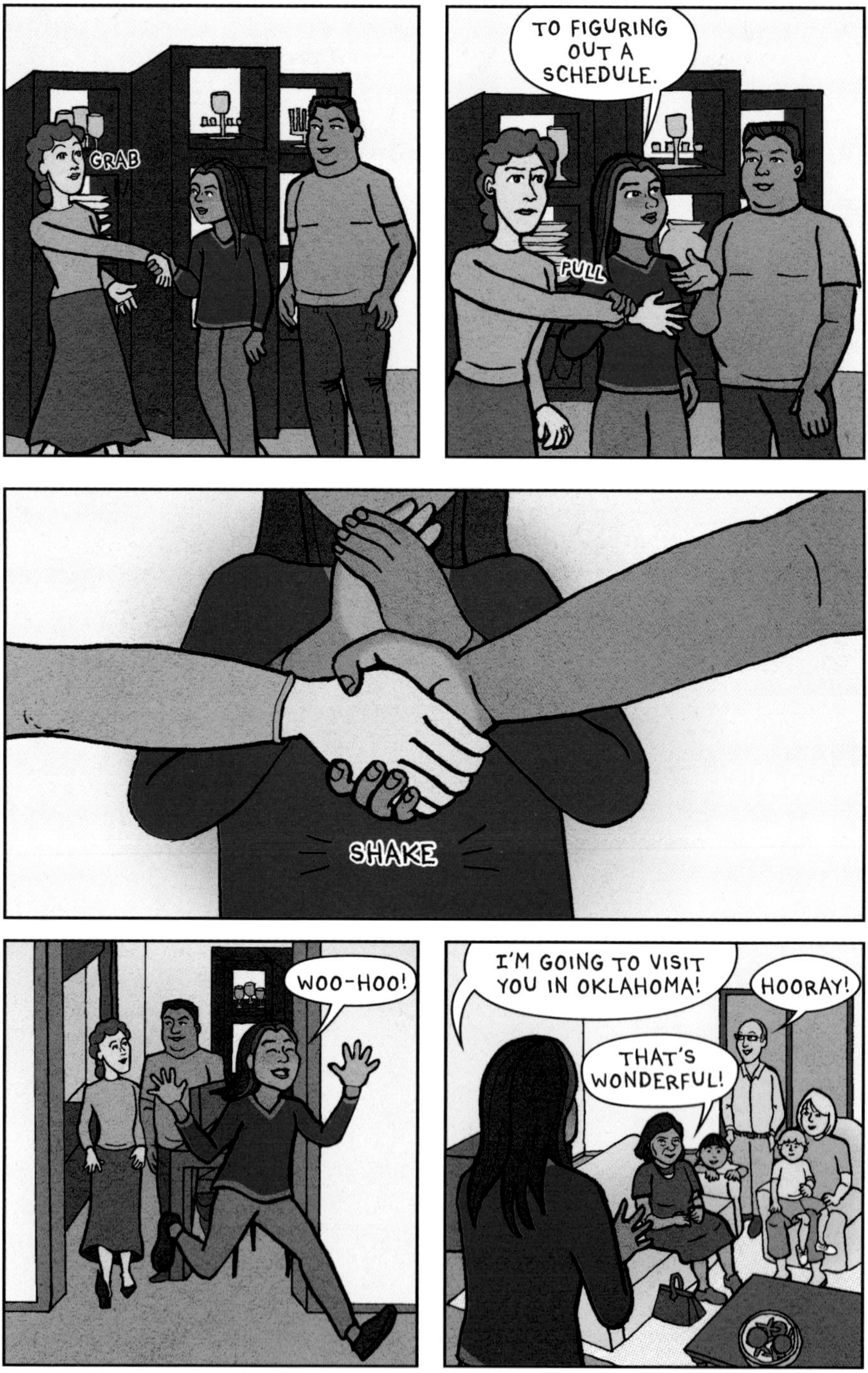
GRAB
TO FIGURING OUT A SCHEDULE.
PULL
SHAKE
WOO-HOO!
I'M GOING TO VISIT YOU IN OKLAHOMA!
HOORAY!
THAT'S WONDERFUL!

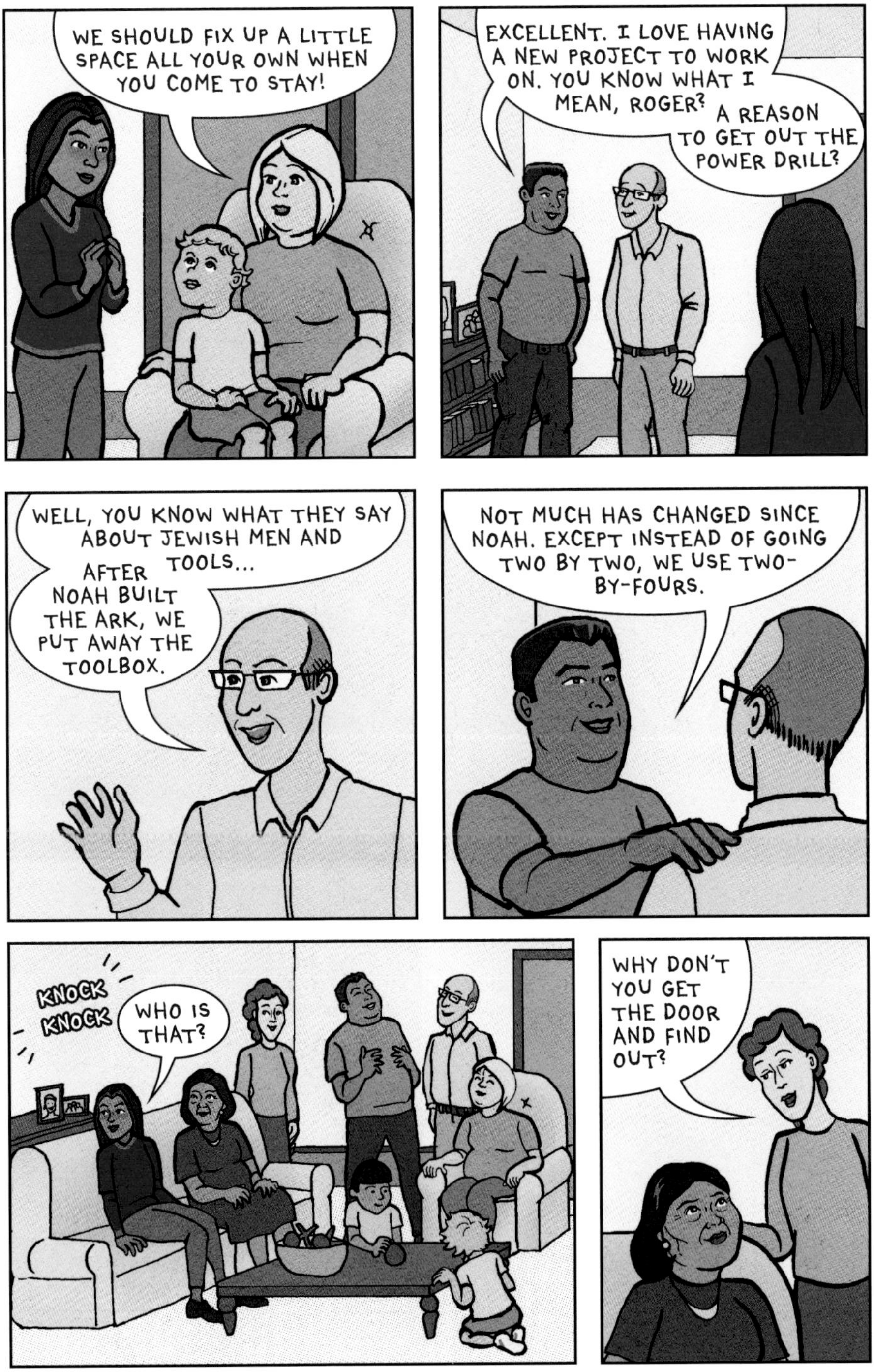
WE SHOULD FIX UP A LITTLE SPACE ALL YOUR OWN WHEN YOU COME TO STAY!
EXCELLENT. I LOVE HAVING A NEW PROJECT TO WORK ON. YOU KNOW WHAT I MEAN, ROGER?
A REASON TO GET OUT THE POWER DRILL?
WELL, YOU KNOW WHAT THEY SAY ABOUT JEWISH MEN AND TOOLS...
AFTER NOAH BUILT THE ARK, WE PUT AWAY THE TOOLBOX.
NOT MUCH HAS CHANGED SINCE NOAH. EXCEPT INSTEAD OF GOING TWO BY TWO, WE USE TWO-BY-FOURS.
KNOCK KNOCK
WHO IS THAT?
WHY DON'T YOU GET THE DOOR AND FIND OUT?

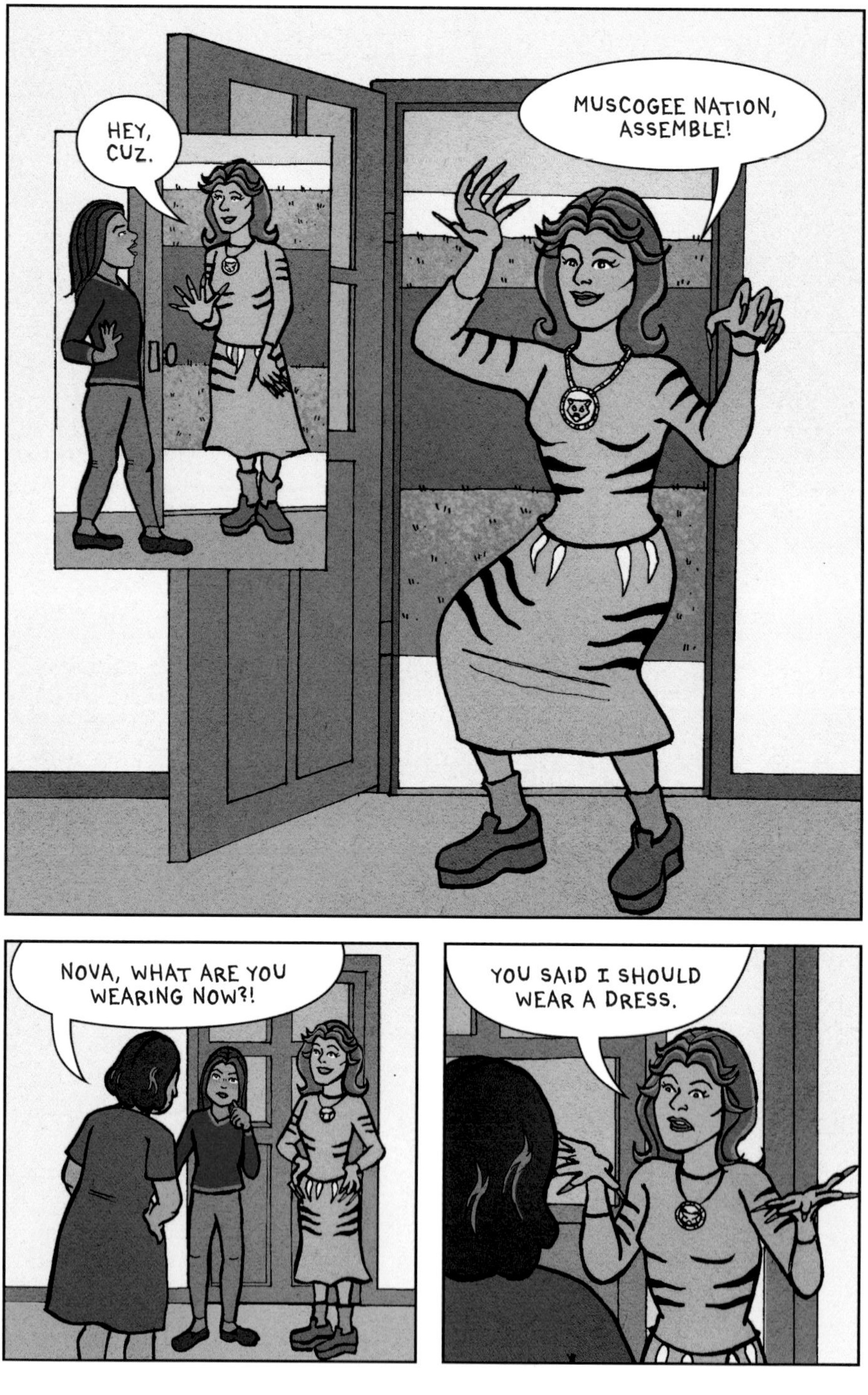
HEY, CUZ.
MUSCOGEE NATION, ASSEMBLE!
NOVA, WHAT ARE YOU WEARING NOW?!
YOU SAID I SHOULD WEAR A DRESS.

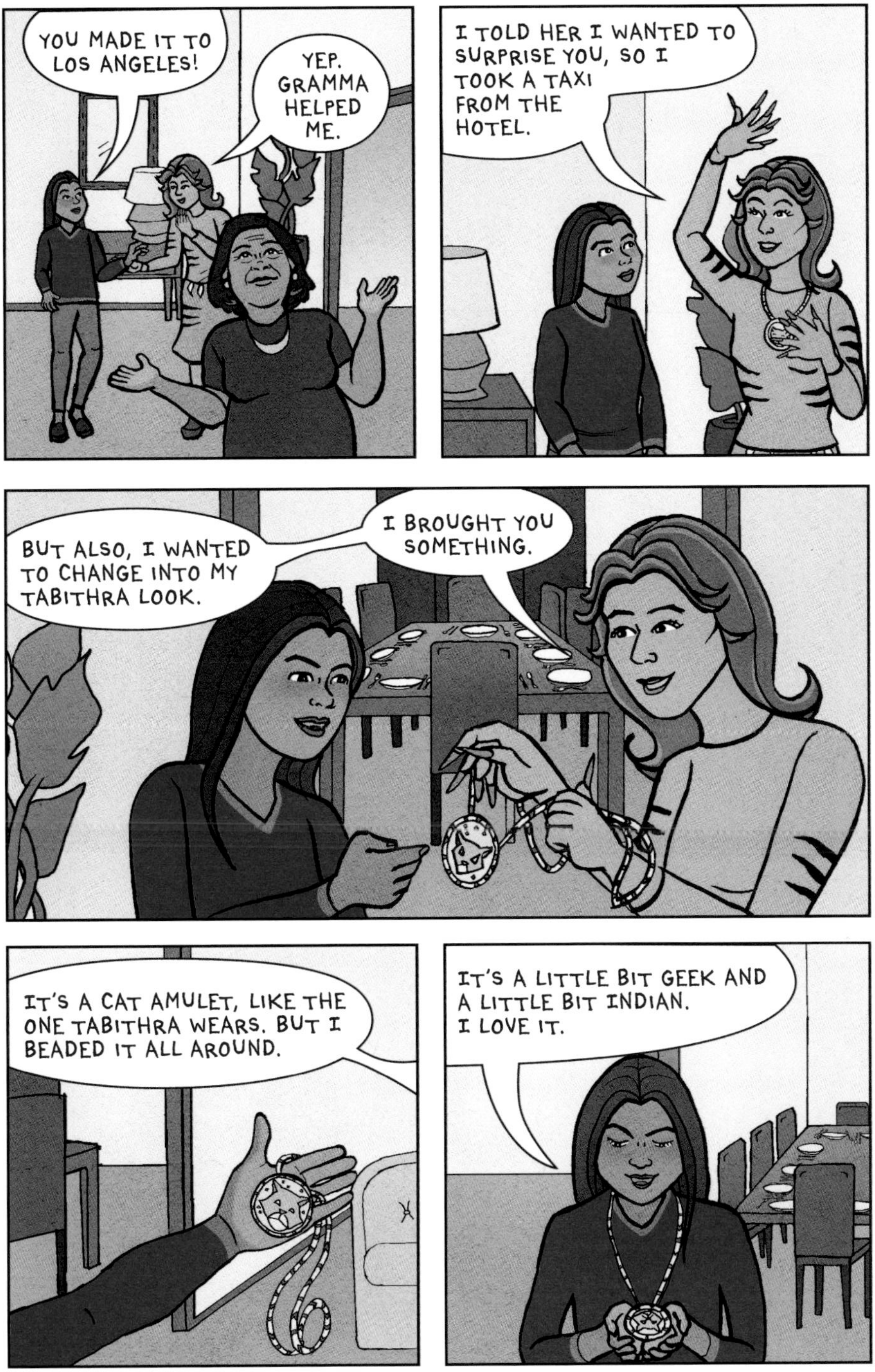
YOU MADE IT TO LOS ANGELES!
YEP. GRAMMA HELPED ME.
I TOLD HER I WANTED TO SURPRISE YOU, SO I TOOK A TAXI FROM THE HOTEL.
BUT ALSO, I WANTED TO CHANGE INTO MY TABITHRA LOOK.
I BROUGHT YOU SOMETHING.
IT'S A CAT AMULET, LIKE THE ONE TABITHRA WEARS. BUT I BEADED IT ALL AROUND.
IT'S A LITTLE BIT GEEK AND A LITTLE BIT INDIAN. I LOVE IT.

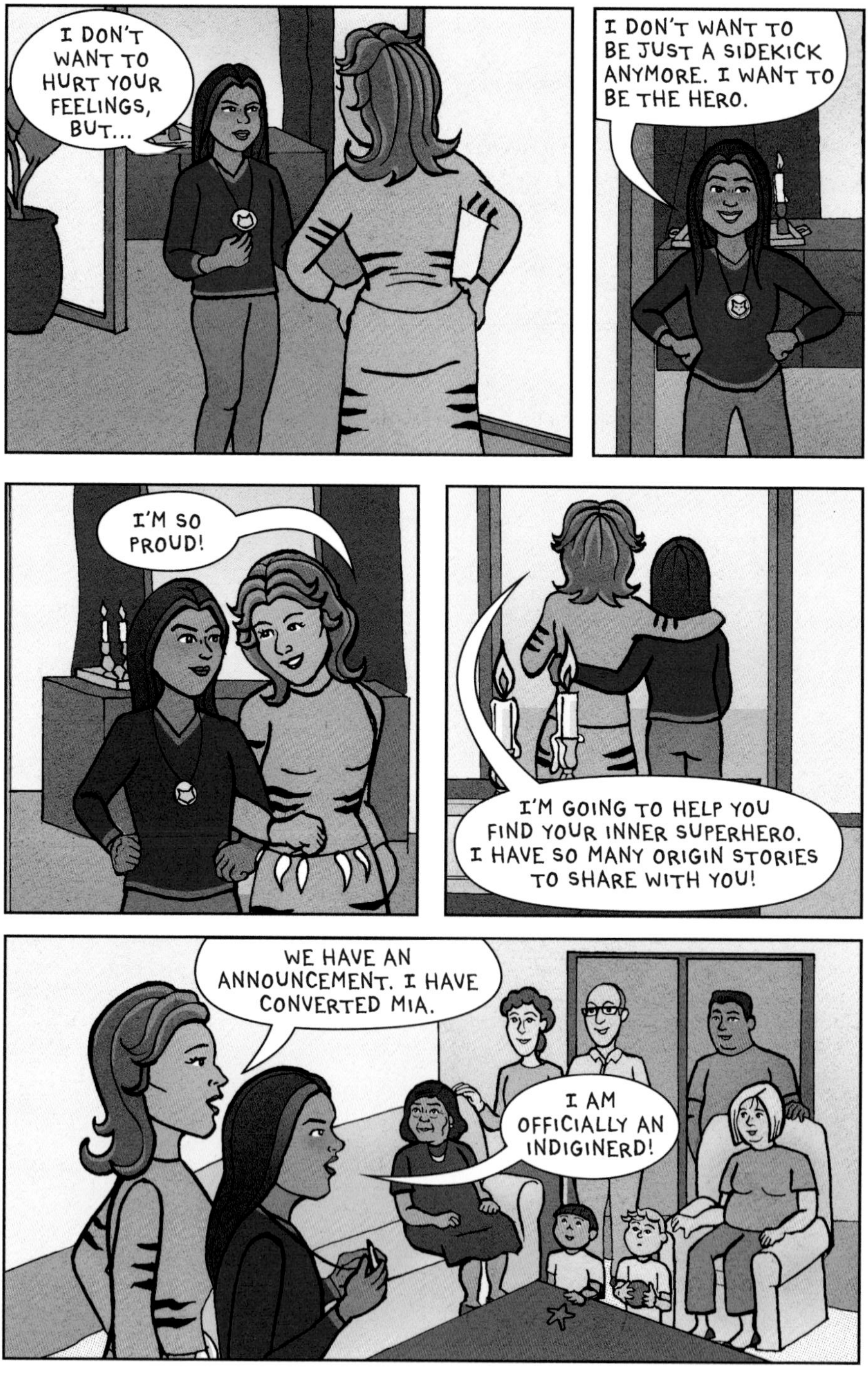

I DON'T WANT TO HURT YOUR FEELINGS, BUT...
I DON'T WANT TO BE JUST A SIDEKICK ANYMORE. I WANT TO BE THE HERO.
I'M SO PROUD!
I'M GOING TO HELP YOU FIND YOUR INNER SUPERHERO. I HAVE SO MANY ORIGIN STORIES TO SHARE WITH YOU!
WE HAVE AN ANNOUNCEMENT. I HAVE CONVERTED MIA.
I AM OFFICIALLY AN INDIGINERD!

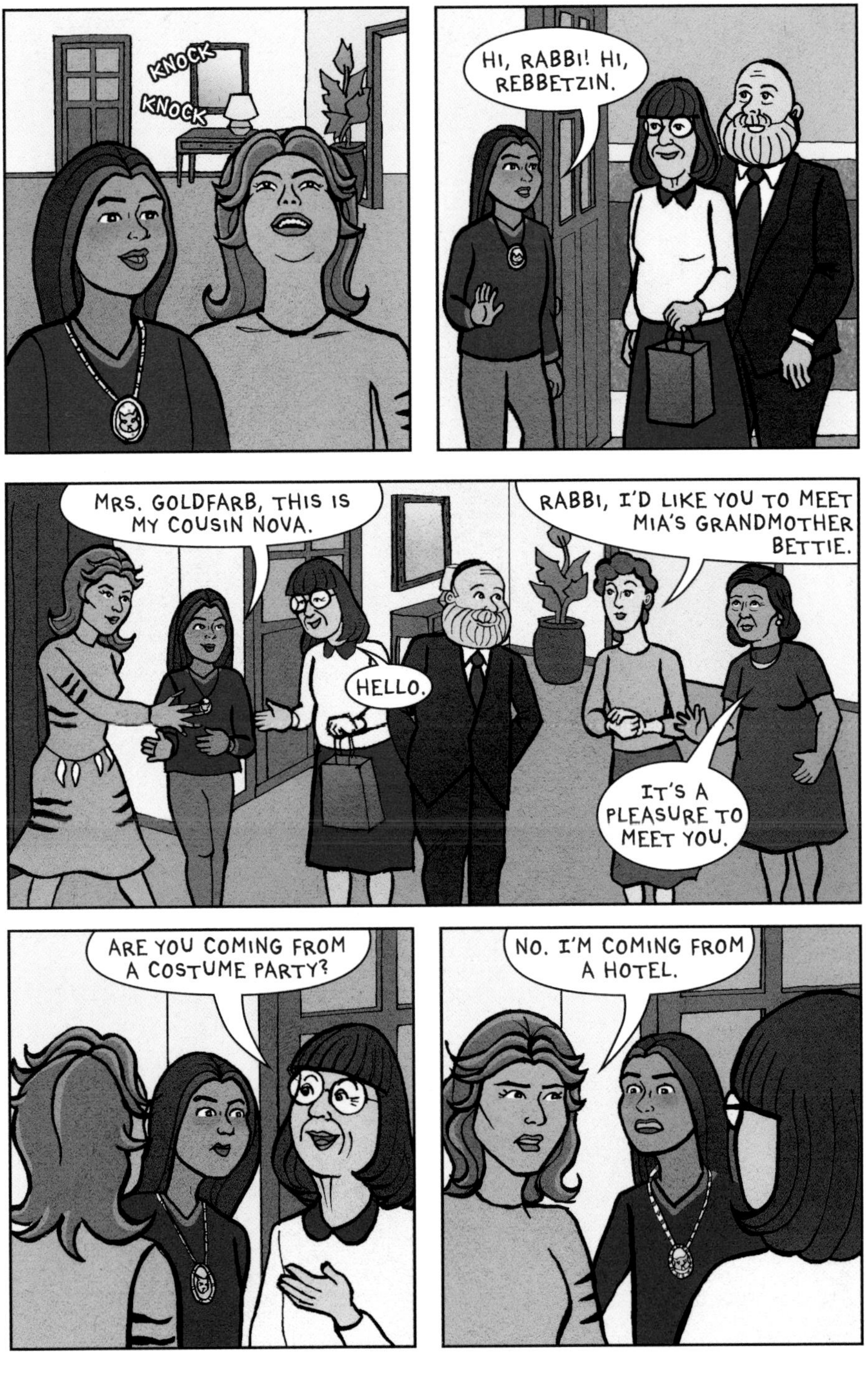
KNOCK
KNOCK
HI, RABBI! HI, REBBETZIN.
MRS. GOLDFARB, THIS IS MY COUSIN NOVA.
HELLO.
RABBI, I'D LIKE YOU TO MEET MIA'S GRANDMOTHER BETTIE.
IT'S A PLEASURE TO MEET YOU.
ARE YOU COMING FROM A COSTUME PARTY?
NO. I'M COMING FROM A HOTEL.

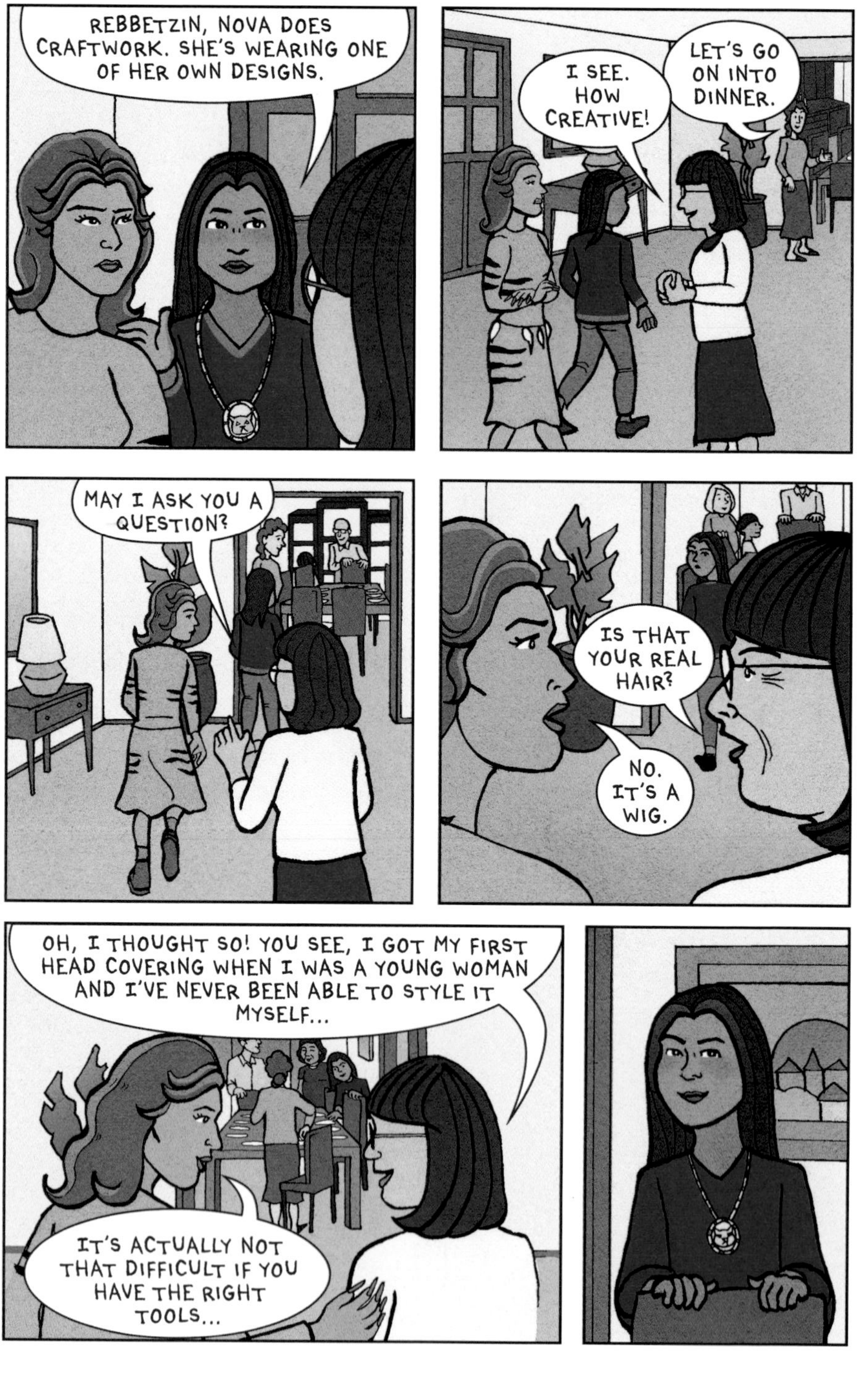
REBBETZIN, NOVA DOES CRAFTWORK. SHE'S WEARING ONE OF HER OWN DESIGNS.
I SEE. HOW CREATIVE!
LET'S GO ON INTO DINNER.
MAY I ASK YOU A QUESTION?
IS THAT YOUR REAL HAIR?
NO. IT'S A WIG.
OH, I THOUGHT SO! YOU SEE, I GOT MY FIRST HEAD COVERING WHEN I WAS A YOUNG WOMAN AND I'VE NEVER BEEN ABLE TO STYLE IT MYSELF...
IT'S ACTUALLY NOT THAT DIFFICULT IF YOU HAVE THE RIGHT TOOLS...

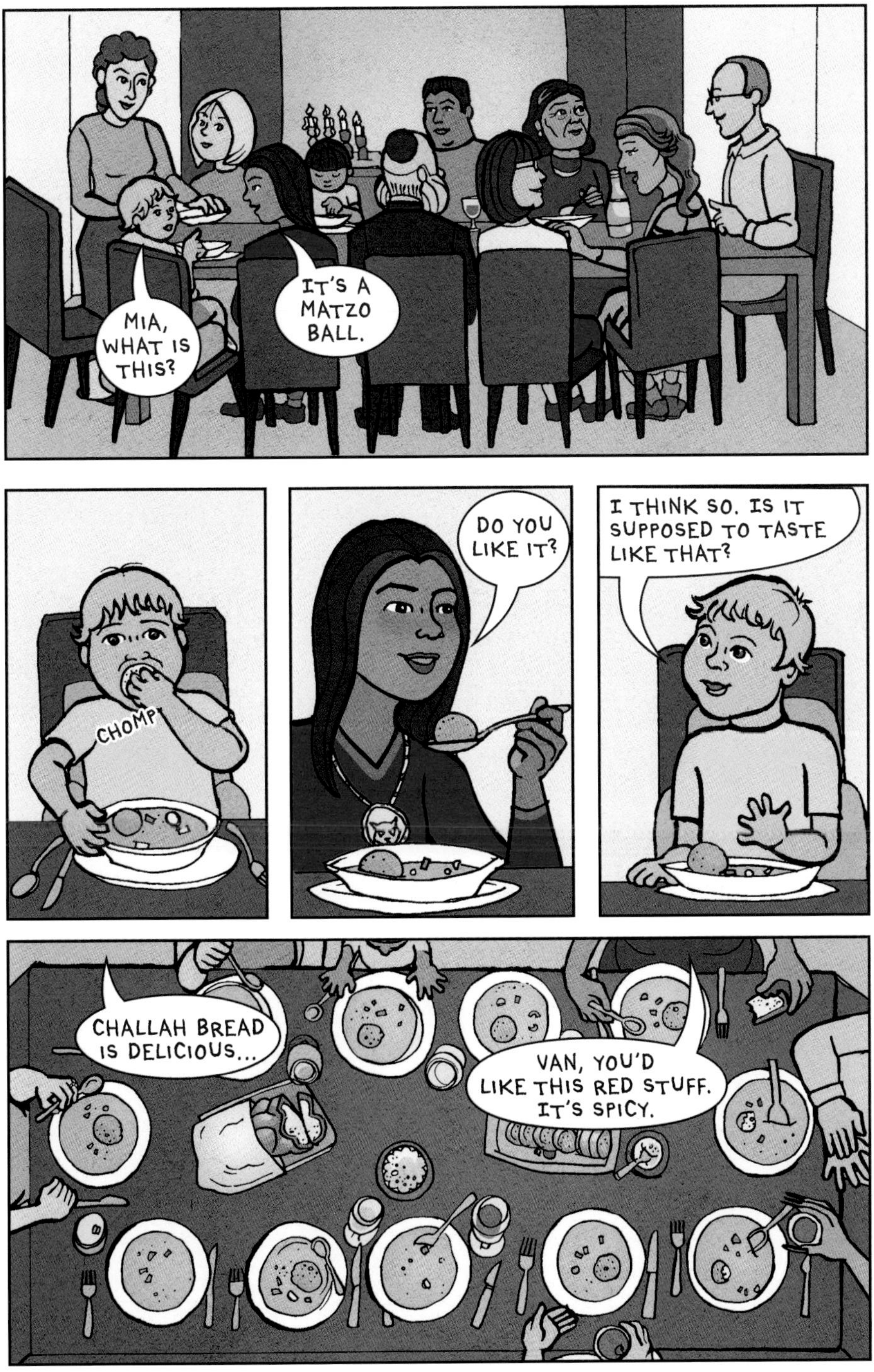
MIA, WHAT IS THIS?
IT'S A MATZO BALL.
CHOMP
DO YOU LIKE IT?
I THINK SO. IS IT SUPPOSED TO TASTE LIKE THAT?
CHALLAH BREAD IS DELICIOUS...
VAN, YOU'D LIKE THIS RED STUFF. IT'S SPICY.

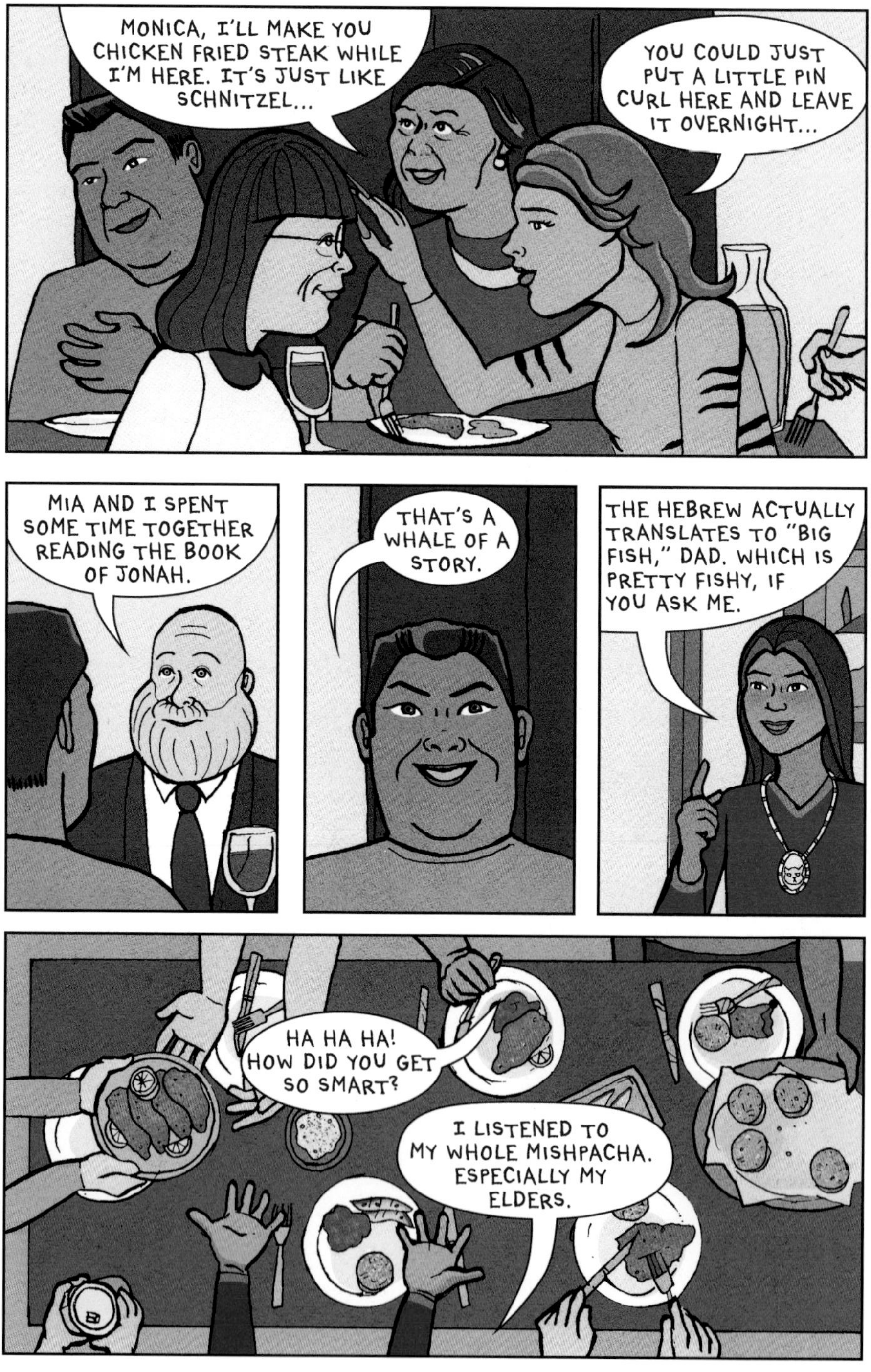
MONICA, I'LL MAKE YOU CHICKEN FRIED STEAK WHILE I'M HERE. IT'S JUST LIKE SCHNITZEL...
YOU COULD JUST PUT A LITTLE PIN CURL HERE AND LEAVE IT OVERNIGHT...
MIA AND I SPENT SOME TIME TOGETHER READING THE BOOK OF JONAH.
THAT'S A WHALE OF A STORY.
THE HEBREW ACTUALLY TRANSLATES TO "BIG FISH," DAD. WHICH IS PRETTY FISHY, IF YOU ASK ME.
HA HA HA! HOW DID YOU GET SO SMART?
I LISTENED TO MY WHOLE MISHPACHA. ESPECIALLY MY ELDERS.

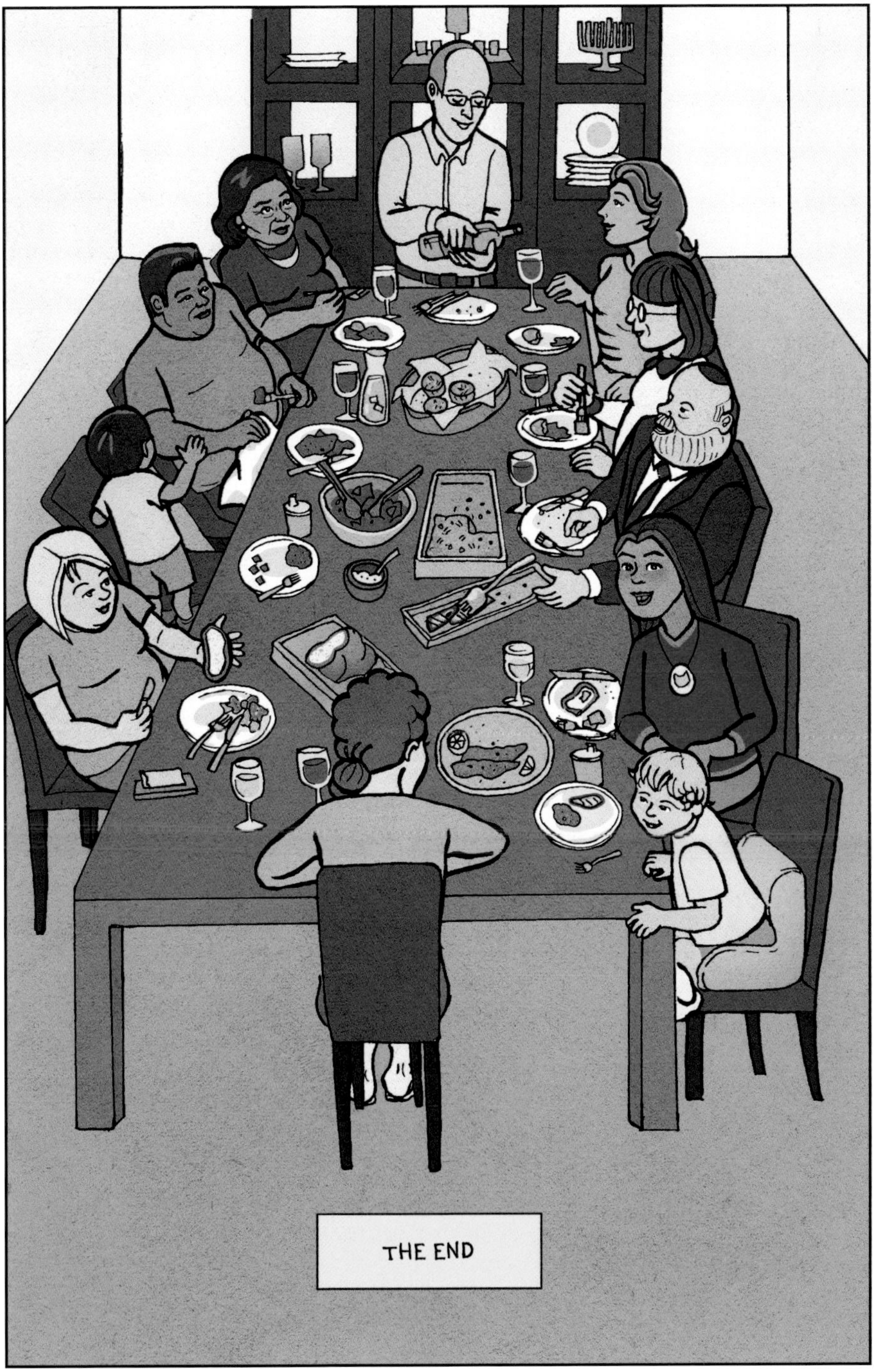
THE END

A NOTE FROM THE AUTHOR

Just like Mia, I am Muscogee (Creek) and Jewish. The name of our tribe has changed over the years. European settlers knew the tribe as Creek, so you sometimes see that name in parentheses. However, our tribe prefers to be called the Muscogee Nation.

My father, Dr. Don Bowen, from whom I get my Indigenous background, died when I was nine. After his death, my mom, my sisters, and I moved to New Jersey. We were separated from my father's family for many years. Throughout that time, I yearned to be closer to them. Finally, twenty-five years after my dad's death, we reunited. I wish I were as courageous as Mia and had traveled to see them when I was younger!

Even when we were away from Oklahoma, my mother made a point to take us to powwows. I am grateful for her wisdom. The swirling dresses, the dances, and the drums were a crucial tie to my Native heritage. Luckily, I now live in Los Angeles, which has one of the largest urban Indian communities in America. I continue to take my own children to powwows as well.

I want to note a few language choices I made when creating this book. I use the word *Indian* to refer to Mia's friends and family. It is not polite to call Indigenous people Indian. However, within the community, it is part of everyday language. It felt natural to use the word when Mia's family was speaking among themselves.

Later in the book, there is another use of the word *Indian* that merits longer discussion. Mia's cousin Nova dresses as a video game princess while wearing a traditional Muscogee ribbon skirt. Nova jokes that she is dressed as an "Indian Princess." Nova is making fun of non-Indigenous people dressing in stereotypical Native American costumes. Playing "dress-up" degrades the cultural significance of traditional regalia. Nova purposely calls herself by a name that is outdated and offensive to communicate her discomfort.

I also want to mention the respect that should be given to the Muscogee story told in the book. Nova shares a traditional account of the creation of Muscogee clans. It is important to note that our creation stories are considered sacred and belong to the Mvskoke people. They should not be minimized or dismissed as "folktales" or "legends." They should be shared with as much reverence as Rabbi Goldfarb shares the text of the Old Testament.

ACKNOWLEDGMENTS

Thanks to . . .

My cousins Melanie Frye and Marianne Frye, who shared sofke with me at Durango's seventieth birthday party. Like Mia, I didn't grow up with the traditional Mvskoke food and traditions, so I am grateful for their generosity. A big hug to my grandmother Mary Smith Colbert, who loved me so much I can still feel it today. All my relatives in Oklahoma showed me the same love when I returned so many years later. I am indebted to them for sharing stories and spending time with me.

Growing up in Oklahoma, I remember hearing about wild onion dinners. My twin sister, Jenny, and I used to pretend to make wild onion dinners from weeds in our backyard. Our big sister, Anna, was the kind taste tester. My mother, Michal, always filled in the gaps of my memories of Oklahoma. My children, Dani, Beverly, and Maccabee, have become proud Muscogee citizens and Jewish people thanks to all their cousins, aunties, uncles, and grandparents. My in-laws, Beth and Steve, have always made me feel like a blood relative. I would never have had the courage to go back to Oklahoma or write this book without the love of my husband, Etan.

My agent, Judy Hansen, for years of dedication and encouragement. My editor, Rosemary Brosnan, and the author-curator of Heartdrum, Cynthia Leitich Smith, for their kindness and impeccable sensitivity. Andrew Eliopulos, for his guidance. My supportive friends who helped this book along the way: David and Nily Steinberg, Jeremy Dauber, Miri Pomerantz Dauber, Katherine Fausset, Laurie Santos, Roni Brunn, Andre Hudson, and Logan Alexander.

MVSKOKE GLOSSARY

In the Mvskoke language, the letter *v* makes a *u* sound, as in *tub*.

Ekv—head

Esakpv—arms

Mvto—thanks

Pvrko svkpoluke—grape dumplings, a traditional Muscogee food made from cornmeal boiled in grape juice

Sofke—sour corn drink

(Spelling courtesy of the Mvskoke Language Program app)

A NOTE FROM CYNTHIA LEITICH SMITH, HEARTDRUM AUTHOR-CURATOR

Dear Reader,

You are a prism! Yes, really, you're a living embodiment of your ancestors' legacies, the places you call "home," your interests and allegiances.

Perhaps, like Mia, you're a member of a community of faith or a citizen of a tribal Nation. Perhaps you are blessed by the wisdom of Elders like Mia's grandmother, or spiritual leaders who will work with you through life's tough questions like her rabbi. Maybe you're more like Mia's cousin Melinda, who honors her culture in a traditional way—by stomp dancing—or like her cousin Nova, who pays tribute to her heritage in her own way—through cosplay.

There's no one right way to be who you are, just as there's no one right way for Mia to be Jewish and Muscogee. She has the power to embrace her whole self on her own terms every day.

Have you read many stories by and about Native people? I'm sure *Two Tribes* will inspire you to read more. The novel is published by Heartdrum, a Native-focused imprint of HarperCollins Children's Books, which offers stories about young Native heroes by Native and First Nations authors and illustrators. I'm delighted to have this book on our list because it's a wonderful read and because it celebrates the diversity within Indigenous Nations, too.

Whatever your cultural or religious background might be, I'm sure you're reflecting on various elements of your identity. It's all part of growing up and becoming confident in who you are and the person you aspire to become.

We hope that you enjoyed *Two Tribes* and remember that you're a beloved member of our human family, valued for every aspect of your identity and the wholeness that is you!

Mvto,
Cynthia Leitich Smith

ABOUT THE AUTHOR

EMILY BOWEN COHEN is a member of the Muscogee Nation. She spent her childhood in Okemah, Oklahoma, and her teen years in Montclair, New Jersey, before graduating from Harvard University. She and her husband, filmmaker Etan Cohen, live in Los Angeles. They have three Jewish Native American children. You can find her memoir-style comics at memberoftwotribes.com.

CYNTHIA LEITICH SMITH is the bestselling, acclaimed author of books for all ages, including *Rain Is Not My Indian Name*, *Indian Shoes*, *Jingle Dancer*, *Hearts Unbroken*, and *Sisters of the Neversea*. She is also the editor of the anthology *Ancestor Approved*. Smith is the author-curator of Heartdrum, a Native-focused imprint at HarperCollins Children's Books, and is the Katherine Paterson Endowed Chair at Vermont College of Fine Arts. She is a citizen of the Muscogee (Creek) Nation and lives in Austin, Texas. You can visit her online at cynthialeitichsmith.com.

In 2014, We Need Diverse Books (WNDB) began as a simple hashtag on Twitter. The social media campaign soon grew into a 501(c)(3) nonprofit with a team that spans the globe. WNDB is supported by a network of writers, illustrators, agents, editors, teachers, librarians, and book lovers, all united under the same goal—to create a world where every child can see themselves in the pages of a book. You can learn more about WNDB programs at diversebooks.org.